THE DEREK & MELISSA BOXED SET

THE ONE

One to Hold
One to Protect
One to Save
One Immortal - Exclusive Bonus Content

TIA LOUISE

ONE TO HOLD

DEREK & MELISSA

BOOK 1

TIA LOUISE

Derek Alexander is a retired Marine, ex-cop, and the top investigator in his field. Melissa Jones is a small-town girl trying to escape her troubled past.

When the two intersect in a bar in Arizona, their sexual chemistry is off the charts. But what is revealed during their "one week stand" only complicates matters.

Because she'll do everything in her power to get away from the past, but he'll do everything he can to hold her.

A STAND-ALONE, ONE TO HOLD NOVEL. Adult Contemporary Romance: Due to strong language and elements of erotic romance, this book is not intended for readers under the age of 18. (M/F)

For the real-life hero who inspired this story.

ONE

A ONE-WEEK STAND

IN THE COOL DARKNESS OF the semi-crowded bar, I could allow the last year to dissolve into a hazy fog, a far-off memory. Each low thump of bass that disappeared into the dull roar of voices beat it further down. With a little more alcohol, it could even become a dream—something that never occurred in real life. Something that could be brushed aside like a phantom, not a true form. Not a reality that burned shame, low and deep in my stomach.

Bars had become a thing of my past, along with flirtatious passes from unfamiliar men, but sitting alone in this hotel club, hundreds of miles from home, I felt wonderfully liberated. I could be anyone. Any anonymous woman having a drink before bed. I could pretend to be free.

My eyes traveled to the dance-floor where younger women in shiny slip dresses and chunky stilettos twisted and swayed, their smooth blonde or red hair matching their movements. They squeal-laughed when songs they liked came on, and the lines around their eyes disappeared as soon as their cheeks relaxed. They could dance all night and still make it to work tomorrow, eyes sparkling.

A bitter laugh slid from my throat as I stared back into the amber drink I'd ordered. The thought of dancing all night made me tired.

The bartender didn't notice me. I'd stood for almost five minutes trying to get his attention to order this drink, and it was gross. "Seven and seven" was all I could remember from the days when I used to order drinks for myself. It was a popular combination then, but I never liked the flavor. Refreshing citrus dragged down by a heavy undertone of bitter syrup. I took a long pull from the tiny red straw and winced.

I should've gone back to the room with Elaine. My best friend since childhood said what I needed was a trip to the desert. She'd booked us a week at the Cactus Flower Spa in Scottsdale, where we could get massages, sit in steam rooms, soak in mud, and let our tensions melt away with hot-wax pedicures. She said it would break me out of my "funk," as she called it.

I didn't have anything else to do this week.

It was with those sunny thoughts in my head that I saw him. At first I thought it was an accident, my eyes flickering across the square-shaped bar at the same time as his. Blue eyes, strikingly blue because of the way they stood out beneath his dark brow, coupled with collar-length, thick dark hair. He had a beard. I didn't like beards—not even close-trimmed ones like his. He was huge. I could see his muscles from where I sat. His chest strained against the tight, black shirt he wore, and his biceps stretched the sleeves. I preferred smaller men, long and lean model-types.

But he didn't look away. And like a deer caught in headlights, I couldn't either. My breath stilled as my eyes stayed on his, as I waited for him to release me. He would release me. I knew he would. I simply had to wait.

Men in bars were after those baby-faced innocents on the dance floor, not me. They wanted energetic young ones with their tight bodies, high-pitched breasts, and even tighter vaginas. Those were the girls men wanted to fuck. They would scream and moan all night and tell them they were the best ever, the king. I wasn't looking for a king. Still, in the next moment, when the mountain of sex holding my gaze stood and began his slow glide in my direction, all I could think was *maybe* . . .

I watched as he passed the patrons facing each other, talking and laughing. Some were more animated than others, waving their arms and putting their drinks in peril. They all shone in the yellow lights hidden above, in the recesses of the wooden shelves that held dozens of upside-down glasses in all shapes and sizes. Liquor bottles were arranged on the top shelf. For some reason, though, the lights didn't seem to reach him. Or me. We were in our own secret, shadowy place.

When he rounded the final corner and I could see him in full, my breath caught. My eyes traveled quickly from his broad shoulders to his narrow waist, down his grey pants ending in sleek, black loafers. Just as fast, they were back to his face, and he was in front of me. I'd never been confronted with so much male presence focused on me in my life. He had to be six-two and twice my size.

"Can I buy you a drink?" The low vibration of his voice shot a pleasing charge right between my legs, and my cheeks warmed.

Blinking back to my glass, I poked the half-empty contents with the straw. "I have this," I said, my voice softer and higher in contrast to his.

"But you don't like it." A small smile was on his lips. It made him the slightest bit less intimidating.

"How do you know?"

He leaned against the bar in front of me, bringing his face closer to my level, his body almost touching mine. A faint scent of warm cologne swirled around me, tightening my chest.

"You make a face every time you sip it," he said. "I've been watching you since you walked in with your friend earlier."

My brows drew together. "Why?"

His tongue touched his bottom lip, and my jaw dropped. I

quickly closed it, thinking how insane it was the way my body responded to him.

This was not me. I did not fantasize about hooking up with strange men in bars. And a cocky alpha who studied me like I was a frontier landscape he was ready to conquer had never been my type. He probably wanted to tie me up or handcuff me to something. A delicious shiver passed through me at the thought. I put my eyes on my drink.

"Maybe I should introduce myself," he said, holding out a large palm. I stared at it a moment. "Derek."

My eyes lifted to his blue ones, which were still holding me in that intense gaze. He had a small nose and a full mouth. A million pornographic images flooded my brain of that nose nudging into my dark spaces, of that mouth kissing areas long-neglected. That beard scratching the insides of my thighs as I moaned and twisted in white sheets, threading my fingers in his silky hair. I cleared the thickness in my throat, feeling heat everywhere in my body.

"Melissa," I said, placing my noticeably smaller hand in his. His fingers closed over mine, and instead of overwhelming, it felt . . . right.

"Sweet Melissa," he said with a little grin. The side of his mouth lifting the way it did made me want to kiss him.

"I'm not so sweet," I said, taking my hand back.

"Aren't others supposed to make that judgment?" His eyes never left me as he motioned to the bartender, who immediately came to us. Apparently it wasn't only the perky blondes who got instant service.

"Two glasses of your best cava," Derek said, giving the boy a quick glance before turning back to me.

"Cava?" I did love the crisp, Spanish sparkling wine. Why I hadn't thought to order that instead of my tan cocktail-disaster? "That's sort of a celebratory drink, isn't it?"

"So let's celebrate."

"Did you get a promotion or something?"

He leaned closer, bringing his eyes to my level. My throat tightened, but I didn't move away. "I met you," he said in that low tone I felt in all the right places.

Two slim glasses were placed in front of us, but I wasn't sure I could lift mine without my hand trembling. Derek picked up both and handed one to me. I took it and carefully sipped, watching as he did the same.

"Are you here on business?" I asked, trying to diffuse the ridiculous amount of sexual tension between us. I considered the possibility I was the only one feeling it.

"Banker's conference this week," he said, taking another, longer drink and then setting the glass back on the bar. His muscles fought against the thin fabric restraining them with every movement.

"You're in banking?" I hated the tremor in my voice. It made me sound like a little girl, when I was striving to be an independent woman. A strong woman who was bigger than her past.

For once, I wanted to forget what happened last year. Let it go and be somebody else. I was out of town, in the desert, in a bar being hit on by a gorgeous stranger. Fate was giving me my chance.

"More like upper management," he said, not seeming to notice my distraction. "I'm doing a workshop on international trade and finance tomorrow. You?"

"Spa vacation," I said. "My friend Elaine said it would be a week to change my life. Or at least my outlook."

A little spark hit his eyes, and I bit my lip. Did I just proposition him? Did I want to? It had been a long time since I'd wanted to be close to anyone in that way. Was I brave enough to let him in?

Internally I shook myself. *Yes.* If that was what I wanted, of course I was. I had always been strong before, and I was still strong. I wouldn't let that be taken from me, too.

"Elaine is who you're here with?" he asked.

I nodded, taking another, longer sip. I allowed my mind to

release the past and return to better thoughts, like those of him removing that shirt and setting that massive physique free. My desire to see what was under it grew stronger by the minute.

"Will she worry if you're out late?" he asked looking directly into my eyes.

I barely shook my head No. Elaine wouldn't mind. She might even throw a party if I got laid. My breathing had become shallow, and all rational thought was quickly taking a backseat to desire.

"I have a key to the conference room," he said quietly. "There's a small, outdoor patio just off the side. It's very private."

"Why do you have a key?"

"So I can set up in the morning." With that, he straightened up and placed two bills on the bar beside his drink. "Let me show you the desert sky."

"That sounds like it might be dangerous."

His hand touched my arm. "I'll keep you safe."

Safe. It was a word almost erotic to my ears. My eyes traveled from his waist up his torso to his broad shoulders to his lips, past that perfect nose to his darkening eyes. The temperature in my body rose with my gaze.

"You're not safe," I whispered.

"And you're not sweet." His low voice caused my tongue to press against my teeth. I was dying to kiss him. "I'll only do what you let me."

As he said it, I already believed him. His tone was calm, and his eyes said he wasn't lying. Somewhere in my head, the voice of reason was telling me to slow down, but either the cava or the anticipation of what might happen had me floating up, out of my body as I watched him take the slim glass from my hand and help me off my stool. I followed him from the bar, past the dancing girls, and out the narrow exit. Against everything I knew to be prudent, I was doing this.

DESERT HEAT WAS STILL HOT. Everyone called it "a dry heat," but it was like opening an oven and getting that first blast right in the face. I'd thought about it when we'd arrived in Arizona earlier today, but now all I was thinking about was the fiery heat blazing through my thighs as Derek held me against the secluded outside wall.

He lifted me as if I weighed no more than a doll, and the hem of my skirt rose all the way up as my legs straddled his waist. His full lips were as soft as they appeared, and they contrasted pleasingly with the scuff of his beard against my skin.

Our mouths opened together, his tongue gently curling with mine, and my hands fumbled to his collar, my fingers threading into his thick hair. Soft and rough forged a fiery trail from my cheek down my jaw to my neck. Little moans rose in my throat with every kiss, and I gasped as my hazy eyes opened to the black sky behind him dotted with thousands of stars. It was a gorgeous view, but I didn't linger on it. The outside patio was secluded—we were completely alone—and my attention was focused on the progress of his mouth as he explored every part of my neck and shoulders with his lips and tongue.

He unzipped the back of my dress, allowing the sleeves to fall down around my elbows as his mouth covered the swell of my breasts. My nipples tingled for his touch, and the only sounds were my rapid panting punctuated by little noises of pleasure. Electricity flew through my body, warming the space between my legs, and I was surrounded by the woodsy scent of his cologne mingled with the growing smell of sex.

His mouth returned to mine, and my fingers dug into his flesh. He was firm and tight, and the way he rocked me against the wall, the swell in his jeans massaging my clit, had me on the brink of orgasm. I wanted him inside me. Desperately.

"Take off your shirt." My voice was a hoarse whisper I didn't recognize. It sounded almost animal.

He lowered me to the ground, his blue eyes now dark navy, as he quickly grabbed the back of his shirt and whipped it over his head. Energy flooded my core then surged low into my pelvis. His smooth skin was the color of coffee with cream, and a whisper of hair covered the top of his chest. I reached out to run my fingers slowly down the cut, muscular lines on his stomach, and he shuddered slightly before catching my hips and pulling me up against him again.

My legs went back around his waist. I was still in my black push-up bra, but I wanted everything off. I wanted my bare breasts pressed against that gorgeous chest. I quickly reached around and unhooked it, slipping my arms from the straps as his mouth covered one hard nipple. Low noises came from his throat as he kissed and gently bit. It was a tense, almost primitive demand, his hands tightening their hold on my ass. A trembling moan ached from my throat. The coarse fabric of the balcony curtain was against my bare back, and his musky scent almost pushed me over the edge.

"I'm clean, but I'll use protection," he said in a rough voice.

It was a foregone conclusion—we were having sex. Only my thong stood between me and what was coming. His mouth traveled back to mine, but I placed my palms lightly on his cheeks, holding his dark eyes for a moment.

"Why me?" I gasped. I had to ask. I wouldn't be me if I didn't.

His hands squeezed my bare bottom. "I love long dark curls and blue eyes."

It was enough. Our mouths crashed together again, and his fingers slid inside me. Two thick digits pressed in and out, exploring what was wet with need. My mouth broke from his and I moaned against his shoulder, gripping his waist with my thighs as his fingers left me and quickly worked below his waist. The sharp metallic clang of a belt buckle was quickly followed by the sound of a wrapper tearing.

I held my breath, my heartbeat, everything. My mouth opened, and he slid into me with a loud groan.

"Oh my god," I gasped. He was huge. I'd never been so full. It was amazing and erotic, and I was about to come. High whimpers gasped from my throat as my orgasm grew stronger, his enormous shaft stretched and massaged every erogenous zone between my legs.

I lay my head back against the wall and let go, savoring the sensation. I was weightless in his arms. He lifted me up and down against him in perfect rhythm, and the tightness in my belly grew stronger. Stronger. More high-pitched whimpers came from me, now joined by his low groans. Every muscle in my body tightened, and then . . . exploded. He bucked me hard as I cried out loud. My legs shuddered with the intensity of my orgasm.

Two more deep thrusts and he was still, gasping, his face pressed into the crook of my neck. We stayed that way several moments. I didn't want him to pull out. The spasms of my orgasm were still tightening the muscles inside me, and with every movement, residual flickers of delicious energy touched me. I held him with my eyes closed. I'd never been fucked like that in my life. I was actually wondering if I'd ever fucked at all after that.

His hips thrust up slowly, gently, and I whimpered again. "I love that sound," he murmured against my neck. "So fucking hot."

His lips pressed more burning kisses against my shoulder, and my nipples tingled at the light brush of his chest hair. All of my senses were heightened as he wrapped huge arms around my waist in an embrace. Slowly rocking his hips again, I tightened my thighs. My orgasm was still fading, and I pressed my face against his neck. Every time my inner muscles would spasm around his cock he'd give me another, gentle thrust and I'd make a little noise, until at last my body seemed satiated. The trembling subsided, and I could think again.

He lifted me and slid out, lowering me to my shaky legs. "Thank you," he whispered. My forehead rested against his cheek, and I felt almost as if it were a dream.

"Thank you," I repeated, stepping back carefully. I located my bra and put it on before pulling the sleeves of my dress back over my shoulders. I slid the zipper up slowly as I watched him restore his pants, fasten his buckle.

I couldn't take my eyes off him. I'd never done anything like this in my life, and I was at a total loss—what now? Did we shake hands and walk away? We'd already thanked each other, another thing I'd never done—thanked a man for sex. Of course, this guy had completely earned it.

He stopped before putting on his shirt and took a step toward me, blue gaze catching mine. "We'll both be here all week?" he said, and the intoxicating scent of his woodsy cologne flooded my senses.

I nodded, knowing what he was getting at.

"I'll be tied up with meetings and networking during the day," he said. "But every night, I'll go to that bar."

I studied him. A one-night stand was one thing, but a one-week stand? With him? After that? It felt like a recipe for disaster. It was going to be hard enough to move past what just happened between us, but adding five more days on top of it? I might never recover.

"I'll be on some regimen at the spa, I guess," I said, my eyes never leaving his.

He put one palm on the wall beside my face and lowered his. Our mouths were a breath apart. "I hope I'll see you again."

I almost melted on the spot. My eyes blinked slowly. "It's a nice bar. And I like cava."

That small grin lifted the side of his mouth, and he kissed me lightly before straightening up and slipping the shirt back over his head. His hair was now in messy waves, and I wanted to run my fingers through them again. Instead, I stepped into my wedge stacks and took the hand he offered as he led me through the dark room and out the side door. He paused to lock it and then turned to face me.

"Shall I escort you back to your room?" he asked.

I shook my head no. I didn't want him knowing my room number yet, although he could easily ask the front desk for it, I supposed.

"Then adieu," he said, lifting my hand and kissing it. "Til tomorrow night."

I watched until he released me, then I turned and walked as steadily as possible to the exit, to the spa side of the resort where we were staying.

TWO

NOT AVAILABLE IN ANY WAY

THE TENDERNESS IN MY THIGH muscles combined with a feeling of calm satisfaction deep inside me were the first indicators what happened last night was not a dream. The next was the scent of his woodsy cologne in my long, dark hair. I lifted a lock and pressed it to my nose, closing my eyes and enjoying his warm scent. It triggered a damp flicker of memory between my legs.

For several long moments, I lay in the soft hotel bed, replaying how last night even happened. Elaine and I had gone to the bar straight from checking in and dropping our bags in our room. We were tired after a long two-days of travel that started with me in Maryland and her in North Carolina. Our first night was spent in Atlanta, where we'd shared a room and stayed awake almost all night talking and catching up. Then we'd flown cross-country to Arizona, and even though it felt early, the day of switching airplanes, running through airports, and hauling bags after our late night had us both tired. I was doubly weighed-down by the problems I'd left at home. One drink, and Elaine wanted to sleep. But I'd wanted to have another. I needed the alcohol to deaden the nonstop pain of my shattered life.

And then he'd appeared.

Images of me pressed against the patio wall, his huge cock thrusting into me, both of us groaning loudly as we came flashed across my memory, and my eyes flew wide. I blinked at the ceiling, thinking about how insane that was. How stupid and potentially dangerous. Clearly the last year hadn't only left me depressed, it also left me engaging in out-of-character and unbelievably risky behavior.

A shiver of longing moved through me at the memory of being held against his firm chest. I sighed. Risky, yes, but how incredibly hot and amazing he was. And he didn't hurt me. He was actually very attentive. He held me all the way to the end, and he even thanked me. My nose wrinkled as a sneaky grin passed over my lips. I thanked him back. What was *that* about?

Then I thought about tonight. Him at the bar waiting. Would I go back? My immediate answer was *yes*, but was that smart? I had a hot memory of the most incredible sex of my life. Maybe it was best to preserve it and not tempt fate with something I'd only leave behind in one short week.

"What time did you get in last night?" Elaine stepped out of the bathroom interrupting my thoughts. She wore one of the thick, white terry robes, and she patted her damp, blonde hair with an equally plush towel.

"I don't remember," I said, rolling onto my stomach. "It wasn't too late. Are we hitting the spa today?"

"I've got us scheduled for massages at eleven, then we'll have lunch in the quiet room, then we can hang around the deck pool. I've heard the waiters there are panty-dropping hot."

I smiled, thinking they'd have to be off the charts to top what I'd had last night. "Sound like the perfect, relaxing day."

Elaine sat on the edge of the bed, drawing her brows together. "You look pretty relaxed right now. What'd you do after I left?"

"Just had another drink. People-watched."

She pressed her lips together in disbelief, but she didn't pursue it. "You'd better get moving if you're going to shower first."

"Don't they just cover us in oil anyway?" I pushed myself to a sitting position.

"That's part of the detoxification."

"Then I'll just do a quick rinse and shower after." I hated the residue of oil on my skin all day, although in the desert, it would probably be a welcome relief from the dryness.

Elaine's tone grew serious. "Have you heard anything?"

My troubles at home came threatening back, and I looked down at my hands as I shook my head. "I emailed everyone that we were out of town for the week. Taking a mental health break. It should be enough."

She exhaled and patted the top of my hands. "You're doing the right thing."

My eyes flickered to hers, and tears threatened. She was the first person to voice support for me since the ordeal began, and it meant everything. I scooted forward to hug her, and she hugged me with a deep inhale. Instantly she jerked and pulled back, studying my face with narrowed eyes.

"What's that smell?"

My face flushed bright red, and I pulled away. She caught my long hair and pulled it to her nose. "That's a *very* nice man-scent if I've ever smelled one."

I shook my head. "I don't know what it is. Just some old cologne."

"Not *your* old cologne. What else happened after you finished your drink?"

Jumping off the bed, I quickly grabbed yoga pants, a bra, and a tank before stepping into the bathroom.

"Melissa?" Elaine was hot on my trail. I pushed the door closed, but she caught it in a crack.

"I just slow-danced with some guy," I lied, coiling my hair into a knot at the top of my head. "It was nothing."

"Just slow danced? He wears a lot of cologne, then." Her voice rose. "Unless it was more like dirty-dancing."

She had no idea. I turned on the shower, holding my hand

under the spray to test the temperature. "Seriously, let's just drop it," I said. "You know I'm not interested in meeting anyone. And anyway, I'm not available."

"Maybe not emotionally available."

I pulled the glass shower door closed. "Not available in any way."

WARM, OIL-COATED HANDS SLID DOWN the length of my back, pushing all the pain down and out through my torso. I lay on a crisp white sheet atop the firm massage table, entirely naked except for a second sheet draped across my bum. Water trickled softly in the desktop fountain, creating a relaxing ambience, and soft beach noises played on a track overhead. The room was dark, and incense lightly filled the air.

I'd never been one of those people who moaned and groaned through massages, but I was on the verge today. When the female masseuse began working on my thighs, the fresh ache from last night's unexpected workout flooded my mind with memories of Derek. I wanted to see him again. I wanted his huge fullness inside me again, stretching me and coaxing every sensitive spot. I wanted to shoot over the edge in another incredible orgasm with him. But what I'd said to Elaine was true. I was *not* available.

Still, he hadn't asked me for a commitment, and from what I could tell, he wasn't looking for anything. One week, he'd said. We could share one week of pleasure, couldn't we? It could be our little secret. Or was I too old-school for that?

The masseuse gently helped me roll over, keeping the second sheet over my private parts. Her expert hands moved to my shoulders, pushing the stress away as her strong thumbs circled, traveling up my neck to my scalp. I remembered the sensation of Derek's lips, his scratchy beard traveling down my neck to my breasts. Moisture was growing between my legs, and I could feel my nipples harden. Luckily the sheet was doubled thick across my chest.

The masseuse gently placed her palms flat against my shoulders.

"Rest until you're ready to come out, Ms. Jones," she said softly before leaving me alone in the small, dark room.

With my eyes closed, I remembered his touch. My hands were flat on the table beside me as I lay on my back. I remembered him gripping my bare buttocks, squeezing them as he rocked me against the curtain, covering my body with his. I remembered pulling off my bra and his ravenous kisses, his gentle bites. I remembered his thick fingers pushing inside me, and instinctively, my hands slipped to my now-tingling clitoris, massaging circles over the sensitive spot. With my eyes closed, I felt his enormous cock push inside me, and in that instant, my body shook with the orgasm I'd provoked. My legs trembled, and I pressed my lips together to keep from moaning loudly.

I wanted him again. Oh, god, even if I wasn't available in any way, I wanted him again so badly.

OUT BY THE POOL, I lay back in the lounge chair, hiding behind dark sunglasses. My hair still had residual oils in it from the massage, but I hadn't washed it. Behind the magazine I held, I casually lifted a lock and sniffed his warm cologne lingering in it.

In my head, I scolded myself. What was I doing? I had to stop this immediately. I slammed the magazine down and stripped off the terry robe I was wearing. In my red bikini, I was still mistaken for being younger than thirty. My stomach was flat, and my skin was tight. No cellulite on my thighs, and my favorite exercise, running, kept my derriere lifted. I'd always just called it good genes, although this last year of pain had taken the once-happy glow from my eyes. My former, easy smile seemed permanently a thing of the past. It was a big part of what made observers think I was younger, and now it was gone. Stolen from me.

Stepping up on the diving board, I fixed my chin. I strode across the plank and did a perfect jackknife dive into the pool, allowing the cooling water to wash away the final remnants of last night. I was *not* available in *any* way.

TWILIGHT IN THE DESERT WAS a beautiful sight.

Elaine and I held glasses of wine as we watched the huge sky turn from blue to pink to dim purple, the fire-pit in the center of our circle of lounge chairs keeping us from getting chilled. As always, I was amazed how the temperature could drop from the 100s to the 70s so fast.

"Wasn't today perfect?" my friend asked as she stretched out, covering herself with one of the complimentary Indian-designed blankets folded across the backs of each chair.

"Perfectly relaxing," I agreed, taking another sip of my wine and forbidding my mind from drifting to the small bar situated between the two halves of the sprawling resort.

He would be there waiting, I was sure of it. And I wondered what reason he would tell himself when I never appeared. He was an amazing lay, and I knew he knew it. I'd been clearly satisfied last night. I took a deep breath and exhaled, drinking another, longer gulp of wine. I couldn't imagine what he'd think.

"Still nothing from home?" Elaine asked, studying my profile.

A missed call had been on my phone, and I'd listened to Sloan's message, demanding to know where I was as I fought the pain his voice now twisted in my gut. I was making a mistake, he kept saying. I was being too hasty, too judgmental. Every message was a lecture in why I shouldn't trust my instincts. I pushed his words and their meaning behind me.

"Nothing important," I said.

"You know, Mel, we've been friends for years." She sat forward in her chair, tightening the blanket around her shoulders. "Something's different today. Won't you tell me what it is?"

My eyes flickered to hers, and for a moment, I considered telling her about the amazing man who'd appeared at the bar last night. Who'd only wanted me, even with all the shiny, happy options twisting and giggling on the dance floor. He'd singled me out. Crossed the bar to be with me.

With damaged me.

Even in the old days when I was whole, no man had ever approached me that way. All of my relationships got serious after the groundwork of friendship had been laid. Either I'd had a project with a man, and after our personalities had meshed, we'd grown into dating. Or even back in college—I'd been in clubs, socializing for weeks with guys before they'd asked me out. It wasn't that I wasn't attractive, and I'd had my share of sexual encounters. I was just never the girl men sought out from across a room crowded with other options.

Until last night.

I felt special, but at the same time, it made me hesitant. Was it possible I was singled out because I was an easy mark? A woman alone, clearly unhappy would easily fall victim to the charms of such a handsome seducer.

Again, these were the not-so sunny thoughts my now-cynical brain conjured when I thought of myself and love. Would I ever be open again or would my heart forever be searching for the hidden truth, the other side of the coin?

"I'm tired," I exhaled, unfolding my legs from beneath me. "I think I'll turn in early tonight if that's okay."

With her question unanswered, Elaine frowned as she watched me rise. "You've been dealt some heavy disappointment this past year," she said. "Try not to give up, okay?"

I nodded, leaning forward and kissing her forehead. "Don't stay up too late. Mani-pedis in the morning?"

She smiled and nodded. "The calf massage will make you come in your chair, from what I've heard."

I laughed. "You've heard a lot about this place."

"Bulletin board reviews. They're unexpectedly erotic."

THREE

THE ADDITIONAL OPTION

CALF AND FOOT MASSAGES KEPT pedicures at the top of my list of all-time favorite spa-treatments. It was the one procedure that almost made me forget my "silent spa" etiquette. Holding the magazine, I leaned my head back in the chair and closed my eyes. The gentle kneading of my tired lower leg muscles had me conceding to Elaine—this week very well could break me out of my funk. Even without the Derek encounter.

My eyelids drooped with fatigue. Last night, I'd tossed and turned for an hour before finally falling into a restless slumber. I kept seeing his blue eyes turned dark navy with desire. For me. The thought made me shiver. Until 2 A.M., all I could do was wonder if he was still there. How long would he wait? Was I making a huge mistake?

Elaine returned about an hour later, and my sterner nature prevailed. I remained in my own bed, in my own room the entire night. Today, she was a little bleary herself.

"What kept you out so late?" I asked, wondering if she might've had her own decadent encounter.

"Fell asleep on the lounger by the fire pit," she said, propping her newly buffed and polished feet on the empty tub near mine.

The clinician had finished my massage and was now scrubbing my heels with a pumice stone. "It's so gorgeous here, I might never go home."

I thought of Baltimore and how I hadn't wanted to move there a year ago. I'd lived just outside Wilmington, on the North Carolina coast for years, and I loved it there. But Sloan had insisted a change of scenery would help us, and when his father died, he needed to be closer to his family's business.

Since I'd gone freelance with my marketing work, and we were moving to another bustling, urban location, there was no reason to fight the move. Other than I loved my hometown. Elaine was there, along with all my old friends.

"I know this is only Day 2, my friend, but I have a confession to make," she said, giving me a serious look. My brow creased. I couldn't imagine what she was about to tell me. "I can't eat another meal of raw foods."

I snorted a laugh, rubbing my forehead with my hand. "What did you have in mind?"

"Let's sneak over to the dark side and order a burger in the main restaurant."

I hesitated. Crossing from the spa resort to the main hotel would increase my chances of running into Derek again. But if he were tied up in conference meetings like he claimed, it was possible we could get in and out without being seen. Still, the thought of bumping into him after my no-show last night made me uneasy.

"Maybe we should just drive into town," I suggested. "I think there's some big thing going on next door and it's probably crowded."

She played with the massage-chair controller while she waited, and didn't notice my worried expression. "A banker's convention," she said, not looking up. "Can you imagine a bigger snooze-fest? Probably a bunch of accountants."

"Probably," I said, remembering Derek saying he was in upper management. "But I'm sure there are other executives there as well, don't you think?"

She glanced up at me then. "Sounds interesting. Maybe we can meet someone and have a little bonus treatment. Some sexual healing?"

"What about Brian?" Elaine's boyfriend back home had been a fixture in her life for years.

She shook her head. "That book's coming to a close, I think."

I sat up quickly, "You never told me this. What happened?"

"Nothing." Her lips pressed together. "And that's just it. I don't feel anything toward him. It's been five years. *Five years!* And I still can't imagine marrying him." She released an exhale. "Sadly, it seems he is not my one true love."

Reaching across the space, I clasped her hand. "I'm so sorry, Lainey. I had no idea. I've been so self-absorbed."

Her hand covered mine with a squeeze. "Please. You've had damn good reasons to be preoccupied. And honestly, I can't even work up the energy to cry over it. I just want to be done. I think he feels the same."

I shook my head, but she winked. "So let's find something new, yes? A desert memento?"

The clinician was finished with my feet and slipping the thin foam flip-flops against my now-smooth soles. "At least let me get changed first."

THE MID-DAY ARIZONA HEAT SWIRLED around us as we walked from the spa lobby across the short, circular drive to the huge, main complex. The resort consisted of three large towers and was all bronze glass, blending nicely with the terrain. Palm trees lined the drive and rocky fountains stood in front of each entrance. I'd slipped on a black skirt and beige tank top and pulled my hair into a low, side ponytail that sent dark curls spilling down my chest. Elaine was wearing a little green dress that made her green eyes glow, and her straight blonde hair hung loose down her back. We both wore flip-flops to preserve our bright salmon pedicures.

The restaurant was crowded as I'd expected, and I tried not to appear to be scanning every face for signs of him. So far, he didn't seem to be here. As we waited for the hostess to return and seat us, a fellow about our age walked up and requested a table.

He was handsome, with honey blond hair and hazel eyes. He wore khaki shorts and topsiders without socks, and I noticed his biceps were well-toned. He also seemed to have a defined chest under his short-sleeved polo. I had to wonder when the banking industry had gotten so sexy. Elaine noticed him, too, and smiled.

The second hostess marked the plastic board in front of her and handed him a square pager. He stepped back and joined us staring into the enormous tropical fish tank that separated the waiting area from part of the dining room.

My friend glanced at him. "Here for the convention?" she said, switching into full flirt-mode.

His eyes lit when he saw how pretty she was, and he turned to face us. "Yeah," he said. "You?"

Elaine shook her head. "We're here for the spa."

He glanced over her shoulder at me and nodded with a smile. I smiled back, and he returned his attention to her.

"I'm Elaine," she said, twisting a lock of her hair around a finger as she leaned into him. "And this is my best friend Melissa."

"Patrick Knight," he said, shaking her hand and taking a step closer as well. "Nice to meet you both."

"Are you waiting for someone, Patrick?" The defining difference between Elaine and me was her complete lack of hesitancy around men. Of course, she'd never been given a reason to hesitate.

"Just my business partner," he said. "We were at the gym earlier, and he's still in his room."

"Is he a banker, too?"

"Nah." Patrick had a charming smile with straight, white teeth. "Neither of us are, really. More freelance consultants. Knight and Alexander."

He handed her a business card, and she took it. But Elaine's eyes moved from the cream rectangle to Patrick's torso. "That sounds fascinating," she said, allowing her eyes to travel slowly up his chest. "I'd love to hear more about your work."

He cleared his throat, obviously appreciating her admiration of his body. "Why don't you ladies join us?"

"Oh, we can't," I quickly jumped in. I wasn't ready to meet yet another banking convention attendee. "We've got a treatment this afternoon, so we're kind of on a schedule."

"Dinner, then," he insisted.

"Perfect," Elaine cut me off before I could block her action again. "What time?"

"Eight o'clock? Here?" Patrick once again had Elaine's hand in his.

"See you then," she said.

The hostess appeared, perfectly timed to escort us to our table, and as we followed her, I carefully scanned the large dining area for his face.

"Yum!" Elaine caught my arm and leaned into my ear, speaking in a low voice. "Wouldn't it be lovely to add him to our treatment schedule?"

"Hmm . . . I think my schedule's full," I said, taking a seat at our table.

I cautiously glanced behind me after giving my drink order, but I still didn't see any sign of him. As far as I could tell, he wasn't having lunch here.

"Maybe this Alexander guy is equally hot," she said with a wink.

I shrugged, sipping my iced tea. "Wouldn't matter."

The corner of her mouth curled up. "We'll see tonight. This might be the additional option you need."

Her words provoked a little laugh from me. She had no idea what additional option I'd already had, and I doubted this Alexander person would be able to top it. That flash of memory caused me to inspect the restaurant once more. Not seeing him, my stomach unclenched enough for me to eat our non-cleansing lunch of cheeseburgers and fries.

FOUR

SPECIAL FORCES

EVEN THOUGH I HAD NO interest in Patrick's partner, when I saw Elaine putting on her strapless, ruched-top dress, I pulled mine out of the closet as well. They were perfect for the weather—handkerchief print, knee-length, and flowing. We'd bought them in the spa store together. Elaine's was black with purple swirling designs, and mine was a bright red with hot pink accents. We each had a glass of the in-room white wine as we made up our faces and dressed.

Using a large brush, I dusted translucent powder over my nose and up my temples to my forehead where my eyes landed on a faded pink scar at my hairline. My lips pressed together, and that old pain twisted inside my chest. I lowered the brush as my hand fumbled to my wine glass. Taking a long sip, I waited a moment for the feelings to pass.

It was over, I reminded myself. That part of my life had ended. I had put all the wheels in motion before I even stepped foot on the plane to come here—before I'd even known I was coming here. Now it was time to let healing take place. I had to let go of what had happened to me and move forward.

A few cleansing breaths, and my control began easing back. Tapping my finger against the pot of concealer, I touched the flesh-toned makeup over the thin pink line, and it was gone. For a split second I imagined a concealer for heart scars. Instead I shook my head. *Over*, I repeated in my brain. Another deep inhale, and I was ready to emerge from the bathroom.

Elaine was leaning down, fastening the buckle on her sandal when I walked out. Her straight, blonde hair spilled like silk around her shoulders, and when she stood, we both caught our breaths. "You're beautiful!" we practically said simultaneously. Then we laughed.

"Oh, Mel," my best friend said, coming over and wrapping her arms around me. "It's moments like these when I know you're going to be okay. Just give it time."

I nodded hugging her back and pressing my lips against her temple. The clean scent of the spa-signature cactus flower toiletries flooded my senses. It was a relaxing smell, and I imagined if she disappeared with Patrick, he'd love it.

"I'm doing my best," I said. "I know holding onto the past is the worst thing anyone can do."

My psychologist mother would be the first to have me on her couch reciting these axioms to me if I dared let her know what had happened. As it stood, only three people knew the whole story—me, him, and Elaine, the closest person I had to a sister. It was a cliché not to tell anyone, but I didn't have the energy or the willingness to involve the authorities. And I didn't want everyone knowing my tragic tale.

It was finished. I'd made my decision, and I was putting it behind me. My instincts said to cut my losses, cut all ties, and move on. I'd made my first step before leaving Baltimore. This trip was the second, and when I got back, I'd take the third.

What happened with Derek might be extended as part of me cutting ties, my declaration of freedom from my past . . . But more likely it was just a blip on the radar screen. An incredible distraction, that was now through.

Walking to the restaurant, the dry breeze blew our hair back. I lifted the weight of my dark locks around one shoulder and linked arms with my friend.

"We should do trips like this more often," she said, looking up at the desert sky. "It's wonderful being together, and there's nothing stopping us now. I had a long talk with Brian this afternoon, and that's done. Clean break. We're both free agents."

My arm tightened on hers, and I pulled her to a stop. "Are you okay?"

She nodded and smiled. "It really was over before I even called you about coming here. It's sad, but I promise, I'm so relieved we've finally made it official. It was turning into the longest goodbye on record."

"Was Brian part of the reason you planned this spa retreat?"

She pulled me, and we started walking again. "Only a small part. I knew how much you needed it, too. I could hear it in your voice every time we talked."

Another deep, cleansing breath. "Well, I think your idea sounds fantastic. Let's plan our next trip as soon as we get back."

"Will you be coming home to the shore now?" her delicate eyebrows pulled together.

I bit my lip and nodded. "Definitely. The best part about working freelance is it goes with me anywhere. And I have lots of contacts in Wilmington."

"Oh, that makes me so happy," she beamed, doing a little skip. "We are definitely planning our next trip. What do you think? Is Thanksgiving too soon?"

I laughed as we entered the restaurant, glad I'd had that glass of wine. I was at ease and far less nervous about accidentally bumping into Derek this time. Elaine told the hostess we were with Patrick and Mr. Alexander as I hung back beside the aquarium.

When she motioned for us to follow her, my friend clasped the crook of my arm and leaned in to my ear. "If this is the 'Mr. Alexander' I found online, it should be a very interesting dinner."

I shook my head and smiled. Her nonstop online

investigations were becoming an entertaining distraction.

"Why?" I whispered, picturing a grey-haired old gentleman with a name like *Mr. Alexander*.

Just then, my eyes found Patrick sitting at a large round table in the back. It was covered in a crisp, white tablecloth, and a vase of bright yellow sunflowers formed the centerpiece, corresponding with the gold décor.

Elaine's words were just meeting my ears when my breath disappeared from my throat. "Derek Alexander is a leader in the field of online investigation. And he's hot as hell."

My brain scrambled as his blue eyes caught mine, and I involuntarily took a step back. "Oh," I said softly, feeling my chest tighten at the sight of him.

There he sat, wearing a light-blue, short-sleeved polo that stretched across that chest that had been pressed against mine less than forty-eight hours ago.

"What's wrong?" Elaine said, stepping between me and the table, studying my face.

I shook my head, attempting to breathe normally. "It's nothing!" My voice was too high, and behind her, I saw his dark form rise to his full height. But I couldn't look. I was afraid I might faint.

"Elaine!" Patrick's happy voice cut through my whirlwind of emotions. "You look great."

She beamed, turning quickly to him. "Thanks," she said, stepping around to catch Patrick's hand and leaving me to face the man I'd stood up the night before.

Derek's eyes flickered with a hint of amusement and definite satisfaction. "Melissa," he said in that low voice that rattled me to my core.

I blinked down to the table. "I didn't know . . ." Actually, I had no idea what to say at this point. Nothing in my life up to now had prepared me for this situation.

Elaine stepped back around to extend her hand to him. "You must be Mr. Alexander," she smiled.

Derek stepped forward to take her hand, then leaned in to kiss her cheek briefly. "Derek, please."

Elaine's eyes widened. "I love your cologne," she said, glancing at me with knowing eyes. "What is it?"

Heat flooded my cheeks. Again, I was having difficulty breathing.

Derek laughed. "You know, I'm not sure. I transferred it to one of those plastic travel bottles for airport security a while back, and now I can't remember."

"It's so familiar," Elaine said. "Almost like something I smelled yesterday . . ."

He shrugged. "I rarely wear cologne, but I liked the scent. Fresh, not too overpowering."

"But lingering," my friend said.

She wouldn't stop, and I wanted to die as I pulled out the chair directly in front of me. It formed an awkward arrangement—Elaine sitting next to Patrick, Derek across from me a few chairs down from them. A waiter appeared ready for our drink orders, and Derek immediately ordered a bottle of cava for the table.

"It's a favorite, I believe," he said, turning his blue eyes on me.

I glanced down to my lap, attempting to stop the flood of images of us together on the secret patio. Every time I looked at his face, I remembered the brush of his lips against mine, the scratch of his beard, the sensation of his chest hair against my bare nipples. I was certain the entire room could see me flush or at the very least, how fast I was breathing.

"So tell me," Elaine said, "Are you *the* Derek Alexander, top internet piracy detective, ex-Marine, and former cop?"

"*Retired Marine* and *police officer* are preferred," he said with a wink as the waiter appeared with a dark-green bottle. "And I'm not sure I'm the top, but I am hired to speak at conferences quite a bit."

"Fascinating," Elaine said, and I could feel her eyes moving to me.

I continued to study the place setting in front of me. Detective? Marine? Former cop? Great. All of those labels only complicated my situation.

The cork popped and four glasses of sparkling wine were served. Derek lifted his. "To the little things," he said.

"Meeting up with pleasant acquaintances," Elaine said, lifting her glass.

I brought mine to my lips and took a long drink.

"So you didn't tell me what you do," Patrick jumped in with his sunny voice. Everything about him was happy, and I figured Elaine could do much worse for a spa-vacation fling. Or transition guy. Unlike me, who only seemed destined for trouble.

"Mel's a freelance marketer," she said, nodding at me. "I teach middle school."

"What?" Patrick laughed. "That's the worst age ever!"

Elaine joined him in laughter. "They're just a misunderstood bunch. All raging hormones. But they want to be loved and accepted just like everyone else."

I could feel Derek's intense gaze on me, and I didn't dare look at him. Instead I faced Patrick, a far less intimidating table mate. "So you work in internet security?"

Patrick's hazel eyes twinkled. "That's right, and don't worry. We've already done complete background checks on both you lovely ladies."

My throat tightened, but Elaine laughed loudly. "Liar! You don't even know our last names."

"You got me," he smiled, taking a drink of cava. "But I will after tonight."

"Maybe I'll keep you guessing," she said.

Their easy banter was making my head hurt. Especially in view of Derek's continued silence. I took another drink, finishing my glass.

"So if all the bad guys are virtual now, why are you two so buff?" Elaine said, touching Patrick's biceps lightly. "I'm pretty sure Derek's arm is the size of my thigh!"

My eyes flickered to his upper arm, and I remembered how easily he lifted me against him, as if I weighed no more than a doll. My cheeks heated at the memory.

"Occasionally Big D has to use intimidation tactics," Patrick said as if revealing an insider secret.

"Big D?" Elaine's nose wrinkled.

I could hear the smile in Derek's low voice. "It's a joke."

The pressure was too much. I stood, placing my napkin beside my empty plate and now-empty cava flute. "Excuse me," I said softly.

Elaine frowned up at me. "Mel? Are you okay?"

She started to rise, but I held out my hand. "Please stay. I just . . . I need to go. I'll have dinner in the room."

"But you don't have a key!"

"I'll get one from the front desk. Please . . . just stay." I turned and hastened to the restaurant exit.

Elaine spoke again, and the low sound of male voices joined hers, but I didn't stop. My heart was flying, and I was out the door, fast-walking through the convention center hall in less than a minute.

I'd intended to exit the way we'd come in, but somehow, I'd gotten turned around. Now I was headed in the direction of the small bar from our very first night. Between me and it were three signs for men, women, and the large "family" bathroom. I paused, trying to remember the quickest way back to the spa side of the resort. Just then, I felt a presence approaching quickly. I started to go, but Derek's voice stopped me.

"Wait," he said, touching my arm.

I turned so abruptly, he bumped into me, catching me in his strong embrace, his familiar woodsy scent all around me. "Oh," I said, clutching his solid arms, looking up into his intense blue eyes. Energy rushed through me so hard, I was sure he could see it. I almost felt like I could see it reflected in his own eyes.

"Here," he said glancing around quickly before pulling me

into the family bathroom.

I only had a moment to observe how very clean it was before he had me against the wall, pinned by his huge physique.

"You never came." His voice was a low, husky whisper. "I waited all night."

My hands rested on his chest, and heat flamed through me with every heartbeat. My eyes traveled up, up, up to his. They were darkened now, and I was certain he was thinking the same thing as me. He remembered how fantastically our bodies came together two nights ago. I barely registered him reaching out to lock the door.

"I'm sorry," was all I could say.

"When you walked in the restaurant tonight . . . god, you're so beautiful." He spoke against my skin as his lips pressed into my brow, his beard roughing my closed eyelids. "Are you feeling bad?"

"No," I managed to say despite the heat surging through me as his lips moved to my temple. "I . . . didn't think I could eat."

"Good," he said in a thick voice before covering my mouth with his. Mine opened quickly, drawing him in. Our tongues entwined before his lips moved to my jaw then down my neck. "I thought about you all day." His breath whispered across my skin, and I couldn't stop a surge of desire low in my stomach. "Will you let me have you here?"

"Yes," I barely spoke, and he dropped to his knees.

He gathered the thin fabric of my dress, shoving it up to my waist as he caught the side of my thong with his thumb. Large, strong hands gripped my inner thighs, opening them, and his nose touched the crease in my leg as his tongue explored my now-wet folds. A whimper trembled from my throat. It was the exact fantasy I'd had in the bar, and he pulled back, pressing his mouth against my thigh.

"I had to hear that sound again." His voice was a sexy vibration against my skin, his beard scratching my charged, sensitive areas. I shuddered in his strong hands that held me as if I weighed nothing at all.

His mouth returned to my clit, and his tongue began making slow strokes punctuated by little sucks. My head dropped back with a moan, eyes closed, as my hips rotated in time with his movements.

"Oooh, god," I sighed, threading my fingers into his thick, dark hair, never wanting him to stop. My back arched against the cold stone wall, and all I knew was his mouth, his tongue, tasting me, teasing me to the very edge. Pressure grew hot and tight low in my belly, tighter with every pull of his mouth. My hips bucked as my orgasm began, and another high-pitched whimper escaped my throat. My shudders were uncontrollable as I came.

I was still finishing when he stood quickly, fumbled with his pants a moment before I heard the familiar tearing sound, the clink of a belt buckle. In one swift movement, he lifted me easily, then slid me down, thrusting into my dripping-wet passage, filling me completely like before, stretching and massaging every place that ached for him. We both groaned loudly, and he pushed into me again, harder. My hands fumbled to the collar of his shirt, down his back, pulling the fabric up, desperate to feel his skin.

He groaned low as I managed to get his polo higher, the strapless top of my dress now pushed down around my waist, my bare breasts tingling for his touch. Our skin met, and I moaned with satisfaction.

"Fuck," his low voice groaned as his hands gripped my butt, moving me up and down his shaft in the most amazing rhythm.

My second orgasm was building rapidly as his large cock moved in and out repeatedly. His mouth covered mine, and the small whimpers coming from my throat were like fuel to his fire. Our pace increased. The tightness in my stomach grew more intense, and my nails dug into his skin. My heart was beating so hard, and my brain had switched to repeating one phrase, *Don't stop. Don't stop.*

Finally the tightness reached its peak and burst through me—shaking my thighs again and making me moan.

"Fuck me," he groaned, thrusting hard. "You're so fucking hot."

"Derek," I whispered against his ear, and he let out a breath.

"Say it again," he ground out, lifting me and slamming me hard against his hips, his rock-hard cock filling me entirely.

"Oh, god," I cried. "Derek!"

With that, he pushed me against the wall, banging into me three swift times before holding the fourth so deep inside me, I felt his heartbeat pounding. A shiver moved through his body, and he groaned soft and low.

We didn't move for several moments. He only held me against him, both of us panting hard.

Our location came seeping back to me through the delirium of love-making. We were in a bathroom in a five-star hotel fucking our brains out. This was nuts. I gently pushed against his arms, and he released me. As I lowered my legs, I adjusted my thong. I slid the top of my dress back to its proper location and I smoothed my hair.

I turned to the sink, unsure if I felt insane or fantastic. My legs trembled from exertion and sensation. One thing I couldn't deny, my fears of ruining the memory of our perfect first time were unfounded. Our second time was even hotter. I turned on the water and touched my fingers under the stream as I listened to him straightening his clothes.

In a moment he was back behind me, bending down to wrap his chiseled arms around my waist and whispering in my ear like before, "Thank you." Then he kissed the top of my shoulder.

No man had ever thanked me for sex like this, and I wasn't sure if I liked it or if it made me feel like a call girl. I decided to go with the first option. He wasn't offering me money, after all, just gratitude. It was a gratitude I shared. He fucked me better than anybody had in my entire life.

My eyes met his in the mirror. "Thank you," I said back.

For a moment our gaze held each other's. I wasn't intimidated or afraid anymore, but I was completely bewildered and still not sure what to do with this. I barely knew him, and my situation hadn't changed. I was not available in any way. Well, except in the way that led to flaming-hot fucks in five-star bathrooms. It was like we were animals or something. Very pampered animals, I supposed. I blinked down as warmth filled my cheeks and turned the water off.

We had to exit, and I wasn't sure what might be waiting on the other side. Neither of us had attempted to control the volume of our voices. Had someone alerted the management? I wouldn't even have heard if someone knocked during what just happened.

"Would you like me to go first?" His deep voice spoke to the fears in my mind.

Without answering, I reached forward and flipped the lock back, pulling the handle down and walking out casually. The passage was empty, and I exhaled with relief. No one was waiting outside, no hotel security, and the only persons I saw were hastening in our direction—but not to us, to the bar behind us.

I walked over to the water-fountain on the opposite wall. Just as I reached it, I heard the metallic door open, and I knew Derek was emerging. I stood and wiped my mouth, turning to face him. When my eyes hit his, my chest clenched. My type or not, he was gorgeous. The light blue shirt stretched across the top of his perfect chest made his eyes glow, and his dark, wavy locks were pushed back from his face. He caught my gaze with an expression of true appreciation, and my whole body warmed. What was I doing? For that matter, who was I? I had no answer.

"We should probably head back to the restaurant," I said as he stepped toward me. "Patrick and Elaine might wonder."

"I told them I'd be sure you got back to your room safely."

I nodded, exhaling a short laugh, thinking of Elaine's plans. "They might actually be glad we're gone."

He lifted my hand into the crook of his muscled arm. "You

need to eat. Would you let me buy you dinner?"

We were slowly approaching the place where we first met, and I still wasn't sure I had much of an appetite. "Let's see what they're serving at the bar."

Only a few steps and we were there, but the music reached us outside, loud and pulsing. It sounded like a party, and not at all what I was in the mood for.

Derek stopped, placing his large hand over mine holding his arm. "Maybe we can see what they'll bring us outside? Beside the fire pit?"

He turned and led us out the side door to lounge chairs and an arrangement that mirrored ours on the spa side of the resort.

"Will this do?" he said, holding out my hand and stepping around the wooden loveseat, over which an Indian-designed blanket was thrown.

"It's lovely," I said, stepping forward and sitting.

"You're lovely," he said softly. "I couldn't take my eyes off you when you walked in tonight. I think red is your color."

A feeling I would not acknowledge warmed my stomach. It was something I couldn't allow to develop for him, not now.

"Thank you," I said, and my mind filled with images of what prompted our last exchange of thanks. The sensations flooding my insides grew stronger.

"If no one comes out, I'll walk in and order whatever looks good," he said.

I nodded, and for several moments we only sat watching the orange flames dance over the coals. It was hypnotic and very relaxing. Derek was beside me on the love seat, and our sides were pressed together. After what felt like many long moments, but what was probably only five, he tugged on my waist. I glanced at him and a smile touched his lips. At that, I leaned against him, resting my head on his firm chest. His muscular arm went around my shoulder and down my side.

We were so familiar with each other's bodies. We knew exactly how to touch one another to provoke the strongest response. But how did we relate in a casual setting like this? With our clothes on?

"Where did you grow up?" I asked, watching the fire.

"South Louisiana," he said. I felt his fingers lifting clumps of my curls and holding them. "And you?"

"Atlanta," I said. "But only until I was nine. Then we moved to the coast, just outside Wilmington, North Carolina. That's where I met Elaine."

"You've known each other that long?" He was still playing with my hair, and I found it unexpectedly soothing. Even though we barely knew each other, I felt incredibly safe with him.

"She's the closest thing to a sister I have. She's always been there for me."

We were quiet again, and at last a waitress appeared. "Can I bring you a drink?" she asked.

"Yes," Derek's voice was full of authority. "A bottle of cava, two glasses, and two of your olive-salad sandwiches."

The young woman nodded, and hastened away.

"In south Louisiana, those are called muffulettas," I said, resting my head back against his chest.

"You've been to New Orleans?"

"No," I smiled, "but I read a lot."

His hand traced circles on my upper arm, and I could feel my eyelids drooping. Sitting here with him, under the desert sky with the temperature dropping, watching the fire in the pit and waiting on olive-salad sandwiches, I could almost pretend we were a couple. That I was a normal person on a holiday with my boyfriend, without a care in the world.

But I wasn't.

I stirred and started to move away, but his arm tightened over me. "What's wrong?"

"I really should head back to my room. It's late."

He released his hold on me, which was good because he was a thousand times stronger than I was. I couldn't have fought him if I tried, and for a moment, I considered that might be the reason I'd always avoided such muscular men. Not because they weren't attractive, because he was damn sexy.

"Just stay and have your dinner first," he said.

As if on cue, the young waitress appeared with a tray holding a dark green bottle, two clear silicone wine glasses, and two large sandwiches. She placed the entire load on the small table in front of us and handed it out.

"Shall I charge this to your room?" she asked.

"Two thirteen," he said.

I didn't want to remember the number, but it seemed the harder I tried to forget it, the more firmly it was imprinted on my brain.

"I thought hotels always skipped thirteen," I said. "Bad luck."

"I don't believe in luck."

A popping sound announced the opening of the cava, which the waitress poured into the glasses for each of us. I took mine and waited until she'd put the bottle in a small stoneware bucket and gone.

"Are we still celebrating?" I asked.

His dark eyes met mine, and for a moment we didn't speak, he only studied my face. I was starting to grow self-conscious when he broke the silence.

"Every day's a celebration, right? We're alive?"

I smiled and nodded, tapping my glass against his. He put his down on the table and picked up his huge sandwich.

"We could've split one," I said evaluating the size of mine. "Half would be plenty for me."

He smiled. "But not for me."

I gingerly took a bite and set the savory concoction back on the plate. The sharp cheese flavor filled my mouth, and I thought it was the perfect blend of tangy and salty.

"So you're a Marine?" I asked, watching him chew.

He nodded, swallowing. "Did my tour in Iraq during the first Gulf War."

"You must've been just a boy!"

"Eighteen," he said, lifting the glass and taking a sip of cava.

"And the special forces?"

"Did that for a while after, before I retired and went to the police academy."

I nodded. "How long were you a police officer?"

"I wasn't," he said with a smile.

"But . . ."

"I bypassed that and got my private investigator's license. In college I studied finance, and with the Internet taking off, I wanted to hunt down cyber-criminals. I worked in Law Enforcement Online a bit."

"What's that?" I studied his dark hair in the moonlight, imagining him in uniform, in the desert, fighting terrorists. It was an extremely attractive image.

"LEO is a branch of the FBI."

"So you're a special agent?"

He laughed. "No. I just worked there a little while."

"What do they do?"

"It's pretty complicated, and much of it's classified. How about we just leave it as is?"

"But you don't do it anymore?" I pressed. Then I wondered why I even cared so much. I didn't need to know all of this about him. We were just in this for a week. He could put himself in as much danger as he chose. I'd never see him again.

The thought made my stomach clench painfully.

He shook his head. "Now I'm freelance. I work with banks to hunt down cyber criminals. People who would steal customers' money or attempt to make fraudulent transactions. Hack into online bank accounts, phishers. Things like that."

I pressed my lips together and nodded. "Still a hero."

He shrugged. "I travel a lot. Do these conferences. I'm as much an educator as anything."

"And do you have a girl at each stop?" I froze. I didn't know where that question came from. "I'm sorry," I said quickly. "It's not really my business—"

"No." He cut me off, staring straight into my eyes. "I don't have a girl anywhere. Actually, I've never done anything like this before."

Suddenly we were both very quiet. I looked at the half-eaten sandwich on my plate and realized I was finished. I didn't want any more wine. I needed to get back to my room, to get my head straight. We were venturing into impossible territory now.

I stood quickly. "Thank you so much for dinner," I said, dusting my hands together.

Derek stood just as fast, towering over me in the night. "Please don't go," he said. "It's still early."

I shook my head. "It's late, and I'm tired. And . . . well . . . I think we both know it's for the best."

Just as I turned to leave, I felt his touch, light at my elbow. "See me tomorrow. Don't stay away. It's just for a few more days."

His words, the tone in his voice, caused a sharp pain in the center of my body. It was as if a sword were thrust into the space below my ribs, above my stomach. I glanced back at his blue eyes, bright and open. It was impossible to believe I could have any power over him at all, but it seemed in this one request, I did.

I nodded. "What would you like to do?"

He smiled and lowered his hand. "What's your last name?"

I shook my head. "My room is 323 in the spa tower. Call me that way."

The crease in his brow told me he didn't understand, but if he truly had access to all of our background information like Patrick had teased, I didn't want him knowing what my year had been like. I didn't want anyone knowing. Having not gone officially on record, I wasn't sure if he could find anything out, but I couldn't be too careful.

"Goodnight," I said leaning forward to kiss his cheek, cutting off any further discussion. Just as I was about to pull back, he caught the back of my neck and pulled my mouth to his for a better kiss.

I didn't resist, allowing his soft lips to part mine. I placed my palms on his strong shoulders, bracing myself as our tongues entwined. His kiss turned hungry, and my mouth matched his pace. I wanted him to lift me again. I craved the connection of our bodies as much as he did. Heat flared between my legs, but I resisted, stepping back, inhaling deeply, eyes still closed.

"Goodnight," I said, this time in a shaky whisper.

My eyes blinked open and only briefly caught his before I turned and walked away, not giving him a chance to respond.

FIVE

LITTLE BOXES

OUR ROOM WAS DIM AND empty when I arrived. The turn-down service had left organic dark chocolates on our pillows and soft track lighting ran around the walls behind the head-boards. Beach sounds were coming from the little music station between the two beds, and the air smelled faintly of the signature cactus flower perfume. Everything was designed to cultivate a relaxed, spa vibe. I actually liked it.

Elaine was still with Patrick, I supposed. I went to the bathroom and flicked on the soft yellow lights, and for a moment, I was stunned by my reflection. My cheeks did seem rosier, and although the faint lines were still visible at the corners of my eyes, even my eyes were different. The smallest hint of that old brightness was fighting to return. Was it all the spa pampering? The easy, schedule-less days of sleeping in and then relaxing by the pool, allowing the nonstop tension to drain from my body?

Or was it him?

I shook my head and tied my long dark curls back so I could wash my face. Once I was finished and had smoothed a thin line of moisturizer under my eyes and across my lips, I turned and walked back to the large, queen-sized bed where I slept. My phone lay discarded at the foot. I hadn't even thought about taking it with me. I didn't want to check emails or texts. I was in a bubble, and everyone had been informed I would be unavailable for the week. I had auto-respond messages set up everywhere.

But still he called.

Sloan's picture and number sat there staring at me like the cat that always came back. Tonight I didn't listen to his message. I didn't want to hear his lectures. I tossed the phone on the small sofa in our room and slipped between the cool, crisp sheets. I considered deleting his contact information, getting a new phone, a new number. But no. I needed to know where he was. At least for now.

Pushing aside those dark thoughts, I inhaled Derek's warm, woodsy scent again in my hair. A little smile teased at the corner of my lips when I thought of how wild our encounters were. I slid my dark locks across my face, closing my eyes and imagining his strong arms around my waist, remembering him pushing me against the wall. The feel of that huge man trembling in my arms when he came. The sound of his groans.

Lying in the dark alone, I did the one thing that would drive my mother crazy. I compartmentalized it all. With my eyes closed, I imagined taking Sloan and putting him alone in his own, cold plastic box. I slammed the lid and shoved it on a back shelf in my mind. Then I gathered all the events of the last year as if scooping up scattered blocks and dumped them in another box, which I shoved under Sloan's.

Stretching out in my bed, I took a new box. I imagined lining it with satin and flower petals. I took little pillows and made a soft bed. That's where I put Derek and his memories. I pictured myself small, climbing into the box with him. He was lying back on the cushions in his grey slacks. The button-down he wore was open, and I could see every line on his sculpted torso. That little smile was on his lips as he watched me approach. I ran my fingers along the lines of his stomach, gazing into his eyes that darkened as I touched him.

His kiss, the same one he gave me beside the fire pit, was gentle but hungry. Our pace grew faster as we kissed each other again and again, tongues entwining, heat growing between my legs, until he pulled me under him. My breathing was fast, my whole body tense with anticipation, so wet, so ready for his awesome fullness. I felt his tip pressing into me, filling me, as a thought drifted through my mind. *We'd never done it in a bed . . .*

SCUFFING SOUNDS AND THE LOUD noise of someone trying to be quiet woke me. I looked at the clock. It wasn't even eight yet. Elaine was hurrying around the room, filling a bag with her bathing suit, a towel,

"What are you doing?" I asked, my voice thick with sleep.

"Oh," she exclaimed. "I'm sorry! I didn't mean to wake you."

I sat up slowly, rubbing my eyes. Looking around, I almost expected to see Derek in bed with me. I'd drifted to sleep in our box, wrapped in his huge, protective arms.

"Did you spend the night with Patrick?" I asked.

A giggle was followed quickly by a throat clearing. "Yes," she said, unable to hide her beaming face. "Oh my god."

My lips pressed into a smile. "Good?"

"Holy fuck," she flopped across the foot of my bed. "I think I came five times last night."

I grinned, smoothing her now-messy blonde hair. "Is it possible to meet your soul mate in one day?" she asked, looking up at me.

"No idea," I said, not wanting to think about questions like that. It made my stomach hurt. "I'm not sure I believe in soul mates. But you like him? Sounds like poor Brian is definitely toast."

"Don't even say the B-word. Patrick is the hottest thing. And that body." She did a little shiver. "First we just talked all hours.

Oh! You never came back. Did Derek find you? He said not to worry, and I figured since he's practically a cop and a Marine . . ."

I bit my lip, still not sure how much I wanted to tell her about Derek's and my . . . relationship? Agreement? I didn't have a clue what to call it. I'd never had a fuck buddy before. Were we even buddies? We never saw each other outside of patios, bars, and family restrooms.

"We . . . bumped into each other," I said. Then I suppressed a grin at how that "bump" went. And how hot and noisy it was.

"Did you get any dinner?"

"I did, but tell me about you and Patrick."

"Mmm," she smiled again. "Okay, like I said, first we talked all hours, really got to know each other. Then we went down to the pool. It was completely dark, so we sneaked in—"

"You went skinny dipping?"

She giggled. "Have you ever had sex in a pool? It is *amazing*. Everything's all wet, and the water was the exact right temperature."

"I hope you used protection." I mentally wondered at how many public decency laws these former cops of ours broke.

"Of course!" Elaine jumped up and went back to filling her bag. "He's going to blow off the conference today, and we're spending it together. When I told him this was my first trip to Arizona, he had all these places I just *have* to see."

"Sounds like fun," I sighed, rolling onto my side.

Then her expression changed. "I'm sorry!" she cried. "I'm the worst friend ever! I need to stay with you and do our treatments. Our mental health regimen."

I sat up and shook my head. "No way! Get out of here! I'm the one who needs a mental health regimen. You can catch up with me tonight."

She bounced over and kissed my cheek. "Thanks," she cooed. "I'll make it up to you. Promise."

ONCE ELAINE WAS GONE, I lay back in the bed again, remembering my little box with Derek and wanting to climb back inside and wrap myself in his arms. Last night he'd entered me from behind, kissing my neck, his scruffy beard teasing the sensitive places around my shoulders. His large fingers massaged my clit until I came so hard . . .

I blinked at the ceiling a few times acknowledging it was all a fantasy—at least that version of us together was. It had been *my* small fingers doing the massaging, and nothing teased the sensitive areas of my shoulders, although the idea of that still made me shiver.

I threw back the covers and got up, shaking the crazy out of my brain. Everything in my life had been upended, and now I was thousands of miles from home, having sex with a practical stranger and inventing an entire fantasy-life around him. Maybe I did need some time on Mom's couch.

As if on cue, my phone flashed her photograph, silently vibrating in the chair where I'd tossed it last night. I'd been avoiding her calls, not wanting to tell her what was happening. But I couldn't hide forever.

I slid my finger across the face. "Hi, Mom."

"Melissa, where are you?" Her stern voice was tinged with worry. I was almost sure I knew why.

"I'm with Elaine, Mom, why?"

She exhaled into the receiver. "You're at the beach? Why didn't you tell me you were headed this way?"

I bit my lip, choosing my words, still fishing for why she might be calling. "What's got you so worked up?"

"Sloan called this morning looking for you, and I didn't know what to tell him."

My chest clenched. *Bingo*. "I'm just taking a mental health break. You're a big advocate of those, right?"

"Do you need to make an appointment? Maybe with Robin? I know she could work you in if you're in town."

Talking to Mom's partner was actually a great idea. Dr. Taylor was compassionate and didn't take sides. Although everyone had already taken sides in my case it seemed.

"I'm actually not in town, Mom. I'm in the desert."

"What? Where?"

"This spa resort . . . somewhere. It's really nice."

She didn't answer, and I could tell she wasn't happy with my evasiveness.

"Look, I'm really trying to get away from everything for a few days, get my head together," I said. "I'm with Elaine, so I'm fine. Let's just leave it at that."

She finally spoke slowly. "I don't like it. What if something happened? I wouldn't even know how to find you."

"You just did," I sighed. "Please. Trust me?"

I heard her matching my exhale. "When will you be back?"

"We're only here a week. I'll be in Baltimore on Monday."

"Call me when you get there."

I agreed and hung up, but the image of me back in Maryland was almost too painful to conjure. Every time I tried, all I could see was me walking, shoulders stooped, as if an invisible weight were strapped to them, dragging me down, lower and lower. This trip had been an escape I needed more than even I'd realized. Elaine had seen something I couldn't see. I was desperate, and it was only getting worse the longer I stayed there.

Being here was like taking a deep breath of fresh air, like standing up straight for the first time in a year. Now I wasn't sure if I'd be able to return to that old life, even for a day.

I rubbed my forehead and went into the bathroom. But I had to go back, at least to get my things, close up my office . . . I'd worry about those details when the time came. As it was, I still had three more days, and if I were counting time with Derek, they would be pretty incredible.

I lifted the red bikini off the bathroom hook and swept my hair into a high ponytail. If Elaine was gone all day, I was spending it at the pool.

SIX

ALL SORTS OF OPTIONS

AFTER AN ENTIRE MORNING IN the desert sun, I was now under the umbrella, sipping a wine spritzer, my plate of raw-food "lunch" devoured. Elaine's review boards were entirely right about everything at the Cactus Flower Spa. The pool boys were sexy, the massages were divine, and the raw food menu was for the birds. Literally. I was dying for a luscious steak dinner with all the trimmings.

Holding my magazine, I noticed a change in the light and glanced up expecting another visit by my server. I didn't expect to see Derek, looking fantastic in navy swim shorts and a maroon tee, holding a spa-issued towel. His blue eyes were hidden behind aviator sunglasses, but his dark hair moved easily in the dry breeze. A smile of approval was on his lips, and my entire body lit up like a firecracker.

"Red is definitely your color," he said in that low voice that made me wish for the nearest family bathroom.

"Hello," I said, pushing myself into a sitting position on the lounger. My cover-up was on my shoulders, but it was open, revealing the swimsuit he obviously admired. "Finished for the day?"

"Maybe," he said, sitting on the chair next to mine. "I was

craving a dip in the pool. Or something."

I smiled, almost, but not quite sure of his meaning. "I'm surprised they let you in the way they guard this place. Did you bribe one of the clinicians?"

"Yes," he said, pulling off his shirt. "A cool fifty, and the doors flew open."

The sight of his perfect chest and lined stomach caught my breath. Less than twenty-four hours ago, I'd been wrapped around him, and I was growing slick at the memory. I blinked down to the shimmering pool water, my whole body flushed.

"How did you find me?" I managed to say.

"I'm a detective, after all."

I returned his grin at that. "Oh, really?"

He chuckled. "Last night you told me your room number. I called and they said you were here."

I wasn't pleased with them giving out my location to unknown gentlemen callers, but in this case, I'd let it slide. My eyes drifted to the round tattoo near his shoulder. It was an anchor design blended with a skull over an *SF*.

"And that's for . . . ?"

He seemed confused then glanced down. "Oh. Marines." He shook his head. "Rite of passage, I guess."

"It's cool. Unique."

"I really enjoyed dinner on the patio last night," he continued, leaning back. "When Patrick said he was blowing off the day, I considered doing the same."

I slanted my eyes at him, confident enough to flirt. "Why didn't you?"

"Had a workshop at ten. But it was hard to concentrate."

One of the slim, tanned pool boys who just moments ago I'd conceded was "sexy" walked up. Now he looked like a child to me. "Drink, sir?"

Derek glanced over at the table beside me. "Two of whatever the lady's having."

The boy nodded and quickly left.

"It's just a wine spritzer, I should warn you."

That grin was back on his lips, making me want to kiss them. "What's with you and ordering drinks?"

I bit my lip unsure of how much to reveal. Then I shrugged. "It's been a while since I've done it for myself."

His blue eyes flickered to my face behind his glasses. I could tell his interest was piqued, and he wanted me to say more. "Sounds like a story."

I lifted the glass from the table beside me and finished the rest of my drink just as the server returned with two new ones.

"Maybe I'll tell it to you sometime." I was relaxed from the alcohol, and wanting to stay in this place of bliss with him. "But not now. It's too depressing."

He nodded. Then he sat up. "I'm taking a dip. It's warmer than I expected."

I watched as he stood and walked to the pool. He was literally perfect, and I noticed many eyes following him into the water. He submerged beneath the crystal blue surface and shot to the other side of the long pool.

Up until now, he'd been the initiator of all our encounters. Elaine was gone for the day, our room was empty. Would I invite him up? Did I want to get that close? As I pondered the question, he surfaced on the other side of the pool. Wiping his eyes he turned, then went under and shot back in my direction. In moments, he was back, surfacing in front of me, and when our blue eyes met, a loud *Yes!* echoed in my head.

Standing, I let my cover-up slide off my shoulders, and I tossed it on the lounge chair. My hair was still in a high ponytail, and as I walked to meet him in the pool, his eyes tracked my progress. He leaned back against the side, stretching his arms out, and his focused attention set my pulse humming under my skin. With every step, desire throbbed stronger in my core, and by the time I lowered myself into the pool, it was all I could do to keep my hands to myself. I pictured drifting one under the water to his waist, running my fingers down the front of his swim trunks, coaxing him to an erection. His face said it wouldn't take much. But I kept my expression neutral.

"The water's nice," I said, leaning against the wall beside him.

He nodded. "Refreshing."

"This morning I was thinking how little we know about each other."

His eyes were still on me, traveling from my face to my hair then back to my mouth, where they lingered. My lips tingled for his touch.

"What do you want to know?" His tone had become low and sexy.

"I don't know," I said, trying to think of neutral things we could share. Questions that wouldn't lead to subjects I didn't want to discuss. "What's your favorite color?"

"Red," he answered quickly.

I smiled, and my cheeks warmed. "Seriously."

He leaned forward, returning my smile as he lowered his arms into the water. "I've never really had a favorite color until now."

I turned and bent my elbows on the side, resting them on the mosaic tiles leading into the pool. We were so close, my upper arm touched his shoulder. It was electric.

"Okay," I said slowly, thinking. "What was your favorite game as a boy?"

"Football."

A little laugh escaped my lips, and I lay my cheek on my forearms. "You're not giving me anything memorable."

His hand drifted under the water to my side, where he lightly ran the back of his fingers down my skin from my ribs to my hip. My eyes closed as desire flooded into my lower abdomen, and I fought a moan.

"I'll tell you something memorable," he said in that sensual voice. "But I'd rather do it in private."

My eyes opened slowly, and I wondered if he could read my

thoughts. He turned and pushed against the tiles, his muscles flexing as he rose out of the water. Little droplets ran down his torso, and an image of me licking them off almost made me burst into flames. I quickly followed him out and back to our things on the lounge chairs. Our wine still sat on the small table between them.

"Should we take our drinks upstairs?" I said.

"I was waiting for you to ask."

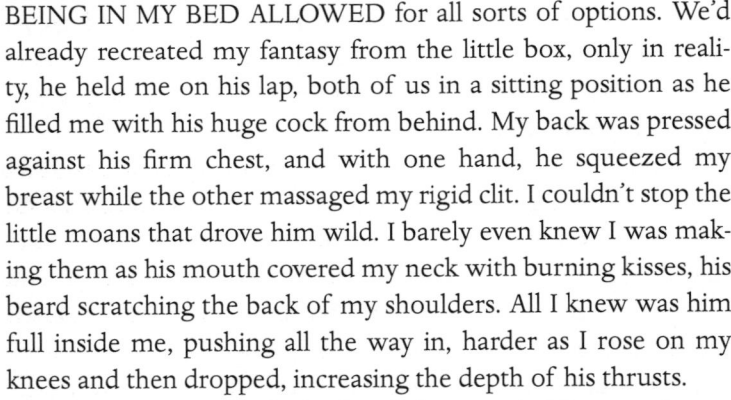

BEING IN MY BED ALLOWED for all sorts of options. We'd already recreated my fantasy from the little box, only in reality, he held me on his lap, both of us in a sitting position as he filled me with his huge cock from behind. My back was pressed against his firm chest, and with one hand, he squeezed my breast while the other massaged my rigid clit. I couldn't stop the little moans that drove him wild. I barely even knew I was making them as his mouth covered my neck with burning kisses, his beard scratching the back of my shoulders. All I knew was him full inside me, pushing all the way in, harder as I rose on my knees and then dropped, increasing the depth of his thrusts.

"Fuck," he groaned, the hand that was holding my breast now moved to my stomach, pulling me harder against him. Our thighs crashed as I moved on him, and the sensation of his rock-hard dick hitting my G-spot while his expert fingers massaged my clit conjured images I'd seen of women coming like men, wet and everywhere. Three more hard thrusts, and I was flying to the moon.

I dropped my head back and came so hard, my whole body shook. He kept pushing, and I gripped his hands, squirming and moaning, desperate for him to keep going, but unsure if I could take any more of this intense pleasure.

"Ooh, god," I wailed, and we both slid forward onto the bed.

He was still inside me gently thrusting, and I rubbed my thighs together, shaking but easing down from the rocket high I'd just hit, savoring the feel of his huge cock massaging my return.

I lay on my stomach, Derek propped behind me, watching me, his pace slowing. We were both breathing so hard, I could feel his warm breath against my back. As much as I hated losing our connection, I slipped off him and turned, resting my cheek on his chest and wrapping my arms around his waist. His strong arms went around me, holding me securely several long moments as my body calmed. Inhaling him deeply, I placed a small kiss against his skin.

"Did you finish?" I whispered.

He chuckled. "If I hadn't been wearing a condom, it might've shot out your ears I came so hard."

My nose wrinkled, but I had to laugh. "That's a lovely image."

"You drive me crazy." His hands went to my shoulders, and he eased up to look into my eyes. "I don't know what to do with you. With this."

I blinked down, not wanting to start this conversation with him. He wouldn't like the way it ended. I didn't like the way it ended in my mind.

"You seem to have a pretty good idea what to do with me," I tried deflecting.

I pulled away from his gaze, resting my cheek against his chest once more. His fingers traced lines down my back, and I closed my eyes, loving this moment, wanting to permanently brand it on my memory so I'd never forget it. Never forget him.

"That night you didn't meet me, I was pretty frustrated," he said. "All day I'd caught your scent on my hair, my beard . . . then I showered before going to the bar, and you were gone."

I chewed my lip thinking how I'd done the same—lifted my dark curls to smell his warm woodsy scent that was now all around me, filling my bed.

"I was desperate to see you one more time just to get that

luscious scent on me again," he finished.

I lifted my head, teasing. "Are you saying you haven't showered in two days?"

He caught my cheeks and pulled my lips to his, covering my mouth in a gentle kiss. My lips parted and the tips of our tongues touched lightly, setting off a little spark below my waist.

"I'm just giving you a peek at what you're doing to me," he said, his voice low.

I slid down, resting my cheek on his firm pectorals, tracing the lines with my fingers. We were quiet a moment, then I thought of us at the pool, our unfinished conversation. "You were going to tell me something memorable," I said.

His hand returned to my back where he lightly touched my skin. "Yes," he murmured, and my head rose with his inhale. "What do you want to know?"

Everything, my stubborn mind answered. Instead, I said, "You were telling me about when you were a boy. Your favorite game. Start there."

He was quiet, thoughtful. "My dad was in the military. A few times when I was pretty young, he was sent on missions where I knew he might not come back."

He paused, but my interest was piqued. "How did you know?" I asked.

"I could tell by the way my mom cried when he left." His hand continued stroking my back. "It scared me so bad I couldn't sleep at night."

In my mind, I pictured a kid-sized version of him, dark hair, blue eyes, lying alone in the dark. Afraid. It was an image I could relate to well, and instinctively, my arm went around his waist.

"What did you do?" I said.

His tone remained calm, comforting. "I made up a game. I thought about my favorite thing to do with my dad. And I decided as soon as he got back, we'd do that together."

"What was it?"

He inhaled deeply. "Different things. Sometimes it was as

simple as throwing a football together. But focusing on us doing it, having fun, smiling, helped me know I'd survive the pain of waiting."

My eyes were damp. "It's a very sophisticated approach for a little kid."

I felt him shrug. "It didn't solve the problem. It just gave it an end point."

I thought about what he was saying, and I thought about my situation. "But what if it feels like the pain will never go away?"

His hand stilled on my back. "It will. Eventually. Sometimes you're not even aware it's gone and then something happens, something unexpected, and you realize it's no longer there."

I lifted off him, sliding my fingers under my lower lashes before propping my head on my hand. He wrapped a dark curl around his finger as his gaze traveled from my lips to my eyes. I wanted to know what he meant, if he had experience with pain like that, like mine, but we were venturing far too close to off-limits topics. Instead I changed directions.

"So you followed in your dad's footsteps and joined the military," I said, looking back at his beautiful blues. "You were so young. What was it like in Iraq?"

His lips tightened. "Lonely. Scary at times."

"Did you use your game?"

A small smile touched his lips. "Sometimes."

"Did it work?"

His eyes moved away from mine, and he didn't answer. Then it struck me—he might have things he didn't want to share as well.

"I'm sorry," I said. "We're probably breaking the rules of a one-week stand."

"Probably," he said, but his tone was different. "I wouldn't know."

We'd gone too far, and it was my fault. I had wanted to ask questions. I wanted to know everything about him. But I'd forgotten I couldn't. No matter how my heart craved knowing him, what we were doing couldn't last beyond this week. When I left this place, I returned to everything I was pretending didn't exist, and that was no place for him.

The thought pressed on my mind, threatening to spoil our private escape. So I lowered my hand and moved up to kiss him, to take us back to what we were able to share. My hands cupped his cheeks, and his fingers that had been tracing lines on my skin began massaging, moving lower. I rolled onto my back, tugging his shoulders as I did. He readily complied, rising above me, deepening our kiss.

My hands moved from his shoulders, down his arms, finding his hard stomach. His lips pressed mine apart as his tongue swept inside to curl around mine. My legs opened automatically, allowing him between them, and in a breath, he pushed inside me, hard and full. We hadn't done much foreplay, and we'd only just come down from our last shattering climax. But it didn't matter. I was already wet. The little we had shared deepened my desire for him, and the fullness of him pushing into me, combined with his mouth covering mine, moving to my jaw, lightly nibbling on my neck, sent heat shimmering down my legs. My insides bonded to him, melted into him, wrapped around him, holding him to me. But I couldn't name what I was feeling.

Never in my life had I dreamed I would enjoy being with someone like him so much, and now I couldn't imagine having anyone else in my bed. He was enormous over me—I was only five four, almost a whole foot shorter and just at 120 pounds—and I knew I'd never be satisfied with anything less again.

"You're so quiet," he whispered against my ear before kissing it, still rocking into me slowly.

I was holding him, loving the feel of his fullness sliding in and out of me. He kissed my neck again, and I wrapped my arms tighter over his shoulders. I never wanted to let him go.

"Mmm," I breathed. "It's even good slow."

His hands moved to my buttocks and together we rolled

over so that I was on top. But I stayed with my torso pressed against his, kissing his mouth, kissing a trail down his neck to his chest.

A low groan vibrated through his upper body, and I sped up my rocking. Instantly, the friction triggered my climb, and I increased the pace. I sat up fully then, bucking my hips against his pelvis as he watched me. My dark curls spilling all around me.

"Fuck, Mel," he gasped. "You're so hot. I'm fucking about to come again."

He gripped my butt, easily lifting me up and down and he seemed to grow larger. I was moaning now as the pressure built in my legs, tightened through my lower abdomen.

"Fuck," he murmured again, increasing the speed as he lifted me, slamming me back down against his hips. "I can't hold it."

I felt him shoot off and instantly my orgasm exploded through my legs. He was still lifting me up and down, and I collapsed forward, pulsing in his arms. He gently stopped lifting me and held me as we rolled back to him on top, still inside me.

"I'm sorry," he breathed, lifting up and fixing his blue eyes on mine. "I wasn't expecting that. I didn't have a chance to prepare."

For a moment, I didn't want to move. The sensations humming under my skin were so strong, so sensual. My eyes slowly opened, and I studied his beautiful face, tracing a finger over his dark brow, thinking how fantastically our bodies worked together. I had a hard time wrapping my mind around it.

"It's okay," I whispered. "I'm still on the pill."

The dark brows I'd just caressed drew together. "Sounds like I had a lucky slip."

A tiny laugh slipped out with my exhale. He had no idea. "You could say that."

"When I told you that first night I was clean, I was being honest," he said, the powerful hands that were so strong to lift me—and probably anything else—gently traveled up my body, smoothing back my hair. "It's been a while since I've been with anyone, and last time I checked, I was all clear."

I nodded. "I've never done anything like this before," I whispered. "But I've had a reason to keep up with things. You're safe with me."

He lowered his face to kiss me gently and right then it was inescapable. The seemingly endless kiss he pressed, soft lips lingering against mine, tongue lightly touching my tongue, sealed it for me. He was everything I wanted. He *was* safe with me, I felt safe with him, and I wanted him to hold me forever so badly.

But in that simple acknowledgment, my heart sank in my chest. This blissful paradise we were sharing, our strange arrangement, was drowned by my dismal reality. I was not one he could hold.

SEVEN

WHAT I'D GIVE YOU

ELAINE AND PATRICK MET US for dinner in the hotel restaurant. They were beaming like blissed-out honeymooners and seemed unable to stop touching each other in little ways, laughing easily and holding hands. I figured they'd spent the day doing at least a little of what Derek and I'd shared, and I wished I was free to look at him that way, to share my passion for him so overtly.

Everything in me was falling in love with Derek, but that didn't change a single thing about my situation. About my unavailability. Add to that, he hadn't said anything to indicate he wanted more than our original week. It felt like he might want more, every time we were together I was sure his feelings were growing as intensely as mine, but he hadn't said anything to confirm it.

Following our last round this afternoon, I'd fallen asleep in his arms and vaguely remembered waking as he slid from my side, lightly kissing my head and whispering that he'd see me at dinner. I'd continued sleeping another hour before I'd risen to shower.

Tonight, I wore a short, black dress with thin spaghetti straps. A sterling silver cuff bracelet was on my wrist and large silver hoop earrings were the extent of my accessorizing. As always, Derek smiled, clearly pleased with my appearance. The three were already sharing a bottle of wine when I joined them, Derek stood to help me in my chair.

"You look beautiful," he said softly, his breath whispering over my shoulder, causing a shiver to tingle through me.

Neither Elaine nor Patrick even noticed, and I was pretty sure they were oblivious to the connection between their dinner mates. All they were focused on was the growing connection between the two of them.

Derek poured me a glass of wine, and I took it with a little nod of thanks. Patrick broke his nonstop gazing at my best friend to greet me.

"So it seems you had a fun day?" I said, teasing.

Elaine flushed. "You could say that."

I tried for a neutral subject, something we could all discuss, and since Patrick had told us so much about their work last night, it seemed a safe option. "You never told me where you two are based, where your office is located," I said.

Patrick smiled, sipping his wine. "Princeton."

"New Jersey?" I asked, slightly stunned. Princeton was an easy two-hour drive from my office in Baltimore, as I knew well. The accompanying thoughts his words conjured made my stomach burn.

"Derek teaches a few classes at the university."

"You do?" Elaine asked.

"We're hardly there," Derek added quickly, and for a moment, he almost seemed annoyed at Patrick's answer.

"I had a client at Princeton once," I said, not sure how those words managed to creep out. Elaine's eyes cut to mine.

"Really?" Patrick said. "Who was it?"

"Sloan Reynolds." Saying his name left a foul taste in my mouth, and I wished I'd never brought it up. I wanted off this train of thought. "I did some work for his family, actually."

The conversation momentarily stalled as Patrick seemed to

think. "Don't know him," he finally said. "Sorry."

"It was several years ago." I finished that topic, taking a sip of my wine to cleanse my palate.

Patrick looked down then held his wine glass aloft, turning back to Elaine. "To unexpected surprises."

My friend beamed at that. "Isn't it the truth?"

They clinked glasses and Patrick covered Elaine's hand with his again, smiling.

I looked back at Derek, giving him a tight smile. "It's so bright in here."

His eyes were warm now, focused on me. "The fire pit is a much nicer setting, I think."

"And you're in Wilmington," Patrick said to Elaine.

"Yep," my friend replied. "Been there all my life. It's where Melissa and I met."

Derek glanced at me. "But you're not there now."

"No," I said softly, wondering when I'd been so unguarded to tell him that. My home location was definitely a one-week stand rules violation.

"She's hours away in Baltimore," Elaine complained.

"It's only six hours. Don't exaggerate." Now I wished I'd thought up a different topic of conversation. I wanted this exploration into my personal life to end. "So tell me about your day. What all did you do?"

That did it. Instantly she was off describing their hike up Camelback Mountain. They'd found a secret cleft in the rocks, she continued, and from the way my friend grinned at that detail, it seemed they'd done more than hike while there. Patrick smiled and squeezed her hand, a little spark in his eye. Our waiter took our orders, and I selected the steak I'd been craving earlier. Derek followed suit.

"At least your food orders are better than your drinks," he teased.

I smiled. "I never stopped choosing my own food."

"Shall I pick a wine to go with it?"

"Please do," I said, wishing I could reach out and touch his hand the way our dinner companions kept doing. His eyes flickered to mine, and it seemed he might be thinking the same thing.

Elaine continued detailing their day, a tour of Taliesin West, a visit to one of the nearby ghost towns. I was amazed they'd been able to fit it all in.

"Tomorrow I was thinking we'd drive to Sedona," Patrick said, looking at Derek.

Derek waved his hand. "Do what you want. We're pretty much finished as far as the conference goes."

His words made my heart sink, knowing the end was so near. I lifted my glass and took a long sip of the pinot noir he'd ordered—perfect for the petite filet I was having. I felt him studying my reaction, and I wondered how he felt about the end of this week. Did it sadden him as much as it did me?

"We're pretty much done here," he said, rising. "I'll ask the host to put it on my bill if you'd like to take a walk outside with me?"

Elaine's eyes flew to mine, and she gave me an encouraging smile.

"Sure," I said, standing.

"I think you can take your glass if you'd like to finish it," Derek said, holding my chair.

"That's okay," I said. "I've had enough."

Patrick and Elaine stayed behind, and she smiled in a way that I knew meant she was dying to give me two thumbs up. If she only knew how behind she was. I just shook my head and took Derek's arm, allowing him to escort me from the large dining area.

It was another beautiful twilight, the sun slowly setting, turning the desert sky a myriad of dusky autumnal shades. I couldn't stop my mind from counting the time we had left—only two nights. We'd fly out early Sunday, and I'd return to my situation in Maryland.

We strolled along the path lining the resort's large golf course. I had so many things I wished I could say, and none that I could truly act upon. I wanted to exchange contact information, make plans to follow up when we got home, to be together, to hold onto him . . .

Derek wasn't speaking either. He seemed a million miles away, and I wondered if his thoughts were following a similar course as mine. As always, he was incredibly handsome in grey, tailored slacks and a navy, short-sleeved sweater. It was thin and hugged the lines of his torso.

"Patrick and Elaine seem to be enjoying the trip," I finally said, holding his arm as we walked.

"Hm," Derek nodded, but he didn't say more.

"Is anything wrong?" I asked, not sure if I wanted to know his answer. If something was wrong, and it was anything like I suspected, I wouldn't be able to ease his mind.

His forehead creased, and he looked out at the horizon, speaking quietly. "This afternoon, being with you . . . It wasn't what I expected."

"It wasn't?" My chest sank. To me this afternoon had set the bar on intensity so high, I was pretty sure I'd never top it. Hearing he might've thought less of it almost killed me.

He exhaled then gave me a sad little smile. "It was intense." We took a few more steps, and he added just above a whisper. "Too fucking intense."

My breath returned, and I gently squeezed his arm. "I've made some pretty lasting memories with you this week."

He stopped then and faced me. "Patrick's got a big mouth. He's said things about me I thought were best left off the record."

I looked down, not wanting to meet his eyes, not wanting him to see the tears forming in mine. "Elaine, too."

"In my line of work, when people don't want you to know their story, they usually have a damn good reason."

I wasn't sure if he was talking about himself or me, but I had to agree. "You're right."

"And pursuing that story only leaves everyone, well, pretty damaged." His voice wasn't angry, but it had a definite tone. I just couldn't tell what he was getting at. Was he saying he understood my need for privacy? Was he trying to tell me his? Or worse, was he trying to cut the week short? Had it gotten too intense for him?

The last thought sliced painfully through my heart. "Sometimes, the damage is already done."

"Listen to me," he put his hands on my cheeks and tilted my face up to look at his. When he saw my eyes glistening, his expression changed. His eyes closed and he lowered his forehead to mine, exhaling the words. "What have I done?"

My hands clasped over my aching heart. "What have you done?" I managed to say.

He'd fucking made me fall in love with him is what he'd done, and now I'd return to Baltimore worse off than when I got here. But I couldn't say that out loud. It wasn't his fault I'd lost control. He'd said one week. I was the one who'd ended up wanting everything I couldn't have.

He lifted his head and then kissed me, softly at first. His lips held mine a moment before the softness turned less gentle. His mouth moved, opening mine and finding my tongue. Heat flared through me as they touched, and his hands moved to my butt, lifting me against him. Easily my legs went around his waist, my arms around his neck. I was kissing him back in spite of the pain.

How could I waste time on self-preservation when our time together was so short? He broke our kiss, dropping his forehead to my cheek. His hands were securely holding my rear, and I moved my hands to his face, making him look up at me again. His brow was creased and his blue eyes were so earnest, yet so full of all the things he wouldn't tell me. How could I be angry when there were so many things I wouldn't tell him?

"If things were different," I said. "I'd tell you I love you right now."

His forehead relaxed, and his eyes closed. The smallest hint of a smile tried to form on his lips, but I wouldn't let myself see it. Instead I leaned forward and kissed him hard on the mouth. He kissed me back with an equal amount of passion, then I pushed against his chest, lowering my legs. He released me, brows pulled together again not understanding. I didn't stay to explain.

I turned and walked fast, not looking back. A few more steps and I was jogging across the grassy area that separated the patio from the spa hotel. He didn't follow me. He let me go back to my room, where I collapsed into the bed, tears rolling from my eyes.

ELAINE DIDN'T COME BACK TO the room that night, and when I awoke the next morning, a note had been slipped under the door.

Please call the front desk. A parcel has been left for you.

Curiously, I picked up the in-house phone and pressed 0. Alerting the hostess I was awake, she said she'd send the parcel right up, and I went to retrieve one of the thick robes that hung in the bathroom. I paused, checking my reflection. My eyes were only a little puffy from crying. I picked up a washcloth and wet it with cold water, holding it gently to them.

All night I'd dreamed of him. We didn't stay in the little box in my mind, we jumped out of it and ran free and clear all over my life. Derek carried me back to Wilmington, and we made love on the beach in my old hometown. We ran hand in hand through all of my favorite places from my memory, and everywhere he fit in as perfectly as if he was always meant to be there. It broke my heart. My dreams could be so cruel.

Just then the tapping started on my door. I jumped out of

bed and ran across the room. The girl handed me a small package, and I handed her a tip. Then I closed the door and went back to the bed, ripping off the paper and pulling out a black velvet box.

For a moment, I hesitated. Then I carefully pulled the top open. Inside was a delicate gold chain on which a floating heart hung. A small note dropped out, and I opened it.

What I would give you. If you hadn't already stolen it.–D.A.

My lips pressed together as my eyes misted. Gently pulling the chain from the box, I fastened the necklace around my neck. The tag indicated it was 24 karat gold. It would never tarnish. I could leave it on forever if I chose. In the mirror in my room, I saw the delicate charm sat just at the base of my throat, in the little hollow between my collar bones where he'd often kissed me. I touched it gently.

He'd survive without his heart. He had mine to use in its place.

EIGHT

SOMETHING TRULY MAJOR

ELAINE CALLED TO SAY SHE and Patrick were driving to Sedona as planned and wouldn't be back until late. I assured her I would be fine in her absence.

"Did you make any progress with Derek," she asked eagerly. "The man is sex on two legs, don't you think?"

Yes. "What are you saying?" I replied. "Aren't your eyes only for Patrick?"

"Of course! Patrick is amazing, and I'm not interested in trading at all. But I'm also not blind."

"Derek is very sexy."

"Very alpha," she said in a tone like she was reading my mind. "And ex-military. I know you tend to shy away from those."

I almost wished that were true. "He is a lot of man, but at the same time, he can be tender."

Her voice rose in excitement. "So you did get to know him better? Oh, Mel, if you got laid on this trip by that hunk of—"

"Hey," I cut her off. "Have fun today and be safe."

"You, too," she said. "Please do everything I would do."

I laughed, fingering the little heart floating at my neck as I hung up the phone. "Okay."

WHEN I'D RUN OFF LAST night, leaving him at the fire pit, I'd also left without a plan for us meeting today. At the same time, when I reflected on our conversation up to that point, I wasn't sure if the door was still open to us meeting today.

Yes, I'd kissed him and told him I wished I could say I loved him. And he'd sent me this lovely gift, but the words we'd said before that . . .

Was it best to leave these tokens as our last goodbye?

Everything in me screamed *No!* If he was within steps of me, I had to try and find him. I considered going to Room 213 and pounding on his door, but I hesitated. If I did that, I'd be sending a message I couldn't live up to. I'd be saying I was his, and I couldn't say that.

I lay across my bed, again touching the floating heart on my neck. My eyes warmed. But I wanted to see him so badly. What could I do? As if on cue, my room telephone rang, and I snatched it up without hesitation.

"Good morning," his low voice touched me through the wires.

"Good morning," I replied softly. "I was just thinking about you. And you called."

"Did you get my gift?"

"I love it so much." My voice was tight with longing for what we couldn't have.

"I wasn't sure if you'd want to see me—"

"I do!" I sat straight up, clutching the receiver against my face as if it were his. "When? Where?"

He breathed a laugh. "Want to meet at the pool again?"

"Why don't we meet at the main hotel pool? Then you can save the fifty."

"It doesn't matter," he said. "I'd spend it again gladly."

"Give me thirty minutes," I said, throwing the covers back.

"I'll be there in five."

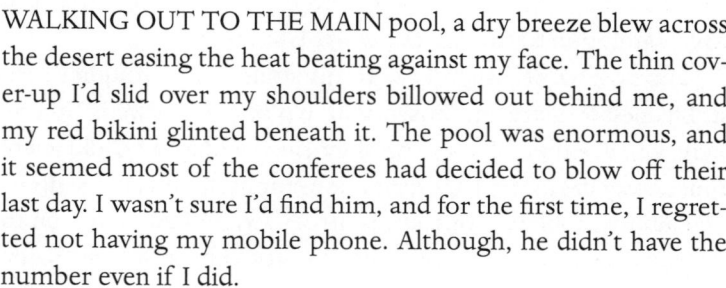

WALKING OUT TO THE MAIN pool, a dry breeze blew across the desert easing the heat beating against my face. The thin cover-up I'd slid over my shoulders billowed out behind me, and my red bikini glinted beneath it. The pool was enormous, and it seemed most of the conferees had decided to blow off their last day. I wasn't sure I'd find him, and for the first time, I regretted not having my mobile phone. Although, he didn't have the number even if I did.

I paused, scanning every face, when I felt a warm presence behind me.

"Looking for me?" His deep voice caused my eyes to close automatically in delight.

I spun around smiling. "Yes," I breathed.

His blue eyes smiled back, flickering down to the necklace, his heart still sitting at the base of my throat. He blinked, and I saw the sadness I felt mirrored in his eyes, but only for a moment. As if he'd made the same resolution as me, he quickly pushed sadness away. We still had twenty-four hours together.

"Come this way," he said, taking my bag. "I've got us a few chairs near an umbrella."

I followed him past rows of loungers occupied by humans of all shapes and colors smiling, drinking, laughing, or relaxing. It was clearly the end of the week, and while for most, that was cause for celebration, for us, it was a sadness that kept trying to sneak in.

"Wine spritzers," he said, leading me around the lounger.

I laughed. "Why?"

"They're surprisingly refreshing in this heat." He stretched out on a chair, lifting a silicone wine glass and tapping mine. I watched him toss back the sparkling beverage and sipped mine.

I didn't want to be fuzzy. I wanted to remember everything.

He rolled to his side, watching as I slid the cover-up down my shoulders. I almost felt shy as his lips curled up slowly in approval. "Red," he murmured.

"It's funny," I said, fumbling with my towel. "I've never paid much attention to the colors I wore. Until now."

His nose curled slightly with his smile, and I couldn't help it. I leaned forward and kissed him. No one here cared. No one here knew either of us. The only two people who did were miles away exploring rock formations (or each other) in Sedona, and all my problems were even further away. I had no reason to hesitate in showing my affections. We could be as free as Elaine and Patrick.

Pausing before I straightened up again, I slid my fingers into the side of his thick, wavy hair. "I love this," I whispered.

He caught my waist, pulling me to sitting on the side of his chair then he sat up as well, swinging his legs around and pulling me close to his body.

"You can't do things like that," he said, planting his lips against my shoulder. I shivered as he made his way up my neck, behind my ear. "I thought about you all night. I almost knocked on your door."

My pulse beat fire under my skin, and everywhere his lips touched seemed to ignite. The slickness between my thighs had me wanting to lead him into one of the cabanas, where I could slip off my bottoms and straddle his lap. We could easily come together and no one would ever know.

"You could've," I breathed, my eyes closing. "Elaine never came back."

"Patrick's a lucky bastard," he said. But I paused. My expression caused him to laugh. "I only mean he has no reason to hesitate."

"And you do?"

That stopped his progress. He looked into my eyes for a moment, not speaking. Then he said softly. "Everything you've done tells me I do."

I bit my lip looking down. He was right. I'd been secretive and distant, putting up boundaries around questions we couldn't ask, paths we couldn't follow. Even if he didn't know why, he knew I was hiding something, and it was something big enough that no amount of fantastic sex could break down the wall.

"We only have one more day," I said. "Can we stay off that path just a few more hours?"

He nodded. "Of course."

I kissed his lips once more, then I stood and spread out my towel on the second lounger in the sun. Lying back with my aviators on, I took a deep breath. I lifted the glass and took a drink, cooling the fire he'd lit under my skin.

The sun was hot, but it felt good to me. The constant breeze kept it from being unbearable.

"I'm getting in for a bit," he said, and I watched him walk to the pool, his perfect physique turning many heads.

How had I managed to capture his affection? How long could I hold onto it outside this secret oasis in the desert? My situation wasn't forever. Would it be possible to find him once my problems were resolved? Was it realistic to think he might still be available? Waiting for me? Asking him to do so would mean having to explain why, and considering his line of work, that would open a whole kettle of complicated fish.

My eyes squeezed shut, and I lay my head back. I could only conquer one problem at a time. Getting back, I would put my plans in motion, then once everything was complete, perhaps I could pay a visit to the Alexander offices in Princeton. It was a short drive, and if he was as well-known as Elaine said, he should be easy to find.

I took another long sip, finishing my glass, and when I looked up, Derek was headed back in my direction. He was dripping from the pool again and looking so sexy. Without his sunglasses, I could see his eyes travel from my toes, up my calves to my thighs, to my breasts where they lingered before meeting my eyes. The dark blue hadn't faded, and the closer he got, the more I wanted to satisfy his hunger. He sat on his lounger facing me.

"I thought that would cool me," he said.

"Did it?" I asked, studying his expression.

"No." His eyes traveled down my body again.

"What can we do about that?"

At that opening, his eyes snapped back to mine. "My room's the closest."

Without another word, I sat up and slid my cover-up back over my shoulders. His brow relaxed, and he grabbed his shirt off the top of the chair. I picked up my bag and followed him past the rows of sunbathers, admiring the movement of his firm butt as he walked. Every step flexed a different muscle, and I grew tense with anticipation the closer we got to the elevators.

I hoped we'd have the space to ourselves, but no such luck. An elderly patron boarded the lift with us as we made our way to the second floor. It was probably for the best. We might not have made it to our destination otherwise. Room 213 wasn't too far down the hall. I watched as he slid his door key quickly in and out of the silver box, the tension of waiting those final seconds taunted my desire for him.

The door closed behind us, I dropped my bag, and he turned, lifting me against him and bruising my mouth with kisses. My arms were wrapped tightly around his neck, my mouth open and eager to meet his. Tongues collided, and he walked, carrying me to the king-sized bed filling the room. I felt him drop to his knees and opened my eyes as he slid me back on the amazingly soft white linens.

I helped, easing myself to the center, but he stayed at the side, reaching forward and taking hold of my bikini bottoms. In one quick pull they were off. His smile was hungry, and he caught the backs of my knees, pulling my wet opening to his mouth. My head dropped back, and I moaned deeply as his warm tongue slowly circled the little spot that drove me wild. It was hot and gentle then rough and sucking. My hips followed his movements, and when his beard scuffed my skin, I flinched, thrilled by the added sensation. My muscles were so tight, and the little noises he loved were coming from my throat. In two more little pulls, his mouth covering my clit, I was flying. His fingers slipped inside me, and he groaned.

"You're so wet," he said, kissing the inside of my thigh.

"I want you so bad," I moaned. "Please . . . Don't make me beg."

He stood up fast, slipping down his shorts, and for the first time I saw his enormous cock before it entered me fully erect.

"Oh, god," I hissed, reaching out to wrap my fingers around him. "You're huge."

His lids drooped as my hand slid down his considerable length and then back up it. I couldn't resist. I put the tip into my mouth and sucked. I couldn't take him all in, he was far too big, but I ran my tongue around him, teasing his ridges, enjoying his sharp intake of breath followed by his low moans. I pulled his tip in and out, sucking and taunting him with my tongue, pulsing my hand up and down his shaft. His hips rocked slightly as he made a low groan, gently touching my cheek. After only a few moments, he caught my hair and held my face back.

"I need to be inside you now." One glance at the large muscle I'd been playing with told me why. A tiny white drop escaped his slit, and I shivered knowing what that meant.

Quickly unfastening my bikini top, I moved back just as he joined me, pulling me down and filling me with his size.

"Ooh," I moaned as once again my body was stretched in the most delicious way possible. My orgasm that had only cooled slightly as I played with him came raging back with every thrust.

He groaned and rolled me on top of him, clutching my buttocks hard and lifting me, gripping me up and plunging me back down. I gasped, reaching forward, placing my palms flat against the headboard, rocking my clit against his shaft. The friction had me blazing and tight. His groans were animal and wild.

In my position, leaning forward, my breasts teased in his face, and his tiny sucks and bites registered directly between my legs. I shook with pleasure. That intense orgasm was on the brink of bursting through me. Two more impossibly deep thrusts and shudders exploded down my limbs.

"Derek . . ." I moaned, and he groaned low in response, still pushing into me. I gasped, my core muscles spasming around his enormous cock again and again, my fingers digging into the headboard as the orgasm radiated through my lower body.

He rocked his hips two more times, going deep into me and groaning loudly in release. Then I collapsed in his huge, strong arms, completely spent. He wrapped them around me, holding me tight against him as we rolled to the side. Our hearts pounded, our breath came so fast. My eyes were closed, and I felt his soft lips kissing my brows, my lids, moving to my nose, down to just gently touching my lips. I blinked slowly, and he smiled.

"You come in the most spectacular way for me," he said.

My first instinct was to be self-conscious, but he kissed me again.

"I've never made love like this," I said softly. "I've never felt it so intensely."

He kissed me lightly again. "It's amazing. You're amazing."

I was wrapped in the circle of his arms, feeling as safe as if I were in a cocoon. "I could say the same to you."

"I only do what you let me. If you weren't into it, none of this would happen."

I thought about that a moment. What was it about him that conjured this wild, sexual side of me I'd never known existed? The side that would follow a stranger to a dark, secluded patio for insane, animal fucking. Or into a family bathroom. That had me screaming in his bed? Was it just chemistry? Was it his confidence? Was it the way he was so sure of what I wanted and so ready to give it to me? I didn't have the answers. I only knew I'd lose something truly major when we said goodbye.

"I guess that's true," I finally said. "But you know exactly how to lead me there. And you're not just willing, you're eager to take me."

"Why the hell wouldn't I be?"

My brow lined, and this time when our eyes met, our expressions were serious, as if we both knew what was on the line tomorrow. I sighed, lowering my cheek to his chest, tracing my finger through the light sprinkling of hair there.

He continued lightly kissing my forehead, my cheek, and I drifted to sleep wishing that I never had to leave this wonderful spot.

NINE

THE END OF THE WEEK

I STAYED IN DEREK'S ROOM all night, and we made love several more times, passionately, gently, each time savoring our final moments together, until at last we *had* to sleep. When I opened my eyes to the sunlight bursting over the low hills, my heart broke. It was here. The end of the week.

Derek was still asleep behind me, his strong arms wrapped tightly around my waist as if he could protect me from what was waiting for my return if I let him. I knew he would, and I was certain he'd do a damn good job. But if that had been what I'd wanted, I'd have gone to the police a long time ago.

No, what I was dealing with I wanted to handle myself, and only involve the very few who absolutely had to know. I took a deep breath, thinking of the packing I hadn't done. Of the plane I had to catch in a few hours. I stretched, placing my hands on his forearms and gently moving them apart.

He released me, rolling onto his back, and I sat up, glancing over my shoulder to see him blinking at the ceiling. Then he turned to look at me. A sad smile in his eyes.

"Every morning this week I woke up wishing you were in my bed," he said, sliding my long dark curls off my back. He sat up and kissed the top of my shoulder, then my smiling lips. His hand slid to my waist then up, cupping my breast. Tingles rose along my legs at his touch, but I was out of time.

"I have to get back to my room," I sighed. "I haven't even begun to pack."

He kissed the top of my shoulder again, wrapping his arms around my waist. "I wish there was something I could do. Start the week over somehow."

I slid forward and picked up my bathing suit, wishing I'd packed at least a dress or something to wear for the walk back to the spa side.

"I keep thinking of all the missed opportunities," I smiled, sliding my cover up over my shoulders and leaning forward to kiss him. "Who needs food? Sleep? Manicures? I should've been with you."

He laughed and tried to hold onto me, but I stepped back. "And now I have to go." But as I said the words, the pain twisted in my chest.

His brow creased, and he stood, stepping into his discarded swim trunks. "Let me walk you back."

"We'll look ridiculous in swimsuits so early in the morning," I tried to laugh. To think of anything to ease the intense misery growing inside me. But it didn't work.

"I couldn't care less." He slipped the tee back over his head and took my hand, picking up my bag.

We caught the elevator down and then walked out into the still-cool morning. Neither of us spoke, but our hands were clasped tightly like two teenagers at the end of a summer romance. Once we reached the entrance to the spa hotel, he stopped and faced me.

"Last name?" he asked, but I shook my head no. I didn't want him investigating me. I didn't want him knowing. He exhaled. "I've been thinking. Maryland's not so far."

"I'll be going back to Wilmington soon," I said quietly.

He nodded, and something flickered in his eyes, thoughtful if still sad. "That's good. I hope you'll be happier there."

A line creased my brow. "What do you mean?"

"That first night I saw you in the bar," he paused, as if searching for the right words. "You were so sad."

I relaxed. "If I'm happy now, I have you to thank."

He reached forward and slid a curl off my cheek. "Thank you," he murmured.

I remembered his odd gratitude the few first times we'd made love. "Why did you? Thank me, I mean. Those first times."

"I knew you were doing something unusual, something you'd probably never have done." He paused a moment, choosing his words. "I kept holding my breath, waiting for you to push me away or make me stop, and when you didn't . . ."

"Thank you," I whispered.

He smiled. "You're amazing. And you let me have you."

He had no idea how much I'd let him have. For a moment we were quiet. I hated this goodbye so much. Suddenly, he reached forward and caught both my hands. He took a deep breath and looked straight into my eyes as if he'd just made a decision.

"I never expected things to go this way. To get so involved so fast." He paused, glancing briefly at our clasped hands. I started to speak, but he continued. "And then I said a week, as if I could just do this one-week thing . . ."

My stomach was so tight, but I only blinked, waiting to hear him out.

"We both have lives back home," he continued, "and maybe you can't share your life with me now. But I'd take your call anytime." He was holding my hands so securely. "I hope this goodbye isn't—"

"Forever," I said softly with him. His childhood game drifted through my memory.

My eyes were warm, and he stepped forward, releasing my hands and cupping my cheeks as he kissed me gently, then deeply. *When we see each other again, I thought, this is what we'll do.* I placed my hands over his, opening my mouth to him for the last time, fighting tears with everything I had. I didn't want his last memory to be of me crying.

When he stepped back, he touched the heart at my throat. "I meant what I wrote."

I lifted it in my fingers. "I'll take good care of it."

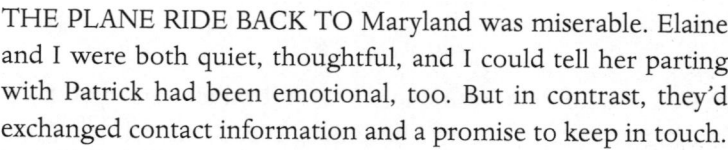

THE PLANE RIDE BACK TO Maryland was miserable. Elaine and I were both quiet, thoughtful, and I could tell her parting with Patrick had been emotional, too. But in contrast, they'd exchanged contact information and a promise to keep in touch. I couldn't do that.

In Atlanta, we parted ways, her headed east and me north. We hugged each other, and it was comforting to know we were close enough to be in this silent place of misery together and not have to question it, pick it apart, or even discuss it.

"So our next trip," she said, her voice quiet. "I'll start planning it the minute I get unpacked."

I nodded, my smile tight. Tears were close in my eyes, but my friend didn't seem to notice. I could tell she had her own tears to manage.

"Have a great start of the school year," I said, squeezing her hands, not wanting to let her go.

She hugged me close. "I'll be so glad when you're finally home."

"Me, too," I breathed. "It shouldn't be long now. I'll keep you posted."

With that we went our separate ways—at least temporarily.

The entire trip to Baltimore, I couldn't rest. I couldn't read. I only stared out the little window thinking of Derek and missing him so much. I was alone, headed back to my unfinished business, and Sloan had been calling the entire time. He was certain to be furious, and when he was furious . . .

I inhaled deeply as the announcer began telling us about the descent into the metropolitan airport. I collected my purse, which held the heart necklace in my wallet. I hadn't worn it because I'd have to explain, but I was keeping it safe and secure, hoping against hope that I'd be able to find him again. And that when I did, it might actually work as well in real life as it had in our little one-week summer oasis.

SLOAN'S CAR WAS WAITING FOR me when I emerged from baggage claim. I wouldn't have even seen it if Hal, his Asian driver, hadn't called out to me.

"Mr. Reynolds said you'll be needing a ride home," he said with a smile, taking my suitcase.

"H-he did?" Instantly my stomach clenched. If Sloan knew when I was arriving and which airline, he must've found out where I went. I wondered just how much he knew. Derek and I'd thrown discretion to the wind our last day at the pool, and my insides tensed at the thought of what Sloan might do if he found out I'd taken a lover.

"Yes, Mrs. Reynolds," Hal was still smiling. "He said you wouldn't be expecting me."

I exhaled deeply and felt my shoulders drop. I was back. "Thank you, Hal. And I'm not going by 'Mrs. Reynolds' anymore. I've told you that."

"Yes, ma'am," he said, but I could tell he was only humoring me. No telling what Sloan had told his staff about me. Probably that I had mental problems. Or at the very least, that the whole thing was my fault.

I took one last look over my shoulder, back at the concourse, and then blinked away the mist in my eyes as I turned and followed the black-uniformed employee to my husband's limo waiting to take me "home."

TEN

CUT THE TIES

NO ONE GREETED ME WHEN Hal dropped me at the front door. If I'd expected Sloan to be waiting with a snarl, I'd forgotten his style. He preferred to play it cool, aloof, much too busy for the childish behavior of his trophy wife. Then he'd strike for revenge once I'd forgotten I'd even done anything.

I hated him.

I slowly climbed the marble staircase to my room. Yes, we had separate rooms. This enormous house with a conservatory, a ballroom, and two formal dining areas—it was like something out of the fucking *Sound of Music*—had plenty of bedrooms, and my husband and I had only shared one for about two months when we moved here a year ago.

He'd complained it was too hot. He didn't have enough room. He suggested we get a California king-sized bed, but it was too late. The damage had been done, and I just wanted my own space. He snored anyway.

Today my luggage would be delivered to my private suite on the east wing of the mansion. The staff would wait for me to unload it and sort my clothes between the dirty and clean. Laundry was sent to an outside service then returned pressed and folded. The housekeeper, Mrs. Widlow met me at the top of the stairs. Her sleek grey hair hung in a straight bob that never moved, and as always, she wore a pantsuit and matching scarf. Today the suit was puce, the scarf lavender.

"Did you have a nice trip, Mrs. Reynolds?" she said.

"It was very relaxing," I answered. "And I've asked not to be called by that name any more."

"Of course, ma'am," she said.

Just like Hal.

They were Sloan's staff, and like the rest, she didn't give a shit what I said. Whatever Mr. Reynolds told them was law.

I continued making my way to my suite. The first time Sloan brought me here five years ago, when I was only twenty-six, everything about his huge mansion knocked my small-town socks off, from the grounds to the stables to the garage filled with all sorts of antique cars. Of course, at that time, it was still his father's mansion.

Back then, the only thing more impressive to me than this house was that Sloan Reynolds, Princeton graduate, mogul, inheritor of his father's export business, had taken an interest in me. I still hadn't figured that puzzler out.

I was simply an ambitious marketing major based on the Carolina coast but participating in workshops at big-wig universities hoping to make bank by snagging some major clients. I was freelance, but in this digital age, I had dreams of managing the world from my hammock on the beach.

My future husband had been on campus that day delivering a check or having his butt kissed by some needy department chair. He'd spotted me making my pitch and invited me to lunch. He was older, but at the time, he was still sexy to me. He was experienced and worldly—rich, smooth, and in control. He took me to the best restaurants, ordered the best wines. The rest was history.

Five years as Mrs. Sloan Reynolds had left me *very* cynical. About everything.

The first months of our marriage were good—he was kind

to me, and we enjoyed being together. Then slowly his interest faded. He seemed to enjoy my company less and less, and he started taking more and longer trips back to Baltimore.

When we relocated, his traveling increased. He said he had to take over his father's schedule, meeting with investors and potential customers in far-off locations. I was never invited to join him, and I later found out why.

He'd asked me to put my marketing career on hold and take his mother's place on her many local charity boards, auxiliaries, and civic associations. Of course, I agreed—anything to help with the transition. His father's death changed everything.

So my marketing business dwindled, and I made few client contacts in the city. Instead, I did what the wives of the super-wealthy did. I attended meetings, had teas, cut ribbons. The only problem was, I didn't want to give up my career. I didn't want to be a lady who lunched. I didn't even know how to play tennis.

I confess—I blamed myself a little for our marriage's "failure to thrive," as the counseling booklets called it. Sloan had swept me off my feet, and he had style. And drivers. And cache into all the best places. But apart from that, we had little in common. I told myself it didn't matter. We would grow into those things.

The opposite happened.

And as if to hasten the decline, our sex life never got off the ground. When we did have intercourse, he at least seemed satisfied. He gasped and groaned and got off, and I sort of followed along. But his hands never drifted below my waist, he didn't like blow jobs, didn't give me head. We would have one disappointing moment, and then months would go by before we'd try again.

Eventually, I quit trying.

I was depressed as hell when I found the receipt in his pants pocket. He'd spent two thousand dollars on a Jessica Black. It only took a few Google searches for me to discover Ms. Black was a high-end call-girl.

He told me it meant nothing. He was having a crisis. He needed to "feel" something again. And after all, she was just a "faceless whore." None of that mattered. I just wanted to be done with it. I wanted to go back to Wilmington and resume my career in marketing. I wanted to restart my freelance business, forget the whole marriage charade, and get back to what made me happy.

Six months had passed, and we'd tried counseling, therapy. I'd even talked to my mom, although I knew her advice before she offered it: All marriages hit rough patches, give it time. It had all been well and good until the night he decided he was tired of waiting for me to "get over it."

Until the night he changed everything.

After that I never wanted to see him again. I filed for divorce two weeks ago—the week before Elaine had taken me to Scottsdale for our spa retreat. I hadn't had a chance to tell anyone but her before we left. I hadn't even had a chance to plan my exit strategy.

As it was, I still had to collect enough money for a deposit on my own place. I still had to decide how I would live—that is, unless I decided to come clean and move in with my mother until I got on my feet again. I wanted to save that option as the very last resort. I still had a few small marketing jobs in the works, and once those clients paid, I'd pack up and leave Baltimore.

Those were the details I was working out when I left for Scottsdale and met Derek.

Derek opened my eyes. He turned my body inside out, and then he set everything on fire. But at the same time, nothing had changed. Derek might've shown me I wasn't to blame, that I could fall in love, that my life could get better. But before any of it could be realized, I had to finish here. I had to get back on my own two feet.

I was still unpacking my suitcase and pondering closure when my soon-to-be ex-husband found me. As I expected, he was not in an understanding mood.

He was ready to get to the bottom of my unannounced trip.

ELEVEN

PORTFOLIO DIVERSITY

SLOAN BREEZED INTO THE ROOM as if finding me here was the last thing he'd expected to happen—as if he hadn't sent his driver to pick me up at the airport. My pulse sped up. My back was to him, and without turning, I cautiously lifted my hand to one of the small top drawers of my dresser. Sliding it open, I casually felt beneath my lingerie, locating the canister of pepper spray now hidden there.

"Well, look what the cat dragged in," he said, dropping lightly onto my bed. He was long and lean, dressed in expensive tan slacks and a pale blue button-down shirt. His light-brown hair was losing its battle against the grey, and I remembered a time when his age had made him seem distinguished to me. "I do love your flair for the dramatic, my dear. Have me served then disappear for a week. *Brava!*"

His words also reminded me of a time when I'd debated whether my husband might be gay. The prospect had softened me toward him. I'd wanted to help him come out, let him know it was okay. He'd grown up in a time and in a world not so understanding of alternate lifestyles. Then I discovered his penchant for prostitutes. Jessica Black had only been the first of many contact slips I'd found. No, it seemed his only problem was having sex with his wife.

"Elaine called and invited me on a spa retreat," I said, keeping my voice calm. I continued unpacking, silently waiting for him to make his next move. "But you already know that, don't you?"

"Spa retreat? Why didn't you tell me," he had the nerve to act hurt. "You know I enjoy a good massage as much as the next guy."

He enjoyed a happy ending. He probably had masseuses all over town ready to jerk him off for a modest fee. The thought made me sick.

"It was more of a friend getaway." The tension was making my shoulders ache. I wanted him to say whatever he'd come to say or do and leave. "You would've been bored."

"No doubt of that." Then as if he'd somehow lost interest, he sat up and went to the door. "As I said, some third-rate lawyer sent your papers. A James Pettigrew or something?"

"James Perry." He knew damn well my lawyer's name.

"Perry, right." He paused in the doorway. "I sent them on to Thomas for a good once-over. Can't have my lady screwing me now, can I."

It would be the first time in a long time, I thought bitterly, but I wouldn't take his bait.

Thomas was Sloan's self-serving lawyer, and if there was anything wrong with the divorce papers, he'd find it. The shocker for both of them would come when they discovered I just wanted out. No alimony, no settlement, just freedom.

"Look them over as much as you need," I said with a smile. "I'm sure you'll find they're completely to your benefit."

He nodded. "Then, welcome home Melissa."

I didn't reply. This was not my home.

ONCE I HAD FINISHED UNPACKING, I walked down the hall to my study. The office was also a library, and when I'd first visited this wing last year, I'd been thrilled with all the books I could read. Little did I know, reading was all I'd end up doing. A desk was placed in one corner, and I saw my small, silver Macbook lying there. I'd left it behind on my trip, not wanting anything that reminded me of Baltimore. As if I could escape that easily.

Tonight, I went to it, lifted the cover and opened the browser. It had only been a day, and already the pain gripped my chest so hard, it hurt to breathe. Quickly I typed in "Derek Alexander" and "private investigator."

Moments later a page of links popped up with the one I sought right at the top. Alexander & Knight, LLC. I glanced quickly at the door then leaned forward, looking as far down the hallway as I could see. No one was coming.

Holding my breath, I clicked on the link. Instantly, I was taken to a plain but professional-looking business site with an A&K logo over an exterior shot of what must be their offices in Princeton. One of the small links across the top said "About Us," and again, my heart clenched as I clicked on it.

The screen changed and there he was. A tiny gasp escaped my lips when I saw his face. It was a professionally posed shot— him in a suit, all-business, just the smallest hint of a smile. His blue eyes seemed to glow, and a knot tightened at the base of my throat. He was gorgeous. I reached out to touch the screen lightly with trembling fingers when I realized I wasn't alone. Quickly I closed the notebook and looked up to see Mrs. Widlow standing in the doorway.

"Mr. Reynolds said he'd be having his supper out," she said, not seeming to notice my suspicious behavior. "When would you like yours?"

I cleared my throat. "If it's not too much trouble, I'd be happy with just a sandwich in my bedroom."

"No trouble at all," the housekeeper said, nodding before

she turned to leave.

Once she was definitely away, I slowly opened the computer again. The screen blinked on, and he was still there. I leaned my face on my hand and studied his image a few moments. He was just as sexy in a suit and tie as he'd been in casual attire—maybe more. A hot tear slid down my nose as his last words flooded my memory. He'd take my call anytime.

I wanted to call him right now. Just to hear his voice again. I took a deep breath and navigated his website. I was impressed by how many services they offered. The financial institution security package was listed most prominently, but they also had plans for identity theft and general investigative work.

Patrick's page listed services including missing persons and domestic issues. I wondered how many of those cases they even took. Neither of them mentioned that line of work, and it seemed the online banking and finance was their primary focus.

I shook my head. As a small business owner, I was all too familiar with diversifying one's portfolio just in case, for backup. I clicked back over to Derek's page, and the image of his face again shot pain straight to my chest. I pressed my lips together, swallowing the lump in my throat. Once more I ran the back of my finger down the screen, remembering his kisses, his strong arms holding me. I felt so safe sleeping in them. Tears were multiplying, but I blinked them away. And with a sigh, I slid the mouse forward and clicked on the little red X.

MY MOTHER'S VOICE HELD ITS usual note of concern. Ever since I'd first told her Sloan and I were having serious problems, she'd urged me wait. And every time she did, I almost told her why that was no longer an option.

But I couldn't.

I couldn't bear saying what had happened out loud.

Especially not to her. The very thought of telling her everything made my stomach roil. If my father were still alive, it would've been even worse.

"So you're moving home," she said. "I guess you have to do what you think is best."

"I've spent as much time as I can trying to make it work, Mom," I said quietly, keeping my voice calm. "Nothing's changing. Things are actually getting worse as time passes."

"Disappearing for a week without a word certainly can't be helping with the reconciliation effort."

My jaw clenched. "I didn't disappear without a word, I just didn't tell him where I was going."

"The results are the same," she exhaled lightly. "So when do you expect to be here?"

"I'm not sure," I said, toying with the sandwich on my supper tray. I wasn't very hungry. "My goal is to find a place and not have to bother you, but it just depends—"

"You're not bothering me, honey. I just want you to be sure you're not doing something you'll regret."

"I'm not," I said, pressing my lips together.

My work with Sloan's family had kept me so busy the first half of the year, I hadn't been able to visit home. Then after the incident, I hadn't wanted to visit. I didn't feel strong enough to see anyone, much less my super-perceptive mother. She would've demanded I do what I didn't really want to.

As it was, I had to be patient with her ignorance. "Just give me one more week," I said. "I'll know something definite then."

"The door's open if you need it."

"Thanks so much, Mom."

We hung up the phone, and I stretched back on my bed. Moving in with Mom was my absolute last resort, but I figured spreading a safety net couldn't hurt. Sloan had become so unpredictable, and now that he had the divorce papers, I wasn't sure what he'd do.

Two months ago, fueled by my determination to get out, I'd

drummed up business with two local clients—a suburban strip mall needing a back to school campaign, and a downtown bakery wanting to test the cupcake waters. Neither of them were particularly wealthy clients, but they weren't poor either. I'd sent invoices to them the week before Elaine and I had left for Scottsdale. My hope was they'd come through and I could go straight to my own place in Wilmington.

Either way, I had to start looking for somewhere to live and transitioning my contact information. The only thing holding me back now were the details. Details I'd see about first thing tomorrow.

TWELVE

A LIST OF NAMES

BEA'S FANCY CAKES WAS LOCATED in an older part of downtown that was now a few blocks off the major pedestrian thoroughfares. The owner, affectionately known as "Aunt Bea," had provided cakes to downtown businesses and residents for almost thirty years, but her sales had dropped as traffic patterns had rotated away from her address.

When she contacted me about helping her market a new line of cupcakes, my enthusiasm lifted her spirits so much, we'd become friends as well as partners. It also earned me a free sample every visit. Today, I hoped it would land an early payment on my invoice, but I knew I had to approach the topic gingerly. She was old-fashioned, and I hoped not overextended.

"That one's a new recipe," she said, sliding over my cupcake *du jour* as she assisted a customer. "Candy corn. I'm testing it for the Halloween market."

Aunt Bea was a fabulous baker, and adding a trendy cupcake line had been a stroke of brilliance to solve her location woes. We simply had to remind the public she was here and convince the downtown foot-traffic to take a slight detour on their way back to the office after lunch. Extending her business hours also picked up after-work employees who'd forgotten a birthday, or

Valentine's Day, or their anniversary. We'd watched with glee as the clientele had grown from one or two customers a day to tens and twenties. I smiled, satisfied as I lifted the little orange, yellow, and white candy off the top of my confection. I'd helped somebody during my time here in a meaningful way.

"It smells exactly right," I said, inspecting the golden-yellow ombre frosting before taking a bite. "Mmm . . ." I couldn't stop a groan of delight as the lightly sweet, toasted-butter flavor filled my mouth. "It's perfect!"

Bea grinned and pulled out a pink and white polka-dot box for the waiting male customer. "Saw the recipe in one of those parent magazines and just tweaked it a bit," she said. "I might make an entire cake from it."

"This will fly off the shelves."

My trip to the desert had coincided with Labor Day, which meant Halloween season had begun. Black and orange ornamentation, cats, and pumpkins were popping up everywhere. It was my favorite time of year with the air growing cooler and the leaves changing colors.

Elaine's return home had put her in full back-to-school mode, and I hadn't talked to her since we'd parted at the airport. I wondered how things were going with her and Patrick, and immediately, I considered sending her a box of this heaven.

"Three red wine velvet, and three tiramisu," Bea repeated, making a note of the waiting customer's order before filling the box. "So what brings you downtown?"

Chewing my lip, I waited as she rang up the fellow, who took the box and hastened to the door. Aunt Bea was short and round, and with her little bun, she actually did resemble the television icon she was nicknamed for.

We were alone at last, and I had to act quickly before another customer entered the bakery. But I didn't want to rush her into a no. "Well," I started, swallowing my heart down. "I'm moving back to Wilmington."

"What!" Her thin eyebrows pulled together quickly as they

rose. "I don't understand. What about . . . ?"

"It's sort of a complicated situation. You see, Sloan and I are getting a divorce." I played with the wax paper lying flat at the base of my half-eaten cupcake.

"Oh, honey," Bea walked around the glass case and pulled me into a hug. "Is there anything I can do?"

"Actually," I inhaled her sugary scent and just said it. "Well, I hoped you might be in a position to pay the invoice I sent over a little early."

For a moment, we were both quiet. Her lips pressed together, and I felt a bead of sweat trickle down my back.

"I'm so sorry to ask you," I continued. "It's just that I'm not sure of my new address, and it would make wrapping up my business here . . . easier."

She shook her head. "I hate to see you go. Mr. Reynolds was such a good man, and you seemed like a perfect addition to that family."

A lump rose in my throat. Sloan's elderly father had been revered as something like a saint by all the downtown residents. He'd held local business in the area through economic ups and downs, and he was a kind man. Despite his son.

But more than that—her words brought me healing. For so long, I'd blamed myself for being a fool, for not seeing the real Sloan before I'd married him. After the incident, I'd assumed I'd been blinded by his family name and the luxury of the life he'd offered. But Bea's words confirmed what I'd believed six years ago, in the beginning. Sloan's father *had* been kind. I *had* seemed to belong. At first.

I'd never dreamed such a dark underbelly could be lurking on that idyllic family life. In that moment, I got a bit of my self-esteem back.

"And I know you would be a great partner in downtown development," she continued. Her voice was tentative. I knew she was trying not to offend me. "I hate to lose my best publicity girl."

My heart filled despite its inner turmoil. Her words were so kind, and I was sure if my situation weren't so bleak, she'd be right. My life might be so different here. But it wasn't, and I was ready to leave this place.

Her words also reminded me why Sloan went on the attack when I'd said I wanted a divorce. Why he was so worried about what public accusations I might make, and why he was so ready to shift the blame for all of it to me.

He had the most to lose in this town, and he knew better than to shit where he ate. If my story became The Story, it would ruin him. He was on the defense, and it was a scary place to have him. He was wicked when cornered.

"I know," I said quietly, adopting my usual line. "But it's just not working out, and we've decided it was a mistake. We'll be happier apart."

She pressed her lips into a smile as she squeezed my upper arm. "Well, that's too bad." I watched her walk back to the register, quietly holding my breath, hoping she'd help me. "Would you be able to give me a week? Is that a problem?"

I quietly exhaled, small tears touching my eyes. "No problem at all!" I did my best not to dance around her bakery—she wouldn't understand. "And thank you so much. I hope we can continue working together."

"How could we do that?" Her face lined.

"It's the digital age! You'd be amazed what all I can do from the comfort of my laptop."

She shook her head, but immediately smiled at the female customer walking through the door. "These computers. They've changed everything."

"Thanks so much, Aunt Bea." I gathered the rest of my cupcake as I headed for the door.

One week. One more week, and I'd be gone. I could feel my lungs straining in anticipation. Soon I'd be able to breathe freely again.

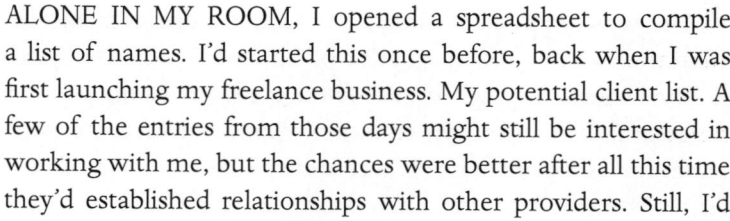

AFTER THAT, I WAS IN full apartment-hunting mode. I focused my search on small condos near the beach. The chances were great I wouldn't find anything I could afford, but I was optimistic. I even started collecting moving supplies.

I'd only seen Sloan once, naturally when I was about to carry two broken-down boxes up the large staircase to my room. I tensed, waiting for how he would respond. The muscle in his jaw tightened, but he didn't say a word. He simply continued to his study and closed the door. I quietly jogged up the steps and then hurried to my solitary quarters in the east wing.

We hadn't dined together, we hadn't had a single conversation since the one in my bedroom the night I'd returned home. I was not complaining. If I never spoke to him again, it would be too soon. But I was nervous. He hadn't agreed to let me go, and he didn't like being crossed.

My nerves were tied up and confused between my growing anticipation of freedom combined with the tension of watching for anything from Sloan. Before Scottsdale, I'd been used to the nonstop pressure, the invisible weights pushing down on my shoulders all the time. But that week-long reprieve had shown me how toxic Baltimore was, and it was all I could do to stay here and wrap up my business.

ALONE IN MY ROOM, I opened a spreadsheet to compile a list of names. I'd started this once before, back when I was first launching my freelance business. My potential client list. A few of the entries from those days might still be interested in working with me, but the chances were better after all this time they'd established relationships with other providers. Still, I'd send them all my contact information once I'd set up my new identity in Wilmington.

Thinking of possibilities, my eyes drifted to the Internet browser window. It had become a guilty habit of mine, a night-time indulgence. My eyes flickered to my door—no one was coming in here tonight—I clicked on the icon and hastily typed in the now-memorized address. Two clicks, and Derek's face appeared on the screen, jolting my heart with a dose of happiness.

I was like a teenage girl gazing at pictures of my favorite boy band. My cheek rested on my hand, and I reached forward to trace the line of his face with my finger as joy pulsed through me with each heartbeat. I still remembered his scent. Closing my eyes, I could still feel the touch of his lips against mine. Only a little time had passed since he'd nuzzled his face into my shoulder, kissed my neck, lifted me against his firm torso. His kiss was my moment, the thing I held onto that helped me know this pain wasn't forever. My lips warmed with longing for the day when I saw him again, when he'd cover my mouth with his and take me.

Rolling onto my back, eyes still closed, I allowed my memory to conjure the sensation of his mouth searching every part of my body. Instantly, I grew wet. My hand slid between my legs as my core filled with heat remembering his mouth being where my hand was now, tasting, exploring, pulling my smaller lips with his. My upper arms pressed my breasts together, and I took us back to our little box. The night he'd held me on his lap, entering me from behind, huge and full. His enormous cock pressed inside, thrusting deeply, rubbing every sensitive place between my legs so well. Driving me crazy.

His hand gripped my stomach, holding me firmly against his chest, easily lifting me up and down. Oh, god, he'd felt so good. A shiver moved through me as my fingers followed the path his larger ones had taken. His phantom whiskers tickled my back, warm lips moving from my neck to my shoulders. He pushed faster, harder, filling me completely, thrusting deeper . . . a little moan slipped from my lips and my thighs shook with the orgasm his memory provoked. Rolling onto my stomach, I moaned again into the pillow, but a hollow ache reminded me how much I missed the real thing. Memories were nice, but nothing matched his body against mine, his lips on my skin, his cock buried deep inside me.

Several moments passed as I waited, eyes closed, breathing deeply. Calm gradually returned, and with it came that flicker of hope I held so dearly. The hope I'd held when we said good-bye outside the resort.

Mist was in my eyes and my stomach tightened at the memory of his words. He'd take my call anytime. Did he think of me this way? Was he waiting for my call, dreaming of our reunion the way I was?

Moving back to my still-open spreadsheet, I quickly typed fourteen letters and ten digits. At the top of my list of names was his.

THIRTEEN

NEVER AGAIN

THE WEEK WAS ALMOST UP, and I could barely breathe waiting for the day to arrive. I was like a convict waiting for my pardon. Every day, I snatched the mail the instant it was delivered, rapidly flipping through the envelopes, straining for my name.

The strip mall had paid their bill, which allowed me to put a large down-payment on a one-bedroom condo near the coast that would be my home. I'd lucked into an amazing deal and jumped on it. I was almost giddy with anticipation. I couldn't wait to be there, but the remainder of my money was eaten up in deposits for turning on services and in rent for a mini storage facility for my things. I needed Aunt Bea's outstanding check to carry me through the transition.

Every day I waited, hoping for that envelope bearing my name, but every day I was disappointed. It never appeared. It was too late to go back and set up direct deposit for her payment—not that my elderly client would've even understood the concept. But I'd learned my lesson going forward. All future accounts would have a direct pay mandate.

The added tension of waiting for Sloan's backlash only increased my anxiety. At least no one back home knew about my pending return. I wasn't sure I could handle nonstop questions of when I'd be in town. My former landlord knew I was returning, as he'd helped me compile the information needed to purchase my new condo. Elaine would've been tripping over herself to help, of course, but for most people, returning after a divorce wasn't cause for celebration. I was happy to be free, but despite it all, I wanted to leave my past in the past. I would tell my friends as little as I could to satisfy their concerned curiosity.

Another day of waiting was another day of taking boxes to the delivery service. I had all my things sent to a mini storage facility in Wilmington that agreed to hold them until I arrived. I did it partly to keep Sloan from knowing my business—if he were investigating—and partly because it was easier than trying to hire a truck. I'd handle an in-town move once I was back home, but I was doing my best to keep all my plans under wraps.

So my delay had an unanticipated upside. My existence here was almost completely packed and moved. It was amazing how little a human being actually needed when possessions were stripped down to the essentials.

STEPPING INTO THE LIBRARY THAT evening, I replaced the hardback I'd never read. I turned slowly, inhaling the scent of books and studying the shelves. My dreams of living in this place had been so different from my reality.

Shaking my head, I left the room. No sense going back down that path. I was moving forward now. And I was ready to curl into bed for my nighttime ritual.

I did not expect to see Sloan standing in my doorway. "I see you're determined to go through with this," he said, a stern line piercing the skin between his brows.

He wore grey slacks, and his top button was open. His hair

was disheveled, and I saw his chest rise and fall. His agitated expression was too familiar, and quickly my mind counted the days. How long had it been since he'd traveled? Why was he here now? My throat went dry.

"I am," I managed to say.

He stepped forward, and I stepped to the side, anticipating the need to move quickly.

"Why are you doing this, Melissa? What could you possibly want that you don't have here?"

My eyes widened. "Is that a joke?"

"Not at all. You live like a queen."

I shook my head not knowing where to begin answering his question. As if he even deserved an answer. "We really don't know each other at all, do we?"

"Apparently not," he said, entering my room. I followed trying to get around him to my dresser drawer, but he stayed between me and my one small protection.

"If we did," he continued, "you'd know I don't believe in divorce."

I flashed at his attempt to take some moral high ground. "I don't believe in husbands raping their wives."

He rolled his eyes, waving a hand. "I didn't rape you."

"You tried," I snapped.

"It was a misunderstanding. And anyway, some women like it rough."

The rage I'd held inside for over three months roared in my chest, choking me with its ferocity. I cleared my throat, shaking my head, trying to stay calm. "Are you saying some women like being beaten?"

He leveled his brown eyes on mine. "You threw the first punch."

Shudders kept moving through my body. We'd never discussed that night since it happened, and my resistance to talking about it had left me unprepared for how it would affect me when I did. I wasn't sure I could do this alone.

"You tried to rape me," I said, my voice small, my throat painfully tight. "I was only defending myself."

"Regardless," he continued, as if enjoying my discomfort. "*You* started it. *I* finished it. And I bet you never hit me again."

I turned to face my open door, ready to run and not caring if I took anything with me. I wanted to leave this place for good. Tonight.

As if reading my mind, Sloan quickly moved from my dresser to catch my upper arm, jerking me against his body. "You're *my* wife," he hissed in my ear. "You belong to *me*. No matter what you think you're going to do, that fact will always remain."

Tears spilled onto my cheeks. I couldn't catch my breath, and a hiccup jerked my shoulders. "Please let me go," I whimpered.

His grip remained tight on my arm. "I'll never let you go. And even when you're gone, I'll know every step you take. You are never out of my reach."

My heart hammered, and I tried to keep my shoulders straight. I refused to cower to him. Still, my body instinctively shrank from his touch. I hadn't wanted to believe he might hurt me again. But now I knew he would.

He loosened his hold and shoved me back before stalking out of my room, slamming the door behind him. I dashed to it, quickly turning the lock, knowing it wouldn't keep him out if he wanted back in.

I ran to my closet and pulled out a suitcase, throwing every outfit I could get my hands on into it as sobs gasped from my throat, fear strangling my voice. The check might be in the mail, but I wasn't waiting anymore.

I SLEPT WITH MY DOOR locked and the pepper spray clutched in my hand all night. I didn't want to take my car—I didn't want to take anything that might be considered community property. Late in the night, once I'd calmed down, I called Elaine and asked if she could come and get me now. I didn't want to tell her why or scare her, but she knew something was wrong. She said she'd be on the road first thing in the morning. I only had to survive six more hours before we'd be gone. Six hours of acting like nothing was coming. I wasn't sure if I could pull it off.

All night my mind kept running to Derek as I tossed and turned, unable to sleep. One thing Sloan had said troubled me— that even when I was gone he knew every step I took, that I was never out of his reach. When Hal was waiting for me at the airport, I'd mistakenly assumed Sloan had figured out where I went. I thought he'd weaseled the information from my mom or found a stray email on my Macbook. Now I knew the truth. He hadn't figured it out. Clearly, he was having me watched.

The perfect person who could help me with this was Derek. If Sloan had hired a private investigator to track me, Derek would know exactly how to handle the situation. It was possible he might even know the person or be able to find him or her easily. The only problem was I didn't want to involve Derek in my disgusting backstory. With everything in me, I didn't want him to know what Sloan had done. Partly because I was afraid if he knew, he wouldn't want me anymore. He'd think I was too damaged, or maybe he'd believe Sloan. He'd think I started it and what happened was my fault. I shuddered at the thought.

But if Sloan was having me watched, and I tried to see Derek, it would all come out anyway. I cringed at the prospect. My story was so humiliating and awful. I wouldn't blame Derek if he wanted to walk, knowing I had a psycho ex-husband lurking around. The pain of these thoughts kept me troubled all night.

BY MORNING, I'D FORMULATED A plan. What if there was a way I could find out who was working with Sloan on my own? What if I could talk to the person, reason with him or her, or even pay the person off somehow? Maybe I could solve my problem without Derek ever having to know . . .

Bolstered by the idea, I crept to my door and unlocked it. It was ten. Elaine would be two hours into her drive if she'd gotten on the road by eight like she'd said she would. It gave me just enough time to try and investigate. I waited, listening. My end of the giant mansion was completely quiet.

I crept down the hallway to the main staircase, but a voice made me jump straight up. A little squeal leaped from my throat before I could stop it.

"Are you ready for breakfast, ma'am?" Mrs. Widlow.

"N-no," I said, my heart hammering in my chest. "I mean . . . Thank you. Is Mr. Reynolds at breakfast?"

Her stern face didn't even acknowledge my fright. Her grey hair was coiffed in its usual helmet, and today she wore olive green. "Mr. Reynolds has already left for the office."

"Of course," I said, pushing my long dark curls back. "It's ten."

I could breathe easily. And I'd be gone before he even returned home. Even better, his personal computer would be sitting in his office unguarded.

"I am hungry," I said quickly. "Would you please see if I could get eggs benedict?" I hoped a complicated breakfast order would buy me some time.

"Of course," the woman said, turning on her heel.

I watched her walk away a moment before quietly dashing down the main stairs and sneaking to the small room behind them at the bottom.

THE DOOR TO SLOAN'S PRIVATE office was unlocked, and I hurried around his large desk, opening his notebook computer. The chances of him leaving anything where I might find it were slim to none. He would expect me to search—especially after last night. He would anticipate me going through his things, trying to find out what he was doing. Still, I opened his inbox, quickly scrolling through all the messages, looking for anything, any kind of lead.

Nothing seemed suspicious. It was all travel arrangements, appointments, luncheons, and follow up messages. My heart beat painfully hard. I was running out of time. Mrs. Widlow would be looking for me for breakfast, and this might be my only chance to access this room alone before Elaine arrived. Not only that, I had to make sure I had everything I needed before Elaine did appear. I was never returning to this house again once I left it.

I sat and stared at the computer several minutes trying to think like my soon-to-be ex-husband. He probably had it all on his phone. My shoulders dropped in defeat. But wait! I realized if it was on his smart phone, there ought to be a corresponding email address. And it was possible it might be an online mail provider . . .

Opening his browser again, I went to the history file and looked for recent mail programs. Hal had picked me up at the airport, so whoever he'd used had been tracking me as recently as that date. I found a link to an Internet mail site and clicked on it, opening a window filled with messages.

My throat closed when I saw the list of names, the numbers, the dates. It was all here—the escort services, the hotel rooms, all over the country . . . All of it.

For a moment, I only stared stupidly as the tears flooded my eyes. The enormity of his betrayal left me weak and wounded. There were so many.

How had I been so trusting? How had I been such a fool? Years of lies, and I'd never suspected.

With a deep breath, I touched my tears away. This was my past. I didn't have to carry this with me, and Derek had shown me love was waiting in my future. Taking another cleansing breath, I realized this was also a gift in disguise. It was the insurance I needed, the backup that transformed what happened from being his word against mine into cold, hard facts. Now I had evidence.

I slid the mouse and clicked the printer icon. Twenty verified transactions later, I didn't want to know any more. It was enough. With these and the other items in my possession, I was sure my case was solid. I had enough to make my soon-to-be ex-husband cooperate. Now all I needed was the name of Sloan's helper. Whoever it was would have to be moved by the physical evidence of my husband's abuse and betrayal. And if he wasn't, well, maybe it didn't even matter anymore.

I was still scrolling when my eyes landed on the name, and I felt all the blood drain from my face. My hand slid from the mouse, taking my strength with it. I couldn't breathe.

There it was, the name of the person tracking me for my husband, *DAlexander@AlexanderKnight.com*

FOURTEEN

OFF THE RECORD

MY VIBRATING PHONE ROUSED ME. I'd sat with my forehead on Sloan's desk for minutes that felt like hours. In one line of text, all the life had gone from my body. My warm light was snuffed out.

I should be crying. The little flicker of hope I'd held so dearly all these days had been cruelly extinguished, and I was left shivering in the cold darkness alone. My entire body braced for the breakdown, but it never came. Only quiet sadness held me unable to move.

The vibrating started again, and finally I lifted my hand to check it. Elaine's face and number blinked at me, but I only stared at her. I couldn't seem to care. I wanted to slide under the desk and stay there forever. Still, my friend persisted.

And even with all the hope sucked out of my life, I knew if she were here, she'd say all the right things. I had to get up. I had to get out of this place and go to the new life I'd been working so hard to establish. Once I was there, I could break down, but not while I was still in this place of danger.

Before I left, however, something in me wanted this last bit of evidence, this last piece of betrayal. I moved the mouse over the print icon and clicked, waiting as the email printed out, not even reading it.

I left Sloan's office quieter and far slower than when I'd entered. I walked down the passage and climbed the stairs to my room before I pressed the button to call my best friend back.

"Melissa!" Elaine's voice was frantic when she answered. "I've been so worried. I couldn't even sleep."

"Where are you?" I managed to ask through the thickness in my throat.

"I'm minutes away. Are you ready?"

Relief washed over me in a wave so powerful, I had to sit on my bed. "Yes, I'm ready. I'm ready now." I felt the breakdown threatening, but I had to be strong. "Oh, Elaine. Thank you so much."

"Oh, honey," she cried. "I'd be there even faster if I could."

I ended the call and pulled myself up by force of will. I had to collect the last of my things. I had to make sure I wasn't leaving behind anything I couldn't live without. I was never looking back.

Opening my closet, I dug through the remaining shoeboxes and old photo albums. The good news was most everything I cared about was in Wilmington now, and as depressing as it sounded, there was very little I wanted to keep from these days in Baltimore. I was just zipping up the large suitcase when I heard the light knock on my door. Looking up, I saw Sloan standing there, a severe line between his light-brown eyebrows.

"What's going on?" he demanded.

I jumped back from the suitcase as if electrocuted. "Why are you here? You're supposed to be at your office."

"Gladys said you were acting strangely, and I should come home."

"Mrs. Widlow," I breathed. As if a switch inside me was flipped, the whole idea that every single person in this house watched me like a rebellious teenager and reported back to Sloan set me off.

The depression I'd been feeling over Derek turned into rage, and I jerked the suitcase off my bed. "There's nothing strange going on," I said, stalking over to my dresser and jerking open the small top drawer. I grasped the pepper spray canister, aiming it straight at his face. "I'm leaving this place. And if you try to stop me, I'll spray you."

Sloan's eyebrow cocked, and he held both hands up as if I'd just pulled a gun. "By all means, leave," he breathed a short laugh. It only fueled my rage.

"Don't test me, Sloan. There's nothing I'd love more than to burn your eyes out."

At that he dropped his hands and walked out. "Have a safe drive," he called over his shoulder.

Just then, Elaine jogged up the main stairway. When she and Sloan met each other, they both stopped. For a moment, I wasn't sure what might happen. My best friend looked at my almost ex-husband as if he were Osama bin Laden, and he looked at her as if she were a witch.

I jerked up the handle on my suitcase and stalked down the hall, rolling it behind me. "I'm here, Elaine!" I called. "Don't bother with him. It's time to go."

Her brow softened, and she turned from Sloan to me. "Let's go," she repeated.

On my way out, my eyes landed on a stack of envelopes sitting on the small table by the front door. The mail! I paused only briefly to spread them out, and my breath caught when I saw it—Aunt Bea's check! It came! I nearly burst into tears at the sight of it. The envelope restored the tiniest bit of hope I needed. I was going to survive this. I was going to be okay. I might be alone, but I was going to make it through.

I snatched it up and walked out the door not looking back. I would never look back.

WE LIFTED MY HUGE SUITCASE into Elaine's car and jumped inside. I watched as she guided us out of the long driveway away from the Reynolds mansion, but when we reached the main road, I put my hand on her arm.

"Wait before we get going." My chest ached with what I was about to ask my best friend, but I didn't have a choice. I had to have closure. "There's something I need to do first. Will you help me?"

Her brows drew together, but she waited. "Of course, what is it?"

I pulled out the three pages that included Derek's email and Sloan's response. "I printed this off Sloan's computer. Would you read it to me?"

Elaine was still frowning, but she took the sheets from me. "To DAlexander@AlexanderKnight.com . . ." Instantly she lowered the pages and looked at me. "Is this . . . Derek?"

"Please just read it," I said, every muscle in my body clenched.

"Derek, I hope you remember your old mentor Sloan." She stopped again, taking a breath and staring at me, brows clutched.

"Keep going," I whispered.

"I found you online, and I hope you might be willing to do a favor for an old friend. Of course, I'll pay you well." Again she stopped. "Oh, Mel. I don't think I can—"

"Please, Elaine." My voice was sharp now. "Just read the damn email."

She took a deep breath and continued. "I'm afraid my wife is having an affair, and I need someone I can trust to verify this for me. Attached is her photograph and information. She is somewhere this week. She wouldn't tell me where. I think it might be with him."

A knot tightened in my throat, and again Elaine paused. But instead of speaking, she took another deep breath and continued. "As you can imagine, this is very sensitive and quite humiliating. I hope we can keep this off the record."

My head dropped at the phrase. It was the same thing he'd said to me after Patrick had revealed the location of their offices. *Off the record.*

"Your friend, Sloan Reynolds," she finished. Then she lowered the pages to her lap.

His friend. I couldn't speak. I had gone numb and nothing felt like it made sense anymore.

"He was spying on you?" Her voice cracked high with disbelief. "Was Patrick in on it, too?"

I shrugged, blinking slowly. Then I forced the words. "He responded. I printed out the whole exchange."

She lifted the pages again and folded the first one back. "Dear Sloan," then she glanced at me, but I was still sitting frozen, unable to feel. "I'm sorry to hear of your marital difficulties. I did observe your wife this week. She was with another female at the Cactus Flower Spa in Scottsdale, Arizona. But I have to confess, I did not observe her with any male guests. As far as I could tell, she was alone the entire week. Sorry not to be more help. No payment needed. Cordially, Derek."

At that she stared at the printout, her brow lined. She flipped the pages back and forth, then she turned to me in her seat. "Weren't you and Derek . . . ?"

For a moment, all I could do was stare at my lap in stunned silence. Then I slowly nodded, finding my voice. "We were together," I said softly.

Her eyebrows flew up. "You *slept* together?"

"Several times."

"But he said . . ." She looked out the front window a moment. "I don't understand."

I reached for the door handle, lifting it, and getting out of the car. I went around and opened the hatchback, unzipping my suitcase and digging through the file folders I'd placed on top until I found the one I was looking for. I walked back to the passenger's side and got in, pulling the door closed. Then I reached down by my feet and dug out the small silk pouch I'd hidden in my bag.

"Would you please do something for me, Elaine?" I looked at my friend with such seriousness, she immediately nodded. "I need you to drive us to Princeton. There's something I have to do."

Her jaw dropped. "But—"

"Please? Sloan can't call the shots any more."

I watched as she chewed her lip. Then she grasped the steering wheel and turned her car toward Interstate 95.

FIFTEEN

THE HUMILIATING TRUTH

THE ALEXANDER-KNIGHT OFFICE WAS EASY to find using the directions on my smart phone, and we were pulling into the corporate entrance in less than two hours. Neither Elaine nor I had spoken much on the drive over. She had turned on talk radio shortly after leaving Baltimore and withdrawn into her own private thoughts. I could only assume she was processing like me, and I welcomed her silence. I wasn't sure how well she was keeping up with Patrick since our trip to Scottsdale, but I was almost certain he hadn't told her about this.

As for me, I was still reeling from my discovery, and I'd spent the entire time thinking and re-thinking what I planned to say. Derek had lied to me, slept with me, known the entire time I was dealing with a pending divorce and a suspicious husband, and he'd never said a word.

Sloan called him his friend. The very thought of them being friends made me sick and angry and nauseated and . . . miserable. I wanted to believe Derek didn't know the extent of Sloan's atrocities, still if he thought of himself as a hero, a gallant fellow who'd protected my honor, I wanted to be sure he knew the full extent of how he had helped his "friend."

Elaine pulled into the front parking lot and sat in the car

looking up at the building. The exterior looked exactly as it did on the company website—limestone and blonde brick, silver windows, four floors. It was one of several office buildings clustered in a pentagon formation and sharing a common entrance and courtyard. In keeping with the season, it was decorated in orange, black, and purple, corn stalks and autumn wreaths. Someone had hung what appeared to be a witch smashing into the trunk of one of the trees. Stuffed arms and legs were splayed on either side of it along with a wrecked broomstick. I was sure it was meant to be funny, but nothing in me felt like laughing.

"I don't think I can go in there," Elaine whispered. "I can't see Patrick right now. I still haven't decided what I want to say to him."

"Well, I know exactly what I want to say." I grasped the door handle and stepped out of the car. "Wait here. I won't be long."

I had the two manila folders in my hands and the small silk pouch. What I intended to do would take less than fifteen minutes.

Stepping into the lobby of Office Building A, I scanned the directory until I located them on the fourth floor. The only thing I hadn't considered was they might be out to lunch, but I wasn't letting anything slow me down. I was acting on pure adrenaline now.

The elevator opened to a sleek, glass and stainless suite. Their entrance had the names Alexander & Knight lasered into the glass doors, and a receptionist's desk was situated right in the center of an open foyer with white leather chairs placed near a low, mahogany table.

Copies of *Forbes*, *Time*, and oddly an *OK!* magazine were arranged on the table. I stalked out, headed straight for his door. The blonde receptionist said something I ignored. I scanned the plaques outside each until I found the one reading *Derek Alexander*. I didn't even knock before entering his huge, corner office. He was turned in his black leather desk chair looking out a wall of windows, but when he heard the door, he started speaking.

"I don't know how you do it, Patrick," he breathed, turning the chair around as he finished. "I can't stop thinking . . ." His eyes locked on mine. "About her."

Derek stood quickly, and seeing him again for the first time since that week, dressed in grey slacks and a dress shirt unbuttoned at the top, blue eyes glowing beneath his dark brow, I had to fight all the emotions warring in my chest. The physical longing, the anger, the betrayal, the unbelievable, gut-wrenching pain. I ignored all of it—including the weakness in my knees at the blaze in his eyes when he saw me. I forced my mind to focus on what he'd done.

"Melissa," he said. "What—" He started around the desk toward me when I cut him off.

"Don't come any closer," I said. My stomach was in knots, and seeing the expression on his face—the frown melting into joy going back to a frown at my words—it took everything I had to control myself, to take it slow and be a professional. To handle him the way he'd handled me.

He stopped. "I don't understand. I'm so happy to see you. I-I want to—"

"Just hold that thought," I said, my hand extended as I walked to the opposite side of the desk from him. "I'm here for a reason."

"To see me, I hope," his voice was soft and low. It made my eyes burn.

My jaw clenched against any display of emotion. I'd had enough of men and their games. "It seems you know my ex-husband Sloan. You did some work for him a few weeks ago? In Scottsdale?"

Instantly his shoulders dropped. "Oh, Mel," he exhaled. "I can explain—" he started toward me again, palms out.

"Not until I've said what I came here to say."

His hands dropped and he studied my face. Then he nodded as if he understood, but I was pretty sure he didn't. "Will you sit?" he asked, going back around to his chair.

"I won't be that long." I pulled out one of the manila folders I'd brought, opening it on his desk and taking out the first document—the printout of their email exchange. "You confirmed for him that I was at the spa resort, but you saw no signs of me with a man? I suppose that was to cover your ass."

"No," he started. "It wasn't. I wanted to let you decide what you wanted—"

"Save it to the end," I continued, pulling out the next sheet. "I guess he told you his side of the story. That he didn't know why I was trying to leave him, that I must have another man somewhere. Maybe that I was crazy? I know he repeatedly told the staff such lies, and he always wondered aloud how I could throw away our life together."

Derek's lips pressed into a line, but he didn't speak. He waited for me to finish.

The next print out was a copy of the confirmation from the first escort service. "He wasn't so worried about our life together when he started fucking prostitutes."

I pulled out another contact, then another. One by one, I put the sheets on his desk, and Derek lifted them. I watched the muscle in his jaw flex as he quickly scanned their contents.

"The first time he said it was the long trip," I continued. "He was missing me, horny as hell, I think he said. And with a prostitute, it didn't count, right? She was just a faceless whore."

His eyes traveled back to me, but I could tell he was waiting, letting me say what I needed to say.

"After that, I couldn't sleep with him anymore." My voice wavered a bit. It was the first time I was saying all of this out loud. And to the one person I had mistakenly thought I could trust.

"That was about a year ago, right after we moved to Baltimore. Six months ago, he decided he was tired of waiting for me to get over it. Marriage counseling wasn't working, and he wanted to fuck his wife, goddammit."

At that, I pulled out the photo I'd guarded so closely. The one I'd never wanted anyone to see. The humiliating truth I still couldn't get my mind around. It had happened to me. *To me!* And I'd always believed I was smarter than that, a better judge of character. Seemed I was wrong twice.

I paused, studying the glossy print a moment, my throat tightening. Then I placed it in front of Derek, shame radiating through my chest.

"Of course, I fought him." The thickness in my voice made it difficult to speak. "And he fought back."

Derek only glanced at the photo before his eyes closed, his hand formed a fist on his desk. The picture showed my battered face. My lips swollen and purple, my black eyes, the cut at my hairline that really should've gotten stitches. It didn't show the bruises covering my torso.

I only had this picture because I'd called Elaine in hysterics. She'd dropped everything and drove all night, six hours to find me in the hotel room. She'd insisted, no, demanded I go to the police. She wanted to call her dad, her brother, every male we knew to beat the shit out of him. But I wouldn't. I didn't want anyone to know what had happened to me.

So she'd insisted I let her take pictures. "For when you come to your senses," she'd said, "and want him dead."

It was the one bit of evidence I'd held onto in case the asshole, bastard, son-of-a-bitch loser I was living with decided he wouldn't let me go.

"The next day," I continued speaking to Derek. "When he saw what he'd done, he laughed and said something about how it wasn't so long ago, raping your wife wasn't even considered a crime."

Derek stood quickly then, eyes blazing. "Melissa, you have to believe me. I didn't know about this. I never wanted—"

"To hurt me? To fuck with me? Well, I guess you did fuck with me. Several times." I walked to the window and looked out. "That's the part I don't understand. Why did you do that?

Was it a little something extra for you? Tap the wayward wife?"

I heard him exhale deeply. "I told you why," he said, jaw clenched. "I cared about you. I wanted to be with you. I still do."

"Were you even there for the conference?"

His lips tightened, and I realized the answer. The conference was just a lucky coincidence. A convenient lie.

I shook my head. "Thanks, but no thanks. You're no hero. You're a liar. And if you were trying to hurt me you couldn't have done a better job."

I stepped back to his desk, turning the photograph facedown and sliding it and the other papers together and into the folders, preparing to leave. But then I remembered. I turned back and placed the silk pouch on the smooth desk's surface. In it was the necklace with the floating heart he'd given me in Scottsdale.

"I almost threw this into the ocean," I said, holding my voice steady. "But that didn't seem harsh enough. Now I simply don't want it anymore. Or you."

His eyes were pleading as he tried to approach me again, but I stepped back, clutching the folder to my chest. My voice shook as I said my final words, and I was afraid I'd over-stayed my ability not to cry. "Don't ever come near me again."

I went straight out and closed his office door, pausing for a moment to lean against it. I exhaled a trembling breath, closing my eyes, but when I heard him approaching on the other side, I quickly walked to the main entrance and dashed out, taking the stairs down instead of waiting for the elevator.

It was over. Nothing he could say could make it right. He'd lied to me. The entire time we were together in Arizona had been a lie. He'd known every time he'd slept with me why he was there, why I was there, and he'd never said a word. I could never trust him again.

All I wanted was to get as far away from him as possible—from all of this. I wanted to go back to Wilmington, back to my old life, and never, never remember my time in Maryland. Ever again.

SIXTEEN

THE ROAD TO ANYWHERE

SITTING ON THE SHORE OUTSIDE my new home, I watched the sun set as the tide gently rolled in against my feet. In the three months since I'd been back, it felt like I had almost completely regained my life. Yes, there were a few scars, a few old wounds, but I was healing. Now I could actually see a time when I'd be whole, unlike before when I was only sinking further into despair.

My old friends were waiting with open arms. Of course, all of them except Elaine got the modified version of why I'd left Sloan. The most I was comfortable revealing was that he'd had an affair. And while there were a few people who didn't understand why I couldn't just forgive him and put it behind us, more people seemed to support me.

Restarting my marketing business proved easier than I'd anticipated. I'd been afraid my old clients had moved on or forgotten about me, but they hadn't. Taking over Mrs. Reynolds' positions on the Baltimore boards had been more beneficial than I'd realized at the time, and now that I was off my "sabbatical," as I framed it, many of them referred new clients to me. In less than a month, I was adding to the spreadsheet of names I'd started that night in my old room in Sloan's mansion.

Only one name had been removed, and I was doing my best to forget it.

I hadn't asked Derek what to do about his childhood game, when the thing you were holding onto for survival was taken away. I supposed the answer would be to simply survive. To keep going. Push through the pain and carry on. Wait for the day when it no longer hurt. He said the pain always ended. I had to believe in this one thing at least, he was telling the truth.

That entire drive back from Princeton, I'd held on with all my might. Seeing him again for the first time that way, after longing for him so hard had been like a million kicks to the chest and stomach. But knowing what he'd done, how he'd deceived me, only twisted all that pain even tighter into a bitter knot.

When I'd finally gotten my keys from the realtor and signed the papers on my new home, I'd thanked my best friend, who had to get back to her work at school, and I'd allowed myself to cry for a long time.

The delay in moving back to Wilmington had given me time to have all my services connected and everything set up from Maryland. My one-bedroom, single bath condo was small, but it was gorgeous, designed for the discriminating beachcomber. The floor-plan was open and airy. It had a gourmet kitchen—complete with brushed stainless appliances and fixtures—a dining area, and a study with a window seat. I even had a private, screened-in porch.

The color scheme was all white and the floors were bright pine, but I'd already decided I'd add color to the interior. Not immediately, as my heart felt like all the color had been drained away. But everything was ready to go as soon as I was ready to pull myself out of the bed.

It was a battle. It took longer than I cared to admit, but I'd gotten back on my feet, and now we were headed into the holiday season.

My only setback occurred a month after I arrived. Halloween

had passed, and I was doing my best to rebuild my client base. Elaine recommended I visit the private school where she worked to leave a card. I hadn't made it over until the end of the day, and walking from the parking lot, I couldn't help noticing a well-dressed, well-built, honey-blond male walking near me. I jumped two feet when I realized who it was.

"Patrick!" I breathed as his hazel eyes lit with recognition.

"Hello, Melissa." That handsome smile crossed his lips, and I felt like an idiot. I should've known they were still together.

Just as fast, I grew tense. "Are you alone? Is—"

"I'm alone," he said. "Had some business in Raleigh, so I figured I'd drop in on my way back. Surprise Elaine."

"This isn't on your way back."

"It can be."

My lips pressed together. Elaine had been kind enough never to mention what happened in Princeton or the guys at all since my return to Wilmington. At the same time, Brian was ancient history, and she never dated anyone to my knowledge, which was very unusual for my flirtatious friend. Now it all made sense.

"I'm sorry," I blinked down, studying my tan pumps. "I hadn't realized you two were still together. Elaine doesn't talk about it."

"I know." We were standing in the parking lot, and he crossed his toned arms over his equally toned chest. "We thought it would be easier if we gave you two some space for now."

"For now?" I shook my head. "You can be as open as you like. Derek and I are through."

His lips parted then closed, and I could tell he was trying to decide what to say. "I'd like to be a little more open with you. If you'll hear me out."

"Patrick, please . . ."

"I don't want to offend you or pick at a fresh wound," his voice turned gentle, "but if you're still deciding—"

"I've already decided." Sadness burned in my throat stronger than the anger I normally used to fight it.

Seeing Patrick reminded me too much of being with Derek, of being held in those strong arms, of that deep sense of safety he'd given me. He had been so comforting after my year of nightmares. Of course, I'd fallen in love with him. I was an idiot.

"Derek's wife died six years ago," Patrick continued. "He wasn't the same for a long time. Not until . . ."

My eyes burned with rapidly forming tears. "Please stop," I whispered.

"He had no idea, Mel. Neither of us knew what you'd been through."

"He should've told me the truth," I said. Two tears splashed onto my cheeks when I blinked, and I angrily wiped them away. "He lied to me. That's all that matters."

"He's sorry."

I spun on my heel and headed back to my car. The last thing I needed was to hear about his regret. Any man who could do what he did, get as close to me as he did, and then lie, hide something that important, was capable of anything. And I'd already been down the road to anything. I wasn't revisiting the location.

Derek Alexander was a thing of my past, and if I never met another man as long as I lived, I'd be happy.

My beach condo was absolutely perfect for my recovery. Just being in it made me feel peace. It also made me feel lucky, like I was getting another chance.

It was part of what had been envisioned as a planned beach community near Sea Breeze that fell victim to the recession. When the developers went broke, they sold off what was left for cheap, and I happened to be on the market at the exact right moment. It was as if all the negatives in my life had managed to twist out one beautiful positive for me.

Since the location was only partially developed, I was secluded from much of the tourist traffic that regularly invaded the area. Most of my neighbors were full-time residents who'd lucked into their properties as well. We were all bound together by sandy paths and picket fences, and we valued the seclusion of our area. Our dunes were untrodden, and the sea oats and beach scrub formed a nice barrier between us and the high-end resorts nearby.

Sitting on the shore, I inhaled the salty air, tasting it on my tongue. I straightened my shoulders and allowed the warmth of gratitude to tingle through every part of my body. I was alone, but I was content in this new, healing chapter of my life.

Except when Elaine visited. Since I'd bumped into Patrick that day, she'd stopped tip-toeing around their relationship. And my former one.

"Patrick said he does nothing but monitor Sloan now," she said, removing the ingredients for our dinner from the brown bag she'd brought with her. I was busy opening a bottle of wine. "He's determined to catch him breaking the law and bring him down."

"I don't care, Elaine," I said in my usual monotone when she got on this subject. "And I'm so tired of having this conversation. Derek and I are through."

"But he's still in love with you," she insisted. "And he wants that bastard to pay."

"And you're a hopeless romantic," I said, pouring us both large globes of red wine. "I'm a little irritated you didn't tell me you were still dating Patrick. He was in on the lie, too, you know."

"He didn't know you were sleeping with Derek," she said. "You didn't even tell me that part until after!"

"You couldn't see anything but each other," I said taking a sip. "Besides, he knew they were there to spy on us, and he didn't tell you. How can that not drive you crazy?"

"Mmm . . . Patrick drives me crazy in other ways." She winked, taking a sip of her wine.

I rolled my eyes. "You're impossible."

"And I think you're secretly in love with Derek."

"I'm not talking about this with you anymore." She couldn't understand because she'd never been hurt like I had. "I won't be with someone who could lie to me like that. So convincingly."

"Patrick said he wanted to stay out of it and let you decide what to do about your marriage. He was hoping you'd come to him once it was over—if it was over."

I shook my head, my voice growing thick. "When the man you love, the man you married, attempts to rape you, then beats you when you try to defend yourself, it makes it impossible to tolerate much from anyone. Ever again."

"Oh, Mel," Elaine crossed the kitchen to me, tears in her eyes. "We don't have to talk about it anymore." She pulled me into a hug, and I held her waist. For a moment we were both silent, remembering that horrible night, how it changed everything. Including me.

"I just care about you," she said, wiping her nose. "And I know Derek's sorry. He's such a good guy."

"Let's have some dinner," I said, going to the bag. I pulled out the box of ziti while she began cutting a pepper.

"Patrick wants to relocate," she said quietly, sliding the ingredients into the waiting sauté pan. "Since their work is primarily online, he'd like to move here."

My lips pressed together as I filled a pot with water and put it on the stove to boil the pasta. Once it was going, I picked up my glass again and leaned against the counter. "Are you two that serious?"

She shrugged. "Maybe. I mean, it's hard to know when we're separated. Distance makes everything so emotionally charged. It's like the first time every time."

"Sounds like you two are enjoying some hot reunions."

Elaine blushed then laughed. "It almost makes me want to maintain the distance."

The water was boiling, and I turned to dump in the ziti. For a few moments, I watched it, poking the dry noodles with a wooden spoon. My mind drifted to the time I'd had with Derek.

Had our intensity all been a product of some feeling of urgency?

He had known the whole time I was married, but he claimed he didn't know how bad my situation was. Was he afraid I wouldn't leave Sloan? Did he think I might decide to stay with my husband?

I shook my head. It didn't matter.

"So the marketing business is booming?" My friend was finished chopping and handed off the raw ingredients to me before hopping up on the counter.

I took her handiwork and pushed it all into the pan, cranking up the heat and stirring rapidly. "It is, and thanks to you, Saint Samuel's has become one of my most loyal clients."

"Good. They need the help." Her little school was trying to grow but struggling against new, free charter options. "Have you heard any more from . . . him?"

I sighed and turned the heat down to let everything simmer. "Sloan tried giving me trouble over the divorce proceedings, but I faxed those emails to Thomas. He said I'd have my final paperwork by the end of next week."

"He's such a prick," Elaine growled, taking a sip of her wine. "I still can't believe you didn't take him for everything he has."

"I don't want anything he has," I said, sipping my own wine. "He's a bastard fucknut, and I hope I never see him again."

"A no-nut sphincter taster."

I snorted and caught my nose with my hand. "A what?!" I cried.

Elaine split into laughter. "I don't know. It's something my brother used to say."

"Come on," I pulled her off the counter. "Let's go eat."

Elaine stayed until after midnight. We enjoyed the spicy ziti and peppers with our red wine and finished it all off with coffee and tiramisu. I asked her to spend the night, but she insisted she had to get up early for a teacher's meeting the next day. So we hugged each other, and she started back for the mainland.

After she left, I walked down to the shore again—this time

using my flashlight. It was a secluded area, and that only increased my risk of getting lost in the dark. But I was careful, and I was learning my way around my new landscape.

At the water's edge, I sat and reconsidered everything Elaine and Patrick had told me. I thought about Derek losing his wife, and the pain he must have felt to spend six years alone. What about me had brought him out of that isolation? Did he connect to a shared sense of loss? Was I able to help him find his way back from that sadness? Could he help me?

I thought about getting away from Sloan. Once the final divorce papers were in, I'd be free and I could truly recover from the disappointment and ultimately the trauma that had been my married life. After that, I could think about maybe talking to people and perhaps giving certain people second chances. If those people were still interested.

Who knew, perhaps it was possible the road to anywhere could turn into a road to somewhere. For both of us.

SEVENTEEN

FINALLY OVER

MY MOTHER WAS VISITING THE day my divorce papers arrived. We both sat at the kitchen table drinking coffee when the postman rang the bell. He carried a package wrapped in brown paper and a long, legal-sized envelope along with assorted letters and bills. I handed Mom the package to open as I pulled the brown envelope apart. She let out an exclamation of delight, but my face fell. In her hands was a box of cupcakes from Bea's Fancy Cakes, but in mine were several long, legal-sized sheets. At the very top of the first page, in bold, all-capital letters were the words FINAL DECREE.

Despite everything that had happened, all the pain and humiliation, a sick lump of failure tightened in the back of my throat. I swallowed it down and blinked to her frowning eyes. She slowly lowered her happy gift.

"Oh, Mel. How are you doing really?" she asked in her best psychiatrist's voice.

"I'm relieved, of course," I exhaled, trying to smile. "But I confess, seeing my name there in black and white followed by DIVORCE in all caps . . ." I shrugged. "I can't help remembering how optimistic I was on our wedding day. I thought my life would be so different."

To her credit, my mother only nodded. Once I'd returned to Wilmington, she'd dropped all suggestions that I try to work things out with Sloan. She immediately switched to supportive mode, and any indications that I might have made a mistake were gone. I assumed she reserved those types of urgings for the pre-divorce discussions, and now that it was over, so were they. Either way, I was thankful. Yet at the same time, I could sense she knew there was more I wasn't telling her.

"Here," she said, putting the package on the counter and going to my refrigerator. She opened the door and pulled out a bottle of champagne I'd stuck in the back—in case of celebration. I'd read a quote that said sometimes just having a bottle of champagne in the fridge could be a reason to celebrate. That was two months ago.

"It's time to open this guy," she said.

"What?" My brows pulled together in disbelief.

"We're celebrating. It's a new chapter in your life." I watched as she twisted the wire basket off the cork and then popped it.

"Talk about pendulum swings."

Mom shook her head. "You were very different when you got back home three months ago. I didn't say anything at the time, but you had a definite look in your eyes."

I pulled two flutes down from the cabinet and placed them in front of her to fill.

"Was it the look of a crazy person?"

"We don't use that term in the profession," she gently scolded as she poured. We waited for the fizz to settle, then she held my glass out. "You looked like you'd been through a long and difficult battle."

I took the sparkling wine from her. "I had," I said softly.

"You looked nearly broken," her voice strained. "It hurt so much to see the remnants of that kind of pain on your face."

My mom's eyes were brown, but she had my dark curls. Our eyes met in a warm understanding, and she stepped forward. "I believe you did the right thing," she said, pulling me into a hug.

"I'm sorry I ever questioned you."

For a moment, I relaxed in her healing embrace. She didn't know the full story; I didn't want her to know the full story. It was enough that we were here. It was more than enough. My head rested on her shoulder, and I held her waist.

A few minutes passed and I stepped back, giving her a smile. I sniffed and wiped my eyes. "Thanks, Mom."

Then she clinked her glass to mine. "Here's to a better future."

I smiled and agreed, taking a sip.

MOM STAYED THROUGH DINNER, AND we had one of our best visits since I'd married Sloan. It was a cold night, and she pulled on one of my sweaters. I lit the gas log, and we sat close together in front of the fireplace sipping coffee and eating the luscious cinnamon-bun cupcakes.

They were warm and comforting and perfectly timed, considering what else arrived with them. Not only that, they were cupcakes like only Aunt Bea could make—moist and buttery cake with a slightly spicy cinnamon ribbon swirling through the middle. On top was a deliciously crusty buttercrème frosting that was the exact flavor of cinnamon bun icing. We were both swooning from the first bite.

"None of my clients send me gifts like this," Mom teased, finishing her small confection.

"Isn't Bea the best?" I agreed, taking another nibble. "She can't figure out the Internet, but I convinced her I could maintain her account from here. And I still get my seasonal treats."

Mom placed her hand over mine and rubbed. "I'm glad to hear Baltimore wasn't all bad."

I nodded. "There are great people there. Bea was one of the best."

Aunt Bea might not understand how small the world had become, but she did know how to show kindness from any distance. Her gifts went a long way toward restoring my faith in both humanity and in one's ability to recover from any setback.

"I need a tree," I said, taking a sip of coffee and hoping to transition the conversation away from the past. Christmas was coming, and Mom loved decorating.

It was the perfect detour, and she immediately launched into the different options I might choose. That led to the topic of gifts, so I pulled out my Macbook. We spent the next few hours looking at pin boards and making lists, until she announced it was late.

I walked her out, promising to drive in and spend the night with her the next weekend—we could complete our lists, do some shopping. For a few moments I stood outside in the cold air, listening to the waves crashing far off and watching the taillights of her car fade into the distance.

Slowly I went back inside and put our dishes in the dishwasher. Our champagne flutes were still in front of the fireplace, but I was tired. I walked to my bedroom ready to wash my face and slip between the cool sheets. Halfway there, I heard a noise in the kitchen. A banging as if a window were falling.

"Mom?" I called, swiftly going back down the hall. "Did you forget something?"

The scream was out of my mouth before a thought registered in my brain. Sloan stood in the kitchen doorway, backlit by the yellow lights. "It's only me, hon."

I dashed into the living room and ran around the couch, putting as much space between us as possible. Quickly, I scanned my room for anything to use as a weapon. All I saw was a lamp.

"S-Sloan . . ." I caught my breath, struggling to keep my voice calm, not fearful. Authoritative and not yielding my ground. "What are you doing here?"

"That's not very a welcoming remark," he said, with a grin, a wicked glint in his eye. "We're supposed to show guests that southern hospitality, aren't we?"

"What do you want?" I reached for the lamp, resting my hand on the neck and waiting.

"Nice place," he said, surveying my new home. "I see you got your divorce papers today. Not celebrating, I hope."

Fear stole the air from my lungs as he quickly crossed the room to me. I snatched up the lamp, but he caught my wrist, jerking it and sending the fixture crashing to the floor. I tried to pull my arm away, but he held it fast, turning me so my back was pressed firmly against his chest.

"You bet I'm celebrating," I grunted, struggling to free myself from his grip. "My time with you is over. Legally. And forever."

He only held me closer, wrapping my other arm around my waist and holding me still. "And what are you telling all your old friends about our divorce? That I slept with prostitutes? That I beat you?"

I shivered with dread as his breath whooshed across the back of my neck. "No," I said, fighting to keep my voice calm, to stay in control. "I figured that was too much information."

He laughed. "I'll say. Especially since it was all your fault."

I struggled so hard to get away from him, my shoulders ached. Finally I gave up. I'd have to out-think him. I wasn't strong enough to overpower him. For starters, I wouldn't fall for his tricks. He knew as well as I did what happened that night. And whose fault it was.

"You still haven't told me why you're here," I said. "What do you want?"

His voice was right at my ear. "I want you, of course. You're incredibly sexy as a single woman. And we never said a proper goodbye."

His grip loosened on my arms, and I jerked them both free. He only caught me by the waist and pulled me back. "I hope you're not planning to fight me again. You know I'll win."

My stomach lurched, and I hated the dread his words

triggered in me. I had to calm my mind, I had to think. Somehow, I had to throw him off and then make my escape.

Taking a deep breath, and closing my eyes for a moment, I relaxed my fighting. I imagined getting a gift on Christmas morning, happy feelings. I tried to make my voice sound like I was having a pleasant realization.

"You're saying you want to spend the night here?" I was all innocence now. "I guess that's a good idea. You're pretty far from Baltimore, and it's very late."

The smile returned to his voice and he released me. "To be clear, my dear, I'm not just looking to spend the night. I'm looking to fuck somebody. Namely you. I vaguely recall you're not too bad in the sack."

I swallowed the tightness in my throat and turned to face him. "But I don't understand. Why me? Why not call an escort service?" My eyes flickering around the room, double-checking for something to hit him with. "You know you prefer them." The words were bitter on my tongue, but I was playing a part, buying time.

"Thanks for your concern about my satisfaction," he said, lifting an empty champagne flute and sniffing it. "But I confess, my interest in you is renewed now that you've added an 'ex' to your prefix. You're still a hot little piece of ass. Oh, and I wanted to let you know, I'm aware you've got someone keeping tabs on me."

My mind was still working, trying to figure out an escape plan, but that made me pause. "I don't have anyone watching you."

"Whatever you say," he breathed, unbuttoning his shirt. "But I'm not an idiot, darling." He pulled the shirt tail out of his pants and started toward me.

I'd given up on finding a weapon. Tomorrow I was buying a bat, but for now, I had to get out of this house. I grabbed my empty flute and headed for the kitchen.

"I'll fix us both a drink. White or red?" My plan at this point was to run for it—even if it was into the dark night, even if it was bitterly cold, and I'd probably end up lost. I'd figure that out once I was away.

"Whatever you're having is fine," he called after me.

My innocent act must have worked. I couldn't believe he let me leave the room, but I hurried into the kitchen, hoping my purse was still sitting on the counter. It wasn't.

I was contemplating my bare feet when a massive arm swept me off the ground by my waist. A hand clamped tight over my mouth to keep me from screaming, and I was held tightly against a solid chest.

"It's me," Derek's voice was barely audible, right beside my ear. "I'm here to help you."

My heart hammered against my ribs as he gently lowered me to my feet again. I was shaking all over as I turned to face him, relief coursing through me.

As always, I noticed how the black tee he wore was stretched tight over his chest, but tonight, my attention was on his biceps straining at the sleeves, his hands clenched in fists. I almost burst into tears at the sight, and just as fast, all I could think was I wanted him to beat the shit out of Sloan.

"Mel?" I heard Sloan's voice from the living room. "You okay in there?"

Derek held a finger over his lips and then circled two fingers around each other as if to indicate "keep it going." He held up a digital recorder, and I bit my lip nodding.

"Yeah," I said, swallowing the knot in my throat. "No clean wine glasses."

"I can help with that," he answered.

"No!" I said quickly. "It's okay. In fact . . ." I went to the doorway and back into the living room. "I've changed my mind. You're not staying here. In fact, it's time for you to go. Now. I don't want you here anymore."

If Derek was doing what I thought he was, I needed to make this count.

"What?" Sloan said, turning to face me, his expression of surprise turning into anger and thinly veiled arousal. He made me sick. "I thought we'd moved past the rough stuff. But I'm happy to revisit it. Whatever you want."

"I don't want any of your *stuff*," I said, wondering if I should speak louder. "Take your shit and get out of my house. We're not married anymore."

His smile was tight over his gritted teeth, and he crossed the room to me quickly, grabbing my arm and bending it back behind me. "You little bitch," he hissed. "You'll take whatever I give you and like it. As much money as I spent on you."

"Ouch!" I tried to jerk my arm away, but he pulled it higher up my back. "You're hurting me," I said loudly.

I was in real pain, but more importantly, I wanted this on the record. This time, I wanted him to pay.

"Then stop fighting," he said, pulling me against his pelvis by the front of my jeans and flicking my top button loose with his fingers.

"Or what?" My voice was still loud. "You'll rape me? Beat me again?"

"It's not rape if you like it," he said, moving in for a kiss.

"I said no, Sloan!" I said his name loud and clear, bracing to have to fight him, to do whatever it took for Derek to get the evidence he needed.

I was just closing my eyes when I felt the swish of air from a fast-moving body followed by a loud *crack!* My eyes blinked open, and Sloan was on the floor. My piece of shit ex-husband moved once before he passed out completely.

It took me a second to register what had happened. Derek stood over him looking down, breathing hard. His jaw was clenched as were his fists, and it looked like he might do more, like one punch wasn't enough to satisfy him. And while I'd have been happy for him to beat Sloan beyond recognition, I didn't want anything to ruin our chances of putting that loser away.

I quickly stepped in front of Derek, placing my hands on his arms. "I'm okay," I said, pulling him gently. My whole body was trembling. I couldn't seem to stop it, but I had to get him to look at me and not Sloan lying on the floor. "I'm okay, Derek."

As if waking, Derek blinked to me and then took a deep breath. His worried eyes traveled over my face briefly before he leaned down to wrap his arms around my waist, pulling me tight against his body. My insides melted, and tears flooded my eyes. I wasn't sure if it was from the close-call, or post-traumatic stress, or if it was just holding him again this way. Maybe it was a combination of all three, but I gripped my arms around his neck and held him as my body shook with sobs.

"It's okay," he whispered, stroking my hair. "It's over. I will never let him hurt you again."

I nodded against his chest, and he held me several long moments. His hands stroked my back gently until I could finally breathe again without jerking out a sob.

Derek straightened up and lifted my chin with his finger, looking into my eyes. "Okay?" he said, sliding his thumbs gently over my damp cheeks.

I sniffed and nodded, wiping my nose with my hand. "Why were you here?" I asked, as he released me to pull out his phone.

"I never stopped watching him." He was touching the phone quickly as he spoke. "Ever since that day you came to my office, I've been keeping tabs on him."

Elaine had told me that . . . I stepped away, going to the kitchen to get a tissue and check my face. "But why?" I called back. "Did you have a reason to think he was going to—"

"I had no idea Sloan had turned into such a fucked up loser when he contacted me about you," he said, following me into the kitchen. "But after you showed me that picture . . ." his lips tightened. "It's a pattern of behavior. I had a feeling he might try it again."

He stepped to the door leading out. "I just need to make a quick call and get somebody out here," he said. "Don't worry, I'll talk to them. I'll keep it out of the media."

His words sent such a wave of relief over me. He'd said the one thing I'd needed to hear, the thing that had held me silent before, without even knowing it.

"Thank you," I whispered.

"You'll still have to answer some questions, but I'll do what I can."

Before he went through the door, I stepped forward and caught his arm, pulling him back. He paused, and I leaned in, pressing a kiss to his cheek. "You are a hero. You're my hero."

His eyes gleamed and he touched my face gently with the back of his index finger. Happiness filled my chest. "I only wish I'd known sooner," he said.

POLICE ARRIVED IN AN UNMARKED vehicle, and Sloan was handcuffed and taken into custody. I had to make a statement, but Derek stayed beside me. His background was a huge assist in corroborating my story, but the real clincher was the recording he'd made. That combined with the picture I'd shown him from before provided enough evidence to form the basis of a solid case.

"We need to ask a few questions," the officer started, but Derek stopped him.

"I know what you need to know," he said. "Would you let me ask her?"

"We have to hear her answers," the man said.

Derek turned to me sitting at my small table and held both my hands. "There's only a few things they need to know."

I nodded, focusing on his blue eyes.

"Do you want to press charges against Sloan Reynolds?"

"Yes," I said softly. "I didn't before, but I do now."

"In the photo from before, clearly you were beaten." Derek paused and stroked the back of my hands gently. "Did he also rape you that night?"

I shook my head. "He tried, but when I hit him, everything changed. After that he only beat me." My throat grew thick as I remembered Sloan's face as he hit and kicked me. The sick gleam in his eyes. I was afraid I might cry, but I pushed on. "It was as if he got off on beating me."

Derek's lips tightened, and I watched him inhale slowly, the muscle in his jaw flexed. "Would you be willing to share those emails with us? It's possible he also beat one or more of those women. I'd like to track them down and see if any of them will talk. Maybe take a plea deal."

Squeezing his hands, I stood and walked slowly to my bedroom, feeling slightly light-headed. I had planned never to share this information with anyone. I only kept it as insurance, in case I needed it to make Sloan behave or leave me alone. I went to my closet and dug out the two manila folders then returned to the kitchen. Derek and the officer were talking softly, the officer was making notes, but when I appeared they both fell silent.

"Here," I said. "There were more. Many more, but these are the only ones I printed out."

The officer nodded and took the stack from me. Derek stood and squeezed my upper arm gently. "Hang tight. I'll just walk these guys out. See if they have any more questions."

Once they were gone, I walked slowly to my living room, dropping onto the couch. I was exhausted and still a little shaky, but at the same time, I felt hopeful. It was possible this was finally over. This horrible chapter was finally closed.

EIGHTEEN

SHARING EVERYTHING

FINALLY, AFTER WHAT SEEMED LIKE a long time, everyone but Derek was gone. Sloan's car was impounded, and the only noises left at my house were the cicadas and the waves breaking softly in the distance.

"They might want to question Elaine, since she was the only person who saw what happened the first time," he said, standing in my kitchen.

I nodded, blinking up at him, seeing him in a new way tonight. "I can't believe how relieved I feel," I said. "I thought I was through with Sloan. I thought once the divorce was final and I was back here it was over. But I see now I was always fearful. And it would never be over while he was free."

He nodded. "I know." Then he straightened, putting his hands in his back pockets and causing the shirt to stretch over his chest. "I'm sorry, Mel. I'm so sorry for my part in all this. I really had no idea when he emailed me—"

I stood quickly. "Please don't," I said. "After tonight, your apology is so accepted. And maybe . . . maybe I've started to understand why you didn't tell me."

His brow relaxed, and a glimmer of hope shone in his eyes. He took a small step in my direction. "I swear, when I saw you that night in the bar, all I wanted was to take you from him. I wanted you to be mine." My heart squeezed at his words, and he continued. "I know that makes me a bad person, but you were so gorgeous. And so clearly miserable. I only wanted to make you happy, to see you smile."

"I was unbelievably miserable," I said softly, remembering the first night of that trip. "But you changed all that. And now you've changed it even more."

He took another small step towards me. "I wanted to tell you what was going on so much, but, well, I felt if there was a chance for your marriage, I should step aside and let you work it out. As much as I hated it, he'd found you first."

I breathed a laugh, shaking my head. "You stepped aside after you fucked me like nobody in the world ever had."

He was right in front of me then, and he cautiously reached out to hold my waist. "If it makes any difference, it was a pretty new experience for me, too."

My hands rested on his biceps, and I met his eyes teasing. "Are you trying to say I blew your mind?"

He smiled for real then and leaned down to my face. "You were the first I'd had in a long time. And you were amazing." Then he kissed my nose. "Thank you."

My arms slid up to his neck, and I pulled him down. "You haven't done anything to thank me for yet."

At that he closed the space between us, covering my mouth with his as he caught my ass and pulled me up against him. I held his neck, threading my fingers into his soft hair. Our mouths opened and our tongues collided, sending heat shooting straight between my legs.

His mouth broke away from mine briefly, "Where's the bedroom?" he asked.

Holding his neck, I looked over my left shoulder. "This way." I loosened my legs from his waist and he lowered me, following me to the small room in the back.

"I might need a bigger bed," I murmured as his hands moved

from my waist under the front of my shirt to my breasts. I lay my head back against his shoulder, releasing a sigh as his fingers slid beneath my bra, caressing my nipples and filling my body with fire.

He kissed my neck, and I turned around slowly, finding his lips again as both our hands worked at our waists, unfastening buttons, lowering zippers. Two tugs and our shirts were off, and he reached out and grabbed me, lifting me up against his chest again. I reached back to remove my bra as my legs wrapped around his waist, my arms around his neck.

For a moment, we simply looked into each others' eyes. "You've had a pretty stressful night," he said. "I'll understand if you just want to sleep."

I slid my fingers through his hair, allowing myself to ac-knowledge for the first time since Princeton, how much I loved him.

"I want you to fuck my brains out," I smiled, leaning for-ward to nibble his lip.

He tilted his head up, quickly covering my mouth with his in a hungry kiss.

His lips moved to my jaw, tracing a burning line to my ear as he spoke. "I want to give you everything you want." Then he laid me back on the bed. I only had a second to wonder when he caught my thighs and pulled me to his mouth. His large hands squeezed my breasts, taunting my nipples as he bit at the front of my thong.

"Ooh, yes," I sighed, twisting with his touch. My eyes closed as my hips followed his movements, the tension in my pelvis growing with every expert touch. Finally, he slid his hands down my torso to my thong, which he removed. From there it was just his mouth kissing and pulling at my throbbing clit.

"Derek," I hissed as two thick fingers slipped inside me. Again, I let out a high-pitched whimper. He increased the pace, thrusting with his fingers as he pulled with his mouth, circling his tongue over my most sensitive parts. All at once the orgasm burst through me, and I cried out, pushing against his mouth and then pulling back.

"I want you inside me," I gasped, and he was up in an instant, dropping his shorts, revealing his massive cock. "Oh, please now." I gasped, but he froze, looking around my bedroom.

"Do you have a condom?" his voice was desperate.

"No," I gasped. His face fell, but I didn't care. I caught his hips and pulled him to me. "I know . . . but nothing's changed for me," I whispered. "There's been no one but you."

He caught my chin, looking into my eyes. "There's been no one but you," he confirmed, covering my mouth with his, stoking the heat raging in my stomach.

He pushed inside my slippery-wet entrance, both of us moaning in satisfaction. "Fuck, you feel so good," he growled against my neck, thrusting again deeper into me.

I nudged his shoulder, and he rolled onto his back, grasping my buttocks in both strong hands and lifting me up and down on top of him.

"I love that," I sighed against his neck, savoring the sensation of him, hot and full, hitting me in all the right places. "I've missed you so much," I gasped.

He groaned and lifted me faster, pounding me harder. I sat up and rocked my hips, rotating the angle so my clit got the full force of his thrusting. In seconds I was moaning and bucking. "Oh, god Derek, oh," I cried.

He rolled us over again so he was back on top, and I reached above my head, gripping the headboard. His mouth dropped to my breasts, and he gently kissed then bit my nipples, pulling another desperate cry from my throat as I shot over the edge, shuddering as I came. He kept pushing through my spasming muscles until in two sharp thrusts he slammed a hand against the wall behind my bed. "Fuck," he ground out as he went incredibly deep, coming hard and hot inside me.

He let out a few more ragged breaths, thrusting with each, and then he slowed, rolling us onto our sides, still buried between my legs. Little spasms continued pulsing through me, holding us together, and Derek hugged me tightly against his chest. My heart melted at the warmth of being surrounded in his arms, back in this wonderful place with him. With each gentle kiss to my forehead, my brow, my closed eyes, my love for him grew stronger.

We lay panting, holding each other for several long moments. It had been months since our last time, but nothing had changed. It was still as hot and breathtaking and beautiful as always. At last he slid out, holding me close in his arms and kissing my lips, gently parting them so our tongues could curl together. I smiled against his mouth, holding onto him, loving all of these pleasing sensations, basking in the afterglow of us together, reunited.

He rolled onto his back, pulling me against his chest and sliding his fingers down my back, tracing the lines in the way I loved.

"I missed you so much," I whispered. "It was terrible to be apart for so long."

He bent his elbow to place his hand under his head. "I felt the same way," he said with an exhale. "Every day, I would stare out the windows for the longest time wondering where you were, what you were doing. If you were happy, if you had made up with him. If you even thought about me."

My eyes grew damp, and I reached up to trace a finger down his perfect nose. "I did something very similar."

He lifted his chin to kiss my fingertip. "You did?"

I nodded. "Only I took it a step further. I would to go your company website and gaze at your picture. You're so handsome in that suit."

He smiled and changed our position, rolling us over and looking deep into my eyes. "I was afraid I'd become obsessed," he said softly. "Your blue eyes haunted me, and the way your voice cracks when you say my name when I'm inside you."

A wave of pleasure rushed through me at his words. He

kissed the little hollow where my collarbones came together. "I still have your necklace," he said, lifting his head to look at my face again. "I hope you'll take it back."

"Do you have it with you? I'll put it on right now."

"Yes, but stay here with me."

He moved to his side, and I snuggled close against his chest. His arms tightened around me as a deep sigh of satisfaction left his lips. Then he kissed the top of my shoulder.

"Melissa," he said, and the note of concern in his voice caused me to lean back and check his expression.

A line pierced my forehead. "What?"

He cleared his throat and looked down, then he pressed his lips against mine briefly. "I want to say this. It doesn't have to be tomorrow, but I need you to know—"

"What is it?" Concern tightened my chest. I had no idea what he needed me to know. I was afraid it might have something to do with the time we were apart. Maybe something he'd done?

He smiled at my expression. "I'm glad you look so worried, I guess."

I pushed back on his shoulder, sitting up in the bed. "If you don't finish that sentence . . ."

He rose to a sitting position beside me, catching my hand and pulling the back of it to his lips. "I want more than a week this time," he said, his voice turning gentle. "Much more." He paused and then held my gaze. "One day soon, when you're feeling whole again, I'm going to ask you to marry me."

My heart turned to liquid. "What?" My voice was a high whisper.

"I know," he quickly added. "You're just out of a bad marriage. You were married to a major league asshole. The ink isn't dry on your divorce papers. I'm not asking you for anything right now . . . But I will."

Tears clouded my vision. "And I'll say yes."

A smile broke across his face, brightening his beautiful blue eyes. He kissed me again, and I caught his cheeks, holding his lips against mine, opening my mouth and finding his tongue.

He kissed me again, longer, and I pushed him to his back, straddling him as I kissed his lips again and again. The heat was growing between my legs, and his palms scratched against the skin of my thighs, gently rising to my butt. My mouth broke from his and I let out a groan. "I want you again," I laughed, breathless.

He caught my hips and guided me down as he slid inside, filling me completely. We were off, and I couldn't stop smiling at the prospect of a lifetime together. Him with me, surrounding me, in me. Sharing everything.

And instead of pulling each other down, we'd be setting each other free.

"One request," I said, placing my palms flat on his chest.

"Oh, god, anything," he groaned, thrusting deeply.

His ravenous desire sent a wave of electricity through me. "I want to honeymoon in the desert."

"Done," he breathed, threading his fingers into my hair and pulling my mouth back to his.

I turned. "And at least once, we have to visit the family restroom together."

He growled a yes, making me laugh before he caught me in a deep, passionate kiss. My back arched and I moaned against his mouth. Wrapping my arms around his neck I rocked my hips, dreaming of that place of warm sunsets and gorgeous, fireside memories. We'd toast to happy surprises, and we'd share many (after)glowing thank yous.

The End

EPILOGUE

Derek

HER DARK HAIR FANS OUT over the white pillow in perfect curls. Lifting one, I gently twist a shining spiral around my finger, sliding my thumb across the silky strand. The only thing more beautiful is her face, smooth and blissful in sleep.

I rest my head on my hand as I watch her breasts gently rise and fall, thinking of our last two months together. Early in December, I'd won her back by having that bastard Sloan arrested. I'd wanted to do more. Standing over his unconscious body in her living room, after he'd tried to hurt her again . . .

It had been years since I'd fought the urge to kill someone. If she hadn't been there, I might've.

Of course, he posted bail and was back hiding in his mansion a day later. He called in his team of lawyers, and Melissa backed down. I wasn't ready to let it go, but she begged me to drop it. She didn't want to be front-page news or dragged through a long ordeal. Reluctantly, I gave in to her. But every time I see that tiny silver scar near her hairline, it takes all my strength to keep from driving to Baltimore and beating him to a bloody pulp.

Only her bright eyes and happy smile calm those thoughts. And now she's having my baby. Our pre-Christmas slip up had been one too many, but I couldn't be happier. When Alison died, I thought my chances at being a father were over. That day, I'd walked away from everything having to do with love and family. I'd shut down, not even interested in trying again. Then six years later, my twisted mentor brought this gorgeous creature into my life.

The night I saw her in Scottsdale, I'd never seen such intense sadness in another person before. She was so beautiful, and yet she was visibly suffering. I knew how that felt. I'd struggled with intense sorrow, but somehow as the time had passed, my mourning period had ended, and I wanted her. I wanted to take all her unhappiness away with my love if she'd let me. And she did.

My hand moved from the curl around my finger to the top of her forehead, right where her dark hair met her ivory skin. Barely touching her, I remembered how incredible that first night had been—that whole week. It was a second chance. Until we'd had to part.

She stirs, dipping her chin the way she always does before opening her eyes. No use thinking about the days we were apart because now we're together, and I'm going to make her my wife.

Her gorgeous blue eyes blink open, and I can't help but smile. "Good morning."

"Were you watching me sleep?" Her soft voice is thick with sleep, and she turns her face into the pillow. Her slim bare shoulder lifts to her cheek, and just like that I have a hard-on. I want to pull her under me and kiss that shoulder, those lips, every part of her, but I control myself. She's just opened her eyes after all.

"You're beautiful when you sleep." I state the obvious, which always makes her blush. The fact this woman can't see how gorgeous she is drives me nuts. At the same time, it's part of the reason I love her so much. She's so focused on her work and her plans and us. She's completely unself-conscious.

"How are you feeling?" My hand travels down the length of her smooth back. Her body hasn't started showing she's pregnant yet. Well, her breasts are slightly larger, but they've always been the right size for me. Perfect handfuls.

She scoots into my chest, and immediately my arms go around her small frame. I love being able to lift her against me when we make love or surround her with protection. But, she's tough as nails. She lived through a year of hell and without anyone's help, she survived and made a new life for herself. That old urge to kill Sloan flickers again in my chest, but she banishes it by lifting her chin and kissing my throat.

"Hungry," she says, answering the question I'd left hanging. And with that she pushes above me, smiling. "I know I'm not really eating for two, but I swear, I don't remember ever craving breakfast like this. I want eggs with cheese and tomatoes and peppers . . ."

I laugh, lifting a clutch of dark curls off her shoulder and planting a kiss there. Her skin smells like roses and the ocean.

"And bacon!" she cries. "I want applewood-smoked bacon so bad right now. Doesn't that sound delicious?"

"You don't have to sell bacon to me." I pull her to me and kiss her nose.

Last night, her body had been wrapped around me in the most amazing way. As always, she'd cried out my name, shaking and moaning as she came hard and full over me. It was all I could do to hold out as she finished, she was so fucking gorgeous. I would do anything to keep this woman happy.

"I'm at a little disadvantage here," I say, sitting up with her in my arms. "You're a local now, but I'm still in Princeton. I don't know the best place to satisfy these new cravings."

Her arms go around my neck and she kisses my lips briefly. "Then let me show you!"

I smile, reaching for her, but she's gone—headed to the bathroom, leaving me to admire her perfect ass and tame this erection she's left me with. My sexual urges have to wait, it seems. Clearly, the mother of my child needs bacon.

"There's this historic little place in town," she calls from the hallway. I step into the boxer-briefs I tossed across the room last night after we returned home from dinner with Elaine and Patrick. Our clothes are a messy trail leading into the kitchen where we started.

Patrick relocated his base of operations to Wilmington last month. It was his early Christmas gift to Elaine, and it looked like he might beat me to the marriage punch. But I have a plan for today. And well, I already laid the ground work for it the night we made junior. Since then idea of us getting married has been theoretical, but today, I'd make it official.

"What's the name?" I call back, studying the picture of her and her mother in a weathered-wooden frame on her dresser. The two smile exactly alike, but her mother doesn't have Melissa's gorgeous blue eyes.

"The Sawmill. It's supposed to be really good," she says, returning to the room. I smile as she goes into her closet, completely unaware of how the sight of her naked, wearing only a thong and my floating-heart necklace affects me. "Did I say it's historic?"

She steps into a black skirt and I watch as she pulls a long-sleeved, faded red tee over her head. The vintage fabric hugs her braless torso in a way I want to. I can't help myself anymore. I go to her and pull her against my chest.

"I love you," I say, covering her mouth with mine. As always, she seems to melt.

She is such an amazing combination to me. This tiny firecracker, strong as a flint, able to survive the shit her asshole ex-husband had put her through. Yet when I kiss her, her entire body becomes fluid in my hands. It's very distracting.

I make sure she's standing before I completely release her to put on my shirt. Her nipples are erect as she grabs my fleece jacket off a chair and pulls it around her body. It's enormous on her, but she tucks her nose inside and inhales deeply.

"I'm keeping this when you go back," she says. "I might sleep in it."

Stepping into my jeans, her bedroom eyes have me fighting

the return of that erection. "So you want to go to the Sawmill or not?"

"Yes," she laughs. "Bacon."

"THERE IS NO APPLEWOOD-SMOKED BACON," I say as we study the menu.

The Sawmill restaurant is a traditional dive. Its exposed-wood interior is covered in tools of the logging trade, and the pages of our menus are covered in plastic. Still, I'm no snob. All the breakfast options look great to me, but I know how Mel's pregnancy has her craving specific things. I'd already been sent in search of Manhattan Key Lime pie the day after Christmas, and we have someone known as "Aunt Bea" on our speed-dial in case of emergencies.

She sighs. "It's okay. Regular bacon will do."

Our eyes meet, and the small, black-velvet box in my pocket feels hot as a coal waiting to be taken out and presented to her. I want to propose now, to claim her as mine, like nothing I'd ever wanted before, but I also want it to be special. So I wait.

"All bacon is wood-smoked, right?" I say as the waiter returns. "And Sawmill benedict? They've substituted gravy for hollandaise."

A little laugh escapes her throat. "Let's get that gravy on the side," she says. "And an omelet and a scrambler. And a juice and keep that coffee coming."

The waiter nods and leaves, and with a chuckle, I gesture for her to come around to my side of the table. As always, she's quick to comply. Sliding in next to me, she slips her arms around my neck and kisses my lips.

"I love you," she whispers. "Last night was . . ."

"Screaming Os, I'm the king and all that?"

I love the sound of her laughter. "I have never—" Our eyes

meet and her tone drops. She pretend-coughs, adjusting her story in an amusing fashion. "You are *always* all of those things," she purrs.

My elbow is bent on the top of the bench behind her. I study her face a moment. "So this is where you want to stay. In this little town."

Our permanent residence is the one roadblock to our union we keep stumbling over.

"How can you even ask me that?" She turns, putting both elbows on the table as she lifts her coffee cup to her lips. "Living at the beach is a dream come true for most people."

"We don't have to sell your house," I repeat my argument, smiling at her cute stubbornness, as if adjusting her position can keep my words out. I move my hand to her waist and then under her shirt, spreading my palm over her bare stomach, thinking about what's growing there. "We can keep it, and you can come here as often as you like for vacations or whatever."

She lowers her cup and leans back, placing her hand on top of mine still covering her flat stomach. Our physical familiarity is another thing I love about her. She's unfazed by my hand against her skin. It's as if every one of my touches is not only welcome, but expected.

"We might as well quit now," she exhales. "If we can't even get through this impasse, I have no idea what makes us think we can handle more serious issues."

I can't help a laugh, and my hand goes from her stomach to her chin. I lift her delicate face and cover her small mouth with mine, tasting the bitter almost-chocolate flavor of the coffee as I part her lips, our tongues lightly touching. I want nothing more than to carry her back to that pretty, miniscule condo of hers and fuck her twenty ways from Sunday. Show her just how strong our love is.

Releasing her face, I look into her now-darkened eyes. "Choosing a home base is actually a pretty big decision," I say. "I think if we can decide on a place where we'll both be happy, it's proof we can handle anything."

She's ready to relent. I know by her expression my kiss has left her willing to do anything I ask. God, I love her so much.

"Derek." When she says my name that way, I can't tell if she's aware I'll do anything she asks. "Sloan asked me to leave here. And it was the most unhappy decision I've ever made in my life. I never want to make that mistake again."

Her words sting, but I understand her fears. I saw what she survived. My fingers trace a light path down her cheek as I exhale. "For one, I'm not Sloan," I say, keeping my voice gentle. "And for two, we don't have to make this decision today."

She blinks and her smile returns. The waiter also returns with our orders, and I kiss the side of her head. As he puts three orders of eggs—poached, scrambled, and wrapped in an omelet—in front of us, all served with sides of sausage, bacon, and ham. We spread out the plates and get ready to sample, share, and devour.

"Delicious," she smiles, lifting a thin slice of salty pork and taking a big bite.

AFTER BREAKFAST WE HEAD DOWN to the shore in front of Melissa's place. My office is still closed for the New Year's holiday, which I spent wrapped in my lady's arms, but I'll be heading back to Princeton in another day.

She inhales deeply as we walk, and the strong breeze pushes her dark hair off her shoulders. It also whips her black skirt around her still-slim hips, and she has my fleece jacket zipped all the way up. It's like a dress on her.

"I have an idea," she says, slanting those baby blues at me, "What if you stay in Princeton and I stay here, and we just met up for conjugal visits?"

I decide to take her challenge and raise it. "That sounds like a reasonable plan. I can probably go a month between visits. How about you?"

Her expression almost costs me my poker face. Clearly she did not expect me to concede to her ridiculous offer, and it appears she might cry. Her brow melts into a frown, which she tries to lift and fails.

"I was only teasing," she says in a voice that twists my insides. "I can barely stand us being apart for a week."

It's impossible to hold out after that, and I scoop her small frame against my chest. "And I can barely stand two hours." I lean forward and kiss her again, and as always, her body melts into mine. It awakens my urge to take her.

"I've been thinking about you all morning," I say. "Let's go back to bed."

Her nose wrinkles as she laughs. "Maybe it is better for us to be separated for now. We're way too horny to get anything done in the same city."

Her use of the pronoun *we* is all I need. My eyes meet hers, and I see that fire brewing in them. It's only grown stronger since she's been pregnant, and I know from our first encounters she doesn't shrink from being risqué.

Glancing over my shoulder, I verify that we're alone. No one is out on this cold, January day but us, and we have the beach to ourselves. Still, I use discretion, leading her away from the open shoreline into a nearby patch of beach scrub. It's not only private, it's out of the breeze and less chilly.

I sit on the soft sand, pulling her onto my lap. Skirts and thong underwear might be my favorite clothing combination. My hands are up her thighs and caressing her clit as fast as our lips can find each other's. Her arms are tight around my neck and her whimpers slip out between passes of my mouth over hers. My erection is straining against the zipper of my jeans, and I want nothing more than to be buried in her tight, wet opening this instant. I've wanted it all morning.

Her hand goes to my waist to unfasten my pants, and when

her slim fingers wrap around me, the memory of her mouth closing over my tip almost sends me off. The first time she gave me head, I almost shot down her throat it was so good. But I fight to distract myself from those thoughts and get her off instead. I've been on edge all morning, and her hand sliding up and down my dick isn't helping. My fingers press into her wet opening as my thumb caresses her clit. I can tell by her breathing, she isn't far behind me.

"Ooh," she moans, sending shockwaves through my shaft. I want to be inside her so badly. Quickly, I slide down the zipper on my jacket and lift her shirt, catching one of her taut nipples in my mouth. Her breasts are gorgeous right now. I give one a little suck, and she sighs with pleasure. I almost lose control.

"I need to be inside you," I whisper, moving my mouth to her ear. I give her lobe a little bite, and she shivers. At once, she shifts her position, moving her thong aside and dropping down on my cock.

"Uuh," I can't help but groan as her warm passage envelops me. I wanted to lay her back and pound her hard on the sand, but I'm not sure she's finished yet. Gripping her ass, I lifted her up and down, keeping my thumb on her clit, massaging her.

Her arms tighten around my neck as her breasts rise under my chin with every lift. It's fucking amazing and almost more than I can take. "Derek," she gasps in my ear, and I know we're hitting the right spot. She's lifting herself on me now without my even helping her.

"Don't stop," she gasps, but I'm barely touching her as she works me. I'm doing everything in my power to hold out while she finishes. Her inner muscles tighten on me as her orgasm begins, pulling and releasing. It's far better than hands or a mouth, feeling her come around my cock.

"Oh, shit," I groan, but I can't stop it. Her inner workings have me shooting off inside her, and the pleasure momentarily blacks out my thoughts. All I know is me buried deep in her gorgeous body, my orgasm primed and extended by hers.

"Will you marry me?"

My eyes travel from her hand to the heart floating at her neck to her eyes, which are now shining. All I can remember is that night in the desert when she'd wanted to say she loved me. I'd gone immediately to the nearest jewelry store still open and bought the first thing they had with a heart on it. She'd stolen mine then, and I knew the only way to get it back would be to marry her.

With a hiccupped breath, her face breaks into a smile. "Yes," she nods. "I already told you I'd say yes, but yes, yes, yes." She laughs, wrapping her arms around my neck. Our mouths meet and my hand fumbles back down only briefly pausing before sliding around her waist, drawing her close against me. I love how our bodies move together so easily. We belong to each other.

"If you want me to move to Princeton, I will," she says, kissing my lips once more before resting her forehead against my cheek. I know right then she's saying she'll do whatever I want, and that's the funny thing with power. When the one you love gives it to you, you start looking for every opportunity to give it back or at the very least, use it for her happiness.

"I don't want you to leave the place you love," I say, my hands moving under her shirt to her breasts. I lay her back on the sand and push up her tee. Her belly isn't the slightest bit round yet, but we've both heard the little heart in there beating so fast.

I kiss her right below the navel. "It's not a bad drive. Let's get this little person here and then we'll decide what to do."

Her slim fingers thread into my hair as she exhales deeply. My wife. My beautiful wife who's given me another chance at a family. Even though my instinct resists, and my inner drive is to be the boss, she has my heart. I'll do anything for her.

I hold her close, resting my cheek on her skin, loving her. She continues lacing her fingers through my hair, and we listen to the soft noise of the breakers. It's as if we're on our own

Instinctively, my grip on her ass tightens, and I'm lifting her harder and faster up and down as I finish.

A hoarse moan scrapes from her throat, and as I continue moving her, more noises follow. Her thighs quiver, her knees press into the sand, and she's riding me now. She's making it, and after several more movements, she drops, arms draped around my neck, head on my shoulder, aftershocks slowly subsiding.

"God, I love you," I murmur, kissing her neck, traveling with my lips behind her ear, causing her to shiver again and laugh.

She sits up and holds my face, her cheeks pretty and pink from her climax. "I love you," she says in a breathy voice.

Our warmth is like our own little world. Sure, we might violate a public decency law every so often, but we take care to keep it secret and unseen. Without moving her away, staying buried deep between her thighs, I reach for my pants pocket.

"I've been trying to find the right time to give you this," I say, fumbling for the black velvet box. Her eyes widen, and instantly she's off my lap, pulling down her skirt and sitting beside me on the sand. She takes the small box, but doesn't open it.

Pulling my jeans up, I catch her eyes on mine, and I can see her enthusiasm. "Is this what I think it is?" Her voice is still breathless.

A smile crosses my lips. "I can't read your mind."

For a moment, she only holds it, and my stomach tightens in anticipation. I took a chance on this ring—it isn't the traditional diamond, but I figured since we've both been married once before, we might be up for something different.

With a quick glance back at me, she pulls the top open and then gasps. Inside is a square-cut blue sapphire ring encased in platinum with tiny white diamonds all around it. It's an art deco style, and it matches her eyes and the sea perfectly.

I take the box back and lift the ring out. Her fingers tremble slightly as I hold her hand in both of mine.

"Melissa Jones," I say, keeping the ring poised and ready.

private island together. After a while, we slowly stand, repositioning our clothes. Our fingers entwine as we walk back to her condo.

"I was thinking if it's a girl, we can call her Edith. If it's a boy, Dexter."

"No and maybe." I say curtly.

As tiny as she is, Mel is unexpectedly strong. She jerks my arm hard, and I can't suppress a laugh. "Edith is a terrible name for a baby."

"It's a family name," she cries.

"And I don't know about Dexter."

"I think it's cute. We can call him Dex."

"I was thinking Scott or Cactus Flower—for where we met."

Her brow wrinkles. "You cannot be serious."

I laugh again. So perhaps we have the housing situation on hold—now begins a new round of debate. Baby names. Knowing how stubborn we both are, I figure we can prolong this argument into the child's fifth birthday when it can decide.

She's still fussing, and I know the one way to win any argument with Melissa. But I'll save my next win for the bedroom.

Thank you for reading!

ONE TO PROTECT

DEREK & MELISSA

BOOK #2

TIA LOUISE

When Sloan Reynolds beats criminal charges, Melissa Jones stops believing her wealthy, connected ex-husband will ever pay for what he did to her.

Derek Alexander can't accept that—a tiny silver scar won't let him forget, and as a leader in the security business, he is determined to get the man who hurt his fiancée.

Then the body of a former call girl turns up dead. She's the breakthrough Derek's been waiting for, the link to Sloan's sordid past he needs. But as usual, legal paths to justice have been covered up or erased.

Derek's ready to do whatever it takes to protect his family when his partner Patrick Knight devises a plan that changes everything.

It's a plan that involves coloring outside the lines and taking a walk on the dark side. It goes against everything on which Alexander-Knight, LLC, is based.

And it's a plan Derek's more than ready to follow.

A STAND-ALONE, ONE TO HOLD NOVEL. Adult Contemporary Romance: Due to strong language and sexual content, this book is not intended for readers under the age of 18.

To the protectors and the lovers.
To Mr. TL.
Most of all to the readers who wanted more.

ONE

A SMALL SYMBOL

Melissa

A COLD BLAST OF AIR steals my breath as I dash through the concrete parking garage, and I remember why I chose my cozy beach cottage in Wilmington over life in the city—even over life in a town the size of Princeton.

The doorman guarding the entrance is another reason.

Hired staff knowing all my moves, my comings and goings, who I'm expecting . . . It's a type of *déjà vu* that's way too close to my old life in Sloan's house, for comfort.

But Walter is nothing like Widlow or Hal, the housekeeper and driver who were basically paid spies in my ex-husband's Baltimore mansion. Walt stands just inside the glass doors in his maroon uniform waiting, and I see the moment recognition crosses his face. Jumping to open the door quickly, he greets me with a warm smile.

"Miss Jones!" His gloved hand covers the handle of my overnight bag as his other arm sweeps away the grocery sack I'm carrying. "Mr. Alexander didn't say you were coming. Let me help you."

His gravelly voice and doting personality remind me of an

elderly relative.

My voice is smooth and high in contrast. "Derek doesn't *know* I'm coming. It's a surprise." I give his shoulder a squeeze, and a whiff of peppermint touches my nose. "I've asked you to call me Melissa."

With a wink, he turns and leads me to the elevator, where he presses the button. I study his salt-and-pepper grays peeking out from under his cap, thinking how perfect he is at his job. "I won't breathe a word about seeing you, then, and management would fire me on the spot if I called you by your first name."

"Ridiculous."

The doors open and he hesitates. "This is a pretty heavy load. Want me to call one of the boys to carry it up for you?"

"I carried it all the way to the front door by myself, no problem."

My eyes are wide, and a chuckle scrapes from his throat. "He's going to be so glad you're here. You're just what he needs."

"I heard it's been a tough week." We're holding up the elevator, but I'm curious if Nikki, Derek's office manager, might have exaggerated the situation.

The building has less than twenty residents, most of whom work the same crazy hours as my fiancé, so I'm pretty certain we're safe for a moment's chat.

"I wouldn't know, but I haven't seen him smile since Sunday."

"Thank God it's Friday then?"

He grins and touches his hat. "Yes, ma'am."

The doors close, and I lean back against the shiny metal walls, thinking about what I know. Late yesterday afternoon, I got a text from Nikki saying if there was any chance I could get away, *Mr. Alexander could use a friendly face. And a hug. Preferably using your thighs.*

I laugh and roll my eyes. Nikki and I have grown close since my *second* visit to the Alexander-Knight offices. On my first, I only had one thing on my mind, and it wasn't making friends.

So much has changed since that day in November.

Now I get regular text updates from her, and her solution to most of her boss's problems is sleeping with me. Frequently. She usually complains he's impossible by the end of our weeks apart, but this time has been different. This time her message sounded worried instead of playful.

The elevator opens at the top floor of the complex, and I walk the short hall to his door. It's almost like living in a hotel, but inside, the condos are huge—only four to a level. Unlocking Derek's, I take a quick survey of the very male space. Leather couch, dark wood furnishings, enormous flat-screen television—make that *gigantic* flat-screen television. I think he said it's 110 inches?

The kitchen is granite and stainless and untouched. The entire condo is spotless. A service comes once a week to clean and do laundry, and his suits are picked up and delivered by the dry cleaner. I smile and shake my head. He probably never even sees the people who take care of him. It's all done by invisible elves as far as he's concerned. He just pays the bills. It's not a home—at least not the kind of loving home I plan to give him once we're finally together in the same city.

Setting the brown bag on the counter, I place one item in the refrigerator, the other in the freezer. I carefully selected both to remind him of a happy night, a night that started in a family restroom. A tingle fills my stomach at that white-hot memory.

Back to the present, I head straight to the master suite. My overnight case is on the dresser, and I quickly remove the few outfits I've brought for the weekend and place them in the top drawer reserved for my things. Then I pull out my toiletries bag and hit the bathroom.

It's only six, and he's not expecting me. No telling when he'll be here, but I want to freshen up after the eight-hour drive. It never gets shorter. We have *got* to get in the same location soon.

The bathroom is smooth beige stone on both the floors and countertops. The shower is matching tile, and is large and recessed like a cave, so there's no need for a door. I shove off my jeans and step in, switching on the dual showerheads while carefully avoiding the blast.

Back out, I lift my long, dark waves up and twist them into a knot then unbutton my white blouse and slide it off my shoulders. His little gold, floating heart sits right at the base of my throat. It wasn't an expensive gift, but when I touch it, my body floods with warmth remembering how he gave it to me. *His heart . . .*

Turning to the side in my matching red-lace bra and panties, my hands spread over my midsection. Still not showing, but my waist is definitely thicker as are my thighs. I've gone up a pant size, and I'm uncomfortable in everything I own besides loose dresses. This baby bump has got to pop out at some point so I can switch to maternity wear and stop looking like a marshmallow.

Underclothes off, I return to the shower-cave, moving under the spray with my head tilted back. It's hot, but not unbearably so, and the massaging motion of the jets soothes all the stress of the long drive away. I wash my face, turn and scrub the scented gel I brought all over myself, taking it easy on my breasts, which are tender these days.

I stand and allow the lovely hot water to envelop me like a soothing blanket. It feels so good after being out in the frigid evening air. Several minutes pass, and I finally shut it off, step out, and catch the towel hanging on the hook.

Quickly rubbing it over my legs and up my stomach, I pause when I reach my face and clutch it to my nose. His fresh, woodsy scent is all over the soft terry, and I inhale deeply. My eyes close as a wave of desire sweeps from my head, past my sensitive nipples, to the growing heat between my thighs. We spent an amazing Valentine's Day weekend together just five days ago, but I can't wait to see him again. The weeks apart are so lonely, even with friends around.

His robe is hanging on the back of the door. It also smells

like him, though he rarely wears it. I pull it around me, leaving the belt untied. It's like an oversized dress on my small frame, and the scent combined with the silky fabric whispering across my private parts piques my longing for him even more.

Only one lamp lights the dim condo as I cross back to the kitchen for a bottle of water. The furniture is bare of any accessories or pictures—I've noted it before—but today something's new. A single wooden frame has appeared on the mantle since my last visit. Picking it up, I recognize the shot of us sitting on the beach. He's behind me, and my head is tilted to the side as he kisses the base of my neck. I love this picture. My best friend Elaine took it a few weeks ago, and I'd sent it to him. I hug the small symbol to my chest, thinking how his place is less the sterile fortress now. He has proof, a loving reminder of my place in his world.

Going to the enormous glass windows to look out and wait, only a few lights dot the downtown area. It's either too early or too wintery for most people to be out. With the tip of my finger, I touch the cold glass and try to imagine where he is right now. How much longer he'll work. When he'll be here with me . . .

A noise from the doorway, and I look over my shoulder. My chest squeezes when I see him enter. His heavy grey overcoat makes him look even taller than six-two, his shoulders broader. His dark hair is longer than usual, and it just touches his collar in gentle waves.

Vibration hums under my skin as I watch him silently, my fingers curl with longing to touch him.

He shrugs off the topcoat and hooks it on the rack, and I almost sigh audibly when I recognize the suit he's wearing. It's the same one from all those months ago when I would gaze at him on my laptop screen. Back then I only had my memories and my hands. Now I have the real thing, and it's perfect.

He doesn't see me, doesn't even know I'm here, and it takes all my strength not to call out to him. I'm waiting, wanting him to see me first. The entry light is on, and the stack of mail in his hand occupies his attention. His brow is lined, and even his shoulders appear tense. The combined effect reminds me of the very first night I saw him—so focused and controlled, so intense and intimidating. Giving in to him was so hot.

Touching my lips with my tongue, I long to peel that suit off him, leave it lying in a pile on the floor as I cover his skin with kisses, massaging his stress away. I remember the band holding up my hair and quickly pull it out. Long, dark waves sweep over my shoulders at the exact moment he looks up. Blue eyes meet mine, and my stomach tightens.

My arm drops, parting the robe, revealing a peek at my nude body underneath, and his confusion turns instantly to desire. Without a word, he tosses the mail on the table and shrugs out of his suit coat. He crosses the dining area fast. I can barely breathe as he gets closer, removing more clothing with each step. Tie off, fingers unfastening buttons, he's in front of me, shirt open, undershirt the only thing between his skin and mine.

Neither of us speaks. It's very possible I'll come the moment we touch, but I snatch the edge of the thin white tank and push it up his lined torso. Pressing my lips against his heated flesh, I slip my tongue out to taste him. Large hands go inside the robe to my bare skin, sliding down and gripping my ass.

A little gasp comes from my throat when he lifts me. I'm off my feet, weightless in his arms. My back is against the cold glass, and his light sprinkling of chest hair teases my nipples.

His mouth roughly covers mine, consuming the noises rising in my throat, and his waist is between my thighs, pressing my most sensitive areas. Firm lips part mine, and his tongue explores my mouth. His kisses are insistent and ravenous, and every time his hips push against my clit, flames of desire shimmer down my legs.

Gripping his broad shoulders, my fingers dig into his flesh pulling him closer as his mouth blazes a trail to my breasts. Soft lips followed by the scruff of his beard teases my skin, and I can't help a moan as my head drops back against the window.

"Oh, god," I gasp as he catches a straining nipple in his mouth and gives it a hard pull. The sensation registers directly to my core. I need him inside me now.

My hands are in his hair, pulling, threading the soft, dark locks, as his kisses climb back up my neck. He pulls little bits of my skin between his teeth as he goes, and his scent is all around me, intoxicating me.

"Now, baby. I need you now." I can't take much more of this or I'll combust. My thighs are already trembling, my inner muscles aching.

I feel him reposition, holding me with one arm as his other works below his waist. Breathless, I fumble to push his shirt further off his shoulders, wishing it would tear. I kiss his skin again; a hint of salt is on my tongue. In one movement, he boosts me up then sinks deep inside.

He lets out a deep groan, and I gasp. The size of him, his incredible fullness stretching me, is always a delicious greeting after being apart. I'm riding on that delicious edge, and by his next, hard thrust my orgasm roars through me.

"Ohh, god," I cry, gripping his shoulders, rocking my hips as best as I can against him.

His breathing is labored. Another thrust, and I'm pulling him closer, unable to get enough. My cries seem to make him move faster, and I clutch his shoulders as he rocks me.

"Deeper," I beg against his neck, my lips just touching his skin. He shudders and grants my request, and a second orgasm begins, hot and low in my stomach.

Powerful waves ripple up my body, and my muscles tighten. It's like electricity, flashing all the way to my scalp, leaving me momentarily blinded. Inside, I'm gripping and pulling him, until with a loud groan, he comes.

His hips jam into me hard, pushing me against the glass, and his hands tighten on my ass, pulling me flush against him. It's a mild pain mixed with the most incredible pleasure, and I never want it to stop.

We push and hold, grind and feel, until gradually our bodies calm, our movements become still. Spent, I drop my forehead against his neck, holding him through the last sparkling waves of pleasure. He's inside me, one arm tight around my waist, the other under my butt. Warm lips touch my head, and I'm in heaven.

As if waking from a dream, I lift my eyes, sliding my hands to his cheeks. At the sight of blue, love bursts inside me. Sometimes it's still hard for me to believe this beautiful man is mine.

"Hi." My voice is soft.

Fine lines pierce his temples in the most attractive way as he smiles back. "You're here." His deep voice massages my insides, and I can't resist kissing those cheeks, his eyes, the tip of his nose, his full lips. They part, and our tongues greet each other again.

Movement stirs below, inside me, and I lean back to meet his loving gaze. "I've been waiting for you to get here."

"If I'd known you were waiting, I'd have left two hours ago."

I laugh, kissing him and whispering, "I love you."

"I love you more." His arms tighten around me. "What made you decide to drive in? Not that I'm complaining."

"I heard you might need a visit."

His brow creases as he considers my meaning. "Patrick?"

Shaking my head, I peck his cheek again. "Nikki."

With that he exhales, dropping his forehead against my shoulder with a groan-laugh.

"What?" I laugh, too, at his exaggerated frustration. "She's not as bad as you make her out to be."

He lifts me and slides out. Standing in front of him, I wrap the robe around my waist as he adjusts and fastens his pants. Then he scoops me to him again, kissing my nose. "For this surprise, I'll get her a little gift."

"Oh! Speaking of surprises, come with me." Pulling him to

the couch, I push him around and make him sit. "Sit here, and don't move. I mean it."

He grins, watching me leaning over him. The robe drifts apart, and of course, he catches my nipple between his fingers, giving it a small pinch. "Ow—stop!" I yelp a laugh. "I said don't move."

"Darlin', I haven' seen you in a week." He tries to grab me, but I dodge.

"Don't pull that southern charm on me."

"I'll pull more than that on you." The devilish twinkle in his eye almost causes me to forget my little surprise.

I manage to resist. "Just wait."

A quick pit-stop in the toilet to freshen up, and I dash to the kitchen. Opening the freezer, I pull out the bottle of cava I brought. Tiny bits of ice float in it, but I pop the cork and pour him a flute—ginger ale for me. Next I take the two large olive-salad sandwiches from the fridge and arrange them on plates. It's all loaded onto a tray, which I carry on my shoulder to the living room where he's waiting.

"What have you done?" His voice is full of warmth as he watches me from the sofa.

"Since you've been working too hard—"

"Exaggeration."

"Since you've been working too hard," I repeat, "I decided to recreate our relaxing spa vacation in the desert."

Placing the tray on the coffee table, I hand him his flute and lift mine. "To family restrooms."

He laughs and clinks back. "To the gorgeous woman who drives me to crazy extremes."

We sip and I crawl forward on the couch to kiss him and tell him again. "I love you."

He leans forward, placing his flute, the tray, my flute, all of it on the coffee table. Then his hands move through the open robe to pull me onto his lap in a straddle, facing him. Just that fast, his mouth is on my neck, nibbling and kissing. My eyes are closed, and I'm powerless.

"I love you more," he says beside my ear with a deep inhale. "You smell so good."

Threading my fingers in his hair, I kiss his temple. "I wore the red lace . . ."

A rumble of approval, and his lips touch that spot behind my ear, a light scruff against my skin, sending shivers flying down my legs.

"My favorite." His voice is thick as I pull his cheeks, reuniting our mouths.

For a moment, we make out like teenagers, hot and breathless, tongues entwining. He holds me against his bare chest, my elbows are bent, and my palms are on his cheeks. His mouth is like some rich, decadent chocolate I can never get enough of tasting. As we kiss, I feel him relax, and my hands slide behind his neck, my lips travel up to his brow. He hugs me against his torso and doesn't move. Neither do I.

This big, strong man saved me twice. If comfort is what he needs, I'm here to give it to him. I'm here to give him anything. After a few more breaths, his arms relax. I lean back and study his face a moment. The robe has dropped around my shoulders, so I'm basically sitting nude on his lap, but I don't care.

"Hungry?" I reach for the sandwich plate and hold it between us, right at our chins. "You probably won't think it's as good as Central Grocery, but I think it's delicious."

His blue eyes take me in before he bites. "Mmm . . ." is all I get.

Giggling, I lean forward and take a bite myself. The tangy, savory flavor of olives and smoky provolone fills my mouth.

"Delicious!" My voice is muffled.

His smile glows as he watches me, his voice full of love. "How's the baby?"

Lowering the sandwich to the plate, I turn and put it on the side table again. "I can't feel a thing, but the doctor said he's doing great."

My last checkup was a week ago, and we both agreed unless something unusual occurred, Derek could miss the routine exams. So far everything has been by the book.

"So he's a boy now?" I love his grin at the prospect of a little son.

Shrugging, I acquiesce. "Maybe . . . it's too soon to know."

His attention moves from my face to my abdomen. Large hands span my bare stomach before he leans forward and kisses me right below my sternum, right at the top of my belly.

"I love you," he whispers to the little bean growing there.

I'm certain my heart melts in that instant, and I catch his face again to cover it with kisses. He's right with me, lifting me in his arms and carrying me to the master suite. A California king-sized bed fills the space, and he spreads me out on the soft mattress, lying on his side next to me.

I trail my fingers lightly over his brow, to his temple, following a line to his strong jaw. He looks at me like I'm the most fragile thing in his bed—another detail he knows isn't true.

We don't disturb the moment, though. The truth might be that both of us are strong as iron, tough as flint, but holding each other, we know how precious it is that we're here, together.

The randomness of chance keeps us both in awe, and for that, we treasure these moments. After working so hard, our reunions are the sweetest bliss. He holds me, and I feel very needed and extremely sexy. This man is like water in the desert to me, and it isn't hard to see the feeling is mutual.

"I'm sorry I interrupted dinner." Leaning forward, he nibbles the skin at my neck, and a surge rises between my legs. "Can you wait?"

My voice is thick as I answer. "I guess so . . ."

His mouth moves to my stomach then lower. My heartbeat quickens, knowing what's coming. A kiss to my navel, his tongue lightly traces the small circle, and I whimper.

"You guess so?" The sly grin in his voice tells me he knows I'll wait. I'm buzzing with anticipation as it is.

One quick slide, one quick lift, and my thighs are open. Toes curled, I let out a little cry as soft lips, scratchy beard, trace a line down my inner thigh to the center where his warm tongue makes a slow pass around my clit.

"Oh, god!" I curl up, threading my fingers in the sides of his hair. "Derek!"

Blue eyes are on me in a grin as another hot, firm circle covers that sensitive bud hidden between the folds. I collapse back with a groan of pleasure.

He sucks and pulls as I writhe, covering my eyes as the pleasure roars through my pelvis. My hips follow the movements of his mouth. He doesn't stop, doesn't let up until I'm bucking and moaning, holding his head and trembling.

Two thick fingers push inside, and my knees rise on their own. One more little pull, and he kisses my stomach, on the way up before thrusting into me, rocking hard and fast.

He's the one groaning now, and I'm holding on, burning in my afterglow as he joins me, his second orgasm even stronger than the first. One large hand grips my ass, and the other is pressed against the wall behind me as he thrusts again and again, harder and deeper, before letting go with a low moan.

For a moment, he's still. I'm lying back on the bed, admiring his lined stomach and broad shoulders. His head drops, and I reach for him. With a swift scoop, he rolls us both to the side, and I'm clutched close against his chest, his arms around my waist. His lips press against my shoulder, and I try to remember what we were even saying before on the couch.

He exhales, speaking into my hair. "You have no idea how happy I am to see you."

That makes me laugh, and I squeeze him tighter. "I think you've shown me twice now."

"I intend to show you several more times before Sunday. I might not let you leave this bed." His tone sends a thrill to my stomach . . . which is followed by a loud rumble. We both laugh.

"Baby is not amused. You'd better run get our dinner before

he starves."

He's up in a flash, pausing to lean back and kiss my forehead roughly before heading to the living room. I admire his tight rear view flexing as he walks out the door to our abandoned dinner. Then he's back, still sporting a semi along with the tray of food and drinks.

My head is shaking. "You're insatiable."

"And you're gorgeous."

"Flattery will get you everywhere." I fluff the pillows and sit back against them while he arranges the tray between us on the mattress.

A quick sip, and he puts the flute on the side table. "I feel bad having cava without you."

"Mmm, I don't mind. It reminds me of the night we met."

"You were the most amazing creature I'd ever seen, sitting at the bar, wrinkling that little nose with every sip." He touches my nose with a grin. "Adorable."

"That drink was disgusting. Seven and seven." I shudder and take another bite of sandwich. "This is much better."

"I was done for the moment I saw you. I couldn't stay away."

Nodding, I swallow my bite. "You were pretty intimidating being so focused, but lucky for you, I wasn't backing down anymore. From anything."

He doesn't speak, instead he traces a line down the side of my face, along my hairline as his lips tighten.

"Or I should say lucky for us," I continue. "Looking back, it was pretty reckless, actually. You could've been anybody." My eyes roam over his darkened expression, and I put my plate aside. "What are you thinking?"

"I had no idea what you were facing." A note of anger is in the background of his tone. "What was waiting for you at home."

My fingers lace with his, lowering his hand to my lap. "We've discussed this. That's all over now. It's the past. There's no point letting it ruin our present."

Being here with him, contemplating our life together, makes it more than easy to forget my old scars. Those are days I can easily let fade into the deep background.

"I know." He pulls me to him, and I curl into his chest. Showered, stomach full, sexually blissed out, my eyes start to drift.

He might be the one needing comfort, but in this moment, in his strong arms, I'm feeling as safe as a queen—and as sleepy as an expectant mother.

Derek's arms are tight around me, and his lips press a gentle kiss to the top of my head. It's the last thing I remember before drifting into happy slumber.

TWO

SPECIAL SKILLS

Derek

ONLY TWO HOURS HAVE PASSED since I told Melissa good-bye, and already that tightness is creeping across my chest. It's a mixture of anger and needing her in my sight where I know she's safe.

She didn't press the subject, but all weekend I could tell she wanted to know what I was working on, what was "bothering me."

Damn Nikki. If I weren't so pleased by the luscious surprise of finding Mel waiting for me half-nude in my condo Friday night, I'd reprimand her for keeping tabs on me. I don't need an office manager who doubles as my mother, or who reports my behavior back to my aunt—or my fiancée.

Melissa stayed to this morning, Monday. She's so different than when we first met. Even back then she had that confidence, but she's happy now. She's also a little rounder, with our baby on the way. It's a killer combination. I love it, and every time I'd bury my face in a new curve, she'd shriek and complain loudly. I almost couldn't let her leave.

Smiling at my desk, I look out the window at the bare winter landscape of the courtyard, thinking of her. This morning as I watched her sleep, I couldn't help breathing a little prayer of thanks. I don't pray, but with that angel in my bed, how could I not? She was curled up facing me, her delicate hand under her chin and her dark hair spread behind her on the pillow.

It was like our own world, secure and full of love. She'd stirred, and meeting her beautiful blue eyes, another quiet *thank you* echoed through my mind, only this time my memories were on our first encounters. How incredibly sexy she was giving in to me, and how breathless I'd been waiting for her to push me away. She never did.

"How long have you been awake?" She'd touched my cheek then smoothed her fingers into my hair.

"Not long." I'd caught her hand and brought her palm to my lips.

She touched my brow, smoothing it back. "You're less tense than when I got here, and now I have to leave again."

"You forget, I'm trained for periods of separation." Even as I said it, I knew nothing would make telling her goodbye easier.

She pushed up into a sitting position and moved me onto my back. "So being a Marine means you don't miss me?" Her elbows were bent, and one cheek rested on her palm.

I couldn't help laughing at her eyes narrowed in disbelief. I wasn't fooling anyone. "I miss you like the worst pain in the world. Like the desert misses rain."

"That's a song." She kissed me lightly. "And something you have experience with."

Catching her neck, I pulled her forward for a better kiss, but she arched away before I could take it further. "I want to know more about your training. What are your special skills? Besides not missing me when we're apart, of course. Can you fly a plane?"

I shook my head with a chuckle. "Sorry, darling. No piloting for me, but I think Patrick did some flying—"

"I don't believe it. You know things. Tell me!"

Pressing my lips together, my eyes moved down to her chin then to her slim neck where my heart dangled on a thin, gold chain. *Yes, I know things.*

"You keep so many secrets from me," she sighed. "What are you thinking now?"

"The things I know aren't things you want to hear about." Reaching over, I slid my palm over the curve of her waist.

She caught my cheeks in her hands and drew my gaze back. "I want to know everything about you."

For a moment I hesitated. Then my eyes were drawn to the scar, that tiny silver line that starts at the top of her forehead, just above her temple, and disappears into her hairline. "I can kill a man with my bare hands."

Our eyes met again, and I could tell she knew where my thoughts had gone.

"Have you ever done it?"

When I answered her, my voice was quiet. "I've had to kill people."

She hugged herself close against my chest. "I'm sorry. I'm not trying to bring up painful memories. We don't have to talk about it."

Wrapping my arms around her, I pulled her up slightly so I could kiss her neck. "Have I told you how amazing you are?"

A laugh bubbled in her throat. "You always say that. I'm not so amazing."

Rolling us so she was on her back, I looked down into her beautiful face. "You're smart and beautiful. You're incredibly busy, but you make time to show up here—"

"When I know you need me." Leaning down, I kissed her jaw as she continued. "You'd do the same for me. Besides, I can work from anywhere."

"Then work from here."

"You can work anywhere, too."

Our old argument. Neither of us chased it any further— not on our last morning together. We were counting down the hours before we'd be apart again, and instead, I focused on trailing my lips down to her collarbone, past the floating heart, lower to her breasts until we were lost in our special place once more.

Now, sitting at my desk remembering, the only thing strong enough to spoil the afterglow of our weekend is this new case . . . and her old scar. That damn silver line, a constant reminder of what that fucker did to her. Even worse, it reminds me he's still out there walking around free.

In my line of work, I know how those assholes are. They all have some fucked up notion their victims belong to them—only them. My fist is clenched on the desktop, and I focus on relaxing it.

Sloan will pay for what he did to Mel. I intend to make sure of it, but she's right. Letting him spoil our present gives him too much power. I'd rather put that aside, in my "To Do" file, and focus on my weekend with my little family—sheer red lingerie, loads of sex, and nonstop affection—hell, I should have a shitty week more often.

Shitty week . . .

I turn to my computer and stare at the report on the screen. As much as Mel wants to know, I can't bring myself to tell her what I'm investigating. It's not that I want to hide my work from her. She could probably help solve half the cases on my desk. I don't want her to be afraid, and I don't have a reason to make her worry yet.

Patrick's in Wilmington watching over her for me, being the guard he is when I'm not there, and I've got tabs on Sloan. We'll know if he leaves the city or makes any threatening moves. Privately, I wish he would. Nothing would make me happier than taking him out in an act of self-defense. With his record, not a jury in the world would convict.

Nikki snaps me out of my reflections. "I'm headed to the coffee shop. Can I get you anything?" She's standing at the door in one of her usual, too-tight wrap-dresses.

It takes me back to her first day here, assigned by my aunt Sue's temp agency. I was still grieving Allison. Three years had passed since my first wife died, but time didn't matter. I didn't want a replacement wife or a girlfriend or an outlet or *anything*, and the idea that my aunt might've selected this woman for any of those reasons got under my skin like nothing else. I didn't need help getting over my wife. I had no intention of getting over her ever, and Nikki's appearance pissed me off.

The reality is, despite her former, inappropriate assertions that I needed to "get laid," she never once made a pass at me. She'd actually seemed more interested in Stuart, my first partner and Patrick's older brother.

I suppose after all this time I should put the past behind us. It doesn't make sense anymore now that I have Melissa. Everything has changed.

She's waiting, and I exhale. "No. Thank you." The departure from my usual, impatient tone makes her pause, and I continue. "You're always thoughtful, Nikki. I appreciate it."

Her mouth drops open and then quickly closes. "I'm . . . um . . . well." She stops stammering, pokes her lips out duck-face style, then nods. "Okay, then. You're welcome."

Turning on a stiletto heel, she heads out of the office, and I grin. That may be the first time I've had Nikki at a loss for words.

Back to my computer, I pull up the file I've been studying for ten days—the one that's had me so distracted. I keep telling Patrick we don't do domestic work, yet I always end up being the one old friends or acquaintances call when they need help.

That's how it started—a runaway case for a friend of a friend.

I was culling through mug shots of beat-up teens and file photos of dead girls. Patrick would say this is the worst part of our job, but truthfully, I don't mind it. I can see past the tragedy to my role here, giving people closure. I know what it's like to need it, and I don't mind helping people get it.

Then I saw *Jessica Black*. Dead.

The name was so familiar, but I couldn't place her at first. Staring at the photo, trying to think, I'd been struck by her appearance—fair complexion, petite frame, and long brunette waves. She looked a lot like Melissa—minus my fiancée's bright blue eyes.

I'd clicked on the thumbnail to read the report. Runaway. Missing five years. Arrested for prostitution several times. Found beaten once. Badly. Now deceased under mysterious circumstances.

Minutes passed as I stared at her photo. Why was she so familiar? She wasn't from Princeton. Her hometown was listed as Raleigh. Shaking my head and chalking it up to overprotectiveness spurred by her similarity to Mel, I closed the document and went back to searching for the runaway.

Nikki had interrupted me that day as well, stopping in with a BLT from the cafeteria.

"I know it's your favorite." She placed the thick sandwich in front of me with a smile. "You need to eat."

I only nodded. "Thanks."

She didn't leave. "Remember the last time I brought you lunch? It was the day Melissa showed up here so angry and unexpected. I was sure I'd never like her, but now she's the sweetest . . ."

Nikki continued talking, but I wasn't listening. Cold realization flashed in my brain like lightening striking a tree.

Jessica Black. It was the name on the email Melissa had put in front of me that day she visited our offices. The day she dropped a nuke on all my dreams of a life with her, when she revealed my former "mentor," her ex-husband Sloan Reynolds's secret double-life. He had high-end escorts all over the country, and Jessica Black was his first careless slip. Melissa had found it.

Nikki was still reminiscing as I spun around in my chair, shaking my computer awake. Fingers flying over the keys, I pulled up all the information I could find on the dead girl.

She'd been living in Baltimore for a year. I wondered if she followed him from wherever they'd hooked up the first time. *Why would she do that? Was it possible she was in love with him? Was it for the money? Had he promised her anything?*

It didn't matter. She'd disappeared off the police blotter from the time she arrived there until now, when she'd turned up dead.

Reasons scrolled across my brain of all the possible causes of death, but looking at her beaten face, all I could see was the photo Melissa had put in front of me all those months ago.

My instincts were on high alert. Sloan was getting antsy, and I knew what he wanted. Jessica Black might look like the real thing, but she wasn't it.

Substitutes would never fill the possession he felt. I'd followed enough of these twisted fucks to know. He was coming for Melissa, and it was just a matter of when.

All last week, I'd tracked down every misstep I could find on him, looking for anything that would stick, that would get him off the streets or at least keep him in Baltimore. I hoped to find a recent paper trail linking him to Jessica, but every lead came up cold. He was either too slick, or his people buried everything.

Even the guy I had watching Sloan in Baltimore had nothing. Jessica disappeared a week before I'd hired him, a month after Sloan had broken into Mel's beach cottage and then gotten off with a slap on the wrist. Apparently I'd moved too quickly when he waltzed into her home threatening to rape her. We had to wait until he actually committed the crime for his money and position not to matter.

The thought clenched my jaw. It was the one thing above all that caused the "stress" Nikki kept texting Melissa about. Only "stress" wasn't what I felt. What I felt was flat-out fucking rage.

The best part was when he threatened me in court with police brutality charges. I'd nearly brutalized him on the spot, but Melissa held me back. I'll never forget her face. She went still as a stone, as if it was the ending she always expected. It was like a heel-kick straight to my gut. I couldn't let her down that way.

Now all she'll say is she wants those memories left in the past. *Just let it go*, she tells me.

Fuck that. That asshole is a threat to my family, and it's clear he's dangerous. Priority 1 is devising a plan to bring him in, and it has to be something that won't ooze off his slimy back.

Snatching my phone off its base, I hit the speed-dial button.

Patrick answers, cocky as always. "Don't tell me. You've come to your senses and realized life at the beach is the only way to live."

"I need you to up the watch on Melissa."

I appreciate how his tone becomes immediately serious. "What's going on?"

"I have to finish a few details for our new Houston client, and then I'm headed your way, possibly for a while."

"This can only mean one thing. Or one asshole."

"I'm emailing a report and mug shots to you now. The name's Jessica Black." Fingers clicking on the keys, I shoot everything I've found to him. "I've exhausted all my sources here. See if you can do anything from there with it."

"Sure." He's silent for a moment, reading. "Jessica Black . . . Raleigh? That's just down the road. I'll rattle a few cages."

"If you do find anything, I need to know why she moved to Baltimore. What she was doing there. If she was seeing anybody and who."

"Did you tell Melissa about this?"

Pressing my lips together, I rock back in my chair. "No."

"Think that's a good idea?"

"Not really, but I'll tell her when the time is right. I don't want her to be afraid."

Sitting forward again, I pull up the report for our Houston client and read over what's still outstanding. A full system analysis is due Friday. I lost a significant portion of last week searching all the police databases for information on Miss Black.

"If I pull some extra hours, I can have Houston wrapped up and out of here by Wednesday." I start a log on my desktop of what's still outstanding, what jobs are lined up next, and what I can handle from Wilmington in case I can't get back right away.

Nikki's thank you gift can be a week off with pay, maybe a Spa Finder mini-holiday. In the middle of planning my getaway, I realize Patrick is still on the line.

"Sorry to keep you in a holding pattern."

"No worries. I can tell this is serious. Somehow. Even though you haven't told me any details."

Patrick can turn any situation into a joke, and I alternate between being pissed and being glad about it. At the moment, I'm too focused on closing the office and getting to Wilmington to lose time on it.

"I'll tell you everything when I get there. Just keep your eyes on Mel."

"She'll be as protected as the crown jewels."

It doesn't satisfy the tightness in my chest. "Maybe Elaine could invite her to stay in your guest room til Thursday."

"You're joking, right? You know Mel won't leave that cottage without a mandatory evacuation order."

Studying my notes, I wonder how many boxes I'd have to pack if I left for Wilmington today. No, I have to wrap up this damn Houston case here, where I can focus.

Frustrated, I push the laptop back on my desk. "We're professionals, dammit. Get creative."

He laughs. "What would work if you were Melissa? I'd say we invite her over for dinner and mix her drinks too strong, but she's pregnant. And even if she were still drinking, we couldn't keep the party going for three nights. Just tell her what's up."

"If I can be there on Wednesday, I will."

"Fine, but will you at least tell me what's going on? Who is Jessica Black? Or who *was*, I guess . . ."

"Jessica Black was a high-end hooker, an escort. She was also one of Sloan's regulars. A few years ago, she was beaten pretty badly, but she wouldn't report the guy. Then she moved to Baltimore. I don't have anything concrete, but my gut says she fell in love with him. How, I can't imagine. Now she's dead."

Silence meets my ear for several moments. When Patrick speaks again, his voice is sober, all joking gone. "And she looks a helluva lot like Melissa."

"Right."

"I know what to do."

In that one sentence I hear my partner lock into closer mode, and it's right where I want him. Patrick can be a royal fuck up when it comes to women, but he's damn good at his job. And to her credit, Elaine seems to have put an end to his screwing around.

"I've got an idea," he continues. "It's something I floated past you a while back, but now with this . . . Raleigh . . . I might have a connection to what you need."

"I didn't expect anything less. See you in a few days, and Patrick? Thanks. I owe you one."

"It's nothing more than you'd do for me."

"You know it."

THREE

BACKUP PLAN

Melissa

EIGHT HOURS SEPARATE PRINCETON, NEW Jersey, from Wilmington, North Carolina. Eight long, boring, tedious hours.

I've been hesitant to push the relocation issue on Derek—I want him to be as happy in his hometown as I am in mine—but one more of these long drives, and I might have to rethink that approach.

The only interesting part is keeping track of the cars I pass. One silver Honda seems to always be with me, a few cars behind, but Hondas are pretty common. As tired as I feel, I'm practically seeing double at this point.

Stopping for a fourth bathroom break and to walk around, I'm halfway through Virginia when I send Derek a quick text. *Made it to Richmond. Only four stops this time.*

It doesn't take five seconds for him to text back. *Thanks for letting me know. Never stop in Baltimore without me.*

My nose wrinkles at his overprotectiveness. *The whole city isn't off-limits. Aunt Bea is there.*

Will take you to see her soon. Her cupcakes are my favorite.

I can't help a laugh imagining what my old-fashioned client, a sweet little baker, will say when she meets my fiancé. *She'll love you.*

I love you. You're so beautiful in my bed. It's hard to let you go.

Those words erase all the exhaustion—and the mild irritation at being treated like a china doll. Warmth floods my middle. *I didn't get enough sleep this weekend.*

Wasn't that the point?

Hmm . . . the point had actually been to find out what's got my future husband so tense and distracted, but between his mouth and my hands and that new red lingerie, that plan had been all but forgotten.

Suddenly the thought of three nights without him seems unbearably lonely. *See you Friday?*

Maybe sooner.

Sooner? A line pierces my forehead.

While I love the idea of not having to wait four whole days to see him, I know he's setting up a new client, and their reports and analyses usually take a month to prepare. Patrick's complained about it before.

I'll explain when I get there. Kiss yourself, kiss baby.

That would be some trick. Love you, Xoxo

Love you more. xxx

I toss the thin phone into my bag and top off my tank before climbing in and getting back on the road. I'm on the Interstate again, and a quick glance to my mirror says Silver Accord is, too. Whatever. Next stop will be my cozy cottage on the most beautiful stretch of beach north of Miami.

My phone buzzes just as I'm pushing through the front door, holding my overnight case and trying to juggle my keys and bag. Inside, I drop everything and look at the face. Elaine. Voicemail dings.

Hitting the button, I put the audio on speaker and set my phone on the counter before unzipping my luggage and digging out my laundry.

"Where are you?" Elaine's bossy, middle-school-teacher

voice is a mixture of concern and amusement. "I know, I know. You couldn't leave him. If Derek Alexander convinces you to move eight hours away from me, I'll never speak to either of you again. You know I hated that drive to Baltimore."

And Princeton's even further, I mentally add.

"So I have this whole supper made up for you, and you're going to come over and give me the scoop. I don't want to hear about how tired you are—you were supposed to be home last night. I spent the whole day cooking."

Laughing I shake my head. More like the crock-pot spent the whole day cooking while she was at school.

"Call me. Love you."

Hitting her name on my phone, it doesn't ring once before she answers. "Are you home?"

"Yes, and it was a long drive, and I'm—"

"On your way here to have a nice, comfort-food dinner. I made beef stew, and you don't even have to change. Patrick won't mind."

"Lainey . . ."

But she's off the phone before I can argue. My stomach grumbles, and I concede. This baby keeps me starving—he'll probably be as big as his daddy—and I don't feel like cooking or eating whatever I can scrape together here.

Catching the strap of my bag, I toss it over the shoulder and head back to the car. At least her place is close.

The savory aroma of celery and garlic, meat and potatoes fills my nose when I open the door. Elaine's got the top off her slow cooker, and the golden boy is right behind her, lifting her light-blonde hair and kissing her neck.

"Okay, knock it off," I complain in a loud, teasing voice.

Elaine drops the lid with a cry and crosses the room to hug me. "How are you feeling?" She leans back and studies my face with a frown. "You look tired."

"I am tired! I told you that." I hug her back. "You dragged me over here, now give me food. And I won't sit and watch you two making out all through dinner."

Patrick leans against the counter smiling at us. His arms are crossed over his lined chest, and he's perfectly handsome in faded jeans and a dark green tee. His sandy-brown hair is shaggy in his hazel eyes.

I've never been happier about my best friend's love life. Elaine used to play it safe when it came to men, which doesn't suit her personality at all. She was miserable with Boring Brian, and I'm glad she took a chance and stepped outside her comfort zone. Patrick is just the sweet bad boy she needs.

"Hey, girl." His voice always sounds like sunshine. "Ginger ale?"

"Sure." I nod, dropping my bag on the counter and allowing Elaine to pull me to the couch in their living room.

"So what did you find out?"

I shake my head as Patrick hands me a white wine glass filled with light amber soda. "Nothing."

"He didn't tell you anything?" Cutting my eyes as I take a sip, she squeals a laugh. "You horny pregnant lady! What exactly were you doing with your mouth all weekend?"

Ginger ale almost comes out my nose. "Shut up!" I pinch her arm and set the glass on the side table.

"Oh, please. You think Patrick's shocked?

He just laughs, going back to the kitchen. "How is the big guy?"

Chewing my bottom lip, I opt for "Energetic."

"No wonder you're so tired. Come on then." My slender friend hops off the couch and pulls me back to the kitchen. "This beef stew I cooked smells delicious."

"Does it count as cooking if you buy all the ingredients premade?"

"Don't be grouchy."

Elaine pulls down three bowls while Patrick slices French bread. He glances up at me. "How was the drive?"

"Long." My elbows are bent, and I rest my forehead on my

palms, rubbing away my exhaustion. "I had the strangest feeling . . ." I shake my head with a little laugh. "I'm sure it was just road fatigue, but I kept thinking I saw the same car behind me the whole way."

Patrick's hand pauses mid-slice, then without a word, he starts cutting again. Elaine's suddenly quiet, and I look around to see what just happened.

"That's silly, right?"

His sunny smile is back in a flash, and Patrick tosses the bread in a bowl. "Yeah. Probably just somebody headed the same direction as you."

Right when I turn away, I'm certain I catch a look pass between the two of them, but when I glance back, it's gone. I am seriously exhausted and seeing things.

"You should spend the night here if you're so tired." Elaine puts a steaming bowl of stew in front of me then sets hers at the place across from me where she sits.

Taking the large spoon from beside my bowl, I dip out a carrot from the yummy-smelling broth. "Mmm . . . I want to sleep in my own bed tonight. But thanks."

Patrick joins us, handing us each a piece of bread before he sits. I rip out the center of mine and dunk it in the dark brown gravy. "This really is delicious. Thanks for making me come over."

Elaine exhales a little laugh and then falls silent, eating. We're all three pretty quiet, which is unusual for our group. I'd complain if I weren't feeling sleep trying to roll over me in giant waves. Instead, I take another warm bite of savory meat.

"At least let me drive you home, then," Elaine says.

I shake my head. "Then my car would be over here, and you've got school—"

"I'll spend the night."

"Then I'd have to get up and drive you back in the morning before school." Shaking my head, I lift my soft-drink-holding wine glass and sip. "I'll be fine, and I want to sleep in tomorrow."

Patrick stands and goes briefly into the kitchen before returning with his phone, which he sets on the table between him and Elaine. My bowl is now empty, and I'm just about to announce my departure when it buzzes. Elaine's head turns, and she snatches it up, springing out of her chair.

"Toni Durango?" Her voice is too loud. "Who the HELL is Toni Durango? Patrick! What the FUCK? Is this a stripper?"

I'm fully awake now, and completely bewildered at both the volume of her voice and what she's saying.

"Lainey—" Patrick stands, but she cuts him off.

"NO!" She shoves the phone hard into his chest. He tries to catch her but she pushes him again. Elaine is unusually strong, take it from me. "I'm not listening to your bullshit! Fuck you, Patrick!"

She storms to the bedroom, and I'm frozen in my spot. My mouth is open, and I'm sure I look like a guppy. *Would a stripper call Patrick? How would she have his number? Did Patrick give his number to a stripper? Could it be part of a case?*

He doesn't wait for me to intervene. He's headed to the bedroom after her, just as a heavy, black combat boot flies through the opening. I scream and he ducks, avoiding the headshot.

"Honey . . . Don't throw things at my head." Somehow his voice sounds scolding instead of pleading.

"Don't touch me!" Elaine's still yelling, and my heart's beating too fast. I've never liked confrontations like this, but I hesitate before leaving.

"Lainey?" My voice is high and soft, and I stand, cautiously going toward the bedroom. I don't want to be hit by any flying objects either, and my coordination isn't as good as it was pre-pregnancy. "Are you okay?"

A flash of blonde hair, and she's out of the bedroom, cheeks pink and a small suitcase in her hand. "I'm staying with you tonight. Let's go."

"Uhh . . ." I'm certain I could win the Most Helpless Award at that moment.

Patrick goes to the fireplace and rubs the back of his neck as he studies the orange flames. I watch as my best friend storms past me and out the door.

"Okay, then." I shake my head and follow her, picking up my bag. Elaine's already in my car, sitting with her arms crossed, when I open the driver's side door.

"Honey?" I have no idea what to say right now. These guys are *not* having problems. It's impossible.

"Just stop. Patrick was a player before we got together, so what makes me think he'd stop being a player now?"

"Because he loves you? Because he left everything in Princeton behind to be here with you? Is it possible you're being a little hasty?"

I can't tell if she's about to cry or not. Somehow it doesn't seem like she is. With a deep exhale, I get in and push the key into the ignition. I almost jump out of my skin when she shrieks again.

"Wait!"

"You're going to send me into premature labor—"

"Forgot my glasses." She's out the car and running back inside as I sit in the idling vehicle.

My shoulders drop as she disappears through the door. This whole situation is weird. Elaine isn't flighty, nor does she jump to conclusions. And from what I've observed, she has Patrick whipped pretty well.

I continue waiting, wondering what the hell's taking so long, when a low throb like heartburn starts in the center of my chest.

What if she is right, and Patrick *is* cheating or whatever? He always seemed so sweet to me. The self-doubt creeping up the back of my neck is even worse than the *déjà vu* of being watched. I think Patrick is a great guy. I also thought Sloan was a great guy. Is my ability to judge character still so warped?

I think Derek's a great guy . . .

Elaine's back, jumping into my car before I can go any further on that crazy-train of mentally exhausted thought. In the brief, dome light, her lips appear pink and slightly swollen . . . like she's been kissing someone. Then it's dark again.

"Let's go," she snaps.

That does it. "Don't be all bossy with me. I don't know any strippers." Now I'm frowning.

"I'm sorry." She drops back against the passenger seat and turns to face me. "Thanks for letting me sleep over. It can be like a girls' night."

I shake my head. "I'm going to bed when we get home. You can work out whatever this is on your own."

I'm asleep before my head meets the pillow. Elaine's snug in my little guest room, and as yet, she still hasn't shed a tear. She doesn't even seem mad anymore.

I'm about to accuse them both of pulling some inexplicable role-playing stunt, but I hesitate. I could be wrong.

Still, I know my friend has a wild side. I'm just too tired to delve into it tonight. Lainey's like my sister, and if she needs to crash here, that's fine. We'll sort it out tomorrow.

Somewhere past midnight, I wake with a jolt. The house is quiet, but I throw back the covers and go to my bedroom door. My heart is beating so fast as I pause and listen, but everything sounds peaceful. *What was it?*

I stand a few moments in groggy silence, trying to remember what might've woken me. It's been a while since I've slept on edge, sleep so near waking it could hardly qualify as restful, and it often involved clutching that small can of pepper spray under my pillow. It was how I usually slept when I lived in Sloan's house.

Elaine's voice comes from the guest room, so I tiptoe down the hall. The yellow-pine floor is soft and warm beneath my feet in spite of the cold, and the cottage is new enough that nothing creaks. I'm quiet as a cat sneaking around.

"I swear I heard something." Her voice is a shaky whisper. She pauses, listening to whoever's on the line . . . I'm pretty certain I know who it is. "Maybe." Pause. "I guess I was asleep, but come over and spend the night anyway." More waiting as she listens. "We'll worry about that tomorrow. I need you here."

Rolling my eyes at the pleading tone in her voice, I'm fully prepared to find Patrick in my kitchen in the morning. They're both about to make my shit list for whatever's going on. Still, I'm smiling as I crawl back into my bed.

Lainey's not used to being here, and I'm not used to overnight guests in that little room. We most likely disturbed each other, but I'll sleep better with Patrick here. And the truth is, I'm relieved to know they're okay, no matter what I witnessed at their condo tonight. I drift back to sleep, my shaky self-confidence restored.

SURE ENOUGH, DEREK'S BUSINESS PARTNER is standing in my kitchen when I stagger in for coffee the next morning. He's in a white tee and the same faded jeans, and he's cute as ever with his messy bedhead and scruffy cheeks.

"Good morning," I say with a squint. "I guess we're all made up again?"

"Hey, babe." He steps forward and pecks my forehead. "Sleep okay?"

"All except for a few moments after midnight . . ."

His body goes on visible defense. "Did you hear something?"

I feel like I'm calming a German Shepherd. "I heard Elaine on the phone begging you to come over."

His broad shoulders drop. "Oh."

Jamming my hands on my hips, my voice is raised now. "What the hell is going on here? First Derek's wound so tight, now you and Elaine are acting like . . . I don't know what. Like you're auditioning for community theater—"

"Hang on." He steps toward me and then looks around.

"She's still in the guest room, but she'll be flying in here any minute. She has to be at school in an hour."

He catches me by the shoulders and pulls me further into the kitchen. "Just between us, okay?"

I nod, unsure what he's about to say.

"Derek wants to tell you himself. So just be cool."

He's quiet again, and it actually appears he's done. That's it. All I get.

I push his hands off me. "What! That's the most . . . I thought you were about to tell me something I can use."

"And risk the wrath of Derek? No fucking way. That's one ass-kicking I've somehow managed to avoid, and I plan to keep it that way." He laughs, and turns to the fridge, pulling out the OJ. "But Elaine's spending the night with you until he gets here, okay?"

"Which means you are, too?"

He grins and does a little shrug.

I'm frustrated, and my throat feels tight. "This doesn't make any sense unless he's afraid of me being alone . . . which means—"

In that instant it all clicks together. It couldn't be anything else, and I feel like an idiot for not seeing it sooner. At the same time, my stomach drops as I acknowledge what it means.

Just then Elaine flies into the kitchen, as predicted, whizzing around the room and gathering her things fast. She sees me and freezes, guilt filling her green eyes. "You're awake."

"And you two aren't really fighting."

Her pink lips twist, but a car horn sounds outside. "Oh, that's my ride. Sorry, Mel. Have to get to school." She pecks me on the cheek and Patrick on the mouth—followed by him grabbing her waist and pulling her back for a longer, open-mouthed smooch.

I leave the kitchen, headed for my bedroom with a boulder in my chest. The case that has Derek so tense, Patrick turning into my live-in babysitter . . . I'm standing by my bedside thinking when it all clicks together.

"You okay?"

I squeal and almost throw my coffee across the bed. "Patrick! Jesus!"

He tries not to laugh, putting a hand on my shoulder. "That's exactly what he wants to avoid. He doesn't want you to be afraid."

My heart's still flying as I set my coffee cup on the dresser. "So you're really not going to tell me what's happening?"

"No."

Dropping onto the bed, I look up at him. "How long will you two be staying here?"

"Until Derek arrives on Thursday."

Thursday. Despite it all, knowing he'll be here so soon makes my heart rise. "That performance last night really wasn't necessary. You could've just insisted I spend the night."

"It was a last-ditch effort." He walks over and sits beside me on the bed, patting my knee. "We tried everything to get you to stay at our place. You're stubborn as a damn mule."

"I am not!" My eyes widen, and he laughs more.

"Have you met yourself?"

I want to laugh, but my realization kills the levity. "This is about Sloan, isn't it?"

Patrick's smile fades, and he looks down. No answer.

The truth of what's going on beats painfully in my chest. The change must be clear on my face because in one quick move, his arms are around my shoulders, and I'm pulled into Patrick's embrace.

"It's going to be okay." His voice is soothing, his hug warm. "I've got you covered until Derek gets here, and then he'll take over."

"I'm fine." I push back and clear my throat. "Sloan doesn't scare me anymore. Look." Going to the closet, I open the door and reach inside, pulling out a wooden baseball bat. "Backup plan."

His grin returns at the sight of it. "Think you could use it on him?"

"I *know* I could use it on him."

He walks over to me. Then he taps me on the nose with the tip of his finger. "Glad to hear it, because I have to drive to Raleigh today. I'm pretty certain you'll be okay while I'm gone, but I feel a little better now."

A line pierces my forehead. "What's in Raleigh?"

"Not what, who. Toni Durango."

"The stripper?" I'm right behind him as he heads to the door. "Elaine was right?"

He pauses before leaving. "No and yes. No, she's not a stripper. She's a former escort. And yes, Elaine knows. I'm hoping she'll help us. Wish me luck."

"Don't get lucky!"

"Too late."

My mouth drops open as I watch him climb in the waiting Charger and drive away. The sound of my phone buzzing snaps me out of it, and I see a text from Derek.

Sleep well?

I pick up the device and quickly type back. *Two house guests last night. You've got some explaining to do.*

See you soon.

We exchange *I love you; I love you mores,* and it appears that's as much information as I'm going to get. And it's pissing me off.

FOUR

A PHYSICAL REMINDER

Derek

FUCKING HOUSTON TOOK LONGER THAN I planned.

Between filtering through their myriad of networks and users and their lax social media policy, half the computers had viruses and the other half had unnecessary virus protection added. I don't finish the analysis until late Wednesday.

Nikki is sitting at the front desk waiting, perky as ever, when I present her with the package.

"Happy leap year." Keeping the frustration out of my voice is difficult.

"What's this, boss?"

Remembering my new leaf, I soften my tone. "I need you to mail that to our new Houston client. And I've got a surprise for you."

Her dark brow arches.

"Take the rest of the week off. With pay."

Instead of squealing, she leans back in her chair. "Is it that bad?"

I feel my own brow furrow in response. "What?"

"Look, I know you think I'm just a dumb blonde, but you're

wrong. Something's going on, and it's something with Melissa."

For a split second, I almost lose it, but I recover fast—poker face back in place. "Melissa's fine."

"I know she's fine. We text pretty regularly. But whatever has you so edgy is about her, and don't try to tell me it isn't."

Fuck. The tension creeps up my back again.

Why didn't I go solo after Stuart left? Patrick was a real test of my patience, but Nikki might push me over the cliff. I don't need an office manager. I handle my own travel plans now, and half the time I even answer my own damn phone.

But Melissa likes her.

"I'm working on something," I say, calming the adrenaline spike in my veins. "And I'm handling it. There's no need to worry Melissa."

Her blue eyes roam around my face searching for clues. Nikki has pretty much pissed me off since Day 1, but if she can keep her mouth shut now, I'll let all of it go.

We face each other for a few, tense seconds before she nods. "I won't say anything."

"Thank you."

"Only because I know how much you love her. You'll do anything to protect her. Right?"

I can't believe she even has to ask, but I guess some women see a lot more shitty guys than good ones. "Right. I won't be back in this office until I'm sure she's safe."

Standing, she collects her coat, purse, and the package. Then she gives me a little salute. "Take as long as you need, boss. I'll be on standby if you want someone here."

And with that, she's out the door. I lean against her desk, gauging my level of exhaustion. If I leave now, I'll be in Wilmington by morning. If I fall asleep at the wheel, I won't be any use to anybody. My phone buzzes, and when I see the face, I make my decision.

PM check in! Melissa texts. *P&E are here. You home or work?*

Just finished Houston, leaving work. Miss you.

Tomorrow?
ASAP.
Be careful driving. Love you.
Love you more.

THE COTTAGE IS DARK WHEN I arrive at 6 A.M. Elaine is the only one with an early wake-up call, so it's possible I can get into Melissa's room before they're up and stirring. Driving all night might not have been the most restful approach, but with the energy surging through my chest, I knew I wouldn't get any sleep anyway. I'll nap a few hours this morning and be ready to go without losing a day.

Dropping my duffel by the stainless fridge inside, I ease off my boots and place them one at a time by the door doing my best to keep quiet. Grabbing a water bottle, I head to Melissa's bedroom, but I nearly slam it against the skull of a half-dressed Patrick. He's right around the corner, holding a wooden baseball bat high, like he's about to use my head for the winning homer in the World Series.

"*SHIT!*" we both whisper-shout.

"What the fuck?" Patrick lowers the bat and breathes.

I recognize the energy surging through his muscles. It matches the rapid tweaking of my own, and I need a second to recover.

"You could've shot me a text," he groans, dropping onto the couch. "Did you fucking drive all night?"

"Couldn't sleep." I clap his shoulder as I pass. "Glad to see you're on your toes. You're officially off guard duty."

"Hey!" I pause, and he tosses me the bat. "Happy to help. I'm going back to bed."

Catching his "weapon," my brow lines. "Think you'll be able to sleep?"

"Nope." That grin spreads across his face. It's the same one that used to tick me off because I knew it meant I'd be cleaning up his shit sooner rather than later.

"Just keep it down. I don't need to hear you getting any."

He points back at me as he heads down the hall. "Right back atcha."

Shaking my head, I turn Melissa's bedroom door handle as softly as possible. Unlike my younger partner, I don't plan to wake her this early. I know the pregnancy makes her tired, and I'll be content to be beside her. It'll be the first good rest I've had in four days, knowing she's with me and safe.

She's curled in her familiar sleeping position, and I can't help a smile as the warmth of love fills me. I will never get tired of watching this woman sleep.

Jeans off, I whip the thin, navy sweater I'm wearing over my head and slip into her king-sized bed. She doesn't even stir, and I'm happy she feels so secure with Patrick in the house. He might have been a pain in my ass in the past, but he's more than made up for it with this assignment.

Easing closer to her, I lift her long, dark waves off the pillow and replace them with my head. She makes a soft noise and stirs, but she doesn't wake. My arm goes above her, and our bodies are so close, I can feel the warmth radiating from her ivory skin.

Wrapping a dark curl around my finger, the tension slowly drains from my body. Being with her is enough. She's home and comfort and warmth and all the good things I thought I'd never have again. She's my future and my desire and my love, and the notion that some dickwad might try to hurt this woman, might threaten what I cherish . . .

She sighs and scoots closer to me, still asleep. The idea that she knows I'm here is incredibly satisfying. My own eyes are heavy, and I lower my head.

In three breaths, I'm out.

IT'S DARK, AND I SENSE his presence. He's hiding like the coward he is, waiting for me to let my guard down so he can strike, so he can try to hurt her again.

Sensations of being back in battle engage my reflexes. I can't see the enemy, but that doesn't mean he can't see me. I have to move forward, keeping the one I'm charged to protect covered by my side.

A noise, and I know where he is. My fists are clenched. This time I'm not sure I'll have the presence of mind to stop until he's eliminated. Permanently.

Energy is building in my core, preparing for a fight . . . And the scene changes.

Softest velvet touches my skin. Whispers like a butterfly's wings feather over my cheeks and the sensation moves to my brow. Now it's on my temple, causing my eyes to blink open.

I'm in Melissa's pale green room. Sloan's gone, and the butterfly wings are her hair falling in my face as her delicate lips cover me with kisses.

One swift movement, and she's on her back with a shriek and a laugh. I want to cover her mouth with mine, but first I'd like to swish with some water—or preferably mouthwash. Instead I opt for devouring her slim neck.

Her fingers thread into the sides of my hair. "What time did you get in?" Her voice is breathy and high, as I follow a trail with my lips along her collarbone.

"Just before six. I tried not to wake you." My mouth is moving up into her hair, behind her ear. She smells like roses mixed with the ocean, and I inhale deeply as she makes one of those little noises I love.

"Patrick said he almost batted you into next week." A laugh moves through her torso.

"He did a fantastic job." I kiss her jaw, pulling little bits of skin between my teeth, tasting her. She's delicious. "I'm giving him a bonus. Something major. A Rolex."

She's squirming, trying to catch my lips with hers, and I lift up long enough to grab the water bottle and take a quick hit, swishing it around and then diving back into her arms. She pushes my shoulders, flipping me onto my back and straddling my waist as she forces my lips apart, finding my tongue.

She's wearing a skirt, and the way she's sitting, I can tell she's not wearing panties. Fuck me. Her heat is flush on my bare stomach, and between that, her hands in my hair, and her mouth moving mine, my morning wood has turned into a full-fledged tree—one of those giant redwoods.

"You're overdressed." I pull up the sweater she's wearing, and my brow collapses with appreciation when I discover she's also braless.

Her breasts are firm and round and a few sizes bigger these days. *Gorgeous.*

Holding them, I massage my thumbs over the dark circles before pulling a beaded nipple into my mouth. She lets out a moan, and the chances are great I'll last about as long as a teenage boy once I'm inside her.

Melissa is not helping the situation. She slides down my stomach and jerks my boxer briefs to my hips. The beast is unleashed, and she covers it with that hot velvet mouth.

"Fuck." I arch back and try to think of baseball. Cold showers. House fires . . .

Her small hand pumping my shaft. Warm lips caressing my tip then moving lower, followed by the slow sweep of her tongue. *Shit.*

In a move fast enough to rival Superman, I catch her under the arms and pull her up and over. I'm inside, sinking deep into her slippery-wet body, in less than two seconds.

"Derek!" She cries and holds on, but I can't stop.

She's lying on her back, but I'm on my knees leaning into her, needing to be as deep inside her as possible. Her moans drive me crazy as I grip her ass, pulling her against me. *Harder, faster . . .* My stomach tightens as the explosion builds. A ragged groan scrapes my throat as the orgasm blazes through me, shaking me to the core. It's so good, I have to hold her a few moments to recover.

Releasing my grip on her backside, I lean on the headboard as I catch my breath. These last several weeks, I've been doing my best to avoid putting pressure on her abdomen, where the baby is, but she's crawling up, lips following the lines on my stomach, kissing her way up my chest until she wraps her arms around my neck.

"You're so sexy when you let go." Her voice is a husky whisper, and when I open my eyes, her beautiful mouth is inches from mine. I can't resist kissing it.

"You didn't finish. I'm sorry."

Her blue eyes narrow, making her look even more like the sex kitten she is right now. "I guess you have to make it up to me then."

I manage a weak laugh. "You might have to give me a minute."

She makes a teasing pout that melts into a smile she presses against my lips. Her breasts touch my chest, and it's possible I might have a little something left.

My hands roam down her sides, exploring her curves. She's still up, but I move lower, kissing the sexy crease at the bottom of one breast, inhaling the scent of her body. Fresh-air flowers.

"Mmm . . ." The vibration of her voice moves through her torso as I kiss her skin. My fingers go between her legs, my thumb circling the tiny bud while my middle fingers push inside her. She moans again, and her hips rock as she rides my hand. I catch her up with a few practiced movements.

Her eyes are closed as she savors the sensations. Her nipples bounce near my chin, so I pull one into my mouth, which earns me another little cry.

"Derek, oh . . ." Her sighing my name like that is enough to get my semi all the way to ready, and I lie back, pulling her onto my lap so she can ride it out.

Her hips buck against mine as her hair swishes around her waist, and I'm glad I got the edge off because I wouldn't miss this sight for the world. Her gorgeous body is like a goddess rising above me, sexy and full of life. I'm holding back now, enjoying the beauty of her ecstasy. She's mine to cherish and to love and to protect, and if my past has taught me anything, it's how to do that.

Her insides are pulling me, massaging and milking, and now my own instincts kick in. I catch her waist, rocking my hips against her.

"Yes . . . oh, shit!" She wails, shoulders shuddering with my thrusts, and with a groan, I let go.

It's pure bliss the second time I come. One last push, and she collapses in my arms, a broad smile on her face. Her cheek is on my shoulder and she starts to giggle.

"What?" Smoothing back her hair, I smile as her blue eyes blink open.

"That was incredible." Then she laughs again. "I'm such a stereotype. The horny pregnant lady."

Kissing her eyes and face, I hug her close against me. "You're not a stereotype. You're amazingly sexy and everything I want."

She stretches up and kisses my nose. "I thought I'd have to wait a while after that first round."

"No way." My hand is cupping her breast, my thumb circling her nipple. "I can't have my lady frustrated."

"Thank you." Then she giggles again, sitting back and wrapping the sheet around her body, eyes sparkling. "Saying that makes me think of our first time. I was sure I'd gone crazy being with a complete stranger like that. And then you thanked me."

She covers her eyes and laughs again. I love seeing her so happy.

"You have no idea what a game-changing moment that was

for me. It was pretty major." My thoughts go back to the reason for that encounter and the reason I'm here with her now, and my tone grows serious. "You were always safe with me. I'm sure you sensed it even then."

Another laugh and she shakes her head, dropping her chin. "I'm pretty sure the only thing I sensed was how incredibly sexy you are."

Catching that chin, I rub my thumb over her soft skin. "I should've done better research before agreeing to help him."

"Stop." Her hand covers mine, pulling it down and threading our fingers. "We've covered that. And anyway, if you had done better research, you probably would've turned him down, and we'd have never met. It was ultimately for the best."

I can't argue with that.

"Now," she continues. "Since we've caught up physically—"

"I wouldn't be so sure—"

She dodges my attempt to pull her to me again. "Tell me why I've had house guests all week. Why you're here early. It's about my ex-husband, isn't it?"

Her attempt at being bossy is adorable. "What makes you think that?"

"Patrick is a terrible liar."

"There goes his Rolex."

I start to get up, but she catches my arm and holds me. "Tell me what's going on."

Her blue eyes are serious, and I sit back against the headboard again. "Okay, yes. It's about Sloan, and this time I'm not giving up until he's behind bars."

Or in hell, I mentally add.

Anger or frustration—it's hard to tell which—flashes across her face. "I told you I wanted to put the past behind us."

"I'd be happy to do that if he weren't still a threat."

"What threat?" Her voice goes high. "He's back in Baltimore. He wouldn't dare touch me. Sloan's pretty sick, but he's not stupid enough to cross you."

"I wish I could agree, but I've seen too many cases like this. I know how they go."

She tries to leave the bed, but I catch her and bring her back. "You have to trust me on this, Mel."

"You mean I have to live in fear all the time, looking over my shoulder? I won't do it. I can't."

"I'm not asking you to live in fear."

"And I won't have you jeopardizing our future by doing something potentially illegal just to . . . what? Get revenge?"

My lips tighten at her words. I know she's saying these things because she wants to convince me, but she's only partially informed. Reaching up, I rest my palm on the side of her face and run my thumb lightly over her scar.

"Every time I see this, I want to kill him. I know exactly how I'll do it, too."

She reaches up to take my hand and fold it in both of hers. "My scar reminds me of how strong I am. What I can survive."

A familiar anger tightens in my chest that she would even need a physical reminder of such a thing.

"I wish I'd never shown you that picture." Her voice is quiet as she traces her fingertip over the back of my hand. "It was unfair, and now you can never un-see it."

"Jessica Black is dead."

Her body goes still. For a moment I'm not sure if she's breathing.

"Mel?"

Now when her eyes travel up to mine, they're worried. "How . . ."

"I don't know, but I have a hunch."

Blinking quickly, her head moves side to side as she's processing what I'm not saying. "He didn't . . . he wouldn't . . ." She squeezes her blue eyes closed, and I'm worried she'll cry. She doesn't. Instead when she opens her eyes this time acceptance is in her voice. "But why?"

"Have you ever seen a picture of her?"

"I never saw pictures of any of them."

"I'd be willing to bet they all have a similar look, and it's long, dark waves, petite with fair skin."

She's off the bed now, scooping up my shirt and wrapping it around her body. Her arms are crossed over her midsection, and she's pacing the room still shaking her head. "No. He's an abusive, controlling son of a bitch, but he's not a murderer."

Picking up my jeans, I quickly step in and pull them up my hips before crossing the room to pull her into my arms. "You say that, but you didn't believe he'd hurt you either."

I feel the tremors moving through her, and I hug her tighter against my chest. "Shh . . . I'm here now, and I'm not leaving until he's no longer a threat to you. Or the baby."

Another shiver moves through her, but she's fighting it. "Do you have some reason to believe he's responsible? The girl was a hooker. She lived a dangerous life. She could've been killed for any number of reasons."

"She was living in Baltimore. She'd moved there a year ago, and it appears she was one of Sloan's regulars. It's probably why he got careless, and you found out."

"That's a big leap with no evidence."

"Police records have a mug shot of her beaten. It's what caught my attention in the first place. The image looks . . . very similar to what you showed me."

"Oh, god." She covers her face with her hands.

Guiding her back to the bed, we sit on the foot. I pull her onto my lap and wrap my arms around her, preparing to hold her for as long as she needs. Not surprisingly, it isn't very long.

She pushes back and seems to shake herself. Standing again, I see her find that strength I know is inside her. It's amazing to watch.

"Fuck him." Her voice is calm. "Let Sloan Reynolds try to come here. I have a Louisville slugger for that very purpose."

Grinning, now I'm the one shaking his head. "I love you so much, and there is no fucking way I'll let you be a sitting duck out here."

She stops moving and faces me, hands on hips. "So you have a plan? Patrick's in on it?"

"Yeah. I'm heading to Raleigh with him to meet someone he says will help us."

"Toni Durango. You're hiring a hooker."

"He really lost that Rolex this time."

"I saw the name on his phone. He told me what she does."

Standing, I cross to where she is and put my hands on the tops of both her shoulders. "I don't know what Sloan might do, but at this point, I'm willing to consider any possibility. After last week, I was willing to hire someone to take care of him for me—"

"Don't let him win." Her eyes are round and serious. "If he took you away from me, I'd have lost something I can't live without."

"Enter Patrick, our man with the plan."

"And his friendly call girl."

A little groan rises in my throat. "I'll let you know how it goes. I haven't committed to anything yet."

FIVE

AMERICAN MUSCLE

Derek

THE SKINNIFLUTE SALOON IS ABOUT the type of dive I'd expect from a Patrick source. A wood-paneled biker joint with perforated steel plates on the lower half each exterior, the only windows are small and near the ceiling, and the dark interior is lit by single-bulbs hanging over the small booths lining the walls. Fluorescent lights and neon beer signs add illumination behind the bar in the center of the room.

As instructed, I'm wearing dark jeans, boots, and an inconspicuous black tee and leather jacket. Patrick's in a similar get-up, but he's added a bandanna tied over his light brown hair.

"Should I be expecting a fight?" I quip as we slide into the wooden booth to wait for Toni.

"Hell, no. These guys are pretty mellow. Didn't even look up last time I was in here."

"How often are you in here?"

He shrugs. "Third time."

A waitress, who resembles Amy Winehouse in hot pants and a tight sweater, appears with a small, round tray. Her dark eyes move quickly from Patrick to do a slow sweep over me. I don't return her interest.

"Hey, Brian. What can I getcha?"

My eyes cut across the table to my partner's. "Vodka rocks and this guy will have . . ."

"Coke is fine. I'm driving."

Her eyebrows rise, and she spins on her heel before sashaying away. I'm pretty sure her exaggerated hip movements are for our benefit.

When she's far enough away, I lean forward on the table. "Brian?"

"First time I was here, I didn't want Toni to know I was looking for her, so I told Lylah my name was Brian."

"Lylah?"

"Just go with it."

We straighten up as she returns to put the drinks in front of us. Patrick puts a twenty on her tray. "Keep an eye on this for me."

"You got it, babe."

She saunters off again, and I settle in to wait for our contact. "So you've explained the situation to Toni?"

Patrick shrugs. "Only in a roundabout way. I wasn't sure how much you wanted out there, but she's willing to help us. She has some bad blood she wasn't ready to tell me about on Tuesday."

"Maybe she'll talk about it now."

I glance up as another brunette enters the bar. She's tall and slim and dressed similarly to Lylah. I wonder if it's the standard uniform for this place.

"Yeah, that's her." Patrick follows my gaze, and I see their eyes connect. A slight nod, and she says something to Lylah before heading in our direction.

My lips curl into a frown. "She's too tall."

"She likes to wear those stilts." Sure enough, she's wearing stripper heels.

"Do you have a shoe fetish or something?"

Patrick gives me The Smile. "Nothing's hotter than a naked woman in heels."

Lifting the Coke, I can't resist a small jab. "Especially when she's got your dick in her mouth."

"Nope." He shakes his head, serious again. "Elaine's the only woman for me now."

"You've got some incredible good luck, partner."

"Don't I know it." He slides down as Toni approaches the table.

Her eyes graze over me as she takes the spot Patrick's created, and she returns my frown. "You look like a judgmental asshole." Her voice is low and smoky.

This is getting worse by the second, and I'm losing interest fast. "And you look like every con artist I've ever helped put away."

"Well," Patrick laughs, doing his best to salvage things. "This is getting off to a great start. Can I get you a drink?"

She shakes her head. "I'm on the clock. What's this about, Patrick?"

"My partner here . . ." He pauses for introductions. "Derek Alexander, Toni Durango . . ."

We nod, still displeased at the prospect of working together. Patrick continues. "My partner here has a problem, and I think you can help. It's about the situation we discussed on Tuesday."

Pushing a lock of straight, dyed-black hair off her shoulder, she takes a sip of his vodka. "You didn't tell me much, and I only said I'd listen. I haven't agreed to work with anybody."

He nods. "Fair enough. Derek? You want to explain the situation?"

It makes sense, as I know more about what's going on than anybody. "It's like this . . ." But my phone cuts me off. It emits the special tone I've set up for my man in Baltimore, and I pull it out fast to read the screen, my current meeting forgotten.

Subject AWOL. Sorry, boss, he must've left in the night. Can't find him.

I'm on my feet before I've even finished reading, swiping Patrick's keys off the table.

"Derek?" Somewhere behind me, I feel Patrick struggling to get Toni out of the booth so he can follow, but I'm in a tunnel. My brain is miles away, focused on one objective—getting back to Wilmington. Fast.

I'm out the door with my heart thundering painfully. Jamming the key into the ignition, Patrick's Charger roars to life. Satisfaction surges through my legs. It's going to be a tough drive, but for once I'm thankful for Patrick's bravado. American muscle is exactly what I need to cover the miles at top speed.

Shoving the stick into reverse to back out, I slam on the breaks and put it in gear before punching it. Rocks fly as I spin out of the lot, and I only vaguely hear Patrick yelling for me to wait. He'll figure out a ride back. I've got to get to Melissa.

I try calling her, but it goes to voicemail. I send her a quick text. *Call me please.*

While I wait, I hit Elaine's number, voicemail. She's in class. I try Mel's mother, voicemail again. *Dammit!* She's probably with a patient. Why don't I have her office number programmed in my phone?

I throw my cell on the passenger seat and grip the wheel again. Both hands hold it so hard, I'm surprised it doesn't bend in half. It's like my body is trying to push the car faster by brute force.

How could I be so careless? Bennett's been watching Sloan for weeks, and nothing's happened. He's been quiet, going about his routine, obeying the law. I should've known he'd make a move now.

Melissa said his behavior was cyclical, and she could tell when it was time for him to either leave town for a hook-up or for her to start sleeping with her door locked and the can of pepper spray under her pillow. The very thought of her living like that grinds my jaw.

After all my work closing the office, driving all night, I left her alone, out there in that little cottage unguarded. *Fuck!* My fists tighten harder on the thin, metal ring guiding Patrick's sports car. I'm pushing ninety, and car after car flashes past.

Traffic is light this early-afternoon Thursday. It's the one small advantage I have. I'm making the most of it and wishing I had a portable siren. Once more the smallest prayer sneaks from my brain. *Not again. Please don't let it happen again.*

I'm too far from her. If she needs me, if she's afraid or in danger, I'm not there. If the unthinkable happens . . . Memories of the pain of that loss scorch through my chest. The mind-numbing helplessness is back. I can't bear it a second time. I can't lose Melissa.

Glancing down, I'm at a hundred now. I'll be there soon, but it still feels too long. My breath is fast, and my brain is repeating the word *No.* It's all I've got, the force of my will, demanding that she be okay.

SIX

FIRST PRIORITY

Melissa

WORKING FROM HOME AT THE beach is possibly the absolute best outcome I could've ever imagined. Waking up to find Derek in my bed only makes it a million times better.

Leaning back on my sun porch as the waves crash a short distance away, I smile warmly remembering our incredible morning. Now he needs to stop being so stubborn and relocate.

It's chilly, and I'm wearing fleece pants, a long-sleeved red tee with a fuzzy blanket wrapped around my shoulders. In my thick socks, I'm cozy enough to nap, but I'm working on a marketing plan for Aunt Bea to take her cupcake bakery online. She's completely baffled by how it all works, of course, but with her skills and built-in clientele, she'll take off in no time.

I've just hit *send* on the email explaining it to her in as simple terms as possible, then I wrap the cozy blanket a bit tighter around my shoulders and drift into a pleasant slumber, hoping that when I wake, my sweet love will be by my side again.

MY SLEEP IS TROUBLED, AND even with the blanket, I shiver. A sound like scissors flicks near my ear, and I flinch. *Cutting . . . Something's cutting . . . My hair?*

No, that's wrong.

The expression "someone walked over my grave" drifts through my hazy brain, and I feel so afraid, I might cry.

Derek . . . where is Derek? I need him here. I need him to protect me.

It doesn't matter if I tell him I'm strong, and I can take care of myself. I'm afraid. The terror holding me won't let go, and all I want is my big man.

It's dark. My heart is thundering in my chest, and with a cold certainty, I recognize the sound of his footsteps, the spicy smell of his cologne. It stings my nose and makes my throat close up.

Sloan.

He's here.

I can't catch my breath.

The baby. I have to protect the baby . . .

Footsteps pound louder, closer, and with a loud gasp, I bolt upright on the couch.

But I'm alone.

It was just a dream.

"Oh, my god!" My trembling hand goes over my face, and I can't stop the tears streaming down my cheeks.

"Melissa?" Apparently the footsteps weren't a dream. Derek bursts through the side door, and without hesitation, I fly off the couch into his arms. Instantly they surround me as he kisses my head, speaking against my hair. "You're okay. I'm here now. You're safe."

His voice is tense as he holds me tightly, and gradually, my shaking calms. He eases me back and bends down to look in my eyes. "What happened? Why are you crying?"

Even though his voice is soothing, his entire body is on edge. His muscles seem larger, like he's ready to fight. That's when I find my strength. Shaking myself, I place my palms flat against my cheeks.

"I'm sorry." *Breathe, Melissa, breathe.* "I . . . I had the most vivid dream. I thought someone was here . . . I-It scared me."

My fingers curl, and he holds me close again. I bury my face in his chest, and the last of my terror slowly recedes.

Derek isn't satisfied. He covers me with the blanket. "I'm going to look around, make sure you weren't picking up on something in your sleep."

He steps to the screen door and turns the little latch, locking it. My brow lines. "What do you mean? Did you see something?"

His face is stoic, but it softens with a smile when he glances down at me. "No, but I want to check the place out just in case," touching my cheek lightly, "you're very attuned to your surroundings."

"For a while I had to be."

He continues into the house, his mouth in a firm line. I stay on the couch, pulling the soft blanket tightly as I wait.

It's later in the afternoon than I normally nap, but having Derek here causes my sleep patterns to shift. More specifically, I don't sleep as much at night—even though he tries to let me. It's hard to care about rest with him in my bed.

The sounds of him moving around inside drift to me on the sea breeze. He's opening closet doors and looking for any signs of disturbance. It's very comforting, even though I feel silly worrying him so much over a bad dream, which was probably induced by all the preoccupation with my ex.

Further down below us the waves crash against the shoreline. One of the things I love about my new home is how secluded it is from the rest of civilization, but I confess, Derek's current obsession with Sloan's whereabouts has me spooked.

I can't tell him what my nightmare was really about.

Joining me on the side porch, he pulls me close against his chest again. "Nothing seems out of place, but I don't know what all you did while I was gone."

"Just worked, came out here. Then I was tired and took a

nap."

I can see him thinking, and I almost jump out of my skin at the very loud and completely unexpected roar of a motorcycle engine. We're both up, but I beat him to the door.

"Why is Patrick on a Harley?"

Derek's lips tighten, and he catches me by the waist, pulling me back and flipping the lock on the door. "Stay here."

Frowning, I watch as he stalks out to meet his partner.

Patrick's royal blue Charger is in my driveway next to Derek's black Audi, and I can only assume they got separated somehow. *But how?* I can't hear what they're saying. Patrick's expression wavers back and forth between irritation and relief, and they talk for a few minutes longer. Then Patrick walks over and straddles the bike once more. He pulls the black helmet over his head and kicks the engine to life. Derek gives him a nod, and with a roar, his partner heads toward town.

Derek turns and heads back to the house. His brow is furrowed, and he studies the ground as he walks. One arm is crossed, and he's holding his bicep, the other hand is a clenched fist.

Stepping back, I let him in the door, but he pauses to flip the metal lock again before taking my hand and leading me into the house.

"I feel like I'm the one out of the loop." The blanket is still clutched over my shoulders as I follow him.

He doesn't answer.

"How did you and Patrick get separated?"

We're in the kitchen now, and I watch as he pulls down an unopened bottle of Scotch. "Patrick invited us over for dinner tonight."

He cracks the seal and pours a small amount into a glass and shoots it back. A little wince creases his eyes, and he puts the glass in the sink.

"I've never seen you drink in the afternoon."

I'm back in his arms, and his face is buried in my hair as he inhales deeply. A warm shiver travels up my arms despite my concern.

"I've never been so worried about you." His voice is low against my neck. "But you're okay now. And I'm here."

I'm unsure how to pursue this. My dream-inspired panic is fresh in my memory, and now he's behaving so strangely. I want to argue. I want to fight this type of existence, to insist this *isn't* how I'm going to live, dammit. I won't be afraid in my own home.

But anxiety is still holding my shoulders tightly. With a sigh, I step back and manage a smile. "If we're having dinner at Elaine's, I want to shower first. We always stay late."

He smiles in response, but it's not as bright as usual. "Not too late. I know you need your rest."

Stretching up on my tiptoes, I kiss his lips. "Thanks." Then I head back to my bedroom to get ready. For the short-term, I'll trust him and put this discussion on hold.

THURSDAY NIGHT ALWAYS FEELS LIKE the start of the weekend, even though Friday is still a workday. Elaine stands by the stove, a glass of white wine in her hand when we arrive. The room smells like tomato-ey deliciousness, and my friend is still dressed from school in a navy pencil skirt and a pink sweater-set. She's also barefoot, and her light-blonde hair is pulled up in a messy bun.

"Come in!" She calls, giving the pot one last stir before dropping the wooden spoon and stepping over to hug me. "I hope you're in the mood for Italian. Oh, Mel. You're absolutely glowing!"

She squeezes my arms before smiling up at Derek. "You're now officially my third favorite person on the planet."

He laughs and leans down to kiss her cheek. Her head tilts

toward him. "I guess third is better than thirtieth."

"Well, I have to count Patrick first, Melissa second—"

"I've been replaced!"

She laughs, and just then Patrick emerges from the side room, his arms full of laundry. "Hey, guys." The sunshine is back in his voice, and it's very reassuring.

"She's got you doing laundry now?" Shaking my head, I glance up at Derek.

"I've got a service that comes once a week." He almost sounds apologetic, which makes me laugh more.

Patrick pauses to speak low in my ear. "Not all of us are as set as Mr. Alexander."

"Wait!" Elaine stops him and pulls a dress out of the load. "This is dry clean only."

"Sorry, babe, but it's got a little stain on it." He gives her a wink, and she shakes her head.

She doesn't notice that when she pulls out the dress, a gold silk tie goes with it. It hits the floor, and I pick it up, noticing how horribly misshapen and nearly torn it is. "Oh, no!" Flipping it over, I see an Armani label.

Patrick reemerges from the laundry room. "What?"

"Your tie is ruined. What happened to it?"

"Oh!" Elaine charges back and snatches it out of my hand. Her cheeks are flaming red, and Patrick laughs loudly.

"Elaine, tell number two what happened to my best tie." That devilish gleam is in his eye, and it takes me a second to catch up. "My kinky fiancée thought she'd play dominatrix, but I had to set her straight."

"Patrick Knight!" My best friend's voice is a loud command as she returns from dropping both items in their bedroom.

"There she goes again."

Derek coughs a laugh, and my eyebrows fly up. "Well, okay then." I'm trying not to laugh, too. "TMI, number one."

"Good work." Derek gives him a fist bump. I elbow my own fiancé sharply in the stomach. He grunts another laugh. "I mean . . . sorry about your tie?"

Elaine's voice is high, and her back is turned while she stabs the wooden spoon in the pot repeatedly. "We can all just stop talking about it now!"

"I'm only teasing you, babe." Patrick goes behind her and holds her waist before kissing her neck. "You know I love your little stunts."

I cross to the cabinet and pull down another wine glass. "On that note, we should have drinks. Derek, wine?"

He nods, and I go to the fridge to pull out the bottle of pinot grigio Elaine's having and a root beer. "You got my favorite."

She glances over her shoulder past Patrick. "Yeah, I figured you were getting sick of ginger ale all the time."

Derek takes the wine glass from me and follows Patrick into the living room. They immediately launch into a discussion, but Patrick's speaking so low I can barely hear him.

"I touched base with Toni and assured them we'd be back tomorrow. Gabe wants his bike now, but he'll give me twenty-four hours."

Derek's voice is equally low. "I don't like leaving her while he's still MIA."

Frustrated, I go to where they're talking. "Please tell me what's going on. You know I don't like being in the dark."

Derek's shoulders drop, and Patrick turns to me. "Sloan's gone off the radar. We don't like it in view of what happened in Baltimore. We still don't have answers, and we're not ready."

My brow lines. "Ready for what?"

"We've been working on a plan since the Jessica Black report turned up. Derek was trying to establish a financial connection, but it was going nowhere. Sloan's too experienced at covering his tracks."

I look up at Derek, and he catches my hand. "Patrick's idea could work, but we hadn't started talking about it when my man in Baltimore alerted me that Sloan was missing."

The dream, the memory of feeling like he was there

watching me, causes a strange roaring sound to grow in my ears. Shivers fly up my shoulders, and I understand the meaning of Derek's panicked appearance, Patrick's following behind on the motorcycle. "You drove back today because you were afraid—"

"He left me stranded in Raleigh," Patrick tries to laugh it off, but it isn't working. "I had to borrow Lylah's boyfriend's bike, and that is *not* something those guys do lightly. I had to leave my watch with him."

"Your Tag?"

"I'll get it back."

My eyes move to Derek's, and I can't decide which of the emotions surging through me is stronger—the intense love I feel for him or the intense hatred I feel for my ex.

The noise is pushing against my temples, and I step into the loving arms waiting for me. I hold his waist, and he holds me tightly until my trembling subsides.

"I hate this so much." My voice is barely above a whisper, but he hears me.

His voice is a low vibration in response. "I'm going to fix it. You'll never be afraid again."

Hidden in his arms, inhaling the clean-woodsy scent I love, I find calm. Until finally I'm able to look around again, and I notice how quiet it is in the room. Patrick is back in the kitchen talking to Elaine.

Lifting my chin, Derek smiles before kissing my lips. "I'm not going anywhere if you don't feel safe. You and the baby are my first priority now."

Shaking my head, I push my hair behind my ears, working hard to regain my composure. "I can go to Mom's office tomorrow and work. I'll be okay. It's like I keep saying, he cannot win. I won't let him."

Elaine calls from the kitchen. "Feel like eating something?"

Touching his rough cheek, I nod. "Let's have dinner. You and Patrick keep your plans for tomorrow."

His lips press into a smile, and he takes my hand in his, kissing the backs of my fingers before walking with me to the table. Elaine smiles and steps around to squeeze my shoulders. "If you ever want to hang out with me at school, I can always use an extra set of hands."

"Thanks." I pat her back. "I think I'll spend the afternoon with Mom tomorrow, but I'll keep your offer just in case."

"We'll have the information we need by tomorrow, I expect." Patrick joins us at the table. "Then it'll just be a matter of timing. We can plan it all out from here, where we can keep an eye on you."

He winks at me, but when Derek speaks, his voice is serious. "I appreciate you watching her for me these past weeks."

Shaking out my napkin and putting it in my lap, I pretend to be offended. "All this time, I thought you kept inviting me over because you enjoyed my company."

Elaine passes the basket of bread. "You've been eating us out of house and home. Jeez! I'm glad Derek's finally here."

"I have not!"

She bursts out laughing. "I was only teasing! But I want some beachside dinners at your place now."

"You got it. I love having you guys over."

The rest of dinner conversation is devoted to easy subjects—the weather, Patrick's newfound desire to own a Harley, Elaine's loud protests over the dangers of motorcycles. It's not very late when we call it a night, and as we say our goodbyes, I catch Patrick's arm, pulling him aside. Derek and Elaine continue talking.

"Thank you for watching over me."

He smiles and shrugs. "I promised Derek. Besides, it wasn't any more than he'd have done for me."

My eyes narrow. "You say that, but I know better. I also won't hear anything bad about you ever again. Everybody'd better look out."

"That might be hard. There's plenty of bad about me that's

true."

"Not for me. It's all good now." He breathes a chuckle, but I'm not through. "Would you promise me something this time?"

Golden-hazel eyes meet mine. "What?"

"Promise you'll look after him now. For me." I touch his arm. "Don't let him do anything . . ." *What's the right way to say it?* "Anything that could mean he'll be taken away from me?"

His warm hand covers mine. "You mean anything illegal or potentially deadly?"

"Exactly."

"I promise. I've got his back." Patrick isn't smiling, and I know I can trust him. He means what he says.

Derek's with us, and we drop the subject, acting casual, like we were just discussing how to get Elaine onboard the Harley train.

My fiancé takes my hand, pausing before we go out the door. "I'll meet you at ten. We should be there by noon to wrap this up and make a plan."

"See you in the morning."

The cottage is dark and quiet when we arrive. Derek stops in the kitchen to check his messages, but I go straight through the house, flipping on lights, refusing to be timid in my own place.

I go to the bathroom and switch on the hot water. An over-sized, jetted bathtub is one of the perks of living in an intended vacation residence, and tonight my whole body craves the comfort of a steaming, swirling bubble bath.

Digging under the cabinet, I find the jar of foaming bath salts I bought at the spa in Scottsdale and add several scoops to the stream rushing from the faucet. Once the temperature is right and the bubbles have risen, I strip out of all my clothes, tie up my hair and slide down into the cactus-flower-scented jets.

The water is the perfect level of hotness. My head rests on a foam pillow attached to the side, and I close my eyes, allowing the swirling water to soothe away the night. I don't realize I'm asleep until the soft press of Derek's lips against my forehead followed by the light scruff of his beard against my brow wakes me. My eyes flutter open, and he smiles down, fully dressed and leaning over the tub.

"Tired?" His voice is gentle.

Nodding, I lift one hand out of the now-warm water and touch his cheek. "Join me?"

I watch as he unbuttons his sleeve and rolls it up to his elbow. One hand on the wall behind my head, he leans forward and captures my lips as his other hand slides beneath the foam to cup my breast.

A breathy moan slips from my mouth into his, and keeping my eyes closed, I cover his hand with mine, following his movements from one breast to the other, his thumb slowly circling my hardening nipples.

He leans up and our eyes meet. "Good news." My eyebrows rise with curiosity, and he continues. "Sloan's back on the radar. He's in Charleston. Bennett's watching him and promises to keep me updated."

"Now you don't have to worry." My voice is thick from napping followed by all the steamy kisses and touches. "I can stay home and work tomorrow."

"I'd still like it if you had someone with you." His voice is soft with a touch of sexy, fanning the heat he's aroused in me.

"*I'd* like it if you were less clothed and in here while we discuss it."

"I'm not sure we'll do much discussing that way."

Sitting forward in the tub, I carefully unfasten his buttons with the tips of my fingers until his olive chest is revealed. A scattering of dark hair covers the top of his lined torso, and I chew my bottom lip remembering how it feels against my breasts. With the pad of his thumb, he touches my mouth.

"Don't bite your lip." He leans in and brushes his against mine. "Let me do that."

He gives me a little nibble, and I'm coming undone. "You're taking too long."

In a flash he stands, pushes his dark jeans down his hips, taking his boxer briefs with them. My breath catches at the sight of his gorgeous body nude in front of me. He's fully erect as he steps in and slides beneath the foam at the opposite end of the tub.

"Mmm . . . warm." Large hands slide to my waist, pulling me onto his lap as he leans back in the water. I'm already slick, so it doesn't take much. I reach around behind me and guide his tip into my throbbing opening. We both sigh as he rocks deep into me.

I lean forward, holding the tub on each side of his head while his mouth covers my breast, sucking a tight nipple.

A loud moan from me, and he moves up, his voice cracking in my ear. "We'll probably get water everywhere."

The sound of his growing desire sparks mine even hotter. "That's what towels are for."

His lips consume my words, his tongue sweeping in to find mine, and his hands grip my ass beneath the surface. Holding my body still, his hips rock into mine. Our mouths break away with a groan, and the water is swaying with us, splashing over the side. His mouth is at my shoulder, and he gives me another little bite. I tremble, holding him as his thrusting increases in speed and depth.

My orgasm mounts, and I feel my brow tense in ecstasy as he moves. The tightness below my navel becomes unbearable until at last it breaks, leaving me crying out his name. His movements don't slow, and I clutch his shoulders. The sound of me coming seems to push him over, and after a few final thrusts, he groans low, shooting off deep between my quivering thighs.

His hips move slower, and I kiss him along his rough jaw. My body is so relaxed and satisfied. I make my way to his ear, whispering my love for him as his arms wrap tightly around my waist. He kisses my neck, moving his hands out of the water to cup my cheeks, bringing my face so our eyes are level.

"Nothing is going to take you away from me." His blue eyes

are intense, and his brow lowered.

Nodding, I lift my own hands out of the water, lightly holding his neck, my thumbs at the corners of his mouth. "Nothing."

An inhale, and he pulls me against him, my cheek at his forehead, his face against my chest. For several moments we hold each other, until I notice the water is growing cold.

Lifting my head and sliding back down to kiss his nose, I smile. "Let's move this party to the bed, okay?"

A sexy grin spreads across his lips. "I'll have to get used to being with you longer than three days. We don't have to be so urgent, trying to make the most of every moment."

"Hmm." I can't help a frown. "I'm not sure I like the sound of that."

"You won't always be the 'horny pregnant lady,' as you like to say. I'm sure you'll appreciate me pacing myself."

My lips poke out as I consider this suggestion. Then my eyes roam from his thick dark waves tipped with bath water, hanging sexy in his blue eyes, his scruffy beard and full lips hiding straight white teeth. His amazing body . . .

"I think we should just play this whole 'pacing ourselves' thing by ear."

He laughs and pulls me against him, rolling us in the tub so that we're chest to chest, our bodies touching from head to toe under the water. I shriek and laugh, loving his possessiveness.

"*Nobody.* Is taking you away from me." He emphasizes the words softly before covering my lips again with his.

Chasing his kisses, laughing as happiness radiates through my core, it's hard for me to ever imagine having enough of him. But I wiggle, struggling to free myself from his vice grip. At once, he releases me.

"We're going to catch a chill if we don't get out of this tub. Not to mention turning into prunes." Standing, I reach for a fluffy white towel as his hands slide up my leg.

He sits up and kisses the side of my thigh. I reach back and slide my hand through is hair before stepping out. "Come on."

The grin on his face as he watches me dry myself tightens my stomach. His expression is a mixture of raw desire and pure appreciation. And love. Always love.

I can't help feeling a little self-conscious about my new figure as I drop a few towels around the tub to soak up the spilled water. "Meet you in the bedroom."

I head down the hall, hurrying to my dresser. I have something red and lacy in mind, something I know is Derek's favorite, but I pause in front of my mirror, my eyes searching my neck in the reflection.

A flash of panic hits me, and I quickly feel all around the dresser top. I don't know how I didn't notice before. The excitement I was just feeling is gone, and I grasp my neck. *Where is it?*

Running back to the bathroom, the towel still tied under my arms, I pass him headed in my direction.

He steps back against the wall. "Melissa?"

Confusion is in his voice, but I can only think one thing. "No!" I cry, plunging my hands into the receding water and feeling around frantically.

I can't find it. I sit back on my heels watching the water disappear. "No no *NO!!!*" Diving forward, I plunge both my hands in the half-inch left, frantically sweeping dying bubbles aside, feeling all over the bottom of the large tub.

Derek grasps my upper arms. "Mel, you're scaring me. What's wrong?"

"It's not here." My throat is so tight, I almost can't speak the words. Jumping up, I run to the kitchen, my eyes sweeping every inch of the floor as I go.

My bag is sitting on the counter, and I grab it, flip it over and dump the contents all over the bar. Lipstick, wallet, keys, pens, peppermint, loose change, dental floss . . . I sweep my fingers through it all, desperate. "No!" I whisper, my voice cracking with tears.

Derek's right with me as I run out to the side porch, flipping on the light. So much adrenaline is pulsing through me, I don't even notice the cold. Shoving my hands into the cushions, I grasp and feel . . .

Nothing. *Nothing* . . .

It's not there.

"Oh, god!" I collapse against the small couch, a flood of tears streaming down my cheeks. "I've lost it . . . I've lost it."

"What, baby?" Derek's voice cracks now. "What have you lost?"

"Your necklace . . ." A sob hiccups in my throat, momentarily stealing my words. "Your heart . . . I lost it. Oh god . . ."

More tears soak my cheeks, and he pulls me against his chest. We're both sitting cross-legged in towels on the floor of my screened-in side porch. It's freezing, but I can't tell if I'm shaking from the cold or the heartbreak.

One large hand holds my waist, the other smooths my back, but even Derek's massive strength can salvage what's happened.

I lean back to look at him, but I can't speak. The shivering and crying have stolen my words.

I can tell he's lost. His brow creases with helplessness. "But . . . It wasn't really my heart. It was just a symbol—"

Shaking my head, my chin drops. "No. You gave it to me. It was the first thing you ever gave me, and I loved it so much." Tears are streaming down my face. I can't stop them.

I'm on the verge of ugly crying, and I don't even care. That little necklace was more precious to me than the most expensive piece of jewelry I might ever get in my life, and now it's gone.

"Melissa. Stop. Look at me." He lifts my chin and pulls my face close to his, kissing the tears on my cheeks. "My heart is here, with you. You always have my heart, even without a symbol. I'm always yours."

I slip my arm around his neck, burying my face against his shoulder, and he gathers me to his chest and stands, holding me. For the briefest second, I wonder at his ability to do that so easily. Then my memory floods as he walks us back to the bedroom and fresh tears come.

"You're so tired." His voice is quiet and soothing as he places me on the bed, pulling back the blankets. "We'll look for it tomorrow. It'll turn up. I promise."

I want to believe that, but somehow, I'm certain it's gone.

Untying the towel still under my arms, he removes it then lifts my legs and puts them between the sheets. We're both naked when he slides in beside me. Hugging me close, he strokes the top of my arm slowly.

"Just rest, and trust me. We'll find that necklace." His voice is warm and comforting, and I must be more tired than I realized. Or the sadness has taken my strength.

Either way, it's not long before my heavy limbs relax, and I succumb to sleep.

SEVEN

PATRICK'S PROPOSAL

Derek

ONLY A FEW TIMES IN my life have I felt completely helpless, and the top two occurred in the last twenty-four hours. Watching Mel fall apart last night was almost as bad as that fucking drive from Raleigh. Holding her now as she sleeps, I think about what happened.

As if dealing with Sloan isn't enough, she's completely undone over a necklace, a trinket that cost me less than two hundred dollars. You'd think it was made of pure platinum encrusted with diamonds.

If I remember correctly, she threatened to throw it in the ocean once when she was angry with me. Now it's more valuable than what we thought was hidden in Al Capone's empty vault, and I can't console her.

At the same time, I adore her so much for it.

The fact that such a small thing, the only thing I could find that late night in Scottsdale to give her—the night when she'd first wanted to tell me she loved me but couldn't. I'd wanted to tell her I loved her, too . . .

It *had* been pretty important that night to do something to mark the moment. Everything in me demanded I make her mine forever, but I knew what we had in the desert was tentative. We hoped for so much more, but we couldn't have it then. I didn't know if I'd ever see her again, yet she'd stolen my heart. That necklace was the only thing I could give her to make it real.

With a deep exhale, I accept what she's feeling right now over losing it. It's pretty heartbreaking, and as much as I mean it when I say it doesn't matter, I know how sentimental that delicate piece of 24-karat gold is.

It'll turn up. I reassure myself as much as her. And dammit, if it doesn't, I'll fucking buy her another one. Maybe the new one *will* be platinum encrusted with diamonds. I can even have it delivered with the original message.

She stirs, and I hold her closer. She's upset, but asleep, she looks peaceful. I want her to feel calm and not worry.

Her blue eyes blink open, and her voice is a soft whisper. "Hi."

The familiar squeeze of love hits me right in the stomach, and I never want it to ease, no matter how many years we pass sharing the same bed. No pacing ourselves, only love, as much and as often as we want it.

"Feeling better?" I smooth my palm over her forehead, back into her hair, but her soft lips press together.

"Not really."

I roll forward and kiss that ivory forehead, right where my hand just was. "I'm sorry I have to leave with Patrick today, otherwise I'd stay here and tear the house apart until I found it."

"It's okay." She pushes me onto my back, resting her cheek on my chest, hugging my torso. "I know this job is important, and I don't mind searching by myself. It'll probably be easier because I know where all I've been."

My phone buzzes, and I glance at the clock. "I've got to get moving, or I'll be late meeting Patrick."

We both sit up, and she wraps the sheet under her arms as

her eyes travel around the room, scanning all the baseboards. I know she'll do it—the whole day, searching.

Cupping her jaw, I kiss her lips lightly. "Try not to worry. I'll make it right. No matter what."

Her eyes flicker to mine and she manages a little smile. "Be safe today."

MELISSA IS ON MY MIND the entire drive to Raleigh. I want to be there with her and make sure she's not sad, or worse, crying again. Patrick's ahead of me on the borrowed bike, and I follow him off the Interstate in the direction of the seedy bar.

Once we're in the parking lot, he slows down and motions for me to find a spot while he manages the bike. I meet up with him heading into the Skinniflute, but he holds my arm before we enter.

"When we meet with Toni this time, hang back. Let me take the lead." His brow is tense, and I notice his jaw flex. "She wasn't too thrilled about working with you."

Glancing away, I exhale a laugh. "That makes two of us. Sloan Reynolds is used to high-class action, not part-time hookers."

My partner releases my arm and jerks the metal door open. "She cleans up well, and she owes me a favor. Just let me handle it."

Following my abrupt departure yesterday, Patrick set up a meeting when she wasn't on the clock. As a result, Toni Durango is sitting in the same wooden booth waiting when we enter the dive.

As directed, I hang back while Patrick strides over, smiling that cocky grin of his. "Thanks for meeting up with us today."

A cup of coffee is in front of her, and she sits up, leaning forward over the table. "What I wouldn't give for a cigarette."

"You quit?" He slides in next to her, and I take my place across the table, hands on the bench at my sides.

"For the fiftieth time. I don't expect it to stick." She has the voice of a smoker, low and husky.

I try to picture her "cleaned up" as Patrick put it. Today, she's wearing thick black eyeliner, fake lashes, and velvet red lipstick. Her black hair is pulled back in a ponytail, and I fully expect to find tattoo sleeves if the leopard-print cardigan she's wearing over her black tank comes off.

Sloan will *not* go for this.

Her brown eyes meet mine. "Patrick said the reason you ran off yesterday was about this guy."

Sliding a glance at my partner, he's still wearing his lady-killer grin, but his eyes are telling me to take it easy. Like this is my first job.

"He's an abusive asshole, and I suspect a murderer. My concern is he's coming after my fiancée, who happens to be his ex-wife."

This girl has either seen a lot of shit or she's used to handling it, because her expression never falters.

Her lips press together then, and her eyes narrow. "They always come back. You think they're gone, the law is on your side, but there's no stopping those motherfuckers." Her hands tighten around the mug in front of her. "The only good abuser is a dead abuser."

"Sounds like you have experience with guys like this."

"Not me." She shakes her head and looks down. "My step-sister was shot by her ex before they finally put him away. Lylah's aunt was almost beat to death . . . If there's one kind of trouble I *do* avoid, it's creeps like that."

Patrick leans forward as if on cue. "He's into sex for hire. Our plan was to set the guy up. Use you as sort-of . . . bait."

"We'll be there the whole time," I add. "You wouldn't be alone with him ever."

She blinks down to the table. "What's in it for me?"

As much as I'm sure we have nothing in common, I'm on her side this time. I wouldn't ask any woman to play prostitute—even ones with experience, and I'm about to call the whole thing off when Patrick cuts in.

"Five thousand dollars, immunity . . . and knowing you helped get a killer off the streets."

Poker face or not, I saw her eyes spark at the mention of money. We didn't discuss it, but I'm slick with his proposal. I'd gladly pay any amount for the peace of mind Melissa and I will gain knowing this guy is dealt with.

She studies the coffee cup as she appears to be turning the prospect over in her mind. "Why can't you get him yourself? Without me?"

I answer this one. "He's not your average, run of the mill lowlife. He's connected. He's got money, power, and lawyers who can get him out of anything."

"Escorts," Patrick adds. "He uses *escorts*."

Straightening her arms out in front of her, she examines her fingernails. "In that case, I'll need some of that money up front. Mani-Pedi, hair, body makeup to cover the tats . . ."

"What tats?" Patrick's brow creases, and she smiles like he's so naïve.

We both watch as she removes her sweater, and just as I suspected. Sleeves.

"Well fuck me." He laughs. "I had no idea."

She laughs, too. "I did fuck you. It was pretty fucking hot."

"Okay." That's the last thing I'm interested in hearing about. Their whole connection still pisses me off. "We can give you a thousand up front. Do the works. Hair, wardrobe—"

"I know my job." Her eyes flash at me, and her voice is sharp.

I put a lid on it. Patrick's right. She responds better to him.

"This guy prefers wavy, light brown hair." He reaches inside the leather bike jacket he's wearing and pulls out a folded sheet of paper. "Something like this."

When he puts the sheet on the table, smoothing it open,

you would've thought it was on fire. Toni jumps back then she stands quickly out of the booth, snatching up the page.

"What . . . Where did you get this?" She seems panicky now, and Patrick's out of the booth just as fast.

"It's the Baltimore police report. It's who we think is his last victim. It's what put Derek on the alert."

"No." She's shaking her head, and I can see her eyes flying down the page as she reads. "No . . ."

The first indication she's crying are the lines. It's like an invisible hand draws two black stripes down each of her cheeks from the outer corners of her eyes to her chin.

She straightens up and spins on a mile-high heel, headed for the bar. "Lylah!"

The younger girl pops up at once. "What's wrong?" She passes over napkins, waiting for a response.

"I need a cigarette." One of the regulars, hunched over his lunch stretches out a soft pack of Reds, and Toni takes one. Her hands are trembling as she lights up and pulls in a deep drag.

Patrick and I exchange a glance before we follow her over to the bar, where she's now dabbing her eyes with the small napkins.

"And a whiskey."

Lylah is quick to set her up.

We're all waiting for an explanation, but we don't get it until after she's shot the brown liquid and glanced at the paper once more. Her voice is husky. "He killed her?"

Carefully, I answer. "I'm almost certain he did."

Patrick puts a hand on her shoulder. "Did you know Jessica Black?"

She pushes a bitter laugh through her lips and shakes her head no. "When I knew her, she was Tiffany Cedric. She was just a kid working in Myrtle Beach, thinking she could pick up some cash as an escort. An *escort*, as you say." She takes another long drag and taps the shot glass. Lylah's quick to hook her up. "She wanted me to show her the ropes. Thought she'd put herself through college and then walk away."

She sips the second shot then slowly turns and carries it back to the booth where we started. Patrick and I follow.

Toni's shoulders are hunched as she slides into the seat. This time Patrick is on the outside. "When's the last time you talked to her?"

She sniffs and pours the remainder of the whiskey into the thick, white mug. "Don't remember . . . more than a year ago. She was so proud she got in at State, a scholarship even. But it wasn't enough. She couldn't pay all her bills."

Patrick's brow is lined, and I know he's trying as cautiously as possible to see if there's anything here we can use. "Is that all you know?"

She circles the mug with a finger, holding her cigarette away from the table. "I got arrested in Myrtle Beach and moved back here. We lost touch, but one of the other girls kept up with her. Last I heard she'd met a daddy."

I'm not certain I understand. "A daddy?"

"A sugar daddy, a rich old guy. They said Tiffany followed him wherever he went." Her voice drops. "They said he liked it rough—bondage, strangling . . ." She takes another deep drag and exhales the blue smoke. "I guess she liked it that way, too."

For a few moments, we're quiet. Toni's studying the sheet; I expect she's thinking about her dead friend. I'm thinking about how betrayed Melissa felt when she discovered her husband was cheating. I wonder if she knows the extent of his private practices.

Toni breaks our reverie, and her voice has a hard edge that I confess is pretty powerful. "I'll do your fucking job. I'll help you get the fucker who hurt her."

"We'll need to work out a timeline." Patrick is focused, in closer-mode. "He's not in Baltimore at the moment—"

"Probably looking for a new girl." It's a bitter retort, and I can tell Toni's going to do a good job for us. She's got a dog in this fight now. Just like me.

Patrick continues. "When he gets back to Baltimore, we'll work out a chance encounter. Maybe you can meet him at a bar."

Reaching into his jacket a second time, my partner takes out a white, business-sized envelope that's thick with bills. He pulls out ten Benjis and slides them across the table. "You'll get the rest when we settle up."

She picks up the money and folds it, slipping it into her bra. Classy. "You have my number."

And just like that. The plan to capture Sloan is set in motion.

PATRICK DROPS ME OFF AT Melissa's beach cottage, and we discuss heading back to Baltimore for the next—however long it takes. On the road I'd gotten confirmation that Sloan is back in Maryland. It's time for us to act, but we need to scout out a secure hotel for Toni that's inconspicuous and somewhat high-end. We also need to be able to be in the next room or somehow in close proximity to where she'll be.

"I'll look for two extra rooms wherever we put Toni," he says. "Will Melissa come with you?"

"No." I'm standing outside the car, talking to him through the window. "I don't want her there, and I'm sure she doesn't want to be there."

"You might run that past her before deciding." He looks out the windshield, away from me. "Melissa's tough. She might surprise you with what she wants."

"She wants to put all of this behind her, and as much as I hate leaving her here alone, at least her mother and Elaine are nearby. We'll be watching Sloan."

He glances back. "Elaine might be with me."

That's not what I want to hear. "What about school?"

Patrick laughs, shaking his head. "She won't admit it, but she doesn't like me working with Toni."

"I can't say I like it myself, but if she helps us, I can overlook a lot." For a moment, I consider assuring Elaine I'll keep an eye on my partner, but I know it's not necessary. Elaine's got him tied up in more ways than one.

"If she decides to stay, I'll ask if she'll bunk in with Mel while we're gone."

Nodding, I pat the top of the car. "Will you be ready tomorrow, noon?"

"With bells on."

He takes off, and I walk slowly toward the little cottage. It's the only residence for several hundred feet, secluded in the sea grass, far enough away from the water that storms aren't a problem, but close enough to run down and enjoy the surf easily.

It's a great place. The only thing I hate about it is she's completely alone out here, and no one is close enough to check on her. The thought twists a sick feeling in my gut.

Through the screen, I can see her sleeping on the small couch on the side porch again, but this time the side door is locked. Somewhat relieved, I pull out the key she gave me and unlock it. She doesn't stir as I cross the small space to where she's curled up on the pillows.

Dropping to my knees, I smooth her hair off her cheek and give her a light kiss there. She's such a heavy sleeper now. Still, a little smile plays at the corner of her mouth.

"Melissa," I whisper, running my thumb across her cheek. I hate to wake her, but it's after six. Kissing her cheek again, I whisper in her ear. "Wake up, beautiful."

She inhales quickly and pulls back, eyes flying open. "Oh!"

"I'm sorry, did I scare you?"

Covering her face with her hand, she laughs. "I was dreaming . . . about you."

That sounds promising. "Something dirty?"

Her hand lowers, and she gives me those eyes. "So judgmental. I would never call what we do dirty."

Grinning, I wrap her in my arms. "Now I feel challenged. How can I change your mind about this?"

Her elbows are bent, and she's threading her fingers in my hair still smiling. "Whatever we do, I won't be able to call it dirty. I love you too much."

There's no getting around it. She gets a kiss for that, but just as I push her lips apart, tasting her sweet mouth, finding her tongue, she puts her hands on my cheeks and moves me back.

"Tell me about today. Were you and Patrick successful? Everything work out?"

Remembering how today went, what we learned about Jessica Black and what's coming provokes a frown I can't hide. Melissa is on it fast. "Did she not agree to help you?"

"She agreed to help us." Releasing her, I rise from my knees to sit on the end of the couch, pulling her feet in my lap. "And I'm more convinced than ever we're doing the right thing. Even if it bends a few rules."

"Sloan's built his life around bending rules and deception."

I'm surprised by this response from her. "So you're not against what we're doing anymore?"

She sighs and pushes herself up to a sitting position. "The more I've thought about it, the more convinced I am that even if he leaves me alone, he'll just find a new victim. How can I let that happen?"

I unwrap the blanket and find one of her soft feet. Massaging it, I nod my agreement. She had to come to this decision on her own, and I'm glad she did.

"He *would* find another victim, it seems. Based on what Toni told us today."

Melissa's eyes drift to the screen facing the ocean and beyond it. "He was so charming in the beginning. Kind and generous."

"You never told me how you fell in love with him, but I assumed he had to be different."

She looks back at her lap, and I know this is hard for her. She once told me what happened with Sloan was her "humiliating truth." I want her to know she can trust me with this. I would never judge her. Her small foot is still in my hand, and I give her arch a deep rub.

"That feels good." She gives me a small smile, and I return it. "He reminded me of my dad a little. Not in a creepy way. But my father was much older than my mom. I'm sure they had a passionate relationship, but all I saw growing up was how he took care of her. How she would go to him for advice, and how good he was to her."

"You said Sloan was one of your clients."

"His father was. Actually, it was the family business, so I interacted with Mr. Reynolds, Sloan, and other executives there. Sloan's father was probably what clouded my judgment. I saw him treat Sloan's mother—"

"He treated her like your father treated your mother, and you assumed like father, like son. It's perfectly reasonable."

Her eyes are full of gratitude when they meet mine. "It felt so familiar and good. Until it didn't."

I fish out her other foot to rub. "Don't want you walking funny the rest of the day."

"Unless it's from sleeping with you?"

It's hard to ignore the stirring below my belt when she makes suggestions like that. "I think you have a type, darling. You like older men."

She pulls her foot back and crawls across the sofa into my arms. "You're only a little older—"

"Ten years."

"Compared to twenty." Her arms are around my neck, but she drops her chin. "I was such a dumb little girl when I met him."

"You were twenty—"

"Six. Almost twenty-seven and completely swept off my small-town feet by his wealth and sophistication."

Catching that chin, I lift her face to kiss it. Her skin is so soft. "We all make mistakes every now and then." I think about the brief period I knew Sloan years ago. "He did my orientation when I started at Princeton, so we spent a little time together. I never saw any sign of his true character."

My lips move from her cheek to her temple, to her hair, where I inhale deeply. Something is definitely on the rise down below, aided by her hand finding its way under my shirt and sliding across my stomach.

"That was a mistake." Her voice is thick with desire. "You were a surprise. A gift."

Speaking of gifts, I notice one gift is still not around her neck, but I'm not about to spoil this moment. "I hope you were able to relax today."

Her head drops to my shoulder, and I kiss her again, noticing that wandering hand is unfastening the button of my jeans. An ache moves through my groin, anticipating her touch.

"You must think I'm terribly lazy always being asleep when you get here." Her hand is inside my jeans now, small fingers wrapping around me, sliding slowly up and down.

My voice is a husky groan in her ear before I kiss it. "I'd never call you lazy." I pull her up, so I can attend to the skin around her neck. She shivers in that delicious way as I consume her.

"Every day at three, just like clockwork, I'm falling asleep." She gasps as my hand travels under her sweater, pushing her bra aside so I can caress her breast. "I've never done that before."

"It's the baby." Moving her completely onto my lap in a straddle, I push her sweater and bra all the way up, pulling her breasts together and taking them in my mouth. Her head drops to mine with a moan.

My dick rises out of my pants, but I'm not sure if she's ready until I notice her grasping at the hem of her skirt, pulling it up quickly. She's on her knees in front of me, and in one quick movement, she shoves her panties to the side and drops hard and fast on my aching cock.

"Fuck!" I can't help groaning it feels so good. My hips are pushing into her, and she's riding, both hands against the wall behind my head.

"Oh, god!" She's riding hard and I'm pushing fast, fueled by the gripping and pulling of her inner muscles.

I'm about to blow, and I grab her waist, moving her up and down, my thumb circling her clit.

"Oh, Derek!" She cries out, and I lose it. It seems my timing wasn't far off because her knees clutch my waist, and she's holding onto me, moaning in my ear. I only lightly touch her ass now, letting her ride it out, not wanting to disturb her pleasure. It's fucking sending me to the moon, and I drop my head back, savoring the sensations of her coming over me.

A few movements more, we hold each other for a bit, coming down. God, to think I have a lifetime of this to look forward to. She falls forward, smiling contentedly.

"Nothing about that is dirty." Her hands go to my cheeks, and she kisses all around my mouth. "It's pure . . . and real . . . and gorgeous . . . and fucking hot."

I'm still inside her as she moves around, and damn if her sexy mouth isn't about to have me ready to go again. "You won't catch me trying to change your mind."

A small laugh, a little nibble, and I have to carry her inside for more.

EIGHT

NO GHOSTS

Melissa

FOR ONCE I'M AWAKE BEFORE Derek. This silly pregnancy is about to drive me crazy with all the exhaustion and the weight gain and the hormones, and now this morning I can't sleep.

Okay, the hormones aren't so bad. If we hadn't started out sharing some pretty hot moments, I'd say we were setting the bar on being insatiable teenagers. A little laugh pushes through my throat as I lie on my side watching him sleep. He's so gorgeous, and I won't lie, this surge of protectiveness he's displaying is incredibly sexy.

I've managed to wiggle out of his embrace—it always takes me forever to get used to sleeping alone after he's been here. He holds me so close against him all night. Now I'm facing him, studying his relaxed profile, small nose, full lips. The first flecks of grey are appearing in his dark beard. It's so few, I can almost count them, and they make him even more attractive in my eyes.

Lifting my hand quietly so I don't wake him, I lightly move a dark wave off his eyes. He'll start complaining about needing a haircut if he stays with me much longer. Just then his violet-blue eyes blink open, and my insides flood with the most amazing sensation—my friend, my lover, my savior . . . the father of my child.

"I love you," I whisper.

He leans forward to kiss my forehead before pushing up on his elbow to reach the bottle of water on his nightstand. "You're awake early."

I span his large bicep with my hand. "You haven't been working out as much."

His head ducks with a laugh. "Are you saying I'm out of shape?"

"Of course not!" I dive into him. "You're perfect! I just . . . I don't want you to be unhappy spending so much time with me. I'm messing up your routine."

His arms go around me, and I'm propped on his chest, looking into his eyes. "Darling, I'd give up any routine to have this time with you."

"I love it when your New Orleans comes out."

"I have another thing that would like to come out."

"Is that so?" Scooting my hips in line with his, I slide myself down, onto his morning wood. His head drops back and his eyes close with a groan.

Nibbling the base of his neck, my voice is thick now. "I can take care of that situation."

Minutes later, we're panting and sweaty and so satisfied . . .

Except I'm hungry.

I'm on my back now, and he's kissing the line of my collarbone as I think. "Remember that place that didn't have the Applewood smoked bacon?"

He chuckles, still inside me. "The Sawmill?"

"You have a very good memory. Much better than mine these days." I push against his shoulder and he rolls back. "Give me a second to get cleaned up, and we can go get some breakfast."

Hopping out of the bed, I skip over to the bathroom. He's

lying on his side, elbow bent, head resting on his hand, and I can't help it. I run back over to kiss his lips, but I scoot away before he can catch me again. We'll never leave the bedroom if that happens.

"I think you're starting to show," he calls after me.

I stop before getting in the shower and turn to the side, looking in the mirror. I think he's right. Finally, my stomach is starting to round out a bit. Smoothing my hands over the small bump, I'm so happy.

"You're right," I call back, before stepping into the stall.

In no time, I'm showered and fresh, and we're heading out the door to the old restaurant designed to look like a lumber-jack's shop. Tools of the trade hang on the wood-paneled walls, and the menus have pictures of all the selections in them.

"I know you appreciate our fine dining options here." I can't help teasing his refined palate. "But I truly love their breakfast."

A waitress appears. She's in her fifties, and her hair's piled in a bun on her head.

"Hey, Melissa. Haven't seen you in a while." She smacks gum as she waits for our order—no notepad required.

"Hi, Peg!" My voice is cheerful. I've known her since I was a teenager.

Derek scans the laminated menu. "I'll have a Sawmill Eggs Benedict. Gravy is my favorite hollandaise."

Giggling, I scan over all the selections. "I want eggs every way. And regular coffee . . . just this once."

He shrugs. "I can't tell you no."

Peg nods and then shakes her head. We're sitting on the same side of the booth, which I know is so silly and young-lov-erish, but I can't help it. I don't know if it's hormones or what, but the situation with Sloan, losing my necklace, none of it seems to dampen how I'm feeling this morning.

Scooting closer to him, I slide the dark hair away from his face as he sips his coffee. "I love having you with me longer than two days at a time."

He puts the cup down and stretches an arm around my shoulders. "We really need to find a compromise solution to our home-base situation."

Our blue eyes meet, and I can't help kissing him. "Then stop fighting me and move here."

"Melissa . . ." he groans.

I sit back, crossing my arms. "What's wrong with Wilmington?"

"Other than the fact there's not a decent airport for miles, it's cut off from everything—"

"Like living in Paradise. A dream . . ."

"For a serial killer. Or any other criminal or societal dropout hoping to escape the long arm of the law."

"You've been working in justice too long."

"I've been very happy Patrick's here to watch over you for me, but I agree with you." He lifts my long, dark hair and kisses my cheek. "Being with you even one extra day is so good. I want us to decide now."

Why did I bring this subject up? I know it's the one thing we can't agree on, and it's also the one thing that could kill my mood. Luckily, the busboys show up at that perfect moment with all our food. Peg's hanging behind them, making sure they deliver the dishes correctly.

"He's having the Sawmill B, she's having all the rest."

I can't help laughing as they unload four plates of eggs prepared in a variety of ways for me to sample. "And my bacon!" A plate of bacon appears in front of me.

"Can I get y'all anything else?" Peg waits chewing her gum, unimpressed.

"We're good, thanks!" I say brightly, and she disappears.

I allow our impasse to give way to the lusciousness of home-cooked breakfast, and we dig in, touching each other every so often as we eat.

"I want to walk on the beach after this," I manage to say around a bite of bacon and eggs.

He nods. "We'll need it." But then his expression turns serious. "I didn't want to tell you this last night, but Patrick and I need to get on the road for Baltimore by noon."

And just like that, my happy mood is gone. Disappeared. He's leaving me in . . . my eyes wander to the enormous clock hanging in the center of the back wall . . . two hours.

My chin drops, and his arms are around me just as fast. "I'm sorry." His breath is against my neck, and it's almost torture knowing all of this will be over so soon and for who knows how long this time.

"This is part of the plan?" I hear the highness of my voice, the crack as I say the words. It's pitiful and pathetic, and I don't care.

He inhales deeply and leans back, concern all over his face. "It is. And I think this time it's going to work. I'm going to make sure it does, or I promise—"

"Where are you staying? You don't have a place in Baltimore." I won't let him finish what he was trying to say. I also know Patrick won't let him finish it—we've discussed the fact that neither of us will let Derek risk his reputation or his future on someone as worthless as Sloan.

"Patrick started looking for a place last night. I'm sure he's found something nice."

Sadness weighs so heavy on my shoulders, I'm no longer hungry. "Let's get out of here. I want that walk on the beach with you."

He nods and fishes out his wallet. Dropping three twenties on the table, he takes my hand and pulls me out of the booth.

I try to protest. "I'm sure that's way too much—"

"Peg's an old friend of yours?" I nod, and he continues. "We'll give her a special tip then."

Moments later, we're on my beautiful beach. It's cold, and I'm enveloped in fleece, hanging on his arm as the waves pound against the shore. It's windy, and my hair pushes hard away from my face.

"Yesterday, I told you about Sloan." I pull him down to sit beside me on the cool sand. "Tell me about Allison."

His expression changes, and for a moment I think he's going to find that one thing he'll say No to me on. But he doesn't. "Why?"

Shrugging, my hands are in my lap. "I love you. It's an enormous part of your history . . ." I look out at the waves. The white breakers hit the sand with such force, spray shoots straight up into the wind before it's whipped back out toward the ocean. "Whenever I visit your place, and there are no mementos of your life together, I can't help wondering why."

"I put the pictures away when she died. I guess I've never thought about taking them out again."

"How did you meet her?"

He looks down then puts an arm around my shoulders, drawing me closer to him. "We went to high school together."

A knot forms in my throat. It's silly to feel insecure about a memory, but I need to know his past. "Did you date in high school?

He nods. "She waited for me when I did my first tour in the Gulf. The war broke out, and they all tied the yellow ribbons around the trees . . ."

"I'm so sorry." Bringing up the subject suddenly feels like the stupidest idea I've ever had. "We don't have to talk about it."

But he catches my face and turns it back to his. "Hey," his voice is a whisper. "I can talk about her with you. I never could with anyone else, but with you it's different."

"How?" I'm wondering if he can ever love me as much as someone he grew up with, someone he'd planned a life with. A woman who'd waited for him to come home, tied ribbons around oak trees for him.

A woman who'd loved him as much as I do.

"Because when Allison died, I gave up. I was so angry. I hated people . . . God, country, everything that had stolen the time we should've had together. The family we might've had. The family I thought I'd never have."

Tears are in my eyes. I love this man, and even as he's telling me about the broken dreams he had with another lover, it twists pain in my chest to think he felt such loss. "Oh, Derek. I'm so sorry."

To my surprise, though, his voice is optimistic. "Stop." He catches me around the waist, pulling me onto his lap. His hands are at my neck, and his thumbs sweep the tears from my cheeks almost as fast as his lips smooth them. "Please don't cry. I know . . . what happened was unfair. I spent so many years bitter about it."

Nothing seems right to say, so I only nod, looking down.

"Melissa, listen to me. You were . . . you *are* something I thought I'd never have. And our baby . . ." He pulls me closer, and he's holding my neck with his head resting above my heart. "You helped me forgive the past and find peace. I love you so much. Why do you think I'm so hell bent on protecting you?"

I understand what he's saying. It's beautiful, and it mirrors the hope he gave me that short week in the desert. "I can't bear thinking of how you suffered, losing her like that."

"During that time we were apart—the time before you came to me with what Sloan had done, when I was only waiting, hoping you felt the same—I realized love isn't something you can give away or shut off when it doesn't work out. When love is taken away, it creates a vacuum that has to be filled with new love. You were a gift I wasn't looking for, a gift I didn't deserve, and maybe that's why you're so precious to me. You're my second chance . . . and you gave me a second chance. Twice."

My arms are hugged between us, and I slide my hands up to hold his face. "You've never told me this before."

"I don't want you to be threatened by my past." He turns his head to kiss my palm. "You're strong and beautiful, and it's what I love about you. I can't wait to see what our future will be."

His words wash away my fears in a flood of understanding.

He said exactly what I needed to know. Our love isn't a competition. There are no ghosts lurking in the background, only memories. Some are good, some bad, but we're something new. We're building our future together, and in my heart, I know it's right, because as much as I love him, I would never want him to go through life alone, and I know anyone who felt the way I do about him would say the same.

"I want to go to Baltimore with you." I don't have to think about it. "We shouldn't be apart anymore."

"No. I want you to stay here. Elaine can stay with you and—"

"Sloan doesn't scare me. He doesn't own me, and he can't win—"

"Anything with the power to take you away from me scares me."

I'm shocked by his answer. Derek isn't supposed to be afraid of anything. "Nothing is taking me away from you."

He catches both my hands in his. "I won't risk you or the baby being hurt. We'll end the long distance arrangement after we finish this job."

"How long?" After all he just said to me, I feel our pending separation more acutely than ever.

"A week? Two tops, and I'll keep in touch with you the entire time."

"Two weeks? That's longer than we've spent apart since Christmas."

"Believe me. I'll be doing everything in my power to make it end sooner." His phone buzzes, and when he looks at the face, he starts to rise. "It's Patrick. We've got to get moving."

Tears heat my eyes as I follow him back toward my house. I'm not sure I'll be able to hold it together until he's away. "It hurts more than ever this time." My voice is soft, and I'm fighting as hard as I can. It's difficult between my fears for him and what he just shared—and a healthy dose of pregnancy hormones. Still, I don't want his last sight of me to be crying.

I follow him back to my bedroom, where he stops and hugs

me close. My face is against his chest, and his fingers thread into my hair at the base of my neck. Several seconds pass and we only hold each other, sharing our breath, melting together. Another buzz from his damn phone, and he releases me.

Quickly he pushes his clothes into his duffel and takes the keys. In the kitchen he stops and pulls me close again. "I promise not to prolong this." Turning me to the side, he puts a large hand over my tiny baby bump. "Love you," he whispers, and I catch his cheek, guiding his lips to mine.

I'm off the floor in his embrace. Mouths open, tongues unite, I'm kissing him like he's headed into battle, which in a sense he is. My only comfort is Patrick's promise to have his back.

Another buzz, and I almost forget I'm on Team Patrick now. "I don't want you to go." I whimper.

"I know." He sets me down and gives me a peck on the nose, another on the forehead as he inhales deeply. "I love your scent."

"I love you."

"Love you more."

And with that, he's gone.

NINE

NOT THE GOOD GUYS

Derek

BALTIMORE IS COLD AND WINDY when we arrive. Patrick's booked us three rooms in the Four Seasons on Harbor East—perfect for our setup, and close to potential hook-up locations. I've promised Melissa to make this happen as quickly as possible, but the truth is, we've got to establish ourselves in this location, make a plan, and scout the best place for the ultimate encounter.

Toni arrived the night before, and she's asked to go by Star Brandon again for this gig. Seems that's her go-to alias. We meet at the bar for our first planning session.

"You don't think Star sounds too . . . hooker-ish?" Patrick is frowning as he studies the drink menu.

Toni . . . or Star is wearing a cream, Calvin Klein dress that hugs her slim body and ends mid-thigh. Her long hair is now wavy and colored light brown, and she's wearing about eighty percent less makeup than at the Skinniflute. Light-brown eyeliner and mascara, pale pink lips. I hate to admit it, but she does resemble Melissa. She's hot.

"You fell for it." Her mouth is the only thing that gives her away—and her husky smoker's voice.

"You were also a blonde." Patrick laughs and has the decency to appear ashamed of himself.

I lift the tumbler of Scotch I ordered. "You're going to have to fix your delivery to catch Sloan's interest."

Instantly, her voice turns soft and high, slightly breathy. "My delivery? Is this what you mean?" She blinks up at me with doe eyes.

"Shit," I sip the beverage. "I don't get to say this very often, but Patrick was right. You're good."

She smiles and lifts the vodka she ordered, holding it out to clink my glass. "Trust me, big boy. I'll nail this bastard for you."

"That's the only reason I'm here." I give her tumbler a bump.

Patrick lifts his drink off the bar and takes her elbow. "Let's find a place where we won't be overheard."

In a corner booth near the back of the hotel bar, we group close together to strategize. "Bennett is keeping tabs on Sloan, putting together a schedule of his week, his favorite haunts."

"Why am I here?" Star's watching me. "I mean, what reason do I give for being in the city?"

Fuck, she's smart. "I can tell you've done this before. What are you comfortable doing? What's familiar?"

"Patrick fell for me being a temp. I could say I'm with Contemporary Staffing?"

My partner leans back to sip his drink. "Is that classy enough for our guy?"

Thinking about what I know, I study the table. "It's probably the best thing. It's why you need extra money. Perhaps you've come up from DC?"

"Where I was shagging a senator." Her dark eyes twinkle, and I'm mildly disturbed that her alibi is so believable.

"Yes. It'll appeal to his ego. You're good enough for the powerful."

Patrick nods. "Now we just need to work out the initial encounter and hooking him."

"I'll hook him." Star's eyes slide over to my partner. "I give a hell of a hummer, remember?"

Clearing his throat, Patrick stands. "I need a fresh drink. Anybody else?"

I nod. "Thanks." When he's away, I turn back to Star. "You'll probably have to meet him more than once to get us what we need. I doubt he gets rough the first time. How do you feel about that?"

"I want to work out with you guys."

That wasn't the answer I expected. "What does that have to do with—"

"Yes." She's dead serious, so I hold back and listen. "I'll probably have to fuck him at least once before we get what we need, but I've been taking kickboxing classes. I want you guys to help me get stronger."

My eyes narrow. "What's on your mind?"

She doesn't miss a beat. "Revenge."

THE WORKOUT ROOM AT THE Four Seasons is state of the art, as to be expected in a five-star hotel, but I catch a cab to the Druid Hill YMCA instead. Patrick takes the city bus; Star takes the Metro. We don't want to be seen together too much around our location.

Bennett has verified we can stage an encounter with Sloan easily in Little Italy. It seems our target is a Thursday night regular at the Oceanaire Seafood Room. It's perfect, and gives us a few days to scout more secluded spots nearby. Somewhere Star can take him where Patrick and I can be in the shadows, waiting.

"I can't wear a wire." Star is curling the bar I've loaded for her with fifty pounds. "If he starts exploring under my clothes, it's too risky."

We're in a somewhat private area of the gym, but we still

need to be speaking in code. "The last thing I'm interested in is hearing you *interact* with him, but you're all we've got in terms of capture."

Patrick's nearby curling dumbbells. "It's true, and I don't like you getting too far out of our reach with him."

Star curls one more time and puts the bar down. "So you two get a peep show." She shrugs. "I've done worse for an audience."

My partner puts down the weights and picks up his towel, holding it in front of his mouth as if he's wiping away sweat. "What are you planning? I expect it'll take two . . . maybe three encounters before he'll show his true colors. Hopefully, not more."

"First night, drinks, making out, BJ most likely." She's holding her towel in a similar fashion as Patrick, over her face, pressing it to her forehead. I'm sitting on the bench, leaned forward doing curls, pretending not to listen as she continues. "Second night, more of the same, penetration. Third night, kick his ass."

Sick fills my stomach. All of this is messed up, and it's the only way we're taking my fiancée's stalker off the grid. His lawyers will have a hard time arguing against a battered hooker full of Sloan's DNA. I can't wait to see them try.

"You sure you're okay with this?" Regardless of her past experience or what she claims, I can't help asking one more time.

Her expression is hard and flat when she answers me. "Yes. I'm helping you, but I'm also doing this for Tiffany. Now let's hit the bags."

Kickboxing.

THAT EVENING AT THE HOTEL, I'm dead. Strength training is one thing, but strength training combined with two hours of kickboxing is over my limit. My phone has a few missed texts from Melissa, but instead of texting her back, I call.

The sound of her eases the tension in my chest. "Where have you been all day?"

"At the Y. Strength training and kickboxing."

"Kickboxing?" Her voice goes high. "Honey, I wasn't implying anything yesterday morning . . ."

That makes me laugh, remembering our conversation in bed. "We're helping our bait get better prepared to defend herself."

"You sound tense again." Her playful tone is gone. Worry and guilt are in her voice, and my arms long to hold her. "I hate this so much. I hate remembering he's out there, thinking of that poor girl facing him alone. For me."

"Star is *not* a poor girl, trust me."

"Star?"

Lying back on the bed, I rub my forehead. "That seems to be her stage name, so we're going with it."

"I guess if she's taking the risk, she gets to call a few shots."

"I don't like it any more than you do." Sitting up, I study my hand, clenching it into a fist and relaxing. "I've gone over it so many times in my mind, trying to find another way."

She exhales. "What if you're wrong and I'm not in danger?"

"I'm not wrong, and I won't let him even think about coming near you."

"Okay, but just for a moment . . . what if he's moved past me?"

Everything in my experience knows that's not true. Melissa belongs to Sloan in his eyes, and he'll be back for her. But I know it's important for her to feel like she's not the only reason we're here.

So I give her something else to think about. "You said it yourself—there's always another Jessica Black. He's got to be taken off the streets."

She doesn't answer, and for a few moments, we're quiet. "How much longer will you be away?"

"Thursday night will be our first contact. We expect it'll take a few meetings before he relaxes enough to get rough." I look out at the setting sun, thinking of all the people living normal lives, doing regular things right now. One day soon, that will be me again. "I expect it to be like I said, two weeks tops."

"I miss you." Her voice is sad, and I want to lighten the mood.

"What did you do today?"

Sounds of her moving through her house fill my ear. I can almost see her walking, her dark waves swaying down her back. "Had lunch with Mom, finished Bea's online storefront. If I were there, I could meet with her in person and be with you."

I shake my head, even though she can't see me. "It's too risky, and if you're seen here, it could put him on alert. It could jeopardize the whole plan. Just hang tight, okay?"

"Elaine and I'll probably trade off spending the night together."

"That's a great idea. You can keep each other company."

"She'll be sexting with Patrick the whole time."

My eyebrows rise. "I'll keep you company then."

"I'd rather do it in person. I could be waiting for you when you get in. Massage that stress away . . . kiss your skin . . . naked." Her words register right below my belt, causing me to shift in my seat.

"Forget the sexting, let's talk it out now. What are you wearing?"

"Maternity clothes at last!"

I laugh. "How's the baby?"

"It seems like I'm showing even more since yesterday." Sadness gone, I can hear her excitement rising. "I really want us together when he starts moving."

Closing my eyes, I can see her gorgeous body, full breasts, stomach just starting to round out. "When can we find out if you're right?"

"Twenty weeks is when they usually do ultrasounds for

gender."

It's getting close. "I'll be there. Take care of you both."

The warmth is back. "Love you."

"Love you more."

We say goodnight, and for a moment I lie on the bed thinking. If there were any way she could be here, damn straight I'd have her here yesterday. In the meantime, I'll hit the shower. We're on our own for dinner, and since my partner is apparently occupied, I want to check out a local jewelry store for something platinum and diamond encrusted.

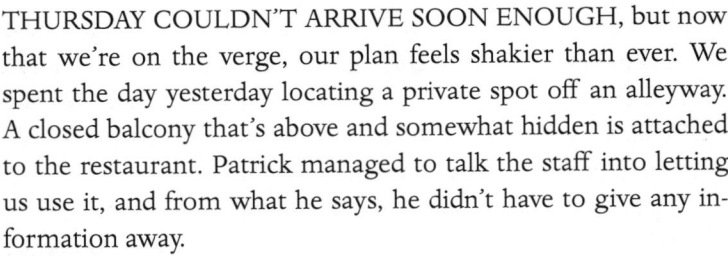

THURSDAY COULDN'T ARRIVE SOON ENOUGH, but now that we're on the verge, our plan feels shakier than ever. We spent the day yesterday locating a private spot off an alleyway. A closed balcony that's above and somewhat hidden is attached to the restaurant. Patrick managed to talk the staff into letting us use it, and from what he says, he didn't have to give any information away.

He and I will be up there monitoring, where we can drop down if needed. Star will lead Sloan into the dark alley and do whatever she needs to do. Once the ball is rolling, we'll tune out unless she gives us the signal.

The real action shouldn't occur before next week. I'm actually hoping it will, but I have nothing to base it on besides my gut. The true timeline could be longer or shorter.

While we'd waited for Patrick to work his magic on the restaurant staff, Star and I had checked out the access in and out of the small lane that runs behind the businesses.

It seems to have been intended for deliveries, but most the doors are welded shut or appear unused. She watches as I try them, one after the other.

"You don't approve of me." She's following me a few steps

behind, and today she's in black leggings and boots, topped off by a short bomber jacket and white sweater that doesn't even cover her ass.

"You came into my office, set up my partner . . ." I grunt as I push on another sealed door. "No. It's safe to say I *don't* consider you one of the good guys."

She pulls her long, brown hair over her shoulder in an elegant sweep. Again, I'm impressed at her ability to shrug off the white trash so easily. "I'm sorry I fucked with Patrick, but I didn't have the whole story. And I needed the money."

"You fucked with my business, my reputation. It's the same as if you fucked me."

"I think I'd remember that." Her voice is soft, and she smiles up at me.

I shake my head. I'm not sure if she's attempting to mend bridges or flirt, but I'm not interested in either option. "You'll need to be here for us to see you." Pointing to the black metal door with the orange band across the bottom. "Can you remember this door? It's pretty distinctive."

"I think I'll remember it."

"Okay." I nod and head back up the alley to where Patrick's supposed to meet us. This should work.

Once we're together at the top, she tries again. "I've never seen a man like you do that before."

My brow lines. "What are you talking about?"

"That day in Raleigh, when you left so fast and took Patrick's car." Her arms are crossed and she looks genuinely concerned. "It's hard to believe someone like you can feel fear."

"Everyone feels fear." I look at my hands again. "Just target the one thing they can't live without."

I close my fist, and I can't help thinking I could end this, no charade necessary.

She touches my arm. "I decided that day I'd do whatever you asked. What do you want me to do?"

For a second, I'm confused. Then I realize she's talking

about Sloan. "Oh. I don't know." I exhale deeply. "I'm not looking to be judge, jury, and executioner here. I just want whatever it takes to put him away for good."

"If you're not judge, jury, and executioner, then you don't want him out of your life permanently." Her dark eyes hold mine, and I can see she's waiting for me to say the word. It's hard to believe this small woman might be capable of doing anything more forceful than turning state's witness.

"You're wrong. I do want him out of our lives permanently."

She's still holding my gaze when I hear Patrick approaching.

"Okay!" His breezy voice breaks through the tension. "I've got it all set up. Derek and I'll be on the balcony. It's closed, so you won't hear us, but we'll be there . . . What's going on?"

He stops in front of us, and I know my partner's too smart to be fooled. "What's the plan if Star gets in over her head?"

"I won't." Her voice is sharp and argumentative. "You two just stay back and let me handle it. Don't fuck up our case being overprotective."

Patrick nods. "Safe word. You need a safe word, T."

"What the hell?" She's confused, but I see where he's going with it. He's right.

"What's something you can yell that you'd never say during sex?"

A laugh bursts from her mouth with an exhale. "Sangria?"

"Can you yell that?" Patrick's running it over in his mind, and I can tell he approves already. "It's good because it won't alert the other patrons. They'll think it's just some drunken diner . . ."

"Hell, it won't even alert him if he's not paying attention." I'm irritated that Star's smart. She could do more with her life than this.

"Sangria it is." Patrick leads us out of the alley. "Now we just have to get changed, head to the bar and wait."

―――――――◆―――――――

HOURS LATER, WE'RE BACK AT the Oceanaire.

Patrick is the only one in the bar with Star. He's not even with her; he's down a few seats nursing a vodka tonic. Sloan knows me, so once they're situated, I head to the secluded balcony to wait.

The staff doesn't even look up when I pass through the side hall off the kitchen and dash up the narrow flight of stairs.

I've only seen this spot from the outside. Inside is a whole different story. It's technically *not* a balcony. It's more like a closet with a window that opens. It's tight and cramped, and it smells like musty socks and body odor. I cover my nose with my hand, thinking this is going to be a long night. What I'm pretty sure is a used condom lies discarded in the corner.

Apparently this is a hot spot for hookups. My first thought is we should've put Star here, but then she would've been too inaccessible. My second thought is what the hell did Patrick say he and I would be doing up here? Fuck it. I can't worry about that now.

I text him to turn on the surveillance app, so I can hear what he's seeing. His phone will be out on the bar, and the technology's not perfected. I'll get plenty of noise along with the conversation through my earbuds, but I'll be able to follow what they're saying.

He texts back they're not in place yet, and I have to wait. Tension tightens the muscles in my abdomen. Fucking surveillance. I've never liked how much waiting was involved in this part of this job. It's a big reason private investigative work lost out over corporate when Stuart and I set up the firm. I feel around the one small window looking for a latch to release it. If we have to get down there fast, one of us can jump. Pushing it open and looking down, I decide that'll be Patrick's job.

A blip on my phone, and I know the subject's in the building.

I'm so tense, the muscles across my upper back ache. Star's competent. She's demonstrated her street smarts and experience. She's committed to this job for more reasons than just helping us. But right now is our most important moment. If this blows up, we could lose our licenses. We could be arrested for entrapment . . .

This has to work.

I slip the earbuds in my ears. Noise.

The ting of ice against crystal, crash of liquor bottles against racks.

Voices are speaking, but I don't hear anything familiar.

Finally, a voice I do recognize cuts through the din.

"I'm sorry." Star's tone is breathy and high. Marilyn Monroe. "Do you mind if I wait here? I'm supposed to be meeting someone."

"Of course not." Sloan is casual, but I'm a guy. There's a spark of interest there.

Tonight, she's wearing a filmy black dress that ends at her knees. It's got a high slit on the side and thin straps over her shoulders, so it's clear she takes care of her body. We got her a very light golden spray-tan and her hair is styled loose down her back. A silver cuff bracelet, thin necklace, and small hoop earrings are her only accessories. She's classy, but also sexy enough to get the wheels turning.

The noise of the bar is loud in my ears, and I can only imagine what's happening. Bartenders moving fast, patrons waiting to put in drink orders. Finally, Sloan orders a Manhattan. Star already has a cosmopolitan—a drink she says is for wannabe little bitches. Whatever. So long as she keeps all that to herself.

"Oh," more Marilyn. "I'm sorry again. It's so crowded here tonight. Is it always like this?"

"Thursdays are the busiest night here." Sloan sounds relaxed—I'm not sure if that's good or bad. "They get the local crowd combined with the tourists just arriving."

She breathes a soft laugh. "I wonder which of those I'd be."

"You're not from Baltimore?"

"No, I'm a tourist hoping to become a local."

"So you're relocating."

It's pretty banal stuff, but at least she's got him talking.

"I hope to. I'm supposed to be meeting someone from Contemporary Staffing, but it looks like they're not coming."

They're quiet for a few minutes. Did she lose him? Fuck. If he walks away, we're left with nothing. A desperate hooker is way too suspicious for his taste.

Another agonizing minute passes.

At last a voice, but it's not either of the ones I want to hear. "Your table's ready Mr. Reynolds."

Shit.

"Well, good luck to you, Miss . . ."

"Brandon. Star Brandon."

"Sloan Reynolds. Nice chatting with you."

It's quiet again, and my gut sinks. Now what?

Just as I was pulling out the earbud his voice comes back. "If you're still here in a little while, I'll be back at the bar after dinner."

Star's voice is a sexy purr. "I won't go anywhere."

Now it's back to waiting. And hoping he doesn't have second thoughts and order dessert.

TEN

ALL I SEE

Melissa

CHANNEL AFTER CHANNEL PASSES ON the screen, but nothing interests me. I can't help wondering what might be happening miles away in Baltimore, and I chew my lip as I watch the talking heads blink and disappear, one after the other. I'm about to give up and start Internet shopping when my phone buzzes.

Snatching it up, I touch my best friend's picture on the face. "Hey, what's up?"

Elaine's voice is pouty. "Are you as frustrated as I am?"

I fall back on the sofa. "Not yet, but I'm used to the weekly drought. Check with me tomorrow. I'll be climbing the walls I'm sure."

"After being with Brian you'd think I'd be used to it. Hell, I think my hymen grew back when we were dating."

That makes me laugh. "You're so crazy. That doesn't happen."

"Now I'm completely screwed." She crunches something in my ear. "I've gotten used to Patrick being in my panties every night—I don't know what to do when he's gone."

"Haven't you been doing it over the phone?"

"Mmm . . ." Another crunch. "That's actually *more* frustrating. He tells me all this dirty stuff he wants to do to me, and he's a million miles away! It's awful!"

"You're supposed to finish while you're on the phone, dum-dum."

"I'm still all achy and needing him." I hear her sit up fast. "Do you have a dildo?"

Laughter bursts out of me then. "I have Derek."

"Not all week! What are you hiding? I bet you have a stash."

Picking up the remote, I start the kaleidoscope of channels again. "I hate to disappoint you, Miss Gold Tie, but I'm not hiding a toy collection."

"Hmm. Neither am I. We should do some research tomorrow night when I'm there."

"What are you eating?" I'm back to watching the faces flash past on the screen.

"Popcorn. Do you want me to run by the store before I come over? After school?"

"Yes. Get chips and salsa, guacamole, tamales . . ."

"Real and virgin margaritas." She pauses for a moment. "Are you doing okay? Really? This has to be bothering you."

I stop switching channels on a talent competition and hit mute. "I'm not sure how I feel. Derek's so convinced I'm in danger, and I can't change his mind. I won't let my mind travel to what he might do—the lengths he might go to."

"Patrick's there. He won't let anything happen they can't sit on. Or get out of."

I know she's right, but I know something more. My mind drifts to my conversation with Patrick a week ago. "He promised me . . ."

Elaine keeps talking. "I gotta be honest, I don't know how you two can keep up the long distance. I *hate* it."

"No shit. I'm starting to remember how obnoxious you were before Patrick relocated." Bending my elbow so I can prop my head on my hand, I gaze out the window at the swaying sea oats. "We've agreed to end it after this job, but even if that means more time for me in Princeton, I'm not giving up my place here."

"I love your cottage. I wish it were warm enough to sunbathe all weekend. You've got the best spot for going topless."

Lying back, I stretch my arms over my head. "One more month and you can attempt to get arrested on my beach all you like."

She laughs. "I have a feeling your beach sees plenty of risky business without me. Besides, we've got connections. See you tomorrow."

"Night, Lainey."

For a few minutes after disconnecting, I lie there and flip through photos of Derek on my phone until I can't decide if it makes me feel better or worse. I stand and go to the kitchen to heat water in the kettle. Maybe chamomile tea will help me relax.

Turning my back to the counter to wait for the whistle, I type up a text. He's probably not in a position to reply, but I want him to know . . .

Miss you so much. It's hard to sleep outside your arms.

Holding my phone, I think of his lovely face on my pillow. At least the bed still smells like him, even if I'm not clutched tight against his chest. My phone vibrates.

Miss you too. Hope to finish here soon.

Imagining our reunion provokes a little tingle. *I have a special red nightie waiting for you.*

You're beautiful in red.

You're beautiful in everything.

You're beautiful in nothing. My favorite.

A pouty sigh escapes my lips, and I'm as frustrated as Elaine. I want him here now. *Please be careful. Remember Dex and I need you.*

No matter where I am, you are all I see.

My insides melt, and I kiss my phone face before typing. *I love you.*

Love you more. Sleep. I'll be there soon.

I'll try. xxx

With a deep breath, I look once more at the images on my phone trying not to feel miserable. My thumb pauses on a shot of me Derek took a while back. I'm smiling, and my hair's blowing across my face from the side. The little gold heart at the base of my throat catches the light.

Placing my phone on the counter, I snatch up the flashlight and run out to the side porch. Shining it all around, I get down on my hands and knees and feel under the small sofa one more time. Again, I come back with nothing.

Frustrated, I sit back on my heels and look out at the dark night toward the shoreline. The doors are all locked, and I promised Derek I wouldn't do any more night walks until he's back. Still, I can't help wondering if I lost it out there somewhere. Maybe a metal detector . . .

Just then the whistle starts loud from the kitchen. I push up from the floor, and walk slowly in the direction of the noise as my thoughts travel across the miles to where he is. He's taking a huge risk. Everything could go wrong, and he could lose his license, his business . . .

Exhaling a tiny prayer to Saint Michael, I take the kettle off the fire and pour the water into my waiting mug.

ELEVEN

OPENING ACT

Derek

TIME FEELS LIKE IT STRETCHES on for hours as we wait, wondering if our target will come back or move on. I want to call Mel, but I also want the kitchen staff to forget I'm here. So I keep quiet. Until she texts me.

All the reasons I'm here come rushing back in just a few lines—to protect her, to keep her safe. We say goodnight, and just like that, everything starts to move.

Patrick shoots me a text. *Switch on. We're back in business.*

I quickly put the earbuds back in just in time to hear Sloan talking to Star. Two more martinis, and she's making progress.

"I only waited to tell you goodnight." Her disguised voice is suggestive but tentative. "My rep never showed up, so I guess I'll head back to my hotel now. Alone."

A few seconds pass, and he doesn't respond. I'm hanging on the sounds of glasses clinking and the low roar of voices. He finally speaks.

"How long are you in town?" I'm not sure, but it sounds like a nibble.

"Just a few days." She releases a sad sigh. "I'll head back to

DC and look for a new job there, I guess."

"What were you doing before you left?"

"I was an intern for Senator Daltry."

Silence, more noise from the bar. Muffled talking. I can't tell if that was them or what happened. Then they're back.

" . . . wouldn't mind a little company." I missed the first of that, but it sounds promising. "We can discuss it tomorrow night if you'd like to have dinner with me?"

"Oh, I'd love to!" The gushy sound of her voice worries me. She doesn't need to be too easy. "I really want to stay in the city."

The noise is muffled again, and then the voices vanish altogether. I'm straining against the tiny white headphones. *What's going on?*

Footsteps outside the door, and it pushes open. Patrick shoves inside, and I realize he put his phone in his coat and headed up here.

"She did it." He hangs by the window, scanning the alley. "This is good. One of us can get down there fast if anything goes wrong."

"I'll let you take that route. I'll use the stairs and the kitchen exit."

He chuckles. "Thanks."

"So what'd I miss? You apparently shoved your phone in your pocket at a critical point."

Pulling it out again, Patrick checks the face. "Our man offered her a job 'keeping him company' while she's in town. Strictly a test-run, of course."

"I heard they're having dinner tomorrow night?"

"Gives us one more day to prepare."

THE NEXT DAY WE HIT the gym again, but not too hard. Star doesn't want to be tired, but we all feel better knowing we've polished her self-defense moves.

"The first night will probably just be hummers and finger-ing." Her tone is as casual as if she's tending bar. "Probably don't need to worry too much about martial arts."

"I like knowing you're more prepared." Wiping my face with the towel, I grab a bottle of water.

Her attention turns to Patrick finishing up a set of curls. "What made you take off last night?"

He exhales loudly and drops the weight, going to lean against the wall. We're alone in the small room, so we're being less guarded with our speech. "Did it seem like he was on guard to you? Like he kept looking around?"

She frowns. "Not really. He seemed pretty relaxed, actually, but I guess he does this all the time."

I can tell Patrick's not satisfied, and I know my partner pretty well.

"What did you see?" I move closer and lower my voice.

Patrick shrugs. "It was probably me being paranoid, then. I don't do this all the time."

"Still, what was it?"

"A few times it seemed like he was looking my way. Like he had his eye on me."

Star has joined us in the huddle. "I don't think he's bisexual."

"That's not what I mean. More like he was . . . curious or something."

"It didn't stop him from propositioning me."

Pressing my lips together, I think about what Patrick is say-ing. "Sounds like tomorrow night you should be somewhere else. Is there another place you can observe and not be seen?"

"I'll go over early and try to find a spot." He turns to Star. "You'll be in the exact same place?"

"That's the plan."

Nodding, Patrick starts to go. "I'm headed back. Don't wor-ry if you don't see me tonight. I'll be there."

I know he will. It's almost three, and we all go our separate ways to reconvene at eight.

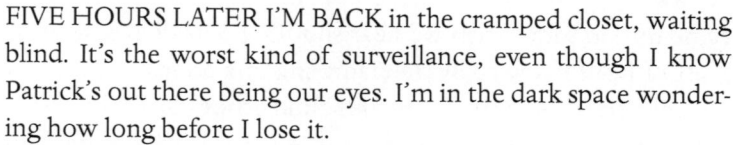

FIVE HOURS LATER I'M BACK in the cramped closet, waiting blind. It's the worst kind of surveillance, even though I know Patrick's out there being our eyes. I'm in the dark space wondering how long before I lose it.

I check my watch. It's eight-thirty now. Pulling out my phone, I read back over the texts Mel and I sent back and forth today. Elaine's spending the night, they're having a Mexican fiesta, a few suggestive exchanges involving red thongs and sheer nighties. I smile.

I'd give anything to be there with her tonight, my unpleasant task behind us. But this problem won't take care of itself, and I'm here to see it through to the end.

More time passes. I lean my head back against the wall and try to rest. There's no fucking way I'm sleeping, but I'm not much for playing with apps, and looking at photos of Mel only gets me more keyed up.

Another thirty minutes pass. I think about what's to come, and what we've got to get through to pin this on Sloan. Then I think about him behind bars and what Star said about wanting him out of our lives for good. We could do all this, and he could still get out on parole. Then what?

My eyes squeeze shut. Now isn't the time to worry about that. It only distracts me from our plan, from what we have to make happen here.

Checking my watch, I'm sure they've had dinner at this point. It's after nine, and it's getting nice and dark in the alley. Just then the door pushes open and my adrenaline kicks up a notch.

"Show's starting." Patrick pauses to catch his breath. "Crack the window. We should be able to see them."

I move to the small window and give it a push. Straining into the night, I locate the black door with the orange stripe across the bottom. It's almost directly below us.

"That's the spot. She knows where to go."

We hang out a few minutes, and I'm about ready to ask if he came up too soon when we hear shuffling outside below us. A scuff of heels followed by the slamming of a door.

The acoustics are bad, and the sound echoes up to where we are louder than I expected—or wanted. The click of heels on pavement is clear as a bell, and shortly after, we're bathed in a soundtrack of female moans and gasps. *Shit.*

"This is great," I grumble, but Patrick shoves his elbow in my torso.

He communicates in gestures. "If we can hear them, they might hear us."

Shaking my head, I turn away from the window, but listening is going to be unavoidable, it seems.

Pulling out my phone, I stare at the face again. Patrick stays by the window watching.

Just kissing. He texts.

I'm not really interested in the play-by-play, but I suppose we do need to keep tabs on whether the events are consensual or not.

More gasping punctuated by little moans. "Touch me," Star whispers in an urgent tone. "Touch me."

So far it sounds about as consensual as this setup was intended to be.

A loud moan.

Fingering. My partner texts again.

Great. Just fucking great. My eyes roam up to the ceiling, and I try to think of a million other things.

"Oh, god, yes!" Star's voice breaks the silence. "Oh, god! Don't stop!"

Looking at my hand, I think about how much easier it would be if I just beat him to death.

"Don't stop . . . oh please . . . pleeease . . ." Her voice is high. I'm going to need a workout after this. "Ohh . . ."

Cries of what I can only assume are an orgasm continue to fill the small space where we're hiding. I can't tell if it's real or fake, and I deny the tightness across my fly. Even Patrick drops his gaze to his shoes, but what comes next snaps us both back to attention.

"On your knees." Sloan's voice is sharp as he gives the order. It's the sound we've been waiting for. "My turn."

"But . . . I . . ." She pretends to be confused. Patrick and I both frown at each other . . . *Is she taunting him so soon?*

Sloan's undeterred. "You came all over my hand, now I intend to fuck your mouth."

The tone in his voice sparks a burn of rage in my stomach. He starts that shit on the first night, it seems. I'm ready to go down and kick his ass, but I feel Patrick's hand grip my arm. His thumb is moving over his phone.

Mine lights up. *She's prepared for this. Let her lay the groundwork.*

Adrenaline is spiking my heartbeat. All I can think of is Melissa being subjected to this fucker's shit, but I hold it together. Shuffling noises meet our ears, and I step forward to see what's happening.

The asshole has his back to the brick wall, and he leans back as Star's head bobs up and down at his crotch. *Shit.* She's going at it.

Stepping back to the wall again, I rub my neck and revisit the plan. It's only the first night. We prepared for this to happen. As many times as I remind myself, this is what she signed on for, I still don't feel any better about it.

Low groans fill the air now. A male hiss, and I'm glad I haven't eaten. Patrick's still watching the whole thing, his hand held out in a "Wait" motion.

Muffled sounds come from Star. A popping noise, and she gasps, laughs a little.

"Good girl," Sloan murmurs to her. "Now all the way . . . All the way."

More muffled hums. It's quiet a few moments then loud gagging. Patrick straightens up like he's ready to go through the window, and I touch his arm. His thumb flies over his phone face.

Holding her in a deep throat. Can't tell if she's okay.

Coughing, she gasps and laughs again. It's shaky, but *fuck*. I don't know what to do.

"Good?" His tone is condescending, like a coach or a teacher. I want to bash his head against the wall.

"You're so big." Her voice is shaky, but I hear her smile. I rub my forehead, wishing to be anywhere but here.

"Almost there . . ." His voice is strained and punctuated by the sounds of Star working him. Scuffing of shoes, low groans, then a deep "Ahhh . . . Drink it all. Fuck yes," which I know is him finishing.

Patrick's lips are tight when I glance up at him.

Star's back to high, breathy Marilyn. "Good?"

"Very good. You can really take it, can't you?" The note of ridicule in his voice makes me hate him even more. I didn't think that was possible.

"I guess." Star's doing the best imitation of timid I've heard in a while, and I'm ready to nominate her for an Oscar.

"No guessing, you can. Next time we'll see just how much you can take, and then maybe we'll discuss my apartment downtown. I'm looking for someone new."

"What does that mean?" She actually sounds excited, and my stomach turns.

"It means treats. And tricks."

"Tricks?"

Sloan's clothes are back in order, and Star leans beside him against the wall. Her black dress is smooth, and only her hair is messy from their encounter.

"You'll see." He touches her hair lightly. "I recently lost

someone . . ."

Tenderness is in his voice. I don't believe it for one fucking second, but we all strain forward anyway, hanging on what he might say next.

"Want to tell me about it?"

Her hand slides across his torso, and for a moment, I think she's going to embrace him—then I notice her black-lace thong peeking out from his pants pocket. He seems to remember as well, and it snaps him out of whatever moment he was just having.

Sloan catches her hand with a menacing smile. "I'll hang onto these. You can have them back tomorrow night."

"When we meet for something more?"

"We'll meet at the bar. Or where are you staying?"

"I'm nearby. The umm . . . Bridgestreet."

I can see him thinking. "We'd better start at the bar. Here, since you came first, you only get half."

"That wasn't the deal." She slants her eyes like he just told a joke. "What will I do with you?"

He hands over a white envelope. "Just so we're clear, I intend to fuck you tomorrow night. In interesting ways."

"Crystal, and I'll expect the full amount." She rolls forward as if to kiss him, but he pushes up and past her, going back toward the restaurant.

"You'll be full. Don't worry." With that he pushes through the door, leaving her alone.

Bastard.

She rolls back against the wall and looks down at her shoes. I can't tell what thoughts are going through her head. Warring in my chest is a tangle of rage and frustration overwhelmed by a strong need for vengeance.

Star looks up at the window, and her face is serious. She gives us a discreet thumbs-up, then turns on her heel, heading out of the alley.

BACK AT THE FOUR SEASONS bar, nobody speaks as we wait for our drinks. Star passes the envelope containing Sloan's money to Patrick, and he puts it in his jacket pocket like a pimp.

My scotch is the first to arrive, and I consider shooting it. Instead, I pick it up and walk to the square table in the back corner where we can talk privately. The other two join me once they've gotten their drinks.

We're quiet until Patrick finally breaks the awkwardness. "Well, that went about as we expected."

I don't know how the fuck he does it, but with those few words, we're all breathing again.

"He's smooth." Star sounds like she's conducting an autopsy. "And attractive. I can see why the girls go for him."

"You're fucking kidding me." I can't believe she just said that.

Her eyes cut to mine. "He's also rich and confident, and he knows his way around a clit." She lifts the glass and takes a sip. "I wasn't faking."

"Well, that's helpful for you, I guess." Patrick follows suit, taking a hit from his drink.

She stares into her vodka. "I see why Tiffany would follow him here."

Her words soften me—now she's speaking language I can understand. For a while at first, I was preoccupied trying to find a reason for this guy's continued success with women. Then I just wanted him gone.

I mutter into my drink. "He apparently has a deceptive opening act."

Patrick keeps us moving forward. "You're all set for tomorrow night. Good work. What's your feeling? Are you ready?"

She shakes her head. "Hope so. He's definitely got a side to him. I wasn't going anywhere without finishing the job tonight.

I don't know what would've happened if I'd said No."

"Okay, so that's our plan. Tomorrow night you push back. See if he gets rough." This was Patrick's idea from the start, so I let him lead.

"Is it too soon?" As she speaks, her finger circles the rim of her glass.

"Impossible to know. But I was worried about you tonight. He's one cold-hearted prick."

She looks up and smiles at my partner. "With you, it was fun. With him, I confess. I'm scared."

That does it. "If you want out, say it, and it's over. I don't like any of this."

She looks up, and with her sitting here fucking looking so much like Melissa, I'm about to call it regardless of how she feels. "That's not what I'm saying."

"What are you saying?" Patrick's tone is calming. "We can call it off and walk away. Figure out another option."

"Haven't you tried that already? Isn't that the reason you came to me?" Her glance catches my eyes, but I look down.

It's true, but I don't want to say it right now. I've tried legal methods, and Sloan's slipped out of the noose every time.

"That answers my question," she continues. "I'm doing this for Tiffany. I'm not calling it off. I shouldn't have said I was scared. I'm not."

"You were right to say it." My partner reaches across the table and holds her hand. "Sangria. Okay? We'll be right there."

She nods and looks down again. I'm pissed. "You should be in college or trade school. Why the hell are you even in this line of work?"

And just like that, Toni Durango's back. "Fuck you, Mr. Derek Alexander. What the fuck do you know about what I should be doing?"

I shake my head. "Screw it. I'm getting another scotch. Anybody else?"

Patrick nods, but Star's still nursing hers. "Two drinks it is, then."

I walk up to the backlit bar. It's elegant with dark wood counter tops and recessed lighting. The liquor bottles are arranged in groups all the way to the ceiling by color. They're backlit as well, and it's an impressive mosaic. While I wait for our refills, I look at the two of them sitting, leaning forward over the table.

Whatever he says makes her laugh. She touches his arm, but he pulls away, I know, because of Elaine. Still, he has a connection with her that I don't have—one I don't care to have. I linger a bit after the drinks are placed in front of me before heading back. I'll let Patrick mend that bridge a bit longer.

She's right. We're worlds apart, and I don't have the right to come in and ask for her help then start passing judgment on her lifestyle. It just pisses me off. All of it. I fucking fought for this country. I'm supposed to uphold the law. Turning to the bar, I know I can't go down that path—not if I'm going to do what needs to be done here.

When Star seems more settled, I walk back and retake my seat.

"Okay, we decided we'll have to find a better place than an alley for tomorrow night's rendezvous." Patrick takes his drink and stabs the skinny straw in it a few times. "I'll scout the area and see if I can find something close to the Oceanaire that we can get in and out of discreetly. Maybe this Bridgestreet will work."

"Sounds like tomorrow's assignment."

Star stands and ducks her head in our directions. "I'm heading up if you don't need me for anything else."

"You're off the clock." Patrick's still going for casual, business-as-usual, but I can't do it.

"I'm sorry you had to do what you did tonight."

She blinks a few times and nods. "I'm sorry I went off on you."

"Water under the bridge."

Once she's gone, Patrick leans forward, and speaks low. "Now will you get off my case about fucking her at the office? She's a fucking pro."

"I will never get off your case about that, but you're right. And it's a damn shame." I think about subcultures and the world of the street. How people get trapped in a life of alleyways and dark closets. Most of them stay there until they're dead.

Then I remember my question from earlier. "What did you tell the kitchen staff we were doing in that closet?"

Sitting back in the chair he laughs. "I didn't tell them anything. I just asked if my partner and I could use the room."

Fucker. "That's what I thought."

"Hey, you're a hot piece of ass. I'd do you. If I went that way, I mean."

"I hope I don't have to kick your ass one of these days."

"Get some sleep. We've got to work fast tomorrow."

———————◆———————

DOWN FROM THE OCEANAIRE ARE two Bridgestreet hotels. Patrick and I choose the closest one to enter, posing as bankers in town planning a conference. While getting the tour of their facilities, we find a smallish meeting space with both an outside door *and* an adjacent tech room—complete with two-way mirror. It's perfect. Bonus: It's soundproof.

While the hotel's conference director describes their state-of-the-art networking system, Patrick pockets the extra door card to the room. We'll come back after hours and go over the best way to get in and out. We'll also be sure that outside door is left ajar. Security will be another problem, but I'll see if I can hack into their computer systems and get a feel for his rounds.

All of it has to be perfectly choreographed, but we're ready by the time eight rolls around. Patrick slipped a hand-drawn map under Star's door earlier in the day for her to take and go over alone. We'll be in the tech booth waiting when they arrive.

Star calls my cell, which is unexpected, to let us know she's heading out, and I feel the need to say it one more time. "If there were any other way . . ."

Her soft exhale passes over the line. "Stop. I agreed to help you for my *own* reasons. Reasons I'm sure you're too noble to understand."

"I'm not so noble. I understand revenge." We're quiet a moment. "Patrick has the lead here, but I don't like putting you in this position."

"Patrick understands me. I fucked him. I messed with his head. I'm not worth you feeling sorry for."

Their history still ticks me off, but with this, I'm ready to forgive. "You're a human being. You're worth my concern, and you shouldn't have to sell your body."

"Don't confuse sex with intimacy, Derek. My body is not my heart. I can separate what I choose to allow happen to me from who I am."

The rationalizations of the hooker. I've heard them before. "If that's what you want to believe, it's not my business."

"Look, let me use my choices for something good. It's a small sacrifice. And by helping get justice, I can find some level of redemption."

I do understand that, even if it turns my stomach. "We'll be there if you get in trouble."

"Sangria."

TWELVE

TOOTHLESS MONSTERS

Melissa

MY FEET ARE IN ELAINE'S lap and she's massaging them while we watch *Pitch Perfect* for the thousandth time.

"I think I can do that cups trick." Speaking of cups, Elaine's on her third margarita, while I've almost finished the entire chips and salsa by myself.

"Don't. You're drunk and you'll just make a mess."

She swats my foot. "I am *not* drunk!" She struggles to get up, but I push down with my legs, pinning her in place. "Let me up!"

"Seriously, can we please just finish the movie? I told you tequila would make you wild."

"All the little kids do it at my school." She's whining now. "I've been wanting to try."

"I don't have any solo cups."

Pouty face. "Fine. But you can't crush my dream. I'll do the cups!"

I grab the remote to rewind the scene we've missed while she was talking, but the movement pinches my stomach. "Oh, shit. Why did you let me eat all those chips? I'll have heartburn."

"I'm not about to get between a pregnant lady and her snack foods." She takes another wobbly sip of margarita. "Besides, you're in that lucky 'eating for two' stage. Live it up!"

"That's a myth. My doctor said I shouldn't gain more than fifteen pounds with this pregnancy."

She leans forward and scoops up some chip particles from the bottom of the bowl. "Have you seen your fiancé? He's a giant. That baby needs food."

"Not sure chips and salsa count as real food."

She flops back, and we're quiet again, watching. She takes another, longer drink, and my eyes cut to her face. She's not smiling. She's been down since she got here, and I know Lainey well enough to tell it's more than just missing Patrick.

"You okay?" I ask as gently as possible.

A few moments go by, and she blurts it. "I did something really bad."

My brow lines in confusion. I can't guess what in the world she might have done, but I can tell it's seriously bothering her. "Do you want to tell me about it?"

She sits up and puts her margarita on the coffee table, then flops her arms at her sides. "Just . . . don't lecture me. I *know* it was wrong."

Eyebrows raised, I nod and take her hand. The anticipation is almost too much.

She takes a deep breath and then lets it out. "I stopped taking my birth control pills last month."

My head ducks forward. "What?"

Her grip tightens on my hand. "You heard me."

"Does Patrick know?"

"No. And I *know* it was wrong. I was having a really hard month, and then Kenny called, and it made me so depressed. I just felt like . . . I'm going to lose him, Mel." Her voice cracks, and her green eyes are so round when she looks at me. "I panicked."

"Oh, Lainey!" I reach forward to hug her, but she pulls away, shaking her head.

"I know, it was manipulative and all that . . . and there's more."

Sitting back again, I chew my lip. Now I'm nervous. "Okay?"

Her voice is thickening, and I can tell she's going to cry. "I pulled this stupid stunt, and . . . nothing happened. *Nothing!* We must've had sex a hundred times last month, and I started today just like clockwork."

I begin to breathe again. "But that's a good thing, right?"

She nods, but she doesn't answer me.

"Hang on." I roll my awkward self so I can put my feet on the floor and then scoot closer to her, wrapping an arm around her shoulders. "What are you thinking right now?"

"That I'm broken?" She puts her head on my shoulder as the tears fall. "What if I can't get pregnant? I really will lose him . . . then what will I do?"

At that moment, the show's enormous musical performance erupts from the screen. We both jump, and I scramble for the remote to mute it.

My heart is thumping, but I go back to where she is, taking her hand. "I think you should talk to Patrick about it. He might want to wait on another baby, considering what's happening with Kenny—"

"Yes, Kenny. *She* can have his babies." She cries harder, falling into my lap. "He's going to leave me for her."

"Oh my god, he is not! For starters, Patrick doesn't love Kenny, he loves *you*. And jeez, Lainey, it was only one month! Come on . . ."

Sitting up and shaking her head, she wipes her nose with the back of her hand. "I know it's true. I can feel it in my gut. This is just what I get."

"What you get for what?"

"For being jealous? For thinking evil things about Kenny and her baby . . ." She sniffs. "I actually hoped—"

"Stop. You have *always* been dramatic. Just because you

thought something about your fiancé's baby mama doesn't mean you actually meant it."

"I meant it." Her voice is low and her chin drops. "I'm a horrible person, and now I'm getting what I deserve. I'll never have Patrick's baby, and he'll leave me for her. Just wait and see."

"What the hell! Of all the—I am never letting that boy leave town again! And you're cut off. No more margaritas."

She falls back on the cushions to cry. It's possible she's on a jag, so I try for counter-maneuvers.

"In fact, I might text him right now and tell him you've gone nuts, and it only took one week of him being out of town for it to happen."

She flies back up then. "Don't you dare! I don't want him to know what I've done."

"So far you haven't done anything but play pregnancy Russian roulette and talk like a crazy person."

"He's going to leave me for her, Mel. He doesn't know it now, but he's going to take one look at his little baby boy, and it's going to be over for me."

Catching her cheeks, I lift her face. "Look at me. Yes, Patrick is going to fall in love with his son, but he is insanely in love with you. Nothing is going to change that. He's drawn to you. He can't fight it. You're the candle, and he's the moth."

She blinks tears, and I pull her to me, rubbing her back. "Trust me. I can see what you can't, and as much as I know Patrick would love it if you got pregnant, you need to include him in the planning."

"I know," she sniffs, holding my waist. "I want to believe that."

"Then believe it."

We're quiet for a few moments as her sniffles gradually subside. My thoughts drift to the young woman I've only met once. "Why did Kenny call?"

Elaine sits up and grabs a napkin off the table, blotting her cheeks. "She needed him to cosign for her to get a car loan."

I nod, pressing my lips together. "I thought it might be something with the baby."

"No." She folds the napkin and then unfolds it again. "He called the dealer the next day and just bought it for her, said she doesn't need to worry about a car note."

That makes me smile. "He's really sweet to her." My smile quickly vanishes when I see Elaine's chin drop. Her brow crinkles again, and I grab her hand, hoping to derail any more tears. "They're *friends*. It's a good thing, Lainey. What if she were a raging bitch?"

Her lips press together as she studies the napkin. "You're lucky. You don't have anything threatening your relationship with Derek."

As much as I want to argue she doesn't either, I pause and think about it for a few moments. Even though she's drunk and irrational at the moment—or maybe *because* she is—I let my guard down. "I used to be afraid he'd never love me as much as he loved Allison."

Her face jerks up to mine. "What the hell? Whatever would make you think something like that?"

Shrugging, I look at our hands. "She was his first real love. They dated in high school, she waited for him to come back from Iraq. I can tell she was this wonderful, amazing person, and I—"

"Now who's talking crazy? Derek Alexander is the most threatening man I've ever met in my life, and when you're in the room, he completely changes. It's like he's your personal tame lion."

"Still, she had his heart first, and he mourned her for so long."

"Okay, so you said you *used* to be afraid. What changed?"

"Oh! That's why I'm telling you this." For a moment my old fears had tried to creep in again, but I scoot forward. "I finally just told him. I said it out loud to him."

"And?"

"And it was the best thing I've ever done. He opened up and told me things . . . I don't think he would ever have said to me otherwise. You know how guys are."

"Patrick will talk, but only when he's in the mood."

"Right!" I relax, leaning back on the cushions. "You need to talk to him about how you feel when he's in that mood."

She shakes her head. "I don't know. It just feels different, and you don't have anything else to be afraid of with Derek. No dark secrets."

"I'm afraid of what might happen tonight." Once the words are out, I wish I'd never said them. Elaine's brow creases, and it's clear she hasn't connected the dots on what could happen if things get out of hand in Baltimore.

"What do you mean? You think Derek might do something—"

"Illegal. Something that if he's caught, he'll be taken away from me. You know how protective he is. He's done things . . . And I'm afraid he'll do them again, and then I'll lose him."

We're quiet, and Elaine's green eyes travel over my shoulder and out the window. Up and away across the miles to where we both know they're waiting. She blinks, and she's back here with me.

"Patrick won't let that happen. I know he won't. Derek's like a brother to him—a brother he *likes*—and he won't let him . . . get caught."

She didn't say *let him do it*, I mentally note. "That's what I'm counting on."

Quiet again, we hold hands until she pulls me into a hug. "Isn't there a saying about how if you speak your fears, they lose their power?"

A knot is in my throat, and I'm not sure I believe it. Still I go with her. "It sounds familiar."

"Well, we've said it then. Now our fears have to disappear."

I hold onto my friend. She holds onto me, and we settle in to wait, hoping against hope that our fears are now nothing more than toothless monsters.

THIRTEEN

TO SLAUGHTER A PIG

Derek

TONIGHT'S WATCH IS DIFFERENT FROM last night's. Unable to find a way to get Patrick from the restaurant to our hideout without being caught, we'd decided he'd be with me from the start, leaving Star alone with Sloan.

We both sit in silence in the tech booth, waiting. Neither of us knows what's happening in the Oceanaire, and we can only hope she manages to lure him here on her own. If anything else happens, we won't know until it's too late.

It's the worst-case scenario.

"When you were in country, did you ever do a night watch?" Patrick is sitting on the floor, his back against the wall. He's got one of his gloves off, and he's rolling a quarter back and forth across his knuckles. "This reminds me of night watch."

"More like being in the advance party." Going ahead of the battalion into a location, no way of knowing what might happen or what surprises might be waiting. "It's a little like that. Minus the IEDs."

My partner exhales and pulls the glove back over his hand. Then he pushes off the floor and steps over to lean beside me against the counter. "You're right. Military deployment is way fucking worse than this. This is plain old detective work, pure and simple."

"Or police work. Waiting around for what's coming."

Glove back off, he starts with the quarter again, back and forth. "Why'd you become a Marine? Other than you were born to play the part?"

"That's pretty much it." I watch the quarter rotate over his knuckles and think about being a kid, waiting on my dad to come home, hearing my mother softly cry herself to sleep at night. "My dad was a Marine. His dad was a Marine—"

"Phew, sounds like a fun group."

"They weren't so bad."

Patrick exhales. Both gloves are off, and he switches the coin to his other hand, continuing the trick. "When Stuart said he was joining the corps, I wasn't a bit surprised. He'd been perfecting that fucking attitude for years."

"Your brother is a great Marine. He had my back more than once." Checking my phone, it's after ten. I don't know how much longer this could take or when to worry if they don't show.

"You'd better keep the gloves on in case we have to move fast." He stops fidgeting, and puts the quarter back in his pocket, nodding as he pulls on the gloves. We can't afford to leave fingerprints.

I'm pretty sure I've asked before, but this wait is mind numbing. "What made you join the Guard?"

"College. I wasn't academic enough for a scholarship, but my parents couldn't afford to send four kids to school. It seemed like the safest alternative."

I chuckle. "And then you got deployed."

"Yep. Thank you, War on Terror."

"I'm sure you were good at it. I've seen your work."

He nods and for a few minutes, we're quiet. Then he shifts and clears his throat.

"Look, I know what we're doing is pretty raw. I'm sorry I couldn't come up with a more elegant plan, but you've got to get some mud on you to slaughter a pig."

I exhale a laugh. "How long have you been saving that line?"

He grins and his shoulders relax. "A few days."

Then I shake my head, serious again. "I couldn't control what took Allison from me. There was nothing I could do." I pause remembering that sick, helpless feeling as she slowly left me forever. I'd never felt that way in my life, and it almost broke me. "I'll be damned if I sit back and let something take Melissa. Especially if I have the power to stop it."

Just then the outside door creaks, and we both jump. Patrick hits the lights, and I instinctively feel my body preparing to fight.

Patrick's the only one armed. He'd insisted, strike that, *demanded* I leave my gun in my room's safe to "avoid temptation." I'd only agreed because he played the Mel card. It's possible he knows me a little too well.

The door creaks again, and in a fumble of hands and staggering steps, Star backs into the room. Sloan's plastered to her mouth, and from this angle, we can see his hands moving up her thighs, dragging the hem of her skirt with them, quickly revealing her thong. *Shit.* This again.

"Here we go," Patrick says in a voice one click above inaudible.

The pair roll against the wall, and the outside door slams shut. The noise breaks their kiss, and Sloan looks up and around, surveying the small, empty conference room. It's dim-lit by small, emergency lighting and the green glow of the Exit sign.

"How did you know about this place?" His voice is thick.

"Passed it on my way to the restaurant tonight." Star's back to breathy-high Marilyn. "I peeked my head in, and when I saw the side door, I thought of you."

He turns back to her with a greedy smile. "Good call." Then he covers her mouth again with his.

His hands return to her ass, and he lifts her against the wall. A memory of me lifting Melissa in a similar way knots my stomach, and I turn my back. We can hear it. I don't have to watch.

Star's voice. "What if I worked for your company? Then I could see you every day. Or every afternoon?"

Glancing over my shoulder, I see Sloan lower and turn her so that her back is against him. "Not a bad idea." He moves her legs apart with his knee, and his hand goes between her thighs in front, pulling up swiftly.

"Oh!" She lets out a shocked noise, but her cheek is pressed to the side so we can see her face. She isn't in pain. In fact, her expression is just the opposite. It's impossible to know when she's acting. I'm fucking listening for *Sangria*.

"You feel that?" Sloan leans into her ear. "That's where I'm going to fuck you. Right in that tight little hole."

She inhales sharply. "I don't do that for clients." Her hips are following his movements, rocking back and forth. "It's too risky."

His hand appears to be moving all over her crotch, and she lets out a little moan. "Your tight little ass loves what I'm doing, and if you want your money, you'll fuck me like I say. How do I know you're on the pill?"

With a shudder, she moves to the side, quickly evading his hand. "Use a condom if you don't believe me. I'm not getting pregnant."

Anger flashes on Sloan's face, and he steps in front of her, pinioning her. Her resistance is good, but it's too soon. We need his physical evidence in her body before he hurts her.

"Don't fuck with me. I'm going bareback, and I'm going where I want."

Rage tightens my throat. The way he's standing, blocking her face, she could easily be Mel facing down this bastard. It takes all the willpower I possess to stay in this small room and not go out there. I have to distract myself from the photos I've seen, the one of Jessica Black, the one of my beautiful bride's battered face.

Patrick's leaning over the counter near the door, and I see his hand twitch. From his tense stance, I can tell he's ready to intervene as well.

"Look, I don't have any lube." Star steps to the side and around so her back is to us again. "I won't ass fuck without lube."

Rage burns cold in Sloan's eyes. He's controlled, but barely, and by the way his lips part over his teeth, I know tonight will definitely be the night.

"I know where to get lube." He grabs her by the neck and spins her back to the wall, slamming her head hard against the plaster.

Star pushes against him, but it's a clumsy effort. Patrick and I both know her skill at self-defense, and I wonder if she was injured just then. He's back on her just as fast, and with a grunt, she pushes away again. Then she rears back and slaps him hard across the face.

The *SMACK!* echoes in the dark space, and my muscles tense up, ready to take action.

But everything stops.

Sloan steps away from her and turns to face our direction. He looks like a freaking psycho killer in the pale green light, and I swear I can see the wheels going as his eyes travel around the dark room.

Hidden in the small tech booth, neither Patrick nor I breathe. This fucker is smart. He wouldn't have gotten away with his tricks so long if he weren't. My stomach muscles tighten. I have no idea what's about to happen.

He speaks into the darkness. "Where are you . . ." It's a whispered taunt, and he takes a few steps toward us before whispering again. "I know you're there."

What the fuck? How could he possibly know we're here? Maybe he really is crazy. My heart's slamming in my chest, and tension pulls an ache between my shoulder blades. Patrick's tense; the air is crackling.

"You're playing with me, using my weakness . . ." My brow lines as I listen to his sinister coaxing. "You know I was there. I got to her when you were gone, and I'll do it again. I'll do it every time, any time I wish . . . She's *mine.*"

Anger blazes low in my stomach, and I hear him. His message is meant for me, whether he's certain of my presence or not. It's a threat he's sending out, and I know the only way to answer it.

I'm ready to answer it.

He waits a few moments longer. Star's got her back to the wall, breathing heavily, watching him. Finally, he shakes his head, looks down, and turns to her. "You're a beautiful woman. Everything I like in one neat package."

A line pierces her forehead, and I can tell she's as confused as we are by this change.

"Thank you?" She tries breathy-Marilyn as she watches him pace back and forth in front of her.

"You remind me of a past lover. One I remember fondly." He smiles, and a creeping dread moves through me. "Would you like something that belonged to her?"

Star blinks rapidly, and I can tell she's on edge as much as we are. Is he talking about Jessica? Can she handle it if he is?

It doesn't matter. I'm just waiting for an opening, any excuse to make my move.

"A gift?" Her voice only wavers slightly. "But we barely—"

"Something *everyone* might find interesting."

Patrick and I exchange a glance.

Sloan's hand goes into his front pocket, and all three of us brace ourselves. The quiet in our small room is broken by the soft scrape of Patrick's gun coming out if its holster. My partner's ready if Sloan pulls out a weapon.

But when we see what has in his pocket, Patrick lowers the gun.

Sloan's "gift" is significant only to me, and for a moment, I stare dumbfounded at the thin gold chain with the tiny heart dangling from his outstretched hand. Melissa's necklace. He *was* there, and he took it.

His meaning is complete. Message received.

In that moment something in me shifts, and two things happen at once: I lunge for the door, and Patrick throws his body in front of me, blocking it. The two of us are locked in a power struggle that I'm about to win.

"What is it?" Star's Marilyn-voice floats to us, unaware of the battle happening behind the glass.

"It's what I would give you if you hadn't already stolen it." Those words drop a veil of rage over my vision, and I'm about to throw my partner out of the way.

Patrick's legs are braced against the door. "Derek! Don't blow this," he grunts in a whisper. "Don't let him bait you."

I'm so fucking insane with fury, I can barely see, but somehow I mange to find control. I know Patrick's right. We don't have evidence yet, and Sloan's fishing. If he knew for sure we were here, he would've already bolted.

It takes all the willpower I possess to step away from the door. I'm breathing hard, and I pace the small room, waiting. Just waiting. Counting slowly as I step—left, right, left . . . One, two, three . . .

Slowly coming down.

"It's a heart." Star takes the necklace from him. "I stole your heart? Are you joking?"

"Are you?" His voice is ridiculing again, and he shoves her back against the wall, his forearm pressing against her collarbone and throat. "Do you think I'm that easy to play?"

Her face begins to turn red, and her eyes squeeze shut. His forearm is right across her esophagus, and a gasping wail comes out. We wait on edge as he rams his hand in her crotch working her hard.

"You think you're going to fuck with me?" His face is leaned close to her ear, and it looks to me like she's fighting tears. "You like that?"

In an instant, Patrick and I are once again locked in a power-struggle for the door.

"Let me go, Patrick, it's too much." My voice is a strained whisper. I could overpower him, but he stops me.

"She can get out of that hold." Patrick hisses back. "Don't blow the job. Just give her a chance."

She snorts louder, and the dim light catches moisture on her upper lip. My chest collapses. I'm not sure she's getting out of this, and I'll be damned if I fucking let him kill her with us steps away.

"*Move*, Patrick." I push against him once more, but his legs are braced. His entire body is levered against mine, and I can tell he's using all the strength he has to keep me in this room.

Sloan's voice cuts through our struggle. "You like that, don't you. Fucking cunt. I have all the power here."

Star's face is turning purple, and I'm about to lift Patrick off the ground when we both hear her mumbling. We stop fighting and wait, looking intently through the two-way glass.

Sloan also pauses, loosening his pressure on her neck. "Are you begging, my love?"

She mumbles again, repeating the word in a whisper. "Sangria . . ." Her knees buckle, and she crumples to the floor.

Patrick is weightless in my grasp, and I realize he's off the door, spinning toward it. I follow him through faster than Sloan can react.

My partner's headed for Star. Light reflects off the gold chain in her limp hand. I'm headed straight for Sloan.

The last words out of the bastard's mouth are. "What the fuck?"

In one practiced motion, he's in my grasp, both my hands on the sides of his skull. Heat radiates between his skin and mine, and I don't waste a second doing what I know to do, what I'm trained to do.

To end this.

To answer his threat and protect her forever.

A swift twist, and a deeply satisfying *SNAP!* travels through the bones of my wrists, up my arms, over my shoulders to my brain. I release him, spreading my hands wide, and Sloan Reynolds drops like a stone, dead at my feet.

My breath is coming in pants, and my arms lower to my sides as I stand over him. The entire room seems to have moved out from me, and I'm alone in a space looking down on what I've done. Waiting to feel something.

Waiting.

Seconds tick by on the clock, and at last it comes.

Satisfaction unrolls like a slow wave in my chest, unfurling like wings through my arms and legs, down my torso to my fingers and toes.

In my peripheral vision, I register Patrick moving swiftly, his voice low. "Fuck fuck *Fuck*. Okay. Well, good riddance. Now we've gotta act. *Fast*."

I step over and gently take Melissa's necklace from Star's weak hand. She's breathing more normally now, despite the tears trickling down her cheeks. Still, she's not weeping. She seems to be recovering, rebuilding her own tough exterior, getting the shield back in place. I'm familiar with that.

Straightening again, I watch as Sloan's body twitches like a dead snake.

Patrick helps Star to her feet and gives her a hug. "Enemy combatant handled," he whispers and pulls off one of his black gloves. Handing it to her, he gives a gentle order, "Take this. Wipe every place you touched him, and get those pants good and down, soldier."

I can't seem to move as they work. It's not out of guilt, because I know with every ounce of certainty I possess I'd fucking do what I just did again and again.

A strong hand grips my shoulder. "Hey. Snap out of it and get the fuck out of here. We're behind you."

Patrick's back to wiping everything with his one glove and

Star's slowly doing the same. *"Go!"* He hisses.

With a black-gloved hand, I grasp the outside door and wait, listening. The only sound is the two of them cleaning, punctuated by a quiet sniff every few seconds from Star.

I rub my hand up and down on the doorframe and handle, wiping it clean, but just as I'm about to step through it, a dull thud comes from behind me. It's followed fast by another, and another. *Whop whop . . .*

Turning back, I see Star kicking Sloan's dead body in the stomach hard. Her voice is cold with anger, and tears stripe her cheeks. "That's for Tiffany, you fuckwad. I hope you're rotting in fucking hell right now." Then she lands a stomping blow to his chest, adding in a low whisper. "That's for me."

She pivots slightly and pulls back to make another blow, but Patrick catches her leg. "Not the head. It might fly off."

Her eyes cut to me, and my brow is creased as I nod. I guess we're more alike than I'd care to admit. I understand her primal need. I know the satisfaction she feels kicking him. She'd probably enjoy punting his head across the room.

Rubbing my eyes, I force these macabre thoughts to stop. I come back out of the rabbit hole, and continue out the door. Patrick's right. We've got to go.

I silently make my way down the hedge-lined alley along the back of the hotel. We have a long stretch of conference-room windows to get past before we're out of range, and I'm hoping Star's recovered enough to walk normally by the time they make it to the end of our leafy covering.

Dark window after dark window, I'm moving fast, thankful it's way after hours. Patrick and I are both trained for stealth, but our injured colleague isn't. I hold up at the edge of the building, where the tall shrub ends and listen.

It seems I've made it, and I yank the black gloves off my hands, shoving them into my pockets. Looking back, Star's leaning on Patrick's arm as he basically carries her down the hidden path. He stops when he reaches me, and leans her against the wall. She watches as he pulls off his gloves and puts them in his pockets.

His voice is low. "We need to act as inconspicuous as possible. The Four Seasons is only a few blocks. Can you make it?"

She nods barely, and it does nothing to ease the adrenaline surging through my veins.

I don't know how to place what I've done, where to put it in my mind or how to wrap my head around it. I've had to kill before, but in this case . . . What I've done is something outside the law. It's vigilante justice, and it's a cold fact that I'm not sorry.

How can I ever explain this to Mel? What will she think? She says I'm a hero, but I don't know if she can love this side of me. The side that won't back down, that will kill without hesitation.

I can't worry about that now—it has to wait, and we have to move. I step out from behind the hedge, walking straight, hands in pockets. I don't slow or look around.

Bodies pass me, but nobody appears to pay attention to another random person heading to his hotel. No one knows what I've done. I keep going straight. Patrick will wait several minutes before following me out, and we'll rendezvous at the bar and decide what to do next.

YEARS SEEM TO PASS BEFORE we've got our drinks and are secreted away at the small back table.

Patrick takes a long hit of vodka before cutting the tension with his usual levity. "I think it's safe to say that did *not* go as expected." He pauses, studying our shell-shocked expressions. "And shit, I will *never* fucking get used to that sound."

My eyes cut to him, but I can't answer. Breaking bones *is* a sickening sound. Only this time, for me it was a sick satisfaction.

"We're lucky that prick's parents are dead," he continues. "He ran Melissa off, and apparently he killed the only remaining person who loved him. I need another drink." He turns to Star. "You okay?"

She nods, and we're both silent as he leaves us alone again. My eyes are on the amber liquid in my glass, and I feel her eyes on me. No telling what's going through her mind right now. We don't even try to address it. We're both in that place of trying to sort out what just happened, how we feel about it, and what to do with it.

It seems quick when Patrick's back, dropping into his chair, slapping me hard on the shoulder. "You are one strong-assed motherfucker, you know that? At one point, I was sure I couldn't hold you any more. I should've known I wouldn't be able to stop what was coming."

I shake my head and actually laugh. It's kind of a loose laugh, but Patrick is such the fucking little brother I never had.

At last, Star speaks, and she's back to her normal low, smoky contralto. "What happens now?"

Her question snaps me to attention. It's time for me to shake it off. Man up, and be the leader I am. Scooting forward in my chair, I reach for her hand. Our next steps have been circling in my mind since we left the Bridgestreet.

"The best thing would be for you to go to the police. Tell them you were hooking up with some guy you just met, robbers broke in and attacked you both. You ran away scared— don't even mention you know what happened to him."

"If I don't know what happened to him, why would I go to the police?" She's not challenging me, just curious.

"She's right." Patrick leans forward on the table. "I think we should lay low and see what happens. If she thinks he's alive, why would she involve the police? She could get herself in needless trouble, and I wiped everything I could find."

For a moment, I press my lips together and think like a cop. I replay the whole scene in my mind again. "I ran my gloves over all the door handles. Unless he's got her DNA on him somehow."

"He hit me, but he didn't scratch me."

"He had his hands all in your snatch, in your ass . . ."

She chews her lips, and her eyes drop to her glass.

"That's okay," Patrick cuts in. "He's in a place he shouldn't be with his fucking pants around his ankles and his dick out. Nobody at his company's going to want that publicity. They'll cover that shit up, you watch."

I glance around the small bar, and for now, we're the only ones in it. *Is it possible we could get away with this?* I'm still calming my thoughts, but it seems like we might actually walk.

"The best way for a crime to be discovered is to have more than one witness." My gaze travels from Patrick to Toni, a.k.a., Star. "Patrick and I have done things; we have experience keeping things to ourselves . . ."

Toni's eyebrows shoot up. "Are you saying you don't trust me?"

I work to even my tone. "There's nothing stopping you from one day using this—"

"Other than the fact I'd be incriminated as well. I can't fucking believe you." She pushes her drink away and sits back in her chair. "Look, I've had to sit on crap. Shit, I've probably got more garbage locked in the vault than you with all your battle scars. You don't have to worry about me. I told you I was in this for Tiffany. As far as I'm concerned, you're the Angel of Justice."

I exhale and polish off my scotch. "There's no such thing."

Toni shakes her head and stands. "I'm taking off. You don't have to worry about me. I think you did the right thing. The *only* thing."

Patrick calls after her. "I'll check in with you in a few days."

She keeps walking, and we sit for a moment in silence then I look up at my partner. "We're finished here."

He tips his glass and kills his vodka. "Fuckin A. I don't think I've ever wanted to see Elaine this bad since I've known her."

Remembering my tension all those weeks ago and how good it felt to find Melissa waiting for me in my condo, I know he's right. The best thing to soothe this pain away are her sweet arms, the reason I'm here.

My love.

FOURTEEN

WHAT NEEDS TO BE DONE

Melissa

WARMTH SURGES ALL AROUND MY body, and that fresh, faintly woodsy scent I love touches my nose. Pressing my cheek into my pillow, I'm so in love with this dream, I don't want to wake up. It's so vivid, and I miss him so much.

At last, after hours of tossing and turning all night, being restless and worried, tension gripping my shoulders, not knowing if I'll sleep again . . . my whole body is relaxed. I'm so cozy, I want to stay here all day in this lovely fantasy of having him in my bed.

If only the morning light weren't pressing against my eyelids. If only I didn't have to work . . .

Stretching my arms wide, my eyes fly open when my fist makes contact with a warm, hot body. *It's not a dream!*

"That's some left hook you've got there." Derek's low voice ignites a burst of heat through my chest, down to my toes, and I dive into his arms. I love the sound of his laughter as he kisses my head

"You're back! When did you get in?" My stomach is on his chest, and I'm holding his face as I kiss his nose, his cheeks, his eyes, his eyebrows.

He rolls us so that I'm on my back beneath him, and he's propped above me, his forearms on each side of my head. "Early this morning." Another (thrilling) little kiss. "Patrick and I agreed—no more hotel beds. We wanted to be with our ladies."

Nodding, I slide my fingers into his dark waves as he peppers my ears, eyes, nose with kisses. "That six-hour drive is a little better than starting in Princeton."

"A lot better. Especially now." He dips his head and covers my mouth with his. The scuff of his beard against my skin is so sexy, it makes me laugh. I turn my cheek and wrap my arms around his neck, holding him close. Soft lips move up to my jaw then to my ear, where he whispers. "I can only think of one thing I like more."

"Hmm . . ." I play coy. "I wonder what that might be."

His head pops up, and sparkling blue eyes meet mine. "Applewood smoked bacon."

"What!"

He laughs and claims my mouth again, tongues twining, heat flaring between my thighs. I want him so much. My chin pushes up, and I break our kiss. "Seven days is over my limit."

"I agree." His mouth is moving down, following the line of my neck. I'm in a sleep shirt and PJ pants, but that doesn't stop him. Catching my breast through the thin material with his lips, he pulls my nipple, and the effect is excruciating.

"Derek!" I gasp, and in one swift movement, my top is off and his mouth is back on my now-bare breast. He pulls hard again, causing the tip to lengthen, and I'm so wet already. He's got me right on the edge with only his kisses.

"Yes, seven days." My voice is a shaky gasp. "Too long."

Large hands span my belly, and he pulls up, inspecting the size. "Look at you!" He leans down to kiss the swell of our little baby. "How is your luscious mom treating you?" He speaks into my navel, and then he turns and presses his ear against it as if listening.

I can't help a laugh, threading my fingers into his hair again. He looks up at me and smiles, the corners of his eyes lining in the most handsome way.

"You look very happy," I whisper, holding him as his head rests on baby. "More than you have in a while."

He rises back up beside me, resting his cheek on his hand and smoothing my hair off my face. "I feel like a weight's been lifted."

"Is it over?"

My question changes his expression to serious. "We handled the problem. You're safe. It's the only thing I've wanted since that day in October."

I know what day he means—the day I went to his office so angry with him. I'd forced him to look at the evidence against Sloan.

It was an emotional act I've often wished I hadn't committed. I'd filed away what happened to me in my heart, and I hadn't considered how deeply that photo of my battered face would affect him.

"What happened?"

For a moment he doesn't answer me. His eyes travel from mine up to the little scar and back again. "Will you accept for now that we fixed it so he can never hurt you again?"

My lips press together as I think about it. He's here, safe in my arms. My fears over what might happen did not come true. Most of all, he wouldn't tell me things were fixed if they weren't.

I consider all of it and make my decision. "I'll accept that for now." Reaching up, I smooth my hands on his cheeks. "I love you so much."

He leans forward and kisses me, gently at first, growing more forceful. He lifts up slightly and catches my lip between his, giving it a little pull. It sparks the desire that had only paused, and I'm pulling him to me, consuming him in a kiss so desperately hungry, it's never satisfied.

He lets out a low noise and circles his arm around me, lifting and turning me so that my back is to his chest, my ass pressed into his pelvis. I barely have time to note his erection before he catches my thigh, moving it up and to the back slightly, allowing him to fill me with his enormous length from behind.

"Aaah!" My head drops back, and he grasps my clit, massaging as he thrusts into me.

"Oh, god!" I can't stop another cry as his lips touch my neck, his beard scratching across the tops of my shoulders. I shiver at the intense eroticism.

He pushes into me hard as his fingers move nonstop over my sensitive bud. His mouth follows a line down the back of my neck, and sizzling waves of fire shoot down my inner thighs. I'm on the verge of screaming the pleasure is so strong. He doesn't slow, and I'm hurtling toward the edge, eyes closed, only waves of pleasure shimmering through me.

"Come now." His lips are a low vibration at my ear, and I moan. "Come." And with his next thrust, my legs erupt into orgasmic shaking. I cry out, overcome by the powerful wave of ecstasy flashing through me.

My body tries to fold together with the pull of it, but he holds me up, still thrusting as my inner muscles tense and pull. I'm arching back against him moaning, unable to endure much more. He's not far behind, and with a loud groan, he shoots off deep inside me.

Strong arms move from my shoulders around my ribcage, just above the swell of my stomach, and he's holding me tight against him, hips gently rocking. My eyes are still closed as we move together, riding it out, gently slowing as we ease down from the stratosphere. A few more deep breaths, and we both curl forward like two hands closing together in a perfect embrace.

"Seven days." His voice is low beside my ear, and a delicious wave of contentment moves in my torso.

My arms go on top of his, and soft lips touch the side of my neck behind my ear. Another wave moves across me. "I never want us to be apart again."

"I meant it when I said we'd be together permanently after Baltimore."

I scoot forward and roll onto my back to face him. "What will that look like? Will you be here?"

His soft lips press together, and I touch them with my fingertip. I know this is a difficult decision. "What if we split the time for now? We can each stay a week in both locations."

"Will that work for you in Princeton?"

"If we start the week on a Wednesday. It'll work in the short-term, and it'll give Nikki a chance to find another job."

My lips twist then. "I hadn't thought of that. I hate for her to lose a good job."

He exhales a laugh. "Working for me is a good job now?"

"You're a very generous employer. Even if you are a hard-ass."

He laughs, and I snuggle back into his arms smiling. We hold each other a few moments, savoring the afterglow. My entire body is completely relaxed and quiet. I'm in heaven in his embrace with notes of happiness pulsing through me on every heartbeat.

That's when it happens.

I feel the faintest stirring below my navel like a little fish. Or it's more like gas moving in my stomach, which should be embarrassing, but this is different. A second passes, and I feel it again. It's unmistakable this time.

"Derek!" I pull back and grab his hand, pressing it hard against my lower abdomen.

"What?" Concern is etched on his face, and he props up on an elbow watching me.

"Just wait . . ." I whisper.

We're both quiet, heads tilted as if we'll hear a noise. Then I feel it again, the faintest little nudge.

"Did you feel it?!" I'm practically bouncing in the bed, I'm so happy.

His brow crinkles. "No?"

It doesn't matter. I know it's too small for him to feel anything yet, but I lunge forward, hugging my arms tight around his neck. "I felt him move! I can feel him moving! It's just the faintest flutter, but I know you'll be able to feel it soon."

He hugs me back, pulling me tight against his torso. "I can't wait." I can hear the love in his voice, but when I look again, there's a shadow over his eyes.

"What's wrong?"

I ask, but I already know. I agreed we'd wait to discuss Baltimore, but I can sense what went down had to be pretty major. I'm sure it's on his mind, and I confess, I want to know so badly. At the same time, I kind of don't.

He blinks and whatever it was is gone, hidden behind the shield I know he's learned to cultivate. We've only been together a few months, but already I've learned to hate that barrier that keeps me at a distance, away from what's hurting him.

"Not a thing, darling, I'm excited." Whatever just happened might bother me, but when he smiles at me that way, I melt. "I'm sorry I can't feel him yet. When's your next appointment?"

"Today, actually." I push the side of his hair away from his cheek. "Dr. Mel works around my schedule. Want to tag along?"

"I wouldn't miss it."

❤

THE DOCTOR'S EXAM ROOM IS warm, and I'm lying on the hard, leather table with my knees bent, turned so I can face Derek. He's sitting at my head, elbow bent on the back of the table, smoothing my hair back.

"Seventeen weeks isn't a particularly exciting visit." I smile up at him, not wanting him to be disappointed.

"You forget. I haven't been to as many of these as you have."
His touch is so comforting, I feel like I should've insisted on having him with me every time.

"I've only been coming once a month. You haven't missed much."

Just then Dr. Mel enters the room. She's a bit older than me, with black hair and olive skin, and a personable disposition. We laughed at having the same nickname, even though her first name is Linda. Her last is Melendez, or Mel for short.

"I see you brought Daddy along this time." She smiles, her dark eyes dancing as she shakes his hand. "Nice to see you again."

"I was just saying it's not such an exciting visit." My voice is apologetic, and she snaps to business.

"We can move things up if you'd like. It's early, but we can do the ultrasound, and I need to test for Down's and other abnormalities."

Now I'm sorry I said anything. "Why are you doing that? Do you think something's wrong?"

She pats my arm in her confident way. "Not at all. It's strictly routine. But we do have to draw blood."

My nose wrinkles. "How much?"

"Three vials. We can save that part to the end. Let's get started."

She measures my stomach and takes my blood pressure, checks my hands and feet for swelling, and declares me fit as a fiddle. Then we're off to the ultrasound room. The lights are dim, and Derek is close by my side as we prepare for the scan. We've opted for the 3D imaging, as it's the most likely to show what we're looking for.

"I've warmed the gel, so it shouldn't be uncomfortable." She spreads the clear medium across my belly and presses the probe against my skin.

We're all quiet. I'm holding my breath waiting, and then it appears—his little face all beige on the screen.

"Oh!" My heart floods along with my eyes. His features are blurry, but I'm sure he looks just like Derek. Reaching over, I pull his daddy close. Derek's eyes are shining, and he kisses me gently before turning back to the screen.

"Hang on and let me see what we can see here." Dr. Mel moves the gun lower on my pelvis pushing against my skin and turning it to the side. The image on the screen shifts and wobbles, what looks like bananas pass rapidly in front of us.

"Legs . . . umbilical cord . . ." She studies the screen, brow creased, watching. We're all fixed to the sepia-colored show. "Come on, baby . . ."

We're waiting on the edge of our seats when she finally gets the view she wants. "All right! Here we are. Can you see this area?" She circles the screen with her pen, and we nod. "This is the spot."

The probe moves almost imperceptibly against my skin and the doctor nods. "That's it. Clear as a bell."

Derek and I look at each other, and I hold my breath, waiting for his response. It's not a word. He only catches my face in both hands and covers my mouth with his.

Dr. Mel laughs as our lips part, but just as fast, he's kissing me deeply, again and again, and I can't help laughing, too.

ELAINE DECIDED WE *HAD* TO celebrate. I didn't tell her the sex—only that we knew, and she insisted on throwing a huge "Privates Unveiling" ceremony at her house. She even invited my mother.

By seven, the four of us are gathered in the Merritt-Knight kitchen raising glasses of sparkling wine in a toast. All except me, of course. I have my own personal bottle of sparkling apple cider.

"Take it easy on that stuff." Patrick teases. "You know you're a lightweight."

"I'll pace myself." I wink as I toss back the glass and wince. It's too sweet, and I'll be switching to ginger ale for my next toast.

"Your mom said to start without her. She'd already scheduled a late appointment when I called her." Elaine's at the stove stirring fast, sautéing vegetables in a wok. We're having her specialty Thai-fusion tonight because it's my favorite.

"I'm surprised you're doing all this. I thought you didn't want to know." I pick up a carrot and snap a bite off the end while I watch her work.

"No way! I have to know! How else will I plan the shower?"

"Are you feeling better? About your . . . situation?" I'd been afraid to say anything about the ultrasound since our sleepover and her big reveal. Of course, then I acknowledged she'd kill me if I stopped giving her my baby news.

"Actually, I am." Her tone switches to controlled problem-solver, a.k.a., normal Lainey. "You were right. One month is way too soon to know anything. It's also possible I was suffering from baby fever, between you and Kenny—"

"Did you say anything to Patrick?" My voice has dropped and I glance toward the living room, where Patrick and Derek seem to be having a serious conversation. They aren't listening to us, and now I'm intensely curious to find out what they *are* saying. I want to know if it's related to Derek's mood this morning.

"He's been busy wrapping up details from Baltimore, so we haven't communicated much. Outside the bedroom." She winks and lifts the wok, shaking the julienne-sliced vegetables onto a platter. Next in the wok go the long noodles.

I shake my head. "Has he told you anything about what happened?"

She stirs the noodles quickly in the vegetable stock. "He said it would be better not to tell me about it. We're not married yet, so I'm not protected by any statues."

"Lainey!" My voice is a cracked whisper. "That sounds really bad."

She shrugs, continuing to stir. "We knew it wasn't going to be good, right? They had to play dirty to find something to stick to your slimy ex."

Closing my eyes, my chin drops. My brows clutch together. "I hate this so much. I can't help feeling like it's my fault. Derek was an honorable man before he met me, a hero—"

"Hey." My friend catches my chin and lifts my eyes to hers. "You didn't make Sloan hurt you. You didn't send him to prostitutes. This is *not* your fault. And Derek *is* honorable. He's so honorable he would never let some criminal get away with hurting you like that."

Pulling my chin away, I turn back to the living room where the guys are still deep in conversation. "I was the one blind enough to marry him."

"He tricked you just like he tricked the rest of us. It's not your fault." She spoons the noodles out on top of the vegetables. "You're lucky you have a wonderful man now. One who won't back down from doing what needs to be done."

No words come to me, so I let it go. "Ready?"

"Help me set the table."

FULL STOMACHS, GLASSES OF WINE, we're all in the living room lounging around the fire when my mother joins us. She takes a glass of red and sits on the couch next to Lainey. I'm standing in front of the warm, orange glow with Derek at my side beaming.

"So how shall we do this?" I look from one expectant face to the next.

Lainey pipes up. "How about two fingers it's a girl, one finger it's a boy?"

A quick look up at Derek and he grins, giving me a wink and

a little nod.

"Okay . . . are you ready?" My hands go behind my back, and a huge smile spreads over my face.

"I think my heart is beating too fast." Mom laughs and sets her wine glass on the end table.

"Just fucking tell us, dammit!" Patrick shouts, and then his eyebrows dart up. "Shit, I'm sorry, Mrs. Jones."

"I was thinking that exact same thing, dammit!" Mom's voice is a loud reply, and we all laugh then.

Derek leans close by my head. "On three?" I nod, and he counts.

One . . .

Two . . .

. . . Elaine squeals when he pauses.

Three!

Squeezing my eyes closed, I shoot my hand out in front of me. The whole room explodes with screams, congratulations, shouts, and laughter, and Derek's arms are fast around my waist in a hug.

My arm is straight in front of me, and I'm holding up one finger.

It's a boy.

EPILOGUE

Patrick

ELAINE'S HANDS ARE PRESSED AGAINST the shelves in front of her, and she rocks her ass in a slow ride, sending my dick even deeper into her tight opening. She's so wet and beautiful. I'm in fucking heaven.

The entire group is waiting back at our place, and she insisted I drive her to the only bakery in Wilmington to get a cake "because she'd had too much wine."

Of course she knows the owner, who said we could help ourselves to the supply closet. Our excuse is needing more blue decorations. I should've known when I saw that wicked gleam in her eye it was a ruse. I didn't expect it to be no panties under the skirt that's now shoved over her backside.

Her ass is so gorgeous and soft. I span my hands over it as she rides my cock, wishing I was flexible enough to lean down and kiss it. Instead, I give her a pinch. She lets out a squeal, and I lean toward her ear.

"Shh . . ." I whisper, sliding my hands under her shirt to tease her nipples. "He'll hear."

She moans again, rocking faster when the bell on the front door sounds, and loud voices greet each other out front.

"I think we've got another minute." Elaine's voice is thick, and at this point, a minute might be all the control I've got left.

I brace the door shut with my foot, and Elaine bends forward, sending me even deeper inside her.

"Fuck me," I groan, releasing my grip on the door in favor of her hips.

Seven days—you'd think it had been seven years as insatiable as we've been since I got back from Baltimore. We've done it six times, in every room of the house, in the shower . . . I'd forgotten how fucking shitty being separated was those few weeks we tried it. I don't know how Derek and Mel have kept it up for so long.

God, Elaine is so beautiful riding my cock. She arches up against my chest, and her silky blonde hair spills all around me, surrounding me with the scent of little flowers. I slide my hands under her shirt again to circle my thumbs over her breasts, and we're laughing and groaning at how risky and fucking hot this is.

One of Elaine's long, gorgeous legs props on a shelf, and she groans. "Harder, Patrick . . ."

"Yes, ma'am." I'm banging as hard and fast as I can, and she moans louder. I cup a hand over her mouth, because dammit, she's too loud. And if she says *harder* once more, I won't be able to wait for her to finish. Her lips part, and my finger slips inside. She gives it a suck, and I almost shoot.

Her body begins to jerk, and I know from experience that's the signal. She's with me, and I can let go, ride this wave of pleasure all the way home. "Oh, god, Patrick, Oh, god!"

Both arms braced on the shelves in front of her, she pushes back, and I finish balls-deep in her hot pussy doing my best not to groan as loud as she's been doing.

"*Fuck.*" My voice is ragged as we collapse together. She's giggling again, and I've got her hugged tight against my chest. One hand's still clutching her breast.

"You're insane." She arches, turning her head to kiss me and shoving her tongue into my mouth. This fucking woman! I spin her around and kiss her good, her back is flat against the shelves now, and she's got both hands on my neck, pulling me closer.

My fingers thread in the length of her hair, and I gently pull down, breaking our kiss. "Damn, I fucking love the shit out of you."

Her green eyes sparkle. "Patrick Knight, you have a way with words."

We both laugh quietly. Elaine covers my mouth, and I hear a loud voice from out front calling our names. The voice gets closer, and we both scramble to put our clothes back in place. It would not do to get caught fucking in the back of the Sugar Plum Bakery in Wilmington. Or hell, maybe it would.

"Are you having trouble finding it?" Franklin, the owner is opening the door and pulling the cord for the light just as we're back to normal. Well, all except for the bright red marks on my fiancée's cheeks and neck where my lack of shaving scuffed her skin.

Yeah, we're pretty much busted, but Franklin pretends not to notice.

"Look, here they are." He grabs a box off the shelf right in front of Elaine and then turns, heading back up the hall to the front of the store.

We duck and laugh, stealing another kiss before following him.

"Tell Melissa 'Congratulations from Frank,' okay?" He rings up the bag of blue flowers, blue mini presents, and little blue balloons, and just before he hits *Total*, I grab two "It's a Boy" cigars from a rack by the register.

"These, also."

He nods and adds them to the bag, and in less than five minutes, we're back at the Charger. I unlock Elaine's door and hold it. She starts to get in but instead steps up on the doorframe, putting her slightly taller than me.

"What are you doing?" I laugh, but she wraps one arm around my shoulders. The other hand holds my face.

"Don't you ever leave me again, Patrick Knight." Her lips just brush mine, and dammit if this woman doesn't know how to get me going. "I get too sad. And a little loopy."

I toss the bag in behind her and grab her around the waist, pulling her even closer. "Baby, I hope I never have to leave you again."

She kisses me hard before dropping onto the car seat. "I guess that'll have to do. Now hurry up, or they'll think we're not coming back."

"Hmm . . . Mel's mom's there. We could take a detour past the beach."

"Don't you want cake?"

My eyes travel from her face down to her gorgeous legs in my car. "I'd much rather have you."

She reaches up, and I lean in for another kiss. "What did I do before I met you?"

"From what I've heard, you almost died of boredom."

"Patrick!" She pushes me back, and I laugh. "Come on!"

BACK AT THE CONDO, DEREK and I leave the ladies inside eating cake, planning showers, and talking nursery themes to step out on the back porch and smoke our stogies.

I can't resist. "So. Another little Alexander Marine on the way."

He shakes his head and looks down at the cherry. "Maybe he'll take after Melissa."

"You mean by being as stubborn as you are?" I inhale, holding the smoke in my mouth before letting it go. "Watch out USMC."

He takes another brief pull. "These aren't too bad."

"They're not too good either."

A short laugh is all I get, and I know he's not okay. From the deflection of a little military son to the shadow covering his smiles all night, I know what's bothering him. I've known it since the night we sat at that little table in the Four Seasons drinking the adrenaline away. As horny as I'd been for Elaine, I'd actually insisted we come back early for him. I've seen it before, guys forgetting why we're doing what we do. He needed to see Melissa.

Rolling the cigar in my fingers, I have an idea. "I'm headed down to Raleigh tomorrow. I need to pay Toni, and I'd planned to give her that other money as well, be sure she's okay."

He still doesn't respond, so I continue. "Heck, if she forgets Baltimore as easily as she forgot the number she pulled on me, we're fine. Want to ride along?"

That catches his attention. "Sure. What time you leaving?"

"Nine?"

He nods. "I'll be ready."

We're quiet again, watching the trees and smoking. I know he's not one to open up, but I'll give it a shot.

"You did the right thing."

He only continues staring out at the woods around us. At some point, he'll have to trust me, and I'm pretty sure after what happened, that point is now.

Plus I'm right.

"According to who." It's not a question, and disgust is clear on his face. "So I'm a fucking vigilante? How can I build a home around that? Dex deserves a better dad."

"Fuck that shit." I'm getting pissed now. "You're the most law-abiding guy I know. What happened was unavoidable. It had to be done, and you know it as well as me. You'll be the best fucking dad to that kid."

"Vigilante justice is not what America is about. We have laws and ways of doing things." He rubs the back of his neck. "I'm over here acting like the guys we fought against. What's worse is I allowed some girl to prostitute herself for it. I stood by and let her take it."

"Goddammit, stop fucking over-thinking it." Tossing the cigar on the brick floor, I grind it out with my boot. "Toni did a job. Just like she did with me. It was all business for her. You want to make it personal. Well, it's not personal. Sloan was a threat to Melissa and your son, and we handled it. Let it go."

It feels quieter after my outburst, and Derek doesn't reply. We're back to looking out at the trees, not speaking. Only now the cicadas have started, so it's not completely silent.

The door slides open, and we both turn at once. It's Melissa, looking ethereal in her thin white top. It's loose to allow her body to grow, and her dark hair hangs in waves over her shoulders. She really does look like a fucking angel.

"Hey." Her voice is soft. "I hate to break up the pow-wow, but I'm getting tired."

Derek's at her side like he's about to carry her to the car if need be. I guess I shouldn't judge him too hard, since I'm probably the same damn way about Elaine.

"I'll pick you up in the morning." I say as they head back inside. He gives me a small nod, and I look back out at the trees. I might be the younger partner, but tonight, I feel years older.

MY PARTNER'S MOOD HASN'T IMPROVED when I pick him up for the drive to Raleigh. He's quiet and brooding, and I can't help wondering if Melissa's noticed the change.

She hadn't seemed concerned when she told him goodbye this morning. The weather's gotten warmer, and she'd followed him out wearing a smile and one of his dress shirts over her bikini.

"Elaine's coming over later, right?" She'd asked me.

I've got to get Derek's head back in the game. Melissa's too cute with her baby belly just starting to extend for him to be so distracted. "Yeah, she was getting ready when I left."

She nods and catches Derek's arm. "You guys don't be gone all day, okay?"

"We'll be back by three." I call to her before climbing in the car.

Derek pulls her close, and I start the engine. Once we're on the road, and he's scrolling on his phone, I test the waters.

"Good night?"

He only nods without looking up.

"Checking on the office?"

That at least makes him speak. "Mel and I've decided to split the weeks on Wednesday. We'll head back to Princeton in a few days, then we'll be back next week."

"How long you plan to keep that up?"

He goes back to whatever he's doing. "As long as we need to."

I give him another glance then just say it. "I've been monitoring the police scanner. They found the body."

Derek's eyes cut to me. "I know."

"I figured you were keeping tabs. Looks like it's going just like we'd hoped. The media hasn't been alerted. Company executives are sitting on it."

My partner's mouth forms a straight line. "For now. I'll be curious to see if they can pull it off."

"I bet they do. Reynolds Corp doesn't want that juicy scandal getting out to their shareholders *or* their competitors." My grip on the wheel flexes then relaxes. "You're all good. The police know what he was doing there. That scene had hook-up gone wrong written all over it."

"As long as they don't decide to pursue it."

"They won't. We cleaned it up too well. There's nothing to pursue."

He's quiet again, that darkness back. I know he doesn't want to talk, so I switch on the music and let it fill the space for our drive south.

THE WOMAN WHO GREETS US at the Skinniflute is not the Toni Durango I'd expected. Instead of being back in her usual biker gear of hotpants, jet-black tease and velvet-red lipstick, she's maintained the light-brown waves. She's wearing a modest dress, and she actually looks somewhat professional, despite her inked-up arms.

"I figured you earned this." I slide the large brown envelope across the table to her. "It's a grand extra. That should give you a boost."

She picks it up, and for a few moments she seems nervous—a first.

"I was thinking . . ." Her voice is a little higher as opposed to the usual smoky deep. Dark eyes flicker from me to Derek. "I might try going to community college. See if I can be a secretary for real. Or maybe a police dispatcher."

The shift in my partner's demeanor is almost palpable. "Sounds like a good plan."

Satisfaction shines in Toni's face, and I have to blink twice. *Did I miss something?*

"I thought . . . since I have some experience doing undercover work, I might try working my way into criminal justice. Maybe I can help there."

I'm nodding, wondering how that might play out exactly, but Derek is more than encouraging. "If you need a reference or have questions, let me know. Here's my card."

She takes the thin rectangle, and holds it, staring at it a few moments. "The way you handled that guy . . . I guess I saw not everybody in this business is perfect. All it takes is having your heart in the right place."

My partner shifts in his chair, and I'm not sure her words have the intended effect.

He clears his throat. "You shouldn't use me as a role model."

Her eyes flash up at him, and I can tell she's confused. "You're saying you did something wrong?"

"Yes. I did."

"I don't know that I agree with you. I was on the receiving end of that guy, and you gave him what he deserved."

Derek shakes his head. "That's not how our country is supposed to work. And if you do go into criminal justice, you'll see why I'm right."

She scoots forward in her seat and reaches across to grab his arm. I lean back and watch this play out.

"I know you don't trust me. Hell, why should you? But you're a good man. So you did something questionable. I know why you did it—it was to protect me. And her."

"And what would she say if she knew the whole story?"

"Don't tell her." Toni releases his arm and straightens in her seat. "If you love her, you won't let her take that blame on her shoulders."

His eyes go to hers, and he's frowning. "Blame for what?"

"For being the reason you did it."

The two of them regard each other a few moments in silence. I can tell that statement had an impact, and I'll be damned if Toni doesn't have real potential in some legitimate field. What the fuck it'll be, I don't know, but I'm impressed.

Standing, I drop a few bills on the table. "It's after noon. We'd better take off if we plan to be home by three."

Derek studies her a bit longer. "Good luck to you. You're pretty tough."

"Mata Hari." She stands and follows us to the door.

I stop before leaving and give her a hug. "Thanks, girl."

Derek holds out his hand, and she gives it a shake.

Then she holds it a beat longer. "I won't let my past get me down if you don't."

His lips tighten, and then he nods. "Thanks."

THE GIRLS ARE CAMPED OUT on the side porch when we

get back. They don't see us, and I take the chance to try one last time. "You going to be okay?"

He lets out an exhale and looks out the windshield toward the house, were Melissa and Elaine are sitting on the small couch just inside the breezy anteroom.

"I will be."

"Listen, what you did was wrong, it was illegal, but dammit, somebody had to stop that prick."

"That doesn't make it okay."

Looking toward the place where the girls are sitting, I exhale. "Sometimes it does. It's like when we're in battle and lives are lost. It's for the ultimate good."

He doesn't respond for a few moments, and I think it's possible I finally found the right combination of words to help him see how he can still be a hero.

When he speaks again, his voice is reflective. "At some point, I'm going to have to tell her the whole story."

I take a quarter out of the console and put it on the back of my hand. "Maybe."

Derek watches as I turn the coin slowly over my knuckles, thinking. A few more passes, and I say it. "I think you should give it some time. See if it can go into that place we have to put things like this."

He leans forward and rubs his face with both hands then he looks at his palms a moment. He turns them over and closes his fingers in a fist. "At some point she'll have to know. She'll have to decide if she can forgive me. If she wants to be with someone like me."

"Mel will never turn on you." I can't help a laugh. "She might turn on me. I was supposed to stop you."

He's still contemplative, so I clap his shoulder. "Just do like I said for now. Sleep on it. Give it time. Don't burden her with the worry. Enjoy your wife and son."

That's as far as we get before Melissa sees us and comes bursting through the door. "Derek!" She's running, and her face is beaming. I can't imagine what she's about to say. "I found it! I found it!"

She laughs, and he steps out just in time to catch her as she jumps, spinning them both in her excitement. Elaine follows her and walks around the car to give me a hug. I kiss her head, completely preoccupied by what Melissa's about to say.

Derek holds her waist, and he doesn't seem as bewildered as I'd expect. She pulls her hand from behind her back, and an item I recognize all too well drops down, dangling from her fist.

"Tah daah!" She swings the gold chain with the floating heart in the air then bounces up to catch him around the neck again. "Can you believe it?"

He hugs her back, and I watch his eyes close slowly. "Where was it?"

My brow lines. I fucking know where it was as well as he does—and who had it—but it's clear my partner is working an angle.

Melissa pops back again. "In the cushions of that damn couch! As many times as I tore it apart. I can't believe it was there all the time!"

"I'm so happy." His voice is low, and he puts both hands on the sides of her head, smoothing her hair back with his thumbs. I never got the whole story on why that particular item of jewelry made him snap in Baltimore. I probably never will.

"You guys coming over tonight?" Elaine walks around to her car. "I'll follow Patrick back. I want to shower."

She gives me a little wink, and I'm ready to let Derek and Melissa ride off into the sunset. It's time for Elaine and me to get dirty while getting clean.

"Yes!" Melissa turns to us. Derek's hands are on her shoulders. "Oh, and Patrick?"

I squint back at her. "Yeah?"

"Thank you."

I tip two fingers at my forehead and give her a little salute. "I'm the Guard, baby. Protection is what I do best."

She gives me a smile, and even Derek's expression softens. They're going to be fine. In that moment, I'm confident we all are.

ONE TO SAVE

DEREK & MELISSA

BOOK 3

TIA LOUISE

Some threats come at you as friendly fire.

Some threats take away everything.

Family won't let you go down without a fight.

The Secret isn't as secure as Derek's team originally thought it was, and a person on the inside of Alexander-Knight is set on exposing him, breaking him, and taking away all he holds dear.

Refusing to let anyone suffer for his crimes, Derek takes matters into his own hands. He's exposed, he's defenseless, but his friends are determined to save him.

A STAND-ALONE, ONE TO HOLD NOVEL. Adult Contemporary Romance: Due to strong language and sexual content, this book is not intended for readers under the age of 18.

For Mr. TL, always.
And for Derek & Melissa fans everywhere:
another sexy, exciting adventure for you to enjoy.

♥

ONE

GAMES

Melissa

IN THE COOL DARKNESS OF the semi-crowded bar, I study the glass in front of me and consider my journey, how many steps I've taken in the last two years, how far I've come. Memories of my old life fade like smoke in a glass. The shame that held me so tightly now dances at the edges of my mind like the whisper of a bad dream, a flicker of shadows that no longer make sense in my world.

Young women in shiny slip dresses twist and laugh on the dance floor, but instead of resentment, my lips curl into a smile. My old self—cynical, bitter, defeated—is a memory I have to work hard to recall. These days I could dance all night with them, but I'd rather spend my energy on other things.

The slim glass holds a pale amber liquid, and I can't resist taking a sip. An involuntary wince pinches my eyes as I put it down. Seven and seven. Refreshing citrus dragged down by the heavy undertone of whiskey. *So gross.*

Sliding my palms over my thighs, I realize my outfit isn't much different from the girls' on the dance floor. The deep red silk is fitted at my waist, and drapes loosely over my torso. My long, dark hair is swept over one shoulder revealing a thin spaghetti strap. I lightly touch the delicate gold chain around my neck leading to the floating heart pendant that sits between my collarbones, and light glances off the thick gold cuff on my wrist.

Unlike that night almost two years ago, I'm alone. My best friend Elaine is miles away with her new husband, most likely indulging in that blissful honeymoon period of early marriage. Make that, most *certainly* indulging. I know those two well.

No, I came by myself to this bar in Princeton after finishing my business with a client in town. My infant son is in Wilmington, spending the weekend with his grandmother. Studying my hands, I admire the deep blue sapphire ring on my finger, but I have no wedding band.

At thirty-two, I'm an unmarried mother of a beautiful little boy, and I wouldn't change a thing . . . Yet. The tiny silver scar at my hairline reminds me of what a bad marriage looks like, and with my successful marketing business and the gorgeous cottage at the beach I own, I'm satisfied with my life. Calm, not desperate. I'll take my next steps deliberately, with certainty.

All these thoughts preoccupy my mind when I blink up and catch him watching me from across the square-shaped bar. Blue eyes, strikingly blue because of the way they stand out beneath his dark brow, coupled with collar-length thick dark hair.

He's massive, at least six-two, and elegantly dressed with a thick stainless watch on his wrist. I can spot his type a mile away—rich, powerful, accustomed to getting what he wants. I can't deny the hum his gaze sets off under my skin. *I know what he wants.*

Catching my lip in my teeth to stop my grin, I know what I want, too, and it's no coincidence I happened to look up at that exact moment to meet his stare. Still, I'll make him work for it.

He starts to move, his eyes never leaving mine. I don't look away either. Thick cords of muscle ripple beneath the thin black sweater he wears as he glides past the oblivious patrons talking and laughing. Some are more animated than others, waving their arms and putting their drinks in peril.

Yellow lights hidden in the recesses above the bar illuminate rows of liquor bottles in all colors and shapes. Glasses hanging upside down above also catch the flickering light. It's a raucous atmosphere, but this man and I are in our own secret place of longing and desire.

As he rounds the final corner, and I see him in full, my breath quickens. My eyes drift from his broad shoulders to his narrow waist, grey slacks and black shoes, then back up just as he reaches me. A close beard shadows his face, and the muscles low in my pelvis tighten at the thought of how it feels brushing the soft skin of my inner thighs.

"Can I buy you a drink?" The low vibration of his voice touches every part of me, and the intoxicating hint of his cologne surrounds me.

Casually, I motion to the glass. "I have this." My voice is softer and higher compared to his.

"You don't like it." A tease twinkles in his eyes, and I almost forget my line.

"How can you tell?"

He leans in close, "You make a face every time you sip it. I've been watching you."

Soft lips graze my skin, and I catch his forearm to steady myself. "Why?"

The tables have turned, it seems, and now I have to work to stay focused. My body is like a spoiled child accustomed to instant gratification, and my insides are clenching, demanding him.

He straightens and clears his throat. "Maybe I should introduce myself. Derek Alexander."

I slide my noticeably smaller hand across his large palm. "Melissa Jones."

"A last name, Miss Jones?" A sexy grin curls his small nose, and a million pornographic memories flood my mind of that nose nudging into my dark spaces, those lips plundering areas of my body he knows will drive me wild as I moan and twist in white sheets, my fingers threading in his dark hair.

Clearing the thickness in my throat, I say under my breath, "I messed up."

His fingers close over mine. "Sweet Melissa, that's impossible."

At once I remember, and I take back my hand. "I'm not so sweet."

"Let's skip the cava." His eyes are dark, but I'm back to coy. "Aren't we celebrating?"

"We can celebrate after I show you the stars."

"Where exactly are you planning to do this star gazing?"

"I have the key to a condo just across the street. It has a private balcony."

For a moment, I consider how intimidating this mountain of sex standing in front of me is. At the same time, I've never felt afraid. Thrilling anticipation, yes, but never fear. "Why do you have a key?"

"Because I used to live there."

"That sounds dangerous." My elbow is in his firm grip, and I allow him to help me off my barstool. Even in my tall stiletto heels, my head only reaches the top of his shoulder.

"I'll keep you safe."

"You're not safe." My voice is a low purr.

Straight white teeth are revealed with his smile. "And you're not sweet."

DEREK'S CONDO HASN'T CHANGED—SPARE, LITTLE to no accessories on the very masculine furnishings, which are dark with stainless accents. It's all hardwood and straight lines. A massive flat-screen television hangs on the wall above the gas fireplace. Only a few low lights are on. The air surrounding us on the balcony is slightly chilled, but it can't compete with the blazing heat flooding my thighs as he holds me against the secluded outside wall.

He lifts me as if I were a doll, and our mouths open and move together, tongues touching, breaths mingling. With every kiss our panting grows faster. As many times as we've been here, the tension could be visible it's still so hot.

"You wore red," he groans moving to my jaw, tightening my stomach muscles. "You're beautiful in red."

The hem of my dress is pushed all the way to my waist, and his large hands grip my bare ass. My fingers slide into the sides of his hair, and I pull his face back to mine, consuming his mouth. His teeth pull my bottom lip before he moves to my temple, inhaling deeply the side of my hair.

"I don't do this," I gasp, still playing the game. "One night stands are incredibly risky and dangerous."

My legs are around him, and he jerks my thong aside. "I won't tell anyone."

A moan scrapes my throat as he invades my core, testing my wetness with two large fingers as his thumb circles my clit.

"Oh, god . . ." He knows just how to touch me, and the metallic *Clink!* of his belt meets my ears.

Anticipation tightens my stomach, and opening my hazy eyes, I catch his reflection in the large mirror facing us from the guest bedroom. His slacks drop around his thighs, and the dim light highlights the planes of his ass.

"Mmm . . ." I slide my hand from his shoulder down, leaning into him so I can clutch that perfect muscle.

Just then he thrusts into me. We both moan loudly. He's so big, it's always a surprise. Flexing my thighs, I push myself higher, catching his shoulders so I can ride him. The movement slams my clit directly against his pelvis, driving him deeper into me.

"Shit, Melissa," he gasps.

He's always the lead, the aggressor, but tonight, I feel power-ful. Our little pretense helped me remember how far I've come since the days when I was the victim. That time is over. I sur-vived, and now I am strong.

He clutches my hips, jerking me forcefully against him. "Fucking amazing." It's the same movement only now he's in charge, and he's right. It is amazing.

"Oh, don't stop!" I cry. He's driving deeper, hitting me hard-er, and we truly let go, riding the waves, oblivious to our shouts and moans of pleasure. It's a privilege that's become less fre-quent now that our little son is old enough to be disturbed by us.

My back is pressed against the rough fabric of the patio drapes, and I look again at his body in the mirror. His ass flex-es as he drives into me, over and over. It's erotic, and the sight combined with the friction of our touch, the force of his move-ments, has me dancing on the edge. One last thing—I reach around to unfasten my bra and arch up. His lips clamp firmly on my beaded nipple, and with a tender bite, I fly over the edge.

"Oh, god!" My orgasm shatters my core. He doesn't stop, and in three more hard thrusts, my entire lower body is shud-dering. I'm coming again, and the intensity of the pleasure radi-ates under my scalp. "Oh, god, Derek."

He keeps going. His forehead is at my brow, and I notice the faint sheen of sweat touching his lip. Pulling forward, I run my tongue over it, pulling it between my teeth as he sinks deeper.

With a flick of his chin, he consumes my mouth, and the moan of his orgasm fills me. His body tenses as he takes one last, slow thrust.

Salt is on my tongue as I hold him. His arms surround me, and his kisses move to my neck. We're locked in an embrace, our bodies touching everywhere, as we melt together. It's the most intense satisfaction combined with such familiar comfort.

"I love you so much," I whisper.

Slowly he kisses me again. "I love you more." A gentle suck, a light nibble at my jaw. His lips sweep my cheek before our eyes meet. "Happy anniversary."

Smiling, I trace my fingers along his beard. "Our anniversary is in the fall."

"It's our mid-year anniversary."

"It's spring. That time when men's thoughts lightly turn to—"

His sexy grin is irresistible. "What I've been thinking about all winter."

We both laugh, and he slips out of me. My lips poke in a pretend sad face, but I lower my legs to stand in front of him. "I'll freshen up. You owe me a cava."

As I step through the balcony door, he playfully lands a *Slap!* on my bare backside. "Don't be long. I'm not finished with you Miss Jones."

Shaking my head, I make my way through the large master suite. It's practically empty since Derek's been with me full-time in Wilmington almost a year. Stuart Knight, his original business partner and Patrick's older brother, briefly lived here before getting his own place—the identical condo across the hall. The only personal items left are a photo of us together on the beach and a new one of me holding Dex.

Stopping, I lift the small frame. Derek took it of us, and my love for him glows on my face. I'm looking up at the camera, and our son is holding my shoulders. His big blue eyes, more the color of mine than his daddy's, gaze out at the ocean.

Warmth stirs behind me, and two strong arms wrap around my waist. "Miss him?" Derek's voice is at my ear. His chin rests on my shoulder.

Turning my head, I kiss his cheek. "I do, but I'm glad we have this weekend."

"Me too." He kisses the top of my shoulder before releasing me. "Meet me in the kitchen?"

"Be right there." Setting the frame down, I step into the bathroom to quickly clean up. My thong is ruined. "I should buy these in bulk," I mutter under my breath.

Returning to the bedroom, I pull open the top drawer that was designated as mine when we lived apart. A few outfits and luckily, panties are still here. I'm refreshed and joining him seconds later.

"Do you think we should still keep this place? It feels like bad luck."

He's just finished pouring two slim flutes of cava. His lined torso is on full display, and the recessed light under the bar casts shadows, making the cut of his muscles appear even deeper. *Sigh.*

"It's good that I have somewhere to crash when I'm in town. If I need to check in at the office."

I take the glass he hands me and sip the crisp, sparkling wine. "I'm sure Stuart wouldn't mind if you stayed in his guest room the few times you come here."

His dark brow creases. "With Mariska sleeping over? That's not very considerate."

"Hmm." My thoughts travel to the beautiful girl who only recently captured his stubborn partner's heart. "I guess you have a point."

"Besides, I like my place. Walter takes care of things, and if we need a quick getaway, we don't have to deal with hotels and luggage . . ."

"Yes, I'd miss Walter." The friendly doorman-slash-butler is like a doting grandfather to all of us. "I'm convinced. For now."

With a grin he kisses my forehead. "How was Aunt Bea?"

"Lovely as always. She's sending you a box of her recommendations for your groom's cake." He smiles, but as he turns, I see that shadow in his eyes again. Lately I've been seeing it more and more.

"Is that a problem?" I nudge.

He's back with me in a blink, shadow gone. "The only problem will be trying to pick one."

It's not a satisfactory answer, and I take another slow sip as I watch him thumbing through takeout menus. "Hungry?"

He nods, still flipping. "Nothing here looks good."

"Walter could order something. I'm sure he knows what you like."

Steel blue eyes flicker to mine, and he's hesitating, holding something back. It's confusing after the way we just made love. Everything about the way he's been acting these last weeks has been confusing. One moment he's with me, the next he's distracted, and it always happens when I start talking wedding plans. Derek has never been mercurial, and I'm trying not to let it spook me.

My visceral reaction is to remember how quickly Sloan went from doting fiancé to cheating and later, abusive husband. But Derek's not Sloan, my heart argues. I know he's not, yet I shudder remembering how Derek has kept secrets from me before. How we originally met because Sloan had hired him to track me—a fact I never knew until I found the emails on my ex-husband's laptop.

"I think I'll take the car and see what I can find," he says. Scooping his black sweater off the couch, he leans forward to kiss my mouth briefly. "Sure you don't want anything?"

I watch as he straightens and pulls the thin material down his bare chest. He's still wearing his black loafers. "I ate so much cake this afternoon with Bea, I might burst if I eat another thing."

With a wink, he's headed to the door. "When I get back, we'll see about working off those extra calories."

Despite the tension, I can't help smiling at his suggestion. "If I'm still awake."

"I seem to recall you like the way I wake you."

He's out the door before I can make another quip. It's probably for the best. He's right, after all. I do love the way he wakes me, especially when he starts with slow, lingering kisses below my waist.

Warmth curls my toes and I sigh. "Oh, Derek. What are you hiding now?"

TWO

THREATS

Derek

I'M NOT HUNGRY. MANEUVERING MY black Audi through the empty streets of Princeton, I pass under traffic lights blinking yellow, block after block, taking me further away from what I have to do. I've never run from a problem, but the reasons driving me on are inescapable.

They're a woman who smells like roses mixed with the ocean, who fulfills me in a way nothing else does, and a little boy with round, sapphire eyes just like hers. My fiancée. My son. The second-chance I thought I'd never have that dropped in my lap one week in the desert. The future I could lose just as fast.

Gripping the steering wheel, images trickle from the corners of my brain—a dark conference room, Patrick and me cramped in the adjacent tech booth, fighting with all my strength. On the other side of the glass is our target. He's holding a woman—our bait—by the throat, strangling the life out of her while he hisses his poison in her face.

Star's cheeks go from red to purple as he grips her, and the sound of her sniffs, her nose running as her life is twisted from her body, is a noise that still ignites an explosion of rage in my chest. *He touched Melissa that way . . .*

The necklace was the final nail in his coffin. When that fucker pulled it out, holding it for all of us to see, I knew I didn't have a choice. He'd been in her cottage and taken it from her somehow. She didn't even know he'd done it.

I'm at the Alexander-Knight building. I don't remember driving here, but I park the car near the front entrance and kill the engine. That night is like a dream. With one word, *Sangria*, Patrick released me. The shock and recognition barely registered on Sloan's sick face before I had him in my hands.

Closing my eyes, I can still feel his wretched skull against my palms. No hesitation. Immediate action. The satisfying *Crack!* of his fucking neck as I twisted it echoes in my brain. In one motion, I ended his threat to my family forever, then I stood over his dead body and smiled, the warmth of satisfaction flooding my veins like hot liquid.

I have to tell her. I have to do it before the wedding. It's not like she loved the guy. It's not like she probably didn't wish him dead. It's not like he didn't beat her, leave her with that scar at her hairline . . . My jaw clenches so hard at the memory of the photograph she showed me. Her beautiful blue eyes rimmed in ugly purple bruises, the jagged cut extending into her scalp, gaping open like a blood-red mouth. A tiny silver line is all that's left to remind us what he did to her, yet the memory of him hurting her that way . . . I've never felt such consuming wrath.

I'm breathing too fast. I need to get out and think. I need to calm down and clear my head. I walk under the security lamps to the obelisk fountain in the center of our courtyard. It's cool out, but not frigid. Spring is breaking all over, and the fresh scent of new growth fills the air.

Dropping onto a nearby bench, I lean forward and jam my hands in the sides of my hair. I know why this is so hard. Lowering them, I study my palms. With malice aforethought, I placed my palms on the sides of Sloan Reynolds's head and murdered him. It wasn't wartime. He wasn't an enemy combatant. He wasn't even coming at me with a weapon.

I charged out of that tech booth with one thing on my mind, and I walked straight up to him and snapped his neck like a twig. Then I stood over him and allowed the sick satisfaction of what I'd done to wash over me like some fucking psychopath. I reveled in that revenge. I drank it in like the finest Scotch.

How can I tell her that? It's a side of me Melissa has never seen. It's a dark and brutal part I'm not sure she could love. It's useful in combat, but it doesn't make me proud. Clearly, I can't even control it.

Patrick, Toni . . . or Star, and I have never talked about it directly. None of us has ever named what I did. We only reference it sideways. It's our secret. The variable we didn't plan for. The thing we're all so ready to sweep under the rug and forget.

Patrick's position is to walk away. He and Star both say it was justice, and telling Melissa will only make her blame herself. For a little while it worked. I'd believed my only reason for keeping it from her was to protect her from somehow adopting the blame for my actions.

Time has pulled the curtain back on that half-truth. Protecting Melissa is only part of why I can't tell her. The other part is much more basic, more black and white. In one moment of authoritarian rage, I turned my back on everything I believed, everything I dedicated my life to defend. I sank all the way to his level that night. I became the monster I killed.

With a growl, I clench my fists, and I know with painful certainty Melissa won't understand. How could she? Over and over she begged me to put it behind us. She wanted to move on and be stronger than her past, and now I've chained us to it forever.

No statute of limitations applies to what I've done. I didn't simply take the law into my own hands, I put our family in jeopardy. I'm a felon, a murderer. No matter how many years go by, how far we get from that night, how old we are or how much she might need me, if I'm ever discovered, I'll go to prison.

Depending on the circumstances, I could get the death penalty.

"Fuck." Pushing against my thighs, I stand, staring out across the courtyard. "He deserved it," I try, but the words ring hollow.

Who the fuck am I to decide what anyone deserves? When did I buy into vigilante justice? I'm a Marine. I took an oath. I trained as a cop. Everything I've ever done has been to uphold the laws of this country. I put my life on the line over and over to defend our way of life, yet in one moment, I turned my back on all of it.

I'm no anarchist. I'm an American hero. At least, I was.

"Melissa . . . Melissa." Closing my eyes, I say her name like a prayer for forgiveness. Will she forgive me? Will she understand?

I killed a man in cold blood with the very hands I use to touch her . . . with the same hands I use to hold our son.

"God dammit!" My shout echoes off the concrete walls, and I know what has to happen. I have to look what I've done in the face. She has to know the truth and decide if she's willing to live this life with me. If she can marry me knowing what's hanging over our heads.

If she wants me to turn myself in, I will. If she can't love me anymore . . . *Shit*. I can't even think that.

Either way, I have to say it out loud to the one person who makes everything real, and I have to do it soon.

———❤———

WHEN I RETURN TO THE condo, I've mentally prepared myself to say it, and she's in my bed asleep. Lying on her side, curled in her familiar sleeping position, I can't bring myself to wake her. It would ruin her night, and a few more hours won't make a difference.

Climbing in beside her, I pull her into my arms. As always, she melts into me as if she belongs there.

She always belongs there.

Since that first night in Scottsdale, I've known she belongs to me. Yet . . . that night I'd been hired by her husband to watch her. Is it possible the wheels I set in motion, taking her instead of doing my job, doomed us from the start?

Pressing my face into her hair I inhale deeply, allowing her scent to relax my mind. These thoughts will drive me crazy if I let them. Sloan tricked me as much as everyone else, and my role in this has always been to save her from him.

Still, my mind can't let it go. How will our beginning appear to a jury? I can only imagine how a prosecutor will take our situation and run with it. I've worked on prosecution teams. Shit, I'd been the key witness in the case against Slayde Bennett. They'll crucify me.

I followed her to Scottsdale, seduced her, then killed her ex-husband.

It would drag all of Melissa's past out of the closet and expose it to intense media scrutiny. She once called Sloan her humiliating truth, and now thanks to me, it could all be put on display for the world to see. The beatings, the prostitutes . . . adultery, murder. It's a sensational, juicy story. The press would eat it up.

Tightening my hold on her, I hug her to me as my chest collapses. The weight of the position I've placed her in destroys me.

When morning finally rolls around, I'm exhausted from wrestling with my thoughts all night. Melissa's still asleep, so I slip out of bed and go to the kitchen for coffee. Just as I've sat down, my phone buzzes. Stuart.

"What's got you out of bed so early," I ask.

His voice sounds surprised. "I was planning to leave a message."

"Now you don't have to. What's going on?"

He clears his throat, and it sounds as if he's been wrestling with his thoughts all night as well. "Nikki gave her notice on Friday."

My brow rises. Not what I expected. "Didn't you just get

back to the office?"

"Yeah. She said she only stayed to keep things running until I came back."

She could've told me, I think but don't say. "What's her reason?"

A soft voice sounds in the background on his end, and I hear a brush over the phone as he answers what I assume is Mariska. A few moments pass before he returns to the line.

"Hey, I can't really talk about this now. I'd rather discuss it Monday. Suffice to say, it's because of something I did."

Shit. Nikki has never been one of my favorite employees, and I'm ready to let her go without a fight until he says those words.

"You've been in Saudi three years. You were in the office in Princeton a week. Now you're with Mariska. What the hell could you have done?"

"When I get to the office Monday, I'll call and explain." His tone has an urgency that makes me relent.

"Fine. Monday. Enjoy your weekend."

We end the call, and I sit back to think as I sip my coffee. I can only find one reason why Stuart would call me early on a Sunday morning to discuss Nikki resigning, and that reason is Mariska. He doesn't want her to know. She should've been asleep, which leads me to believe it has something to do with sex.

I can't believe it. Stuart is as committed to professionalism and following a code of conduct at work as I am. At the same time, when he came back from Saudi, he was addicted to narcotic painkillers and basically hitting rock bottom. Patrick and I feared he might take his life.

As much as I can't imagine Stuart crossing a line, I can't imagine Nikki suing us. The lion's share of her duties has been working with me, and I've always treated her with respect. She and Melissa are close . . . Still, I know she carried a torch for my partner for years, and when he got back, well, he didn't go to her. Mariska had been the woman to heal him.

Finishing my coffee, I stand and walk to the sink. I'll figure out this problem, solve it, and return to handling my shit. I'm just passing the table when my phone buzzes again. Patrick. *Isn't anybody sleeping this morning?*

"Why the hell aren't you in bed with your wife? You're supposed to be in your fucking honeymoon period."

"We've got a situation." My younger partner's usual cocky greeting is absent, his tone tense. "Will you be back tonight?"

"We'll probably leave in about an hour. Melissa needs to pick up Dex at her mother's—"

"Toni called. She's in trouble." My chest tightens at his words. This fucking snowball just keeps getting bigger. "It's better if we discuss it in private, but it can't wait."

"I'll drop Melissa off and head over as soon as we get in."

"Meet me at the satellite office in town."

Disconnecting, I notice Melissa has joined me. She's standing at the large windows gazing out over downtown. Based on her expression, I know she's curious about my early calls. Melissa is one of the smartest people I know, and the fact I've been able to keep my shit from her so long blows my mind.

"Everything okay?" She gives me a little smile, and dammit, she's so beautiful. Her dark waves ripple over her shoulders, and she's wearing a satin pajama top that displays her long, smooth legs.

I can't tell her what Patrick said, so I say what I can. "Stuart called. Nikki gave her notice Friday."

Her mouth drops open. "Nikki loves working for you guys! What happened?"

"I'm not sure. Stuart's only been in Princeton a week, but apparently there's a story."

Crossing her arms, I can see her brain working behind those beautiful blue eyes. "It doesn't make any sense. Nikki was excited he was coming back. She managed to work it into nearly every text or email she sent me leading up to his arrival." Quiet settles over us, her eyes slowly move to mine. Despite all my conflict, warmth spreads across my chest. Stepping closer, I slide my hands over her hips, around her waist.

"Are you going to let her go?" she asks softly.

"Stuart will have to make that decision." Pulling her closer, I drop my chin and take a deep inhale at the top of her head. Ocean roses. "I know you like her, but trust me. Nikki can be a challenge as a secretary."

Her arms are still crossed, and I can tell by her tone, she's not buying it. "That explains why Stuart might fire her. Why would *she* quit?"

"I'll know tomorrow."

"So you're going to talk to her about it?" Arms uncrossed, she returns my embrace at last. I love holding her this way. I love her holding onto me.

"I'll talk to Stuart first. He couldn't discuss it in front of Mariska."

Again she's quiet, thinking. "You think this has something to do with Mariska?"

I exhale and kiss her head. "If it were Patrick, I'd say yes without hesitation, but Stuart's different. He keeps it in his pants."

Pulling back, she barely hides her surprise. "You think he slept with Nikki?"

"I'm not jumping to any conclusions. The reason Stuart and I agreed to start this firm is because of how alike we are. If something happened, my guess is it was before he left the last time."

"He wasn't planning to come back."

I nod, remembering the night he left. He was pretty jazzed about going overseas. I left him and Nikki alone together at the bar. "Three years is a long time to keep a secret," I say, thinking out loud.

Her eyes narrow, and I realize I've given her an opening. "Even three months is a long time."

One problem at a time. I turn my gaze out the window and watch the bright green trees swaying in the early spring breeze. "Sometimes people have reasons for keeping quiet."

THREE

SECRETS

Melissa

LOUD, IMPATIENT SQUEALS ECHO FROM Dex's room down the hall, forcing my eyes open. Looking around our bedroom, I see no signs of his father. He'd been late again last night after meeting with Patrick, and I wouldn't have known he was back if he hadn't pulled me into his arms in the darkness.

Our son is only playfully complaining, so I take a moment to reflect on last night. It's the second time in a row I've gone to bed alone. Combined with Derek's increasing withdrawal, it's getting to be more than I can take.

Last night, when his strong arms circled my waist, pulling my back against his chest, it wasn't like his usual embrace. His face moved into my hair, against my neck. "Melissa . . ." His voice cracked in a low whisper against my skin.

He hadn't been trying to wake me, yet the sound of that break tightened my throat. Anxiety moved across my chest, and I slid my palms down his forearms to entwine our fingers.

Sensitivity to my environment is a skill I learned the hard way during my final months in Sloan's mansion. I'd slept with a can of pepper spray clutched beneath my pillow, all my senses on alert against any changes as I slept.

Only one thing has ever scared Derek, according to him, and that "thing," that threat—my ex-husband—has been dealt with. How exactly, I still don't know, but I believe Derek's words. So if Sloan is no longer a threat, what's tormenting my love?

I whispered his name in the darkness. Clutching our hands, he wrapped them around my waist as his mouth moved to the top of my shoulder. My head dropped back against him, and we held each other several long, quiet moments, our hearts beating together, our bodies touching head to toe. We were home, our son was in his bed asleep, we were together. What could be wrong?

Releasing one of his hands, I reached up to thread my fingers into the side of his thick hair. I knew how to ease his tension. I wanted to ease his tension.

The climate in Wilmington is warmer than Princeton, so I only sleep in a thin cami and panties. His large hands spanned my bare stomach, tightening my muscles. Derek's touch is a delicious mixture of gentle and rough. Soft lips, scruff of beard; smoothing hands, firm grip. From the first night we were together, his touch has always made me hotter, wetter than I've ever been with anyone.

Shrugging off my lace underwear, my eyes don't open as he parts my thighs. His thick erection sinks deep into me, stretching me. "Oh, god," I gasp. It's so good.

Arching my back to allow him further access, another soft moan scrapes from my throat as his expert fingers find my clit.

Quiet words of desire, love, and appreciation rumble across my skin, and my mouth opens to release another little cry as I buck against him. Pleasure snakes up my thighs. He goes deeper, his length massaging my tightening insides.

I want it harder, and I tell him so. He's quick to comply. Large hands grip my breasts, and we're working together, meeting each other thrust for thrust. Moving faster, gasping and grinding, our bodies tense as we reach the crest of orgasm.

"Come, Melissa." It's a low order I don't need.

I'm riding him as the pleasure lifts me out of myself. A quivering little wail comes from me as he clutches my thighs so hard, I'm sure he'll leave a mark. We ride our orgasm to the end, moaning and trembling, then holding each other, breathing hard.

"I love you so much," he exhales against my skin, yet even in the sparkling afterglow, that tone is still in his voice.

My chest clenches. I don't understand. "I love you more," I whisper back, stealing his usual line as I tighten my grip on him.

He doesn't speak. His arms never loosen their hold. His lips touch the back of my neck, followed by the scratch of his beard. Derek's arms are always a safe place for me—they have been since our first night in the desert. He's sexy, wildly passionate, and deeply safe, the most erotic combination my guarded heart could desire. Whatever's bothering him, I know we can fix it. Our love hasn't changed. The thought comforts me as I drift to sleep again.

Sometime before dawn, my eyes open and he's still holding me. My back is against his chest, and I'm tight in the confines of his strong arms as if I might slip away while he sleeps. I've become so used to it, I practically have to relearn how to sleep alone when he travels, which is rare nowadays.

A more insistent squeal from Dex brings me back to the present. It's time to start the day. Dragging myself out of bed and staggering down the hall, I catch a glimpse of my fiancé in the kitchen already dressed and talking on his cell. His brow is lined, and I can tell we're back to where we left off. With a sigh, I enter our son's room.

He's standing in his crib, holding the side. When he sees me, his blue eyes sparkle and he starts to jump. My worries about his daddy fly away, and I can't help laughing.

"Good morning, pumpkin," I coo, lifting him over the rail. His legs pump against my waist as he struggles to get down, out of my arms. "You want to walk, big boy?"

A week short of his first birthday, and he's already tearing through the house. We've had to move all small items to the top shelves in every room as his favorite thing is pulling whatever he can reach down on his head.

"I can drive to Raleigh if I need to." Derek's voice is low as he speaks into his cell. That makes my brow crease. Raleigh hasn't come up in more than a year.

When he sees me, he smiles, but it's not his usual flood of appreciation at my presence. It's that tight smile, the one accompanying his subtle mood-swings. He gets an impatient smile from me in response.

"We can talk more at the office. I'll be there in ten minutes." He disconnects and walks over to pull me into a hug. "Sorry I was late last night. I hope I made it up to you."

I press my nose against his chest and inhale the warm, slightly woodsy scent I've come to associate with the greatest love of my life. I feel him kiss the top of my head. "Still working on the Nikki situation?" I ask.

Releasing me, he picks up a leather portfolio and grabs his keys. "I'm heading to the office to meet Patrick and talk to Stuart. Are you working today?"

"Later," I say, walking to the coffee maker. I drop in a small, plastic pod, slide my mug in place, and hit the button. "Elaine and I are taking the boys to do their fittings this morning."

His expression is confused, and I'm ready to have it out with him. I knew he hadn't been listening to me on our drive home yesterday. "Their tuxes? For our wedding?"

"Oh, right." He steps back to me and kisses my forehead before heading to the door. "Don't let Dex knock over the mannequins."

I give him a little growl, but his comment still makes me smile. Our toddler is a menace to anything in his grabbing space. Derek's gone, so I grab a baby breakfast bar and a sippy cup of milk. Dex is in front of the flat-screen television attempting to turn it on when I return to the living room.

"Come on, little man, I'll put on your show." Scooping him up, I deposit him in the pack and play in my bedroom, pulling up his show on the Internet television. "Be sweet while Mommy showers!"

My shower is fast, and I listen for any changes in the bedroom as I step into jeans and pull on a loose, charcoal tee. I tie my hair in a low, side ponytail, and drop a few necklaces over my head as I step into black ankle boots.

Running down the hall, I stop at Dex's room and grab his little jeans, long-sleeved polo, and an extra diaper. He can still wear the cowboy boots we bought him for Elaine's Christmas wedding in Montana. He wasn't walking yet, and we intentionally bought them a few sizes too big. He's adorable in them.

When I return to the room, he's engrossed in his favorite train show, and just like a little man, he doesn't even look at me when I enter. "Okay, mister. Time to get dressed."

"May, tank," he says, twisting and pointing over my shoulder as I scoop him up and carry him to the living room.

"Yes!" I nod. "A blue tank."

Flipping on the flat screen, I'm about to sit when I hear banging on my back door. "Guess who it is, Dexy? It's Aunt Elaine and Laney!"

That sends him wiggling again, and I let him down, following him to where they're smiling and waving at the back glass. Shouts and squeals fill the kitchen as the boys greet each other and my best friend and I hug.

"I tell you," Elaine says, stripping off her coat and dropping it on the back of a kitchen chair, "After how cute they were in my wedding, I can't even imagine how they'll look surrounded by the guys in their dress whites."

"Blues," I correct. "Derek told me in spring it's blues."

"Are you sure about that?" Elaine has a sour straw hanging out of her mouth. "I think you have it backwards."

"Hell, you're probably right. I'll have to double-check. Properly addressing the invitations was enough to drive me crazy."

She follows me into the living room where Lane is sitting in front of the television making engine noises as he moves his ever-present truck back and forth across the rug.

Dex is parked in his tiny leather armchair with matching ottoman—identical to his daddy's right behind it. Love spills through my veins as I pause to study his baby profile. He looks so much like Derek.

"So? How was the weekend getaway?" Elaine drops onto the couch.

"It started out amazing, but then . . ." I'm trying to figure out how to end that sentence when she cuts in.

"Stop! Don't say you had a fight. I'll lose all my faith in happily ever after!"

"You're so freaking dramatic." I flop on the couch beside her. "Give me a sour straw."

"Am I the worst mother or what?" She digs in her purse and pulls out two—one for me, and another for her. "Lane loves these things, and I'm completely addicted."

That makes me laugh. "I'm sure you only give him one a day."

"It's true! But only because I've eaten all the rest!" She falls back on the couch, a fresh straw hanging from the side of her mouth. "I'm going to get a cavity, I can feel it."

"What does Kenny think?" Lane's birth mother, a young artist Patrick was involved with briefly before he met Elaine, keeps their two-year old one weekend a month.

After a rocky beginning, she and my bestie bonded last fall over a situation involving Kenny's boyfriend Slayde. Kenny is also how Stuart met Mariska—in a crazy twist of love and fate.

"She's the one who started it! He came back from Bayville demanding sour straws and Coke floats."

"Oh, wow. Coke floats." I try to remember the last time I had that creamy, bubbly deliciousness. "So old-school, and so good."

A sharp kick to my thigh makes me yelp. "I'm trying not to gain a hundred pounds! I'm convinced Kenny has a worm. It's impossible she can stay that skinny with all the crap she eats."

"She's a fitness instructor," I snort laughing. "A worm. You sound like my grandma!"

"I'm not lying. She eats the worst shit!"

Lane's towhead pops up at once. "Mommy, bad word!"

"Good grief." My friend flops back against the couch. "Don't tell daddy."

Lane goes back to engine noises, and I chew on my sour straw. "I thought Kenny was lactose intolerant."

"Goat's milk doesn't bother her. It's been life changing, apparently. She eats goat ice cream and chévre nonstop now." I exhale a little laugh, and Lainey's green eyes blink to me. "So what the heck could've spoiled your romantic getaway?"

Leaning beside her on the sofa, I straighten my legs and rest my heels on the coffee table next to hers. "I'm probably overreacting."

She kicks my leg again. "Spill!"

"Ow!" I cry. "You're so violent."

"Mel."

With a loud groan, I just say it. "He's keeping something from me again, and it's kind of making me crazy."

"Oh, shit." Elaine's eyes narrow.

Lane's little head pops up again. "Mommy, bad word!"

"Mommy said *spit*," my best friend casually corrects him.

I can't help noting the obvious. "Lane's pretty good at spotting the swear words all of a sudden."

"It's Patrick!" she shrieks, slapping her leg. "I said he swore too much, and now all he does is point out when I drop a bomb. I'm ready to kill him!"

That makes me grin. "I love him."

Her bottom lip goes under her front teeth, and she wriggles out an arm to squeeze me. "I know. Now finish telling me what happened."

With a sigh, I lean back. "Derek is wonderful and attentive and sexy . . . and I can't take how he hides things. It's like this invisible shield or something, and it's too . . . It reminds me too much of living with Sloan. I lived so long in his house of secrets and lies. I just . . . I can't do it again, Lainey."

We're both quiet, and in my peripheral vision, I see her chewing a sour straw as she thinks. "I get that," she says quietly. A few more moments pass and she adds, "but you know, the grass isn't really greener. Now that we're married, Patrick wants to tell me all this sh-spit he's working on. You know, because wives can't testify against their husbands?"

"Yeah?" I can't hide the eagerness burning in my chest that she might know something.

"I don't. Want. To know!" She waves her hands over her head. "I'm married to the master of pushing the limits. He's driving me crazy with worry!"

That gives me pause. I sit back and think a moment. I remember my request from Patrick—the promise I'd asked him to make to keep Derek from doing anything "hazardous or potentially life threatening" as Patrick put it.

"I guess that makes sense," I say quietly.

"We both love Patrick, but oh my god. He takes too many chances."

Shaking my head, I catch her hand. "It's not like that. Derek and Patrick are different people, they have different styles." Searching for the right words, I just say what's eating up my thoughts. "Derek's hidden stuff from me before, and it hurt when I found out. It hurt badly."

My friend's eyes are round as she turns to me, all teasing gone. "Derek loves you, Melissa."

"I know that. I know." Pushing up I go and pull Dex out of his baby chair, ignoring his complaints as I strip off his pajamas. "I'm not a little girl, Elaine. I don't want a daddy. I want a partner. I want someone who views me as an equal, not someone who keeps things from me—even if he does believe it's for my own good."

The best part about having the same best friend since child-hood is sharing a deep understanding of each other. Her expression is serious as she watches me. "Have you told him that?"

"No," I confess, standing my son in front of me and pulling his jeans over the puff of his new diaper. He's content to let me change him so long as he can see his trains. "He should know how I feel by now. We've already been through this."

"Wait." My best friend holds her hands up. "Are you saying a *male* should *know* how you feel? Is that what I'm hearing you say?"

"Lainey." I can't suppress my irritation. "This is Derek."

She shakes her head, her light blonde hair spilling over her shoulders. "Who happens to be the most manly male we know? Except for maybe Stuart?"

"Patrick's pretty manly. And stop defending him!" Dex is dressed, and I grab the remote. "We've got to go."

Once the TV is off, both boys get restless, and I can't help wondering about that Y chromosome. We scoop them up, grab our bags and head out the door. They're secure in their car seats, and we're heading to town when Elaine grabs my forearm.

"Stop at the office for a sec."

My eyes narrow at her. "We don't have time for a quickie."

"Just . . . it's not that." She grins, and I can't help it. I have to know.

"What is it, then?"

"Mel."

"Lainey."

She lets out an exasperated breath. "I visited Patrick at the office Friday, and . . . well . . . you know, and I forgot a *personal item.*"

"Do you have a checklist? Shit! Where have you not done it?"

Lane pipes up from the back seat. "Aunt Mel, bad word."

"Lane!" I cry, defensive. "I said *spit!*" Narrowing my eyes at my bestie, I grumble. "You've got me lying to babies now."

"I blame Patrick."

We both snort as we laugh. "Oh my god." I shake my head, turning into the parking lot of the long, one-story building where Alexander-Knight's satellite office is located.

"Besides, we're newlyweds! It's our honeymoon period!" She climbs out of her side, and I call after her.

"That excuse might've worked if I hadn't known you before the wedding."

"Grab the boys. The guys will want to see them."

I lean into the backseat unbuckling them before we all follow her into the rented space, but it's empty. "We must've missed them," I call as she heads to the back office.

I stand in the reception area while our little boys resume their usual positions—Lane is on his knees making engine noises as his favorite truck runs over the tracks on the rug, Dex is beside him watching. It's hard to know how long that will last before my little wrecking ball is up and exploring.

"Hurry up," I call to her as I pick up an issue of *People* magazine. "I can't believe they subscribe to these. Who reads them?"

I flip through the magazine as Dex toddles to where I hear Elaine searching.

"Heads up!" I call. "Here comes my little wrecker."

"I can't find it!" My friend's voice is a muffled reply.

Lane is content being the soundtrack for his truck as it follows the lines on the carpet. I'm scanning a movie review, when the monotony is broken by a *CRASH!* a shriek from my friend, and the slow siren-whine from my son.

"Dex!" I rush to the back.

My little boy's heartbroken cries grow louder, and I drop to the floor beside Elaine who's trying to comfort him. He's rubbing his eyes, and I look around at the scattered photo prints and a large paperweight he knocked off the desk. I'll have to clean this up.

"It's okay, baby," I whisper, shushing him as he pulls my shoulders and buries his face against my chest. "He's only scared, not hurt." I glance up at Elaine. "Did you find what you were looking for?"

"No," she says, but her voice trails off. She's on her knees collecting the photos and looking at them, eyes wide.

"What is it?" I reach out and take one of the prints from her. Turning it over, I have to blink twice to understand what I'm seeing. She hands me another, and my heart starts beating faster. My breath comes in pants as the images click together. I realize what I'm seeing, or rather *who* I'm seeing.

"Oh my god," I whisper as my hands tremble. My stomach turns like I might vomit.

Dex is still clutching my arms, and I hold my lips, taking a slow breath and trying to calm down. *Breathe, Melissa, breathe . . .* Leaning forward, I pick up another photo and notice my hand is trembling.

The images are horrible—a dead man, his face a sick grey color and his neck bent in an unnatural angle, clearly broken. He's lying on the floor in what appears to be a dark, hotel conference room.

"It's . . ." But everything tilts. The room seems to move out, away from me, and I'm afraid I might faint.

I can't finish my sentence. It doesn't matter because my friend whispers it for me. "It's Sloan."

Lane makes a loud engine noise from the front, and Dex releases me, running to see what his friend is doing. I can't move. I can barely breathe. I'm paralyzed and numb—and confused. I don't understand why I'm reacting this way, why I'm so terrified.

My voice shakes like my hands. "Why do they have these?"

Clearly, he was murdered in some gruesome manner. *No.* I stop myself. I'm jumping to conclusions. Maybe he had an accident. *Could he have fallen? But from where? And how?*

This is why Derek has been so preoccupied. Rising to stand, my light-headedness almost makes me fall. Dropping all but one print, I catch the side of the desk.

"Melissa?" Elaine jumps up and holds my arm. "Are you

okay?"

"I have to talk to Derek."

"Of course." Her face is lined, and she holds my arm as we head back out to the front. "Come on boys. Lane, get your truck. Dex, hold my hand."

It feels like a thick fog is wrapping around me, clouding my vision. Derek doesn't want me to know about this . . . But why? I'm afraid I know the answer without needing to ask.

We're in Elaine's car heading back to the beach, and I barely register her telling me she'll keep Dex for the afternoon. When she stops at my cottage, I see his black Audi sitting in the driveway.

"Call me when you're ready for me to bring him home," she says.

Nodding, I glance back to check on my little son before I go. He's happily chattering baby-gibberish at Lane, unaffected by the sudden change in my mood.

"Thanks," I say softly and start toward the door.

Pausing, my eyes close, and I listen to the soft whisper of the waves in the distance trying to find calm. I know I have to talk to him, but I'm so afraid of this conversation. My emotions are all over the place. Sloan was an abusive, sick, evil man, who hurt me and kept me living in fear for more than a year. I should not feel emotional at discovering he's dead. I shouldn't be shocked or disturbed . . . I shouldn't . . . care. Why do I care?

Opening the door, when I see Derek sitting at the table, I know why I'm so torn up and twisted. I care because I know why my abusive ex is dead. I don't have to ask who did it. I know who did it.

That leaves one question: What now?

Derek

I'D BEEN LATE GETTING BACK to the beach cottage last night, and Melissa was already asleep for the second time in a row. I know she's growing increasingly annoyed with my evasions, and she has no idea how her talk of our wedding plans and Dex's first birthday party are killing me. The drive back from Princeton had been difficult, but leaving her as soon as we'd arrived home was worse.

"You have to meet Patrick *now?*" Her hands are on her hips as she follows me to the door.

"He found out about the Nikki situation. He needs to go over a few cases." Lying to her burns in my chest, but it's the last time I'll do it.

"What about Dex? He hasn't seen you in two days!"

"Patrick and Nikki are close." I pull my keys from my pocket. "She's heavily involved in several of his cases. Her leaving probably impacts him the most."

"Then let him convince her to stay." She catches my sleeve in her hand. "I can't believe this can't wait until tomorrow."

Covering her small hand with mine, I look into her eyes. "I won't be long."

I'm going to make this right, I vow as I walk to my car. *I'll make all of this up to her, and we'll never be in this situation again.*

Patrick is waiting when I arrive at our satellite office in Wilmington. Dressed in his usual faded jeans and a maroon, short-sleeved tee, his light-brown hair is a messy bedhead, and if he didn't have his son Lane at the house, I'd guess he came straight to meet me from sleeping with Elaine.

Hell, he probably did that anyway. Those two have been known to leave a house full of dinner guests for a quickie in the bathroom.

Standing in our small office space, I hold the fax and read the typed letter. It's on nondescript, white paper in a basic, serif font. Nothing distinguishes it. Nothing gives us a clue as to who might have sent it.

The message is short and clear:

Ms. Durango:

I know about your involvement in the death of Sloan Reynolds. An item belonging to you, containing your DNA, is in my possession along with digital files of the enclosed photographs.

Lowering the sheet, I glance up at my partner. "Photographs?"

He hands over cheap prints showing Sloan's corpse from a distance, lying on his back, his head cocked at a sick angle. The images gradually move in closer, frame by frame, until the focus is on a black lace thong in his pocket.

My jaw clenches. "Her fucking underwear."

Patrick's bicep flexes as he bends his elbow, pulling a fist to his chest. "We forgot he had it."

I also know about your record and the child in Myrtle Beach. If you want her to remain safe, you'll do as I say.

My next letter will contain instructions. Tell anyone, and you can kiss your baby goodbye.

Signed,
A Friend.

"A *friend*? Is that a fucking joke?" I'm ready to slam my fist through the wall. "What the fuck do they want?"

"Letter number two hasn't arrived yet. Toni called me as soon as she read this. She's pretty spooked, which you know takes a lot." He walks around the only desk in our two-room satellite office. He and I both do the majority of our work on the road or from home, so this space is for the rare occasion we have to meet with a client in person.

Sitting in the chair, his hazel eyes laser into mine. "You get what this means, right? This asshole was there. He or she saw what we did and is looking to exploit it."

"But why go after her?" My voice is flat. "Why not come straight to me?"

"That's the part neither of us can figure." He leans forward, elbows on the desk. "You clearly have more money if it's blackmail. Maybe whoever it is sees her as the weak link in our chain."

Growling, I try to think. "What's this about a kid?"

"A little girl, Camille. She had her about a year ago, but the baby lives with her sister."

Confused, I look up at him. "Could it be the father?"

"My first question." He stands and walks around the desk again. "She says no. He still lives in Raleigh. They're friends, just not together."

Scrolling through my thoughts, I try to remember the last time we've heard from Toni . . . or "Star," depending on whether she's running a con. She'd enrolled in community college and was working toward a degree in criminal justice. I'd offered to help her find a legitimate job when she finished.

"She's sure he's not after the baby?"

"From what I understand, Cammie lives with her sister because of Toni's . . . work history."

"She expected something like this to happen?"

"I don't think she expected Sloan Reynolds to come back from the dead, but apparently she's been involved in some pretty high-risk jobs. She didn't want to elaborate. I think she was afraid I might arrest her."

"So that's it. Whoever is sending this is trying to drag up her past for some reason."

"Maybe." He leans against the desk and crosses his arms. "Only she can't figure out why. As we've both already noted, she's not rich."

"What do you want me to do?"

"The fact this person addressed her as Durango and not

Brandon, her stage name, has her scared. It means he or she knows the real Toni." He slips the letter back in his pocket and grabs a manila envelope. I watch as he drops the photographs in it and places it under a paperweight on the desk. "She's afraid for her little girl."

"How old is the child?"

"Almost a year."

Same age as Dex. "I guess I understand how she feels."

Patrick nods. "She's tough, but you know how it is. Hit somebody where they live, and you can pretty much get whatever you want."

Inhaling deeply, I nod and start for the door. "Speaking of, I need to get home. Let me know as soon as you hear from her. Tell her not to be afraid. We'll take care of this."

FOUR

THE LAST STRAW

Melissa

DEREK IS AT THE KITCHEN table when I open the door to my beach cottage. The images of Sloan's gruesome, broken neck churn my stomach. I'm still holding one of the prints.

"Melissa?" He crosses the room as I step inside. "Are you sick? What's wrong?"

I lift the photograph, holding it so he can see what I know. "Dex knocked this off your desk."

His jaw clenches, but he doesn't speak. I don't need him to. I remember the night he'd told me he could kill a man with his bare hands. We'd been discussing "special skills." He'd said he wasn't proud of that one.

"You did this." My voice is so quiet, yet it feels like the loudest thing in the room.

His eyes close, and for the second time, my head grows suddenly light. Only this time, the whiteness overpowers me. I'm going down, until I'm scooped up in his strong arms at once.

"Hang on," he soothes, carrying me to the sofa and gently helping me sit. "Stay here. I'll get you something to drink."

"No!" I catch his arm and hold him. "I need you to tell me if it's true."

With a deep sigh, he lowers himself beside me. My head hurts. Pressure is behind my eyes, and my limbs are weak.

His voice is quiet, resigned when he answers me. "It's true."

"Oh, god, Derek!" Tears flood my eyes, and my whole body is trembling now. "Oh, god!"

The tears spill down my cheeks, and he gathers me to his chest. I can only clutch his shoulders. Breathing is hard. Thinking is hard—past the one thought of *What now?* Repeating over and over in my brain. My worst nightmare is coming true.

"I'm sorry." His voice remains quiet, and he continues holding me, softly running his hand up and down my back.

"When were you going to tell me?" My whisper is accusatory. I'm angry, but more than anything, I'm terrified of losing him.

I feel him take a deep breath, his hold on me loosens as his arms lower. "In the beginning? Never."

Pushing back, I catch his eyes. "You were never going to tell me you killed a man?"

"I didn't want you burdened with that knowledge." His tone is closed, but his steel blue eyes tell me he's not saying everything.

All the shock and fear that had just been swirling through me binds together in a fist of anger in my chest. I push to my feet, adrenaline driving me now. "You didn't want me to be burdened with the knowledge that you've committed a crime? That my ex-husband is dead at your hands?"

I'm pacing the living room, but he's not moving. His eyes follow me.

Finally, I stop and shout at him. "How could you keep this from me?"

He looks up at me, and his expression is so pained, my chest clenches again. As angry as I am, I still love him so much. His suffering tears me apart.

"Melissa," he breathes my name in a way that nearly melts

me. "I've wrestled with this decision so long—"

"Because you know it's the wrong one."

"Because I love you." He stands and steps toward me. His massive size makes me feel very small. "I couldn't risk you assuming any of the blame for what I did. This crime is solely on me. I wouldn't let him hurt you again."

With that one statement, understanding washes through me. "He threatened me?"

Derek's chin drops, and I reach up to cup his cheek, sliding my palm over his close, dark beard. Our eyes meet then, and his are filled with so much regret. "Yes," is all he says.

Reaching for him, I surrender to his embrace, and for a few moments, we simply hold each other. Our breathing swirls together, and images fill my mind of how something like that would affect this man who spent the first part of his career as a commanding officer, leading men like Stuart on combat missions. It would be like tweaking the nose of a lion.

My cheek is against his chest as I consider it. "How did he do it? How did he make that threat?"

Silence settles over the room, and I lift my head to look at him. He smooths my hair back from my face, his lips tightening as he views the tiny scar at my scalp. "He had your necklace."

"What?" The icy fear is back.

"We were watching him, and he had it. He pulled it out and showed it almost as if he were taunting me . . ." Derek's voice trails off, but I can see the anger darkening his blue eyes. "The idea that he had been here, in this house, close enough to take something so precious to you without our knowing . . ."

Memories of the dream I'd had that day so long ago trickle into my thoughts. I remember the squeak of his shoes, the spicy scent of his cologne burning my nose, the sound of scissors. Shivering, I step forward again to hide in the shelter of Derek's arms.

He only holds me, breathing in the top of my hair. My eyes close as guilt rolls over me like a flood. I'm to blame for this. If

I hadn't been such a stupid fool to marry Sloan Reynolds, none of this would be happening. Derek Alexander, one of the most honorable men I've ever known, a hero, wouldn't have ruined his reputation and possibly his life for me. He'd be free from guilt, he'd be away from this nightmare. It's the horrible truth, my humiliating truth, that started this chain of events.

"It's my fault." My voice is so low, I'm sure Derek can't hear me, but I'm wrong.

He catches my upper arms and holds me in front of him as anger fills his eyes. His dark brow lowers, the muscle in his jaw moving as his teeth clench. In this state I imagine he's intimidating to others, but I feel no fear. He'd never hurt me.

"That is exactly why I didn't tell you," he growls. My eyes start to close, but he gives me a gentle shake. "Look at me, Melissa." I obey and meet his steely gaze. "You are not to blame for this. Sloan Reynolds was a master manipulator. He fooled everyone, including me, and the last thing I'll let you do is blame yourself."

"If I hadn't married him—"

"Stop." Another gentle shake, and I'm back against his chest, surrounded by his arms. "You had no idea what he was hiding. No one did. We've talked about this."

I want to argue, but he won't let me.

"I should have had more control," he continues. "I'm trained to be in control at all times. What happened is entirely my fault."

I don't agree with him. I know him too well, but that means, I also know he's convinced himself of the truth of his words. Only one person is as stubborn as he is, and she's locked in his arms right now. Struggling to get free, I look up at his face again, so strong, so handsome, so intense in his commitment to keeping his family safe.

"We're not going to agree on this." A few beats of silence pass, and for the first time in so long, he smiles. It's small, but it's better than the dark veil that's been clouding his eyes.

"If anything ever happened to you . . ." His voice is soft, and he cups my cheeks. "I can't live without you, Miss Jones."

My anger dissipates as his lips lightly cover mine, but I pull back. One enormous part of this is still unresolved.

"You can't hide these things from me." My voice is low, and I'm deadly serious. "Something this big . . . you have to include me in this, in your life."

"I know." He blinks down. "I told Patrick—"

"Patrick is in a shit load of trouble with me, too! He specifically promised to keep you out of trouble."

"He's already predicted your response." That little smile is back, and he glances at me. For a moment, I forget I'm mad as his sexy gaze holds mine. "What's all this making deals with Patrick behind my back anyway?"

"He promised he wouldn't let you do anything dangerous or . . . potentially life-threating. Nothing that could take you from me forever."

My final sentence is the big question hanging over us now. Our blue eyes meet, and I know the fear twisting my insides is plain on my face. He sits on the sofa and pulls my body to him. I'm standing in front of him, my hands resting on his broad shoulders.

"Nothing can take me from you," he says, placing his cheek against my torso.

We hold each other a moment, before he slides my tee up so he can kiss my skin. The touch of his lips on my stomach, the scratch of his beard pulses need in my lower body, and I lean down to kiss his head, curling my fingers in the sides of his thick, dark hair. He pulls back to unbutton my jeans, sliding them over my hips along with my panties as I step out of my boots.

A deep inhale and he speaks against the crease of my thigh. "You smell so good." His kisses move closer to the center, and my knees grow weak.

"Derek," I sigh. With one slow circle of his tongue over my

clit, I rise on my tiptoes, crying out as electricity snakes up my legs.

"Oh, god!" I'm gasping and clutching his hair as he sucks and pulls at me until my thighs begin to tremble. All at once, I'm off my feet. I clutch his cheeks and cover his mouth with mine. The adrenaline, the anger, the fear, the frustration, all of it is burned away as he carries me to our bedroom.

♥

Derek

MELISSA IS SO BEAUTIFUL COMING apart in my arms. I have her in our bed, thighs parted, and I slide my tongue over her clit then down, tasting her deeply. I don't want her angry. I don't want her blaming herself. I want her to understand nothing in this world is ever allowed to threaten her in my presence. I'll take any chance, any risk to keep her safe.

"Oh, god, Derek!" Her soft moans are shocks of pleasure straight to my cock, which is aching to be inside her. "I'm almost there," she gasps, and I give her another firm suck, resulting in a high-pitched cry.

Her body is soft and wet, like honey on my tongue, and as her legs start to convulse, I rise up to kiss her belly before sinking deep into her. It's the most incredible feeling, her clenching and holding me, hot and wet.

She's in my arms, my weight supported on my elbows. Every thrust piques the pressure growing in me, and I can't stop a groan. I kiss then bite the soft skin of her shoulder. She moans, and all I can do is hold her as the most intense sensation of relief explodes through my body. My orgasm shakes me like blinding light.

"Melissa." Her name is a prayer on my lips.

Two more hard thrusts, she's so tight and willing. Rolling onto my side, I have her in my arms as we slowly come down together. Our breath mingles, our bodies melt. It's beautiful and perfect . . . until she twists away. I release her, and she rises up on an elbow. A dark lock of her hair falls over her ivory shoulder.

Reaching out, I touch her lightly. "God, you're so beautiful."

"That wasn't exactly fair, you know." Her blue eyes sparkle with her tease, and I do a quick internal evaluation of how long it might be before I can take her again.

"What wasn't fair?"

"I'm mad at you, you distract me with mind-blowing sex—"

"Did I blow your mind?" We're both smiling now.

"You must've. I don't feel angry at all."

Pushing myself up to sitting, I gather her in my arms. Her cheek rests against my skin, and I thread my fingers through her soft, gorgeous waves. "You're not angry."

I feel her brows move against my skin. "Oh, I'm not?"

"No. You understand why I did it, why I couldn't tell you, although I'm glad you know."

"Derek," she exhales, frustration in her tone. "You have to include me in things like this. You can't keep them from me." Lifting her head, our eyes meet, concern filling hers. "I'm your wife. Your partner."

"I can't wait to make that official."

Her expression is still agitated. "So what happens now?"

"Nothing."

She pushes all the way to sitting, the sheet clutched under her arms. "You think you can get away with it?"

"Sloan was in the wrong place committing a criminal act. Patrick's theory is his handlers will sweep it under the rug, protect the shareholders and the Reynolds name from what was clearly happening when he was killed."

"What was clearly happening?" Her voice is so quiet, just above a whisper.

"He was engaging in criminal activities with a prostitute."

Her eyes slide closed. "Star." It's not a question, and she doesn't give me time to speak before continuing. "And you killed him."

We're quiet a moment, and I can see her internal struggle. "What are you thinking?"

She shakes her head slowly. "I never understood . . . I guess now I never will."

Catching her chin, I make her look at me. "Understand what?"

"How he could be so duplicitous. Smooth. Seductive even. When we were engaged, he was completely different." Her eyes shine with forming tears, and my stomach tightens. "For the longest time I stopped trusting myself, my ability to judge people."

I reach for her, smoothing her hair away from her beautiful cheek. A tear falls, and I touch it with my thumb. "You lived through hell."

She sniffs and wipes her cheeks roughly. "It was all a lie. He lied to me every day." Taking my hand, she threads our fingers. Her strength shines in her eyes. "You helped me learn to trust myself again. I'm so lucky to have you."

"I'm pretty sure I'm the lucky one in this scenario." She lifts her chin and smiles, and I kiss her hand. "I wanted to kill him for hurting you."

"Shh!" Pulling it away, she lightly touches my lips. "I'm always safe with you."

I'm ready to show her how much more than safe she is, how loved and appreciated she is as well, when her phone rings from the kitchen.

"That's Elaine with Dex." She's up and heading for it before I can do anything more.

Sitting alone in our bed, my eyes drift past the light-olive colored walls, out the window and over the miles, over time, to that night. I can still hear the sounds of Star's life being choked from her body, still feel the rage at the overwhelming knowledge that he'd touched Melissa that way. My jaw tightens, and I know I'd do it again. I'd kill him every time. Control be damned.

Patrick's right. We have to ride this out, track down who-ever's blackmailing Star, handle that asshole, and then put this case to rest.

Melissa's back. Her shirt's over her head, and she goes to the dresser to pull out a fresh pair of panties. Red lace. I smile, think-ing it's only a few more hours until we're back in bed together.

"Elaine's bringing Dex home, so you'd better get dressed."

Throwing back the covers, I stand and catch her by the hips, running my fingers under the elastic of her underwear. "I like where your head's at with these."

She gives me a little grin and a quick peck on the lips. "Later, soldier. For now we have to get dressed."

I smile at her using Stuart's and my favorite "diminutive." It started when we'd first joined the Corps, and a civilian kept calling us *soldier*.

My pants and boxer briefs are where I quickly discarded them earlier. "It's not like Patrick and Elaine ever worry about being discreet," I say, stepping into them.

"Listen." She stops in front of me, and I stand, pulling up my jeans. "I'm serious about what I said earlier. No more secrets."

Her blue eyes are so round and beautiful. I grab her by the waist, pulling her into a hug. Her hands rest on my bare chest. "No more secrets," I repeat.

"Promise me?"

A slow kiss, a little nip on her bottom lip, and I meet her gaze. "I promise."

❤

THE NEXT DAY, PATRICK AND I are in my car speeding to Raleigh. He explains the latest in our evolving case as I weave us through the morning-commuter traffic.

"Toni's getting panicky. She wants us to find a safe place for Camille."

My teeth clench, tightening my lips as I think. "Did you explain to her that's not something we're prepared to do?"

"Whoever this is knows exactly where the little girl goes to daycare, her schedule, everything."

"And we still don't know what this fucking *'friend'* wants?"

"Toni seems to think he's after you."

Silence fills the car. My eyes flick to my partner's. "What the hell?"

His face is dead serious. "Her last letter referenced 'the big guy.' Her idea is you're the biggest guy connected to the case in every way—physically, financially, professionally . . ."

"Then fucking come get me," I growl. "Why go through her?"

"Safety. Insurance." Patrick releases a long exhale. "Our man's smart, which is not good. Going directly to you will only get him killed."

"Damn straight it will." Tightening my grip on the steering wheel, my thoughts go immediately to the ones I've left behind. "You should've told me this before we left today. Melissa and Dex are home, unprotected—"

"I think they're okay for now. I told Elaine to be aware of their surroundings, take precautions if she notices anything suspicious."

"You told Elaine?"

"Of course." His hazel eyes narrow at me. "You need to tell Melissa more than you do. She's a tough chick."

"She's a beautiful, smart woman."

"But you didn't tell her about Toni."

"I'll tell her when we have answers. I'd rather tell her our solution than our problem." My promise to her yesterday lurks in the corner of my mind. "What makes you think they're not in danger?"

"Toni said the letter is very specific. She was too afraid to fax it. Doesn't want it out of her possession in case he goes after Cammie."

"That's not going to happen. This asshole's not going after anyone."

Soon we're pulling into the parking lot of the Skinniflute, the biker bar where Star works and where we've met on several occasions in the past.

"I can't believe she's still at this dump," I grumble as I lock my car.

"Working her way through college." Patrick's dressed in his usual Skinniflute attire—faded blue jeans, a black tee, and combat boots. I'm in slacks and a thin navy sweater. I'm no fucking biker, and I don't have to dress like one.

"She could get a job in an office. Be a secretary or something respectable for a change."

He heads inside the all-wood establishment with neon beer ads shining in the windows, but I take a moment to text Mel.

You okay?

It only takes a moment for her to respond. *The boys are hilarious. Just like little men. Wish you could see them.*

Me, too.

Everything okay?

I pause a moment, considering. *So far nothing new.*

Working on the Nikki problem?

Shit. I made this trip without telling her. *And other things.*

Tell Patrick to call her. She loves him.

I will.

Check this out. A picture of Mel kneeling beside my little boy in a tiny tux appears on my phone, and my chest warms.

I love you both.

We love you more. Want us to stop by the office?

No. We'll talk tonight. Be safe, okay?

This is Wilmington, babe. We're good.

I exhale deeply. I can't believe some new asshole is threatening my family. He'd better be ready for the hell he's inviting.

It takes a moment for my eyes to adjust to the dim interior of the establishment. A few pool tables are situated in the back corner, and the usual cast of regulars in their faded jeans, leather vests, and bandanas are stationed around the center bar.

Lylah, the other Amy-Winehouse-looking waitress, is hanging on the polished wood separating them laughing and talking trash. It's just after noon on a Tuesday.

We slide into a wooden booth and she calls back over her shoulder. "Toni! Got a couple of regulars in your section."

Toni, a.k.a., "Star," walks out, and I'm surprised to see she hasn't changed her look since the last time we saw her. Instead of the blood-red lipstick, jet-black hair, and white tank showing off her matching sleeve tattoos, she's wearing a navy shirt-dress and leopard print cardigan. Her hair is smooth and hanging down her back in chestnut waves, and while she still has the cat-eye makeup, her lips are a pale shade of glossy pink. She's a ringer for Melissa. It's the look we used to trap Sloan. The only thing missing is my fiancée's sapphire-blue eyes.

"Thanks for driving up," she says in her low smoker's voice. "I know it's a haul, but I didn't know what else to do."

"No worries, girl," Patrick steps forward and kisses her cheek. "You look great. How's school treating you?"

She slips in across from us and picks up a cardboard coaster. Lylah appears smacking gum and looking every bit the biker chick with her side ponytail, short shorts and tight tank. She's still sporting the look—Priscilla Presley hair and red-velvet lips.

"What can I get you fellas today? The usual?"

"You bet." Patrick drops a twenty on her tray. "And a little privacy."

Lylah's eyebrows rise. "When have I ever been a concern?"

Star cuts in. "Just get us the drinks, Lyle."

Her friend spins around and swings her hips back to the center of the room. I turn my attention to the woman in front of us. "Show us what you've got."

Her dark-brown eyes flicker slowly over mine, and her face flushes. I don't know what that's about, but she reaches into her sweater pocket. The letter is folded into a small square, and we watch as she spreads it open on the table then hands it to me.

Ms. Durango,

If you follow my instructions, your daughter will be safe, and you can return to your normal life. If you involve the authorities in any way, be sure my offer is null and void. I will make good on my threats.

You have one task: Let the big guy know I'm coming for him. Let him know if he tries to run or retaliate in any way, you and your daughter will suffer for his crimes.

It's time to pay up, and revenge is a dish best served cold.

Signed,
A Friend

Anger fires in my chest at the nerve of this fucker. "This is about money."

Star's voice is soft. "It says revenge. And crimes."

She's looking pointedly at me like all that bullshit means anything. I'm ready to punch whoever this is in the face for harassing a mother and her child.

"It doesn't make any damn sense," Patrick interrupts. "I thought Sloan didn't have any family left."

"His parents died years ago," I say. "Melissa was his only wife as far as I know, and they never had children."

Leaning back in the seat, I try to think. "My job is putting criminals behind bars or turning bad guys over to the cops. It could be anybody."

Star's doe eyes are round with worry. "What do we do?" She blinks and a tear falls. "I can't have this asshole threating Cammie. She's too little. She wouldn't understand. She'd be so scared . . ."

Her voice goes high, and I reach across the table to grasp

her hand. "Look at me." When I've got her attention, I put as much meaning behind my words as possible. "I won't let anything happen to you or your daughter. I promise."

She blinks a few times, eyes glistening with unshed tears, but I can see her body start to relax. "I believe you. I do. I just wish . . ."

Her voice trails off, and Patrick jumps in. "Has your daughter ever lived with you or has she always been with your sister?"

"She's always been with my sister." Star's voice drops a few decibels. "I'm no kind of mother for a little girl."

He sits back with a deep exhale. "Well, that fucks my plan."

"What are you thinking?" Patrick might color outside the lines, but he's smart. He's good at our job, and I've learned to trust him.

"Your condo's sitting empty in Princeton, right?" I nod, and he continues. "I was going to say Toni and Cammie can hide out there until we solve this. Stuart's across the hall, and Walt won't let anybody suspicious past him. The parking garage is secured . . . Unless it's too stressful for the baby."

"It's a good thing you're so fucking smart, partner. Otherwise your screw-ups might be more noticeable."

Star looks from Patrick to me. "I don't understand."

Patrick leans forward and smiles that ridiculous smile of his that makes women act like idiots. "How would you like to live like a queen with your little girl completely safe while we figure this shit out?"

Her brow lines, and I almost laugh. She's unaffected by his charm—probably because she's already been there. "Can you be a little more specific?"

He gestures to me. "This guy has a huge, two-bedroom penthouse condo in Princeton with a doorman, secure parking, and my Marine older brother right across the hall. I think you and Cammie should stay there until we've nailed this fucker. He'll never know where you are, and if by some chance he figures it out, he'll have three layers of security to get through."

Star's eyes flicker to me again, and a note of relief is in her voice. "You'd let me stay at your place?"

"Of course. I don't know why I didn't think of it myself. You're in this situation because of me. This idiot wants me. It only makes sense."

"Okay, then!" She actually smiles, and relief shines in her eyes. "I'll call Nan and see if I can get the baby tomorrow . . . ? Is that too soon?"

"Not at all." I give her a reassuring smile. "Go home and pack. I'm sure you're worried about your daughter."

Her eyes flood again, and she jumps out of her seat, rounding the table and giving me a tight, unexpected hug. I lightly touch her waist as the scent of honeysuckle drifts around us.

"Thank you so much." Her voice cracks.

Star might be a tough girl, but her Achilles is Cammie. Having Dex has shown me the power of children. They can bring even the hardest characters to their knees.

"I gave you my word. I'm going to fix this."

ON THE DRIVE BACK TO Wilmington, my thoughts are preoccupied with what this asshole wants from me, and how I can find him so I can rip his dick off and shove it up his ass. Patrick's preoccupied with his smartphone, and it reminds me of my text chat with Melissa.

"That was a smart move with Star," I say, catching his attention. "I'm glad you thought of it."

"It just came to me as we were sitting there." He exhales a laugh. "I'm glad you're not pissed I volunteered your place without asking."

"Nah, it was good." Pausing a beat, I continue to our "other business." "You had a chance to talk to Nikki?"

He nods, looking back at his phone. "Seems Captain Asshat

is also Captain Hypocrite. He fucked her."

That makes me wince. "Shit. When?"

"The night before he pulled out last time."

Fuck. My grip tightens on the steering wheel. "I can't believe he'd screw up like that."

"Ah, give him a break." My younger partner stretches in his seat. "He never planned to come back from Saudi." We're quiet a moment, and my thoughts go to how messed up Stuart was when he did come back.

Patrick breaks the moment with a laugh. "So I'm officially off the hook. At least my office fuck-up was also a set-up."

"I'm glad you're both on a leash now. Makes my job easier."

"I am a happily married man. That is the truth."

"As if we don't have enough shit going on." I grumble. "Is she going to sue us?"

"No fucking way. It was consensual—apparently very con-sensual. It's why I never made any progress with her. She was hoping to get back in his pants when he came home. Ahhnd now she can't work with him."

"So she's pissed about Mariska?" Jealousy is a fucking night-mare to deal with. I rub my brow, trying to think. "I don't have time to train somebody new."

"I thought you hated Nikki." His laugh irritates me.

"She's a terrible secretary, but at least we know her weak-nesses." Filtering through my options, I land on one. "Maybe if I talked to her . . ."

"Won't work. This is more than simple jealousy. She pulled some stunt in Montana, got Stuart all riled up, ran Mariska off. She said she's too humiliated to stay."

"What kind of teenage drama is this?"

"Don't yell at me. I tried to keep her out of their way."

Frustration twists in my chest. I've got a fucking psycho threatening Star and now the Princeton office is a circus. "I'll talk to Stuart and see what he thinks."

"It's possible if I asked her to stay, told her we need her, the office can't run without her—"

"Just hold off on that. I don't want to make any false claims."

He chuckles as we're pulling into the parking lot of his and Elaine's condo. "I'll run more background checks on Sloan tonight. See if he has any nutjob relatives we overlooked."

"Thanks. I'll see if I can come up with anything."

"You might try talking to Melissa about it. She was married to the guy."

That reminder burns my chest. "Yeah, we'll see."

My eyes flicker over Patrick's shoulder as I pull out, and I catch Elaine standing in the doorway. She's watching me with a worried expression that bothers me, and I drive a little faster than legal to get home. Patrick should have told me this case had gotten so specific. I never would have left Wilmington today if I'd known.

Quickly killing the car in our driveway, I hustle up to the door when I see something that slows my pace. Three large black suitcases and my duffel bag are stacked on the porch. My eyes travel over the house, and I can see the flicker of the television through the sheer blinds in the kitchen. Melissa and Dex are here, but clearly something's wrong.

My chest tightens as I walk toward the entrance. Lifting one of the bags, I notice it's heavy. I pull the zipper down, and inside are my clothes. *What the fuck?* Standing, I push my key in the lock and try to open the door, but it stops short. The metal chain prevents it from opening. I can only see a few inches into the kitchen.

"Melissa?" I shout through the crack. "What's going on? Let me in."

Footsteps thud on the other side, and all at once the door is shoved closed, pushing me back. The sound of the deadbolt locking follows next.

"Melissa?" I shout, banging on the door, but she doesn't answer. I'm simultaneously pissed and confused. All my shit's out here . . . *Is she throwing me out?*

My key is back in the lock, and I open the door again, but again it's stopped by the chain. "Melissa, unfasten the chain."

"No." Her voice is just on the other side of the door.

I can't see her, but I can hear the anger in her tone. Dex's train show sounds in the background, and I don't want to argue in front of him.

Taking a deep breath, I stay calm. "Please open the door and talk to me."

"Oh, *now* you want to talk?" Her voice goes high. "I'm sorry. You're a day late and a promise short."

The muscle in my jaw clenches hard, but my voice stays calm. "Open the goddamn door, Melissa."

"No."

I step back ready to snap that chain with a swift kick, when she pushes it closed and the noise of that fucking deadbolt sounds again.

"God dammit!" I shout as I shove my key back into the lock. I'm turning it open when I hear scraping noises on the other side. This time when I push against the wood, it doesn't move at all.

Resting my forehead against the door, I take another deep breath, fighting for control. "Please let me in."

"You promised!" She yells from the other side. "You looked in my eyes and *promised*."

"Baby, I didn't know how serious this was."

"I won't hear any more lies from you. Take your shit and leave. It's over."

She's crying now, and all semblance of control I had is gone. This is not happening. Stepping back, I hit the door with my shoulder as hard as I can. A low growl escapes my throat on impact. The door doesn't budge.

"Open the door," I repeat.

Again, she shouts. "No."

Stepping back, I kick it with the sole of my foot. The door-jamb shudders, but it doesn't give.

"Don't make me call the police," she shouts from the other side.

That nearly sends me into a rage. My shoulders are rapidly rising and falling as I step back and survey this situation. The woman I love has thrown me out and is now threatening the cops on me. *Am I having some kind of fucking bad dream?*

The only possible way I might get in the house comes to mind. "I want to see Dex."

She's angry, yes, but if we can look at each other, talk it out . . . Maybe she needs to yell at me. I can listen, hear what she needs to say, and everything can go back to normal.

"I'll talk to my mom. We'll work out a schedule for you to visit him."

My fist is pounding on the wood before I even realize what I'm doing. This is fucking idiotic, and I need to get on the other side of this fucking door and hold Melissa in my arms.

"Stop it!" I can hear the break in her voice, and it rips me apart. "You're scaring Dex."

Breathing hard, I rest my head against the wood again. Looking to the side, I can see the cracks that have formed around the doorjamb from my attempts to break it down. Sound filters through the spaces easily. The noise of my Melissa crying is just on the other side. I can't take this.

"Melissa." This time I'm pleading with her. "Please open the door."

"No." She says softly, between sniffles.

My heart is twisting in my chest. "What do you want me to do, baby? Just tell me what to do."

"I want you to go away." Her voice shakes as she says the words.

"I can't do that." I'm breathing hard now. "I love you."

"Not enough to keep your promise."

"I love you more than enough." Gripping the wooden frame, I fight my emotions. "Let me in."

"I'm done talking. Take your bags and go."

Noises on the other side sound like Dex whining. I hear her go to him and attempt to soothe him. Stepping back, I look at the windows and consider breaking one of them. For several long seconds, I visualize myself doing it. I look around the perimeter and see every place I can force my way inside, go in there and gather her in my arms, make her stop saying these things.

But I don't. It would scare Dex, it would anger Mel . . . It would only make things harder for me.

Instead I do what she asks. Ice is in the pit of my stomach as I pick up my duffel and the largest suitcase and carry them to my car. Popping the trunk, I put them inside and go back for the remaining two.

Once everything's loaded, I turn the car back toward Wilmington, stopping briefly at a liquor store for a fifth of Dewar's. It doesn't take long before I'm in a hotel room trying to figure out my next steps. One thing is certain, no matter what she says, this is *not* over.

FIVE

HEARTBREAK

Melissa

TEARS COAT MY CHEEKS AS I rock my whimpering little boy back and forth on my lap. My entire body is shaking, but I'm struggling for control. I have to keep it together for Dex. He's only a baby. He's too small to understand why Mommy can't stop crying, why Daddy has to go away.

Rocking him in my arms, his little cheek is against my chest, and he's sucking on his finger. His little fist grips my sleeve tightly. I shush him and kiss his soft dark hair, rubbing his back until he slowly calms down from the explosion of his father trying to break down the door. Derek's anger is terrifying and his determination formidable. Only one thing is just as strong—my refusal to make the same mistake twice.

The memory cramps my stomach and fills my eyes with fresh tears. A hiccupped breath jerks my throat, and I'm on the verge of sobbing again. Packing Derek's bags had been the hardest thing I'd ever done in my life, but I will not live in another house of lies and deceptions. At least this time I've found out before it was too late.

Elaine and I had spent the day taking the boys for their

fittings. Derek had even texted me to check on us. He'd texted me from Raleigh and never said a word about being out of town or what he was doing. He'd pretended he was dealing with Nikki! I can't believe the extent of his deception, and after just promising me . . .

The never-ending train show makes a cheerful whistle, and Dex wiggles to get free of my arms. At least he's young enough that what just happened is quickly forgotten. Mommy's here, he's safe in my arms, back to the trains.

Standing on shaky legs, I take his little hand and a train and slowly lead him to my bedroom. Upon entering, it appears the same as it did when Derek was here, but if I open the closet, I'll see the gaping hole where his suits used to hang. If I open his drawers, I'll find them empty where his jeans and tees once were. His exercise clothes are gone, his socks. In the bathroom, his toothbrush, razor, shampoo, shave cream . . . All gone.

The pack and play stands waiting as I gently lower my little boy into it before pulling up his never-ending show on the television. He's contented as I crawl onto the bed, silently weeping as devastation tries to pull me under.

My phone rings. It's Elaine's tone, but I'm too weak to pull it out of my sweater pocket. I know what she wants. After the fitting today, we took the boys for ice cream. Lane wanted a Coke float, but Dex only had half his dip cone before hopping down and running to the indoor playground.

"Derek said not to, but we should drop by the office since we're in town." I watched our little boys play. Dex stormed across the top level with such determination, so much like his father, I couldn't help but laugh.

"Did you forget something?" Elaine winks at me, but I shake my head.

"I just wanted to stop in and say hey."

"Wait, what? Stop in and . . ." Her voice trails off, causing me to turn and catch her confused expression just before she tries to hide it.

"What's going on?"

She looks at her lap, and I can tell she's trying to think of an excuse. I'm not having it. "Lainey. What are you not telling me?"

"It's not me not telling you." Her voice is soft, and she won't meet my eyes.

"Then tell me what I don't know."

"The guys drove to Raleigh today."

She doesn't have to elaborate. I remember all too well what's in Raleigh. "Has something happened to Star?"

"She's been getting threatening messages. It's where the photographs came from." Shaking her head, she looks away from me, over her shoulder to where Lane has joined Dex on the playground. "After the last one, she wanted to meet in person. She's scared. Somebody's been blackmailing her about the crime. Using her to get to Derek."

With every word, my throat goes tighter and tighter, and I'm sure I'll start screaming. I've never been this angry . . . *ever!* We made love yesterday—sexy, passionate love—and I forgave him for keeping secrets, for not telling me he'd murdered my ex-husband . . . *Murdered.* My. Ex-husband.

He kept a secret from me so big it could change all our lives. Police could break through our door at any moment as long as we live and take him away, and I would be clueless.

No more secrets. I can still see his steel-blue eyes fixed on mine as he said the words. *I promise.* He looked me in the eye and gave me his word. Yet here I sit hearing he's doing it again. We spent the rest of the day together, we slept together last night, had coffee this morning, and he never mentioned it. Never told me what he was doing today. Didn't say anything in his text. My head feels so hot, I wonder if my face is red.

"I have to go." Standing, I collect my bag, Dex's train.

Elaine is on her feet just as fast. "What are you going to do?"

"More like what am I not going to do." My breath is coming so fast, but at this point it's only anger. I'm unable to be still. I have to move. The tears come later, bathing his clothes in salt water as I shove them into his suitcases. Crying and cursing, unable to believe he would put me in this position.

I never dreamed I'd feel this way towards Derek. At the same time, dancing at the edges of my memory is the day I discovered his email to Sloan. That day long ago in that horrible mansion when I thought I'd lost my last shred of hope.

"Tell me what you're going to do," my friend repeats as we catch the boys and carry them to the car. Both struggle and complain, but I'm too distracted to worry about Dex wanting to stay.

Buckling him in his car seat, I say one word. "Pack."

Now, a half-day and a nightmare later, my phone is ringing again, and I know Elaine won't stop until I answer. Forcing my arm to move, I reach into my pocket and pull out the device. Sliding my finger across the face, I hold it to my ear.

"I'm here, Lainey."

"Melissa?" Her voice is tentative and high. "Are you okay?"

"I'm okay."

"Patrick talked to Derek." She pauses, and my eyes close. Pain twists in my stomach, and I know I'll start crying again if I have to talk about it. As if knowing this, my best friend doesn't make me. "I can come over if you need me. Help with Dex?"

"It's okay. We'll be okay."

"Call me if you need me." She hesitates then continues. "You don't even have to call. Just send me a text—911."

"Thanks. I will."

We disconnect, and I push myself off the bed. I have to make Dex's supper, bathe him, get him ready for bed. He can sleep with me tonight.

MOM'S IN THE KITCHEN WHEN I open my eyes the next

morning. I vaguely recall her coming over last night, having to shove the heavy table I'd moved in front of the door back to its place and unfastening the chain. She'd wanted to talk, but I couldn't do it. I'd been crying off and on all evening, and I'd only just managed to fall asleep with Dex in my arms. Being outside the tight grip of his daddy's embrace would take getting used to, but I'd get there. I had to be strong.

Now I hear her talking to our little boy, and I stretch out my hand to Derek's empty side of the bed. Pain twists in my stomach, and I push my face against the pillow to muffle my cry. It hurts so bad. On my nightstand is the photograph of Derek and me sitting on the beach. His arms are around me, and it's a painful reminder of what a beautiful liar he is.

Oh, god! I jump from the bed and run to the toilet. I barely make it before I lose what little contents are in my stomach. I collapse on the cool tile floor and weep, holding onto the handle. I don't know if I can pick up the pieces this time. I've been through this with him before, forcing myself to get over him, but that was in the beginning. I'd only had a week. Now it's worlds different. So much of his life is woven into mine.

Five minutes pass, and I force myself to get up. Scooping handfuls of water into my mouth, I look in the mirror. My eyes are puffy from crying, and I lean forward to hold a cool rag on them. After a few moments, I straighten, pat myself dry, and take my robe off the hook. I can do this. I *have* to do this.

"I made eggs," Mom says quietly as I enter the room. Dex is already down and in the living room running his trains all over the lines of the rug.

"Thanks, Mom." My voice is thick with unshed tears. "I'm sorry about last night. I just . . . couldn't."

"Derek called me. He's worried . . . He sounded a little desperate."

I can't answer that. I don't even want to hear that. My insides clench, and I'm fighting the crippling sobs as I go to the coffee machine and drop in a plastic pod. Waiting as my mug fills, I know she's watching me for some sign. Anything.

"He said you kicked him out?" she nudges.

Taking my coffee to the bar, I don't look at her as I pour in a dash of creamer. My jaw tenses. *Be strong, Melissa.*

"Was it another woman?" Her voice strains.

I glance up at her worried face and shake my head. I can't tell her about Sloan's murder—I don't know what I can tell her that won't get Derek in trouble with the law. So I stick to the facts.

"He lied to me," I say. "He kept secrets from me and then lied about it."

Her face scrunches as she tries to understand. "Can you give me an example?"

"I don't think so. It involves his work."

Mom exhales and drops into a chair. "Sweetie, I have to say, it must be something incredibly major. I've never seen any man love someone as much as Derek loves you. Your father—"

"Mom." My voice is sharp, and I hope she can tell how serious I am. "You have to trust me this time. Just like you had to trust me with Sloan."

She looks down at the table. I take the chair across from her and hold my mug in both hands. The warmth of it soothes me, even if I don't feel like drinking it. I don't trust my stomach yet.

When she speaks again, her voice is quiet. "I've also never seen you so in love with a man." Her eyes are full of concern even as her words gut me. "Maybe give it time. I'm here to help you any way I can—with Dex, with the cottage. Do you need to stay with me a few days?"

My first instinct is to say no, until I consider the week ahead. One important milestone is coming, and I'm not sure I can get through it alone. "If you can help me with Dex's birthday. I want him to have a happy first birthday."

"Of course!" she answers quickly.

My insides clench at what I have to say next. I feel my stomach again on the verge of losing its contents, which at this point is nothing.

"After that . . ." I pause to steady my breathing. "If you can help me cancel the wedding plans." She makes a little noise of shock, and my grip tightens on my mug. "If it's too much, I can ask Elaine—"

"No! I just . . . What if we just say the plans are on hold?" The flicker of hope in her voice spears the pain in my heart. I want to crawl into a dark place and never come out. I want to turn back time and never have met Derek Alexander. I want to scream and throw things, and . . .

I hear Dex in the other room. Only, I'd never give up my little boy. If all of this means I have him, it's worth it.

Steadying myself, I shake my head. "The wedding is off. I can't marry him."

"Darling, I'm afraid you're being too hasty. You've been hurt—badly, I can see that. At the same time, you and Derek have something so special—"

I can't listen to any more of this. She's killing me little by little and she doesn't even know how or why. I can't tell her the extent of his deception or how deep it goes without risking police involvement.

Holding out my hand, I grasp hers. "Let's focus on Dex right now. Help me get through his birthday. We can deal with the rest after."

She's satisfied, and I'm exhausted. I leave my full mug on the table and head back to my bedroom. I only barely hear her say she'll take Dex for the day before I push through the blankets. I curl into a ball surrounded by the scent of warmth and woods that used to soothe me. The scent of a man I trusted with everything, and who couldn't trust me with anything. It's a scent I used to crave when we were apart. Now it only breaks my heart.

SIX

SAFE HOUSE

Derek

PACING THE SMALL HOTEL ROOM, I pour two fingers of scotch in a glass and call Patrick. I should be at the cottage. I should be sitting in my chair with Dex in front of me playing with his damn trains. Melissa should be sitting beside me with her laptop or ordering takeout. I should be with my family, dammit.

Melissa and I have been a foregone conclusion so long, I can't get my mind around what's happening. It's almost comical to think of me being trapped out of our house with her on the other side of the door telling me to go away. I'd laugh if I weren't so fucking ready to kill somebody.

My phone buzzes, and I snatch it up without even looking.

"Hey, man. I just heard." Patrick's voice is a mixture of concern and his usual swagger. "What can I do?"

"You've fucking done enough," I growl before taking a long drink of scotch.

"What the fuck does that mean?"

My eyes squint and I shake my head. "Nothing. It doesn't mean anything. I'm just . . . I'm fucking pissed as hell. I don't know why Melissa's doing this."

"It's what I told you before. Women don't like being left out of the loop."

I'm ready to strangle him, considering the whole *Don't tell her* approach was his fucking idea. "This is way past a simple tantrum, Patrick. Melissa doesn't make dramatic gestures. This is serious."

He's quiet a moment, thinking. "What are you saying? You think she means it?"

"Fuck yeah, she means it." My fists clench, and I have to count to ten before I slam the tumbler against the wall. Trashing my hotel room won't help me. "What I don't know is if she'll forgive me this time."

"Melissa loves you. That is a fact."

"Sloan hurt her too badly. I fucked up when I didn't tell her about Star. I wanted to have more information before giving her the whole story, but she won't listen to that now."

"Give her some time. She'll come around. You have Dex, after all."

Setting the tumbler down, I pour two more fingers into it. "His birthday is this week."

A hiss of air fills my ear. "Shitty timing."

We're both quiet a few minutes while I think of my little boy, my beautiful bride. Patrick's back in problem-solver mode.

"Or it could be really good timing," he says. "It'll give her a few days to cool off before you see her again. Then you can try talking to her."

"I want to talk to her now." The scotch has my insides warm. My anger is soothed, and I want to hold her, kiss her, love her until she forgives me.

"You need to give her space."

"That's going to be impossible." Being in this shitty hotel room is already impossible.

"I know what you can do." His voice brightens. "Help Toni and Cammie with Princeton. Meet up with them, spend the night, and when you get back, go to Dex's birthday party."

I think about what he's suggesting. At least it will fill these hours. "It's not a bad idea," I agree.

"You can get Toni set up in your condo, make sure she knows her way around, introduce her to Stuart and Walt . . ."

"Us traveling together might attract attention. Reveal her hideout."

"All the better." Patrick has an edge in his voice now. "I'd love that fucker to make a move in Princeton. Get Stuart involved, and you won't have to kill him. Asshat'll dismember him."

"Stuart's pretty ruthless in a fight." I finish my scotch and look out the window toward the beach. My chest is heavy. I want to be home. Still, I know my partner's right. "I'll do it."

"I'll message Toni and tell her you'll meet her in Princeton. She's spending tonight with her sister Nancy and Cammie. She hopes it'll ease the transition."

"Great. I'll get on the road first thing. And Patrick?" He makes a noise in my ear. "Keep your eye on Melissa for me."

"Just like always. I'm the Guard. I got her covered."

THE FIRST THING I NOTICE when I enter the condo building in Princeton is Cammie. She's a tiny little thing, wearing a purple dress with a big white flower pattern on it. Her dark hair is brushed up into a purple bow the size of her head, and she's holding a saggy pink bunny over one arm.

She seems calm, which is in direct contrast to her mother. Star's hands flutter over her daughter's hair every few seconds. She shifts the little girl from one hip to the other, then she digs in her bag and pulls out what looks like a small packet of jellybeans. Just before she hands them to Cammie, however, she pulls them back fast. I enter the double doors and greet Walt, whose eyes are twinkling at this new development, and Star hustles over to me.

"Are jelly beans a choking hazard?" she whispers, blinking huge brown eyes up at me.

"Maybe," I answer in what I hope is a calming voice. She's clearly nervous as hell around her child.

"Right." She nods fast and shoves the plastic package back in her bag. "What the hell was I thinking?" Then she gasps. "Shit!" She gasps again, and grips her mouth with her fingers.

I can't help it. My insides are shredded, my head hurts from drinking myself to sleep last night, but despite it all, this makes me laugh. She's a complete screw up as a mom, and she can't even stop swearing.

Catching her arm, I give it a squeeze. "Relax. She seems okay for now. Cammie's what? A year old?"

"Ten months."

"She won't remember any of this. All she knows is how you feel, so be cool. Let her know you love her."

She's blinking fast, and I'm afraid she might cry. Unsure how my own battered insides will respond to that, I catch Walt's attention.

"Mr. Alexander?" He steps over, ready to serve.

"Walt, this is . . ." I hesitate, unsure which name we're using on the record.

"Star," she says quickly.

"Star Brandon and her daughter Camille." Walt gives her a friendly nod, and as if by magic, pulls a sucker out of his pocket. The little girl takes it and smiles. Her brown eyes are bright, and a little dimple is in her cheek.

"She's a cutie," Walt says, giving her arm a light tap.

Touching his shoulder, I pull him aside and lower my voice. "Star is one of our clients. She's gotten some threats. No one is to come near these two."

He's immediately serious. "I'll alert the other doormen. We'll be on the lookout against any new delivery guys, postmen . . ."

I give his shoulder a squeeze, and the level of appreciation I feel for him at this moment is indescribable. "You're a good man, Walt. I confess, I miss you."

"Ahh, you traded up, Mr. A." He laughs in his warm, scratchy voice. "How's Miss Jones and your little look-alike?"

I can't help the wince of pain at his question, and he seems to notice. "I'm sorry, sir. I hope everything's okay."

Patting his shoulder I nod and swallow back the thickness in my throat. "Everything will be fine, Walt." It *will* be fine.

MARISKA IS AT STUART'S PLACE, and the minute she hears us arrive, she's at my door. As usual, she's wearing some filmy, red handkerchief-print dress, but she's pulled an oversized, drab-grey fisherman's sweater on top of it. It falls off one shoulder, and with her loose, brown waves pulled in a high ponytail, I don't know how she does it. She actually makes her bag-lady outfit look sexy. Stuart's fucking happier than I've seen him in my life.

"Drop off your stuff and come across the hall!" Mariska says, giving Star a huge hug.

"Okay!" Star's tension seems to melt slightly.

"Do you think Cammie will come with me?" Mariska holds out her hands to the little girl, who's sucking a pacifier now and still clutching her limp bunny.

Star and her daughter share those huge doe-eyes. "I don't know." Her mother's voice is hesitant as she studies the little girl on her hip.

"Let's see." Mariska holds out her hands with cheerful confidence. "Cammie! Come here, baby! Come with Aunt Mare Mare!"

Mariska's slim hands are covered in rings of all shapes and colors. The little girl looks up at her smiling face and instantly smiles back, leaning forward. Mariska gives her a twirl, and the baby laughs, losing the pacifier Star had shoved in her mouth on our way up even though she wasn't even crying.

"Oh!" Star jumps forward and grabs it. Mariska doesn't pause. The two of them are out the door and headed to Stuart's place before we even have a chance to respond. All we hear are Mariska's sing-songy coos trailing behind them.

Star looks at me in wonder. "She's really good with kids."

"Kids, animals . . . stubborn jackasses," I say under my breath, heading to my room. "Make yourself at home. After tonight, you can have the master bedroom if you want it."

I stop just inside my old room and drop my duffel on the floor. The photo of Melissa and Dex at the beach is on my dresser, and it hits me like a sucker-punch to the gut. Leaning heavily on my hand, I pick up the mahogany frame and look at my beautiful family as several painful moments pass.

"Melissa," I whisper, touching her face. "What are you thinking?"

"Hey, you okay?"

Straightening, I put the frame back on the dresser. "Yeah. You need something?"

Star's eyes narrow and flicker from mine to the frame and back. "I wasn't expecting you to meet me here. I wanted to say thanks."

"No worries. Patrick suggested I drive up. It made sense."

"Shouldn't you be with your family?" She's watching me, and I remember what I observed the last time we worked with this girl. She's smart. She should be so much more than a fucking part-time hooker. She should be in college, which is what she was doing until some asshole thought he'd start blackmailing her.

"I'm not going to let an opportunistic thug steal your future. Especially not to get to me. They understand."

Her voice softens. "I don't know if I'd understand. If I was your family, I mean."

Not going there. "You'd better get across the hall. Mariska is pretty persistent from what I understand."

She nods and takes off. Finally, I'm alone.

Holding my phone, I stare at Melissa's face on my screen. She's so beautiful, sitting on the beach, the wind wrapping one of her perfect waves around her neck. My body physically aches for her. I need to bury my face in her ocean-roses scent and tell her I love her.

Patrick said not to call. He said he has his eye on her, give her space, give her time. None of that matters. I have to hear her voice. Touching the number, I wait as it rings in my ear.

It rings and rings. I've almost given up when the call connects.

"Hello?" Her voice is so soft. I can tell she's been crying, and it rips through my chest. I want to hold her.

"Melissa." I exhale her name. "Baby, please talk to me."

Silence first, a few moments where I only hear her shaky breathing, then she clears her throat. I know her so well. She's building that wall against me. I can't let her do it.

"What do you need?"

"I need you."

Silence again. The sound of brushing covers her phone, and I wonder if she covered it with her hand. When she comes back, the slightest tremor is in her voice.

"If you need something, please tell me. Otherwise, I'll have to block your calls."

"Don't do that. Just hang on." I think fast, hoping to derail that notion. "I need to know about Dex's party. What time and where."

Another deep breath in my ear. It tightens the knot in my chest. She's so close but still so far. What will it take to get her to listen to me again?

"I didn't realize you were coming."

"Melissa." My voice is low. "It's his first birthday."

"I thought you'd see him another time. Later in the day, I

mean. At Mom's."

I'm not invited to his party? This is fucking getting worse and worse. And it hurts like hell. "I'd like to be there. If that's okay?"

She's quiet again. We were just in bed together less than two days ago. I know this is killing her, too. She can't turn on me that fast.

"I'll talk to Mom." Her voice is quiet. "We can have the party at her house."

"Okay." I'm keeping my tone gentle, like I'm approaching a wounded animal. "Do you know what time?"

"Dex naps at three . . ." her voice breaks off, and I can hear her losing the battle against her tears. I'm on the verge of losing my battle with all of this. A sharp breath, and she's back in control. "I'll text you after I've talked to Mom. I need to go now."

Not so fast. "If you can, give me some lead-time. I drove Star to Princeton so she can stay here. Hide out until we know who's blackmailing her. It was Patrick's idea, but it's a good one. Stuart can watch over her, and Walt guards the door. You know the setup."

She makes a noise, and I go for it.

"I'm telling you everything, Mel. Full disclosure. Whatever you want to know." I wait, but I only hear the soft sound of her breath. She's got to be thinking the same thing as me: *This is so wrong.* "I love you, baby. I miss you so much."

I've gone too far. A whispered, "I'll text you," and the line disconnects.

Setting my phone on my dresser, I clutch my forehead. I've trained for torture, prolonged periods without sleep, food, or drink. I've gone days staring at the desert sand until I thought I'd go blind. I've been in combat, injured . . . Nothing compares to this.

Turning, I go to the kitchen and reach over the stove. My supply of alcohol is relatively untouched. Melissa prefers wine, and nobody's been here for months. I pull down the Johnnie Walker and a tall glass. My front door opens just as I've taken the first sip, and I hear Stuart's voice.

"Hey, man. Looks like Mariska's found a new friend." He rounds the corner, and stops in his tracks when he sees me. "What happened?"

Taking another long drink, I stare at the amber liquid and just say it. "Melissa kicked me out."

"What the hell?" He takes a step forward and stops. "What did you do?"

It's funny because I've known Stuart so long. I can remember a time when his response would've been *Fuck her. There's plenty of fish in the sea. I'll get the boat.* Apparently Mariska's changed everything.

I lean back against the cabinets and take another drink. "She found out about Sloan. Then she found out about Star."

My friend's brow lines, and I know he isn't following me. I'm not making sense. Saying it out loud makes it all sound so stupid to me.

I clear my throat and start over. "She was mad I didn't tell her about Sloan."

"You didn't tell anybody about Sloan. You didn't even tell me."

"The fewer people who know about a problem, the better the chance it *won't* get discovered."

"It's Security 101," he agrees.

Shaking my head, I wonder why women aren't as reasonable as men. "Well, my fiancée isn't in the security business, and she didn't like that answer." Taking another sip, I confess. "In fairness, I understand her being mad about it. I should've told her. My role in what happened to Sloan impacts her and Dex . . ."

Stuart doesn't speak. I can tell he's waiting for the other shoe to drop.

"I promised not to keep her in the dark on these things anymore."

He nods, and I see the pieces click together for him. "And then she found out about Star."

"And then I found all my luggage on her front porch."

"Shit." Stuart leans against the opposite cabinets, crossing his muscled arms. On his face is stunned empathy. "You must be going crazy."

A female voice interrupts us. "What's up with you guys?" Mariska is standing in the doorway watching, and I don't care anymore.

"Melissa and I are . . . taking a break."

"Oh my god!" Mariska swirls to me in an instant, touching my arm. "Is there anything I can do?"

Stuart leans forward and catches her around the waist, gently pulling her back against his chest. "You could order up some food?" His voice is tender, and he leans down to kiss her ear. I turn away from the sight of her touching his cheek and take another long drink of scotch.

"I've done something even better!" She's smiling when I look up. "I made a big pot of sarmale this afternoon. It's the ultimate comfort food."

"Is that the tomato-cabbage . . ." Stuart's still holding her against him.

"Cabbage leaves stuffed with tomatoes and rice and pork . . . It'll warm you to your toes."

"I'm not cold," I say under my breath.

"It's delicious," Stuart says over to me. "Can't have my CO getting his dinner from a bottle."

Mariska kisses his mouth briefly before going to the door. She pauses before leaving and looks back. "Derek?" I glance up at her. "It's going to work out, okay?"

My brows rise briefly. "Thanks."

She's gone, but Stuart's still watching the place where she stood. I'm glad I'm not staying because being around these two still so fresh in love would push me over the fucking edge.

"Take your time," he says before following the trail she left. "Come over when you're ready."

"Thanks," I nod.

"If you don't come over, I'll send a plate with Star and Camille."

"I like that even better."

He nods. "Brothers. Always there for each other."

———————❤———————

I'M SITTING ON MY LEATHER couch staring at the black screen of my enormous television when Star and Cammie bump through the front door.

She doesn't speak, so I look up to see the little girl is fast asleep on her mother's shoulder. I put my empty glass on the coffee table. I've only gone through half a bottle tonight. I'm trying to pace myself knowing I'll see Melissa and Dex tomorrow. I want my head to be clear.

Star motions to the guest room, but I don't respond. I'm tired and numb, and my insides are shredded. I just want to go to bed.

It doesn't seem like enough time has passed before she's with me again in the living room, plate in hand.

"Mariska made this. It might be the best thing I've ever eaten." She's beside me on the couch, but my mind is miles away with Melissa. What is she doing right now? Can she sleep without me? I can't sleep without her.

"Take a bite." Blinking up, I realize Star's been talking, and she's now holding a fork with a square of cabbage roll on it.

Clearing my throat I straighten up on the couch, taking the fork and plate from her hands. "Thanks," I say.

She relents and sits back on the couch. The spicy tomato dish tastes like dishwater. I'm in no mood to eat. If I'm honest, I want to go to my room and finish off that fifth until this fucking pain is gone. The only thing stronger than that urge is me not wanting to look like shit tomorrow.

"I hope Cammie sleeps tonight." I glance up and Star's

chewing her lip. "If she asks for Nan, I don't know what I'll do."

"You're doing okay with her."

"You think so?" Worried eyes meet mine.

"Yeah. You're not born knowing these things. I've learned a lot being around Dex, watching him." I mechanically cut another piece of cabbage, put it in my mouth.

Star exhales, shaking her head. "That's the problem. I've never even babysat. I don't know what the hell I'm doing."

I don't want to say it shows. I'm trying to be encouraging. "You love her. That's what's important. Try to be calm and smile more. Use that voice like Mariska does."

She nods, blinking fast. "I'm afraid I'm going to break her."

"Kids are pretty sturdy."

We're quiet again, and Star watches as I force myself to take another bite. "It's good, yeah?"

"I don't know."

She laughs then. "You've taken four bites. Either you like it or you don't."

Leaning forward, I set the plate on the coffee table. "I'm not really hungry."

We're quiet again, and I'm about to excuse myself when she speaks. "I wanted to thank you for something else."

Sitting back on the couch, I look at her, blinking those brown eyes at me. I'm trying to figure out when she got so vulnerable. "Okay?"

Reaching out, she takes my hand and holds it in both of hers. I start to pull away, but somehow that feels mean. "This is going to sound pathetic."

She does a little laugh, and I confess I'm curious. "Shoot."

"Nobody has ever believed in me like you did." Her eyes move from our hands to my face. "Or do?"

Shifting my position to face her, I take my hand back. "You're a smart girl. I believe you can do better than your past."

"Right," she nods, looking down again. Now her hands are clasped in her lap. "You're the reason I applied to college. I wanted to see if you were right. At the same time, I was scared. You didn't know me or anything."

I'm sorry her life has been such a shit hole. "It's my job to read people. We spent a week together, and I saw your potential. I'm glad if I helped you see it, too."

She smiles, and for the first time I concede she's a pretty girl. Without all the makeup, her features are delicate, and even if her eyes aren't stunning blue, they're lively and full of emotion.

"So I owe you more than I can repay. First with the believing in me," she exhales a laugh again. "That sounds so dumb, I know. Now you let me stay here with Cammie . . ."

"It's the right thing to do. Only an asshole threatens a helpless mother and child."

"I'm not so helpless." She cuts me a look from under her lashes, but I let it pass.

Anger burns in my chest. Star's blackmailer has pulled her out of college, dislocated her and her daughter, wrecked my home.

"You're not as strong as I am," I growl. "I'm ready to kick this fucker's ass. You have no idea."

Her lips press together and she nods. "Either way, you're really special to me."

With that, it's time to say goodnight. I stand and pat her shoulder. "There's more good people in the world than bad. Keep doing the right thing, and you'll meet them."

She touches the top of my hand on her shoulder, but I pull away heading to my room. I don't expect to get any sleep, but I'm hitting the road early. My chest aches at the thought Melissa might not text me, but just as I'm plugging in my phone it lights up.

Mom said we can have the party at one. If that gives you enough time.

Pain mixes with relief at her words. *I'll be there. Thank you.*

She doesn't respond, but I'm still encouraged. I still have a chance of getting back inside that wall, and when I do, I won't fuck it up again.

SEVEN

BIRTHDAY BREAK

Melissa

MOM IS IN THE LIVING room with Dex, and I can hear her playfully chatting with him while he lines his trains up on her coffee table.

"Is this the station?" she asks in a high-pitched tone. "Are the trains wishing Dex a happy birthday?"

His little voice answers a loud *Yes!* And they continue chattering.

My hands tremble as I stand in the kitchen dropping slinkies, tiny containers of bubbles, and toy trains in decorated plastic bags. I'm doing my best to stay calm, breathe through my growing anxiety as I finish the party favors for his few little birthday guests.

They'll all be here in less than ten minutes. Lane is invited, of course, and two little boys from Dex's Mom's Day Out class. They'll only stay for an hour, then I'll be alone with his daddy. Another tremor moves through my stomach at the thought.

I'm not strong enough for this yet. Mom's being very supportive, although she repeatedly slips up and makes some comment about how she can't believe this is happening. She blames herself, saying if she hadn't gotten sick last fall we wouldn't have postponed our ceremony, and we'd already be married. I counter saying yes, and again I'd be stuck in a marriage built on secrets and lies. Elaine also blames herself, which is ridiculous. She didn't force Derek to break his word. I haven't even spoken to Patrick.

A quick glance around the kitchen, and the blue and red train decorations are all in place or draped over the table. His cake is an elaborate blue tank engine with red and yellow piping and a bright yellow *1* on the side. It's a special delivery from my favorite client and baker "Aunt Bea," and a bright red candle is waiting to go on top. It's so cheery, Dex will love it. I can hardly look at it.

I'm not sure how much longer I can take the building tension waiting for his guests to arrive. Silently, I pray Derek won't be the first one here. Then I silently add another prayer that I won't cry during my son's first birthday party. I've been crying every other time of day. My determination is to make it one hour without tears.

The doorbell rings and I jump. Stepping to the passage between the kitchen and the living area, I watch my mom catch Dex's little hand and help him toddle to the door.

"Let's see who it is, Dexy!"

My eyes close as I hold my breath, releasing it in a rush when I recognize the squeals of children and realize it's Hannah and Evan from Mom's Day out. Right behind them are Cheryl and Tatum.

"Hi, guys!" I manage to say, surprised at my ability to act so calm.

I *will* be calm. Dex *will* have a happy first birthday party. Hugs are exchanged, and I take the gifts into the kitchen. The little boys go immediately to Dex's train station setup on Mom's coffee table and start picking their engines.

"Such a lovely apartment," Hannah says, giving Mom a hug. "It's so nice of you to play hostess!"

"I thought it would be easier for everyone if we had the party in town," I lie. The truth is I can't have Derek back in the cottage. I'm afraid he won't leave, and I won't have the strength to force him.

"It is closer to everyone," Mom agrees, supporting my fictitious excuse.

"I suppose it's easier for Derek to pop over from the office, too," Cheryl says.

My breath stutters, and thankfully Elaine and Lane are coming through the door at that exact moment.

"We made it!" she calls cheerfully, and Lane makes a beeline to the little boys. "Where's my mimosa?"

"Good idea," I say, heading for the kitchen.

My hands shake violently as I reach for the cava. It's only a matter of moments before he'll walk through the door, and I'll have to face him. What the hell made me think I could do this? I should've insisted he wait to visit Dex at a later time when I could be elsewhere. Several deep breaths, I have to compose myself. It might have made things easier for me, but I couldn't ban him from the party. It would be too cruel, and Dex would want his daddy.

Tears threaten in my eyes, and I quickly pop the cork. Elaine walks up behind me. "How's it going?" Her voice is low, concerned.

"Okay," I nod as I pour an inch of cava into her glass of orange juice. I take my wine straight, sipping it fast. "If I can make it through this party."

A low voice from the living room interrupts my sentence. My heart stops then restarts beating painfully fast. In a gulp, I finish the rest of my wine and quickly pour another glass.

Elaine's green eyes are fixed, and she holds my forearm. "Ready?"

Taking another sip, I see my hand tremble too much, and I set the flute on the counter. "I don't have a choice."

Holding hands, we start back for the living room. Rounding

the corner, my entire body flushes with heat when I see him. He's wearing dark jeans and a long-sleeved chambray button-down shirt under a brown tweed blazer. The shirt makes his eyes glow and the blazer accents the natural highlights in his dark hair. It's ridiculous that he looks even more handsome than when I saw him two days ago. He's carrying a soft brown teddy bear with a huge blue bow and a bouquet of red and white roses. I have to look away quickly before I lose the tiny bit of control I'm desperately clinging to.

"Oh, Derek, they're beautiful." Mom takes the flowers, holding his arm as if it's a lifeline. "Did you drive straight in?"

"Yes," his low voice cuts through me, and I can feel his gaze on my skin. "Had to get an early start, but I wouldn't miss Dex's party."

"Were you out of town?" Hannah's sitting on the floor near the boys.

"I had some business to take care of in Princeton," he answers, and his long explanation last night on the phone of exactly what he was doing filters through my mind.

It's too late, I stubbornly argue. Am I going to set the precedent that every time I need him to take me seriously, I have to throw him out of the house? My thoughts swirl with frustration and anger, and I realize Mom is asking me something.

"I'm sorry?" I say, blinking up to her.

"I said would you get Derek a drink?" My eyes land on his and lightning flashes to my toes.

"I-I . . ." I'm trying to recover when Elaine jumps in and rescues me.

"I'll take care of it. Mimosa, Derek?"

"Just a soft drink will be fine."

"Anybody else?" My best friend makes her way through the room, and I glance over at the clock. Fifty more minutes.

"We can head into the kitchen for cake if everybody's ready," I say, wishing my voice didn't sound so fragile.

"You ready for cake, Dex?" Derek squats down beside our

son, who suddenly recognizes his presence.

"Day!" Dex squeals and holds Derek's shoulders, trying to climb him. Derek laughs, and my stomach cramps. I turn and head to the kitchen to light the candles.

An hour has never gone by so quickly. The little boys are full of cake and ice cream, goodie bags are passed out, and they're chasing each other around the coffee table as Hannah and Cheryl say goodbye and snag their little guys. Mom sees them to the door, and I busy myself cleaning up.

Elaine has done her best to run interference between Derek and me the entire party, trapping him in the living room with discussions of all things Patrick, Stuart, little boys, buying a condo versus buying a house, car buying versus car leasing, basketball or football, fly fishing . . . I swear to god, if she feels responsible for our present situation, she's redeemed herself a thousand-fold today.

Lane's whining is the only thing able to pull her from between my ex-fiancé and me. "I guess I'd better get him home," she says, and I can hear the worry in her voice. "Do you want to come with me, Derek? I'm sure Patrick wants to see you."

Nice try, I can't help thinking as Derek declines her offer. He's here to see his son, but I know who else he's here to see. Picking up my flute, I take a last gulp of cava. Elaine and I essentially split the bottle.

"I'll walk you out," Mom says. *Traitor.*

Dex is back to playing on the rug, but I can tell from the energy behind his train noises, he'll be crashing soon. I'm standing in the kitchen clutching the counter when I hear him enter.

"It was a great party." His voice is soft, and my insides twist painfully.

"Thank you," I manage in a voice far calmer than I feel.

"Dex seems really excited about his new toys."

"He really likes the stuffed bear you got him." I'm still facing the counter, afraid to turn around.

"Yeah," I hear a smile in his voice. "I know he's a train guy, but sometimes it's good to try new things."

His casual tone makes me glance up at him. It's a huge mistake, because the pain I'm feeling is reflected in his blue eyes. My heart clenches hard, and I have to look away again. He saw my response, however, and he's at my side.

"Mom sure is taking a long time with Elaine," I say around my rapid breath.

"Melissa." The torture of our separation is bound up in one word. I can barely stand it.

"I think I'd better go for a walk or something." I try to pass when he catches me by the arms.

"Wait." His voice breaks on the words, and my eyes flood. "Won't you talk to me just a moment?"

"It's too late for talking."

"It's not too late if you still believe in us."

Cutting my eyes up at him, I let out all the anger I'm feeling. "I *always* believed in us. You were the one who held me apart."

"You know it wasn't like that." His low voice is urgent. "I wanted to protect you."

"That excuse is only good once, not after you promised me—"

"Dammit, Melissa! I wasn't trying to break my promise."

"Still, you lied—"

"No. Lying implies deception. I never tried to deceive you."

"You conveniently omitted the part where you drove to Raleigh because Star was being blackmailed!"

"I didn't want you to feel responsible."

"Responsible? How could I feel responsible? You never let me in!"

"May, tank?" Our voices have grown too loud and Dex toddles in the room. He's holding his toy in one hand and his new bear in the other. I bend down to pick him up, but I have to look away from the break in Derek's eyes.

"I need you to give me your key." My voice is quiet, and I feel my body trembling as I say the words.

Derek steps toward us, but I turn my back.

"Stop this," he pleads. "Why are you doing this?"

"I've lived that life. I've been with someone who acted one way before we were married, and once we said *I do*, everything changed."

"I'm not like that." It's a low growl.

"Neither was he."

"Goddammit! I am *NOT* Sloan Reynolds!"

Dex starts to cry, and I clutch him closer to me. "I need you to give me your key and go."

I'm doing my best not to back down from what I have to do, doing my best to hold myself together. Doing my best not to dissolve into the fountain of tears I feel welling up in my chest. Shifting Dex on my hip, I again try to step past Derek, but again he stops me. "I won't let you do this to us."

"NO!" Now my voice is raised. "You're not putting this on me. You did this to us when you lied to me. When you swore you would be honest with me and the very next day you broke your word."

He's holding my arm too tightly, and I'm about to give in to my tears. "Let me go, Derek."

"I can never let you go."

My voice trembles. "Let me put Dex down for his nap."

His grip relaxes, but he doesn't move. "I'm not finished talking to you."

I push past him speaking softly to my little boy, who's sucking his finger. Once we're in his room at Mom's, I lay him in the crib and pull his favorite blanket beside him. He clutches the bear close and turns his head away, ready to sleep.

For a few moments, I stand beside his crib and rub his back, blinking as the first tears drop onto my cheeks. I have to stay strong. I have to make it through this. I have to believe I'm right.

A few more moments pass. Finally, I feel like I can go back to the living room. Dex is slowly drifting to sleep as I step out and close the door. A mirror hangs in the hallway behind me, and my eyes land on the gold chain around my neck. My breath hitches, my stomach cramps, and new tears flood my eyes. Reaching around my neck, I can barely unfasten it for my trembling fingers.

Holding the necklace in my hand I walk into the living room. "I should give this back."

"You will not." His face looks as if I've slapped him. "My heart is yours. Nothing has changed. You still love me."

More tears flood my eyes until they can't be contained. Drops fall on my cheeks, and I have to turn away. "I do. I love you more than I've ever loved any man."

"Okay, then." He's behind me, holding my shoulders. "I'm moving home."

"No, you're not." I step forward, out of his grasp. "I'll deal with my broken heart the way you'll deal with yours."

"Dammit, Melissa." His words are sharp even if his voice is low, and I appreciate him not wanting to upset Dex any more. "How can you say that?"

"I made a vow when I left Sloan's mansion that I'd never live that way again."

"If you compare me to that bastard again—"

Looking back over my shoulder, I meet his eyes now. "You're not an abusive asshole who frequents prostitutes, that's correct. Otherwise, you treat me the same as he did."

His jaw moves as anger flashes in his eyes. "Nowhere in the fucking universe is that true, and you know it."

"I'm not your equal. You hold me apart from your life—"

"You're so far in my life, I don't know where you begin and where I end. It's why we can't be separated."

From somewhere deep in my heart comes a question I'm not sure I want to ask. Yet out it spills. "Did you keep secrets from Allison?"

"Of course not, but—" His answer is so fast, so automatic, it crushes me.

"I need you to give me my key and go."

His fists clench, and for a moment, I'm afraid he might grab me. His voice grows louder as he speaks. "Stop this goddamn stubbornness, Melissa. I hear you now. I understand what you need, and I'm ready to give it to you."

Dex's whimpering from his room matches the quaking of my own insides. My head is light as I back away. I can't argue with him anymore. I don't have the strength. Putting my necklace on the end table, I clutch it for a moment, saying my final words. "I can't do this anymore."

Holding the walls I make my way to Dex's room. At this point, I'm feeling so broken down, I don't know if I'll make it through this. If I won this battle he wins the war. When I'd said I still loved him, I'd spoken from the depths of my soul. My heart is battered, broken, and torn, and all I want is to crawl into his arms and let him hold me. Take this pain away and come home.

Only how can I say that? He doesn't treat me like he should. He flat out admitted he never hid things from her . . . He knows this isn't the way we should live, and I have to mean more to him than that.

Dex is standing in his crib, blue eyes round, a tear hangs on his little dark lashes. I lift him into my arms and walk to the glider in the corner. He snuggles into me, and the closeness of him, his baby scent eases the bleeding hole in my chest.

It would be so easy to give in, to say it doesn't matter and take him back. At the same time, everything inside me revolts at the prospect of going back to a life of half-truths and double-lives. Even if I know Derek isn't Sloan, I can't shake the ghosts of how my life used to be. The faintest hint of it sends ice water running through my veins.

If I willingly go back and nothing changes, I can only blame myself for making the same mistake twice, and this time, I can't blame it on ignorance. This time I'd be making the decision with my eyes wide open.

Dex scrubs his little head against my shoulder, and I hug him closer. As much as it hurts being away from Derek, I also have to consider our little boy. A baby is something I never had with Sloan, thank goodness.

His little fist grips my sleeve, and I kiss his dark hair. His little humming noises as he soothes himself actually soothe me.

Derek would never hurt me the way Sloan did. His lies are different from Sloan's in that while my ex-husband cheated on me and humiliated me at every turn, Derek has only risked everything to protect me—and then kept it a secret.

My survival instinct says to protect myself from even the hint of how my life used to be. What if my survival instinct and the man I love are on the same team, fighting the same battle? Derek says he'll change, and maybe he will. But if he doesn't, can I overlook this side of his personality?

"I'm going to figure this out, baby," I whisper, kissing Dex's ear. "I'm going to make the right decision for us. I promise."

I just need more time.

EIGHT

HARD LINES

Derek

LEAVING HER IS THE HARDEST thing I've ever done, but I'll be damned if I give that fucking key back. I'll be damned if I give any of it back. Melissa is mine. She and Dex belong with me. I won't back down from that.

Listening to her say those words was like being gutted with a dull knife. She fucking compared me to Sloan. God dammit. The mere suggestion rains acid all over my shredded insides. I would never treat her like that bastard. I killed that fucker because of what he did to her, what he wanted to do to her.

Anger pushes me too hard. I'm at a hundred on I-95, and I don't even see the cars as they pass. I have to drive back to Princeton tonight. I don't know what I'll do if I stay in Wilmington, but I know it won't help my case any.

Melissa is my heart and my soul and my life and my love, and every word she said made me want to grab her and shake her until . . . No. I'd never do that. I've just never been in that position where every word out of her mouth was so impossibly insane. My skull feels like it's coming apart from the pressure in my head.

I've suffered through someone I loved slipping away from me. When Allison had cancer, and all I could do was watch her die, I never thought I'd survive it. Yet, Melissa stands there with our little boy in her arms talking to me like nothing we've done even matters.

"Fucking bullshit!" I shout inside the car, slamming my fist against the steering wheel.

Yeah, getting out of Wilmington is the right call. Staying wouldn't lead anywhere productive. I'll step back, decompress, do some work, and see if I can figure out a better solution than tearing her door down with my bare hands.

The eight-hour drive is done, and I'm parking in my usual spot, heading into the building by eleven.

"Welcome home, sir," Jason, Walt's regular backup greets me.

"Hey, Jase." I pause inside the doors. "Did Walt mention my guests to you?"

"Yes, sir." Jason's overgrown eyebrows pull together like two black caterpillars. "We've alerted the other staff to be cautious of new runners and such. We won't let you down, sir."

Clasping his shoulder, I nod. "I appreciate it. The mother's okay, but her baby—"

"She's a cute little girl." Jason's oval face splits with a smile. "Dark hair and eyes. A real show stopper."

"Thanks." Nodding, I head to the elevator, wondering what Star was doing with Cammie in the lobby. I'll have to talk to her about being more discreet.

My condo is empty when I enter, which surprises me. I can only assume they're across the hall with Stuart and Mariska. It's late, but the little girl could easily sleep on a palette or a bed, and honestly, I appreciate the time alone. I need to recover from Melissa's blistering words.

Opening the cabinet, my scotch is gone. A bottle of Belvedere sits in the background, and I pull it down. Amber last night, clear tonight. My insides are loose and shaken. I haven't felt this helpless in years.

Walking to the couch, tumbler of ice in one hand, bottle in the other, I kick off my shoes and collapse into soft black leather. My phone is in my pocket, and I pull it out. Holding it in my hand, I stare at her beautiful face smiling, blue eyes glowing.

I want to call her. I want to shake her. I want to pull her to me and hold her until these fears in her melt away. Sloan put them there, and now from beyond the grave, his ghost still threatens us. I can barely take the thought, and I pull the cork out with my teeth. God, what am I? A fucking pirate?

Setting the phone on the end table, I pour until the tumbler is full. Fuck control. Fuck sensibility. I'm killing the pain tonight.

Leaning back on the sofa, my head drops back against the leather. I haven't checked in with anybody. I haven't answered the calls from Patrick. I'm sure Elaine told him I was there, but fuck if I feel like discussing it.

Another long pull, and the tumbler is half empty. Behind me, I hear the noise of my front door open. I expect it to be Star bringing Cammie back for the night, but the voice is my partner's.

"Patrick suspected you drove back." Stuart walks into the living room and takes the bergere facing me. "How long you been in?"

Lifting the tumbler, I finish my drink. "Five, ten minutes."

His eyes move from my hand holding the glass to my face. "That bad?"

"Shittier than bad." Leaning forward, I take the vodka and start pouring again.

"Give me some of that." He leans forward and catches the bottle before I've topped off my cup. Walking past he goes to the kitchen, and I drink while he fishes out another glass. "Did you talk to her?"

"She compared me to her fucking ex."

"The abuser?" Stuart's back, taking the seat across from me, keeping the bottle closer to him on the coffee table.

"One and the same."

"She knows better than that."

We're both quiet. He's nursing his drink, but I lean back and polish mine off then reach across for more. Before I grab it, he's picked the bottle up and is pouring more for himself. My brows lower as I watch. *If he's trying to piss me off* . . .

"Why don't you come into the office tomorrow," he says. "It'll take your mind off things."

"Why don't you fucking back off."

He actually has the nerve to chuckle.

"Don't fuck with me, Stuart. I'm in no mood."

"You don't have to tell me," he leans back, holding his glass. "It's been a long time since I've seen you this way."

"Buckle up. It's about to get worse."

"Strike that." He's in my way again, holding the bottle so I can't refill my glass. "I've never seen you this way."

"Fill it up," I growl, slamming down my tumbler.

He opens the bottle, but he only pours a shot. "This isn't going to change anything. It's only going to make you feel like shit."

"I already feel like shit. This is going to keep me from trashing this condo."

He stands and goes to the kitchen. "What about Cammie and Star?"

I'm leaning forward now, shoving my hands into the front of my hair, gripping the sides of my skull. "She asked for the key. She tried to give back her necklace. I'm surprised she didn't think of her engagement ring."

"Give her time. She'll think of it."

"Whose fucking side are you on?"

He walks back and leans against the wall of windows facing me. "I've only been around Melissa a few times, but I can tell she loves you. You crossed a line."

"She keeps saying it's over." Dropping my hands, I stare at my fists. "If she says that one more time."

"Grab the reins, and give her space. At least this time, she's still here. You still have a chance."

My fists open, and I reach for my glass. Only one sip is left, but I've made it through the scorching burn of rage. Now my pain is dulled from the vodka, and all I'm left with is the helplessness.

"Losing Allison is nothing like losing Mel. It was out of my hands. I couldn't do anything to stop it."

"The situations might be more similar than you think."

Glancing up, I study his face. "How so?"

"You can't do anything now. You're going to have to let her come around in her own time."

"I don't know if I can wait that long."

We're interrupted by the sound of the door opening again. Looking back, I see Star enter with her daughter asleep on her shoulder. She does a little wave, and I stand.

"I'm sorry. I needed to come back," I say softly. "Were you . . ."

She shakes her head and points to the guest room. "I'm sleeping with Cammie."

Stuart pats my shoulder and heads for the door, leaving his full glass of vodka by the sink. "I'll pick you up in the morning. Get some sleep."

The two doors close simultaneously, and I pick up my phone. She doesn't want to hear from me, but I'm sticking to my policy of full disclosure.

I drove back to Princeton tonight. I'm going to go in and talk to Nikki, see if Patrick's found any leads on Star's situation, see if I can find anything. I'll be home this weekend. I'll be thinking of you every minute until then.

I hit *Send* and wait. Seconds tick past, and there's no answer. A minute, and I let it go. Stuart's right. It's tearing me apart, but I have to let her take the lead.

———◆———

NIKKI DOESN'T EVEN LOOK UP from her desk when we enter the glass doors of the Princeton office. It's not until I speak that her white-blonde head snaps to attention.

"What's this I hear about you quitting?" My tone is mock disapproval, and her blue eyes go wide.

"Derek!" Her pinup mouth drops open, and I can't help shaking my head. Of all the secretaries I expected to stick around, it wasn't this airhead blonde.

"Can I see you in my office?"

She hops up and follows me in the same too-tight dresses she's worn since Day one. We step inside the office, and I push the door closed.

"What's going on?" I go around and sit behind the desk, and she takes the chair in front of me, not meeting my eyes.

"I got a better offer at another firm. A law firm."

"You don't know anything about being a legal secretary." She's bluffing, and I know it. "Try again."

Clearing her throat, she shifts in her seat, pulling on the hem of her skirt. "Okay, well, I just thought I'd take a break. Maybe go back to school . . ."

"Remember when it was just the two of us in this office?" She nods, and I continue. "I got pretty good at knowing when you weren't being completely honest with me."

"I can't work here with him anymore." She says it so fast, I lean back in my chair. I hadn't expected her to cave in the first round of questioning. "I did everything right. I waited. I . . . I . . ."

Her eyes well up, and she drops her chin, pressing her fingertips to her forehead. "I wasted three years, and now I'm too old to meet anybody." Her shoulders shudder as she cries, and I'm at a loss.

Scanning my former office, I spot a tissue cube in the back

corner. Going to fetch it, I cross back and hold it out to her.

"First, you're young and fit. I'm sure plenty of guys would want to ask you out." Not me necessarily, but I prefer brunettes. I prefer Melissa. "Second, I don't think he was expecting you to wait." It's a shitty thing to say, but somebody has to tell her the truth.

"I know!" She wails, breaking down even more. She's full-on sobbing now, pressing a handful of tissues against her nose, her glittered fingernails catching the light. "I'm the loser here. I'm the one who gambled and lost."

She cries harder, and I flip through my papers trying to think of an excuse to send her home. "Tell you what. Why don't you take the day, and maybe you'll feel better tomorrow."

"No!" She wails shaking her head. Mascara is smeared on her cheeks, and she's starting to look pretty bad. "It's so much worse than that. I have to resign."

"Settle down, now." Walking around the desk, I put my hand on her shoulder. "If you have to resign, I won't stop you. At least stay and train your replacement."

All the bone-headed mistakes I've put up with from her, she can do that much.

"I don't know," she sniffs. "As long as I don't have to see . . . them."

Considering this, I figure we can make it work. "Stuart will be in the office, but if we can get a replacement this week, it shouldn't be a problem. Will that work?"

She nods still looking down, still wobbly from crying. "I'm going to miss you guys. I really liked working here."

Patrick's lines drift through my head, but I don't have it in me to lie to her. "You've been here a while . . . we'll miss you, too."

It's not a lie. Patrick will miss her, and I know Melissa was her friend, whether that still counts, I'm not sure. Nikki's reaction to my words comes out of the blue.

"Oh!" She jumps out of her chair, catching me around the

neck. "I always knew we were friends, even if you are a hard ass at the office."

"Take the morning off if you need it," I say, patting her arm then pulling it off my neck.

"It's okay," she sniffs, straightening up and wiping her eyes. "Let me know if you need anything." She's at my office door when she stops and looks back. "How's Melissa and Dex?"

Doing my best not to wince, I open my MacBook. "Good. Thanks for asking."

She pauses for a moment, and I can see curiosity stirring in her eyes.

"Thanks, Nikki." I pull open files and try to appear busy. She shakes her head and leaves.

The rest of the day, I comb through every file I have on Sloan Reynolds. After Melissa showed up in my office that day in November, I became mildly obsessed with nailing him. I tracked down every dirty deal, every misstep, every possible way I could expose him. Going through all of those files, looking for anything I might have thought insignificant, I'm struck again by how well he'd been able to cover his tracks.

"Fucker," I mutter under my breath. "You will not win. I didn't let you win then, and I sure as hell won't let you win now."

"That's the spirit." Glancing up, I see Stuart standing in my doorway. "It's after six. Let's call it a day."

Leaning back in my chair, I realize I worked through lunch. Brown accordion files surround me on the desk and the floor. "I collected a lot of shit here." My eyes travel over the mess.

"This is why you were better at academia than me." He exhales a laugh, opening one of the files and reading the cover sheet. "I could never bury myself in research this way."

"Don't be so sure." I stand, closing my computer and slipping it into my case. "Let somebody threaten Mariska, and we'll see how much you like research."

A light flashes in his hazel eyes, and he spins his keys.

"Somebody threatens Mariska, that'll be the last fuck-up he ever makes."

Gripping his shoulder, I follow him out the door. "Good answer. Keep in mind we're supposed to uphold the law."

"I never took any oaths." He glances back as the elevator doors open. "Even if I had, it didn't make a difference to you."

"I'm paying for that now."

"This story isn't over." His face turns serious. "Not by a longshot."

❤

THE GIRLS ARE CAMPED OUT in Stuart's condo playing Boggle when we arrive. Mariska has Cammie on her hip, and Star's hastily scribbling words as the egg timer counts down.

I'm feeling mildly better after spending a concentrated day tracking down potential connections to Sloan. It's not getting me closer to Melissa, but I have to believe with every passing day, she's softening. She loves me. She belongs to me. I'll report my progress to her tonight, and even if she doesn't reply, she'll get the message. I heard her, and I'm serious about giving her what she needs.

"This looks fun," Stuart, quips, walking over to Mariska and kissing her.

Cammie lifts her head and pats his face. "Scoot."

"Yes!" Mariska coos to the little girl. "Stuart!"

I can't help a laugh. "Sounds like she's trying to get rid of you."

He grins, and the way his eyes glow at the two of them, I'm surprised he hasn't already proposed. He's clearly ready to procreate.

"Did you look into transferring to Princeton like I asked you?" His voice is low, and Mariska's brow lines.

"I told you, I'm not letting you pay for my college. It's not your place."

"How about I make it my place." He catches her around the hips and pulls her to him, and I realize I'm not as recovered from the pain as I thought.

Leaning forward, I read Star's list. *Toe, roast, leaf, leap, leer* . . ."Doing okay?" I ask, and she shakes her head, holding up a hand.

"I've got to win this time!"

"It's Boggle."

"Mariska's won every time!"

"Sorry, I didn't know you were playing for blood. I'm stepping across to my place," I say, heading to the door.

Mariska looks over her shoulder. "We're ordering Thai food tonight. You'll come back and join us, okay?"

I give her a little wave, unsure what I'll do tonight. Now that I'm outside my office, back in the world of couples and families, I remember the gaping hole in my life where mine should be. I head to my bedroom, slip off my shoes, and loosen my tie. The picture of Melissa and Dex is on the dresser, and I lift it, enduring the pain radiating through my midsection and focusing on my love for them.

"I'm not going anywhere, babe," I say softly. "I'm waiting right here for you."

My phone buzzes, and I see Patrick's face. Touching the screen, I lower the picture. "Hey, man, what's up?"

"Nothing," he says, blowing air into my ear. "Abso-fuckin-lutely nothing. I swear, I feel like I'm beating my head against a brick wall. That fucker hid everything."

"You're talking about Sloan?" Stepping over to my closet, I hit speaker on the phone and put it on the end table.

"Who else? I've spent the last two days shaking every tree I can think of, and nothing falls out. That prick was tighter than Fort Knox."

Nodding, I know he's running into the same thing I faced back when I first tried to investigate Sloan Reynolds. I realize my frustration probably fueled the rage I felt at not being able to keep him from Melissa. It's probably why I killed him. My legitimate options had run out.

"He was a piece of work," I breathe, slipping into relaxed jeans and a navy tee. "Have you gotten anywhere with Star's guy?"

"Until he makes another move, we're just waiting. Since he went directly to her, I don't have a lot of background. She tossed all the envelopes, so I have no postmarks, no DNA, no potential fingerprints . . ."

"Hang in there, partner. These assholes always screw up." I scoop up my phone and head back to the kitchen. "They're not as smart as they think they are."

"Fucking Sloan Reynolds was one smart motherfucker."

"He wasn't so smart. He had money and great handlers." Patrick and I've worked together a while, and I realize this is the first time I've seen him facing a dead end.

The line is silent a beat before he speaks again. "How are you doing?"

It's a question I'm not ready to delve into. I take down the half-empty bottle of Belvedere from last night and grab a tumbler off the drying rack. "I've gone through everything I collected on him the last two years. Nothing stands out."

"That's not what I meant." He pauses again. I know it wasn't. "You going to be okay?"

I've got a nice full glass of vodka, and I take a long drink. Pausing to let the burn pass, I nod. "I'll make it one more day."

"I'm watching her for you. She's safe."

Gratitude warms my chest. Or maybe it's the alcohol. Either way, "Thanks, partner."

"She won't talk to me either if that makes you feel any better. Apparently, I'm in the dog house, too."

Another sip and I rub my forehead with the back of my hand. "It doesn't make me feel worse."

"I think it's a good sign. She's mad, and being mad means

she loves you. If she didn't, she wouldn't give a shit."

It's a good theory. Of course, then I remember her face at the birthday party, the tears in her eyes and the words she kept saying. Leaning back against the sink, I take another long pull. "I hope you're right."

THE LIGHT OF A FEW lamps casts a dim glow across my dark wood floors. My eyes trace the lines of my mahogany furniture. Stainless accents dot the interior, and an enormous flat screen television hangs dark on the wall in front of me.

When I bought this place, I was alone. Allison had died, taking with her my dreams of a home and a family. I was broken and empty, dark and angry. I had plenty of money to buy the ultimate bachelor pad, yet I had no intention of doing anything with it. I chose to be alone.

Then Melissa came. Then Dex. My life became so much more than I ever imagined when I moved in here. I had another chance at my dreams.

Now I'm back in this elegant cave by myself. Dex's cries are still in my ears, and the sight of Melissa refusing to look at me as she demands her key back . . .

I haven't eaten since breakfast, and even then, I didn't have much. An empty bottle of vodka is beside me, and anger twists in my chest. My fingers tighten around the crystal tumbler I'm holding, and I want to break it. I'm ready to smash every piece of elegant glass in the whole goddamn place.

The front door opens, momentarily interrupting my internal firestorm, and Star walks in with Cammie. The little girl is crashed out on her shoulder, and my thoughts travel to Dex. He'd be asleep on Melissa's shoulder right now.

Star deposits her daughter in Cammie's sleeping quarters then goes to the kitchen. I hear her digging in a crinkly plastic bag, and she's headed my way.

"Mariska said Walt knows all the best take-out places in a ten-mile radius." Her voice is too cheerful for how I feel. "I'm convinced. This is the best Thai I've had in . . . possibly ever!"

She sits on the coffee table in front of me, a plate of noodles in her lap. "You need to eat something."

My head is heavy, and I take in her appearance. Tonight, she's wearing tight jeans and a fitted, white long-sleeved sweater with thin black lines across it. Her long light-brown hair is loose and swept over one shoulder, and her face is more natural than I've ever seen it.

"What made you stick with this?" I say, lifting my hand to gesture to her outfit. "I thought you preferred rocker chic."

"I don't know," she smiles and glances up through dark lashes. "I guess I feel prettier this way?"

Nodding, I sit forward. "You look like Melissa."

She doesn't reply. Instead, she takes the glass from my hand, replacing it with a plate. I lift the fork and take a bite of pad Thai. It's good, so I take another.

"You've been driving a lot. Do you feel stiff?" She stands in front of me.

"I feel like shit." Instead of going back across the hall this evening, I'd sent my full-disclosure text to Melissa. As per usual, she didn't reply. All the vodka later, I'm twisted in my thoughts, trying to find any way back inside, through the wall she's built around her heart. It's killing me.

Star is on her knees, climbing behind me on the couch. "Mariska knows massage therapy." I feel her hands on my shoulders. "She showed me some touches. That's what they call them. *Touches.*"

She pushes and squeezes my muscles, and warm relaxation moves through my neck, into my arms. "Feels good," I say, leaning forward to put the plate on the table, resting my elbows on my thighs.

"It does, right?" Star climbs around me and scoots the plate aside, sitting in front of me. "Check this out."

Her voice is soft, but my insides are toast. All I want is one thing . . . one thing 850 miles away. My head is right at her chest, and she slides cool palms to my temples. Slim fingers go behind my ears into my hair. Gentle but intense pressure on my scalp, her thumbs move to my forehead, and the pain eases.

Her voice is different, lower. "Like that?"

"Mm. It's nice."

My eyes blink open, and her slim torso is right in front of me, swaying gently. Long, chestnut waves move over her breasts, covered in that white sweater. She stops massaging my scalp and her hands move down to my cheeks, lifting my face gently.

"Beautiful man." Her thumb lightly touches my lips. "You're tired and you're hurting. Let me comfort you tonight."

For a whole half-second in the dim light, her lips are fuller, begging for a kiss. Her long, brown waves distract me with how much they look like Melissa's. I imagine them falling around me as she straddles my lap. My hands grip her small waist, and as she leans forward, I catch the scent of honeysuckle.

I'm on my feet as my brain's still working out a response. "I'll be across the hall," is as good as it gets.

The next moment, Stuart's at his door in boxers and no shirt, squinting at me in the light of the hallway. "What the fuck?"

"I'm sleeping here tonight." I push past him into the dark condo when I realize I've brought nothing with me. "Can I borrow a shirt? And a toothbrush?"

He stands for a moment, brow furrowed. A quick sweep of my appearance and he shrugs. "You should be able to find whatever you need in the guest room. Nobody ever sleeps there, but I use it for overflow."

"Thanks." I start for the door, but Mariska's with us, wrapped in a silk robe, her hair messy.

"Are you spending the night?" she whispers. "Let me move my art supplies."

I step back and let her pass, catching Stuart's eyes on her ass.

"Art," I say, since we're momentarily stuck facing each other.

"She's taking a class in nudes this semester." An expression flickers in his eyes.

My brow lowers. "If I see you nude, I'll kick your ass."

"Grow up." But he can't stop his grin. "It's art.

"As if your ego could get any bigger."

Mariska's back with us. "It should be safe now." She smiles up at me. "We almost never have overnight guests."

"Yeah," I clear my throat. "Got a little crowded at my place. Cammie or something."

"But you have Dex . . . ?" Her eyes crinkle.

Stuart touches her back. "I figured this was coming. Let's turn in."

Thankfully, they take off. I step into the room and close the door. In view of my new full-disclosure policy, I decide in my next text to note that Star has my place to herself while I crash with Stuart and Mariska.

Stretching across the king-sized bed, I rub my forehead. I must've drunk more vodka than I realized. My body misses Melissa so much, it was ready to go for a cheap substitute to stop the pain. My stomach turns at the thought. Nothing is as good as Melissa. Closing my eyes, I picture her beautiful sapphire eyes, her long, dark waves over her ivory skin, her ocean-touched roses scent. I love her so much.

Even if she's thrown me out. Even if we're in a place where she won't talk to me. We'll get it back. I have to believe that, and when we do, I'll have no secrets from her, nothing to come between us. I won't betray her trust.

NINE

MOVING FORWARD

Melissa

WORK . . . WORK . . . *work*. I've done everything to bury myself in my marketing business, fighting with all I have to escape the pain of this gaping hole in my chest. A local strip mall is hosting a spring promo event, and several of the businesses have combined forces to do an inflatable playground for children with a bounce house and games, balloons and a tiny petting "zoo," consisting of rabbits, a few goats, a pot-bellied pig, and litter of kittens they hope to give away.

It's a solid week of work, collecting the various logos and nailing down exactly what type of promotion or event each shop will be hosting, locations and times, alternate arrangements for bad weather.

Sitting at my laptop, typing out the various press releases and newsletter templates for the stores, my eyes drift to the pin board of wedding ideas still lurking on my desktop. One pin is an ivory satin dress with large lace panels forming the bodice. Another is a white, strapless chiffon with lots of layers and movement in the skirt. Perfect for a beach wedding . . .

"I hadn't chosen my dress." Heat fills my eyes, and I lean my head heavily on my hand.

The board also includes cake ideas, and I realize I've got to stop Aunt Bea working on the wedding cake. "Oh, god." Another twist of pain.

Our engagement photograph is there, and the sight of me in his arms, soft lips touching my cheek, his dark hair moving in the breeze is almost too much. *He doesn't want this*, my mind shouts. *You don't want this*.

Standing I go to the kitchen for a glass of water. My mother has taken care of cancelling the roses, talking to the minister, the caterer, the musicians . . . Since we'd planned a beach wedding, we didn't lose any deposits. All I lost was my heart.

On the counter is a flier design I worked up for Aunt Bea. She wants to try decorated cake doughnuts in her shop. As old fashioned and out of touch with technology as she is, she still keeps up with the latest cooking trends. She's also addicted to the cooking channel.

Glancing at my calendar, I see it's Thursday. Has it been a whole week since Dex's party? Since that crushing day? Derek did not leave his key. He also did not take my necklace. It's back around my neck, actually, and every night I get a lengthy text from him detailing everything he did that day.

It's pretty routine info, and the only one I found interesting was when he made a point of telling me he was crashing with Stuart and Mariska while Star and her daughter stayed in his condo alone.

My hand instinctively moves to my midsection as I try to rub the cramp away. He knew I'd care about that. More heat in my eyes. All this information, all this thoughtful consideration . . . Why did it have to take such extremes to get us here?

An idea filters through my mind, and I pick up my phone.

Mom's gentle voice greets me. "Are you doing okay, honey?"

"Yeah, I need to go to Baltimore." The flier is in my hand, and I turn it over, thinking about what I'm doing. "Aunt Bea is starting a new product line, and I want to take pictures for her website. I'd also like to tell her in person about the wedding cakes. She's done so much, I feel like I owe her a visit."

"Oh, Melissa," she sighs, and I want to hang up immediately. Every wedding detail has been reluctantly cancelled by my mother, and all with repeating "are you sures" the entire time.

I power on. "I'll only be gone overnight. Would you mind keeping Dex?"

"You don't even have to ask." She's smiling now. "I love keeping my grandson."

Nodding, I slide my laptop into its sleeve. "He has Mom's Day Out in the morning. I'll let Hannah know you'll pick him up."

"Drive safe."

We disconnect, and I place a quick call to Bea. Of course, she'll be in the shop tomorrow. It's a fantastic idea for me to drive up and take pictures for the website. She can't wait to see me and show me her ideas for the groom's cake, and when is Derek going to make up his mind? I dodge that last question and tell her I'll be there by early afternoon. All that's left is getting through another night alone.

Evening used to be my favorite time of day. Derek would be home, the three of us would be together. Now the prospect of sleeping in that king-sized bed, surrounded by his warm, lingering scent, with no strong arms to hold me . . . It's become a little slice of hell for me to endure. Lately my endurance has moved to the couch.

Tonight, at least, I have something to focus on: packing.

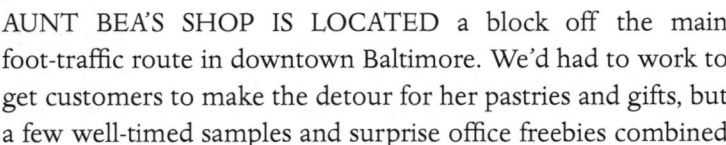

AUNT BEA'S SHOP IS LOCATED a block off the main foot-traffic route in downtown Baltimore. We'd had to work to get customers to make the detour for her pastries and gifts, but a few well-timed samples and surprise office freebies combined with her talent in the kitchen and my ability to spread the word paid off.

Her shop is full of customers when I arrive, and parking in front of the store, I think of how different coming to the city from this angle feels compared to how it was when I lived alone in the Reynolds mansion.

A dark thought tightens my stomach, the empty Reynolds mansion. Sloan is dead. Derek killed him, and somewhere, someone knows about it. Whoever that person is could be anywhere. Glancing over my shoulder, an involuntary shiver moves down my spine.

Derek's nightly check in said they'd had a breakthrough in the case. It was unexpected, and he wasn't sure he believed it. Apparently, the harasser sent a letter to Star at the condo. He'd said it was too long to text, but he'd know more tonight.

As much as I want to be indifferent, I'm on edge waiting to hear what's happening, and hoping it doesn't make his situation worse. My thoughts are distracted as I enter the store, and I make my way past the waiting customers to a side table.

"I've got your special cupcake! " Aunt Bea nods to a little pastry on a small plate. It's a tradition she started before I moved home, and even after I was in Wilmington, she would still send me special deliveries at the holidays. "Drunken buttered rum."

Distractions vanish, my eyes widen as I check out the dark cake topped with white frosting and shaves of coconut flakes and pecans. "It looks amazing."

A male customer curiously inspects my treat as I peel back the wrapper.

"It's something new I'm trying," she says, assembling a pink and white polka-dotted cardboard box. "Cooking channel."

I grin and take a small bite. Rich buttery rum and spicy cinnamon fill my mouth. A hint of nutmeg, and I have to work to suppress a groan.

"How do I get some of that?" The man in the navy pin-stripe suit nods toward me with a wink.

His question is a bit vague, but Bea is on it. "Be my marketing genius and favorite customer." She winks back at him. "Her fiancé is a very lucky man."

His expression drops, and he orders red velvet. I wait until she's finished with him and helped the nanny and kids behind him, and once they're done, we're momentarily alone.

"Good?" The petite, round baker hustles over to me. Her apron is stained with pink frosting, and I can't resist teasing her.

"They think I'm so lucky, but they don't know I'm your test subject."

Leaning back, she crosses plump arms over her ample bosom. "As if I'd ever give you anything bad."

I lunge forward to hug her. "You give me sinfully delicious treats."

"Speaking of sinfully delicious, how's Derek?" A nudge and a grin, and I glance down.

"He's, umm . . . doing great."

Her face turns serious, and she goes to the door. In a flash, she turns the "Back in ten minutes" sign around, flips the lock, and pulls down the shades.

"What happened?"

Damn. I'm stunned by both her quick response and her question. "We sort of had a . . . well . . ." Tears flood my eyes. *I can't believe I'm still crying like this.* Grasping for control, I clear my throat. "We broke up."

Concern lines her face, and she leads me to one of the small tables. "I can't believe it," handing me a napkin, "I saw you together. How is this possible? What did he say?"

Dotting my eyes, I look down at the paper cloth trying not to cry more. "It was me, actually. I broke it off."

"What!?" Her voice is too high, and she collapses into the chair across from me. "Melissa, honey, you have got to explain this to me."

My gaze stays fixed on my hands. "We wanted different things." *No, that's not right.* I shake my head and try again. "We have different ideas about what a relationship means. To me it's a partnership, sharing, including each other. No secrets. To him it's . . . not."

"Can't you find a compromise?" Her voice is urgent but gentle. "You've been married before. You know men . . . well . . . I mean—"

"That's just it!" My eyes flash to hers. "I *have* been married before. It's the whole reason I had to end it."

Her grey eyebrows pull together. "You broke it off because of Sloan?"

"Because of what happened with Sloan. All the lies, the secrets. The double life. I married a man I thought I knew, and then it turned out . . . I didn't know him at all." I pause for breath then quietly add. "I won't make that mistake again."

Bea studies the table in front of me a few moments before taking my hand. "Then why do you still wear this?" The dark blue sapphire ring is on the third finger of my left hand.

My lips tremble as tears threaten, and I move it under my thigh. "I don't know."

It's a lie. I haven't been able to take it off because no matter how my insides twist and fight, it's the last piece of evidence holding me together. I'm afraid if it's removed, all my insides will bleed out.

We don't speak, but I can feel her studying me. I can feel myself unraveling in front of her, and I wish she'd say something.

"Sloan Reynolds was a sneaky young man." She leans back in her chair, and her tone grows thoughtful. "Very slick and always smiling, but always being naughty when no one was looking. I don't know where he got it. His father was a good man. His mother was a bit . . . materialistic, but she wasn't cruel or vindictive. Still, for whatever reason, their son was attracted to the darkness more than the light."

Slowly, my eyes move up to hers. I need to hear this. "You know, I caught him stealing from my register when he was about fifteen." She nods, hands across her midsection. "Why the son of the town's richest family would need to steal, I don't know. He saw me catch him, too, and I'll never forget his wicked grin. Slipped that money in his pocket and walked right out the door as if daring me to call him on it."

"Did you?" I whisper.

"Of course I did! I called Jackson right away and told him his boy had taken forty dollars right out of my cash register."

"What happened?"

Exhaling, she shakes her head. "His father thought it was funny, a boyish prank. He apologized for Sloan and said he'd send the money right around, and sure enough, his driver came by before the end of the day with the money and a little gift."

"What are you saying?" I wait for her next words as if they're the key to some incredible mystery.

"The average male is not born ready to share every thought in his head." She smiles at me now. "Half of them aren't even sure what to make of the thoughts in their heads beyond food and sex."

"Derek's not like that," I say under my breath, leaning back.

"Derek was alone for how long after his wife died?"

"Six years." Reaching out, I trace the wood grain with my fingernail.

"And he works in the security business. Investigations. Things that require the utmost secrecy."

My jaw tightens. "Yes."

"Derek Alexander is a war hero, am I right? A commanding officer? His friends and coworkers trust him? Vouch for his trustworthiness?"

"Of course." Pressure is building inside me, pushing upward in my chest.

"Honey," she exhales a chuckle. "Give the man a chance to mess up once before you throw him out of your life. Especially one as handsome and clearly devoted to you as that one."

"You don't understand. It was more than once, and the secrets he kept were . . ." I can't tell her the whole story. "They were huge."

"Another woman?"

"No!" The very idea burns in my stomach.

Bea's lips curl at my response. "Have you heard from him?"

"He texts me every night . . . telling me everything."

"Oh, sweetie." Her warm tone moves through me like a wave, and I know what has to happen. The truth is clear as a bell. I don't know why I didn't see it sooner.

"Love is a risk," she says. "Putting your heart out, making yourself vulnerable again is scary. I can only imagine how gun-shy you must feel after your last experience. But trust me, you picked the right man this time. Everyone can see it."

I'm on my feet and at her counter collecting my things before her last words are even uttered. "Do you mind if I reschedule our meeting?"

"Only if it's for the reason I hope it is."

"I'll call you next week."

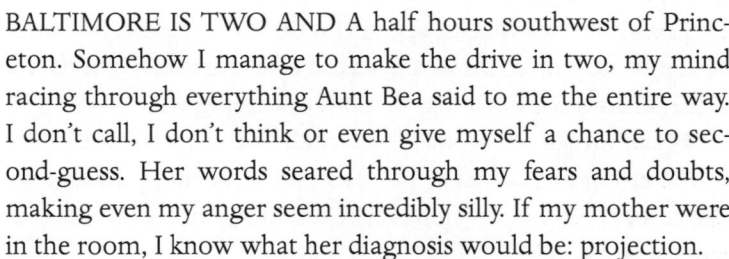

BALTIMORE IS TWO AND A half hours southwest of Princeton. Somehow I manage to make the drive in two, my mind racing through everything Aunt Bea said to me the entire way. I don't call, I don't think or even give myself a chance to second-guess. Her words seared through my fears and doubts, making even my anger seem incredibly silly. If my mother were in the room, I know what her diagnosis would be: projection.

Fear, gun-shyness, whatever was going on, it's over, and now I'm sitting in my car looking up at the Alexander-Knight office building. My heart beats so fast it hurts. A quick glance at the clock tells me it's five-thirty.

"Please be here," I whisper.

Hopping out, I run inside and press the elevator button. It takes an eternity to finally open at the bottom floor. Dashing inside, I repeatedly press the button for the top floor. Finally the doors close, and another eternity as it slowly starts to rise.

Tapping my foot, I pace the small box. "Come on!" I growl, until finally the movement stops. A pause and the doors slowly open.

Running out into the breezeway, I head straight for the glass double-doors and push through. Nikki's not at her desk, and I only briefly wonder if she's even still working here. I'm headed straight for his office, but before I turn the handle, I stop. I'm breathing fast, and I'm actually trembling.

Wiping my palms down the sides of my jeans, I scrub my hair with my fingertips, hoping it looks pretty and not smashed from riding in the car all day. I'm wearing a red sweater, which is a relief. His favorite color. Hand on my twisting stomach, I take a deep breath and open the door.

The sight of him hits me like a freight train. He's behind his desk in his usual charcoal suit and tie. Elbows bent, his forehead is lined. A dark brown wave has fallen on one eye, and his lips are in a firm line making his square jaw stand out attractively. I wonder for a half-second what's got him so focused. His phone is in his hand, and he appears to be texting.

I don't know what to say, so I clear my throat softly. Steel blue eyes snap up to mine, and a rush of energy floods my body.

"Hi," I say softly. "I hope I'm not disturbing you."

Phone down, he's out of his chair and crossing the room to me at once. Just before he reaches me, he stops, hesitating. We're so close, his delicious scent teases my nose, his warmth hints at my skin.

"You never disturb me." The low ripple of his voice squeezes my heart, and I'm so light I'm either going to lift off the ground or faint. "I was just texting you . . . What are you doing here?"

He's holding back. I see his palm twitch, and I can tell he's trying to decide if it's okay to touch me.

"I needed to see you. I needed to tell you I was wrong. I'm sorry. I want you to please come home."

With every word, his brow relaxes more, the shine of love grows stronger in his eyes. I've barely said the word *home* when I'm swept up in his embrace. The strong arms I've been craving for weeks hold me tight, secure, and exactly where I'm supposed to be.

"Melissa," he breathes, kissing my temple, my cheek, until at last our lips crash together, tongues find each other and desire tickles low in my stomach.

A little noise, somewhere between a laugh and a moan slips out, and I'm grasping his shoulders, his hair, his face, trying to pull him to me as hard as I can. I want our bodies touching. I want every cell melting together. I want to be so wrapped up in him, we're like he said, *it's impossible to know where I begin and you end.*

"You're back," he breathes, kissing me again and again.

"I didn't hold out very long." I'm in heaven as his soft lips, that lovely, scratchy beard trace a line into my hair, behind my ear, until he stops and takes a long, deep inhale.

"It felt like a lifetime." Chills skate across my body. "I want to take you home and make love to you."

"Let's go." I grip his arms smiling. "Or here is good . . ."

My back is against the wall of his office, and he kisses me roughly. Heat floods between my thighs, and the only thing left is for our bodies to be reunited. I ache for it.

He pulls away, and our eyes meet. His are so full of love, but there's something else, something breaking. As we hold each other, his expression looks like he's being torn apart, and I'm instantly afraid.

"Derek, what's wrong?"

"Like I said, I was sending you a text to tell you . . ." His arms surround me, pulling me tight against him. His head is against my shoulder, and he only holds me. "Oh, god, Melissa."

I grasp his broad shoulders, trying to move him back so I can see his face. "Baby, what is it?"

"Just let me hold you. I need to hold you right now." His

voice is muffled, and I swallow the knot in my throat. His lips move to my jaw as I hear noises from outside the office. They're loud and pushy, almost as if a team of individuals is forcing their way inside.

"What's this about?" Stuart's voice is stern.

"Derek Alexander?" A male snaps back.

I feel him tense in my arms. His head lifts, and he looks deep into my eyes. "Listen to me. I love you so much. You're my home and my family. You're all that's ever mattered to me—"

The office door slams open, and men in dark blue uniforms surround us. Stuart's voice follows them, demanding answers. Derek's arms are ripped from my body and pulled behind his back, but his eyes never leave mine. One of the men begins to speak.

"Derek Alexander, you are under arrest for the first-degree murder of Sloan Reynolds. You have the right to remain silent. Anything you say or do can and will be used against you in a court of law—"

"NO!" I scream, grabbing his arm. "Stop it! STOP!"

"Miss, I need you to step back." A sharp voice orders me. "You have the right to an attorney. If you cannot afford an attorney, one will be appointed to you."

Tears blind me. "Leave him ALONE!" I shout, and my hands shake as my fingers fumble to the cold metal on his wrists.

"Melissa," Derek's voice is in my ear, his face at my temple. "I have to go."

Pulling back, I find his eyes. Heartbreak is in them, and tears spill onto my cheeks. "I can't . . ." My voice trembles and breaks. "I can't let this happen . . ."

"Stay with Stuart."

Stuart is behind me holding my shoulders as the officer finishes. "Do you understand these rights as they have been read to you?"

"Yes," Derek answers, and my knees give out.

Stuart catches me. "Hang on," he says, and I grab him,

trying to find my balance.

"Take care of her," Derek says.

Stuart nods. "I'll get her to Mariska and be right down."

It's the last they're able to say before the group of cops escorts him out of the building.

TEN

UNMASKED

Derek

IT'S BEEN A WEEK SINCE Dex's party, and nothing has changed. It's driving me crazy. I keep texting Melissa, debriefing her on my days. She continues not responding. I keep digging through these records, looking for any clue as to who's behind the letters. We continue coming back with nothing. It's starting to feel pointless, and the strain is wearing on all of us. Patrick's ready to set a trap, and for the first time since I've known him, Stuart agrees with his brother.

I'm turning over the details of their plan when my phone buzzes. One glance, and I'm surprised to see it's Star. Ever since that night in my condo, I've given her a wide berth. I sleep at Stuart's place and spend most of my time there or here. When we do speak, it's very basic: the latest on the case, if she needs anything, how Cammie is adjusting.

Snatching up my phone, I slide a finger across the face. "Derek here."

Panic fills my ear. "It's over! He knows we're here! Oh god!"

I'm out of my seat, snatching my blazer off my chair and heading for the door as she's still speaking. "Calm down.

Where's Cammie?"

"I'm holding her." Sounds of movement, and the little girl makes a fussy noise.

"Are you in my condo?" Waving at Nikki, I'm out the double-glass doors.

"Yes. We're in the condo, alone—"

"Go across the hall and stay with Mariska until I get there. Can you do that? Is Mariska home?"

"I-I think so?" Her voice cracks, and I hear the tears coming.

"Star, listen to me."

A sniff. "Hm?"

"Don't cry. Think of Cammie. She doesn't know what's going on. You need to stay calm." Fishing in my pocket, I pull out the keys to the Audi.

"Okay . . ."

"I'll stay on the phone with you until you get to Stuart's place. Go ahead."

More rustling noises, another little fuss from Cammie. I hear a door opening and closing followed by soft tapping. Mariska's high voice greets her in the background.

"Are you in?" I'm on the road, making my way through traffic.

"I'm at Stuart's." She already sounds calmer. "We're here together."

"Good. Ask Mariska to lock the door and don't let anyone in until I get there. I'm five minutes away."

"Okay." She speaks to Mariska, but I cut in.

"I'm hanging up now."

"Derek!" She's back to panicky.

My stomach tightens. "What is it?"

"I'm just . . ." Hesitation. "You'll be right here?"

"Less than five minutes now. Don't be afraid. Walt's downstairs."

"Right."

"Hanging up now."

We disconnect, and my teeth clench. This is the break we've been waiting for. If this asshole was stupid enough to send mail to my condo, we can track it all the way back to his doorstep. *Shit!* Snatching up the phone again, I call Star right back.

"What is it!" Her voice is a gasp.

"Everything's fine," I say, trying to ease her back down. "Don't throw away the envelope. Don't touch it any more than you have to."

"I left it in your condo!" she cries.

God dammit. Keeping my voice calm. "We've got to have that envelope, Star. I'll stay on the phone with you. Go back across the hall and get it."

"Hang on . . . Cammie, stay with Aunt Mare Mare. I'll be right back." Door opens, door closes, noise of frantic movement . . . more frantic movement . . . I'm gripping the steering wheel as I wait. Finally, a loud exhale of relief. "It's here! I have it."

"Pick it up carefully by the edges and put it in a plastic bag." I'm pulling into the parking garage. "I'm in the building. I'll be up in less than a minute."

We disconnect, and my next call is to the office.

STUART HAS THE CLOSURE FLAP on the envelope and the stamp in his hands, and frustration lines his brow. "They're all stickers. None of this requires saliva."

"So whoever it is knows better than to leave behind traces of DNA."

We both sit back and stare at the brown envelope and the white sheet of paper. I pick up the letter and read it again.

Ms. Durango,

The time has come, the walrus said, for us to end our game. You've done everything exactly as I expected. Give these instructions to the Big Guy:

Meet me at the Palomino Bar, martini room, tonight at nine. I'll be the one with the Gibson and the gat. If he brings any helpers, my accomplice will turn your photograph, your underwear, and your exact location over to the MSPD.

I look forward to our meeting.

Signed,
A Friend

Tossing the paper back on the table, I exhale and stand. "Fuck it. I'll meet him tonight, and I'll go alone. I'm not worried about any of this. I'm ready to unmask this asshole."

Stuart's eyes flick to the clock then back to me. "That gives us two hours to work out a Plan B."

"I don't need a Plan B. We'll follow his Plan A. I've handled rats like this before. I'm happy to do it again."

"At least wear my Kevlar." He heads to the master bedroom, and I wait, turning his instructions over in my mind. An accomplice.

Star has Cammie in the living room, and we decided they should stay with Stuart and Mariska the rest of the night in case it's a setup.

My partner's back with his black vest in hand. "The perfect double-cross would be to pretend he's after you in order to pull us all away from covering her. Or to lead you out in the open alone."

"You read my mind, partner." I pull my black sweater over my head and take the vest from him. Once it's securely fastened, I restore my top layer and add a lightweight grey blazer.

"I'd feel better having you covered." Stuart hands me a small pistol I slip in my boot. "I don't need a gun to end this."

"You never know how he'll come at you." He steps to the

door and opens it, and I follow him back to the kitchen. "This fucker didn't give us any time. If Patrick were closer, we'd have at least one more set of eyes."

"I give our *friend* credit. He's bringing you two together in a way I never could."

"Extra muscle is always helpful in situations like this. Regardless of whether I agree with him."

Clapping Stuart on the shoulder, I head for the exit. "Don't worry. I'll be back in a few hours."

THE PALOMINO BAR IS ADJACENT to one of the nicer steak houses in town. The main bar is large and traditional. Wooden booths line the perimeter and a matching bar is located in the center of the room. A layer of tall tables with high chairs ring the space between the two, and it's all shiny brass and low lighting. Off to the side is the dim-lit martini bar where I'm looking for an asshole with a Gibson. And a gat.

It takes a few seconds for my eyes to adjust to the change in lighting. For a Thursday night, it's pretty deserted, but it's early.

A couple sits in one corner leaning close together. The female holds a pink martini, a cosmopolitan, I'd bet. Her date has something with a curled lemon peel slivered in it. Lemon drop. A table of three women is across from them, but again, pink drinks. Finally my eyes land on a patron in the very back, dead center of the room. I can't make out the face. Whoever it is has leaned out of the light, but on the table directly in front of him or her is a martini glass containing clear alcohol. In the bottom middle of the crystal is a small, white onion on a toothpick. Our "Friend."

Without hesitation, I walk straight to where he or she is sitting and stop, waiting for the snake to slither into the light. When it finally does, I'm momentarily winded. I have to take a step back.

"Bennett?" Confusion lines my face as I recognize the contract private investigator I've worked with for years. I've trusted him on several cases, and he's been my right hand tracking subjects in remote locations. The last time we worked together was . . . last year. He kept an eye on Sloan for me in Baltimore when I was in Wilmington with Melissa. Anger mixed with betrayal fires in my chest. I'm ready to kill this guy, but for the moment, he has the upper hand.

"Derek Alexander." He leans forward, placing his elbows on the table and giving me a sick grin.

"Robert." I pull out the chair across from him and sit. "I confess, I'm surprised. You're better at your job than I gave you credit for."

His eyes narrow before they travel over my torso. "Credit is hard to come by in your business, Mr. Alexander."

"The bird in the hand is always preferable to theories and promises."

He exhales a short laugh. "You're so fucking smooth. You with your suit and tie, your fancy car, your ultimate bachelor pad, and sexy-assed fiancée."

My fist tightens. "A smart guy would keep his thoughts about Melissa to himself."

"Or what?" He leans back and really laughs. "You'll kick my ass? She's not even yours anymore."

I meet his ice-blue stare. "I'll break your neck."

He takes a long sip of the Gibson in front of him. "Your preferred method of disposal." A pause as he evaluates my response. "Such a rookie mistake, losing control like that. You honestly thought no one would find out? I'm disappointed."

"The feeling is mutual." The waitress puts a short glass of scotch in front of me and sashays off again.

Lifting the toothpick, he slips the tiny onion into his mouth. "Even more disappointing. I gave you the perfect setup. That hot piece of ass right in your condo. You never even fucked her, and I hear she gives a hell of a hummer."

"You're talking about Star?" My eyes narrow. "Is she in on this?"

He shakes his head and frowns. "I'm no amateur. All she could talk about in Baltimore was how you believed in her. It was pathetic, and I fucking thought after the way she played your partner—"

"You asked her to help you?"

His cold gaze lands on mine. "Of course not. I knew she'd never turn on you. She's too in love with you." A disgusted noise, and he takes another sip.

I've heard enough. "What do you want, Bennett?"

"My letter was perfectly clear," he says with a smirk. "I want you, big guy."

Leaning back, I shove my drink forward. "What the fuck? I'm not gay."

"HA!" He says loudly, leaning forward in mock laughter. "Your ego is only outsized by your stupidity." Straightening, all traces of his smile disappear. "I want you taking a dose of your own medicine."

"What the hell does that mean?"

"Let's see . . . You're *Mister* Alexander, fucking American hero, fucking top in your field, fucking paragon of truth and virtue. Am I right? Or do I exaggerate?"

"You exaggerate."

"Maybe, but you do blaze in like the scales of justice ready to put anyone away, ruin his life, without a shred of mercy."

Studying his face, I remember the last letter. *Revenge is a dish best served cold.* "You said you wanted revenge. What have I ever done to you?"

He's collected again, running his finger around the lip of his now-empty martini glass. "Do you happen to remember a young man named Shane?"

Filtering through my memory, I come back with nothing. "No."

His head moves slowly side to side. "You wouldn't. You only knew him as Slayer. Slayer Bennett."

Lightning flashes behind my eyes, but I remain cool. "You're related to Slayde?

"You might say that." He exhales a chuckle and signals the waitress. "You might say I'm the reason he exists."

Another Gibson is placed in front of him, and we both wait until the young, tattooed lady is gone again.

More than any other, that court case is etched in my memory. I remember what they said about Slayde's father.

"Are you pretending to care?" I evaluate the fucker sitting before me. "The court psychiatrist said you beat him regularly within an inch of his life."

"I didn't know about that." Staring into the drink, his voice drops, and for the first time, he doesn't come off as a raving fucking lunatic. "Shane doesn't know I'm his real dad." Bennett's eyes slide closed. "His mother was the most beautiful woman . . ."

"So you abandoned him." My empathy for this guy evaporates as quickly as it tried to appear.

"It wasn't like that. Mary pushed me away." He shakes his head. "When she got sick, she said it was God's judgment for violating her marriage bed."

"Sounds like Slayde's had a lot of crazy to overcome in his life." I take a long drink of scotch.

"But you knew the hell he survived. You had all the evidence. The psychiatrist said he had intermittent explosive disorder. They tried to reduce his sentence. But you wouldn't let them. You had no mercy."

Glancing away, I can't help admitting I still have a problem with that diagnosis. At the same time, I can relate to a father's concern for his son. I have Dex, after all. "So what? You want revenge because I did my job?"

His crazy returns with his rage. "You wouldn't stop until you finished him. He was destined to be a boxing legend, and you took it all away." His voice is a breathy growl. "Look at you. You're no better than him. You fucking hypocrite."

Quiet settles over the table. I think about his words, that case. "I was a lot harder then. I'd just lost Allison—"

"Save the sob story. It's time for payback, and you know the saying. She's a bitch."

"You want money?"

"Fuck no!" A spate of real laughter erupts from him now. "I want you to lose everything. I want your ass in prison, rotting away just like my kid's."

My brow lines. "You know he's out, right?"

"He's a fucking janitor. A nobody living in a shit town."

With an exhale, I lean back. "I don't know what to tell you. It was the right thing to do at the time. Slayde's paid his debt, and from what I understand, he's happy now."

"What the fuck do you know about his happiness?" Bennett shoves his glass forward. "I've been watching, waiting for the great Derek Alexander to slip up, and boy, did you ever."

"You want me to go to prison." I nod, looking at my glass. "What's your plan for making that happen?"

"Easy. You have two choices. The whore goes to prison or you do." He leans back, a calm smile crossing his lips. "What's it going to be, hero?"

Ice settles in my stomach. He's prepared for this. He's crazy like a fox, and he's left me no options. "That will satisfy you?"

"Watching you clean shit off of fucking toilets just like my boy had to? You bet your ass." He leans forward and his voice becomes a hiss. "I'll be fucking jerking all over your fucking photograph."

The image forces a grimace. "Turn myself in."

"You've got twenty-four hours, Big Guy." The smile on his face is testing my ability to not snap him like a toothpick. "I know that look. You touch me, you seal her fate. My accomplice has everything she needs to put Star away for life should anything happen to me."

Standing, he shoves his chair in. "I'm listening to the wire. By this time tomorrow, your ass had better be in a cell."

Sitting back, I watch him walk out of the bar. For the moment, it appears my former PI has the upper hand. I'm not sure how we're going to resolve this, but I have to talk with Stuart and Patrick. Then I have to call the Maryland State Police Department.

ELEVEN

OLD FRIENDS

Melissa

STUART PACES THE OFFICE, HIS fists clenched as hard as his jaw as he shouts into the phone. "Derek is not a fucking flight risk. He turned himself in for Chrissake. I can't believe this bullshit."

I'd spent a restless night at the condo, sleeping alone in Derek's king sized bed, worrying, praying for his safety in Baltimore central lockup. Star was in the guest room with her daughter Camille. It was the first time we'd ever met, but she was demure. Shy and apologetic. Her daughter was beautiful.

Now I'm back at the office with Stuart, and the two of us are trying to think of any way to shorten Derek's stay, to prevent this from going any further. I watch Stuart talking to Patrick.

"We need your ass here now." Silence as he listens to his brother. "Because I can't fucking keep my eye on everyone alone."

My eyebrows rise. I can't help wondering what might happen with these two in the same room and Derek gone. Bolt down the furniture.

Stuart ends the call and turns to me. "How you holding up?

Need anything?"

Shaking my head, I look down at Derek's desk. "I need him home."

"We all need that," he says through an exhale.

Just then, Nikki scampers into the room. Her eyes are red as if she's been crying, and she holds a brown envelope. I smile at her, glad she's stuck around. Having to find and train a new assistant would not be ideal at the moment.

"I'm sorry to interrupt." Her voice is high and quiet.

"It's okay," I say. "What do you need, hun?"

"I just wondered if Mr. Alexander . . . If Derek still needs me to mail these files for him."

"What files?" Stuart growls and doesn't make eye contact.

She's flustered and holds them out. I notice the tremor in her hand. "Bennett? His old PI said it was for a case he handled. He said it should go to the police department in Maryland."

"What the *FUCK*?" Stuart explodes at her, and her eyes widen suddenly before she drops the papers on Derek's desk and runs out the door.

He's right behind her. "You're Bennett's accomplice?"

I jump out of the chair and run after them. Nikki's behind her desk, tears streaming from her eyes in black lines. "I don't know what you mean!" She wails, but Stuart's not stopping.

He rounds the desk and grabs her by the upper arms, shouting in her face. "How long have you been working with that fucker?"

"I don't know!" She's crying harder, her face an ugly red mask. "Two years? H-however long Mr . . . Derek's used him!"

Stuart's face is flushed, and I jump between them. "Hang on!" I shout. "Stuart, *stop*! Let her go!"

He shoves her back, and I catch her arms. "Nikki, what do you know about Robert Bennett?"

She's shaking and grabbing fistfuls of tissues out of the box on her desk. "He's a contract PI," she sniffs, hands shaking as she wipes her face. "He does jobs for Derek here in town. Not as much in the last year, but—"

"Oh my god," I exhale, leaning heavily against her desk. "He knew all our weaknesses. His accomplice was right under our nose and didn't even know it."

Stuart's still fuming, but I can see he's slowly getting on the same page as me. "You didn't know what was in that envelope?"

Nikki's white-blonde head shakes rapidly. "I never look in his files. Derek said they were confidential. I only type up the reports he specifically gives me."

Going back to Derek's office, I scoop up the sealed brown envelope and rip it open. Out drops a photograph and a pair of black lace panties. Digging inside, I pull out the letter that details who Star is, her connection to the murder of Sloan Reynolds, and the address to Derek's condo in Princeton.

"God . . . freaking . . . Stuart!" I shout, and in less than a moment he's back with me. "He knew Nikki would mail this without question. She only asked because of the arrest."

Stuart picks up the letter and reads it briefly before glancing at the photograph and the panties. "Are those—?"

"Only one person can say for sure." I pick up the black thong by an edge of lace and drop it back in the envelope. "It's probably got both their DNA all over it."

"A pleasant thought."

"Tell me about it." We exchange a glance, but it's cut short by both the reality of what's happening and the immediacy of what's out front.

Nikki is crying at her desk, and I spin on my heel, heading for the reception area. When I get there, she's packing her stuff.

"Nikki!" I round the corner and catch her hands. "Wait. Please."

"I can't stay another day here." She shakes her head, tears streaming down her face. "It's all spoiled. I'm nothing but a problem now."

"It's not true," I urge, trying to find the words. "We need you right now, Nikki. It's a crisis situation. We don't have time to find a new receptionist."

"No," she sniffs, touching her face with a tissue. "I'm constantly fucking up everything. I'm a weakness just like you said."

"Patrick will be here tomorrow. Won't you at least wait and see him?"

Another sniff, and she considers what I've said.

"Patrick's your friend," I continue. "Why don't you take off this afternoon, and come in Monday when he's back."

She blinks up at me, and I smile. Leaning forward, I give her a hug. "We need you Nik. You're part of the team."

"The weakest link," she sniffs.

"Not true. You care about Derek, right?"

She nods but doesn't answer. I watch her dab her eyes more.

"That's what matters most. We're all here for him now." Smiling, I hold her hand. "Now you know to be extra vigilant. Anything unusual, run it past Stuart, okay?"

Her eyes flicker to the office where he remained behind. "I'd rather not," she says quietly.

"Okay, then run it past Patrick. He's your guy. Right?"

A wobbly breath and she nods. "Okay."

Releasing her arms, I head back into the office where Stuart is. I'm not crying, and I'm not fainting. I'm ready to find a solution. My Macbook is on Derek's desk now, and I stare at the screen thinking.

"What are we going to do?" I say.

He walks over to the bookshelf and pulls out a thick textbook. "We have to think like a lawyer. Our biggest problem is he confessed to the crime. We have to build a defense, find some precedent we can use . . ."

My mind immediately goes to a person I haven't seen in years. "I've got this." Sliding my finger across the touch pad, I log into my airline account. "I'm flying to Chicago."

Stuart doesn't even question. "I'll see if there's any way to sway the prosecution. I've been out of the game a while, but maybe I still know somebody in the Maryland PD."

"Go for it. Patrick will be here tomorrow." Looking up, I see Nikki preparing to leave. "Nikki! Would you set up the phones before you go? We're closing the office for the rest of the day."

She nods and circles her desk. Stuart's lips tighten, and he narrows his eyes at me. "You should've let her quit."

I'm flicking through flights trying to find the next one I can catch. "I don't know what's between you two, but you need to put it on hold until we get Derek back."

"Her incompetence makes us vulnerable."

My eyes flash to his. "Bennett won. He got what he wanted. Derek's behind bars . . ." My throat tightens, and I have to pause as despair tries to choke me. *Deep breaths.* "We don't have anything left to lose."

Two more clicks, and I've booked a flight. Powering down my laptop, I dig my phone out of my bag to call my mom. Dex will need to stay with her a few days longer.

"Damn, I hate research," Stuart mutters, flipping through the book I now see is a legal text.

"Your brother will be in the office Monday." My eyebrows rise. "I thought you were headed to Maryland?"

He exhales a laugh. "Are you suggesting I pass the buck?"

"Two heads are better than one."

"Travel safe."

THE LAW OFFICES OF MERRITT, Hampton, and Donnelly are located on the thirty-first floor in an office building on Chicago's East Loop. Stuart called his mother during my flight, and by the time I made it in last night, she'd sent a car to pick me up. I hadn't seen Sylvia since Patrick and Elaine's Christmas wedding in Montana, but she had only been back in the city a few days herself. We'd agreed to have dinner tomorrow night, and I crashed—after taking an unexpected call from Derek.

"What's in Chicago?" his voice is warm, and hearing him, knowing where he is, I can hardly keep the tears away.

"Not what. *Who*," I say with a sniff, working for control. "Elaine's older brother Marcus. He's one of the best criminal defense lawyers in the country."

"That's right. Elaine was supposed to be a lawyer when she grew up."

"Edward was such a jerk about that. You'd think she said she wanted to be a stripper instead of a teacher."

He laughs, and I close my eyes. "I miss you so much. Are you doing okay?"

"As well as can be expected, considering." He pauses a moment, and I hear shouts behind him. "I'm not a fan of orange jumpsuits."

"You're much sexier in Gucci. Oh, god! I'm sorry."

He exhales a laugh. "My level of sexiness isn't a problem yet. I have my own cell, so for now—"

"How did you manage that?"

"A guy I did police training with is one of the guards. He pulled some strings."

Slipping my fingers over my mouth, I inhale quietly. "I can't stand thinking of you in jail. Baltimore is horrible."

"It was the right thing to do. We couldn't go on with this hanging over our heads."

"I'm afraid for you."

Quiet moments pass. "I'm a little worried myself," he says. "I'd just gotten you back in my arms, and now . . ."

"Bennett is such a bastard. I want to kill him."

"Hey, don't say things like that on a police line."

"And I can't believe the judge refused to set bail. You're not a flight risk."

"He might not've made the wrong call." His warm exhale feels so close. I hold the phone as if it's his cheek. "I'm not sure I'll get out of this one, and I've heard the French Riviera is beautiful year-round."

"Don't say that." A tone sounds in our ears, and I know our time is ending. "We're going to get you out." I speak fast. "Stuart's headed your way to meet with the prosecutor. I'm meeting Marc tomorrow, and Patrick will be in the Princeton office Monday—"

"I love you, babe."

"I love you more."

It's our last words before we're cut off. My head drops on my arms, and I can't fight anymore. My shoulders shake, and I dissolve into tears.

THE FOOT TRAFFIC IS LIGHT on Michigan Avenue this morning. Lifting my chin, I let the warm sun shine on my face as I take a deep breath of sweet spring air. I'm glad Sylvia's condo is close enough for me to walk. I need to think about what I'm going to say to Marcus. I'm ready to tell him everything, whatever it takes to save Derek. Nothing in my past is more important than getting him back home with his family.

I haven't seen Marcus Merritt in almost ten years—before I graduated from college or even knew Sloan Reynolds. I'm not sure how much Elaine keeps her brother in the loop on my life. When we were kids growing up together in Wilmington, our parents used to hint that Marcus and I might eventually get married. We dated off and on, but he was always a ladies' man. And as much as I loved him dearly, I was always looking for someone "more mature."

Pushing through the revolving glass doors, I shake my head. "Years ago and water under the bridge."

I cross the grey marble foyer leading to the elevators. Stepping out on the thirty-first floor, I quickly scan the polished surfaces of the waiting room. The décor is very traditional. Dark, cherry-wood paneling, stained oak floors, and built in bookshelves surround me. It's Sunday, so the office is closed. The receptionist's desk sits empty.

Unsure what to do, I step across the luxurious waiting area. Wooden doors with glass panes lead to a small conference room. I'm just peeking through when I hear my name and turn.

Marcus is stunningly handsome as ever. He's a bit darker than Elaine, with caramel-brown hair and hazel eyes. He's dressed in grey slacks and a light blue dress shirt with a navy tie. At six foot, he's so fit and polished, I can't help a laugh.

"When did you start moonlighting at GQ?"

He smiles, revealing straight white teeth, before kissing my cheek. "And how is it possible you're more beautiful now than you were in college?"

I hadn't packed for this trip, so I'd had to stick with my dark skinny jeans and red tunic sweater. "Hmm, I think you're winning this morning."

"Come on," he touches my elbow. I follow him through the opposite glass doors down a short wood-paneled hallway to a large, corner office.

"Nice place." My eyes roam the arched built-in bookshelves lining the walls. The coffered ceiling and gold accents create a stunning space. "How do you ever get anything done in here? I'd be staring at the ceiling all day."

He laughs, and the familiar sound comforts me. "Have a seat and tell me what I can do for you."

"Thanks for meeting me on short notice. And on a Sunday." He waves my thanks away, and I drop into a tan leather chair across from him. "I don't know how much you know about my life now."

He leans back and props his foot over his knee. "Seems my little sister said you were happily engaged with a baby on the way." His eyes scan my body. "I guess that last bit is old news. You look amazing."

I smile. "Dex is a year old now."

"He was in a picture she sent me of Lane. Cute kid. He has

your eyes."

"Thanks. They play together pretty regularly. We're all back in Wilmington now."

"And your fiancé is the *Alexander* my new brother-in-law works with?"

"Right. Derek."

He only smiles briefly. "I can't say I'm sorry it didn't work out with Reynolds."

My bottom lip catches in my teeth, but I hesitate. "He wasn't the man I thought he was."

"You were too young when you married him."

I'm unsure whether to charge right into our situation or continue catching up. It's been so long since we've seen each other. I decide to ask one more question I actually want to know the answer to.

"How come you never got married? What's wrong with these Chicago girls, anyway?"

He grins and sits forward, leaning his forearms on his desk. "You know marriage isn't my thing. You're the only girl I *might've* considered settling down with."

"Oh, you *might've*."

"It did take me a while to get over you." His eyes twinkle, and I can't resist.

"No, it didn't. You were dating Jules Ashton the next week."

"Was I?" His brow lines, and I can't help remembering the attractive playboy Marcus has always been. It seems not much has changed. "Regardless, when we were together, I was all yours."

"We had a lot of fun," I say with a nod. "But I did have to go to college."

"Whose idea was that again?"

"College? Or educating women in general?"

He laughs loudly. "God, you always made me laugh. I miss that."

I give his enormous office another glance. "Say what you will. I know you want a little future lawyer running around this place. Pulling all your important papers off your desk and drooling on your furniture."

"Yes. You know me so well."

"I do know you well. That's why I'm here, Marcus." Our eyes meet, and I'm ready to get to the reason for my visit. "I need you. It's a matter of life and death, and you're the best lawyer I know."

He's immediately serious. "Are you in trouble?"

"Not me." Scooting forward in the chair, I glance over my shoulder. "What do we need to do for this to be confidential? Attorney-client privilege and all?"

"You agree to hire me as your attorney."

"I'd like to hire you as Derek's attorney."

His jaw moves, and I watch as he thinks, as his glance moves to my left hand. "You're not married?"

"We were planning our wedding next month. I'd love it if you could be there."

A brief smile, and he's back to business. "I'm not going to write down anything you say. Whatever you tell me could be used by the prosecution against us."

Fear clenches my stomach. "This is so serious, Marc."

"What happened?"

Closing my eyes, I go all the way back, knowing what this is going to do to my old friend to hear the truth. "After Sloan and I were married a few years, his parents died, and we had to move back to Baltimore."

He nods, watching me closely.

"Our marriage grew more and more distant. Months would pass and I'd never see him. We stopped having . . ." I took a deep breath, swallowing my embarrassment. "We stopped sleeping together."

Silence. I forge on.

"I thought maybe it was his age? I didn't know what to think until I found that first receipt." I pause, cringing inside. "Then I found the next one and the next one." My chin drops, and I tell him everything. "He had escorts all over the country, apartments where some of them stayed. I was so humiliated."

I didn't dare glance up at Marc's face. If I saw anything in his eyes—rage, vengeance—I'd never finish.

"I moved to the other side of his mansion. I wouldn't see him. I insisted on marriage counseling, but really, I wanted a divorce. I wanted out." Taking a deep breath, I go for it. "Until the night he decided he was tired of my bullshit. He wanted to sleep with his wife. I fought him . . . I hated him. But I wasn't strong enough. He beat me and almost raped me."

Marcus is out of his chair and pacing his office. "What the fuck . . ." His voice is a low growl. "What the fucking fuck, Melissa? Why didn't I know about this?"

Looking up at him now, I can't stop my emotions. I'm not sobbing, but warm tears line my cheeks. "I begged Elaine not to tell anyone."

His face is pained, hazel eyes intense. "Why? Why wouldn't you let her tell me? I would've buried that fucker."

Shaking my head. "I was so ashamed." He hands me a cloth handkerchief, and I touch my face with it. "I didn't want anyone to know. I just wanted to be rid of him."

"So you left him?"

"We were divorced, and Derek and I got together." The memory of that floods my chest with so much warmth, I actually smile through my tears. "He was so good for me. I love him so much."

Marcus is in front of me now, leaning against his desk. "I like him already."

"That brings us to now." My brow lines as I study the double Ms monogrammed on his handkerchief. "He was working on a case last year, and he crossed paths with Sloan again. He was convinced Sloan was coming for me."

"Abusers never give up on their victims." Marcus's voice is matter of fact. "You belonged to him, regardless of whether you'd moved on."

Nodding, I continue. "Derek and Patrick and this

woman . . . Star, an escort—they were going to set a trap to catch him, to put him away for good."

The room is tense. I can tell Marcus is waiting for me to say the worst. I don't prolong his anticipation.

"Derek killed Sloan. He said Sloan was strangling Star, that she was about to die, and he killed him."

"With a gun?" Marc's voice is quiet.

"With his bare hands."

The tick of his desk clock is the only noise in the room for one . . . two . . . three . . . seconds.

"I don't blame him," he says. "I'd have shot him in the face."

Blinking up at him, I know the desperation is clear in my expression. "He's been arrested for first-degree murder. He's in jail in Baltimore, and we've got to get him out."

My friend's jaw clenches as he rounds the desk. "What's his bail?"

"The judge wouldn't set bail. Said he was a flight risk."

"Fuck yeah, he's a flight risk. If it were me, I'd have your pretty ass and my little boy with me on the first flight to Nice. One-way tickets."

"The French Riviera," I say with a smile. "I've always been a bit partial to Monaco."

"Not sure of their extradition policy, princess. France is safer." He gives me a tense smile. A pause, then he starts moving quickly. "I need you to send me everything, and I mean *everything* you have about this case, everything you have on Sloan and his past, his crimes, all the information about Derek's past, any military honors he's received, recognitions . . ."

"As soon as I get back to Princeton." I'm out of my chair and heading to the door. He's right behind me. "I'll leave today."

"Melissa?" I look up at him and he touches my chin. Marcus has such a beautiful smile. "It's not going to be easy, but I'll do everything I can. I want to be at your wedding next month."

"I knew I could count on you."

A kiss on the cheek, and I'm gone.

TWELVE

MAKING A PLAN

Stuart

MARISKA'S EYES HOLD MINE AS she moves on my lap. Her long, chestnut waves fall over her shoulders in a rippling curtain, and I'm doing my best to hold on, not finish before her.

We've been together four months, and I'm only scratching the surface of making love to this woman. She's sensual and elemental. She likes to feel every emotion, every sensation. It's fucking amazing and impossible all at once.

"Oh, Stuart," she whispers. Her eyes slide closed and she cups my cheek with one slim hand as her movements quicken. Leaning forward, she presses her soft lips to mine and exhales a little moan. *Fuck*, I'm on the edge. She arches back, and I catch a tight nipple in my mouth, giving it a strong pull. I feel her clenching around me as I'm buried deep inside her.

"Yes," she whispers, holding my neck as I kiss a trail across to her other breast and do the same, catching that tight dark bud between my teeth. Her body shudders, and she's almost there.

Again, she leans down and pulls my face to hers, roughly consuming my mouth. I'm right there to meet her. It's her pattern when she's getting close. Her kisses grow more desperate, her little noises wild. She's riding my lap like it's a fucking pony, and dammit it's the hottest thing I've ever known. Tracing my fingers across her ass, she groans, rising up on her knees and slamming back down. The pressure in my pelvis is building, and I've got to stop thinking about how gorgeous she is.

"Come on, baby," I growl against her shoulder, giving her a little bite. "Come for me." That does it. One more rise and fall, her knees scrub against my hips and her insides break into spasms massaging me deep inside her.

"Oh, god!" Her arms are around my shoulders, and she finishes so beautifully. I lean my head back and let go. The force of my orgasm nearly pulls me out of my skin it's so intense.

"Fuck," I hiss, gripping her ass and moving her up and forward on me as she cries out more. Rolling us to the side, she's on her back, and I hold the inside of her knee, spreading her thighs as I drive deeper, harder, finishing those final, blinding thrusts as her fingers clutch my shoulders.

I'm holding the last one, trying to find my way back to Earth, and my eyes blink open. There she is, lying on her back, her hair spread out around her, smiling at me. Those sunset hazel eyes, golden and gorgeous, are filled with more love than I deserve.

I drop onto my elbows above her and kiss the base of her neck. "You are the fucking sexiest woman I've ever known."

Everything about being with this beautiful girl is new for me. I've never done the whole "making love" bullshit. In the past, it went along with my "no relationships" lifestyle. If I needed a release, it was pretty easy to find a willing partner. The women I'd been with liked it fast and dirty—bend over the desk, take it from behind, slap that ass, and we're done. Everyone was happy. Until now.

She laughs, and her fingers curl in the sides of my hair. I feel her lips against my brow, and I hold her as I find my bearings again.

"I'm not sure how I feel about that compliment, Stuart William." Her voice vibrates against my cheek as she teases me.

"It makes it sound like you've known a lot of women."

One more kiss to that fabulous neck, and I lift my head. "Not all of them biblically."

Her nose wrinkles as her eyes roll, and I swear, I could take her again on the spot. Instead, I go back to the question that got us in this position. "You never answered me. Did you fill out the transfer application today?"

She exhales a growling sound and twists in my arms. My hug tightens over her. I'm not about to let her wiggle out of answering this question.

"Let me go, Stuart." Blinking up at me, her resistance is so adorable, I kiss her lips, long and soft. Then I swipe my tongue inside, finding hers for good measure.

When I lean up again, she blinks slowly. "You fight dirty."

"You give me dirty thoughts." Our eyes meet, and I continue. "Princeton is one of the top schools in the country. You might have heard of it."

"It's too expensive, and I have a scholarship at Ocean County College. I like it there."

"You'd rather go to a state school than live with me here."

She starts to struggle again, and this time I do release her.

"I have a job in Bayville. Kenny, my best friend is there. Remember her?" She sits up, wrapping the sheet over her beautiful body. I resist the urge to pull it away. "I won't drop my life to move here and live with you and let you pay for everything like I'm some . . . some . . ."

Her chin drops, but I catch it and lift her face. "You're here almost every day as it is. How would it be different?"

"You know how it would be different." Fire is in those beautiful eyes. I love it. "I'm here because it's an easy drive back and forth, and I like spending my free time with my boyfriend."

"Is that so?" A smile pulls at the corner of my mouth, but I hold on. We're leading up to a question I've been ready to ask since December.

"Besides, it sets a bad precedent if I let you win every

argument by sleeping with me."

"Aren't we supposed to fight it out in bed?"

A little nose twitch, a teasing glance, and I can't take it any-more. Snatching the sheet away, I catch her around the waist and pull her body flush with mine. She squeals with laughter, and I cover her mouth, kissing her deeply until her struggling relaxes and her arms slide around my neck slow and easy.

Pulling back, I hold her body and her gaze a moment. Then I say it. "I want you to marry me, Mariska. I want you to trans-fer to Princeton and live here with me as my wife. Fuck this boyfriend-girlfriend shit."

Her eyes blink fast, and her brows pull together. For a sec-ond, my chest tightens. Sick hits the pit of my stomach when her tears spill over, down her temples and into her hair.

"Baby, what's wrong?"

Her body jerks with a sniff, and she cries more. She pulls herself up to me in a hug, burying her face in my neck, and I'm going crazy until she finally speaks.

"Stuart," it's cut off by another sniff. "Oh, Stuart, I want that so much."

Relief blasts through me, anxiety gone. I wrap her in my arms, holding her close. Her face is still at my neck, and I feel her tears on my skin. I feel all of her against my skin, shoulders to stomach to thigh to knee, and I think about that old idea of becoming one. She's the part of me that's been missing for so long. Inhaling deeply, luscious jasmine fills my senses.

After a few moments, I slide my hands over her bare back, from her soft shoulders to her soft ass. "So is that a yes?" My voice is low and gentle.

She nods against me, squeezing me in her arms.

"Mariska?" I'm smiling now, holding my wife in my arms. Everything has changed. "Look at me."

She takes a moment before pulling back, those beautiful eyes shining with her tears. "Will you please call about transferring to Princeton tomorrow?"

A laugh explodes from her lips, and she pulls up, hugging our faces together. "I guess if you put it that way."

Kissing her jaw, her cheek, I roll her onto her back and prop myself on my elbows. "Thank you for agreeing to be my wife."

Her eyes roll and she shakes her head. "As if you ever had any doubt."

"You are a very strong, independent lady, Mariska Renee." I pause to scoop her lips in another brief kiss. "I wasn't sure you'd say yes so easily. I worried you might think it was too soon."

"With as well as I know you?" Her cat eyes slant.

"I thought you might have some old-fashioned notion about finishing school or us needing to date for a year or something ridiculous."

"Don't give me any ideas."

My brow lowers. "Is that something you want to do?"

"Is that something I should want to do?" How she manages to go from sassy to shy in the blink of an eye slays me. I can't believe how vulnerable she is. Like I didn't just ask her to fucking marry me.

"No." I don't even let that idea hang around five seconds. "I don't want you away from me anymore. I'm getting your ring as soon as I get back from Baltimore. Give your landlord notice and start packing. You'll start Princeton this fall. Summer if you want to start earlier."

She laughs, and her body arches against mine. Her head falls back, and she lets out the most amazing happy squeal. I was above her, but she pushes me back against the pillows. I'm on my back watching her hold her brow and shake her head.

"It's like a dream," she says. Then she catches my face in both hands again and kisses me. I can't help laughing now. "Do you remember how awful you were in Montana?"

"Hang on," I try to act offended and fail. "You came at me out of nowhere."

"You are literally the man of my dreams, Stuart Knight."

"Don't forget," I say, smoothing both hands over her cheeks, sliding her brown hair back. "You're the woman in mine, too."

"Would you make love to me again?" Her lips curl as her hand moves down between us. Her fingers wrap around my cock, and my body immediately responds to her touch, hard and strong.

"With pleasure," I say, before kissing her lips, her chin, her neck, making my way down her torso to the place I know will have her screaming my name.

♥

KISSING MARISKA GOODBYE THIS MORNING was the hardest thing I've done since this nightmare with Derek began. She's dressed in only my white dress shirt, looking like the most beautiful sex kitten who's ever agreed to marry anybody.

"My goal is to hit the prosecutor strong," I say, grabbing my suitcase so I don't grab her.

"Take as long as you need, baby." Her eyes are round and serious, oblivious to how her words affect me. "I'll be here doing my assignments."

"Your assignments?"

"You gave me a list last night. Don't you remember?"

She smiles and my suitcase goes down. I pull her to me and kiss her one long, last time. "Yes. I want all of that done when I get back."

"Or what?" Her expression is coy. "You'll spank me?"

"Hell, no." I exhale a laugh before I kiss her again. "If I say that, you'll never do it."

"Hmm . . . I suppose you have a point."

"If I didn't have to be in Baltimore . . ." One more kiss, and I'm out the door, only pausing once to look back at the beautiful creature who belongs to me. Damn, I'm ready to fast track this week's business and get us all home.

Patrick's in the office when I get there, and he's got three law books out on our shared desk.

"You could take the office down the hall," I quip, causing him to look up.

"You're freakishly happy," he turns back to the book he's studying. "Mariska's a fucking miracle worker."

It's true, and even my annoying little brother can't bring me down this morning.

"Anyway, you left." He's making notes on a yellow legal pad. "Derek gave me this office, and it has all my shit in it."

It's true. When I came back from Saudi, I was put in Derek's old office, but I never felt right about taking my CO's spot, even if he had moved to Wilmington full-time.

"Working behind a desk isn't my thing. What have you found out?"

"Not much." He straightens and tilts his head, stretching his neck. Patrick's five years younger than me, and no matter how much we age, he always seems like a kid. Our little sister Amy is a perennial baby.

"Hit me," I say, loading my briefcase with my pick of the worst reports from Derek's "Sloan files."

"I need to talk to Melissa. She's been pretty pissed at me, but her evidence against Sloan is going to be critical. She's got email receipts of his transactions with hookers, photographs of her face when . . . he beat her . . ."

He pauses to grimace, and I share his sentiment. Melissa's a beautiful, classy woman. She's Derek's fiancée, Dex's mom. The idea of some fucker hitting her makes us all a little crazy with rage.

Clearing his throat, he continues, looking guilty. "I hate to ask her for those things. I know how much she wants to put it behind her. But they'll pretty much make the case for Derek's taking him out."

"You're sure Sloan has no surviving relatives?"

He drops into the desk chair and starts clicking. "Only distant ones, and most of them are older, infirm."

Pausing, I lean against the doorway. "You realize, if this does go to trial, you're an accessory to murder."

His lips tighten and he nods. "I've never been a more willing accessory."

"Tell me what happened that night. How exactly it went down."

My brother's hazel meet mine. His are more green than brown. "It was pretty fast. We were in a small conference room with a tech booth off the side."

"Why?"

"Star was the bait, but Derek didn't want her to be too far from where we could help her if things got ugly." He looks down at his hand and slowly makes a fist. "That asshole manhandled her pretty good. Slammed her head against the wall, then he had her pinned, his forearm against her neck."

"Shit," I exhale, stepping forward into my old office, thinking. I've only known Star about a week. She's a little rough around the edges, but she's sweet with her kid. Despite her painfully obvious crush on Derek, she seems like a smart girl. "So he was killing her?"

"I think so." He's still looking at his hands, remembering. "He had a reputation for liking it rough, and I was pretty preoccupied while it was happening."

For a moment, I'm stumped trying to figure out what my little brother might've been doing besides keeping his eyes on his target.

"Derek fought me to get out there. I held him back as much as I could, but he's fucking strong."

Shaking my head, I can't even imagine. "I'm surprised you could hold him."

"When she said the safe word, I let him go. We both rushed out, but when I went to Star, Derek went straight and finished things."

"So that's how it happened."

I take a step back, turning to face the female voice addressing us. Melissa is standing in the doorway. Her dark brow is furrowed and her lips are tight.

"Hey, you're back." Patrick's out of his seat and headed toward her.

She steps into the office and meets him, giving him a warm hug. "I forgive you for not keeping your promise," she says, leaning back and mussing his hair. "But I don't forgive you for not telling me."

"None of this was supposed to happen." He follows her back to the desk. She steps over to where I'm looking out the window at the highway.

"Marcus is going to help us. He said he'd fly to Baltimore to meet you. He's scheduled a meeting with the prosecutor, but he needs us to send him everything we've got on Sloan and Derek."

Putting the case down, I snap it open and pull out the files I'm taking with me. "Fax these to him now. I want to have them with me when I get there."

She nods and takes them from me, but she stops to speak to Patrick. "Is there any chance Elaine can come here today or tomorrow?"

"She was planning to drive up with Lane on Thursday. Her school's spring break is next week."

"We're going to need her sooner than that."

"What are you thinking?" Patrick sits on the edge of the desk facing her."

"My photograph, the email receipts I printed off . . . I'd say she could FedEx them, but I don't want to take any chances of them being lost."

He nods and pulls out his phone. "She'll do that for you. I need to ask her now so she can find a substitute."

Melissa rubs her eyes. "I wish I could have Dex here with me. I miss him so much."

"She could bring him with her. Lane needs the company."

Shaking her head, she drops her hand with a sigh. "He'd better stay with Mom in case I have to go to Baltimore. I want to be free to do whatever Derek needs on a moment's notice."

God, I hate hustling her right now. I'm concerned as well about the possibility of a long, messy trial. None of us want that.

"I need to get on the road," I say, nodding to the papers.

"I'll fax these now," she says, heading down the hall.

Patrick walks back around the desk and drops into his chair. "Bennett cooked us good forcing Derek to confess like that."

"Let me know if you find anything else useful." He nods, and it hits me he arrived last night. "Why aren't you sleeping at Derek's place? There's no reason for you to be in a hotel."

He glances down and manages to look embarrassed. "Star and I have sort of a past. I don't want to make Elaine uncomfortable."

"That's pretty mature of you, brother."

"Yeah, well, I tested Elaine enough in the beginning to last a lifetime." He glances over his shoulder, out the office window as he says the last bit. "She's the best thing that's ever happened to me."

I'm feeling pretty generous, considering my recent developments with Mariska. "I hear that." We pause a moment. "Stay at my place. Melissa's here now, and Mariska will probably be back and forth to Bayville."

His lips poke out and he nods. "It's a good idea." Turning back, we exchange what is possibly the first warm greeting in our lives. "Thanks, bro."

"No worries."

The door opens and Melissa breezes back in. She hands me the papers. "I'll fax my evidence as soon as Elaine gets here with it."

"She texted she could probably be here tonight," Patrick says, reading from his phone.

"Perfect," she's focused, all business. "Marcus needs everything we have on Derek—medals, service awards . . ."

"I can personally vouch for his conduct in the line of duty,"

I say.

Melissa's brow relaxes, and her eyes glisten with tears. "Bring him home, Stuart."

I touch the salty drop off her cheek. "I'll do everything in my power."

THIRTEEN

INSIDE

Derek

MY LUNCH TRAY HAS JUST touched the long cafeteria-style table when I feel him standing over me. So far it's been pretty quiet, but I knew it was a matter of time before the population would start to feel me out. Without lifting my eyes I wait as the large form takes a seat across from me.

The food is shit. A flat sandwich, bologna on stale white bread, sits in front of me. A banana and a plastic cup of juice complete the meal.

"We've had two new guys since you got here." My lunch guest pauses, but I don't look up. "You still have your own cell."

Silence.

I pick up one half of my sandwich and inspect it. Mayonnaise and what I can only assume is fake cheese join the flat processed meat. My stomach turns and I put it back down.

"You a mole?" The enormous guy isn't deterred.

"No," I say, acknowledging him.

"A snitch?"

"No." My expression is flat. I appear calm, but my adrenaline is ticking up slowly.

His dark eyes inspect me. "You're white collar." A beat, another quick scan. "What you in for?"

"Murder." Returning to the food, I decide it's probably wise to keep my strength up, even if it's crap, and take a bite. The meat is salty and the bread sticks inside my mouth.

The fellow across from me bends a dark eyebrow. "How'd you do it?"

Reaching for the plastic cup of orange juice, I pull the foil off and take a sip trying to get the crap food off my teeth. It takes a moment, and in the meantime, I turn my right hand over, palm up.

His eyes flicker down to it then back up to me. "Strangled?"

Shaking my head, I'm able to speak. "Broke his neck."

Silence falls between us again. He's studying me. "You Italian?" I shake my head no. "Latino?" Another no. "Irish?"

That makes me almost laugh. "No."

"Biracial?"

Lifting my blue eyes, I smirk. "What do you think?"

He watches me a beat. "You're military."

"Good guess," I say, trying the banana. Peel off, I break a piece and put it in my mouth. Mealy.

"I can smell that shit a mile away," he says.

I don't answer. I break off another piece of fruit.

"Okay, soldier," he continues. The reference makes me flinch, but I let it go. "You can call me Chairman. I'm your welcoming committee."

My brow is lowered as my eyes return to his. "I'm not interested in a welcome."

"Shut the fuck up and listen." I'm pissed, but his brow lowers as well. I notice he's expanded a few inches in size, and I decide I'll check out that weight room after all.

Sitting a little straighter, I decide to hear him out. "I'm all ears."

"We do things a little different here. You're not in the joint. You're only in a holding pattern. We don't do white versus black, Dago versus Polack, Mick versus Spick." I resist asking if he writes greeting cards. He leans forward, and his tone turns sinister. "We do bad-asses versus pussies. Looks like you might be one of the bad-asses."

"You're smarter than I thought."

"You want to survive Phase One of your incarceration? Sit at the head table with us." He nods in a direction behind me, over my right shoulder. "We'll protect you."

"If I'm one of the bad-asses, why do I need protection?"

"Because if you're not sitting with us, you're one of the pussies. We don't truck with pussies. Somebody needs to blow off steam . . ."

Our eyes clash, black iron against blue steel. I guess it's time to get affiliated. Glancing over my shoulder, I see the table in question.

Another, equally large black guy is sitting hunched over his plate of shit. Beside him is a skinhead white fellow just as big as he is. In the next seat is a smaller, wiry guy with sallow skin and a black buzz cut.

"Who's the little guy?" I say, turning back.

"Reverend Moon. Rev for short." Chairman leans back and a look of admiration passes over his face. "Don't cross that little fucker or you'll end up in a sling. Or worse."

Taking another sip of OJ, I look at the man in front of me then I look around the room where we're sitting. "This is central lockup. We're not in prison, there's no culture here. How do you know so much?"

He's off defense, and his chest deflates slightly. "You're a rookie." Shaking his head, he acts so wise. "You'll see when you've been around a while, it's one big circle. Maybe you get out . . . Well, you're never getting out, but maybe Rev gets out. He's just a habitual drug offender. He'll be back. After a while, we know you. And you know us."

His eyes laser into mine, and I nod. "Badass."

"Or pussy."

Without another word, he stands and takes the tray off the table in front of him. I watch as he goes, thinking this is my life now. I might not like it, but I'd better get ready.

STUART SITS ACROSS THE GLASS from me, holding a phone. My partner's dressed in a brown tweed blazer over a white shirt, no tie. He's also wearing jeans. I mentally wonder what it is with the Knight brothers and suits.

"How you holding up?" His brown-hazel eyes assess me through the glass.

"Apparently I'm a badass."

A short laugh, and he shakes his head. "I could've told you that. Anybody giving you trouble?"

"Nah, just the usual shit you'd expect."

He doesn't say anything for a moment. "I'm sorry you're in here, brother. You killed a worthless piece of shit. You did the world a favor."

Shaking my head, I don't let that continue. "I broke the law. Now it's a matter of whether I'll find mercy or whether I'll stay here for the duration."

"I'm meeting with the prosecution tomorrow morning," he says. "They're going to try and make the case for why you should stay, but we're ready to fight it. Melissa got you one of the best lawyers in the country, from what she claims . . ."

"Elaine's brother."

"Right. Do you know him?"

Shaking my head, I look down at my hand. "Only by reputation."

"He's flying out here tonight. We've collected everything you put together on Sloan—good work, by the way—and with Melissa's evidence, we should be able to build a strong case for 'defense of others.'"

My eyebrows rise. "I hadn't considered that."

"You can thank my little brother," he laughs. "Seems you're not the only college graduate in the office."

"If you weren't so busy playing soldier, you'd have finished college."

"Somebody's got to defend our country."

It's our old banter, and it takes my mind off the shit I'm living with now. The America private citizens wonder if we should worry about defending. The America they'd rather kill. My mind drifts to the nighttime. The things I miss most.

"Can you get me a picture of Melissa?" I ask, looking down at my hands. "When they arrested me, I only had my phone, which they confiscated."

"Of course." He nods. "You got it."

"And one of Dex."

"I'll get them to you tomorrow. Tonight if I can."

We're quiet a moment, and I can't help saying what's on my mind. "She has to go on record with what happened to her." Wincing, I look down at the Formica space between us. "She never wanted anyone to know. She wanted to put it behind us."

"Look at me." Stuart's voice is sharp, and when I glance up, his brow is lowered. "Melissa is more determined than I've ever seen any woman. She's not angry or backing down. She's doing whatever it takes to get her man home."

"Yeah," I say through an exhale. "Because of what I did."

"You did what you had to do." His tone is more emphatic, and I can't stop the label that floats across my brain: *Badass.* "We're doing what we have to do. Keep your spirits up. It won't be long."

DINNER. I'M IN THE LINE, holding my tray as a blob of what appears to be pulled pork is dumped on it. Turning away, I'm faced with a cafeteria full of men waiting to be convicted, sentenced, and either let back out into the population or sent to prison.

Two young guys who should be in college joke and laugh as they take their seats. An old man who looks too weak to do anything significant passes. He's probably the worst offender of all, preying on those weaker than him. Then my eyes land on the table in the back, the group of thugs waiting to see if I'll join them.

I was a Marine. I took an oath. Now I'm one of these guys, a convict trapped in a holding pen while the system either succeeds or fails. Clenching my jaw, I start toward the same spot where I had my lunch earlier, where I've had every meal here alone. I'm not a pussy, but I'm not a thug. I might be a badass, but I'm not joining the ranks of the repeat offenders.

Nobody speaks as I take my seat, but I feel Chairman's eyes follow me. Regardless of what happens outside with Stuart and the rest, I'm on the inside, and I have to establish my identity. Here it is.

FOURTEEN

THE CASE

Stuart

PACING MY HOTEL ROOM, I study the photographs I printed off at the drugstore earlier. One is Melissa looking up from where she's sitting on the beach and smiling. The breeze is swirling her long hair back, and her sunglasses are pushed up on her head. I nod. It's a good one.

Flipping it back, I have one of Dex. Melissa texted it to me. It's from his birthday party, and he's hugging Derek, climbing into his lap with a big smile. The last is the one from his condo. I've seen it in a frame there dozens of times. Melissa, again, forwarded it to me. They're perfect—loving and sweet—they'll keep his spirits up, remind him of home, help him remember why he has to get out.

It's late or I would take them over tonight. Instead, I'll run them by first thing in the morning before I meet with the prosecutor. My phone buzzes, and I slide my finger across the face.

"Stuart here."

"It's Marcus," the male voice says. "Just checking in about tomorrow. I'm pretty sure we have all we need."

"Did you get Melissa's evidence."

"It was on my computer when I got to the hotel." He pauses, and I hear him struggling for words.

I help him out. "It's tough stuff."

"I've never met Derek Alexander." His tone is serious. "I don't usually take cases where I haven't met the client. Her photograph changed my mind."

"We've got a pretty sound case for defense of others."

"If we can get around the premeditation and entrapment allegations."

"Entrapment would be stronger if it'd happened on the first night. In terms of when it happened, Sloan propositioned her. He was offering her a job, giving her a trial run."

Marcus exhales a laugh in my ear. "You'd make a good lawyer."

"I just know my friend." My stomach is tight, determination burning in my chest. "He doesn't belong in prison. If he made the executive decision to take this guy out, it was the right call."

"Only he wasn't at war. He was at home, a civilian, committing a crime against another civilian."

"Defense of others."

"If that fails, we can go with objective reasonableness." I hear pages flip in the background. "Derek was licensed to use deadly force. He didn't work as a cop, but he was trained as one. He was also a decorated commanding officer, responsible for leading troops. His judgment should be without question."

"It's not the most popular defense right now."

"Still, it should gain more sympathy than an abusive suspected murderer who was in the process of trying to kill an escort while Derek was in the next room."

Adrenaline surges in my veins. "I feel like we've got a strong argument."

"I was going to suggest bringing Patrick in to testify, but at the moment, they have Derek acting alone."

"He'll do whatever it takes to help get Derek out."

"I'm thinking of my little sister. If this doesn't go well, I'd rather not be the asshole who put her husband behind bars."

My fist clenches, and I look at the clock. It's after ten. "They did the right thing. I'm holding onto that fact."

"I'll meet you in jail."

Hanging up, I pace the room again. Bennett had better keep his ass far away from here. If I ever cross paths with that traitorous sonofabitch, I'll kill him.

A SUIT ISN'T MY DRESS code of choice, but today's business calls for a professional image. Tough, no bullshit. I skip the tie in favor of a black dress shirt unbuttoned at the top. Sliding the cuffs forward, I fasten the top button on my grey herringbone two-piece. I'm shaved, and my hair is brushed neat. I look like I'm in fucking *Oceans 11*.

It's a far cry from jeans and Carhartt jackets, breaking horses on my uncle's ranch in Montana, sleeping by a campfire under an endless sky, holding Mariska's body next to mine as the winter wind rages outside that small cabin on the plain. Damn, I miss that.

I give the king suite where I spent the night one final sweep. Marcus is bringing all the paperwork. I have the photographs I'll leave at the desk for Derek. It appears I have everything I need. Door card in my pocket, I head out to face this day.

When I agreed to return to Alexander-Knight, I never expected my first case to be fighting a murder rap against my best friend. I came back unsure what direction I wanted to take. Derek said I could have some time to find what interested me. One week back, and I'm fighting to keep him out of prison, going head to head against a life-sentence for murder facing experienced prosecutors. I haven't been in a pre-trial conference in ten years. Turning my Silverado into the parking lot of the state correctional facility, I consider if this keeps up, I'll have to trade my truck in for a sedan. *Not happening.*

Marcus is at the jail when I arrive, and he's dressed in dark-grey sharkskin holding a black leather messenger-style satchel.

"Interesting," I say, nodding at his suit.

"It's my favorite for defending murderers," he says with a smile. "Classic Rat pack."

"Where the hell did you find sharkskin?"

"Brooks Brothers." He nods at me. "Armani?"

I shrug. "Louis Vuitton." I didn't grow up on a horse ranch. I just prefer it to this.

I pass over the envelope containing the photographs Derek requested while Marc fills out the check-in form. I'm next, then we empty our pockets before going through the metal detector. On the other side, Marcus holds his arms up as the security guard pats him down. It's like going through airport security, but worse. No cell phones in jail, no devices of any kind. If something goes down, we're stuck here just like every other criminal in the joint.

"I spent half the night going over all we've got," he says under his breath, as we follow the guard down the corridor. "Sloan Reynolds has no family, no dependents, and his company doesn't want his shit coming out." His eyes meet mine, and he nods.

I smile and nod back. "You're the best, right?"

"That's what I hear." We pause outside the door before facing the prosecution.

WE ENTER THE SMALL CONFERENCE room and each shake the hand of the prosecutor, a solemn-looking African-American gentleman.

"Earl Mason," he says, taking a seat across the table from us, files spread out before him. "I've reviewed the case against

Derek Alexander, and I have to say, it looks pretty open and shut."

Dark eyes glance up at us, and I can tell he's not finished. "Your client willfully and of sound mind murdered Sloan Reynolds. He said so right here in his confession. As far as I can tell, we have every reason to expect a conviction for first-degree murder."

Marcus places his satchel on the table beside him. "Quite a bit is left out of that confession, which is why we're here today." I watch as he pulls out three thick files.

"And you are?" A salt and pepper brow lowers over Earl's eyes.

"Marcus Merritt, attorney for the defendant."

"I haven't seen you around the courthouse before." He scrutinizes the man beside me, but I don't even sense a tremor from Marc. "Are you licensed to practice in the state of Maryland?"

"If necessary, I will associate local counsel for trial, but we don't think a trial will be necessary." Marcus answers with a swagger that makes me wince. This old man is not one to fuck with.

The prosecutor holds his gaze a beat longer before returning to the documents in front of him. "We're here to informally discuss resolution of the pending charges against Mr. Alexander before pretrial discovery and trial preparation begins. I've told you what I have. What do you have?"

Sliding the first folder across the table, Marcus begins. "My client is, and was, engaged to the ex-wife of the deceased."

"That doesn't exactly help you."

Marcus pauses, and his expression grows stony. "Until you see what's in that folder."

We wait as Earl opens it, watch his brow line as he peruses Melissa's evidence. "What is this?" he finally asks.

"Miss Jones divorced Sloan Reynolds after he beat her to the point documented in that photograph." A pause, and I feel my partner collecting himself. "That battery followed her discovery of his penchant for prostitutes."

A slow inhale, and our opponent closes the folder. "Was this incident reported to the police?"

"No." Marcus's voice is grave. "But she has a witness that can corroborate her story."

"It's weak, but I'm still listening. You're describing a conviction for second-degree murder, a crime committed in the heat of passion. It carries a ten-year sentence with at least five to be served. Do you have anything else?"

Another manila folder crosses the divide. "The defendant was in the process of building a case against Sloan Reynolds when the crime occurred. In this folder you will see evidence, including photographs almost identical to Miss Jones's, of a woman Reynolds assaulted, Jessica Black. My client had reason to believe Reynolds murdered Miss Black."

Again we wait while the prosecutor evaluates the files in front of him. His lips tighten as he turns page after page. "Is any of this on the record?"

"Miss Black did file a police report for battery, which is how we obtained that photograph of her beaten face." Marcus's fingers cross as he folds his hands. "She later backed down from pressing charges. She didn't name Reynolds in her case, but we have evidence that she was in Baltimore as his escort when the crime occurred."

A few moments pass, and the attorney across from us puckers his lips as he thinks. "So Mr. Alexander took the law into his own hands. Voluntary manslaughter."

No one speaks for a moment.

"So there's more. Okay, Mr. Merritt. What's behind Door Number Three?" His eyes are on the last folder Marcus holds.

"It's the heart of our defense of others argument." He slides it across, and the older man takes it. "Inside you see a photograph of the victim dead, and in his pocket is a pair of thong underwear."

"I hope this is relevant."

"We are in possession of that undergarment and believe if it's tested, you will find Reynolds's DNA on it."

"And?"

"You will also see photographic evidence of one Star Brandon, a high-class hooker Reynolds was . . . servicing at the time my client acted in defense."

The prosecutor seems bored at this point. "How is this evidence?"

"As you can further see in the photograph, Ms. Brandon's neck and torso are bruised and battered. Reynolds was in the process of strangling Brandon to the point of death when my client was compelled to use deadly force to rescue her."

"Sloan Reynolds was unarmed at the time of death. Deadly force was not required. Three to five years, one year in prison less time served, the rest on probation."

In that instant, Marcus's tone changes, and I hear why he's the best. "We're not letting our client spend one more night behind bars. We want him out now. He's a decorated veteran, a former commanding officer, a member of law enforcement, respected Ivy League professor, and a leader in the security field. He had objective reason to believe the only way to stop Sloan Reynolds's pattern of abusive murder was to take him out in the line of duty. Sloan Reynolds was a low life using his family's money to fund his lifestyle of abuse and cruelty to women. I think we've got as solid a case as we need, sir."

Silence falls over the conference room. The clock ticks slowly, and mentally I'm standing, spiking the ball, and doing the Harlem Shuffle all at once. On the outside, we're as cool as the minute we walked in.

Earl sits back and sighs. "As you may know, no one has come forward to press these charges on behalf of Mr. Reynolds' family or friends. Only one party seems genuinely interested in the possibility of a conviction."

My insides are tense, and I sense Marcus preparing to hear him out. I can't believe anybody would have anything good to say about Sloan.

"Mr. Reynolds' company took out a sizable life insurance policy on him. The insurance company has been reluctant to pay because of the appearance that Mr. Reynolds might have somehow committed suicide, since he was alone and there was no recorded cause of death. In which case they do not have to pay."

"Makes a difference," Marcus says with a nod.

"On the other hand, if Mr. Reynolds were murdered, the company stands to get a double recovery under the policy."

"Double indemnity." Our attorney half-smiles.

"What is this?" I say.

"Don't you know your classic movies, Stuart?" Marcus turns to me. "If Reynolds is murdered, his company gets double their money under the life insurance policy."

"Correct," Earl replies. "And I've got a company accountant looking to turn a zero-value policy into double recovery if I can get a murder conviction."

"How much is the policy?" I ask.

"Two million dollars."

"Listen," I flash, "I can guarantee you if this case goes to trial, that company is going to get ten million dollars' worth of bad publicity. We'll show the world its CEO was a wife-beating rapist who was killed in the act of choking a prostitute to death. You can't buy enough insurance to protect the company from that level of damage."

Earl seems to notice me for the first time. "What's your say in all of this?"

Sitting forward, I'm glad to have a say. "I'm here both to confirm everything Marcus has said, but also to stand in the place of Derek . . . Mr. Alexander."

"You are?"

"Stuart Knight, founding partner of Alexander-Knight, LLC, and retired Marine. I was under the direct command of the defendant. He's a good man of high character."

"Semper fi," Earl says, glancing down.

"Yes," I agree, meaning every word.

"Well, gentlemen, I'm not interested in going out on a limb for a rich degenerate, who has no one particularly interested in his murder. Especially when it's only to help a company that stands to profit from his death. Speaking of publicity, that's frankly the kind of publicity that gets district attorneys unelected and prosecutors fired." He pushes back from the table and stands, reaching across to shake our hands. "If Mr. Alexander will plead guilty to the misdemeanor charge of failure to timely report a homicide and pay a one-thousand dollar fine, I am inclined to dismiss the charges. I'll speak to the judge and see if we can get the paperwork going to get him home today."

For a moment, I feel like I'm back in a PTSD dream. I'm unsure if what just happened is real or if I imagined it.

Marcus is the epitome of smooth. "Thank you, Mr. Mason—"

"Earl," the prosecutor corrects him.

"Earl," he nods. "I knew once you'd had a chance to see what was at stake, it would be a pretty simple decision."

"Nothing is simple." Earl's expression goes immediately serious. "Murder, vigilante justice, these are not things I take lightly by any means."

"Of course not," Marcus says. "I didn't mean to imply—"

"However, there are also situations in which reasonable, thoughtful men are compelled to act." He pauses as if for emphasis. "In my considered opinion, this was one of those situations."

Rising from my chair, I reach across the table, holding out my hand. Earl seems surprised, but then he takes it, giving me a firm shake back.

"I can assure you," I say, infusing my words with as much sincerity as possible. "This was one of those situations."

Earl nods and smiles for the first time since we've seen him. "Let's get Mr. Alexander back home to his family."

FIFTEEN

BADASS

Derek

BREAKFAST IS OVER, AND I'M facing free time. I know my defiance of Chairman and his band of "badasses" at dinner won't go unanswered. What I don't know is when or how the answer will come. I decide to make my way to the weight room in the interim. It's been years since I've faced the prospect of hand-to-hand combat. I was trained to do it in the Middle East. I never dreamed I'd face it behind bars in my own country.

The prospect of Rev and a shiv flickers through my mind. It could get a whole lot worse than hand-to-hand. It doesn't scare me. It pisses me off. Adrenaline surges in my veins, and I feel myself getting ready. I'm running on three weeks of uninterrupted frustration here, starting the day Melissa put me out of the house. My only break lasted all of five minutes in my office when I held her in my arms again. When she'd asked me to make love to her, and the fucking cops walked in. Maybe a good fight is exactly what I need.

Last night, I'd stood at the bars of my cell. My forearms rested on the door and I looked out at the peeling white paint, the center space filled with round tables bathed in the blue light of the dark hours. None of us would be here for long. Jail was a constant stream of in and out, depending on what happened with the courts. I wondered how much longer I'd have before moving either to prison or being allowed to walk.

Stuart had said he would bring me pictures of Melissa and Dex, but I can only guess he wasn't able to make it happen before visiting hours ended. Closing my eyes, I tried to conjure the scent of ocean roses. I couldn't, but I could remember how it felt to smell them. My body craved hers. Standing in the darkness, I considered the worst—a lifetime of separation. It clenched my insides, and even if I wasn't afraid of the inmates or the horrors of life inside, I didn't know how I'd get through the years of this separation. *Would I ask her to wait for me? Could I be that selfish?*

"Melissa," I whispered into the darkness.

I hadn't been given many breaks since this nightmare began, but the greatest one had been encountering Benjamin Lance at check-in.

Ben is from New Orleans just like me, and even though he's from one of the rougher, African-American neighborhoods while I grew up in the Garden District, we'd bonded over our hometown connection when we did our police training. I can only imagine his shock at seeing me booked for murder. He'd managed to get me my own cell and kept it that way for the several days I'd been in hock. If nothing changed, it'd be the last kindness I could expect.

My thoughts drifted to Slayde Bennett. I could still see him sitting in that courtroom, ice blue eyes full of hate and rage. He was deadly calm as his judgment was handed down. He walked out of the room with a life sentence and never looked back. I never thought I'd see him again. He was a murderer and he could rot in prison for all I cared. It only shows how you never know the moments that will alter your life.

Remembering him last year, standing in that corridor with Kenny, he had changed. I was too angry at the time. The idea of a murderer walking free, getting out of the judgment I'd spent so much effort to secure, hit too close to home. It smacked too much of Sloan's ability to slip out of every charge I'd tried to make stick. All I could see was the system failing again.

Yet now, looking back, I have a different view. He still had the body of a fighter. He still moved like he could take anyone out with one hit. He still had the ink, and he projected aggression. Only the eyes had changed. My first sight of him stands out, the way he looked at Kenny, the tenderness and love. I didn't want to see it that day. I only wanted justice, and I took everything from him again.

Exhaling, I turn and walk into the darkness at the back of my cell. I demanded justice in all things. Why should I escape it?

Melissa's beautiful smile fills my memories, her soft body in my arms and her beautiful hair spilling around us. Closing my eyes, I feel her lips against mine. Placing my fists against the cinder-block wall, I remember her legs around my waist, her soft sighs and little moans as I move inside her, plunging into her depths. Again, the prospect of a life sentence twists my stomach.

She needs to understand why I did this and why I didn't tell her. It's something I could never say before, but now that I'm facing a future without her, I want her to know. I couldn't let it go. I couldn't put it behind me. As much as I love her, it went against my nature to allow him to walk. Jessica Black or no Jessica Black. Star or no Star, none of it mattered. He'd touched her in a way that couldn't be forgiven or forgotten.

It went beyond our beginning—his lying to me about her. It went beyond me not knowing what a loser he'd become when I'd agreed to track her for him. It went beyond her showing up in my office that day she'd learned the truth and shooting all my dreams to hell with one word.

After all I'd lost and all I'd found, the idea of him being alive in the world after what he'd done to her was abhorrent to me. She'd shown me that picture of her battered face, and it was indelibly marked on my soul. The mere fact of it was an underlying driving force I couldn't deny. As much as Melissa was mine, his unanswered crime was like the distant hum of a freight train growing louder and louder until it blasted through everything.

Inevitably, inexorably, as long as I lived on this planet, my future would lead to that moment in a small conference room in Baltimore when I got revenge. The darkness of what he'd done to her overcame me, and somewhere in that darkness I lost myself. No matter how honorable or law-abiding I might be, nothing would satisfy the blood lust in me. Sloan Reynolds had to die.

And now, justice continues its journey. Now I have to pay.

All the thoughts keeping me awake last night press against my brain as I enter the empty gym. I sit on the vinyl-covered bench and the low throb of pain sticks in my chest. *Melissa . . .* my soul cries her name. I want her. I need her. How will I survive if I'm in this place until I die, separated from her forever? *Fuck.*

I grip the weight bar and push up, feeling the burn in the pit of my biceps. I haven't worked out in almost a month. I've been away from home, dealing with the separation, dealing with this situation. Bennett's manipulation was clever. It showed how well he knew me. I wouldn't let Star pay for my crimes. I couldn't value my family above hers, even if she insisted her life was worth less than mine. Who makes those kinds of decisions?

The question has only entered my mind when I realize I'm not alone. I return the five hundred pound load to the rack, and my peripheral vision counts five men in the room with me. Lowering my arms, I sit up, not quite ready to make contact.

A deep inhale. I allow the battle I fought all night to flood my veins with anger. I focus all my frustrations over Melissa, Sloan, my future, to compress into one raging need for expression. I need an outlet. Looks like I have five.

"I got your message, boy." Chairman stands at the head of the bench. "You're a pussy. You'll do real good inside. Lots of cocks to suck."

I don't answer. I only sit up slowly allowing the gates I've opened to flood me with rage. What's about to happen will be sweet release. I can feel the strength building in my fists in anticipation.

"He's a pretty boy." The voice came from behind me, but my eyes are locked on Chairman's. "Hold him. I want him to be my pussy."

Try it, fucknut. The thought tickles in my brain before it closes in like a steel trap. A touch on my shoulder, and my hand snaps over it, clasping the wrist and flipping it around in a move so fast, everyone jumps back. It's the big white guy. He's on his knees with a broken wrist. A scream starts, but I punch him in the face and he drops. One down, four to go.

Only, they're ready now. I might have gotten lucky with the first one, but now two mountains of black flesh have me by each arm. Chairman stands back and watches. Rev is in front of me, and his black eyes narrow like a snake. I don't think, I only respond. A swift kick to the face, and he flies back to the wall.

"You've got to be faster than that, little man," I growl, but the hulks holding my arms aren't finished.

"It's about to get rough, pussy," the one on my left snarls.

My arm is jerked up behind my back, bending me forward, and the asshole on my right grabs my face. I know what's coming when I see him shift his balance to the other leg. I only have one chance. A loud groan scrapes from my throat as I throw everything I've got to the right. His knee flies past my head making contact with the fucker behind me. It's not a hard hit, but it stuns him. His grip loosens a fraction, and I spin around, out of his control.

"Oh, I like this one," Fucker to my left smiles.

Chairman moves his back to the wall and is making his way around the perimeter. I don't have time to wonder why he isn't getting involved. The two are slowly approaching me again, both smiling. What happens next is so fast, the specifics are fuzzy.

One guy lunges at my torso while the other takes a shot at my face. His fist makes contact with my cheekbone, and a flash of white explodes behind my eyes. I was already in the process of shooting a roundhouse kick to the right while driving a punch to the left. The punch misses but my foot makes contact with the other guy's face. I feel the crunch of his jaw in my bones, and I know he's out of commission.

He goes down, but so do I. Puncher is over me ready to start raining blows. A fist like a concrete block slams into my kidney, and I can't stop a groan of agony as pain blasts through my torso. His next punch is right to my gut, and my wind disappears.

I reach out and grab the metal leg of a weight stand near my head. Pulling with all my strength, I drag my body out of the line of his next, finishing blow.

His fist makes contact with a metal rack, and a howl of pain fills my ears. I only have one chance to get the upper hand. Pushing off the floor with both arms, I shoot my leg back, making contact with the soft flesh of his throat. A sick gulp, and he drops like a tree. I don't have time to check, but I hope I haven't added a second murder to my rap.

Panting, I face Chairman. Rev is on his feet against the wall, but he's not making a move yet. Keeping him in my view, I step back until I've got a wall behind me as well.

"Not bad, soldier," Chairman says, nodding. "Maybe you are a badass, but you crossed me. Can't let that pass."

I'm breathing hard, and my eyes move from him to Rev. "Bring it."

A flick of his wrist, and both men lunge for me at the same time. I see the glint of light off the weapon in Rev's hand, but I don't have time to block it before Chairman has my arms. Flexing my muscles, I twist away, but Rev is ready. He stabs me deep in the left side.

"FUCK!" I shout, struggling to get my arms free before he's able to do it again.

I'm too late. He's driving it into me again as I try to shift my weight so I can kick him into next week. Chairman anticipates my plan and jerks my body to the side, knocking me off balance. The movement drives the knife between my ribs. All at once, I can't breathe.

I go down gasping. I'm suffocating. Hot, sticky liquid is flooding around me on the floor. It's my blood. The room is receding . . . moving out from my vision. I feel the clock ticking as my muscles go weak. I can't get air.

Commotion fills the space around me, and I register two things before I blackout—Rev is slammed against the wall, and Chairman's arms are jerked behind him.

"Captain!" The word echoes in my ears, and I remember it was Ben's nickname for me when we were in training.

"You're a cop." Chairman's says, hatred dripping in his tone.

It's the last thing I hear before the curtain falls.

SIXTEEN

THE WORST

Melissa

LANE IS ON HIS KNEES at Derek's long dining room table eating mac and cheese while Elaine sits beside him holding a glass of white wine.

"I hate waiting," she grumbles, picking up a stray noodle that escaped onto the mahogany surface.

I can't help smiling at how a child changes the tone of Derek's single-male penthouse condo. A line of trucks is on the floor in the living room in front of the gigantic flat-screen television that's paused on a little-boy building show.

"At least we're all together," I exhale, wishing Dex were here instead of with my mom back in Wilmington. "If you hadn't made the drive, I'd be bouncing off the walls."

"You could've gone to the office to wait with Patrick."

"Even worse!" I cry, dropping into one of the leather armless chairs arranged around the dark-wood table. "It's nothing but reminders of what's happening."

"Did Kenny say she was driving up?" Leaning forward, I pick up the wine bottle and pour myself a glass.

"She and Slayde had to finish with clients at the gym, and

then they were picking up Mariska at her place." She glances up at the clock. "It only takes half an hour to drive here from Bayville."

I resist the urge to chug my glass of wine, and instead, I'm out of my chair again, pacing the room. "What can we do, Lainey? I'm about to go crazy."

"Want to watch a movie?"

"Not really." Chewing my lip, I walk to the windows and look out on the spring afternoon.

Stuart and Marcus had an eleven o'clock meeting with the prosecutor this morning, and from there they said they'd know if Derek would have to go to trial or if they would commute the charges and sentence him to time served. We've only heard once from Stuart, who said their meeting with the prosecutor was very productive. All that's left is a judge to sign off on their agreement.

"My chest is so tight, I feel like I'm having a heart attack," I laugh. "It's like we've won, but we haven't. One person stands between us and the future."

My best friend is out of her chair and crossing the room as I'm still speaking. Standing beside me looking out, she hugs me, putting her chin on my shoulder. "I don't know a whole lot about this process," she says, "but I think if the prosecutor is on our side, the judge will go with his advice."

"Even in a murder case? What if they get one of those hanging judges?"

"Oh my god, stop!" She cries, shaking her light-blonde head. "Now you're making me nervous."

A sudden knock on the door actually makes me scream. "Jesus!" Rubbing my stomach, I dash across the room to answer. "I'm so nervous, I'm screaming at the drop of a hat."

Star is outside with Cammie on her hip. "Is it okay if we hang out with you guys?"

"Of course!" Holding the door wide, I let them both in.

Star's involvement in the case is over. Bennett played his

hand, and for now he seems to be winning. Still, none of us can return to normal life while Derek is in jail.

"I can hardly stand this," Star says, putting her baby girl down. The little girl immediately crawls to where Lane is driving his truck up and down the lines in the rug. "I wish he'd waited. I wish he'd talked to me about Bennett's ultimatum."

She wrings her hands, and I grab another wine glass. "Wine?"

"God, please," she exhales. "I'm about to start smoking again."

"I might join you!" Elaine says, joining us around the table. "Cheers." She holds her glass up, and we tap our three glasses together.

I take another long pull and walk to where the babies are playing, oblivious to our adult concerns.

"She's so close to walking," I say, as Star's dark-haired beauty pulls up on the coffee table. "I remember when Dex was that age."

With a sigh, I drop my head in my hands. Derek has to come home. He can't miss being with Dex, teaching him to play football, helping him learn to ride a bike. The thought of him getting a life sentence makes my entire body shake.

"How much longer before we know something?" Star asks.

"No idea," Elaine says, taking another drink. "Stuart will call Patrick first, I'm sure. They're just waiting to get an appointment with the judge."

"That time I went to court, it took four hours before I saw the judge," she said, sitting on the floor by her daughter.

My brow lines. "Why did you have to go to court?"

Looking down, she clears her throat. "Just some . . . misunderstanding in Myrtle Beach."

"Oh my god," I say, remembering Star's former occupation. "I'm such an idiot. I'm sorry."

Seeming to read my mind, she shakes her head. "No! It wasn't anything like that. I just . . . it was sort of a wardrobe malfunction, you might say."

Blinking around, I try to place what that might mean. "Oh . . ." is all I can manage.

"They're stricter than I realized on the public beaches."

"Ohhh!" It's clicking into place when another knock on the door makes me jump. Nodding at Elaine I head to open it. "I didn't scream that time."

"It's the wine," my best friend calls after me.

She's right. I'm feeling warm and less panicky for the first time all day. Last night all I did was roll around in Derek's king-sized bed missing him and wishing I could call him. We'd already used our one phone call, so I was left with my stomach twisted and aching, hoping he still had his own cell, praying that he wasn't being targeted. I'd heard stories of prison justice. At the same time, Derek wasn't in prison yet, and Sloan wasn't a helpless victim who needed avenging. Stuart had texted yesterday asking for pictures of me and Dex to send to him, and the request made me simultaneously happy and miserable. Happy that he was thinking about us; miserable at the thought of him needing pictures to get through extended periods of separation.

Kenny, Slayde, and Mariska are at the door, and when I open it, Mariska pulls me into a hug.

"How are you holding up?" She studies me, her golden-brown eyes full of concern.

"It's possible this is the worst thing I've ever had to endure," I confess.

"That's saying a lot," Elaine mutters, taking another sip of wine. "Anybody need a glass?"

"I'll have some," Mariska goes over to her, smiling.

Kenny goes straight to Lane on the carpet, and he's in her lap at once, hugging her and sliding his fingers in her violet hair. "Mommy purple," he says.

"How's my big boy?" She kisses his cheek. Slayde sits on the leather sofa beside her, and watching them makes me want Dex here even more.

"I should have Dex," I say mostly to myself.

Elaine's beside me. "It's better he's with your mom." She slides my hair back from my shoulder. "He'd be fussy if he were here. You're stressed, and we need to know what's going to happen first."

Dropping my chin, I rub my forehead hard. I know what she's not saying. If the outcome is not what we're all straining for, I'd rather not come apart in front of my little boy.

"Oh, Lainey," I say as she hugs me again.

Slayde's deep voice cuts through the tension. It's so calm, I welcome the change. "I know this isn't the most correct thing to say, but why didn't he . . . not get arrested?"

For a moment, I consider the attractive young man sitting in Derek's living room. He's dressed in jeans and a navy tee with a matching navy windbreaker on top. We've only met once before at Elaine and Patrick's wedding. He's the love of Kenny's life, and his past is so mixed into what's happening here, it's hard to fathom.

As he waits for my answer, his dark brow lines, and Kenny looks up at him then at me. I can tell she's thinking the same thing, wondering why I'm hesitating.

Star jumps in from where she sits across from them on the floor, Cammie pulling up in her lap.

"It's my fault," she says, pulling her face away from the baby's grasp. "He was protecting me . . . or us."

"I don't understand," Kenny says, and her large blue eyes flicker from Star to me. "How was he protecting you if he killed Melissa's ex?"

My eyes go to Elaine's, and her expression is worried. I'm not sure how much Stuart's told Mariska, but Kenny and Slayde know nothing about this story. I'm not sure how much Derek wants Slayde to know.

I'm about to answer, but Star continues. "A guy that used to work for him . . . Bennett? He started blackmailing me, saying he was going to turn me in for the murder. But when Derek met with him, he was really after revenge. Derek put his son away for life . . . I think for the same thing."

"Star!" I say, trying to head her off, but it's too late. The words are out before I can distract her.

Slayde's face changes at once. His ice blue eyes cut to me. "Who is this Bennett?"

"I-I've never met him," I say, truthfully, wishing at least Patrick were here to help me explain.

Slayde is on his feet, walking to where I stand, as Lainey pours us another glass of wine. "I need you to tell me," he says.

Kenny follows, standing behind him, one hand on his waist the other holding his hand. She's so tiny, but Slayde's not quite six foot. He's slim and muscular, and everything about him, from the way he moves to the way he stands, underscores his past as a fighter.

"You should probably hear this from Derek," I say, holding his gaze. "I don't know the whole story, and I'm afraid I'll get the details wrong."

"Just . . . try." His expression is so intense, my chest clenches.

"Derek didn't actually tell me," I hedge. "He didn't have time before . . . I got the story second-hand from Patrick."

"Patrick knows?" Kenny's brow lines, but Slayde cuts in.

"Melissa," his voice urges. "Please."

I take a breath and tell him what I know. "Bennett is a contract PI Derek used for cases here after he moved to Wilmington with me."

"He's from Princeton?" Slayde asks.

"I'm not sure. If not, he's from somewhere near here."

Slayde's eyes wince. "Go on."

"Derek didn't know about this. Patrick was floored telling me the connection . . ." I try to remember the exact details. "Derek helped build the case against his son, who he called Shane." Slayde's eyes wince again, and my heart beats painfully hard. "He said Derek put him away with no mercy and he wanted Derek to suffer the same fate."

Slayde exhales a long breath, and covers Kenny's slim arm

with his hand. I can't help noticing the bold *21* inked near his thumb.

"Where is this Bennett?" he says.

"I don't know." Looking up at Elaine, she shakes her head. "It's possible Patrick might be able to find him."

Star and Mariska have slowly walked to where we're standing, and now they join us.

"What's going on?" Star says softly. "Do you know Bennett?"

"No," he says not breaking eye contact with me. "Only one man ever claimed to be my father. He was the worst kind of lowlife." His voice trails off, and Kenny's arm tightens around his waist.

Turning back, a phone rings, and Elaine's out of her chair, dashing to the guest bedroom. "It's mine! It's got to be Patrick."

My head feels light, and I pull out a chair to sit. Mariska runs over behind me, placing her slim hands on my shoulders.

"Hey, babe, what's the news?" We all lean forward listening. Elaine's voice is unbelievably calm. "Okay," she says. She frowns, and the room starts to blur. "Oh shit, Patrick, talk to Melissa. She can tell me what you say." My best friend rushes toward me. "What?" She pauses. "Oh, right! Speakerphone!"

She pulls the phone away, touches its face, and sets it on the table in front of me. Then she drops to her knees beside me, taking both my hands in hers and holding them tightly. I can't breathe waiting for what Patrick will say. Everyone in the room is huddled around my chair. Only the babies play on the carpet in the living room.

"I have great news and then . . . not so great news."

I'm sure I'm going to throw up until Mariska shouts. "Good god, Patrick! Just tell us if Derek is free!"

"Yes—he is! The judge agreed with the prosecutor." We all exhale in a united noise. Tears flood my eyes, spilling over onto my cheeks. I'm shaking as waves of relief rattle my insides.

Mariska and Elaine hug each other, and then we realize Patrick is shouting over the noise of our celebration.

"Hang on!" Elaine says, "Hang on, guys. What, Patrick?"

We all grow quiet, and Patrick continues. "While the meeting was happening . . . well . . . it seems a fight broke out in the jail where Derek was located."

Fear clenches my insides. "Is he okay?" I manage to choke out.

"No . . . he's not. One of the guys had a shiv, a makeshift knife, and he stabbed Derek twice."

A strangled cry, and Mariska's on her knees at my side, wiping my hair from my face. I don't even see her. My vision is blinded, and all I can see is Derek slipping away, needing me. I try to force my brain to understand what he's saying.

"I think I'm in shock," I whisper. Everybody is frozen, staring at the small device on the table, waiting for more.

"Patrick, what's going on?" Elaine shouts again.

"He's in the ICU at Johns Hopkins. I'm in the car headed your way. Can Melissa come down and meet me? I'll drive her to Baltimore."

Pain causes me to bend at the waist. I turn to the side and grasp the chair next to me. I can't breathe. "Lainey," I whisper. "I can't breathe."

"Oh my god, Patrick, you have to tell us if Derek's going to be okay."

"It's still a bit touch and go, but he's at the best hospital in the country. I have to believe he'll be fine."

"She'll be ready," Elaine picks up the phone and switches it off speaker. "I'll ride with you. Text me when you're out front. We'll come down when you get here."

THE DRIVE TO BALTIMORE PASSES in a blur. I sit looking out the back window as Elaine and Patrick discuss what happened up front.

"Marcus convinced the prosecutor Derek didn't deserve to go to prison?" My best friend says.

"Mmm . . . More like nobody would come forward to defend Sloan Reynolds, so why did he want to send a decorated Marine to prison for defending someone against attack."

"Your 'defense of others' suggestion?" Elaine is proud—possibly even a little smug.

Patrick grins. "As much as I want to support you in this Us versus Them thing you're doing, your brother was pretty vital to the case."

She exhales and leans back in the passenger's seat. "Why can't you take credit for doing a great job? Why does everyone have to be a member of the damn bar association?"

"I think you mean the state bar."

"Whatever! You helped. Did he even acknowledge that?"

"He didn't get a chance." Patrick smiles at her, and glancing back, I see so much adoration on his face. "Hey, look at me. I only talked to Captain Asshat, and he was so relieved, he was fucking nice to me. I can only imagine they were shitting bricks waiting for that judge to decide."

My best friend looks out the window. "They should have been. We were all counting on them."

We ride in silence as the music plays on the radio. Patrick finally speaks. "I know your dad and brothers were shitheads when you told them you wanted to be a teacher instead of a lawyer—"

"They still are," she quietly grumbles.

He lifts her hand and kisses it. "I'm not. I think you're an amazing teacher. And I'm really glad you're related to one of the top lawyers in the country."

Her eyes slant at him, and for a moment, I'm not sure if my bestie will make a quip or kiss her new husband. She does the latter, and despite my growing anxiety, I smile.

I might have been mad at Patrick for encouraging Derek not to tell me about Sloan, but I can never be mad for long. He's made my friend one of the happiest people I know. Their love is so strong. Chewing my lip, fear tightens in my chest. I can only hope our love is strong enough to pull Derek through.

------------------------- ♥ -------------------------

WE'RE PRACTICALLY RUNNING DOWN THE polished corridor. Stuart and Marcus are in the waiting room, and the minute we see each other, they stand and head in our direction. Marcus gives me a hug.

"Melissa," he exhales. "We were so sure he was in the clear and now this."

"What happened?" Elaine says from behind me.

I turn and her older brother leans forward to kiss her cheek. "Hey, sis."

Stuart's entire body is tense. "Ben said it looked like they jumped him in the weight room. By the time he got there, Derek had been stabbed twice."

My hand flies to my mouth. Tears blur my vision, and another set of arms embrace me. Elaine hugs me on top of her brother, and for a moment, I take comfort from my childhood friends.

I only give it a moment, however, straightening up and wiping the tears away. "He's going to be okay." My voice is wobbly, and I have to force myself to believe it. I won't give up on him. Not after how far we've come.

"Mrs. Alexander?" A soft voice speaks from behind us, and I turn.

"Here," Patrick says, gesturing to me. I don't correct him.

The doctor joins us in the waiting area, grim-faced. "May I speak to you in private?"

My knees try to go out, and Stuart catches my arm. Blinking up to him, I hold his hand. *Be strong, Melissa.*

"It's okay," I manage. "These are his closest friends . . . and his lawyer."

A tight smile doesn't soften the doctor's expression. His eyes travel over the five of us before he continues. "We moved him to a private room. He's heavily sedated, but he's not intubated. He won't require surgery, since the lung didn't fully collapse. Luckily the wound wasn't very deep or jagged. I took him off the ventilator, and once I see how he responds to treatment, we'll bring him around."

"So he's okay?" Stuart cuts to the chase in his usual, direct way.

"He's developed an infection around the second stab wound that we're monitoring. His fever spiked, and we've started antibiotics in his drip. I'm concerned about sepsis."

The white threatens again, and I'm sure I'll faint.

"Mrs. Alexander," the doctor catches my arm. "I didn't mean to be insensitive. Can I get you something?"

"No," shaking my head, I blink down as tears fall. "So he's . . . not okay?"

His voice softens. "Your husband is healthy and fit. I'd rather be overly cautious. He had some minor contusions, and his body needs rest."

"Can I see him?"

"I'm limiting visitors—as much for exposure as anything else."

My chest squeezes. The tears won't stop flowing, and Elaine passes me a handful of tissues.

The doctor observes me a moment. "Still . . . He might benefit from having you beside him."

Without hesitation or even a look back, I go to Derek's hospital room. I can't see him from the small window. A screen stands between the bed and the door, and inside, the steady beep of monitors fills the air.

Stepping around the screen, a fresh flood of tears spills down my cheeks. He's so pale. Lying on his back, his shirt is off and wide bands of gauze are wrapped around his chest. I can see the thick pads where his injuries are. I can't bear the thought of what happened to him. Stabbed, beaten, jumped by five men . . .

The IV bag hangs near his head. His dark hair is pushed back, and his eyes are closed. That lovely scruff is still on his cheeks, and I want to press my face to his, kiss his lips gently, tell him it's going to be okay. I'm here. I'll never leave him again.

The doctor's concern for infection is on my mind, so instead I pull up a chair at his bedside and sit, sliding my cool hand under his large one. I kiss the top before lowering my face to put my damp cheek against it.

"You're so warm," I say, swallowing the thickness in my throat. "The doctor is giving you something for that. He says it will fight the infection."

No change. The beeping continues, and I continue to stroke his hand, making my way slowly up his forearm. His skin feels so good to touch. I have him with me again. It feels like years have gone by since he held me in his arms. Looking back, I realize how precious our love is, how much I have to fight for it. He doesn't tell me important things. He protects me too much. We can work through these non-problems.

"I'm so sorry we fought," I whisper, smoothing the dark hairs on his forearm. "I'm sorry I was angry. I love you."

Movement behind the screen, and I look up to see a nurse entering. She has dark hair touched with silver, and when she smiles, lines form around her brown eyes.

"How about we wake him up?"

"Is it time?"

"His fever is down, and the antibiotics have been going several hours."

I stand quickly, moving out of her way. "Do you need me to wait outside?"

"Nope. I'm just changing out his bag, reducing the medication. When he comes around, he'll probably want to see a familiar face. He might be a little disoriented."

My chest clenches. "Thank you," is all I can say.

I watch as she works around him. The doctor enters holding a metal clipboard with papers on top. He steps over to one of the large monitors and makes notes. "Oxygen levels are good," he says quietly. "Let me know if anything changes."

The monitor beeps, and I wait. Nothing seems to be happening.

"Mr. Alexander?" The nurse touches his shoulder.

No response.

Her expression changes, and fear cramps my stomach. "Is something wrong?"

"Not necessarily." She steps over to the monitors again and makes a few notes. "I want you to call me when his eyes open. I'll be back to check on you in a little while."

She goes around the screen, and it's just the two of us. I'm on edge near his pillow waiting, straining for him to wake up. A round clock above the small television mounted on the wall says it's almost nine. I hadn't asked if I could stay overnight, but the doctor didn't seem interested in making me leave.

My mind drifts back to when Dex was born. I'd decided to have a drug-free delivery, and my groans and screaming as I worked to get our little son into the world nearly drove Derek out of the hospital. I'll never forget how helpless he looked. A bit like he looks now. Once it was over, he never left my bedside. At one point he climbed in beside me, putting one arm over my head and the other across my waist and around our new baby nestled in my side. It was one of the happiest moments of my life.

Quickly assessing the position of the tubes and monitors to his left, I sit on the bedside in the small space to his right. Slipping off my shoes, I stretch my legs down his. The arm I was just caressing is between us, and I'm careful not to disturb his injured torso. The beeps continue steadily, without interruption, as I place my cheek against his shoulder and wrap my arm across his chest.

For a little while I only hold him, feeling the warmth of his body soothing the fear in my chest. Several moments pass, and my muscles begin to relax. I feel his calm breathing, in and out, and it calms mine. My body melts into his, and for the first time in three weeks, I feel whole again.

"I won't leave until you're back with me," I say, sliding my palm carefully over his shoulder.

SEVENTEEN

FINISHED BUSINESS

Derek

AN IRRITATING BEEPING NOISE IS in my ears. It's dark, and I'm sluggish. My limbs are so heavy, I can't lift them. Confused, I blink up at the ceiling, trying to remember where the hell I am and how I got here. The last thing I recall is lying on the floor of the jail, blood pooling around my midsection.

Clearly, someone called help. Wait. Ben was there. He called me Captain . . . Something is across my shoulders. I try to lift up, but pain sears my left side, and I remember the knife going between my ribs, gasping for air. *Shit*. That fucker must've punctured a lung. So I'm in the hospital? Another beep, and I try to move again, but the slim band across my shoulders prevents me.

Turning my head, everything changes. I realize what's holding me. Melissa. Her soft hair is against my shoulder. I try to lift my arm again, but it feels weighted down. I want to hold her. Straining my neck in her direction, I take a deep inhale . . . ocean roses. Warmth swells in my chest. She's in the hospital bed beside me.

"Derek?" Her voice is thick with sleep, and the sound is so

lovely. Lifting her face, her dark brow pulls over those beautiful sapphire eyes. "Are you awake?"

I try to answer, but my mouth is so dry. "Yes." It comes out a scratched whisper.

"Oh!" She's on her feet at once. "Are you thirsty? Here, let me get you a drink." She runs around the foot to my other side. A plastic cup is on a rolling tray. She grabs it and is back at my bedside just as fast.

"Take a sip." Her hand lightly touches my chin as she holds the straw to my lips.

Fuck the water. I want to drink in her lovely form, standing over me. Her eyes are a little swollen, and I realize she's been crying. My lips part, and I pull the tepid water into my mouth. It's not very good, but it soothes my throat.

"You're here." I whisper. It's all I can think. She's here. After all those nights apart when my body ached for hers, she's right here in this room with me. Then she's up on the bedside again, leaning closer, but holding herself off my torso.

"I'm here," she repeats with a smile, her eyes glistening with more tears.

"Don't cry," I say, but my voice cracks again. She quickly holds the straw to my lips, and I take another sip.

More tears are in her eyes, but she's smiling now. She sniffs as they stream down her cheeks, and she leans forward, pressing her forehead to mine.

"I'm so happy you're awake. I've been waiting to tell you how much I love you. I want you to come home. I want us to never be separated again."

I tilt my chin to kiss her cheek. She lifts up, but hesitates before kissing my mouth. "The doctor is worried about infection . . ."

"Kiss me." My voice cracks, but the order is clear. Her lips press together, and she hesitates. "Melissa," I say a bit stronger. "I'm not worried about infection. Kiss me, dammit."

She breaks into a smile before lightly cupping my cheeks and leaning forward. Her soft lips press against mine, and I curse my inability to hold her. Lightly pulling my lips with hers, it's just a tease of a kiss. I growl and lift my head, kissing her more forcefully, but the movement sends a stab of pain into my ribs.

"Ugh," I gasp, falling back against the pillow.

"Oh my god!" She hops up. "I'll call the nurse!"

"Melissa," I growl. "Get over here and give me a real kiss before I fucking hurt myself."

My words freeze her on the spot. She blinks back at me then exhales a laugh. With a shake of her beautiful head, she's at my side again in the same spot as before.

"You're the most stubborn man," she whispers in that low, sultry voice I love.

"What do I have to do to make you listen to me?"

Her eyes sparkle as she cups my cheek. "I'm listening to you." She touches my lips softly with hers and pulls back. I let out a frustrated growl, and she speaks again. "I hear every word you say."

This time her lips crash against mine with all the longing we both feel. Mouths open, my tongue finds hers and curls with it. Desire floods my veins, and I manage to lift my right arm. It's heavy, but I hold the back of her neck, drawing her body closer to mine. She lets out a little sigh and lifts her chin. Pulling her closer, I press my mouth to her soft throat.

"You have to be careful," she whispers, threading her fingers into the sides of my hair.

"I'll let you know if anything hurts."

Slipping off the bed, she's again beside me. My arm falls and she catches it, moving it under the blanket. "You've had some pretty serious injuries. Let me call the nurse."

All I want is to hold her. I've waited so long for this moment. "Only because I don't want to stay in this bed longer than I have to."

She smiles and leans forward to kiss my forehead. I make a move to catch her and she laughs, dancing back. "Your recovery might be extensive."

"Don't worry. I'm not finished with you."

THREE WEEKS, AND I'M BACK in the Alexander-Knight office in Princeton, collecting the files I'd brought up from Wilmington and sorting through the files I'd dug out while I was here away from Melissa.

The doctor in Baltimore released me a few days after I came around, once my infection cleared up. I had to check in with my doctor here, who put me on bed rest. I still get winded, and at times I feel like an infant learning to walk again.

Speaking of infants, Melissa brought Dex from Wilmington to stay with us, and my ultimate bachelor pad looks more like a nursery than ever. It's exactly the way I like it after those nights alone, hating the sterile single-ness of the place. Today, they're in Baltimore meeting with Bea. Our wedding plans have been restored, and Melissa is taking pictures of doughnuts. I didn't even question her.

"These are the last of the files," Nikki says, taking a stack of accordion folders off my desk. "You want them in the back filing cabinet?"

"We should probably think about scanning them and saving them on the hard drive." I open my MacBook and click on the main directory folder. "As a leader in online security, it's pretty ridiculous for us to keep paper files in the office."

Her chin drops and she pauses at my door. "I'm not planning to stick around and help with that. I've sent my resume to a few offices, and I have an interview with one tomorrow."

Stopping what I'm doing, I push back against the desk and slowly stand. "I guess we never finished talking about that."

"There's nothing to talk about. I don't belong here anymore."

Patrick has returned to Wilmington with Elaine and Lane, and I briefly glance in the direction of Stuart's empty office. He hasn't made it in yet this morning.

"I understand how you feel," I say. "If you need a reference, I'll be happy to give you one."

"I won't make you lie for me," she says with a bitter shake of her head. "I slept with Mr. Knight, I helped a blackmailer trap Mr. Alexander in a murder rap—"

"To be fair, it was an honest mistake." I'm not holding it against her.

"Yes, because I'm such a god-awful secretary, you didn't let me open your mail."

I don't have a good answer for that because it's true. I'm standing in the office trying to think of a nice send-off when the glass doors open, and a face I never expected to see here emerges.

Slayde pauses in the doorway when he sees Nikki and me standing there. "Hi," his voice hesitates. "Hope I'm not inter-rupting anything."

"I was just taking these files away for Derek." Nikki takes off toward the back office, and I'm left facing the son of my nemesis.

"Would it be okay if we talked in your office?" He steps for-ward, and his expression is conflicted. "Star told me what hap-pened. I just . . . I need to ask you some questions."

"Of course." I step to the side and motion for him to enter.

He walks in, but doesn't take a seat. Instead, he steps to the bookshelves and puts his hands in his front pockets as he studies my photographs of Melissa and Dex. I step around my desk and take a seat.

"You hired this guy Bennett to be your private investigator?" He asks, turning to me. "You didn't know anything about him?"

"I knew his work history," I say. "I needed someone to work cases here when I moved to Wilmington. He came highly rec-ommended, and Bennett is a common enough name. I'm sorry, but you never entered my mind."

The young man nods and paces to the other side of my office. "No, *I'm* sorry." He stops and faces me, those ice blue eyes burning with intensity. "I'm sorry for what he did to you, the blackmailing and the forcing you to turn yourself in. I'd never have wanted him to do that. I'm not about revenge."

Nodding, I lift the Montblanc pen off my desk. "I believe you."

"It sounds like a line, but I'm not sorry I went to prison. I was a waste of space, an ungrateful killer." He pauses and rubs an inked hand over his mouth, glancing down. "Doc changed my life. I'd never have met him if it weren't for what you did."

I knew a little of Slayde's story. Patrick had explained his transformation to me when we debated whether Lane should spend time with Kenny now that she was dating an ex-con. Based on how I knew him, the answer was an automatic No. However, since leaving prison, Slayde had started over, taken control of his life. He rescued Kenny then he rescued his entire work crew and was named a hero. We'd decided he was one of the rare success stories of the penal system, and it was obvious Kenny couldn't be more in love.

He looks up at me. "Do you know where this Bennett is now?"

"I haven't had a chance to look into it," I say. "It's only my first day back in the office. But I'm sure I could find him for you."

"Would you?"

I'm just leaning forward to wake up my computer when a cold voice breaks through our conversation.

"No need to look," the man says. "I'm right here."

Slayde spins around just as my head snaps up to see none other than Robert Bennett in the entrance to my office. He's smiling, leaning against the doorjamb. His brown hair—the same color as his son's, I notice—is neatly trimmed, and he's dressed neatly in khakis and a short-sleeved shirt, as if he were just out taking a drive and stopped by the office.

Despite his casual appearance, I'm on high alert. He wanted revenge, and I'm not sure he's satisfied. Momentary silence fills the air as the three of us assess one another. My attitude is angry, defensive, but I can feel waves of rage rolling off of Slayde. His fists clench, as does his jaw. I'm on guard against what he might do. At the same time, I recall his reputation for control.

"What do you want?" Slayde's tone is low.

"Shane?" The man says, pushing off and taking a step toward us. "I wasn't expecting you to be here."

"My name is Slayde," the young fighter replies. "Why are you here?"

An evil smirk crosses my former PI's face, and his dark eyes narrow. "I've been keeping tabs on my old employer, waiting for him to be strong enough to get back to work."

"That doesn't answer my question."

My brows rise. Slayde might be tamed, but a lot of his old ferocity still exists.

"Take it easy, son," Bennett says, stopping in his tracks. "This is for you. Everything I've done has been to avenge your honor."

"I'm not your son."

"Well, biologically speaking—"

"I don't have a father." Slayde's fists tighten again, and I remember his signature move. High-volume punching. "The man who raised me was a fucked up bastard, and you were nothing more than a sperm donor."

Robert frowns. "I wanted to be there for you. I followed all your fights, all your matches. I was so proud of you."

"Once I was an adult. Where were you when I needed you? When I was seven years old being beaten for leaving a fucking Lego on the floor? When I was locked in a closet for hours for not knowing how to make breakfast?"

"My cousin was a fucked up loser," Robert snaps, and for a moment, I see a glimmer of the old Slayde reflected in his face. "Trust me. If he hadn't died already—"

"He was an alcoholic who was broken after the love of his life died." Slayde's demeanor shifts like sand, and I can see how he's changed since I faced him in the courtroom. "At least now I understand why he hated me so much."

"It doesn't excuse what he did to you."

"I never said it did, but you knew about it. You knew who I was and what I was going through. You never did a thing to help me."

"How could I?" Robert holds his hands open in a plaintiff gesture that makes me sick. "I was in no position to raise a kid. I was alone and not in a good place myself when Megan died."

"You could've sent the cops. You could've done something to help me."

Bennett shakes his head, and I see the crazy rage spark in his eyes. "NO! This isn't about me. This is about HIM!" He waves his arm at me. "You survived. You made it out of there and made a name for yourself. You were a star, a rising legend!"

"I was a broken loser just like the drunk who raised me." Slayde's shoulders droop. "I was so full of rage. I went through money like it didn't matter. I went through women like they were worthless whores."

"Until Derek Alexander ended your life."

Slayde's head snaps up at that. "He didn't end my life. He started the chain of events that helped me find peace. It's more than you ever did."

Bennett lunges forward now. "How can you say that? You don't know him like I do!" Sneering in my direction, his level of hatred for me is stunning. "He struts around here like some fucking hotshot, like he's some king."

I would argue, but I'm feeling my injury. My wind is cut in half.

"You're just trying to assuage your own guilt," Slayde murmurs.

"It's time the king was dethroned."

"What are you talking about?" Slayde's voice is an echo in

my ears. Bennett's hand is in his coat, and I see the gun as he pulls it from his pocket.

"You are fucking . . . NO!" Slayde shouts, making a lunge toward the man.

A *BLAST!* rings out, and I flinch, anticipating the bullet wound. In the hair's breath of a second, I know it could very well be more than my body could handle in my current state. Slayde is young and strong, but if it hits him in the chest, in the heart . . .

Gunfire is a sharp, staccato sound. It ends almost as fast as it begins, leaving you to wonder if it truly *was* a gun. *Could it have been fireworks? A car backfiring? No, cars don't backfire in these days of computer-controlled starters*

My first thought upon all these reflections is *I'm in shock.*

My second is *I haven't been hit.*

Looking up, I realize Slayde is standing in the center of my office as well, seeming stunned. On the floor in front of him, the man claiming to be his father is crumpled into a heap. A thick, blackish pool is forming around him, and I realize he didn't shoot at all. Bennett was the victim here.

Wresting control of my scattered thoughts, I look up, and in the hallway, I see her standing there. In her hand is the small pistol Stuart put in my boot the night he dressed me in Kevlar and sent me out to meet our unknown blackmailer. I'd given him the small gun back, and he'd put it in his desk, where for the first time since she'd been a part of our team, our weakest link took control of the situation and changed it for the better.

Nikki shot Bennett just as he was attempting to shoot me. Now he's on the floor at Slayde's feet, writhing in pain, and my secretary stands, blue eyes huge, shivering in the reception area.

♥

THE POLICE HAVE CLEARED OUT by ten. One of Nikki's

friends drives her home, promising to stay with her, and Slayde heads back to Bayville. I send a quick text to Melissa, promising to tell her everything once I get home.

When I meet Stuart at the bar across from our office, he has Marcus on the line discussing the details of the shootout and whether he needs to come in town to represent Nikki. It's the same bar Patrick and I visited the night he decided to drive to Wilmington and take Elaine back, and I can't help remembering that night with a smile. We've come a long way since those days.

"I can't believe she fucking shot him," Stuart says, shaking his head.

"Does it ever calm down around there?" I hear Marcus laugh over the speaker on Stuart's phone. "I'm putting you assholes on a $250K retainer."

"I'm sure you are," I say, noting his Armani style as I take a sip of the Glenfiddich the bartender places in front of me. "You'd be happy letting us keep you on the dole."

"Depending on the timeline, I could probably handle this when I'm in town for the wedding. If it comes to that."

"I'll keep you in the loop. Slayde witnessed the whole thing, and I intend to press charges."

"We're becoming the poster office for 'defense of others,'" Stuart says, sipping his beer. "At least we're not in Baltimore this time."

"He's lucky she didn't kill him," I add. "She said she closed her eyes and pulled the trigger."

"Good god," Marcus says. "My fee just went up."

Stuart stands, polishing off his beer. "It's late. I'm headed home to Mariska."

"Yeah, I've got to get back and tell Melissa what happened."

Marcus is right there to give us hassle. "It's a Thursday night, and you're going home at ten? You fuckers are so whipped."

"Famous last words," I say, finishing my scotch.

"Famous true words." I hear the grin in our attorney's voice.

"Just keep talking, friend," Stuart pays our bill and slips on his blazer. I shake my head, remembering the days when my partner was just as cocky.

"Don't get me wrong," Merritt continues. "I love pussy, but there is no way in hell I'm letting it order my life. I control my destiny."

Yeah, yeah. I've seen enough to know how this story ends. Taking the phone from Stuart, I turn it off speaker. "Hey, before you go, I wanted to thank you for helping me."

"Just doing my job," he says. Then as if remembering, he's back to teasing. "Thank me by paying your bill."

"Don't worry."

The slightest pause, and a serious tone enters his voice. "I'm glad you weren't hurt today. Melissa's a special lady, and she loves you. You're a lucky man."

"Thanks again."

"See you next month. Now I'm headed out for the night."

Disconnecting, I hand the phone back to Stuart. We decide to split a cab rather than driving. Sitting in the back, I look out the window at the passing lights.

"I'm thinking of offering Slayde a job," I say.

Stuart shifts in his seat. "Doing what?"

Shaking my head, I don't know why I feel the need to reach out to these kids. "I'm on the market for a new PI."

"It'll only work if Kenny will move here."

"We might make it work if he doesn't mind commuting." A few quiet moments, and I remember our other unfinished business.

"I was also thinking of asking Nikki to stay on." He looks out the window, and I keep going. "Since she saved my life and all. How would you feel about that?"

"I don't have a problem with Nikki," he says through an exhale. "All that shit is water under the bridge in my mind. She handled things wrong, but maybe I did, too."

Silence again. I'm not sure what to say. "That's pretty

generous of you."

He glances at me, and a smile spreads across his face. I'm confused, but not for long. "I asked Mariska to marry me. She said yes."

"What?" Now I'm smiling. "Well, damn. Congratulations."

"Yeah." He leans back and looks out the window again, still smiling. "None of that past shit matters anymore. It was stupid anyway."

We're at the condo, and my partner slaps my back before heading up the stairs. I'm feeling good as I go to the elevator. Marcus and his playboy swagger cross my mind, and I remember how Stuart was before Mariska came along. I wonder what girl's going to knock our hotshot attorney on his ass.

Jason is filling in for Walt again. He hits the elevator button and smiles, a wistful look in his dark eyes as the elevator comes down. "That little guy of yours is one cute kid. I used to dream of having one of my own."

"What's holding you back?" I glance at him as I wait.

His dark head bows. "You have to woo the fairer sex, and I'm financially challenged."

I can't help thinking his sallow complexion and oversized nose might also be challenges, although the right lady would overlook such things. "Money isn't a necessary evil. Be creative."

Shaking his head, his melodrama continues. "I'm not creative either, sir. It's my curse."

Clapping his shoulder as the elevator doors open, I'm ready to be upstairs wooing my own lady. "Only one person can change that situation, my friend."

"No truer words." He waits as I get inside and hit the button for the top floor "Have a good night, sir."

The condo is dim when I arrive. Dex, I'm sure is sleeping, and as I step through the kitchen area, I see Melissa sitting on the black leather couch in front of the gas log. A glass of white wine is in her hand.

I drop my keys on the oak table, and she looks over her

shoulder. Our eyes meet, and hers are soft and full of love. "How are you feeling?" Her voice is a gentle wave in my direction.

I don't waste any time going to her. She's wearing only one of my white dress shirts, and I'm feeling awake in every part of my body, most of which are located below my belt. Leaning forward, she puts her glass on the table, but I don't want her to get up. I want to scoop her into my lap and hold her.

"I'm not used to feeling weak," I say, sitting beside her and loosening my tie. My eyes never leave hers, and her cheeks flush under my gaze. "I'm ready to be back to normal."

I lift my tie over my head, and she leans forward to unbutton my top button. "I know," she says and kisses my throat. "At least you're here with me."

Her movements give me a nice view down the front of the shirt loosely covering her body. She's bare underneath, and my thoughts are moving away from this conversation to the bedroom.

"We had some excitement at the office today."

"Is that so?" She shifts so she's straddling my lap. "Tell me about it."

My hands slide up her smooth thighs to her ass, and I tease the edge of her panties with my fingertips. "I'll give you the short version."

A little shiver, "Okay."

"Slayde came to see me. He apologized, but he also wanted to know if I could find his dad for him."

"I had a feeling he would want that." Her elbow rests on my shoulder, and her beautiful cheek is against her slim hand.

I can't help thinking the best part of my day is holding this woman in my arms, talking. I understand now she needs this, and damn if I'll give her any reason to put my shit on the doorstep again.

"I was ready to tell him I could when the asshole walked in the door."

Her head lifts, and her expression changes. I was sure she

would've heard this from Elaine who heard it from Kenny by now, but I guess not.

"Derek!" she whispers. "Oh my god. What happened?"

Pulling her to me, I kiss her soft lips. They melt to my pressure, accepting my comfort. "Nothing to me, as you can see. Slayde had the confrontation I think he's always needed . . ."

Her brow lines. "And?"

"Bennett was pretty pissed I'd escaped a life sentence. He pulled out a gun." She slides back onto the couch, both hands cover her mouth. "Nikki shot him."

Jumping up, she paces my living room shaking her hands. "Oh my god, Derek. I don't think I can take any more of this."

Easing to my feet, I capture her in my arms and hold her close, smoothing her long dark hair as I kiss her temple. "He's not a threat to us anymore."

She tenses and pulls back to find my eyes. "He's . . . dead?"

"No, but he's under arrest. They've taken him to the hospital for treatment then I intend to press charges. Marcus said he'd help us ensure Bennett will never threaten us again."

Wiggling free of my embrace, she holds my arms, her eyes glistening with tears. "I'm not sorry." Her voice drops to a whisper. "I hoped he was dead. Does that make me horrible?"

I pull her to me again and she melts against my chest. "It makes you human. Bennett is a psychopath."

For a moment, her small body rests against mine. My hands slide down her waist to her hips, and I pull her closer.

"I have an idea," I say against her hair. "Let's do something to take our minds off the bad stuff." She exhales a little laugh and puts her arms around my neck.

I want to carry her to the bed, but this fucking lung injury prevents me. Instead, I take her hand and lead her to our dim-lit room. Her lacy red bra, pink nightgown, and emerald silk robe are scattered around the room . . . these delicate items break the dark mahogany furniture, stainless accents, and white linen of my male space. I love the change.

Stopping, I turn to face her, watching her beautiful eyes as I unbutton the shirt she's wearing. Sapphire turns to navy as desire builds, and I cup her breast in my hand, teasing a beaded nipple between my finger and thumb.

Leaning forward, I capture her mouth in a deep kiss. My tongue sweeps inside to hers, curling with it as my thumb circles the tip of her breast. I want to sweep her up, throw her on the bed, and climb after her, claiming her in whatever position we land.

Again, I have to be more deliberate. I kiss her slower, pulling her full bottom lip between my teeth. She rises on her tiptoes with a little squeal, tangling her fingers in the sides of my hair as she kisses me again. Her tongue plunges in my mouth, and I can feel the heat rising in her body as it presses against my chest.

Being more deliberate might not be as bad as I originally thought.

Breaking away, she gasps as she quickly unfastens the last of my buttons. I take the opportunity to touch the side of her neck with my tongue then cover it with my mouth, pulling her flesh in a hard suck.

"Oh, god, Derek," she gasps, ripping the last of my buttons free and jerking at the bottom of my undershirt.

A little chuckle rumbles from my throat as I remove them. Another little noise from her, and she spreads her palms flat over my chest, smoothing them up and curling her fingers so her nails scrape my skin. It's teasing and erotic, and I'm quickly unfastening my belt as her breasts press against me.

"You have to take it easy." Her voice is low and sultry. "Let me do all the work."

I can't help a grin. "Whatever you say, Miss Jones."

"Sit back against the headboard."

The remainder of my clothes are gone, and I comply, getting comfortable against the pillows. She stands at the foot of the bed a moment, letting her eyes travel over my body. Fire follows her gaze, and I'm ready to ditch the helpless act.

"You'd better do something or I will," I say with a rasp.

Her eyes widen a flicker and she's on her hands and knees, climbing up the length of my body. Along the way, she ducks her head to plant a kiss on my thigh. It's like a charge of electricity straight to my cock. Once there, she stops again, blue eyes flashing to mine. My stomach tenses, and she dips her head forward, pulling my tip into the hot space of her mouth.

"Melissa," I groan as she begins to suck. Her tongue flickers around the edge, and my head presses back against the pillows as my orgasm roars to life. Her hand grips my base, pumping my shaft, and her head bobs to meet it. Tension builds, and my eyes squeeze shut. I'm panting, but fuck if this doesn't feel like heaven.

"I'm close . . ." But she doesn't stop. I want to be inside her before this ends, so I sit up and catch her under the arms.

She comes off me with a pop, and I fall back, taking her naked torso with me. "Ride me," I groan as she reaches down, sliding my tip into her clenching, hot center. "Come on, baby."

I'm in. My whole shaft is engulfed in her. It's hot and tight, and she's on her knees facing me, rising and falling fast. "Oh, god," she moans, bucking against me.

I can barely take the sensations. "Melissa." My voice is hoarse, and I can't stop thrusting up into her. As hard as she's getting off on me, I'm unable to stop meeting her fuck for fuck.

"Oh, YES!" She cries as I grip her ass. I'll probably leave a mark, but damn if I can help it. She's flying over the edge, and I grab one of her bouncing tits in my mouth, giving it a hard pull followed by a little bite. She cries out again, and it's all I need.

My lung burns, and I don't care. I feel like I'm dying the most fantastic death possible. I close my eyes and hold her, letting my orgasm fill her, pressing up into her as her nails bite into my shoulders. A cough pushes through my moans, and I take a ragged breath.

"Fuck," I gasp. "I think that was the best yet."

She collapses against me, and I rock my hips once more,

allowing the receding waves of pleasure to ripple through my pelvis. Her arms hang on my shoulders, and I feel the smile on her lips.

Then she starts to laugh. "You always say that."

Holding her waist, I roll her onto her back and prop on my elbow beside her. "I mean since I got home."

She arches her back and laughs more, and I catch a nipple in my mouth again, giving it a little pull. "Oh!" She squeals, curving the other way. "You're insatiable."

Nodding, I bend down to kiss the hollow of her neck, making my way up to her jaw. "I will never get enough of you."

"Mmm." Her hands cup my cheeks. "That goes double for me."

We hold each other a moment, looking into each other's eyes. I think about the recent past, our future . . ."Everything straight in Baltimore?"

"Yes," she nods. "And I've been able to restore all our previous arrangements. The only problem was with the caterer."

"No food?"

"It's okay. I talked to the manager of a hotel near our venue, and I was able to reserve their ballroom. Catering included."

My brows rise. "Seems like that was a lucky break."

"It really was." Her slim fingers thread into the side of my hair. "Now all you have to do is show up in your dress blues."

"Whites."

"Shit!" Her eyes blink close, and I laugh. "I always get it backwards."

"Doesn't matter." Leaning down, I kiss the side of her jaw. "I know what to do."

"Me too," her voice is warm. "And I can't wait to do it with you."

That makes me smile, and I capture her lips again. Our tongues touch, and love burns in my stomach, spreading upwards into my chest. We've endured so much, and in only a few short weeks, this woman will be mine forever.

She turns her face and whispers at my ear. "What are you thinking?"

The touch of her lips against my skin stirs other parts of my body. "I'm thinking of something else I'd like to do with you."

A little laugh, a little touch, and our bodies move together in a way I will never jeopardize again.

EIGHTEEN

THAT DAY

Melissa

ELAINE STANDS BEHIND ME AS I lift the delicate band over my hair. I opted for the flowing beige strapless chiffon dress. It's plain with only the tiniest seed pearls scattered across the bodice. A wide, grosgrain ribbon forms an empire waist, and the skirt flutters in rippling waves just like the ocean.

My dark hair is down, but I secured the sides at the back of my head in a barrette, and my best friend-matron of honor stands behind me attaching the veil to it.

"I love this veil so much," she whispers once it's in place.

Sheer tulle hangs from the top, but right at my shoulders, a band of floral lace ripples down and along the edge, curving back up the other side.

"I can't believe this is happening." Heat fills my eyes.

"Hang on!" Lainey cries, dashing for the tissues. "If you start crying, I will, and we don't want to look like raccoons on your wedding day."

That makes me laugh, and I look up at the ceiling, quickly doing some mental math problems to distract my overactive tear ducts. "Hand me a mimosa," I order, taking the tissue from her and blotting under my eyes.

"You're beautiful!" She says, eyes brimming.

"Now you're doing it!" I laugh, touching the tissue under my lashes again.

"One postponement, one cancellation, and we finally made it."

"Two months ago, I was pretty sure this was never going to happen." Standing, I press a hand against my sternum to calm the pain that memory provokes.

"Not me." My best friend's arm goes around my back. She leans her light-blonde head against my dark one. "I never gave up on you two. Derek is the perfect prince for your fairytale."

"He's more than a prince."

"You're right." Elaine smooths her hands down the front of her thigh-length sequined dress. "Patrick's my prince. Derek's more like . . . the king in this story."

I almost snort mimosa through my nose. "Oh my god," I laugh harder. "Don't tell him that!"

She breaks into laughter, and I look up to see Mariska and Kenny joining us looking fresh and pretty. We all spent the day having our hair and nails done. We got pedicures for my beach wedding, and I sprang for everyone to have massages. For the last few hours, we've been lounging and taking our time getting dressed. The wedding starts at six, and a quick glance to the clock says we're in the final countdown.

As matron of honor, Elaine wears a thigh-high, strapless sequined dress the color of sand. Kenny's dress is a one-shoulder sea-foam green chiffon. Mariska's is a strapless chiffon in ocean blue. We all have our hair down in loose, rolling waves, and the effect is stunning. Perfectly blended with our location.

"You guys are laughing way too much," Kenny says, prancing forward in her champagne stilettos. "Give me a mimosa."

"Oh!" I wave my hand at them and pull my skirt up so I can run across the room. Digging in my bag, I pull out a handful of tissue-wrapped parcels. "I have these for your feet. You can't wear heels in the sand."

Tossing them each a bundle, we rip into the packages to find lace-covered elastic foot-thongs.

Kenny's small nose wrinkles. "What is this?"

"It's 'shoes' for a beach wedding," I explain. "Look. Slipping off the Marine-blue heel I'm wearing, I fit the contraption over my foot. The thong portion goes between my toes and the lace overlay covers the top of my foot. I hook the back over my heel. "Isn't that pretty?"

Her face changes. "Yes . . ." she starts to laugh, "It actually is."

With the stiletto queen onboard, the rest of the girls ditch their shoes and start pulling on lace "thongs."

"Have you seen Derek's hair?" Mariska gushes to her friend. "I love it."

Standing up fast, "What did he do to his hair?"

"He cut it." Elaine is next to me and makes an excited face. "He looks amazing."

I'm not sure I'm happy about this. I love threading my fingers through his collar-length dark waves. "Why would he do that?"

"Probably because of the dress whites," Mariska continues, unaffected. "Stuart went with him and got even more taken off his."

"Stuart's hair was already short," I say, looking in the mirror and feeling concerned. I can't imagine Derek high and tight.

Elaine's right with me, placing her hands on my waist. "Trust me. You're going to love it."

"Love what?" My mother enters the room in her rose-colored, tea-length chiffon dress.

"Mom," I step over and hug her then pull back, nose wrinkled. "Where's Dex?"

"Star's watching him. He's having a ball, playing in the sand with Lane and Cammie." She leans toward the mirror and straightens her dark hair behind one ear. "If they weren't so cute, I'd make them stop."

"Is Star okay watching them?"

"She doesn't mind, and Amy's with them."

"Amy's here!" Elaine perks up at the mention of Patrick's little sister. "I'll be right back. I haven't seen her yet."

She runs out, and my mother gives me a serious look. "I have something for you."

"What is it?"

She holds out a cream-colored envelope with my name written on it in brown ink. It's fine linen stationary with a large *A* embossed on the outside, and I recognize Derek's handwriting. Taking it carefully, my lips press together. I look up at her.

"Take it behind the screen and read it," she says with a little smile.

Stepping around the wooden dressing screen, I do as she says.

At first, I only slide my hands over the smooth paper. His script is precise and blocky, controlled just like my man . . . except when he isn't. A tingle of love passes through my stomach, and I turn the envelope over. Lifting the seal, I pull the heavy paper out and open it. He's written me a letter.

Dear Melissa,
(Or should I say "Miss Jones"?)

I'm a bit older than you, so this might seem old-fashioned. I wanted to write you a letter to read on our wedding day. In the future, if you ever doubt me, you can read this and know my heart.

Before I met you, I was in a dark place. I thought this part of my life had ended, and I never expected to have a family or even to find love again. Then you appeared.

You changed my life in ways I can't explain. The weeks we were apart, the nights I thought our separation might last a lifetime . . . It was the worst time of my life.

I can't imagine me without you.

I'm sure I'll mess up again, but please know if I do, I'll be the first one to fix it, to find a way back to us.

I lost myself in the darkness of trying to protect you, but you're my light. In the worst time of my life, your true colors shined through, and you demonstrated how deep your love is. You saved me.

Thank you for being my life. Thank you for giving me a son. I dedicate myself to loving you, to your happiness, and to never letting you feel in the dark.

My love.

My life.

My family.

I'll be the one down front waiting to make you mine.

Love,

Derek

(Or should I say "Mr. Alexander"?)

I sniff a laugh, and it's way too late for tissues. My makeup is ruined. "Oh, Derek," I whisper. "You are full of surprises."

"What's going on?" Elaine is back, and when she rounds the screen, she squeals. "Oh no! We have to redo your eyes!"

"Just forget it," I say, waving my hand. "I'll put on some lipstick and go with it."

"Your veil doesn't cover your face!"

"It's okay. He'll know why I'm crying." My eyes drift to the window, and I share a secret smile. "It'll make him happy."

Elaine shakes her head as she smooths my hair back. "I'm not sure you're going to be happy with these wedding photos in a year."

"I'm already happier than I can ever say."

❤

AT THE FRONT OF OUR line, Kenny holds Slayde's arm. He's

in a dark blue suit that makes his eyes glow silver. Behind them, Mariska holds Stuart's arm. He's in his dress whites, which I now know means white pants, belt, and hat. The coat is the traditional deep navy with red piping. He looks amazing, and my breath catches in my throat imagining how my Marine will look.

Behind them, Elaine absolutely glows in her sparkling dress. Patrick is more formal than I've ever seen him in his Guard uniform. Navy coat and pants, gold stripes down the legs, gold crest on his sleeves and hat. Gorgeous.

Edward Merritt, my best friend's dad, takes my arm. "Your father would be very proud," he says, and I glance up at his salt and pepper hair, remembering a time when everyone imagined I'd be with Marcus.

"I appreciate you doing this," I say softly. "I can't imagine anyone else escorting me."

He gives me a warm smile that crinkles the corners of his green eyes. Elaine looks so much like him. "You're a beautiful, accomplished woman, Melissa. I'm proud to represent your father."

Squeezing his arm, I put my head briefly against his shoulder. "Thank you."

My cousin Ryan appears in a navy suit to escort Mom to her place in the front. He's a cute college guy with messy blonde hair. Mom takes his arm and kisses his cheek before the two head out toward the front.

The strains of Pachelbel's Canon drift to us, and it's time to move. Kenny and Slayde begin the procession, and my chest clenches. Mariska and Stuart are next. I don't miss the warm look that passes between them, and the idea they have a secret only briefly enters my mind before Elaine and Patrick start walking. Butterflies fill my stomach, and I feel like I'll laugh and cry at the same time.

The music gradually builds, but I can't see him yet. Our witnesses all stand by their small white chairs arranged in two sections on the sand. Friends and relatives smile as I pass. A few cover their mouths, and some dab their eyes.

Damn this flat sand. I grip Edward's arm, trying to see him when the procession opens before me. Dex is the first one I see in his little navy suit. He points at once and shouts, "May!" which makes everyone laugh. He starts to run to me, but Mom catches him in her arms. I blow him a little kiss before looking up again.

In a flash, I pan across the groomsmen—Slayde looking like a rockstar, Patrick looking like a model, of course he gives me a wink. Stuart is completely intimidating, but his eyes are on the beautiful girl in ocean-blue chiffon standing with my bridesmaids.

When at last I see Derek, my breath catches. Under the black brim of his white cap, his steel-grey eyes fix on mine. It's as if he sees all the way to my soul, and I feel it catch fire inside me. My vision tunnels. I don't even hear the words of Edward giving me away. I only know I'm drawn to this man watching me with such intensity.

A flash of timidity tightens my stomach as I reach out to take his white-gloved hand, but the moment he pulls me close, all fear melts away. We're facing each other, and I can only gaze at him with all the love expanding in my chest.

The minister leads us through our vows. Everything is very traditional.

For better or worse . . .

For richer or poorer . . .

In sickness and in health . . .

The words are a promise from the bottom of my heart. Derek removes his glove as we exchange rings. Shining, thick gold bands for each of us. Finally we've made it to the part I've been waiting for.

"I now pronounce you husband and wife," the man says. "You may kiss the bride."

My lip catches in my teeth, and Derek reaches up to touch it with his thumb. "That's for me to do," he whispers before slid-ing his hand behind my neck and covering my mouth with his.

Of all the times we've kissed each other, this kiss outshines every one. His warm lips move mine apart, and with the gentle taste of his tongue, my head grows light. I'm afraid I'll faint, but his strong arms hold me. It's amazing and passionate, and I never want to let him go. Until I realize our friends are clapping and a loud whistle slices the air.

He smiles against my mouth and lifts his head a fraction. "It seems we have an audience."

My dazed eyes open and I laugh, cupping his cheek. "I al-most forgot."

We turn as the minister calls over the noise, "I present to you Mr. and Mrs. Derek Alexander."

The applause grows louder, and Stuart steps forward, giv-ing a low command. He and their fellow Marines form a line of crossed swords, and we pass under the gleaming arch. Mom releases Dex, and he baby-runs to us. Derek catches him, lifting him on his arm. I turn and face my guys, and in that moment everything in my life is complete.

THE HOTEL BALLROOM SPARKLES WITH white twinkle lights and dim lamps. At each table are bottles of champagne and small containers of bubbles. I haven't stopped dancing with Derek since we arrived.

"We should probably eat something." His low voice in my ear is a warm massage to my insides.

"I don't want to be out of your arms," I say, resting my tem-ple against his cheek. I feel him smile.

"You never have to worry about that."

Glancing up, I kiss his lips briefly before letting him lead me off the dance floor to where our friends sit at a round table covered in white linens. Close by is the wedding cake, and Aunt Bea outdid herself making a four-layer round cake covered in white fondant. Each layer has a navy bow around its base, and the Marines emblem decorates them all the way to the cake topper—a Marine in dress whites holding a bride in his arms. I smile and rest my cheek against Derek's shoulder.

"Getting tired?" Elaine says to me, from where she's sitting on Patrick's lap.

I shake my head no just as Sylvia joins our group. "Derek," she steps around and gives him a brief squeeze. "The wedding was lovely, but I'm afraid it's late for me. Has anyone seen Amy?"

"We reserved a block of rooms if you'd like to spend the night here," he says, holding her hand.

"We have one at this lovely B&B in town," she says with a smile. "We already unpacked, or I'd stay. Now if I can just find my child."

"Hey, Mom," Stuart rounds the table to where Sylvia is standing. Mariska is right behind him, holding his hand. "Since most everyone is here, we figured it's time to announce it."

"Announce what?" Kenny perks up, her dark brows clutched.

My eyes widen in anticipation. I had a feeling this was coming.

"Mariska has agreed to marry me."

"What!" Her friend is out of her seat and going to them fast. "When did this happen?"

Mariska beams as Kenny takes her hand. "I actually agreed about a month ago, but then he changed his mind."

Kenny's face snaps up, but Stuart grabs Mariska around the waist, pulling her to him and kissing her neck before nipping her ear.

She squeals a laugh. "I was teasing!"

"Mom had to bring me the ring," he corrects her. "It was our grandmother's."

"Oh! Let me see." We all crowd around to examine the

delicate white-gold engagement ring. It's in the shape of a flower lying on its side with a large round diamond in the center.

"It's beautiful," I say with a smile, looking up at Stuart.

"I wanted it to be bigger—"

"That would've ruined the design!" Mariska argues.

"It's perfect for you," Elaine says, giving her a hug. "And now we'll be sisters."

"Speaking of sisters," Sylvia interjects. "If you see your other one, tell her I'm looking for her. Congratulations," She stretches up and kisses Stuart's cheek. Then she puts an arm around Mariska's shoulders. "Best wishes, although you don't need it. You are one impressive young lady."

"Thank you," Mariska laughs.

Stuart gives her another squeeze before answering Sylvia. "I spoke to Amy at the bar a few minutes ago. I'll try and find her if you want."

"Oh, I can wait a little longer," his mother pats his arm. "I'm glad to see my children so happy."

Derek's arms are around me again, and I can't help agreeing with her. So much has happened to get us here. Breakups, secrets, heartbreaking discoveries that turned into blessings or paths to forgiveness, and now the most resistant member of the group has found a home.

"This day couldn't get any better," I sigh, leaning my head back against his shoulder.

His lips touch the side of my neck, sending tingles through my stomach. "It's only the beginning."

I know he's right. We've each made it through the dark times, and we've found the one to hold, keep, love, and save. Another wedding to plan, more babies will arrive . . .

I'm so lucky to be with this man. He's risked his life for me again and again, and all I want to do is make that risk worth taking. When I see the love in his eyes and feel the love in my heart, I know it is. The future is wide open, and our love is strong. I can't wait to see what's next for all of us.

The End . . .
(Or maybe not.)

EPILOGUE

RUNAWAY

Amy

RETURNING FROM PARIS, THE LAST thing I'm in the mood for is a wedding. Still, Derek Alexander is the closest thing I have to a third brother. He's also my favorite of Stuart's friends—and Patrick's, I guess. Anyone who can get those two to put down their arms and stop fighting is a master in my book. Also, Mom insists I go with her so she doesn't have to go alone. I suspect she's hoping I'll meet someone as always. The woman is living for more grandchildren these days.

I've only been to Wilmington once, but it's a precious little beach community. Sylvia, being the way she is, has found an exclusively plush bed and breakfast for us to stay in. It would be the perfect girls' getaway, and I love spending time with my mother—except for the wedding part.

"Melissa is the dearest thing," she says as she unpacks her black and white-patterned Vera Bradley luggage. "She's in marketing, so if you have a chance, let her know that's what you do."

"I doubt she'll want to discuss work on her wedding day." I watch as she fiddles with the navy and red-patterned silk scarf tied neatly at her throat.

She steps back and runs her hands down her sandy-blonde bob. For her age, Mom is still a beautiful woman. It helps that she's Coco Chanel-elegant in all things, the result of her up-bringing. She survived the same elite childhood as my brothers and I. The nice thing is she's not cold-hearted, passive-aggressive, or a materialistic bitch like so many of my friends have for mothers. We had dear old Dad to fill that role.

"How much time before the wedding?" I assess my long blonde hair and decide I won't need to wash it. I would, however, like to freshen up.

"It starts at six, so we should probably leave in a half hour."

"I'll be ready."

I step into the large bathroom and close the door. I haven't had any time to come down from my sudden departure from Europe. I haven't even given myself a moment to consider what Armand is thinking. I honestly don't care to know.

Sinking into the warm bath, I close my eyes and allow the lavender-scented water to relax me. Armand made the fuck-up. I was always completely honest with him. It's probably the reason he hasn't called since I walked out, not that I really care for that to happen either. No, he knew before he even said the words how I would respond. Now here we are, and I'm not looking back.

Promptly half an hour later, I'm dressed and applying red lipstick as Sylvia fastens a chunky strand of pearls at her neck. She's dressed in a beige, sleeveless shift with black accents at the shoulders and hips. Classic Coco. I on the other hand, am wearing a long slip-dress with high slits above each leg. It's white with black leather accents, and I top it with a fluffy mohair vest. Very Valentino.

"You look fresh off the Paris catwalk," Mom says with a smile.

I shrug. "Not much point living in Paris if you don't indulge in the fashions."

We're out the door and headed to the beach in less than five.

———————◆———————

THE WEDDING IS A STUNNING showcase of our nation's finest. I still can't believe both my older brothers are veterans. Patrick most of all. Stuart was always fighting his natural tendency to be exactly like our father, but my favorite brother is so playful and fun. It's still hard to imagine him carrying a rifle, much less actually using it to kill someone. Of course, I'm pretty sure his stint in the Guard was intended to satisfy our father's chauvinistic requirements while avoiding deployment. Poor darling. Talk about backfires.

"Looks like you came back from Europe a woman." The familiar male voice surprises me with its cheerfulness. I turn to see my oldest brother actually smiling for the first time in my life.

"Looks like you came back from Saudi a happy man."

He shakes his head. "I never went back to Saudi. That's what made me a happy man." I wait as he signals the bartender. A scotch neat for him, vodka rocks for me. "Have you met Mariska?" he watches me as he sips the amber liquid.

"I haven't, but she's very beautiful."

"I asked her to marry me."

That almost makes me drop my drink. *"Et tu, Brute?"*

"Yep," he grins again. "Me too."

"I go away and everything falls apart." Taking a long sip of vodka, I watch as he chuckles. He's so fucking happy, I can't believe it. Stuart does not chuckle. Only now it seems he does.

"So what brought you back? I thought you loved Paris."

"Oh, I do love Paris." I take another, longer drink, finishing off my vodka as my mind races to find a suitable answer. I can't say the truth: Armand asked me to move in with him, and I caught the first flight home.

"Even the City of Lights gets old after a while." It's not very good, and I can tell he doesn't buy it. "And Mom's not getting any younger."

Stuart accepts that lie a little better. "Well, I'm glad you're back. It's good to have the family together again." He pats my arm. "Come over and meet Mariska."

"Mmm," I nod, giving him a little wave. "Let me get a fresh drink."

He strolls away, and I turn and flag the bartender down. "Vodka rocks." I slide a tenner across the counter. It's an open bar, but tipping ensures better service. I'll need a few more of these if I have to deal with all the love going around.

Taking my drink, I turn my back to the bar and notice a tall, slender specimen of male waiting beside me. He orders a vodka rocks, and I quickly assess him. Dolce & Gabbana suit, fatigue-green and stainless Tag, light scruff on the cheeks. *Interesting.* Stepping back, he catches my inspection and pauses. I lift my chin and own it. After the house I grew up in, men don't intimidate me.

Apparently, I don't intimidate him either. *Even more interesting.*

He exhales a laugh, revealing nice white teeth. "Are you here for the bride or the groom?"

"Hmm . . ." I realize I'm not sure how to answer that question. I'm equally acquainted with both. "Groom, I guess."

"You guess?"

"I'm friends with both, but I knew Derek first."

"Ah," he nods.

"You?"

"Bride." Then he hesitates, taking a sip of his drink. "Actually, no, that's not right. I guess my answer is the same as yours. Only in reverse."

He looks out at the dance floor where the happy couple hasn't stopped slow-dancing since they arrived. Something wistful is on his face, and I can't resist.

"You have a history with Melissa?"

Blinking hazel-green eyes back at me he seems to wake up. "We were childhood friends. It's unexpected to see them all married."

"I'm never getting married." *Good god, Amy, over-share much?* Looking down at my drink, I realize it's nearly empty. I'm more relaxed than I realized.

My companion doesn't skip a beat. "Is that so?" he chuckles. "And what are you? Eighteen?"

Irritation burns in my chest. Treating me like a baby is *not* a good idea. "I'm twenty five, and I guess that's a compliment?"

"Baby," he exhales, turning back to the bar.

"Old man," I say, waving at the bartender and ordering another.

"Old man?" The guy turns to the side and leans on his elbow facing me. "You think ordering another is a good idea?"

"I can outdrink you any day of the week." *No idea what I'm doing right now.*

He gives me a player's grin. "I'm a lawyer."

"So you're an asshole who's about to be outdrunk by a baby."

Something flickers in his eyes. It's a spark I've seen before, and it usually leads to naughty places. "I haven't played drinking games since college."

"Is that fear I'm hearing?"

"Line 'em up."

He slides a hand to his waist, moving his suit coat back to reveal a trim physique. Yes. Something naughty might be just what I need to get the funk of Paris off me. It is a wedding, after all. Isn't everyone supposed to hook up?

"I have a better idea," I say, waving to the bartender again. "We'll take the bottle."

The well-tipped server is happy to oblige, and I grab it, two glasses, and my black clutch. "This way, lawyer."

A small billiards room is off the main ballroom, and it's completely empty. The reception party is focused on the room where the food, drinks, and band are located. Striding into the cozy, dim-lit space, I place the full bottle of vodka and two slim glasses on a tall table with two bar stools.

"Do you play?" he asks, stepping over and sliding the cue ball across red felt.

"Not billiards." Cracking open the bottle, I pour two glasses mid-way. "You're up."

Stepping to the counter, he lifts one. "*Skal.*" With a clink, he slams the entire contents back.

"Swedish?" My eyes only pinch a little as I do the same.

"No, I only figured if we're shooting vodka, we should keep it real."

I'm pouring another drink feeling looser than ever. "So if you're not Swedish," I glance up and give him a playful wink, "Where is home? Here in Wilmington?"

"Chicago." He takes the glass, openly letting his eyes run all over my body. A warm tingle follows his inspection.

"I don't believe it," I say, sliding the fur off my shoulders to give him a better look.

"Why?" He moves a bit closer. "Too conventional?"

"Chicago is where I live now."

"Now?"

"I spent the last year in Paris."

His eyebrows rise. "The City of Love?"

"I prefer City of Lights."

"Right." He's even closer. Close enough that I can smell the fresh linen scent of his cologne. "You don't do love."

"I do *other* things." It came out as more of a purr than I'd intended, but I'll go with it. I feel good, and I want to bury my face in his delicious scent while I tangle my fingers in those caramel-brown waves.

A pause. Our eyes hold each other's a moment. "What's your name?" I ask.

"Marcus." I like it. Marcus the lawyer. "What's yours?"

"Amy."

"Pretty." Unexpected warmth simmers in my stomach. "What's your game, Amy?"

The sound of his voice saying my name is a delicious vibration under my skin. *What's my game?* It could mean anything, but I go with the less provocative interpretation.

"International trade and finance." I push my lips out just a bit over the *S* sound, allowing my eyes to stay on his mouth. It's a nice mouth, and I love the feel of scruff against my bare skin. "I'll probably focus on PR now that I'm home."

He's not backing down, and a shimmer of excitement moves through my stomach. "Are you experienced at PR?"

"Why don't you find out?" My voice has gone a little lower. It's enough for him.

Another step forward, and our bodies are touching now. He's warm, and that crisp linen fills my senses. Large hands slide up my hips, and I close my eyes, dropping my head back for him to kiss me.

He trails his lips lightly up my skin, more taking in my scent than tasting me. It makes me wet. When he reaches my jaw, he pulls a little nibble in his teeth, and a noise comes from my throat.

"You're good at this," I whisper, finding his eyes.

"I like surprises."

"Surprises are one of my two favorite things."

His hands span my lower back, lifting me onto the stool, before his mouth covers mine. The slits in my skirt allow easy access to my center. His lips force mine open, and our tongues curl together. It's not frantic and grasping, it's controlled and confident. He tastes like cinnamon and expensive vodka, and I feel his erection pressing against my thigh. It's fantastic, strong and demanding. Another shiver moves through me as my fingers quickly unfasten the buttons of his shirt. I'm enjoying this too much for a random.

"Are you cold?" He breathes against my skin, tracing a burning trail to my ear. He pulls the top between his lips, and my insides clench.

When I reach the bottom button of his shirt, I slide my hands down the front of his pants between us. "I'm ready to know you better."

Stepping back, he loosens and removes his tie, tossing it on the table. His shirt is open and untucked, and his lined chest makes my mouth water. Eyes dark, he returns to me and pushes my sleeve down my shoulder. I shrug it off and allow him to unfasten my bra.

"Mmm," he rumbles, cupping my breast and rolling my nipple between his fingers. "You are a naughty girl."

"I think I'm a lucky girl." My voice cracks with desire as he pulls the dark bud between his lips giving it a hard suck that shoots electricity straight between my legs. More wetness. God, this is going to be good.

"I think I'm the lucky one." He kisses back up to my neck, scuffing my skin in a delicious way.

I've managed to get his pants unfastened, and I slide one hand down his cock, curling my fingers around it. *Damn, it's thick.* "Why don't you get lucky then?"

A rustle of pockets, and I help him open the foil wrapper. Our mouths reunite, and I push my breasts against him as he slides on the condom. Light chest hair tingles my nipples, and I'm heady with lust, anticipating the feel of him stretching me. Large hands return to my ass. I hold my breath a moment before he moves my thong and pushes inside.

"Oh," I exhale at the same time he mutters a "Fuck me."

Marcus lifts me off the seat and thrusts harder, going deeper. My legs are around his waist, and I arch so our moving bodies massage my clit. If we were controlled before, we've given in to flat-out carnal enjoyment now. It's crazy and reckless and wild.

He slams my back against the wall, and he's hitting me hard, rocking us both in perfect rhythm. Sizzling electricity vibrates my veins and pleasure snakes up my thighs.

Here it comes, my mind whispers. "Oh, god," I gasp as my

orgasm grows hotter with each thrust.

"Harder," I beg, and he complies. Again and again, he pushes into me until he groans in my ear. He's coming, and the noise of his climax pushes me over the edge. All at once the tidal wave bursts, flooding me with ecstasy.

"Oh, yes!" I cry as the orgasm quivers in my thighs. It's one of the best I've had in a while.

"God, you feel good," he groans against my neck, giving me two more deep thrusts as I ride out the aftershocks of pleasure, my insides tensing around his cock.

A few more movements, and we're on the way down. He's still holding me securely in his strong arms and I like the way he feels.

My insides immediately recoil at that thought. "To the bride and groom," I laugh, pushing against his shoulders.

He eases back, holding the condom as he pulls out, lowering me to my feet. I avoid his eyes as I straighten my top. Protection trashed, he fastens his pants as I straighten my thong and grab my clutch. I don't have time to mess around. I've got to get the fuck out of here now.

"I'd like to have you for breakfast," he says, turning to me with a cocky smile. I'm annoyed that it thrills my insides.

"Tempting." I give him a wink.

"Are you staying in the hotel? I'm on the tenth floor."

"I'm actually here with my mother. She's at a B&B, so I need to be sure she has a way home."

I've made it to the exit, vodka bottle and glasses forgotten. He follows me into the ballroom and pauses. "Check on her. I'll head up and order us some wine. See you in a few?"

"Sure." Stepping forward, I kiss his cheek. He captures my lips briefly, and I curse the damn flutter in my stomach.

"Room ten-sixteen." He holds my eyes then. His are deep hazel-green, and I refuse to acknowledge they're damn sexy. He is a *random*.

"Ten-sixteen," I nod. "Got it."

He heads toward the lobby, and I only briefly hesitate before turning on my heel and making my way to where Sylvia stands chatting with Stuart and Mariska. I'll meet them, say goodnight, and get back to the B&B. In the morning we'll be gone. No shitting where I live.

Surprises are nice, but my second favorite thing? Running.

Want to know what happens when Amy and Marcus collide in Chicago? Keep turning the pages for an Exclusive Sneak Peek at ONE TO CHASE!

Curious about Stuart Knight, former Marine, Derek's first partner, and Patrick's older brother? Keep turning the pages for a Sneak Peek at ONE TO LEAVE right after!

ONE IMMORTAL

DEREK & MELISSA

EXCLUSIVE BONUS CONTENT

TIA LOUISE

Melissa is a vampire; Derek is a vampire hunter.

When beautiful, sad Melissa Jones flees to New Orleans with her telepathic best friend, she is looking for a cure—not an erotic encounter with a sexy former Marine.

Derek Alexander left the military intending to become a private investigator, but with two powerful shifters as partners and an immunity to vampire glamour, he instead rose to the top in paranormal justice.

At a bar on Bourbon Street, Derek and Melissa cross paths, and their sexual chemistry is off the charts. Acting on their feelings, they are pulled deeper into an affair, but Melissa is hiding, hoping to escape her cruel maker.

It doesn't take long before the shifters uncover her secret. Still, Derek is determined to confront the Old One and reclaim her mortality—even at the risk of losing his.

A STANDALONE PARANORMAL ROMANCE with an HEA based on characters from the One to Hold series. Contains voluptuous vampires, alluring alpha military heroes, scorching-hot shifters, beguiling witches, and panty-melting sexy times. Keep the fans nearby . . . Readers 18 and older only, please.

*To all my Derek & Melissa fans, and to
everyone who loves a sexy thriller as much as I do!
As always, to Mr. TL, my One.*

❤

ONE

AN ENCOUNTER

Derek

MY SEARCH FOR THE VAMPIRE has led me home.

It's been six years since I walked the streets of New Orleans—the hot, moldering streets of this historic city time forgot. How well I know these ancient buildings stubbornly hanging on centuries after Napoleon left, the dark green vines climbing every stationary object. The air is heavy with music and spices, mystery and decay.

I'll need a day to get used to the climate, another to ease back into the smooth-talking, greased-palm way of getting information. The little wink and a smile, the lazy request accented with a *darling* or a *cher*. Even among the undead, it's all about the sugar in the Crescent City.

My phone blips, and I quickly pull it out of my pocket. Patrick Knight, my new partner, is checking in from our offices in New Jersey.

Any signs of nonlife?

He's always one with the jokes.

Not yet. I reply. *I'll alert you if anything appears.*

He doesn't miss a beat.

Or doesn't.

Shaking my head, I slip the thin black phone into my pocket. When Patrick first joined his older brother Stuart and me in Alexander-Knight LLC, I thought on more than one occasion we'd made a mistake. As the weeks have passed, however, I've come to appreciate his subculture contacts, and his knack for turning up fresh leads on stale cases. It helps that he has extra-sensory abilities.

The Knights come from a long line of shifters—their preferred form being large-breed dogs, although I once saw Stuart shift into a grizzly. In human form, we're all around the same height, six-foot-give-or-take-a-few-inches, but while I release my tension in the weight room, the Knights prefer working out between the sheets. One thing about shifters, they're horny as hell.

The result is I outweigh them by at least thirty pounds of straight muscle. Still, I'm no match against the undead on my own. My special gifts are my training and my weaponry. If I'm outnumbered, it's best to have an oversized lycan at my side.

On the books, I'm a private investigator and occasional Law Enforcement Online instructor at Princeton University. Much further off the books, in the deep background, I'm one of the top three paranormal detectives in the States, specializing in vampires. When I started I was one of four, but sadly, in this line of work, the fatalities are quick and untraceable. As such, we've established regions. New Orleans is not mine.

Only two people know why I'm here, and it's not because I don't respect our rules. I'm here because this time it's personal. An Old One is at work in the city, and from what Patrick's been able to flush out, it appears to be the one I've sought for a long time.

I'm taking a big chance coming here alone, but I have one more secret—I'm immune to vampire glamour. Acting alone, it's possible I'll catch the killer off-guard. Still, if I'm detected, at least I won't be hypnotized.

Settling in at the dim-lit Korner Bar, I survey the patrons.

College girls clearly looking to get wasted and get laid twist and giggle on the dance floor. Their shiny slip dresses barely cover their asses, and they lick their lips while tossing back their hair, leaving their necks and arms wide open and vulnerable.

One might expect the undead to favor a more historic spot like Lafitte's Blacksmith Shop, or the subculture atmosphere of Oz. One would be wrong. Vampires like the easy kill, the kill that goes down without a fight or that is readily subdued. These women are prime targets.

I consider the foolishness of youth when my eyes land on her. She's alone at the bar, nursing a Sazerac. Her eyes are sad, and while she's young and beautiful, her expression is world-weary. Long, dark hair ripples over one shoulder, and I can't resist the pull of curiosity. She's far too elegant for this bar. It's almost as if she's hiding.

I watch her lift the old-fashioned glass with a slim ivory hand, and her full red lips pull together as she sips. It's a seductive movement, but suddenly she winces and does a little jump. I can't help a grin. It's unexpectedly cute.

Almost as if she feels my gaze, her sapphire-blue eyes blink up, across the darkness, straight into me. It's like a thousand-watt volt of electricity, a Taser blast straight to the brain, and all the years I've spent alone hit me like a medicine ball to the chest. She blinks a few times, and the smallest smile lifts one corner of her mouth. I'm on my feet at once, headed in her direction, my target temporarily forgotten.

The bar is only half-full as I pass behind patrons engaged in animated discussions. Hands wave, drinks are put in peril, but I'm oblivious to the commotion.

My eyes move down her cheek to her neck, and I can see the slight uptick in her breathing. Allowing my eyes to move lower, I linger on the deep V of her midnight-blue dress. Her breasts rise and fall faster, and the fly of my slacks grows tight, until at last I'm standing in front of her.

I wait as her gorgeous eyes travel from my Italian leather

shoes up my grey pants, hesitate at my waist, before blinking quickly to my face. She knows I caught her, and her cheeks flush the sexiest shade of pink.

I don't remember the last time I approached a single woman in a bar, but I guess it's like riding a bicycle. "Can I buy you a drink?"

She turns to face the amber beverage in front of her and gives it several pokes with a skinny red straw. "I have a Sazerac."

Her voice is soft and high in comparison with mine. I want to hear it melt into a moan. "You don't like it."

Her gaze moves to my mouth, and I give her a little smile. It seems to put her more at ease.

"How do you know?" She blinks those gorgeous blue eyes back to mine.

I lean in, as if it's a secret. "You make a face every time you sip it."

"Why are you watching me?" Her eyes narrow, and I see she's smart—and strong. Very sexy.

I ease back just a bit, extending a hand. "I should introduce myself. Derek."

Her eyes hold mine for several moments longer. She's sizing me up, and I confess, I'm holding my breath a little.

With a smile, she places her smaller hand in mine. "Melissa."

My fingers close gently around it, and I resist the urge to pull her to me. I do allow my thoughts to slip out, however. "Sweet Melissa."

"I'm not so sweet." She takes it back, smile fading.

"Aren't others supposed to make that judgment?" Waving the bartender over, I order for us. "Cava. Two glasses. Make it your best."

He nods and quickly retrieves a dark green bottle from the refrigerator at the end of the bar.

"Cava?" Her eyebrows rise. "That's not a very New Orleans choice. Shouldn't you have ordered a hurricane?"

Every sass, every glimpse of her personality, fans my

smoldering desire. She's hypnotic, like the sexiest New Orleans voodoo, and my mind floods with images of us together. I want to be inside her. I want to taste every inch of her body, and fuck her with my tongue. I want to bend her over and take her from behind, pull her dark hair until she screams my name. I want to have her again and again.

Shaking the pornographic images away, I answer. "Cava is for celebrating good things."

"Did you get a promotion?"

"I met you."

The glasses are in front of us, and we lift them. I give her a little clink, and we take a sip of the sparkling Spanish white wine. It's crisp and refreshing. Perfect for what I have in mind. A little tease, the slightest easing of inhibitions, and a night of unbridled passion. I touch my bottom lip with my tongue and her jaw drops. She quickly looks away.

"So," she clears her throat, straightening in her seat. "Are you here on business?"

"Meetings," I hedge. "At the Royal Sonesta."

"Nice place."

"Where are you staying?" Her lips press together, and she blinks down. "Sorry—you don't have to answer that."

She lifts her chin as if defying something invisible. "I'm staying at the Hotel Monteleone. With my best friend Elaine. Girls' weekend."

New Orleans is infamous for such things, but usually the "girls' weekends" on Bourbon Street are fueled with too much alcohol, raucous dancing, shrieking, and showing tits.

Knowing she's staying at a historically traditional hotel off Royal Street tells me a lot—as if I hadn't already deduced Melissa is a bit too classy for such behavior.

"Where is your friend now?" Glancing toward the dance floor, I can't imagine she's one of the kids out there.

"She went back to the hotel. We only arrived this evening. Elaine was tired, but I wasn't quite ready to go to sleep." She gives my torso another slow sweep, and while she might be too classy for flashing her tits, she might be open to a private meeting of the minds. "What's your line of work?"

"Upper management. Investigations."

"You're a PI?" Shifting again, she re-crosses her long, sexy legs.

"Basically." Digging in my pocket, I pull out a twenty. "I should walk you back to your hotel. It's after two."

"I didn't realize I was calling it a night." A sexy smile curves her lips.

"This place is closing soon, and I won't rest unless I know you're safely at your hotel."

A brief pause, and she slides off the stool toward me, putting us face to face. Her palms are on my chest, and that soft lip slips between her teeth. The pressure in my chest grows tighter. I want her.

"Are you trying to make me believe you're safe?" she says softly.

"I'm not safe." My hand moves to her lower back. "But I would never put you in danger."

"I'm not sure I trust you."

Leaning down, I catch her eyes. "You can always trust me."

Melissa

HEAT. I'VE BEEN WARNED ABOUT the oppressive New Orleans heat. I've heard stories about how on his first visit to the Crescent City, Sir Paul McCartney went for a jog and thought he was having a heart attack, drowning in the heavy air.

Now, pressed against the damp, cool wall of Pirate's Alley, my eyes flutter closed from the heat radiating between my thighs.

This gorgeous man wants me. He's one of the last sensual

escapes I might ever have, and damn if I'm not taking it.

I moan at the velvet of his lips followed by the scruff of his beard against my skin. All of my senses are heightened, my nipples hard and tingling.

He lifts me as if I weigh no more than a doll, and I luxuriate in his strength, the width of his shoulders, the way he dwarfs me with his enormous frame.

For a moment, my eyes drift open. The full moon shines enormously white over our heads, casting everything in a pale-bluish hue. Smaller orbs, the ancient streetlamps line the cobbled streets, making rainbow reflections in the puddles.

It's possible these sights are only vibrant in my eyes, but I don't have time to follow that train of thought. Derek catches my chin, pulling my attention back to him.

He covers my mouth with his, forcing my lips apart roughly. Our tongues collide, and I can't help another moan. His virility floods my veins like a drug, so seductive. He's a decadent indulgence, and a dangerous one. He tastes like champagne and mint, and something deeper, meaty and masculine at its core.

My blood races beneath my skin. Desire burns between my thighs, and as badly as I want to fuck him, I want to taste him. I want to drink him in and feel him inside me beating with my heart.

He unzips the back of my dress, and the straps fall down around my elbows. Reaching around behind me, I unfasten my bra. A hungry groan rumbles from his throat, and my breasts strain for his rough touch. I'm dripping wet. I've never felt so wanted, so craved.

We're secluded from the main street. No one can see us. It's possible we could be heard, but it would take some searching to find us.

Now. The word thrums in my ears like an ominous drum. *Now is your time.*

Shoving the voice from my mind, I focus on the moment. Lips brush my nipples, teeth pull them into pebbles. This incredibly gorgeous man is feasting on my breasts.

Feast.

"Take off your shirt," I order in a hoarse whisper I don't even recognize.

He lowers me briefly and whips the thin, navy sweater over his head, revealing a lined torso, olive skin dusted lightly with hair.

Oh, god. My mouth waters, and my gums ache. He's so beautiful. He's the sexiest man I've ever seen in my life.

Take him.

His eyes darken as he watches me appreciate his body, and I see the tent in his designer slacks grow. Energy floods my core, surging through my pelvis. I can smell the strong, healthy blood in his veins.

Take him.

"Café au lait," I murmur, sliding a finger across his chest. "Delicious."

In a sweep, I'm off my feet again. My legs are again around his waist, my back pressed against the cool, damp wall. I pull him closer. I want all of him touching me.

The light hairs on his chest tease my breasts. "Oh, yes," I sigh.

"I'm clean, but I'll use protection," he grinds out, shifting me so he can retrieve a condom. I hear the metallic clink of his belt buckle, and I don't bother telling him it doesn't matter.

Two thick digits plunge into me, and I gasp. "Jesus," he hisses, finding me more than ready for him. All my senses heighten when he gives me a quick lift . . . then plunges deep into my clenching insides.

"Oh god," I moan. He's huge. I've never been so full in my life. I'm not sure I can breathe for a moment, and he starts to thrust. Over and over . . .

I haven't fucked like this in . . . never. And from the sounds of it, neither has he. Only, I can't believe that. Not this mountain of sex between my thighs.

My head drops back, and my mouth opens, savoring the sensation of being stretched and massaged in the most erotic way.

Faster, deeper—he groans with every push, his large hands grip my ass so hard, I know he'll leave marks. Tingles of orgasm snake up my thighs, and I feel the change beginning. My gums ache as my canines grow.

"Don't stop," I gasp. He doesn't.

Sweat lines his brow, a bead trickles down his cheek, and I lean forward to lick it away. His salty flavor fills my mouth, and I almost can't control my urge.

I *must* control it. I can't resist the building pleasure, but I can fight what comes next. Every push of him deeper inside me drives me higher. If he were to stop now, my heart would explode. I'm not sure what would happen then.

"Please don't stop," I beg louder, teetering on the edge of orgasm.

Each hard thrust is punctuated with his growls. "So . . . Fucking . . . Good."

Every muscle in my body tightens into an irresistible ball low in my stomach. Tighter . . . tighter . . . *Too much!* . . . It bursts in shuddering pleasure down my thighs. A cry escapes my throat, and I'm flying through the heavens. My hazy eyes open, and I think the moon is singing. Perhaps it's the stars.

My orgasms are even more intense now. They radiate in my brain, and I never want them to end. Working my legs, I ride him as the waves of pleasure continue rippling through my insides.

His forehead is against my shoulder, and I feel him coming. He bucks and holds me tight. A low groan, and the muscles in his hips flex as he throbs again and again deep inside me. My eyes close as I drink in the energy of his release—another new, intensely erotic sensation.

Two more slower thrusts, and he stills, pressing his face into the side of my hair.

"Fuck me." His voice is ragged.

We stay that way several long moments, riding out the last whispers of pleasure. I don't want him to pull out. I want more, so much more it's overwhelming. Only one thing would be better than this. His salty taste is still on my tongue, tempting me with his flavor. With my eyes closed, I visualize doing it, piercing his skin, feeling him slip down my throat as I swallow all his coppery richness.

Every time he moves, another shimmer of residual pleasure tightens my core. I want to go all the way this time. I want it to be with him, this man between my thighs. His hips move slowly, and I whimper.

"I love that sound," he breathes against my neck. "It's so fucking hot."

His words thrill me. I've never felt this way with a man. Not even with . . . the man who changed me. It's the most I've ever wanted to cross that line of no return. Somehow I'm certain going there with Derek would be unforgettable.

But I can't go there with him. I can't give in. I hold his broad shoulders and measure his strength. It's a striking contrast to how weak I've become. Every day I grow weaker. Perhaps that's why he's so tempting—his incredible strength.

He presses another burning kiss against the top of my shoulder, his chest hair teases my nipples one last time. He's still inside me, holding, until we both seem to have reached temporary satisfaction. Strong arms are around my small waist, and I'm captured in the most secure embrace before he lifts me and slides out.

Lowered onto shaky legs, he waits as I regain my balance, inside and out.

"Thank you," he says quietly, and I've almost decided this is a dream.

Did I doze off at the bar? His steel blue eyes capture mine, and I know it's no fantasy. Lowering my chin, I touch my lips lightly with the tips of my fingers, making sure it's safe for me to speak.

"Thank you," I say back, turning to the side so I can refasten my bra, slide the straps of my dress over my shoulders.

He retrieves the thin navy sweater and turns it right side out before slipping it over his head, leaving his dark hair in messy waves. He's hypnotic.

Looking down at me with that intense gaze, he smiles. "How long will you be in the city?"

"Until Sunday." My voice is soft, and he steps closer.

"I'll be tied up with meetings during the day, but tomorrow I'll be at Mr. B's at seven. I hope you might stop in."

Mr. B's Bistro is across the street from my hotel. It's known for having some of the best cuisine in the city. It also has a nice bar. But that's not what Derek wants. Like me, he's hungry for more.

He places a large hand on the wall beside my face, and his enormous bicep is right at my cheek. A thick vein draws my attention. "I'd like to see you again."

I'm walking a treacherous line, so close to giving in to my cravings. One minor slip could be the end.

"I love Mr. B's," I say, and a small smile lifts the corner of his mouth.

I want to thread my fingers in that glossy dark hair again. I want to taste his mouth one more time. I want that sensual beard roughing my skin. I want more of everything about this moment we just shared, but I know how potentially deadly that would be.

"Shall I escort you to your room?" he asks.

I shake my head no, and walk away from him the half-block to Royal Street. He's still in the alley, leaning against the brick wall, watching me. The streetlight is behind him, and he looks like every fantasy I never knew to have.

"Goodnight," is all I say.

"Goodnight, sweet Melissa," his deep voice touches me through the darkness, and I'm overwhelmed by despair. It drops like a heavy cloak over my shoulders.

My life is over.

He starts to move, and I hasten away, up the block until I'm far from him. A few more steps and I push through the revolving door of the Hotel Monteleone.

I might have escaped my fate tonight, but my grip on control is rapidly failing.

TWO

CRAVING

Derek

RECKLESS. MY ALARM BUZZES ME to consciousness, and it's my first thought. Last night was dangerous and unprofessional. Not only did I blow off my mission, I hooked up with a total stranger—alone, with no one knowing where I was.

In this city, in my line of work, it could've been the last mistake I ever made. And shit if I'm not lying here with a hard-on craving her body all over again.

Turning to the side, an ache pinches my lower back. As much as I work out, I can't believe I could possibly be sore anywhere, yet when I move again in my king-sized bed, I realize it's an ache that would only come from holding another person against the ancient brick wall of Pirate's Alley and fucking her brains out.

Jesus. I sit up fast, marveling again at my behavior. Scrolling back through the night, it's almost as if I were hypnotized by her sapphire eyes.

I shake that shit away. It's a fucking cop-out, or worse—it's the product of working too long in the paranormal field. I'm no amateur. What happened last night was simple math. I saw an extremely beautiful, intensely sad woman sitting alone in a bar, and nothing could have kept me from going to her. We had immediate chemistry, and we acted on it.

Her little moans and breathy cries echo in my ears, and I exhale a growl, remembering how hard I came. Rubbing my large hands over my face, I try to grab the reins.

I need to remind myself who's in control here. Melissa is a strong, sexy woman. Of course, I responded that way to fucking her. I haven't been with anyone since Alison died six years ago. I haven't wanted to. At first, it had seemed like an insult to her memory, but after a while I was too obsessed with my work to deal with starting a relationship or the needs of another person.

Until last night.

Yes, our intensity was off the charts. It was enhanced by my awakened desire. Like flipping a light switch, Melissa revived a need in me long dormant, and damn, if she didn't seem to need it as much as I did. Add to that the push-pull of knowing what we were doing was dangerous and illegal . . . That's all it was. Nothing more.

Throwing the blankets aside, I walk naked to the bathroom and switch on the shower. My brain might know all of these facts, but my cock sure as hell doesn't. Images of her sliding up and down me, riding me hard, falling apart in my arms—the raw hunger in her eyes invades my mind. I've never been with anyone so . . . receptive. I crave more of her like a drug.

I test the water, and just before I step under the spray, I catch a faint whiff of ocean-kissed roses. Her scent is still on me. My eyes close, and I see her pale skin in the blue-shadow of moonlight. Her small breasts and dark nipples, her soft wails as I bit and teased them to stiff peaks. My dick is alert and throbbing, and I lean forward, resting my head against my forearm as I relive the pressure.

Sliding my hand rapidly up and over my cock in the warm spray, I picture her body. She's beautiful, delicate but strong, and her dark waves spill all around us, surrounding me in the luscious scent of flowers mingled with sex. My hand moves faster, and I remember pushing inside her wet heat. She was so tight . . .

"Fuck," I growl as my orgasm spills over and my knees get weak. I'm jacking off to her memory like a fucking teenager.

A few more strokes, and I'm at the end. But I'm not satisfied.

My hand is no substitute for her beautiful body. The water beats down on my shoulders, and I can't escape it. I must have her again.

Melissa

THE SUN BURNS MY EYES when I open them. It's after noon. I'm sleeping later and later as my internal clock becomes more and more nocturnal. The second queen bed in our room is empty, and I hear the shower running.

My best friend Elaine actually planned this trip. It is *not* a girls' weekend. Elaine has been a telepath since we were children. She started communicating with the dead in her teens, and before long, whispered rumors of her powers began filtering through the psychic networks.

Families from as far away as Seattle would make the pilgrimage to our hometown on the North Carolina coast to get answers or to find peace. She would kindly tell them what she sensed, and they would thank her and try to give her money. She never accepts any.

Her abilities have only grown stronger as she's matured. I didn't even have to tell her when I was taken and forced to become a monster that horrible night. She knew when my mind went silent in her perception.

In the past Elaine could see where I'd been, what I'd done. Now our connection is gone.

The night I lost everything, I lay on the floor hundreds of miles away, weeping and thinking as hard as I could, projecting my thoughts across the distance, calling to her. *Help me, Lainey!*

Only, the receiver had been cut off. Signals lost.

She drove all night in a panic to find me, guided only by cell phones and texts. She took me to safety, and a week later, she scheduled this trip to New Orleans.

We're here to meet Demeter, one of the strongest Voodoo queens in Algiers, and I need to get moving before we're late.

And yet . . . in the midst of all the horror I've found an escape—however fleeting. For one stolen moment, I bask in the tingling warmth of last night's memory.

Energy surges between my thighs as scenes of my back slammed against the brick wall, his strong arms lifting me easily, shoving my clothing aside as he ravaged my breasts and body. His enormous cock stretched and plundered my core, and *ohh* . . . with a shiver I remember the bead of sweat on his square jaw. It was so raw, he was so delicious, and I want more of him so badly.

Getting ready for bed last night, I examined my body in the bathroom mirror. Red marks from his beard scuffed my neck and breasts, and large handprints that would normally leave bruises were faint on my ass. His marks would all be gone today. My body can tolerate much harsher treatment now, and actually, I crave the roughness.

Before the change, I would never have engaged in such risky behavior. Now it doesn't matter. Now I can easily lure them in, play with them, tease them to erection . . . Then, in the helpless throes of orgasm, I strike.

"No!" I actually say the word out loud as I sit up in the bed. I've never done such a thing. I *can't* or I'll never escape this.

Oh, how is it possible I've met this man now, at the darkest point in my life? Or is it because I'm at this point I found him? I'm the huntress, seeking the dominant alphas, the ones who radiate power and control, the oversized mountains of sex, with their rich blood pumping strong in their veins. It's what I should be . . .

Yet, for all of Derek's masculinity and aggression, he was gentle and attentive to my needs. He held me all the way to the end, and then he thanked me. My cheeks flush as I remember our parting words, his steel-blue eyes holding mine.

He'll be at Mr. B's tonight, waiting. Only, I'll never appear. He won't understand, but I can't allow myself to explain, not that it would make sense if I tried.

Ultimately it's for the best—even if he never knows it. I've been brought so low. I have to stay away from him. I've never felt so sad in my life.

I didn't ask for this! The cry echoes through my brain again, but I have to shove it aside. Self-pity and wallowing in my tragedy won't help me. Only action can save me now, and it has to be fast action. Before it's too late.

Elaine breaks my musings. "What time did you get in last night?" She's wrapped in one of the thick, terrycloth robes from the hotel, and her light blonde hair is damp. "I didn't hear you."

I look down at my clasped hands. "It was after two."

My clairvoyant friend has always been so sure of everything. Now she watches me like I'm a riddle she can't solve. "What did you do after I left?"

"Nothing much," I lie. "I finished my drink, people-watched for a little while, then I came here."

She drops onto the bed beside me, her pretty face lined with worry. "I shouldn't have left you alone. I was just so tired."

I manage a smile. "I'm not a child, Lainey. You were exhausted. And . . . I don't sleep so well anymore. Not at night anyway."

Taking my hands, she studies them. "Has he tried to contact you?"

I decide not to tell her about the message waiting on my phone last night. His voice was so cold and calm, telling me to return to him.

I can still hear his words when I told him I was leaving: *Go ahead and have your fun, your final moments of humanity. You'll be back. You're mine now.*

My stomach cramps the harder I fight him. The distance helps some, but burning pain drags through my insides the more I resist.

I won't go back. I will break his power over me. These words have become my mantra, yet, at the same time, fear chills my insides. What if he's right? What if I can never escape his power?

My eyes heat with unshed tears at the thought. His voice echoes in my mind as surely as his blood mixes in my veins, and I shiver at the idea he can see me.

I don't know how to say any of these things out loud, so I don't.

"I left messages with everyone," I deflect. "We're having a girls' weekend in New Orleans. That should satisfy them."

"This silence between us is killing me." Her green eyes mist as she squeezes my hand. "I've always known you were safe. Now I'm afraid whenever we're apart."

We move together in a hug, and her body stiffens. She pulls back quickly, lifting a lock of my hair and inhaling deeply.

"What's this?" Her eyes narrow as my cheeks heat. "That's a *very* sexy man scent!"

I hop off the bed moving quickly around the room. "I don't know what you're talking about."

"I think you do! Tell me more about your people watching."

"I only danced with someone, that's all." I grab fresh panties and the other robe from the closet before dashing into the bathroom. She's right behind me.

"Must've been dirty dancing if he left his scent all over you. You had sex!"

Flashing her a glance, I press my lips together before turning to the shower. "It's really nobody's business what I did."

She dances around me, pulling my arm, forcing me to look at her. "You had sex, and from the way you're responding, it was damn good sex. Did you . . . ?"

She leans forward peering into my eyes. I want to pull away, but I know what she's looking for. Her expression brightens, and her voice drops to a whisper.

"It was fucking *great* sex, and you were able to control it." Her eyes sparkle as she bounces in place. "I think that's incredibly significant!"

I test the shower water without answering. She has no idea how close I came to losing control. "Will we have to discuss it with Demeter?"

"Yes." She answers so fast, I glance over my shoulder to meet her eyes. Her expression is serious. "I've never dealt with anything like this. I don't even know if we have a chance, but I know we have to tell her everything."

"I have to shower."

My best friend nods and goes to the door. "As soon as you're ready, we'll get lunch then head across the river."

I nod before stepping into the steamy box. Lifting my hair one last time, I inhale the sensual, woodsy smell of him. Again, intense sadness floods my core. I hate to lose him, yet I know it's for the best. My body might crave him, but I can't give in to my cravings anymore. It's the worst thing I could possibly do.

Elaine and I are here to find answers, not distractions. I have to stay in control. Stepping under the warm water, I pick up the shampoo. In a few moments, he'll be gone. It will be over, and next time I'll be more careful.

THREE

GROUNDWORK

Melissa

MY RED SUNDRESS IS ALMOST identical to Elaine's green one. Both are swishy rayon with thin spaghetti straps and stop just above our knees. New Orleans is hot as hell, and the fewer clothes we can decently get away with wearing, the better.

A blast of cool air greets us as we step through the white arched doorway of the Original Pierre Maspero's restaurant. It's been our favorite lunch dive since college, when we used to take occasional girls' trips to the Big Easy.

Nothing says party like sweating your ass off and drinking cheap beer from a plastic cup while walking through the French Quarter. Too bad that's not the reason for our visit this time. Shaking my head, I try to figure out how it's possible my life could have taken such a turn.

The restaurant is only two blocks west of our hotel, and we wait to be seated at one of the small, dark-wood tables inside the circa-1788 building. The grey stucco outside hides the beauty of the weathered brick interior. It's so gorgeous and historic, I'm overwhelmed with sadness.

Is this why New Orleans is such a magnet for the

paranormal? Am I destined to live alone through the centuries until the memories of a place like this are my sole source of comfort? *God help me.*

Elaine's teasing voice cuts through my despair. "Are you waiting for someone?"

She's further in the dim room than I am. I had drifted to the door as I considered my grim future, and looking back, I watch as she speaks to a handsome man. He's fair with hazel eyes, an easy, sexy smile, and an impressive physique.

I try to walk closer and *WHAM!* I'm hit with a powerful wave of nausea. Reaching out, I grab the old French door for balance.

"I'm here with my partner," I hear him say. "We're working on a case."

"Are you a cop?" Elaine's flirting, and I can tell she's intrigued with him. Squinting up, I see in his eyes he's equally fascinated and bewildered by my pretty friend.

I want to care, but I have to step out onto the sidewalk. I'm afraid I might vomit my meager breakfast of buttered toast. With my enhanced senses, their voices are clear in my ears.

"Close." I hear the smile in his voice. "Private investigator."

"Interesting. Are you in town for long?"

"Through the weekend. You?" He's got a cute, player quality to his voice, and I can practically feel the sexual tension between them.

"We head out on Sunday." The rustle of bags, hands in pockets. I know they're both fishing out business cards. "Elaine Merritt. Call me."

"Patrick Knight, and I will."

Elaine is so endearingly bold, and I know how men respond to her. It helps she can read their minds. She can tell the jerks right away and deflect their advances before they begin. In the meantime, I've got my back against the wall. I'm taking several deep breaths, trying to regain my composure.

"I'm sorry . . . I have to go." She's noticed my absence and is heading my way.

"Hey, wait." Patrick is right with her, but his growing presence sends my insides into another spasm.

I have to lean forward just in case, and I catch the disapproving looks of passing pedestrians. *I'm not drunk!* I want to yell, but I'm powerless.

"What are you doing for dinner tomorrow night?" He's too close. I push away from the wall and stagger down the block to the corner.

On Chartres Street, I can catch my breath. I'm able to stand and breathe deeply when my friend rounds the building fast, worry clear in her eyes.

"Shit, Melissa! You scared the hell out of me. I didn't know where you went."

"I'm sorry." Pressing my eyes closed, I touch the perspiration off my brow. "I don't know what happened back there. I thought I might puke."

She glances back over her shoulder before pushing us both further up Chartres. "Do you still feel like eating? We can go to K-Paul's instead?"

Nodding, we head northeast in the direction of the Louisiana Chef's signature restaurant. My strength returns quickly, still I'm confused by what just happened.

"Who was that guy?"

A little smile curls her lips. "Not sure, but we're having dinner with him and his partner tomorrow night." She gives me a wink. "Try to relax. Before that happens, we'll meet with Demeter and get answers."

Dread floods my insides, but I'm not sure whether it's because we're having dinner with Elaine's new lust-interest, or if it's because I'm afraid of what the old woman will tell us. Or won't tell us.

Derek

PATRICK'S TEXT WAS WAITING WHEN I stepped out of the shower this morning. He'd taken the red-eye and was in New Orleans.

Further intel. You shouldn't be here alone.

Cryptic. It means he's worried our texts are being monitored.

As soon as I'd read it, I shot back a reply. *Preparing. Meet at Two Sister's, dinner to debrief and regroup.*

Then I'd closed the blackout shades in my suite, shut off all my devices, and forced myself to sleep eight hours longer, until late afternoon. The Knight brothers and I have worked together long enough to know our strengths and vulnerabilities. Patrick's emergency trip to the city is significant.

I've been accused before—mostly by my targets—of being a hypocrite for hunting vampires with shifter partners. Two responses: First, I'm not. Second, I don't search out vampires for the thrill of staking them. I seek justice.

The Knights are law-abiding, and in addition to their loyalty and adherence to family bonds, they have heightened senses, strength, and enhanced healing powers.

Patrick's overactive sex drive tests my patience, and it doesn't help that his shifter charm seems to dissolve women's inhibitions. He's been embroiled in two sticky situations in the short time we've worked together. Still, he's smart, and he's a great tracker. I can overlook a few lapses in judgment, but I'll be glad when he finally mates.

When my alarm rouses me, it's after six. It's not yet twilight, still New Orleans feels darker than other cities. The black wrought iron and clinging vines covering every structure add to the shadowy nature of the place. It's sweaty and damp, and everyone is looking for a cool place to escape the heat.

It's also September. We're moving into fall, harvest season, Halloween. It's a dangerous time to be in my line of work, and I'm on full alert. I'm actually thankful my younger partner is here.

Before I leave my suite, I slip a 9mm handgun in my boot. It's loaded with silver bullets, and it's the only weapon I'll carry. Forget sneaking up on immortals. Their heightened senses alert them to your presence, and even if they didn't have that advantage, they're paranoid about attacks.

Patrick is a huge asset, but if our target truly is an old one, neither of us will be a match for him alone. I only hope together we'll be a close equivalent. My flesh is vulnerable, but I've learned a few tricks for staying out of danger. Shifters cause such painful wounds, vampires tend to avoid tangling with them.

Anyway, we only want information. This old one isn't *the* one. Patrick's investigations have indicated they're associates, nothing more. If we don't walk into any surprises, we should be okay.

The sun is behind the clouds, still the air is thick with heat. I'm wearing dark, loose jeans, a light, short-sleeved polo, and heavy black boots. As I walk the few blocks from my hotel to The Court of Two Sisters, I wonder what my partner did today while I rested and prepared. Female laughter and loud music flows out of the Bourbon Street bars, and I can imagine the temptation is great for him here. We're on a job, however, and he's usually focused when we're working.

Returning as a tourist to the city where I grew up makes me feel like a pampered guest in my family home. In short, it feels wrong. My parents still live in their garden district mansion on St. Charles Avenue, but it's close to the sister campuses of Tulane and Loyola Universities—far from here.

I don't intend to visit them on this trip. It's best they don't know why I'm in town. They have no knowledge of my current occupation (obsession?) since Alison was killed. If they even believed what I was doing, it would only fill them with unnecessary fear.

I'm a block from the restaurant, and I can't help glancing in the direction of Royal Street and the Hotel Monteleone. I won't be at Mr. B's tonight. I'll never know if she goes there to meet me.

Her shimmering skin, dark hair, and beautiful breasts fill my memory. Regret twists low in my stomach. I don't even know how to reach her. My fists involuntarily clench, and I consider postponing this job for a second time. Honor won't let me do such a thing.

All I know is somewhere, two blocks from where I stand, is an amazing woman I only hope I'll find again, and when I do, I hope I can convince her to accompany me back to my suite for another taste of heaven.

Wiping that thought from my mind, I step through the white, arched doorway into the restaurant. Nodding to the Creole hostess, I do a quick scan of the narrow interior. The outer walls are lined with large French doors, and the hallmark of the establishment is the enormous, open courtyard situated under a network of thick wisteria vines.

In the spring it resembles a vineyard with the purple clusters of grape-like flowers hanging through the foliage. In the fall, it's more like a jungle. Dark-green canvass umbrellas shelter the tables where the wisteria doesn't grow, and white twinkle lights shine in the dark branches and around black wrought-iron columns. A bright blue fountain adds a trickling noise to the low drone of conversation. It would be relaxing if it weren't for the task ahead of us.

My younger partner is staring at a menu, but he's clearly not reading it. I can't tell if he's preoccupied with our case or something different.

"Patrick," I say before pulling out the chair across from him. He starts, and I frown. I can't afford to have him distracted tonight. "What's on your mind?"

He's on his feet clasping my hand in a strong grip before we both sit. "Sorry." He only pauses a beat. "Unusual lunch."

"Anything you need to tell me about?"

Seated across from him, I scan the menu briefly. I've lost count of the number of times I've dined here through the years, and I already know what I'll order.

He doesn't have a chance to answer before a young woman in black and white arrives at the table. "Good evening, gentlemen." She gives me a wink and a smile. "Can I start you with a Sazerac? It's the signature cocktail of New Orleans."

I do miss the easy nature of my hometown, but my partner and I can't afford any weakness tonight. "Thanks, but I'll stick with iced tea. Unsweetened with lemon."

Patrick nods. "Same."

She gives us a quick nod, and we place our orders before she goes. Turtle soup with sherry to start, followed by crawfish étouffée for me. Roasted half duck with Bourbon praline sauce for my cynanthropic friend.

Our waitress disappears, and my gaze levels on Patrick. "What has you so distracted you didn't even notice me approach the table?"

He leans back and flashes that cocky grin women can't seem to resist. "We're safe here. Even the undead respect New Orleans's finest restaurants. If they forget that—"

"We have to be on guard everywhere in this city." It's as much a reminder to me as to him, and I wait while the busboy places two tall glasses of iced tea in front of us. "Tell me what you've learned."

When the boy leaves, Patrick leans forward, and his fair brow lowers along with his voice. "The one we're after is here, in the city. Now."

Adrenaline mixes with excitement in my chest. Could my hunt possibly be over? Could I possibly end my quest and return to a normal life?

Maintaining control, I lift my glass and take a sip. "How do you know?"

"Sloan told me."

Patrick wins. I'm completely stunned. "Sloan? What the

hell—"

"Keep your shirt on." Again with that grin.

"Patrick." Warning is in my tone. My former mentor is no laughing matter to me. "Explain."

"When you left, I had a little free time, so I dug out Sloan's old research journal. That fucker has some seriously sick shit in his notes."

"He dedicated his life to tracking the paranormal." Fear teases in the back of my mind. *And I'm following dangerously close in his footsteps.*

"Remind me again—what happened to him?"

Mildly impatient, I quickly rehash the story of the man who taught me how to track and kill vampires.

Like me, Sloan Reynolds had been an adjunct professor at Princeton University. With my Marine background and police training, I'd focused on Law Enforcement Online, a branch of the FBI. Sloan was the son of a successful Baltimore importer-exporter and taught students how to build and manage shipping businesses on the eastern seaboard.

In his spare time, he'd become obsessed with the ancient writings of the vampire hunters employed by the Vatican in the fifteenth century. He believed it was God's work, and after a few evenings sharing drinks at a local pub, he pulled me into it.

I confess, I didn't believe any of it at the time, but I was fascinated. I enjoyed studying the old legends and reading the ancient journals, seeing how the job was done centuries ago.

It wasn't long before I was supplementing my income investigating mysterious deaths and unsolved murders across the states. In the beginning it was only a distraction. Sloan taught me all the signature marks of paranormal criminal behavior—bodies covered in Katrina debris, bodies under the twisted rubble of car crashes, bodies added to crime scenes—the only connection being the victims were all drained of blood.

Unlike the savage murders committed by rogue shape-shifters, a vampire killing generally leaves very little evidence of the

attacker. The undead typically do not engage in sexual intercourse with their victims. The act of draining a human mimics
the orgasmic state for both victim and killer.

Occasionally, a fetishist vampire will sleep with a victim,
however they leave no DNA evidence behind. The two tiny pink
puncture wounds are the only indicators of what took place.
The blood is completely consumed.

Time passed, and I was drawn deeper into his world. I began
to see things I couldn't easily explain away. Nine months later,
we spotted our first vampire. The thing was inexplicably hanging around, lurking in the shadows of a kill when we arrived on
the scene.

I could feel its presence. It was unlike anything I'd ever experienced in my life—dread mixed with anger mixed with adrenaline. Sloan stayed behind to check the victim, a young runaway.
I went after her killer, and I finished him.

It was my first kill. I had my gun, and I shot him straight
through the heart with three silver bullets. It was quick and brutal, and I expected to be more shaken by the experience. At the
same time, looking back on it, I was able to see how my Marine
background prepared me for such a moment.

For years we had been studying and preparing to confront
these monsters. Unlike human killers, vampires can't be reha-
bilitated. Murder is their nature. The one I executed was cruel
and remorseless. He was exactly what I expected a vampire to
be, and ridding the world of him was the obvious right answer.

Once he was down, I walked straight to his writhing corpse
and cut the head off then torched the body. Vampire corpses
are highly flammable. When all that remained were his ashes,
I sprayed them away with water. No chance that fucker would
ever reanimate.

Unlike me, Sloan was disoriented when I returned. He said
another creature had appeared and cursed us both. I searched
but could find no signs of anyone else in the area. Knowing
vampires are typically loners, I dismissed it, told him to pull

himself together.

A month later, my wife Alison disappeared. She'd run out for a pint of ice cream and never came back. We found her dead, drained of blood and dumped in the woods of central New Jersey . . .

It's a night I'll never forget. My life changed that night.

I've put away those feelings. I had to or I would never move past it. Nothing in my experience prepared me for the pain of what happened to her. It marked me for a long, long time, and I was convinced I'd never get over it.

I stood over her ghastly white body and swore I'd find her killer. I'd get her justice. From that point on, I was all in.

Patrick and I are quiet a moment as I finish the backstory. All the Knights know what happened to my wife. Their loyalty and commitment to helping me find justice binds us together, makes us brothers. Even after all these years.

Still, my partner isn't satisfied. "He taught you everything he knew, and then what? He simply disappeared?"

The waitress and an assistant set our plates in front of us, and as they work, I scroll back through the years to that awful month and the sudden retirement of my former mentor. Patrick assures the girl we need nothing more, and she retreats, leaving us to resume our conversation.

"Within days of Alison's death, he tendered his resignation and withdrew to his mansion. He refused all visitors. He wouldn't even see me. As far as I know, he's never come out again. His staff takes care of his needs."

Patrick shakes his head, lifting his knife and fork to cut into the duck. "And you never went after him? You didn't demand to know why?"

Stirring the shot of sherry into my soup, I hesitate, remembering my disgust. "I knew why," I say, before tasting the rich, brown roux.

I know he can sense the change in me. Still, he asks the follow-up question. "Why?"

"He fell in love with one of them. Or lust . . ."

Patrick's fork hits his plate with a clang. "You've never told me this!"

"It never seemed important before." I slide my soup aside and take my fork to try the étouffée. "I didn't know you were digging in his old files."

"What did it look like?"

"I never saw her."

"It was a female?" My young partner leans back in his chair, a knowing look on his face.

"I assumed it was. From what I pieced together, he was trying to find a way to change her, bring her back."

"That's impossible."

"Yes," I nod, stabbing my fork into a curled crawfish tail covered in thick, red-orange sauce. "He didn't realize it until the end."

Patrick doesn't say the question plain in his eyes. He doesn't have to. *The end?*

"Somehow, he realized she was beyond redemption." I take a deep breath, remembering Sloan's final notes. He left me his files along with a post-it saying only two words: *It's over.* "He drove a stake through her heart."

"Jesus!" My partner hisses. "What the fuck?"

"He'd dedicated his life to eradicating them. After all our years of hunting, he found her, stood right there on the precipice. It took everything he had to make the right decision."

We're quiet a long time, neither of us eating. It seems appropriate—a moment of silence for the mortal broken by the immortal.

"Well, he left some kick-ass research behind," Patrick finally says. "Why haven't you shared any of it with me?"

Leave it to youth to be able to shake off the gravity of the situation. A small grin lifts the corner of my mouth. "Perhaps I grew a little disillusioned myself."

"Bullshit," he hisses. "You're as focused as you've ever been."

"Maybe I felt it was disrespectful." Returning to my plate, I try and remember why I'd locked up Sloan's notes. Patrick's right. All those years of work should be in our shared arsenal, not my brain alone.

"When he quit, he was tracking a very powerful one," my partner says. "Possibly the one we're after."

Alison's murderer.

My sense of vengeance toward this particular killer roars like a bonfire in my chest. Patrick knows how important avenging her is to me. Her death was a personal attack, and I won't rest until I answer it.

Placing my fork beside the elegant white china, I level my gaze on him. "Tell me what you've got."

FOUR

THE OLD ONE

Derek

LAFAYETTE CEMETERY AFTER HOURS IS an eerie place. The tombs stand six feet above ground, coffins encased in either concrete or ancient red brick. The exteriors are decorated in scrollwork and statues, and they look like gothic cathedrals, their long shadows forming a striped, grey-and-black landscape for us to cross.

It's no surprise vampire movies and television shows are often filmed here. The statues and headstones are a perfect setting for encounters with the supernatural. Even during daylight hours, the legion of crypts is a daunting site. So many dead are housed above ground in this city.

Growing up in the garden district, I've visited this location before, but never did I dream I'd be here on such an errand. Patrick has filled me in on what we're after. The old one is a loner according to Sloan's notes, and it lives here among the tombs when not traveling abroad.

We're disguised as visitors, paying our respects to a fictitious dead relative. In addition to my jeans, black polo, and heavy boots concealing our sole weapon, I'm carrying a small bouquet of lilies.

At my side is a large bullmastiff with thick, muscular shoulders and an intimidating jaw. Patrick's preferred form is a German shepherd, but we agreed size would help us more tonight.

His head is nearly at my chest as we walk. A heavy silver chain is around his neck, but it's only for show. This oversized dog is not a pet.

It's after eight, and the cemetery is officially closed. The sound of insects and running water fills the background. Otherwise, the air is tense, as if drawn and waiting. We walk the weedy path between the tombs, our eyes and ears alert for any change in our surroundings. We don't have to wait long.

The swirl of a skirt catches my eye, and we both stop. A woman steps out from the side of a larger tomb. She's smiling in a friendly way, but I can see the cruel lines around her mouth. Her lips are too red, and her skin is pale as bone. If we had more light, I would wager her brown eyes are in fact burgundy.

My partner's fur bristles, and I'm on full alert. We came here not knowing if our target would be a male or a female, and while I'm pretty sure this isn't an old one, we can never be too careful.

I'm amazed at the audacity of the immortal in this city. Sloan and I searched for nearly a year in New Jersey before we even found a hint of a vampire. I suppose we do live in the land of the Salem Witch Trials, while New Orleans is the land of voodoo and magic.

"You're late to be visiting the cemetery." Her voice is like the shattering of glass or several voices speaking at once. It's unnerving. "Are you lost?"

The way her eyes roam my body, I can tell she's hoping I'm lost. She's hoping I'm an innocent. She'll be sorely mistaken if she tries to attack me.

"I'm here on an errand." My reply echoes among the crypts. Patrick's body vibrates with a barely audible growl, and I place my hand on his head.

The thing's eyes flicker down to him, and she takes another step forward. "Impressive dog." Her hand stretches out as if to pet him, and his growl grows louder.

"Heel, Patrick." I tug the chain at his neck sharply.

He responds with a stinging nip to the side of my hand, and I almost break character. I know how much he hates being treated like a pet.

"Sorry," I take the opportunity to grin, hoping to throw her off-guard. "He's usually very friendly. Especially with the ladies."

Instead of coming straight toward us, she steps to the left, circling, watching. "What is your errand?"

I side step, copying her movements until my back is to a large, open vault. "My father asked me to tend the grave of his sister, my aunt. I just got off work, and I didn't want to let him down."

Patrick has moved to the side, still facing us but away from the path. The woman now walks straight to me, and without thinking, I step back. My boot hits the stone wall of a tall mausoleum, and internally I curse, realizing I'm cornered.

"You're a very good boy," she purrs, swaying slightly as she walks, not stopping until her body is directly in front of mine. Her seductive blend of vanilla and salt drifts lightly around us. They all have a unique odor.

"I'm not a boy," I say. Patrick's growl is low in the distance. "My dog is trained to attack, so I suggest you let me pass."

She laughs like crystals being dropped one after another on ceramic tile. "Are you afraid of me?" Her eyes widen and she runs a narrow, ivory finger down my cheek, through my beard. "A big, strong man like you? With such thick muscles? Such a good red-blooded American male."

Her voice sways with her movements as her eyes narrow. I can sense her glamour surrounding me, but it won't work. It's my sole defense against her dark arts. My immunity. Sloan and I discovered it working on our first case together. We have no clue how or why my mind is able to block it, and it's a closely guarded secret.

"Such a beautiful man alone in the dark night." Her voice is a heavy whisper, her lips full, and she presses her breasts against my chest. I pretend to be falling for her charms. "Would you like to fuck me?"

She says the words right at my lips, and I resist the urge to break her wrist as she slides a hand over the front of my jeans, over my cock. "Would you?"

A rustling noise scrapes against the stones overhead, and I look up fast—just in time to see another pale figure crawling like a lizard, headfirst toward me from the roof of the tomb. A hideous grin distorts his ghastly face, and his long fingernails clutch the cracks in the grey stones.

Shoving the woman back, I push away from the wall right as he reaches for my neck. Through my distraction, I catch the sound of snarling and growling mixed with hissing and champing of teeth, and I realize Patrick is fighting another one. We've inadvertently stumbled into a nest of them, and neither of us is prepared for this.

The thing crawling from the roof is now on its feet, and I can see by his ancient clothes and the tissue-quality of his skin he's the one. He's apparently made these young ones to protect him. Otherwise, vampires usually avoid living in groups.

"Call back your slaves," I shout to the leader. "We're only seeking information."

"You don't order me, boy." His voice is a scratchy hiss. "You're in my territory now."

The hideous smile combined with his rows of sharp, pointed teeth and blood-red lips, makes him look like a sinister, white-haired clown. The woman beside him sways toward me, still smiling as if attempting to hypnotize me.

Patrick lets out a sharp yelp, and I glance fast to see a beefy male vampire has him by the throat. His mouth is open, and his enlarged canines have descended.

In one swift move, I drop to a knee, whipping out the small gun just as the woman lunges for me.

BLAST! BLAST! Her smile transforms into horror as the silver enters her body. Red eyes widen, and she falls back, screeching like a cat. The noise was enough distraction to put Patrick back on top, and he snaps his powerful jaws, throwing his attacker against a crypt opposite the path.

"Patrick, come!" I shout, and he immediately runs to my side. "Stay back!"

We're slowly walking backwards out of the cemetery. I can only hope these two are his only guards.

The old one doesn't move. His smile is gone, but he isn't attacking. Instead, he goes still as a statue, watching us retreat. I have enough bullets if either of them tries to come after us, but he's letting us go.

Before we round the final corner to safety, I see his eyes tracing, memorizing all my features, and I know this isn't over.

Melissa

I'M LYING ON MY SIDE staring into the dark. I haven't left the bed since we got back from Algiers this afternoon. Elaine has run to the drugstore on the corner, assuring me we'll get dinner when she returns, but I can't eat. My stomach aches with emptiness, and despair holds me down against the mattress. I'm unable to shake it off.

We'd taken the Canal Street ferry across the Mississippi River to Algiers Point this afternoon. We disembarked amid beautiful Victorian houses and historic shops. Our objective, however, was deeper in the West Bank community, where the streets were narrow, barely wide enough for one car to pass, and the homes were mostly wooden shotgun shacks.

The live oak trees were thick and low to the ground, and ivy and wisteria covered everything that didn't move. As a result, the atmosphere was dark and heavy, and the noise of cicadas rose in a shrill screech above it all.

Demeter's was a red-painted wooden home hidden back off the road under the shade of several trees. Elaine had parked at the curb and taken my hand.

"No matter what happens in here, I'm not giving up." I knew she was trying to be encouraging, but her words filled me with dread.

A stone walk led to the house, and before we even knocked, the front door opened with a slow scrape. A dark screen kept us from being able to make out the person on the other side, but from the shaky sound of her voice, I knew it was Demeter.

"I saw y'all park at the street. Why you come to Mama Demeter's house without calling? What you after?"

"I'm sorry, Mama." Elaine leaned forward into the screen. "I'm Elaine Merritt. My friend Sabrina Hyatt gave me your name, but she said you don't have a phone."

"Don't need a phone. I hear enough as it is."

My friend went silent, her green eyes focused on the woman through the screen, and I waited. The woman's posture stayed relaxed, as did my friend's. A hint of a smile flickered across Elaine's lips, but she quickly covered it.

I'd only seen Elaine communicate telepathically one other time, and it was equally disturbing then. It felt like I'd slipped into another dimension, or at the very least gone deaf.

All at once, the old woman's eyes flashed to me, and she took a step away, further into the darkness of her old house. As if forgetting her power, Elaine suddenly spoke.

"No! You're wrong! She isn't like them. Every day she fights the change. We came all this way hoping you can help us."

It was silent several moments as the old woman stayed in the shadows of her home. My heart beat wildly in my chest, and I could barely breathe. If she pulled out a *gris-gris* or command-ed us to leave, I didn't know where else we would go. Despair clutched tightly at my throat.

Just then a musical tinkling of bracelets met my ears. It seemed very loud, but I knew it was because of my vampire ears.

"Hello! What's happening here?" A higher voice greeted us from behind, and Elaine and I both turned to see a slim girl coming up the walk.

Her skin was a lovely tan shade, and her long, chestnut hair hung thick down her back in shiny, wavy curls. She wore a flowing, red gypsy-style skirt and white tunic top, and when she smiled, her golden-hazel eyes glistened like the sunset. The treasured sunset I so desperately didn't want to lose.

"Mariska!" Demeter's voice was loud, moving quickly in our direction. "Come inside at once!"

The screen door flew open with a screech, and Elaine and I both stepped back. Mama Demeter was dressed in a navy tunic top with tribal designs on the front, and her dark hair was braided in two thick ropes down the sides of her head. I was shocked to find her not African. Her skin was the same warm Creole as Mariska's.

"Why are you afraid, Yaya?" Mariska stopped and smiled at me. "These women aren't here to hurt you."

"Come inside, child" the old woman said, glancing at me. "*Loogaroo.*"

Mariska's lips pressed together, and her golden eyes grew serious. "Yes," she nodded. "I felt it. Only I wasn't sure what it was."

Reaching for my hand, she pulled me into the dark house. "Come with me. We'll see what we can do."

Elaine followed right behind me as did Demeter, and we were through the dim-lit living room and in the much brighter kitchen when I heard the screen door slam.

"If we mess with her, we invite a rain of evil down on us. Nothing can be done for *Loogaroo.*"

My heart sank at her words, but Mariska jumped in at once.

"You say that, Yaya, but have we ever tried?" She turned to me with a smile and took both my hands in hers. "Your aura is a beautiful indigo, although at times it tends to muddy."

"I don't know what that means." For all my supernatural state of affairs, I was woefully ignorant of paranormal things.

Elaine stepped up behind me, putting her arm around my waist. "It means you're afraid of the future."

The tears that had been threatening all day, waiting for a reason, suddenly flooded my eyes, and my chin dropped. My shoulders shuddered, and I found three tissues handed to me at the same time.

"Now now," Demeter said in her stern voice. "Mariska's right. We haven't tried to solve this problem before. In the past we've only looked for ways to repel or kill your kind."

Her words did not give me comfort, but Mariska placed both her hands on my shoulders. "What is your name?"

Touching the tears away, I lifted my chin. "Melissa."

"Don't you worry, Melissa. I'm going to scour every book we have in this house, and if I can't find an answer here, I'll go down to Philome's and see what she knows about the matter."

"Pfft!" Demeter made a disgusted noise. "Philome don't know anything. She's a greedy, materialistic hack selling *gris-gris* to tourists in the Quarter."

A grin crossed Elaine's lips, and this time she didn't cover. "Thank you." Her voice was warm as she took both of Mariska's hands. "You're going to help us find the answers, I can feel it."

"I'll do my best." I watched as the two of them exchanged numbers and Elaine told her where we were staying.

Mariska followed us to the door of the cottage, and as she held the screen door open she touched my arm. "I won't give up until I have an answer."

"Thank you," I said, and we left, headed back to the ferry.

For all their encouraging words, however, I couldn't shake the dread that my life was truly over, that my maker's words were right and my fate was sealed.

Now I'm lying here hours later, staring into the darkness. Only it isn't terribly dark to my evolving eyes. One of the things I've noticed about my gradual transformation is my ability to go very still. I can think about the smallest thing until it consumes my focus. I'm not sure how long I can maintain it, because my friend hasn't left my side since it happened. She refuses to let me spiral into the despair hovering at the edges of my brain.

"You have to get out of that bed!" She's back, slamming drawers open and closed and jerking back the heavy curtains. "We're not going to sit in this room and brood. We're going out!"

"I don't want to go out." My limbs are as heavy as my voice, and the black thoughts have nearly consumed my mind. "I'm grieving."

Pulling my arm, she pushes my feet off the bed, forcing me to sit up. Anger fires in my chest so fiercely, I feel my gums tingle, and I know my teeth are growing. Another new trait—my emotions turn on a dime.

"Leave me alone!" I shout, and she jumps back, stunned by the ferocity of my voice. I'm a little stunned myself. And ashamed.

My chin drops, and I calm the savagery smoldering inside me. "Please leave me alone, Elaine. You have no idea how difficult this is for me."

She carefully moves to sit beside me on the bed, and I can tell she's a little shaken by my sudden, violent response.

"Oh, Mel," she speaks quietly, touching my arm. "You can't give up. I won't let you give up."

"Didn't you hear what they said?" My voice has switched from rage to intense sadness. "The old woman said there's no cure, and if a voodoo queen says there's no cure—"

"Then Mariska promised to find one." Elaine's voice is strong. "She's going to do it, I can tell. I read her thoughts, and she's passionate about helping you."

The last bit is true, at least. I'd felt the intensity of the girl's commitment. It confused me. "Why?" My voice is soft. "What makes her want to help me so much? She doesn't even know me."

Standing, Elaine goes to the closet and slides hangers across the brass bar. "She's not psychic, but she has gifts. She could tell you had been forced against your will. Her sense of justice is incredible."

"She's very generous."

Elaine turns to face me, and her shoulders drop. "If you could only see yourself. The reality of this hangs on you so cruelly. Still, you're so clearly a good person."

"I'm not so good," I mutter. "Every day, I feel the evil growing inside me. Every day it's harder to fight."

"You can, and we will! We're going to wait for Mariska, and in the meantime we're going out. We'll have drinks, laugh and dance, and then we'll come back here and sleep."

For a moment I think about her words. I weigh the options of lying in bed versus going out, forgetting these dismal circumstances for one more night. It can't get any worse.

With a deep inhale, I find the strength in me to rise, to force a smile. "If you say so. I can't sleep anyway."

"That's the spirit!" She pulls out a strapless, ruched-top dress made of thin rayon and hands it to me. "I'll wear mine, and we'll head over to Bourbon Street. Tomorrow will be a new day with new answers. I promise."

I stand and take the dress, hoping with everything in me she's right, yet at the same time, I hear his whispered laughter in my head.

Enjoy it while you can.

FIVE

TASTING

Derek

PATRICK SWEARS AT HIS WOUNDS while I nurse my scotch. "Fucking god damned motherfucking blood suckers." I watch him wince as he binds the gaping slice of a vampire bite on his forearm. "Their saliva burns like acid."

"You'll be healed in less than an hour," I mutter, sipping the amber liquid. "You're lucky you're immune. Nothing more to worry about."

"You're lucky you're immune."

"It isn't the first time." I take another pull off my glass of scotch. It's taking longer than usual for me to calm down after a hunt. "I'm only immune to their hypnosis. If I hadn't brought that gun . . ."

My partner's lips press into a tight line. "We need Stuart here."

I nod. I'd already thought of that. "He'll be here tomorrow." That's how it is with Stuart and me. I call, he appears, and vice versa. "Did you have any idea what we were walking into?"

"Are you seriously asking me that right now?" Patrick isn't one for sarcasm, and I only laugh.

"Then we really are a couple of lucky sons of bitches."

"Damn straight."

An icy chill passes down my spine at how wrong tonight could have gone. It isn't often an unprepared vampire hunter and a weredog—even a young, strong shifter like Patrick—walk into a nest of vampires and make it out with only a scratch. I'm wrestling a mixture of fatigue, relief, and uncanny amusement.

"We are so fucking lucky." I exhale, rubbing my hands over my face.

"Sazerac," Patrick says to the bartender. We're sitting at the bar in Razoo's off Bourbon Street, and my partner is jumpy. I can't stop drumming my fingers on the shiny wood in front of me.

"What exactly did you read in Sloan's journal?" At this point it doesn't really matter. Still, I'm curious, passing the time, waiting for us to come down. I can't shake the image of that nightmarish clown-face, that grinning undead fucker coming down the wall at me headfirst like a giant fucking lizard. *Shit.*

"Nothing like what we encountered." Patrick shakes his head, taking a sip of his cocktail. "Sloan's notes said 'an old one with answers' lives in the crypt in Lafayette cemetery. It said if we went with flowers, played the role of gracious mourners, he'd talk to us."

"Looks like he got bored with gracious mourners. Decided to turn a few."

"No shit."

Razoo's is also a karaoke bar, and a young south Asian-looking woman approaching the mic draws my attention. She's sexy with long, wavy black hair. I try to let her swaying and singing ease my mood, but it isn't working. Her dark eyes only make me yearn for sapphire blue. I want Melissa. I want to burn off this excess energy in her arms.

"We should've stayed close tonight, done more research." *I should've been at Mr. B's.*

"That sounds like you're second-guessing me." Patrick's

itching for a fight, but I'm not interested.

"I'm not," I answer honestly. "Just post-mortem."

A group of drunken college kids stumble through the doors, laughing and adding to the crowd coming in off of Bourbon Street. It's so late in the evening, I have no reason to believe any-one I'd want to see might come here. Melissa would be with her friend Elaine, most likely dining at Brennan's or Galatoire's, then heading back to her hotel to sleep, her beautiful dark waves spread out over her pillow.

"Fucking no way." Patrick's hiss cuts through my distrac-tion. "It can't be."

Snapping to attention, I can't help wondering if our friends are back. "What is it?"

He doesn't answer, and I follow the line of his sight to the door. A beautiful blonde stands just inside, off the street. She seems a little lost, as if she's looking for someone or trying to decide if she'll stay.

I'm ready to guess she'll leave, but her eyes move as if direct-ed by an invisible guide directly to my partner.

I turn and look at him as well. His posture is as confident and strong as ever, but his expression is stunned. He's trying to play it off, but something is happening to him.

"Do you know her?"

"No." He looks down at the bar, his voice barely controlled.

"She's headed in our direction." Looking up, I see the con-fident smile on her lips. It's as if she's aware of her power over him. "You sure you've never—"

"It's Patrick, right?" Her tone is happy, like she's found some-thing she lost.

My partner straightens, facing her, and though I've never seen it before, I know exactly what's happening.

"Yes," he says in a husky voice. "Elaine?"

"Yes!" Her green eyes sparkle, and she touches his arm. His entire body stills at her caress. "We were walking by, and I knew you were here."

She laughs, but he only smiles.

Fuck me, Patrick's imprinting. If I thought we needed Stuart before, we sure as hell need him now. I have no idea how finding his mate is going to impact his performance.

As much as I've wanted this to happen, it irritates the shit out of me it's happening now, until I glance up toward the entrance and my entire body snaps to attention. She's there, just outside the door, watching this woman with my partner. Her brow is lined in frustration, as if she can't enter—or she doesn't want to.

"Melissa . . ." The word is a whisper on my lips, and I'm on my feet.

Elaine and Patrick are talking. He's turning on all the charm, and she's falling for it hard—or maybe she's already fallen for him, and all his charms are sweet icing on the cake. She sure walked into this bar and straight to him as if she knew full well the strange transformation happening in his mind.

None of it matters. I'm consumed by the discovery of Melissa. She sees me. Her sapphire eyes hold me, and a mixture of deep longing and cautious optimism moves through me.

I want her. I've wanted her all day. From this morning in the shower to every other minute of this long-assed day, I've thought about her luscious lips, her gorgeous breasts, her long legs wrapped around my waist. I'm at the door where she's standing, keeping the glass between her and the bar as if it were a shield.

"Hello," I say with a smile. "I'm really glad to see you again."

Blinking down, she seems almost guilty when she answers. "I wasn't able to be at Mr. B's tonight. I'm sorry if you waited."

She wasn't there. The idea sends a wash of relief through me followed quickly by disappointment. I debate my next words.

"It's okay," I say. "I'm really glad you're here now."

Her hand trembles a bit, and I can't help wondering if I make her nervous. Is it possible this small, beautiful woman who holds my entire breath in her hands is nervous?

"Did you come here after dinner?" she says.

I decide to be honest. "I wasn't at Mr. B's tonight either." Her eyes blink quickly to mine. "A job took me away from the city, and I couldn't make it back in time. I'm so glad you weren't there."

"And what if I had been there?" The defiance in her tone fans my smoldering desire even hotter. She's so fucking strong.

"I'd do everything in my power to earn your forgiveness."

I've stepped outside, closer to her, and she inhales sharply. Her gorgeous eyes blink up to mine, and I want to taste her so badly my mouth waters. The scent of ocean-kissed roses, her scent floats around us. I want it all over me again.

She exhales a little sigh, glancing toward the bar. "Lucky for you, I've had a really shitty day. I'm in a forgiving mood."

"I had no idea it was going to be such a lucky day for me."

A hint of a smile crosses her lips, and I want to gather her in my arms and love the shittiness away. Lifting my finger, I lightly trace a line up the smooth skin of her arm to her shoulder, and she shivers. Her breathing shallows, and it's almost too much for me. I mentally calculate how far we are from Pirate's Alley. The Royal Sonesta is closer.

"Let's go to my hotel."

Her eyebrows pull together. "You want to—"

"Spend the night with you." I reach for her hand. "Yes, I want to spend the night with you . . . like before."

Shaking her head, she moves out of my reach. "I'm sorry. I don't do the walk of shame."

"I would never let you walk home alone."

Her back is to the glass doors and she seems to consider my offer. I take a chance, rubbing my hand across my chin. "A bed would be more comfortable, and I would do anything to see your gorgeous body spread across my sheets."

She blinks up at me through her lashes, and desire spikes in my veins. I know she remembers last night. I glance quickly back in the bar to see Patrick dirty-dancing behind Elaine. She's smiling with her blonde head thrown back on his shoulder, and from the looks of things, they'll be in a bed together before long.

Closing the distance between us, I speak softly, right at her temple. "Can I have you tonight. Please?"

Only a brief hesitation, and she whispers, "Yes."

Relief mixes with desire and urgency as I take her hand. We're only steps from our own heaven, and I plan to spend all night with her there.

Melissa

MAYBE IT'S BECAUSE I HAVE nothing left to lose, or maybe it's because nothing can really hurt me anymore—at least no more than I've already been hurt. Most likely, it's because Derek is so damned determined and delicious . . . and sexy. As soon as I saw him in the bar, my teeth ached. Everything we did in the alley flooded my mind, and I flushed with need to have him again.

None of that matters. I don't need justification anymore. I want him, and he wants me. The half-block to his hotel passes in a haze of anticipation. My skin is on fire, and my breath comes in little pants. Above the corner entrance, the word *Desire* is lit up in vaudeville lights, and it makes me want to laugh. After everything that happened today, all the disappointment, I can't believe I might even consider laughter, but this man changes everything.

We cross the marble-tiled lobby straight into an open elevator. It's empty except for us, and Derek presses the number four repeatedly.

Close, doors . . . Close! Anticipation buzzes in my chest, until they finally start to move. They barely touch when he has me against the wall, pinned by his huge physique.

"God, you're so beautiful." His breath is a hot whisper across my cheek just before he claims my mouth, forcing my lips to part and finding my tongue with his.

A little whimper aches in my throat, and he lifts me against the shiny, wood-paneled wall. Breaking apart, his lips move down my jaw, velvet followed by scratchy beard. Another moan. My lust for him is at an epic height.

He lifts his head and our eyes meet. "I want to taste you."

"Okay." My voice trembles.

I'm thinking the same thing, when all at once the box we're in stops. The doors open, and he looks over his shoulder. We're on his floor.

He gives me a little wink. "Hold that thought."

In a flash we're out, headed down a narrow hallway. He swipes the door card, it emits a little tweet, and we push inside the room. I barely have a chance to notice the gold walls, marble-topped coffee table, or wood and brass accents of his suite before he's got me in his arms.

My hands rest on his chest, and heat flames through my core with every heartbeat. My eyes travel up, up, up, to his blue ones now darkened with desire, and I know he's remembering the same things as me—how fantastically our bodies came together only twenty-four hours ago. It seems like a lifetime after this day.

"When I saw you tonight . . . I couldn't stay away."

I smooth my palms over his shoulders, down his rounded biceps. He cups my cheeks, studying my hair, my chin, my lips, as if memorizing every part of me. It's incredibly seductive, and I almost can't bear the anticipation.

He gently kisses my brow, and my eyes flutter shut. "When I realized I wouldn't make it back tonight, I was sure I'd lost you." He traces a fiery line across the bridge of my nose to my other brow. "Why did you stay in the street? Were you feeling sick?"

"No," I manage, despite the thickness in my throat. "I . . . I didn't want to go inside."

"Good," he says before covering my mouth with his.

Our lips part quickly, and our tongues entwine before he continues his progress down my neck. Tasting. He wants to taste me. I'm burning with the same desire.

A swift pull and the top of my strapless dress is at my waist, revealing my bare breasts. A low noise of approval, and he rolls a hard nipple between his thumb and forefinger.

"Oh, god," I gasp, as he leans down to give it a little suck, a teasing bite.

Heat floods my panties, and with every inhale, my need for him rises. Only tonight something is different. My heated lust is burning at both ends. My core is throbbing, begging for him, but something else—a consuming hunger is in my throat.

"Take me," I barely speak, and he drops to his knees.

With one powerful lift, I'm off my feet, my back pinned against the wall as he holds my legs, pulling my thong to the side with his thumb.

Large, strong hands grip my inner thighs, opening them, and his nose touches my skin as his tongue covers my clit. A cry trembles from my throat, and he pulls back, pressing his mouth against my leg.

"I had to hear that sound again." His voice is a sexy vibration against my skin, his beard scratching my most sensitive parts. I can't help another shudder.

He holds me with strong hands, as if I weigh nothing at all, and his mouth returns to my center, his tongue making slow, languorous sweeps mixed with little pulls.

"Ooh, god!" My head drops back against the wall as my eyes roll closed. I thread my fingers in his soft, dark hair never wanting him to stop.

My back arches against the textured wallpaper. My entire focus is on his mouth, his tongue, slowly massaging, tasting and teasing me to the very edge. Pressure builds tight, low in my pelvis, then expands, snaking down my legs with every stroke of his tongue.

Another deep kiss, it slides lower, plunging into me.

"Ah, yes!" I cry as he does it once more before returning to my clit. The circles quicken, and my entire lower body explodes in fiery orgasm.

"Oh, Derek! Oh, god!" My hips buck against him. I can't stop the shuddering in my legs. I'm wailing and shaking and grasping his shoulders as I come.

He strokes me a few more times until I can't take the sensation anymore, then he gives me a quick kiss, stands, and sweeps me into his arms. I'm in a daze of euphoria as he crosses the small space to his enormous, king-sized bed.

My dress is quickly removed along with my panties, and I push to the center, watching him with hooded eyes as he steps out of his boots while unfastening his belt. *Yes*, I'm thinking, *Oh, yes.*

I want him inside me again, stretching me, filling me. His pants are finally off, his navy eyes never leaving mine, but I break away to admire his full erection. *So big.* Crawling toward him, I grasp his thick shaft, flickering my tongue across the tip before pulling it into my mouth.

"Shit," he hisses, smoothing my hair off my cheek with a large palm as I suck him.

I lower my head as far as possible, grasping the base and pulling it into my throat. I'm rewarded with a deep groan, and I pull back, looking up at him with a naughty smile. His lips press together in a stern line, and he shakes his head.

"I'm not coming in your mouth." All at once, he's got me under my arms, pushing me back on the bed forcefully.

Excitement flashes in my chest. I want him to be rough. I want him to show me his strength. He only pauses a moment to whip his dark shirt over his head before crossing the bed toward me.

"What do you want?" I say in a low voice, rising to meet him in the middle. The white cotton sheets are as soft as silk, and I grip his strong arms in both hands. "You want to fuck me?"

His eyes cloud with desire, and I turn around quickly, leaning my back against his bare chest. I drop my head onto his shoulder and grind my ass against his rock-hard dick.

"Fuck," he growls, grasping my breasts in his large hands. Scratchy kisses tease the backs of my sensitive shoulders as he glides a large palm down my flat stomach. Two thick fingers plunge deep into my core, and I moan loudly.

"You're so wet," he groans.

"Fuck me hard," I whisper. "Don't be gentle."

An animal sound fills my ears, and he lifts me quickly before lowering me firmly onto his lap, onto his cock. His sudden invasion is shocking and erotic, and I cry out from the pleasure tinged with pain. The back of my head is against his shoulder as he lifts and lowers me again, thrusting further into me.

I have to help. I rise on my knees and drop, sending him even deeper. A ragged groan coughs from his throat. "Jesus . . . So fucking good."

His forehead is pressed to my back as he grips my hips, slamming me up and down his shaft. I feel a trickle of his sweat roll down the line of my back, and it's as if I go into a trance.

The memory of his taste floods my senses, and it begins. Something more powerful than my will takes over. The hot pressure of my orgasm tightens low in my pelvis, but the drive of hunger burns hotter in my throat.

My jaw drops open, and I let out a long wail as my canines stretch from my gums. "Ahhh!"

It's like fuel to his fire. He's pumping harder, faster, and I fumble one hand to the back of his neck. His muscles are rippling and strong. Turning my head, he's right at my mouth. I lick the sweat from his skin, but it's not like before. His taste overwhelms me. I must have more.

Feed. The low voice of my demon speaks directly to my soul.

No! A small voice whimpers back.

Derek's heartbeat is loud in my ears, drowning out everything. The strength of his blood fuels my orgasm. He releases my hip with one hand and touches my clit, circling quickly with his fingers, and all my control is lost.

Another burst of intense pleasure scrambles my brain, and my hips begin circling with his movements. *Don't stop. Oh, god, please don't stop.* My brain repeats the phrase like a mantra as my legs begin to shudder and jerk.

FEED! It's a direct command I can't resist. My extended canines burn.

"I'm coming," Derek grinds out. So much raw hunger is bound up in his words.

"Yes, Derek, yes."

I arch my back, grazing my razor-sharp teeth lightly across the skin behind his ear, right at the base of his hairline. A little pinprick, and I pierce him. As my teeth sink into him we're both swept up in a powerful orgasm.

"Fuck!" He shouts, coming deep inside me.

My body goes rigid, as if electrocuted. The onslaught of erotic pleasure blanks my mind. My mouth is attached to his skin as his blood pulses into me. He doesn't seem to notice I'm drinking him. He groans, and I can feel his cock deep inside me, throbbing.

I swallow, and my eyes squeeze shut. I'm on another plane where sound and sight—nothing exists but this man. He penetrates me; I penetrate him. It's the most intense experience of my life. Had I known it would be this way, I'd never have been able to resist it last night.

His ragged groans are little after-shocks of pleasure. He's still coming; I'm still coming as I drink. Until, from somewhere, some other place inside me—a place filled with sadness and loss, a place still clinging to the smallest hope of mortality—a word appears: *STOP!*

It's my voice, not the demon's. I have to stop. I don't want to kill him. I don't want to lose him. Pulling out quickly, I swallow the last drops as the haze breaks. As if released from a trance, he pushes us forward into the pillows never once breaking body-contact. His hips rock twice more before we both are able to control our breathing and slowly start to come down.

"Jesus." His voice is a hoarse whisper at my shoulder as he makes another slow thrust.

I can't move. I'm floating in space, attempting to manage the legions of emotions spinning and warring in my mind. His blood races through me, a slight burning at first. *Curious.* The discomfort passes as it mixes with my blood in my veins. It's in my brain, filling my mind with everything about him.

Derek Alexander. Strong . . . so strong . . . so incredibly strong. He's a soldier. No . . . a Marine . . . A commanding officer . . . There's something more. Something different. Something . . . like me? No . . . it's not like me, but it's supernatural. What have you done, my Derek?

I pull my lips between my teeth to capture any last essence of him lingering there. *I want more.* I want to swallow every drop of his sensual blood. *I want more.* I want to fuck him all night. I never want him out of my sight. I want him to be a part of me always. *Mine.*

My eyes are pressed closed as all these messages flood my brain, but I realize he's above me now. He pulls out slowly, moving to his side. I feel his absence intensely. His large palm smooths my skin from my shoulder, down my torso.

"That was . . . incredible." His voice is husky, but I can't answer yet. I'm still trying to find my feet. "You make me crazy."

I make him crazy? He has no idea what he does to me. He sends me to another galaxy. Focusing all my strength, I force my teeth to retract. He can't know what I am.

When he speaks again, I hear a smile in his gentle tone. "Did I break you?"

I have to move. My chin dips, and I push up onto my elbows, hoping to buy time for my mouth to return to normal. I'll be able to face him in a moment. In the meantime, I allow my long, dark hair to form a glossy curtain between us.

"I'm not broken," I whisper. As I say the words, I realize how untrue they are.

He kisses my lower back, and the scruff of his beard is almost painful against my hypersensitive skin. "Good, because I hope to repeat everything we just did a few more times tonight."

It's safe, and I lift my heavy locks over my shoulder. "A few more times?" I give him a coy smile, and his gorgeous blue eyes twinkle.

"Naturally, the number of times is up to you, Miss . . ." His dark brow furrows. "I don't know your last name."

I quickly scan the suite looking for something I only vaguely spotted when we entered—before he had me against the wall. *There it is.*

"You have a Jacuzzi." My chin drops and I lift an eyebrow. "We should test it out."

He smiles, revealing straight white teeth. He really is perfect. I feel a strange surge of pride over the few ounces of his blood I've stolen, a peculiar possessiveness of him buzzes in my veins.

"So it's like that?" He levels that steely gaze on me, and it's breathtaking.

"You're a private investigator?"

"Yes, Melissa."

"Last names aren't a good idea." I can never explain the fucked up nature of my existence, and anyway, it doesn't matter. He's my last fling, my final heavenly indulgence before I accept my fate and return to Baltimore to die.

He doesn't move as he watches me. I wait while he weighs my words against the mind-blowing experience we shared only moments ago. He'll either insist on knowing more, in which case I'll leave, or he'll accept my answer.

"You want to test out my Jacuzzi?" I release the breath I'm holding with a grin and a nod. "Give me a sec."

He pushes off the mattress, and I watch his perfect ass flex as he crosses the beige marble floor to the large tub. Two low steps lead to it, and he sits on one as he opens the faucets.

No need to worry he'll change or be like me. We didn't complete the ritual. I only have him inside me. He doesn't have me in him. I didn't force him to drink from my veins the way I was forced. I didn't rape his only hope away.

I, on the other hand, am running out of time to complete my transition. I have to kill or die. I've already decided which it will be.

Leaning on one elbow, he reaches out to me, and I stifle a gasp. His body is Michelangelo's Adam, reaching out for the hand of God. Only he's reaching out to a devil.

Horror and guilt hit me like a freight train. My chin drops, sending a dark curtain across my cheek, but I know he saw the change in my expression. I hear him crossing back to the bed at once.

"What's wrong?" Concern fills his voice. "Melissa, look at me."

He catches my chin, and my eyes travel over his olive skin, his smooth muscles, the light dusting of hair on his chest. I have to leave. *Now.*

I can't believe I would risk my one hope at escaping my fate—not only that, I risked his very life! Has my animalistic nature truly become so strong? I stole from him. I bit him. I can't rationalize this away any more. I'm too weak to fight my lusts. I'm lost.

His hands are on my shoulders, pulling me onto his lap. "Stop," he orders.

I try to resist his arms, but he's stronger than me. Or I'm too weak to fight him.

His stern voice continues. "Whatever you're saying to yourself, stop it."

I shake my head. "We can't do this, Derek. It's wrong."

"It's not wrong. It's fast." His chin drops, and I watch as he collects his thoughts. I confess, I'm incredibly curious as to what he might say next. "I'm sure this is new for you. Hell, it's new for me." His eyes fix on mine, and his expression is so earnest and lovely. "Don't shut us down yet. Give us a chance."

"You don't know me," I argue. "We don't know each

other—"

"So let me get to know you." He takes my hand carefully in his. "I want to know your mind the way I already know your body."

His blood sings in my veins, and my eyes close at the sensation. Tasting him has only made him harder to resist.

"We don't have time."

"We have plenty of time." He smooths my hair back, cupping my cheek with his large palm. "My life has been so empty these last six years. This is the first time I've wanted to live."

Oh, god, the terrible irony. "You want to live?"

"I'm not explaining it right. I'm jumping ahead." He takes both my cheeks in his hands, and looks deep into my eyes. "But you feel it, too. I know you do. Please stay."

I want to cry. My heart is breaking because I can't tell him we don't have a chance. I can't tell him that if he wants to live, he needs to run as far and as fast away from me as possible.

I'm either the worst coward or his blood is making it impossible for me to say no, because this beautiful man holding my face overwhelms me with his words.

"Okay." My voice is soft, and I feel my cheeks turn pink. It's a ridiculous response. I know all of this is a fantasy, yet I want to indulge it so badly. "What do you want to do?"

He glances over his shoulder at the now-full Jacuzzi tub and pushes away to walk over and shut off the water. Reaching into the pool, he tests it. Then he smiles and dries his hand.

Returning to me, that sexy grin is on his lips. "First, we finish what we've started tonight." Catching me by the legs, he roughly pulls me across the sheets, making me squeal a laugh. I'm in his arms as he carries me to the tub. "Tomorrow, I'm going to buy you brunch."

"Brunch? So I'm sleeping in?"

He laughs as he steps down into the swirling water, me still in his arms. It surrounds us in bubbling warmth, soothing away my tension, making me believe I could be a normal girl with a normal life, who only needs to give this incredible man a chance. As if we have a future. As if I get a happily ever after.

"You'll probably be tired after tonight. I wasn't planning to wake you."

I'm on his lap, straddling his waist, our faces close. My hands are on his shoulders, and I wouldn't push him away for anything.

"And then?"

He leans forward and captures my lips with his. Our mouths open to let our tongues touch, and I feel a stirring low in my pelvis. At the same time, energy surges through my chest. His blood is in my heart making me burn for him.

He pulls back, nipping my lip. "We take it as it comes."

I hope you enjoyed this EXCLUSIVE SNEAK PEEK at the newest Derek & Melissa love story, One Immortal.

Get One Immortal *Today!*

YOUR OPINION COUNTS!

If you enjoyed these novels, please leave a short, sweet review wherever you purchased your copy. Reviews help your favorite authors more than you know.

Thank you so much!

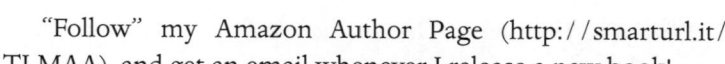

"Follow" my Amazon Author Page (http://smarturl.it/ TLMAA), and get an email whenever I release a new book!

Get Exclusive Text Alerts and never miss a SALE or NEW RELEASE by Tia Louise!

Text "TiaLouise" to 64600 Now!

Sign up for my New Release newsletter, and get a FREE Exclusive Bonus Scene from One to Love! (http://smarturl.it/ TLMnews)*

*Please add allnightreads@gmail.com to your contacts so it doesn't bounce to spam!

EXTRA! EXTRA!

Check out these Fun Freebies:

- Hear some of the music that inspired *One Immortal* on Spotify! (http://bit.ly/1MpcWd1)

- See the images that inspired *One Immortal* on Pinterest! (https://www.pinterest.com/AuthorTiaLouise/one-immortal/)

- "Runaway" is the FREE, specially packaged SUPERHOT Prequel to *One to Chase* (Marcus & Amy). Grab your copy wherever eBooks are sold! "Free" signed copies (+ shipping) are available in my online store: http://mkt.com/TLM-Productions

- Join "Tia's Books & Babes" on Facebook and chat about the books, post images of your favorite characters, get EARLY exclusive sneak peeks, and MORE! Go here: https://www.facebook.com/groups/TiasBooksandBabes

- Keep up with the guys on their Facebook Page: *The Alexander-Knight Files!* (https://www.facebook.com/pages/Alexander-Knight-Files/1446875125542823)

THANK YOU
FOR READING!

Dear Reader,

I hope you enjoyed the Derek & Melissa love story!

I confess, I fell in love with Derek and Melissa, and it was exciting and heartbreaking to go with them through the challenges I knew were coming. I hope you enjoyed all the moments in their journey. I hope you were surprised, I hope you swooned, and I hope you even shed a tear. Most of all, I hope you felt the love between these two great characters.

When readers begged for more after *One to Hold*, I was excited to keep going with *One to Protect* and *One to Save*. Then when they wanted EVEN MORE Derek & Melissa, I decided to have some fun and write *One Immortal*, which is a paranormal re-imagining of their story.

Writing that book was like going home to me, since I'm a south Louisiana native, and I grew up going to New Orleans and experiencing the culture, music, and FOOD!

Some readers think *One Immortal* is even Hotter than the original three! I don't know how that's possible, but you can let me know what you think after you read the Exclusive Bonus Content in this set and hopefully get the book!

Readers often ask me, "What's next?" or they want more, and I'm happy to report *more is out there!*

One to Keep is Patrick and Elaine's love story. Patrick's a bit younger than Derek, and a little wilder, but readers seem to love him just as hard. I hope you will too!

Kendra "Kenny" Woods is a favorite character from *One to Keep*. She's a young woman with a broken past, and in her book *One to Love*, she meets an injured ex-boxer (Slayde Bennett) with secrets of his own.

One to Leave is Stuart Knight's story. (#SexyCowboy) Stuart and Derek are like brothers since they were Marines together; however, Stuart is hiding some major PTSD issues. He's also a dominant alpha, but he meets his match in sexy little gypsy Mariska. If you love sizzling romances under the Big Sky of Montana, *One to Leave* is right for you!

After I introduced Marcus Merritt in *One to Save*, it was time for Amy Knight to make an appearance. You got a taste of Marcus and Amy in the *One to Save* epilogue "Runaway." Don't miss their blazing hot love story all set in Chicago in *One to Chase*.

As always, let me know what you think of my books! Email me your thoughts, feedback, what you liked—even what you didn't like! I really like hearing from readers. I also hope you'll leave a short, sweet review on Amazon and/or wherever you purchased this book! Reviews help indie authors more than you know.

You can write to me at allnightreads@gmail.com or visit me on Facebook at *www.facebook.com/AuthorTiaLouise*!

Join my reader group, "Tia's Books and Babes" to meet other reader-friends and get all the scoop FIRST:

www.facebook.com/groups/349265091949486/

Thank you again for spending time with me. I hope to hear from you soon!

Stay sexy,

<3 Tia

ONE TO CHASE

MARCUS + AMY

Marcus

AMALIE KNIGHT.

Amy.

The girl from the wedding.

What are the chances?

I guess the chances are pretty damn good, considering our families are connected. She's just back from Paris, and she's living in Chicago. God, she was so fucking gorgeous walking in here, throwing out that confident act same as the night at the bar when she called me an old man. It still makes me chuckle. Old man. Baby.

Picking up my phone, I look at the little red indicator saying I have a text. Sliding my finger across the face, I stare at her number and without hesitation save it to my contacts.

I don't need to read her resume to know she's good at what she does. She sat in that leather chair across from me in that silver business suit looking as fierce as her older brother Stuart when we faced the prosecutor together, hoping to get his business partner off the hook for murder.

She's smart, sexy, and bold. It's a killer combination. I had to divert my eyes when she crossed her long legs. I barely heard her words for fighting the memory of them wrapped around my waist. Every detail of that night in Wilmington had raced to the front of my brain.

Amy Knight. She left me hanging at that hotel in Wilmington, but perhaps we can revisit what happened between us. In the meantime, I'll check with Paul and Chris. Perhaps it's time Merritt, Hampton, and Donnelly revisited our corporate marketing plan.

Shaking my computer awake, I flip over to the firm's website. Looks pretty dated. Maybe we should add a short interview section with the founding partner, i.e., *me*. Perhaps we need a slogan.

A total brand revamp such as this requires full-time work, planning, meetings. Lots of meetings. Brainstorming over dinner and drinks, and perhaps a visit to my loft. I like this idea more by the second.

The way she left puzzles me. Women don't run from me. Not when I want to catch them. She projects a hotshot image in her power suit and heels, but one thing I know about runaways. They're afraid.

What are you afraid of, beautiful? What will it take for me to find out?

Get One to Chase Today!

ONE TO LEAVE

STUART & MARISKA

Mariska

"WHAT ARE YOU DOING?" STUART'S voice was level, but I could sense a change.

Looking back at him, my braid flipped over my shoulder. "More than one of us can leave."

With that, I set off toward the cabin. We'd strolled here at a leisurely pace, but I took a fast, determined stride. Minutes later, I was back, pushing through the door and grabbing my bag. When Stuart made me drive over in the truck, I'd been sad because I'd wanted to ride with him again. I wanted my back pressed against his chest, his strong arms around my waist, our hands clasped. We were at the start of this mini-escape, and my brain was full of romantic dreams.

Today, I realized my head was just as hard as his, and I was glad I had a truck to drive back to the ranch. I almost wished I had a plane ticket as well. All of my things were quickly shoved into the duffel I'd brought, and I reached for the door when it opened on its own.

Stuart stood in my way, water dripping from his hair, eyes blazing. "You're not leaving."

As angry as I was, my breath still caught at the site of him, towering over me, seeming twice his normal size.

"Yes, I am." My voice was annoyingly small.

He surveyed me a moment before stepping into the cabin and pulling the door closed behind him with a slam. I was trapped. "Why?"

My brow lined. All the reasons I should go and never look back crowded together in my mind fighting each other to get out. The result was me stuttering. "You . . . Are you? Seriously . . . ?"

In one quick move, Stuart caught me, pulling my face to his.

"Stop!" I cried out, slapping his hand off my cheeks.

I was angry. He was angry. I pushed at him, trying to get past, and he caught my arm, jerking it behind my back.

"Ow!" I shouted, twisting to get free. "Let me go!"

"No." His eyes were dark, and something wicked, low in my stomach tingled in response.

I pushed and fought harder. He blocked every blow, holding my wrists, turning them away, lifting me off the ground, pulling me closer to him. We were both breathing hard, our chests moving together.

My voice was low and angry. "What do you want, Stuart?"

In that moment, I saw the break in his eyes. "You."

Two blinks passed between us before our mouths crashed together. His large hands were on me, tearing my sweater, grasping my breasts. I whimpered, desperately holding on, chasing his kisses with mine, trying to hold him as his mouth moved over me. It was rough and painful, and my insides throbbed for him.

Get *One to Leave* today!

BOOKS BY TIA LOUISE

Signed Copies of all books can be purchased at: http://mkt.com/TLM-Productions

All books available in eBook and print.

All are stand-alone novels.

Mature content warning: Readers 18+ only.

One to Hold
(Derek & Melissa)

Derek Alexander is a retired Marine, ex-cop, and the top investigator in his field. Melissa Jones is a small-town girl trying to escape her troubled past.

When the two intersect in a bar in Arizona, their sexual chemistry is off the charts. But what is revealed during their "one week stand" only complicates matters.

Because she'll do everything in her power to get away from the past, but he'll do everything he can to hold her.

Also available in audiobook format.

❤

One to Protect
(Derek & Melissa)

When Sloan Reynolds beats criminal charges, Melissa Jones stops believing her wealthy, connected ex-husband will ever pay for what he did to her.

Derek Alexander can't accept that—a tiny silver scar won't let him forget, and as a leader in the security business, he is determined to get the man who hurt his fiancée.

Then the body of a former call girl turns up dead. She's the breakthrough Derek's been waiting for, the link to Sloan's sordid past he needs. But as usual, legal paths to justice have been covered up or erased.

Derek's ready to do whatever it takes to protect his family when his partner Patrick Knight devises a plan that changes everything.

It's a plan that involves breaking rules and taking a walk on the dark side. It goes against everything on which Alexander-Knight, LLC, is based.

And it's a plan Derek's more than ready to follow.

Also available in audiobook format.

One to Keep
(Patrick & Elaine)

There's a new guy in town...

"Patrick Knight, single, retired Guard-turned private investigator. I was a closer. A deal maker. I looked clients in the eye and told them I'd get their shit done. And I did..."

Patrick doesn't do "nice."

At least, not anymore.

After his fiancée cheats, he follows up with a one-night stand and a disastrous office hook-up. His business partner (Derek Alexander) sends him to the desert to get his head straight--and clean up the mess.

While there, Patrick meets Elaine, and blistering sparks fly, but she's not looking for any guy. Or a long-distance relationship.

Patrick's ready to do anything to keep her, but just when it seems he's changed her mind, the skeletons from his past life start coming back.

Also available in audiobook format.

One to Love
(Kenny + Slayde)

Tattoos, bad boys, love...
Boxing, fame, fortune...
Loss.

It's the one thing Kenny and Slayde have in common. Until the night Fate throws them together and everything changes.

It's a story about fighting. It's about falling in love. And it's about losing everything only to find it again in the least likely place.

One to Leave
(Stuart & Mariska)

Some demons can't be shaken off.
Some wounds won't heal.
Until a pair of hazel eyes knocks you on your ass, and you realize it's time to stop running.
#SexyCowboy

One to Save
(Derek & Melissa)

"I lost myself in the darkness of trying to protect you..."

Some threats come at you as friendly fire.
Some threats take away everything.
Family won't let you go down without a fight.
The Secret isn't as secure as Derek's team originally thought it was, and a person on the inside of Alexander-Knight is set on exposing him, breaking him, and taking away all he holds dear.
Refusing to let anyone suffer for his crimes, Derek takes matters into his own hands. He's exposed, he's defenseless, but his friends are determined to save him.
#SaveDerek

One to Chase
(Amy & Marcus)

Paris fashions,
Chicago nightlife,
Secrets and lies...
Welcome to the North Side.

Marcus Merritt doesn't chase women. He doesn't have to. But when the spirited and sexy blonde who left him wanting more shows up in his office looking for work, little things like the rules seem ready to be rewritten.

Amy Knight is smart, ambitious, and back home in Chicago to care for her mother. A courtesy meeting with one of the top lawyers in the city should be a boost to her career...

Until the polished green-eyed player turns out to be the same irresistible "random" she hooked up with at a friend's wedding in Wilmington. Bonus: He's the brother of her older brother's new wife. What the hell?!

Who's chasing whom? It all depends on the day. Or the night. #SexyLawyer

**Get a taste of Marcus and Amy FREE in "Runaway": A *One to Chase* prequel! Available where eBooks are sold!

One Immortal
(Derek & Melissa paranormal)

Melissa is a vampire; Derek is a vampire hunter.

When beautiful, sad Melissa Jones flees to New Orleans with her telepathic best friend, she is looking for a cure—not an erotic encounter with a sexy former Marine.

Derek Alexander left the military intending to become a private investigator, but with two powerful shifters as partners and an immunity to vampire glamour, he instead rose to the top in paranormal justice.

At a bar on Bourbon Street, Derek and Melissa cross paths, and their sexual chemistry is off the charts. Acting on their feelings, they are pulled deeper into an affair, but Melissa is hiding, hoping to escape her cruel maker.

It doesn't take long before the shifters uncover her secret. Still, Derek is determined to confront the Old One and reclaim her mortality—even at the risk of losing his.

#SexyVampires

One Insatiable
(Koa & Mercy)

One wounded panther, one restless lynx, one insatiable hunger.

Mercy Quinlan is a whip-smart lynx and the youngest in her shifter clan. She's tough and independent and dreams of escaping her alpha sister's control and living life on her own terms.

When a lone black panther shows up in her hometown, Mercy is intrigued. He's just passing through, which makes him perfect... Along with his broad shoulders, defined muscles, and sexy fighter moves.

Koa "Stitch" Raiden is picking up what's left of his broken life. Exiled from his black panther clan, he's running from Princeton to Seattle when he's drawn to Woodland Creek.

He's aware Mercy is watching him. What he doesn't know is the sexy little vixen who sneaks through his window each night is both the trouble he doesn't need and the hope he can't live without.

One to Take
(Stuart & Mariska)

Stuart and Mariska head back to Montana, but our strong and silent cowboy is still learning how to communicate with the gypsy girl who stole his heart.

It's setting up to be just as hot and volatile in Big Sky country as it was in One to Leave. Don't miss it~

#MoreSexyCowboys *Coming Jan/Feb 2016!*

ABOUT THE AUTHOR

TIA LOUISE IS THE AWARD-WINNING and International Bestselling author of the "One to Hold" series.

From "Readers' Choice" nominations, to USA Today "Happily Ever After" nods, to winning the 2015 "Favorite Erotica Author" and the 2014 "Lady Boner Award" (LOL!), nothing makes her happier than communicating with fans and weaving new tales into the Alexander-Knight world of stories.

A former journalist, Louise lives in the center of the USA with her lovely family and one grumpy cat. There, she dreams up novels she hopes are engaging, hot, and sexy, and that cause readers rethink common public locations.

CONNECT WITH TIA:

Website: www.AuthorTiaLouise.com

Email: allnightreads@gmail.com

Twitter & Instagram: @AuthorTLouise

Pinterest: AuthorTiaLouise

Facebook: AuthorTiaLouise

17439172R00373

Printed in Great Britain
by Amazon